The Carthage Chronicles: The Original Trilogy

Marcus J. Mastin
Black Bird Literary Company
New York USA
MarcusJMastin.com

Illustrations By: Ed and Joe Turck & Clay Dumaw
Cover Design By: Marcus Mastin

The first **3** stories of the 'Carthage Chronicles'

Dedication

This is book is dedicated to the memory of Mary B. Honer.
Not only was she an avid fan and staunch supporter of my
writing career, she was also a wonderful teacher who
I respected very much.

Thank you for everything.

Carthage Chronicles Volume I

Acknowledgements

As I mentioned in my previous books, any imperfections in the story that managed to slip through are of my own mistake and should be addressed as such.

As always, I would like to gratefully acknowledge the help of my father, James P. Mastin, for assisting me with the layout of my stories. He also contributed to the imaginative descriptions of the characters as well as many of the places referenced. Many long hours were spent discussing ideas, and he helped push me along when my confidence began to wane.

In addition to my father, a special 'thank you' goes out to those who helped improve my manuscripts. Edwin Thompson is a former college professor of mine who set aside hours of his own personal time to read my first two manuscripts and make them more unified. Shane Dayton is a fellow writer and a literary editor who set aside hours of his own personal time to read my Revenge manuscript and make the storyline more thrilling and cohesive. Together, these gentlemen acted as my proofreaders, editors, and suggestion makers all in one.

I also have much appreciation for the wonderful artists who designed my creepy cover art as well as the eerie illustrations that enhance the pages inside. Clay Dumaw designed the covers for my Ferryman and Reaper novels as well as provided many illustrations. Edward and Joseph Turck also contributed many spectacular illustrations throughout the mystery series.

Over the duration of the project, there were others who were instrumental in helping me with support, research, and additional important areas. They are:

James A. Mastin
Kyle G. Moody
Tammy Sue Mastin
Jeffery P. Mastin
Christina A. Mastin

Throughout this book, you will find plenty of individuals with some degree of mental problems or illness. However, not all of these characters are dangerous or go on to become a serial killer. Here is a list by Dr. Phil McGraw of the 14 most common traits that a serial killer may possess.

1. Over 90 percent of serial killers are male.

2. They tend to be intelligent, with IQ's in the "bright normal" range.

3. They do poorly in school, have trouble holding down jobs, and often work as unskilled laborers.

4. They tend to come from markedly unstable families.

5. As children, they are abandoned by their fathers and raised by domineering mothers.

6. Their families often have criminal, psychiatric and alcoholic histories.

7. They hate their fathers and mothers.

8. They are commonly abused as children — psychologically, physically and sexually. Often the abuse is by a family member.

9. Many serial killers spend time in institutions as children and have records of early psychiatric problems.

10. They have high rates of suicide attempts.

11. From an early age, many are intensely interested in voyeurism, fetishism, and sado-masochistic pornography.

12. More than 60 percent of serial killers wet their beds beyond the age of 12.

13. Many serial killers are fascinated with fire starting.

14. They are involved with sadistic activity or tormenting small creatures.

CONTENTS

Book I: Don't Pay the Ferryman

Book II: Don't Fear the Reaper

Book III: Revenge of the Reaper

Book 1

Don't Pay the Ferryman

Original Concept design of Louis Ferr
By Clay Dumaw—June 2003

The Ferryman

Lightning strikes and streaks dance across the sky.
The colors that once frightened now seem magical before my eyes.
Across the river, I see a ferryman and his boat heading my way.
In the back of my mind, I hear words an old woman used to say.

Her warnings of caution chill my spine and cause my ears to burn,
Speaking of the many who have boarded his vessel, never to return.
My pulse quickens and my breathing grows heavier as he comes near.
In the distance a wild dog howls; my apprehension turns into fear.

The lantern on his boat and a full moon supply the only light to see.
A fierce storm brews overhead as a thunderous boom rattles the trees.
I am the watcher and watched alike, keeping one eye on the ferryman,
     And the other on a cautious crow
Suddenly I notice the ferryman is surrounded in fog, following him
wherever he goes.

(over)

From under his cloak, he extends a bony finger to motion me aboard.
Feelings of dread and anxiety arise as we pull away from the shore.
Storm clouds form and he insists upon payment, screaming his demands twice.
But I refuse to pay the ferryman before we reach the other side, or even fix a price.

I thought no one else could send chills down my spine like the ominous gatekeeper,
But the eeriness of my host has me feel as though I'm in the presence of the Grim Reaper.
His voice is so hushed, I can barely make out what he is chanting.
If my knees weren't trembling, I'd surely be upon them praying.

The boat proceeds ever so slowly; frustration causes the cloaked stranger to become enraged.
To the ferryman's dislike, we arrive safely with my soul unscathed.
With a sigh of relief, I quickly pay my fee and run away fast as I can.
I've become just one of the few who has survived a ride...
      With the Ferryman.

By: Marcus J. Mastin
Survivor of a ferryman encounter
June 11, 2002

Prologue

Nestled in the foothills of the Adirondack Mountains in Northern New York is a small town by the name of Carthage. It is a town much like any other small community with the exception that its lifestyle is about to be changed forever because an 'Evil' has come to town.

The Village of Carthage began as a small, simple town and was incorporated May 26, 1841, with a charter that called for the election of five trustees who would choose one of its own to serve as president. The original members of the Carthage Town Council, referred to as "The Corporation," served without pay and felt that such service was considered a citizen's public duty and responsibility. Those founding fathers made a pledge to turn Carthage into a productive and well-respected community that would thrive and prosper into the future.

While the village never did quite live up to its primal expectations, Carthage (and its surrounding areas) developed into a favorite place for tourists to visit in recent years. The community has become somewhat of a famed attraction because of its beautiful scenery and its Norman Rockwell style of living.

Carthage is still a relatively simple town, supported mostly by the farmers living on the rural outskirts of town and the local mill workers. Although its residents have remained true to their roots and traditions, Carthage has also been no stranger to bizarre events. Throughout the town's history, there have been several devastating fires in the past one hundred and fifty years, many of which nearly leveled the town to nothing but ashes. The baffling circumstances of what ignited these fires were rarely ever determined and have ultimately added to the village's mystery as town folklore still speculate on those historic occurrences.

One particular fire, known as the Great Carthage Fire of 1884, destroyed everything in town with the exception of the St. James Catholic Church. Miraculously, the church was untouched by the fire, even though every building around it burned to the ground.

On February 20, 1955, the village, with its unfair share of fire losses in history, suffered yet another tragedy. It was during that particular fire in which town realtor and Council President, Jacob Gordon, perished trying to rescue a 41-year-old woman from a burning building. Not only was the fire mysterious in nature, but an eerie ghost-like figure was seen in the vicinity. It also marked the first and only time that a member of the town council was killed by one of the fiery disasters.

In spite the catastrophic fires that have plagued the village, Carthage has continued to rebuild each time and forge ahead. Because of the strong will and determination the townspeople possess, Carthage has kept its rich history intact. Carthage is generally known as a picturesque and peaceful town as well, which has seen only rare occurrences of crime and only a handful of murder cases since 1841.

Over the years, many people of notoriety have visited the area for its relaxing atmosphere and beautiful countryside. Artists of all kinds come to Carthage and its surrounding areas each year to sketch, paint, and photograph all the spectacular landmarks and scenery. Because of these aspects, Carthage is recognized as one of the safest and most pleasant places to live in the entire state.

Carthage's rich history dates all the way back to the early 1800s. For almost a century, it was a bustling Port situated on the Black River Canal System, which was part of the New York Erie Canal System. However, with the coming of the Catskill Mountain Railroad in 1870 which expanded to the neighboring town of Watertown first, Carthage was no longer the thriving village it had been. A few years later, with the continued development of the railroad industry, New York State stopped funding the canal system altogether, a crushing blow to Carthage which left it a struggling community.

However, the residents of Carthage, determined as they were (and being conveniently located near an Army base), decided to draw on the opportunities offered by Fort Drum.

The military installation, now known as Fort Drum, began as a military training site in the 1800s under the name Pine Plains. Then, in 1908, Brigadier General Frederick Dent Grant, son of General Ulysses S. Grant, was sent to Northern New York with several thousand troops (totaling 2,000 regulars and 8,000 militia). General Grant found Pine Plains to be an ideal place to train troops. The following year money was allocated to purchase the land and summer training continued at Pine Plains through the years.

With the outbreak of World War II, the area (which had been renamed Pine Camp) was selected for a major expansion and an additional 75,000 acres of land was purchased. With that purchase, 525 local families were displaced. Five entire villages were eliminated, while others were reduced from one-third to one-half their size. By Labor Day 1941, 100 tracts of land were taken over. Three thousand buildings, including twenty-four schools, six churches and a post office were abandoned.

Pine Camp became Camp Drum in the summer of 1951, named after Lt. Gen. Hugh A. Drum who commanded the First Army during World War II. Throughout the entire World War II, as well as during and after the Korean War, a number of units were stationed and trained at the military base to take advantage of the terrain and climate.

During the late 1950s and continuing through the 1960s, Carthage was a notably attractive village. Every commercial edifice was occupied with well-known department stores such as Woolworths, Newberries, and WT Grant Company. However, after the dangers of war had subsided, Carthage began to decline again as factories and jobs left the area and Camp Drum was used very little, mostly as an Army Reserve and National Guard training area during the summer months.

Carthage eventually became a shadow of its former self as downtown businesses closed their doors due to lack of shoppers. Nowadays, large stately buildings remain vacant where thriving businesses used to be, and there are empty lots stand where buildings have burned and were never rebuilt.

With the late 1970s and on through the 1980s came new interest in the Army base. Camp Drum was renamed Fort Drum in 1974, and in 1984, the base saw a large expansion project that lasted straight through the 1980s and into 1990s.

With the expansion and upgrade of Fort Drum, Carthage saw a rapid increase in population; however, the job situation around Carthage and throughout the North Country still remained bleak. Some new businesses started to enter the community, buying land from the local farmers and building new structures on the outskirts of town instead of renovating older, vacant ones that already stood within the village boundaries.

Today, downtown Carthage has no department stores and only one grocery market. The only shops that seem to thrive in town are the ones that cater to the tourists during the warm summer months. In recent years, however, even the once-profitable tourist season has dwindled considerably. Inadequate lodging, second-rate restaurants, and lack of exciting activities have prompted tourists to pass by Carthage rather quickly or skip the town altogether.

Although the town's residents are too prideful to admit the town is in despair, their thoughts are filled with the belief that something evil has taken over and damaged the moral fiber and resilience of this village. The citizens of this once bustling, picturesque community go on with their daily business and act as though everything is fine, but deep down in their hearts and minds, there is hidden fear and feelings of hopelessness.

Most of the new inhabitants in town are military personnel and their family members. These transplanted residents have little knowledge of Carthage and its historic past, or the many tragic fires that have plagued the little town over the years and still wreak havoc sporadically.

As the town of Carthage enters the new millennium, a sense of optimism has entered the residents' thoughts, hoping that the worst of times are behind them. However, a mysterious stranger has now arrived as the town's new ferryman, and shortly thereafter, peculiar happenings begin to occur around town—including several bizarre disappearances and a weird, unexplainable behavior sweeping through the neighborhood.

A powerful force, determined to destroy the very essence of this town, will challenge the courage and faith of the citizens in this small community. As a couple of townspeople band together to search for clues to solving the mystery, the answers to several of their darkest fears and secrets will be revealed. The most unlikely people will show true characteristics of heroism whereas others who are more renowned will fall from grace.

While the intentions of the stranger keep the townspeople wondering, his motive will not remain a mystery for long. And when the puzzle finally unravels, the conclusion will be catastrophic for all.

PART ONE:
Evil Comes to Town

Chapter 1:

An Unfortunate Dilemma

"Thomas!" a woman's voice shrieked. "What in blazes are ya doin'? Are you comin' or not?"

With a grumble and a groan, he hollered out, "Damn it, Stacey! Leave me be!"

"Don't you holler at me, Thomas Parker! We're all waitin' for you. Get in the car this instant so we can leave."

He waved her on and said, "Go ahead without me."

"When will ya be home? How'll I know what time to have dinner on the table?"

"Be gone, woman!" he snapped. "I'll be there when I'm damn well ready!"

Thomas Parker walked over and sat on a grassy knoll along the bank of the Black River, recalling the events that had taken place over the past couple months. As he loosened his black tie and unbuttoned his suit coat, his sad face softened and a heavy sigh was heard as it interrupted his peaceful surroundings. He closed his eyes and smiled as a cool breeze brushed against his freckled face and through his wavy red hair.

Though Thomas was in his late thirties, his pale complexion and lack of wrinkles made him appear much younger than his years. Thomas looked like a brawler with his six-foot frame and stocky build, but to the contrary, he was quite gentle. He was a quiet man who kept mainly to himself and walked with a bit of a limp that was hardly noticeable. Hampered with a crippled left hand, no one knew whether it was a result of something that happened to him during his

Air Force days, or if it occurred after Thomas was discharged from the service but before moving back to Carthage.

The circumstances which transpired during that period are believed to be known by no person in town other than Thomas himself, and he tensely refers to them simply as "The Lost Years." That was a mysterious time in his life and a topic of discussion which he did not care to share with others. Not even his wife.

As Thomas sat alone, thinking to himself, he could not believe that the horror which terrorized the little town of Carthage had finally ended. He tilted his head back on the cool grass and began to fall into a deep sleep. Within minutes, Thomas was dreaming, and his dream took him back roughly two months earlier.

The dreaded events Carthage endured over the past several months had etched themselves into history as a period that will be remembered as one of heartache for this tiny little town in upstate New York. Many of the townsfolk's worst horrors were confirmed while other residents had to confront their own fears alone. It was a time when panic consumed a town that was generally oblivious to the perils of the outside world. This town boasted unity and balance, but soon all that would change and the once amicable little town would be turned upside down.

It all began during the middle of May in the year 2000, and the town's citizens increasingly described it as an unusually hot season for the North Country. Traffic had become a major political issue because the increased congestion had brought the town to a standstill. Too many motor vehicles converging on the tiny village resulted from the expansion of the local Army Post, Fort Drum.

Mayor Patrick "Pat" Jordan was a fifty-year-old former entrepreneur with an intuitive nature. He kept his shoulder-length curly black hair pulled back into a ponytail and often wore a gray, wool fedora to hide the fact that his hair was thinning on top. Pat was just over 5'7" tall with a lean physique who liked to keep fit by canoeing along the Black River in the summertime. Although he had scrawny arms and chicken legs, his unquenchable craving for Italian pasta had left him with a plump face and a potbelly.

Back in the early 1980s, Pat lobbied heavily to bring big businesses into town to offset the mill closings, declining industry, and high unemployment. Even though Pat didn't achieve the success he had hoped for, he did single-handedly convince such companies as McDonalds and Starbucks to bring their businesses to Carthage.

Pat was born and raised in the North Country and loved everything about the area. Like so many other children who grew up in upstate New York during the 1960s, Pat Jordan grew up on a dairy farm. His family's farm was located five miles outside of town and it was during that time in his life when he learned about the misery of poverty, the struggle to cope during times of financial strain, and how to survive after the family business was gone.

Over the years, Pat had seen Carthage evolve from a simple farming community of approximately 8,000 people to what he considered a booming metropolis of nearly 20,000 residents. Fort Drum was the primary reason for this huge influx of people. The Post had been home to only 5,000 troops, however, the infamous wisdom of the state politicians arranged for an expansion of the military base which resulted in an additional 10,000 troops to be stationed near Carthage's small and placid community.

Many of the incoming soldiers lived in barracks on the Army base; however, those in the military who were married often preferred to live off-post with their families, and so they purchased homes in the neighborhoods surrounding Fort Drum. Consequently, since many of the soldiers who lived off-post made their home in Carthage, Mayor Jordan decided it would be beneficial to get an opinion on how to relieve the traffic congestion brought about from the Fort Drum expansion and their added personnel. Pat took the initiative to set up a meeting with the Post Commander, Colonel Mark Gaines, to discuss the situation affecting the community.

Colonel Gaines was a kindhearted, friendly gentleman who was approaching his mid-forties and was known by the other soldiers as being a firm but fair man. The Colonel had given over twenty years of his life to the U.S. Army, and on top of being completely devoted to his job, he also loved the North Country and all of its many charms.

Although Mark had a desk job and developed a stout build from his lack of physical training over recent years, he still enjoyed going for long walks along the many streams in the Adirondacks. He had explored a majority of the forests and state parks, and one of his favorite summertime activities was going for camping trips with his kids in the surrounding areas on the weekends.

Mark Gaines was raised in an ordinary middle-class family from the Midwest who, upon graduation from Ohio State University, moved back in with his parents. Initially, he wanted to take a year off from entering the job market in an attempt to find out what he wanted to do with his life. However, sometimes in life, things don't always work out like you thought they would.

It was a hot summer day on Mark's 23rd birthday, and because of his rash actions, some have wondered if it wasn't just a little *too* hot that day. Mark's folks had often joked that the sun was so hot on his birthday it baked his brain and clouded his judgment, which might explain why he abruptly left his birthday party and drove to the recruiter's office to enlist in the military. Nevertheless, Mark remained loyal to his decision, and throughout the years, has dedicated himself to be the best at his job. He was always grateful to the military for helping him straighten out his life and provide him with the motivation he needed to excel.

Pat Jordan arrived at Colonel Gaines's office late on a Friday afternoon and hurriedly rushed up to the door before the office closed for the weekend. When Pat entered the building, he immediately noticed the vacant chair at the front desk; however, he could distinctly hear the faint sound of someone typing on a keyboard coming from down the hallway. Pat followed the clanking noise, which eventually led him straight into Colonel Gaines's office.

Pat stood in silence as the silver-haired serviceman rapped at the keyboard. Once Colonel Gaines finished typing his report, he looked up and saw Pat standing in his doorway. The Colonel smiled and motioned for Pat to sit.

"You're secretary wasn't at her office," Pat stammered, "but I *do* have an appointment to see you. I hope you don't mind that I walked in here unannounced."

"Not a problem, Mayor Jordan," the Colonel replied. "I've been expecting you." Colonel Gaines put a folder labeled 'Trioxin Report' back in his desk drawer and sat up straight. "You seem a bit nervous, Mr. Mayor. Are you feeling okay this afternoon?"

Pat exhaled as he began to feel more at ease. "I'm feeling fine, Colonel; thank you for asking. And please, call me Pat. After all, I'm just a small-town Mayor; there's no need to be so formal with me."

"Okay, Pat," the Colonel voiced with a wink and a grin. "So tell me, what can I do for you today? From the message you left with my secretary, I was under the impression there was an important issue you wanted to talk over with me."

"Yes, Colonel, there is, Pat began. "I'd like to discuss the topic of congested street traffic in my town."

Colonel thought for a moment and said, "Maybe I'm not on the same page as you are, Pat. Give me an overview of the general problem, okay?"

"Well, with only one bridge linking the east side of Carthage to the west side, and what used to take roughly a few minutes to get to and from work, could now take up to an hour or longer."

"Now, Pat, I realize that is a major inconvenience in your town; however, you're going to have to understand that these types of problems are going to arise from time to time. This always happens whenever a large number of people move into a small area within a relatively short amount of time."

"We're all dealing with the problem the best that we can, Colonel, but with automobile accidents mounting and no relief in sight to ever-increasing traffic congestion, I need to hear some possible options and alternatives to alleviating the traffic problems. I'm afraid that if something isn't done soon, someone is going to get killed...maybe even one of *your* soldiers."

The last remark seemed to get the Colonel's attention. "Is it financially possible to build a second bridge across the river and link it to a different street that connects out of town?"

"Not really." Pat responded. "You see, for nearly thirty years, the entire district has been repressed due to the high unemployment and very little industry. It is because of these financial problems that money is in short supply; therefore, the town's options are *very* limited."

"Well, what did Carthage residents use to cross the Black River years ago...y'know, before the bridge was built?"

Pat took a deep breath, then tilted his head back as he tried to recollect. "There was a ferry service in town about a hundred years ago. I heard stories about it from my great-grandfather when I just a young kid."

"Now *that's* something to consider!" the Colonel replied boisterously. "Talk it over with some of your friends, Pat. If they think it's a good suggestion, maybe you should spread the word around about bringing back the ferry service...updated and expanded for the 21st Century."

"That's not a bad idea, Colonel." expressed Pat, nodding his head in agreement. "I'll see what I can do."

The colonel grinned. "When you come up with a definite plan, Pat, let me know. I'll try to help out in any way I can."

After several days and much deliberation over several reasonable proposals, the people of Carthage called for a town meeting and made a motion to the town council to invest in a modern ferry service rather than pay for the expenditure of a costly second bridge which would undoubtedly raise property taxes throughout the community.

A few residents stood up to speak, brought in maps of the area, and explained their idea to the council members. They stated that a ferry service could conduct its operations one mile downstream from the existing bridge. The ferry would begin on an old, unpaved side street off from Academy Street and connect to West State Street, thereby allowing the commuters to jump on Route 126 with ease.

Colonel Gaines, who was in attendance at the town meeting, stood up to speak. "I realize I'm not from this area, but y'all don't mind, I'd like to put in my two-cents."

Everyone on the council nodded in agreement.

"Seeing as how this town is financially in a pickle, I don't see how a second bridge *could* be built without raising taxes, applying for a grant from the state, or having some other type of fundraiser to get the money you need. With that being said, I agree that a ferry service is the most economically sound idea."

"Thank you for your insight, Colonel," Pat Jordan uttered as the colonel sat down. "I'm sure the residents and council members value your opinion as much as I do."

Since Mayor Jordan came from humble beginnings himself, he prided himself as someone who listened to voters' ideas and always made an extra effort to help his community. Pat recorded notes during the town meeting and was very attentive to the residents' concerns about costs, manpower, and swiftness to resolve the situation.

After some careful thought, Pat coincided with the residents' suggestion to hire a ferry service between the east and west side of Carthage. However, the decision would ultimately rest upon the three-men, two-woman town council.

The board members consisted of five longtime residents of Carthage. First was Scott Patterson, Chairman of the town council, and the person with the longest tenure. Scott was also President of the Carthage Savings and Loan, one of only two banks in town. Mr. Patterson, a short man in his forties, was moderately overweight and had light-brown hair, though it appeared to be slightly balding. He had a booming voice and his face always seemed to have a reddish hue, which gave his eyes a bloodshot appearance behind his wire-rimmed glasses.

Scott cleared his throat, adjusted his glasses, and bellowed, "I'd like to come to a final conclusion by the end of tonight's meeting. But before I call for a vote, I'd like to ask the other council members what their assessment is of our two options."

The man sitting next to Mr. Patterson was the twenty-seven-year-old, attractive bachelor Dave "Bucky" Morgan. The townsfolk all knew him only as Bucky, a nickname given to him as a kid after his favorite New York Yankee baseball player, Bucky Dent.

Bucky was the only one on the town council with any formal education in business, obtaining a Bachelors Degree in Political Science and a Masters Degree in Business Management from nearby Syracuse University. At an even six feet tall and 165 lbs, Bucky, who had played basketball during his college years at Syracuse University, looked like he could've been a professional athlete.

Aside from his athleticism, he was exceedingly popular with the young women on campus with his shiny black hair and sparkling light blue eyes. Bucky was broad-shouldered with a barrel-shaped chest and an extremely toned body; yet, he kept himself fairly slender from jogging three miles every day around the Carthage Athletic Field.

After Scott finished talking, Bucky got up and said, "Though I think a bridge is the better decision for the long term benefits, I understand money is in short supply. I'll agree on the ferry service and propose that the board create a savings account we can add money to over a period of time with donations, tax money, and anything else. This account would be for the sole purpose of generating money for the construction of a bridge within the next five to ten years."

Bucky sat down and tapped the man on the other side of him on the shoulder, letting him know that he was done with his speech.

The final man on the town council was mild-mannered Bryan Harsha, who was never much for words. Bryan's appearance sort of resembled a half-stuffed scarecrow because he was scrawny and feeble looking, had a pale complexion, and had much too large feet and hands. He also had a bit of a spare tire around his midsection, a by-product of his insatiable addiction to dark chocolate.

Several seconds passed after Bucky tapped his shoulder before Bryan actually stood up and addressed the crowd. It was apparent he was uncomfortable being the center of attention. Bryan kept his head low and spoke softly.

"If the others think the ferry service is a good idea, then so do I."

And just like that, he sat back down and put his hands upon his lap.

The first of two women on the town council was Cristina Boyd. She was considered the town bitch because of her brazen demeanor and uncompromising conduct during town meetings. Although an angry woman at times, Cristina was well educated and had a very good head on her shoulders.

Cristina was a very alluring woman with raven colored hair and dark brown eyes. Wherever she went, she liked to wear tight revealing clothes, which would show off the curves of her gorgeous body that she developed from many hours working out at the Carthage Y.M.C.A. each week.

When it was time for Cristina to voice her opinion on the bridge-or-ferry debate, she placed both hands on the table and exhaled deeply before rising.

"I don't even know why we're *still* discussing this topic," she said rather brusquely. "Anyone with even a *little* common sense can tell you our town *can't* afford another bridge. And unlike my colleague, Bucky, I don't believe we will *ever* be able to fund such a project."

Bucky took notice at Cristina's not-so-subtle jab at him and raised a brow.

"We're having a hard enough time keeping jobs in the area," she continued, "as well as keeping our residents from moving away. Raising the price of *anything* right now would only drive more people to leave. So let's just do the *smart* thing and take a vote already. Then we can get started on bringing a ferry service here for Christ's sake."

Cristina plopped back in her chair, crossed her arms, and stared ahead with an annoyed expression on her face.

The last member of the town council who spoke on the matter was a sweet, yet naïve woman, Rebecca "Becky" Taylor. Becky joined the council a few years ago after retiring as a fifth grade teacher for the Carthage School District.

Ms. Taylor was a mature woman in her mid-fifties, yet she was still exceptionally attractive for a woman her age. Becky sported black curly hair that was showing traces of gray, which she wore short up to her ears. Ms. Taylor was a uniquely classy lady who liked to look flawless and wore just a hint of make-up to accentuate her features.

The crowd, as well as Bucky, was silent after Cristina's little speech. Becky patted Cristina on the hand to calm her down and smiled as she stood.

"Although I would've worded it a little differently, and said it with a little less hostile tone," Becky said with a wink, "Cristina's assertions are basically true." Becky glanced at all the faces among the crowd and noticed them nodding in agreement. "It seems we're all thinking along the same lines, so I propose we take a vote right now."

By the end of the board meeting, the votes had all been tallied with the decision being unanimous. And the judgment was to bring in a ferry service to Carthage.

Chapter 2:

Planting a seed of Evil

The groundwork for terror was set into motion during the beginning of June. It was at that time when Mayor Jordan and the town council wrote up an announcement for the invitation of bids and inquiries for the ferry boat project. After it was agreed upon, the solicitation for bids was then forwarded to the local papers and expanding regions. In the invitation, it stated that Carthage's Town Council was seeking any and all ferry owners who would potentially be interested in bringing a company into Carthage and starting a new ferry service.

By the time the ad expired at the end of the week, a total of three bids were received, with one being so strangely low that every member on the council was boggled. While the other two bids were as much as four times higher than bid number three, Bucky was the only council member who questioned *why* the bid was so much lower than the others. He also wondered why the bidder did not send along a copy of his credentials, any prior work history, or mention any job references for the town council to contact.

After many hours of debating his concerns, Bucky was finally supported in his protest of the bid from Bryan Harsha; however, the other three board members had no problem with this ridiculously low bid. Then, in a three-to-two vote by the town council, the decision to award the contract to the lowest bidder was made under strong protest and objections from Bucky and Bryan. Even Bucky's live-in girlfriend, Cristina Boyd, stated Bucky's concerns were blown out of proportion.

Bucky and Bryan wanted the council to conduct a thorough review of the lowest bidder's records, reputation, and methods being used to conduct the ferry service, and why the bid was priced so ridiculously low. Consequently, the remaining council members did not want to hear these arguments and were not concerned with those issues; for they were only concerned with price and how much they were saving the taxpayers and themselves. As a result, a majority agreement was reached, and by the middle of June, work began to put this business on contract.

The bottom line to the majority council members was price. By their actions, it appeared as though certain council colleagues were acting scrupulously and turning a blind eye to potential problems...such as problems that sometimes occur when you bring an 'outsider' into your home.

The council members in question did not seem as concerned with the public's well-being as Bucky and Bryan were. They were only worried about saving the townspeople money and looking good in the eyes of the taxpayers and voters, no matter what the consequences were.

Bucky, on the other hand, was not interested in being 'admired' by the townsfolk, and he let his opinions be known—(no matter how many voters he alienated in the process). Not only did the integrity of the bid make Bucky feel uneasy, the name of the ferry service was highly suspicious as well.

The owner of the ferry service registered his company under the DBA of "The Mephistis Pheles Ferry Service," but no one in town really knew what the meaning of the ferry company's name actually meant. Unfortunately, everyone would soon find out with horrific effects.

The ferry owner was an elderly and feeble man who had recently moved into this quiet town—a person who said hardly a word to anyone. He was a tall and lanky man who stood about 6'2" and could not have weighed more than 160 pounds. Although his appearance was mostly obscured by a black broad-brimmed hat that draped over his eyes, a closer view showed that his face was pale and drawn, with a scraggly white beard and thin lips. His frail body made him appear sickly; however, he had an aura of wealth and education about him that overshadowed his appearance.

When the old ferryman actually *did* converse, he spoke with a distinct European accent and carried himself as if he had royalty in his blood. Even the name of the ferry owner seemed to have a regal lineage quality—Mr. Louis Charles Ferr. It would become a name that had much more meaning than anyone ever imagined…and a name no one really paid much attention to until it was much too late.

Mr. Ferr's initial appearance seemed to be non-threatening, and a person could almost feel at ease in his presence. That is, until you looked into his eyes. The ferryman's narrow eyes were so black and cold that it sent sharp chills down the spine of anyone who dared to gaze directly into them. The only thing worse than the old man's eyes was his rugged touch. With his long, bony fingers and blackened fingertips, it made shaking hands with Louis Ferr feel as if one was in the presence of the Grim Reaper himself.

In his younger days, Mr. Ferr may have been a very attractive man, someone that all the women would have wanted to spend time with. Now he looked like a man who has seen a lot of what the world has to give, and may pass away at any time from just being tired of what he has had to endure for so many years. The ferryman was unmarried, and as far as anyone knew, he didn't have children or any other family members. He did, however, have an aide that followed him around everywhere.

The name of Ferr's aide was Mr. Steve Jensen, a simpleton who tagged along with his boss while catering to his every need. Mr. Jensen seemed more like a bodyguard instead of an assistant ferryboat operator because of his short, stocky build, and scruffy appearance. His face was haggard and plump, with a large nose that was as wide as it was round.

At five feet five inches tall and one hundred ninety-five pounds, Steve's waistline was larger than his chest and, along with his unsightly face, made him resemble a troll rather than a human being. Looking ever the part of a bum, Steve also appeared as though he had not shaved in several days and possibly hadn't bathed in a while either. In fact, to put him and Mr. Ferr side by side, you wouldn't have thought these two men had anything in common…except that they possessed the same black, cold eyes.

Although Mr. Ferr was unmarried, he certainly knew how to handle himself around women. He had the uncanny ability to make all the ladies in town become weak in the knees, especially when he greeted each woman by kissing her hand. And when he spoke, the women were like pudding in his hands. His power over people was quite apparent when Mr. Ferr arrived at the Carthage Town Hall to accept the ferry service contract being awarded to him.

Louis Ferr seemed to be very casual about the award, almost as if he expected to be offered the contract all along. He was a smooth talker and seemed able to convince the majority of the townspeople that he was a kind and gentle man. He spoke convincingly of how he only had the community's best interests in mind and that he wanted to assist the townsfolk's in any way he could.

Ever the skeptic, Bucky wondered if what Louis Ferr stated was the truth, or if he was trying to cover for some ulterior motive and simply restating what the townspeople wanted to hear. Everything Mr. Ferr had said about his business seemed to be too good to be true, but everyone was too oblivious to notice or care. The remaining council persons melted like butter on hot corn on the cob and were on the edge of their seats eagerly waiting for the next word the old ferryman had to say. Even Cristina, the woman with the biggest attitude in town, was quite pleasant with the elderly ferryman and even commented to Bucky that Mr. Ferr seemed to be a very kind and gentle man. She had even gone as far as saying that Mr. Ferr was an attractive man in his own sort of way.

All of the residents were entranced by Mr. Ferr whenever he was near; however, the praise for the stranger did not end when the crowds dispersed. All of the local newspapers wrote lengthy articles praising Mr. Ferr for his generosity—for coming into town to save them from the severe traffic problems brought upon by the expansion of the Army Post. Furthermore, the *Carthage Republican Tribune* editors, Ty Harris and Eric McGary, made Louis Ferr out to be the second coming of Jesus in nearly every news article.

Of course, that wasn't much of a surprise to residents because the two editors had consistently been of one mind when it came to any articles they wrote or deemed worthy enough to put in their newspapers. Besides agreeing on social and political issues, they also dressed alike, styled their hair the same way, and even wore the same fashionable style of glasses.

Many of the townsfolk found the editors' behavior to be quite peculiar, and it was even rumored that the two editors were living together, leaving people to wonder if there wasn't more than just a working relationship between the two gentlemen. Therefore, as long as one of them was going to write articles glorifying Mr. Ferr, you could be certain that the other would do the same. It was only through the efforts of Mr. Joshua "Josh" Roberts, a reputable young man and the *Tribune's* top reporter, who prevented the newspaper from containing more tributes to the ever-charming, ever-enigmatic, Louis Ferr.

Josh Roberts' main purpose in his stories about the ferry service was to try and offset other articles written by brown-nosing reporters who tried to get in the editors' good graces by depicting Louis Ferr as the next great Messiah sent from heaven. Even though Mr. Roberts' articles were not derogatory towards the ferryboat or its owner, Josh *did* question whether the ferry service would actually do anything for the economy of the community.

Before Ty Harris and Eric McGary took offense to Josh's opinions and assigned him to cover other news stories, Josh's thought-provoking editorials began to leave an impact with some members of the community. Josh had a gift for words and knew how to phrase his opinions to leave readers question their own views of the ferryboat project and wonder if Louis Ferr actually *was* worthy of all the praise he received.

It wasn't until after a couple weeks of endless praise, both on the TV and in the newspaper, that Bucky was becoming nauseated at what was going on. He was not without his suspicions either. There was something eerily familiar about Mr. Ferr, but Bucky couldn't put his finger on it. Also, Bucky was eager to get these praises justified and he knew just who to talk to about getting this accomplished.

Then, on a Tuesday morning in late July, Bucky set aside some free time and put his paperwork away so that the first opportunity he had, he could go over to see Becky Taylor at her office. He hoped to have a one on one conversation to try and convince her that his concerns about the community's safety were genuine and his uneasiness about the new ferry service was valid.

Bucky always enjoyed his conversations with Becky. She had a grandmother-quality to her that made him feel comfortable in her presence. A part of him felt sorry for Becky as well because she had an uncommonly difficult life, having had two husbands pass away on her rather suddenly.

Becky's first husband was killed in the Vietnam War during the summer of 1969. They were high school sweethearts at Carthage Central High School who married right after graduation, and had only been married three years before his untimely death.

Upon learning the news that her young handsome husband had been killed in Asia, Becky was devastated and emotionally distraught. It took Becky more than five years before she was able to date again; however, as time passed, she fell deeply in love for a second time. She gave her heart to a kind man who understood her uneasiness regarding relationships as well as her reasoning for wanting to keep her maiden name.

After a whirlwind courtship, they were married exactly nine years to the day after the death of her first husband. However, husband number two was killed in a terrible car accident only two years after being married. Since that time, Becky remained single. She sensed she had horrible luck when it came to relationships and did not want to experience another tragedy again.

Becky's office door was half open when Bucky walked in. She was so wrapped up in the correspondence and documents in front of her that she was unaware Bucky was standing in her doorway. Bucky cleared his throat, hoping the noise would get Becky's attention and not startle her, but still she did not notice. After a few more seconds, he tapped on the glass of her door while pushing it completely open and against the wall.

"Hi Becky," he said in a low-key voice. "I was wondering if you had a moment to talk."

Becky glanced up from her desk with a welcoming smile and replied, "Sure Bucky, come on in. I've always got a minute for you."

Placing her pen down on the desktop, Becky removed her glasses as Bucky made his way over to the leather chair that was positioned in front of her desk and sat down. Becky nonchalantly set a notepad over some notes she had been working on, and then laid her arms crossed over her desk so that the papers could not be seen.

"I'm delighted to see you," she said. "It has been a while since you've stopped by my office for a visit. Lately it seems that we only get to see each other at council meetings and haven't had a chance for a social chat in a long time."

Bucky nodded and grinned courteously.

"So tell me," she continued, "how are your folks doing? I haven't seen your mother at bingo for at least a month or two."

Bucky scanned the room to take in his surroundings before he spoke, and then he answered casually. "Oh, they're doing fine. It seems like I never see them anymore either. They rarely get a chance to call me with all the traveling they've recently done. At the moment, my folks are visiting relatives in Tucson, Arizona."

"That's such a beautiful area." Becky said with a gleam in her eye. "I went there years ago with my second husband—on our honeymoon. During our trips into the desert, we witnessed some of the prettiest sunsets I've ever seen." She turned toward Bucky again and uttered, "I hope your folks are enjoying themselves."

"They have been in Arizona for about three weeks and are having the time of their lives. My father wants to move away from this area eventually, mostly because of our long, bitterly cold winters. So, right now, they're checking out various locations and states as potential places to move to."

"That's wonderful," she replied, still smiling. "I'm glad to hear that they're having such a great time. Tell me, how's your father taking to retirement? I never thought I'd see the day when ol' Donnie Morgan quit being a lawyer."

"He seems to be handling it okay." answered Bucky. "Dad has gone fishing with his brother at least three times this summer—and he seemed to *truly* enjoy himself instead of complaining about it." Bucky chuckled and stated, "I'd love to see those two retirees out on the lake together, trying to reel in a big fish!"

With an astonished expression, she asked, "When did your uncle retire? I can't believe I didn't hear about one of Watertown's best police officers leaving his post!"

"Uncle Luke retired this past spring after thirty-five years on the job. But from what my dad told me, Luke's son, Grant, is following in his father's footsteps."

Becky sighed as she looked away. "Still, I don't know how *I'll* ever adjust to retirement. I think I'll miss the routine of getting up and going to work every day." She paused briefly and said, "I guess I'm afraid I'll get bored."

Bucky nodded. "I'm sure that concern weighs on many retirees' minds; however, my father hasn't had time to be bored—at least, not yet. When I last spoke to Dad, he told me that he doesn't miss the hustle and bustle of being a prosecuting attorney. He indicated that he didn't have the stomach to deal with a faulty justice system anymore. I guess he and my mom have made plans to spend a portion of their retirement money and see the world before finally settling down in a warmer climate. More than likely, it will be somewhere out west near our relatives."

Becky grinned and nodded slightly before changing the subject. "So, anyway, is this visit today for business or personal reasons?"

Bucky cocked his head to one side and scratched the top of his head. "Well, as a matter of fact, I'm here concerning business. Actually, it's regarding our newest business in the community."

Becky nodded again as she pushed her chair back from her desk, placed both her elbows on the arm rest, and leaned backwards.

"Okay, you have my full attention. What's on your mind today?" she asked.

Bucky bent forward in his chair and gazed directly at Becky with a determined look on his face. "I wanted to talk to you about Mr. Ferr and his ferry service. He's been here for several weeks now, and we still haven't seen any of his credentials. If he's not going to provide us with references, then shouldn't we at least do a background check?"

"That will not be necessary," Becky said as her smile faded and her tone turned harsh and defensive. "In fact, I'm overseeing the ferry project personally, and I couldn't be more pleased with our choice. Bucky, I don't want you going around trying to cause trouble and making our new patrons feel uncomfortable."

Bucky's eyes got wide from the belligerent statement he received from Ms. Taylor. "That's not my intent at all, Becky. I just want to make sure that he *is* the best man for the job. Believe me; I have only the town's best interests in mind."

"As well as I do." Becky snapped back. "Louis Ferr has stopped by my office on several occasions, and I can assure you that he *is* a trustworthy individual."

"That may be," Bucky retorted, "and I respect your opinion as well as your recommendation for the guy; however, you have to admit, we hardly know anything about him. And that's what bothers me the most!"

By now, Becky's tone had changed from defensive to contemptuous. "Let me tell you something, Bucky. I may not have been born here, but I have lived in this community for more years than you have been alive. I know what it's like to have very little money and see relatives out of work."

Bucky's cheeks became flushed and he appeared almost shamefaced.

"Now, maybe I haven't been a member of the town council as long as others," continued Becky, "but I have worked as a teacher for twenty years and have been a contributing member of our society for a long time. This town is finally turning a corner after many years of hardships, and I am **not** going to have you scare off a generous man like Louis Ferr just because you have frivolous doubts about his credentials."

"Frivolous?" Bucky uttered, visibly stunned. "Look, Becky, I'm not questioning your actions or sincerity. All I'm saying is…"

Becky cut him off. "Bucky, I'll have you know that the money we're saving by hiring Mr. Ferr can be put back into our community to help the people in this town get jobs and help families receive the financial assistance they need."

Bucky stood up and put his hands on top of her desk, leaning over towards her. "But it's *not* my objective to try and scare him off, and you know it!" he shouted. "Why are you getting so defensive over this subject? This is standard procedure for all new companies that come into this town. We've *always* asked potential businesses to supply a list of credentials to the town council, and Louis Ferr is not above our rules and regulations!"

"This matter is closed, Mr. Morgan," she said strictly. Then she put her glasses back on and looked down upon her desk, shuffling though some junk papers and placing them neatly in a pile off to the side of her desk. "Now then, if have nothing more to say, Bucky, I have plenty of work to do today and must ask you to leave."

For a moment Bucky continued to stand in disbelief. He said nothing as he turned toward the door with simply a befuddled look upon his face.

As Bucky walked away, he could not shake the perception that Becky was withholding something while they were talking. Although he couldn't quite put his finger on it, he was certain it was *not* something favorable. After all, why would she get so edgy all of a sudden? Now, more than ever, he began to get an uneasy feeling about what was happening around town.

Chapter 3:

Suspicious Feelings

That night, Bucky was walking the streets of Carthage. He needed to be alone for awhile so he could reflect on what transpired throughout the day and clear his mind. And Bucky reckoned that strolling aimlessly about was the best solution. So many questions kept popping into his mind—such as where did this Louis Ferr come from and why did he pick Carthage to start his ferry service? Bucky also wondered how Mr. Ferr could possibly operate his ferryboat at such a low bid and still make a profit for himself. Most of all, he couldn't understand why Mayor Jordan and the majority of the town council were going out of their way to help this man start his business.

All these questions and more were haunting him, and he just could not get a handle on the events of that strange day. Not only did he have a disastrous conversation with Becky Taylor, but practically everyone else on the council believed he was suffering from delusions of grandeur over his feelings about the new ferryman and his mysterious ferry service. With a streak of bad luck such as this, Bucky started to feel somewhat distraught.

During times such as these, Bucky wondered if he should have even bothered joining the council or why he tried to help the community. Though Bucky had a big heart and good intentions to facilitate Carthage's prosperity, he wondered if his talents were appreciated or if he would ever see the progress he hoped to achieve.

Although Bucky had numerous commercial offers and opportunities to advance his career in other cities, he decided to return to Carthage upon his graduation from college. He wanted to become involved in the business and political aspects of his hometown and give something back to the community.

Bucky was not without his flaws; he had a long history of being the town flirt and had the reputation of dating nearly every attractive, available, and unavailable woman in Carthage and its surrounding areas. Slightly conceited, he thought of himself as a 'ladies man' and would sometimes laughingly refer to himself as a Clark Gable look-alike. However, despite his shortcomings, Bucky was the most well liked individual on the town council, and the most level headed of the group.

Bucky continued walking around lost in thought for over an hour when he eventually wandered over to Liberty Street and entered Kitty's Bar, one of the town's local pubs. What a pleasant surprise it was to see his good buddy, Roger Fasick, sitting at the bar and enjoying a beer.

Roger Fasick was a twenty-three-year-old college student and a senior at Syracuse University, entering his final year to obtain a Bachelors Degree in Ancient History. Roger was very intelligent and expected to pursue a career in Anthropology upon graduation. He had been working as a Research Assistant on Fort Drum between semesters, and after working there for two years, Roger had obtained great respect from the local patrons and was now making fairly good money for only a part-time job. Unfortunately, Roger needed every penny of it since he planned to marry his very beautiful, yet materialistic girlfriend, Nellie Spencer, early next spring.

Roger and Bucky were very good friends, and the two had much in common. Often, they would get together at the local bar to drink and talk for hours. Roger had been close to Bucky since the disappearance of Roger's older brother, Paul Fasick, who vanished during Roger's senior year of high school when Roger was only seventeen. Paul, a twenty-one-year-old college student at that time, was in Florida for spring break with his buddies when he disappeared without a trace.

Paul Fasick had been captain of the football team in high school and was voted class clown during his senior year. He was also blessed with the wild, outgoing personality in the Fasick family. Paul's extroverted persona complemented Roger's more quiet and subtle behavior, and the two of them were very close. Although he had many acquaintances and was courted by several ladies, he always remained a devoted one-woman guy and a level-headed individual who was loyal to all his friends.

The investigation into Paul's disappearance was difficult from the beginning, leaving the police department in Florida with no leads to his whereabouts. The absence of clues, combined with no witnesses, eventually left the police with no other choice but to give up, so the case was never solved.

Roger had a hard time coming to terms with the tragic loss of his brother and has suffered from regular periods of anxiety and depression ever since. It was because of his deep, intense depression that made it impossible for him to function in everyday tasks. This ultimately prompted him to start college a year later than anticipated while he spent most of his time cut off from the companionship of friends and family, as he remained inside his house alone. Bucky had been the one true friend to Roger and stood steadfastly beside him, helping him throughout his difficult times.

Even though Bucky and Roger were not related, they were very close and acted as if they were brothers. They had many of the same interests, such as sports and exercise, and could be found many evenings at the schoolyard playing one-on-one basketball for hours. Another similarity they shared was an appreciation for old music from the 1960s and 1970s era. After they finished playing basketball, they would always journey over to the local watering hole with a handful of quarters so they could sit down, drink a couple of beers, and listen to some classic rock & roll.

On occasion, people even told them that they had a slight resemblance because of their comparable facial features; they both exhibited dimples when they smiled, both had square jaws, and both men had deep penetrating eyes. Roger was 5'10" tall and weighed 180 lbs. He was in excellent shape and was slightly bulkier than Bucky from his years of weight-training and working outdoors for his job in anthropology.

His ash-blonde hair hung almost to his shoulders and had sideburns down below his ears. Roger usually sported a Vandyke-style beard with a moustache, which looked good with his ruddy complexion and green eyes. On his left shoulder, he had a tattoo of an Ankh, which is the Egyptian symbol for 'Life,' as a token of devotion to his brother.

Bucky's demeanor changed from agitated to relief when he saw Roger inside the bar. He walked over to his friend, sat down on a stool next to him, and motioned for the bartender to come over.

"I need a couple of beers over here for the two of us." Bucky announced.

"Comin' right up!" yelled the bartender. "Do ya want a glass to drink your beer, or are ya goin' to sip it from a bottle?"

Roger spoke up and said, "We'll take some of the cold bottles you have in the beer fridge, Bob."

The bartender, a scruffy-looking middle-aged man by the name of Bob Earle, set up another coaster, put two bottles of Budweiser in front of them and said, "Here ya go, fellas. Lemme know if yous will be needin' anything else, okay?"

"Sure thing, Bob, we will." Roger said with his eyes glossy from the amount of beer he had already consumed that evening.

"So, Roger, what are you doing in here on a Tuesday night?" asked Bucky.

Before he could get an answer from Roger, Bucky took a sip from his bottle and noticed two rather bizarre characters sitting at the other end of the bar. They were both dressed in late 1960s throwback attire, with long, baggy bellbottom pants, leather sandals, and Tie-dyed T-shirts with a skeleton symbolizing the Grateful Dead on the back. One of the individuals was wearing a rather unusual multi-colored Jamaican Tam hat that was too big for his head. In fact, it was so large that he looked like the Dr. Seuss character, The Cat in the Hat.

After a few seconds, Bucky turned away and directed his attention back toward Roger. "So, as I was saying, Roger, you hardly ever stop in here anymore on a weekday, and when you do, you never stay out more than a couple of hours."

"Uh huh," grunted Roger.

"I was going to give you a call around supper time to see if you wanted to hang out tonight, but I thought you'd probably want to stay home with your girlfriend since both of you have to work in the morning."

"Nah, I could care less to hang out with that pain in the ass." Roger belched as he took another large gulp of beer. "I needed to get away from the pint-sized psycho for awhile and just relax without her bitching at me all night."

"Is something bothering you?" asked Bucky in a cautious tone. "You seem *very* irritated tonight, and I've *never* heard you talk about Nellie like that before."

"Nellie and I haven't exactly been seeing eye-to-eye on things lately," Roger replied solemnly.

"Anything you wanna talk about?"

"Well, it's just that recently she seems to want to argue about every little thing. At first, I thought it was me, that possibly I was the cause for all the friction. Now, I don't know what to think anymore. It

41

seems like the more I do for Nellie, the more she expects from me, and I can't live up to her expectations anymore. I have been thinking of calling it quits, but I can't bring myself to ask her to leave."

"Do you *really* want her to leave?" asked Bucky.

Roger shrugged his shoulders. "I don't know. I keep hoping that she will get over her moody attitude and things will go back to the way they used to be. Even though things are distressing right now, I still don't want to give up too soon on our relationship. I did that once before and ended up hurting a very special person to me...I don't want to make the same mistake twice."

"I'm sorry to hear this, old friend." Bucky said in a low, uneasy voice. "I didn't know that things have gotten so bad between you and Nellie."

Roger looked up for an instant, and Bucky could see tears in his friend's eyes. Then Roger looked back down towards his half-empty bottle and said, "Nellie and I used to have great times together."

"I know you did, bud. I remember how happy the two of you looked together."

Roger forced a smile and then continued. "I used to think we had so much in common. We both liked art and the same kinds of music. We even enjoyed the same foods and liked the same restaurants. I don't understand how my perception could've been so wrong. I've even suggested that the two of us take a trip together, but she keeps making excuses why she can't go."

"I know how hard it is to keep a relationship together," Bucky told him, "so I can understand what you're going through. I don't want you to think that you have no one to turn to if you are depressed or stressed out. You're like family to me, and I'm always there for you."

Roger put his hand on Bucky's arm and replied, "Thanks, your support means a lot to me."

Bucky glanced down at Roger's arm and noticed a metal bracelet on his left wrist. "Are you going to church, Roger? You didn't tell me you were getting back into religion again."

"Huh? What are you talking about?" Roger said, quite confused.

Bucky pointed toward Roger's wrist. "Your bracelet. Isn't that one of those '*What would Jesus do?*' bracelets?"

Roger erupted in laughter. "No, this is something Nellie picked up for me at a flea market she was at in Watertown last week. The WWTJD stands for '*What would Tom Jones do?*' He's a worldwide celebrity!"

"Did you say 'Tom Jones'?" Bucky asked, biting his lip to hold in the laughter.

"Hell yeah!" retorted Roger. "I have all his records. He's got the best singing voice in the entire history of modern music."

Bucky gave him a pat on the back and chuckled. "I like your enthusiasm, old pal, but let's not get carried away here."

Roger smirked and said nothing more about the topic. For the next few minutes, the two friends sat in silence, nursing their beers. Finally, Roger spoke up and said, "By the way, I was hoping you might drop in."

"Why?" asked Bucky, "Is something else on your mind?"

"No, not really." answered Roger. "I haven't talked to you in a while and wanted to catch up on what's been happening in your life."

"As a matter of fact, I'm all stressed out over the new ferry service in town." Bucky said with a sigh.

"What do you mean?" inquired Roger, "I've heard only good things about it."

"That's just it!" Bucky exclaimed. "To me, it seems too good to be true, and when I told Becky Taylor I wanted to do a background check on the old ferryman, she turned me down flat."

"I thought background checks were standard procedure."

Bucky nodded. "Yeah, they usually are."

Bob was standing off to the side cleaning beer mugs as Roger and Bucky conversed. He lifted his eyes off the glasses and looked over to the guys as they talked but did not join in on their conversation. Always a good listener with lots of advice, Bob had many people come and discuss their problems or their life stories while sitting at the bar. By the expression on his face, it would seem as though something they said sparked his interest, but at that moment, he was content to just pay attention.

Roger placed his beer bottle up on the bar as Bucky tipped his drink up to his mouth and finished off the last of his Budweiser. "We need a couple more beers over here, Bob, when you get a chance," Roger said with a bellowing voice. "And this time, give us some of those frosty mugs instead of a bottle, okay?"

"No problem guys, I'll be comin' right over." Bob answered back with a grin. Bob put down the mugs he had been cleaning, walked over to pour a couple glasses of draft beer from the keg and set two frothing brews in front of them.

"How much do we owe you, Bob?" asked Bucky.

"Don't y'all worry about it," said Bob. "You two are some of the bar's best customers. Besides, bein' as how it's practically dead in here tonight, I kinda like the company. I'll use some money from the tip jar to cover the beers."

"Thanks!" Roger yelled out as Bob walked away.

"We really appreciate the hospitality!" added Bucky.

Roger grabbed his mug off the bar and turned to face Bucky. "I'm still amazed Becky was so brusque with you. I've known her since I was three years old, back when she was my Sunday school teacher. After that, she was my teacher in fifth grade as well. Believe me, I've spent a lot of time with her over the years and that doesn't sound like her at all." he said as he guzzled down his beer. "She's usually a friendly lady…and a stickler for the rules!"

"Y'know something, you're right!" Bucky yelled out in a commanding tone. "Not only is Becky acting different, but so is the whole town."

"What do you mean?" Roger asked.

"I just think it's unusual how some mysterious man just waltzes into our neighborhood with no references and sweeps the townspeople off their feet!" Bucky shouted in a distressful tone of voice. "And the worst part of it all is that nobody seems to care or even question it."

"Have you mentioned your feelings to Cristina?" Roger asked, understanding Bucky's point of view for the first time.

"Yeah, I did." replied Bucky, grimacing. "She suggested that I 'get a life' and forget all about Louis Ferr. She also mentioned that until there *is* something to be worried about, then I should mind my own business and just accept the fact that the town of Carthage is finally seeing a much deserved and long awaited return of prosperity and rise in industry."

"That was pretty harsh!" Roger said with a slight laugh. "What'd you say to her after that?"

Bucky took another swallow of his beer. "Well, I wasn't in the mood for an argument so I reluctantly agreed with her comments and decided to go for a walk to clear my thoughts. That's how I ended up here tonight."

Roger just smiled and reached into his pants pocket. "I'll be right back, bud."

Roger pulled out some quarters, gave Bucky a pat on the shoulder, and went over to the jukebox. Bucky, on the other hand, kept looking over at the two 'Deadheads' still sitting at the other end of the bar, unable to shake the feeling that he knew one of them. Suddenly his eyes widened, and he shook his head in disbelief as he realized that one of them was his cousin, Adam "Red" Richardson, who he had known since they were kids. Red, as he liked to be called, earned his name from his fiery red hair and was teased about it when they were all much younger.

Red and Bucky were related through their mothers (who are sisters) and six years apart in age. Although there are several years between them, they were together quite often when both were kids and Bucky always thought of Red as the little brother he never had. They remained close friends for many years, but eventually drifted apart when Bucky went away to college. Even though Red grew up in a very conservative family, he looked much different now. Constantly reeking of cigarettes and beer, Red had long greasy hair, which was parted in the middle along with a shabby appearing goatee.

Bucky walked down to the end of the bar and tapped one of the men on the shoulder. "Adam, is that you?" he asked with hesitation.

"Hey, cuz!" Adam answered in an excited tone. "It's been a long time since I've seen ya, man. Hell, I think it's been close to three years, or something like that."

"You're right, Red." Bucky replied. "The last time I saw you was during your high school graduation. Gosh, the last three years seem to have just flown by!"

As Bucky and Red conversed about old times and families, Roger saw a small piece of paper attached to the bulletin board on the wall near the restrooms. It seemed out of place as it hung there and had only a single word written upon it, which was written in Old English style handwriting. Although Roger's eyesight was blurry, he could make out that it read...*Beware.*

After several minutes of jabbering, Red remembered that his friend, John, was still sitting beside him. Red turned and nudged his drinking buddy to get his attention.

"Bucky, I'd like to introduce you to a friend of mine. His name is John Sears."

"How are you doing?" Bucky asked as he shook John's hand. "I'm Adam's cousin, Dave Morgan, but you can call me Bucky."

John faced Bucky with a half-dazed stare and smiled, exposing his yellow, rotted teeth. "What's up, dude? It's groovy to meet some of Red's family. He's talked about you many times."

Ol' John had long dreadlocks that he covered with his multi-colored Tam and looked as though he had just woken up. His hair was black and thick, reaching the middle of his back. He was of Indian ancestry and once lived on the Oneida reservation as a teenager with his mother. John had stubble all over his face, and seemed to have dark circles under his eyes, looking as though he hadn't slept or shaved in days. However, smelling of sweet ganja and incense, it appeared to others that John was a little on the wasted side.

After Bucky and Red exchanged a few more pleasantries, Bucky looked around and saw that Roger had returned to his seat. He turned his attention back toward his cousin, looked down at his empty bottle, and said, "Well, I have to get back over there and order another beer. It was great to see you again, Adam. Hopefully, it won't be another couple years before the next time we chat. It was also a pleasure to meet you, John."

By the time Bucky returned to the other end of the bar, Roger had already ordered both of them another beer and two shots of Rum. "Hey, Bucky, what's the name of that ferry service again?" inquired Roger.

"It's called The Mephistis Pheles Ferry Service," answered Bucky as he pulled out his wallet and sat down. "Why do you ask?"

"I don't know," Roger said in an unsure voice. "It seems that I've heard that name, or some part of it, somewhere before."

Roger put down his mug and pulled out a pen from his back pocket. He reached over to the napkin in front of him and wrote the name of the ferry service upon it. "I think I still have some of my old college books lying around the house. I'll look up that name and tell you if I find anything."

"So...you agree with me?" asked Bucky impatiently. "Do you think there's something fishy about our new ferry service and its enigmatic owner?"

"Whoa, hold on a second!" Roger blurted out quickly. "That's not what I meant at all. All I'm saying is that if this situation has you so worked up over it, then *maybe* it's worth my time to assist you."

Bucky looked confused. "Assist me with what?"

"In verifying the genuineness of the ferryman's motives," answered Roger. "And in the process, perhaps we can ease your mind of any shenanigans."

"Great!" shouted Bucky. "I think I'm going to do a little research on my own, too. I'd like to see if I can find anything about Mr. Ferr's past *or* his ferry service."

"And how are ya goin' to do that?" Roger inquired.

"I'll check out the local library's newspaper clippings from the past fifty years. I'll pull all the information there is on mysterious occurrences within the neighborhood and the surrounding areas."

"That's fine, I guess. You might get lucky and come across a similar incident from the past that may shed some light on what's currently happening in our town. But I plan to go in a different direction."

"Really?" asked Bucky. "Like what?"

"I'll concentrate my efforts to finding the origin of the ferry's bizarre name. I'm sure there's a blurb contained within the mountain of books and papers from my college days. With all the money I spent on them, you'd think there should be *something* useful hidden in there."

Chapter 4:

The Terror Begins

Friday nights were always busy in Carthage, especially at the local pubs. Kitty's Bar was the hot spot for the under thirty crowd, and was usually packed with wall-to-wall people trying to unwind from the daily grind of the workweek. It was the best place to catch up on the newest town gossip and socialize with friends.

Kitty's Bar was a sports bar that had been owned by Kitty Dunn and her family for nearly fifty years. She was a perky, yet sophisticated woman who was in her late thirties, and known throughout town as "Miss Kitty." Her family was originally from Ireland and moved to upstate New York in the early 1940s for better opportunities and a better life. Her grandfather, Alton Dunn, worked many different odd jobs for several years before he saved up enough money to purchase the bar. He patented the style of the bar after the pubs he frequented in Ireland as a remembrance to his life back home in the old country and as a type of novelty to the local residents who had never experienced Irish culture before.

Even though it had been known as Dunn's Pub since her family first owned it, Miss Kitty renamed the bar after herself when she took over the business several years ago in order to give the bar a fresh look and attract new customers. Although she changed the name, the great pride she felt for her Irish heritage prompted her to keep the style of the bar in the rustic setting her grandfather instituted with many Irish artifacts to show off their family ancestry. These days, most of her clientele were the younger populace in town because they went there to enjoy the two big screen TVs for watching sports and other variety of games such as billiards and darts.

Miss Kitty had strawberry blond hair and was about five foot eight with long, shapely legs and a great smile. Though it may have seemed as if she was always in a good mood and smiling, it was best not to be deceived by the beauty of her external appearances. Whenever someone had too much to drink and was causing trouble, she was fully capable of handling herself and anyone who got out of hand.

Once, a burly trucker feeling a little too frisky reached across the bar to grope Miss Kitty's well-developed breasts. Before he even made contact, she quickly grabbed him by his scraggly beard and sharply pulled down. The trucker slammed his chin on top of the bar, and slid off his stool and onto the floor, unconscious. Needless to say, this reputation kept many a rowdy patron in line but put a crimp on Miss Kitty's social life, even with her good looks and funny sense of humor.

Bob Earle worked every Friday night from 5 pm until 2 am at Kitty's Bar. In fact, Fridays were usually so busy at the bar that Bob always arrived two hours early for his shift. This gave him a chance to fully stock the beer fridge, take inventory on what liquor's were in low supply, and make himself a quick dinner consisting of ketchup on a slice of bread and a handful of stale peanuts. He would then wash down his meal with a glass of expired milk—something that Miss Kitty was going to dump down the drain anyway.

Bob had been employed as a bartender at Kitty's Bar for more than sixteen years. He was a quiet and friendly man in his late-thirties who never had much. Bob grew up in Carthage, the town where he had resided all his life. He was set to join the military and see the world once he turned nineteen, when fate stepped in and changed his life forever. His young wife, Tracy, who he married only six months earlier, had been diagnosed with cancer. Therefore, Bob put his military plans on hold so that he could be by her side. Bob even sold his car and only rode a bike back and forth to work so that he could pay for his wife's medical bills.

Unfortunately, there was nothing the doctors could do to help her, and after thirteen months of battling the disease, it finally overtook her and she passed away. After her death, Bob was heartbroken and decided not to join the military so that he could be close to his wife's resting place.

At present, Bob was living in a one-bedroom apartment on the opposite side of town from Kitty's Bar, but he continued to ride his bike to work. Even though Bob was a person that was very health conscious and enjoyed rigorous exercise, it can also be asserted that Bob had never been much of an overachiever. He barely made it through high school and barely made more than minimum wage as a seasoned bartender. However, what Bob lacked in education and motivation, he made up for in generosity and compassion. Every year at Christmas he organized a food drive for the needy and homeless; he also went from house to house every night in the month of December singing Christmas carols with members from his church choir.

On an average day it ordinarily took Bob twenty minutes to ride to work. However, sometimes it took longer when the weather was inclement since his bike was his only means of transportation.

On one particular Friday, however, Bob was standing at the sink in his bathroom getting ready for work. He had just finished shaving the stubble off his face when he leaned over and splashed ice cold water over his cheeks; then Bob straightened and gazed at the hexagonal mirror that hung on the wall. A mirror so small, in fact, that it could've fit inside a woman's wallet. After inspecting his face for any nicks or deep cuts, he glanced at his wristwatch, noticing that the time read 2:37 pm.

"Shit! I'm runnin' a little late!" Bob said to himself. "I better get my ass in gear and move a little faster if I'm going to make it there on time." He veered his head toward the bathroom window. "Just great. The sky is turning gray and dark storm clouds are approaching fast!"

Bob let out a sigh. "If I don't get outta here soon, I'm goin' to get stuck ridin' my bike out in the rain!"

Bob burst out of the bathroom and over to his weather-beaten dresser. He rushed to get dressed, throwing on a dingy white T-shirt and wrinkled blue jeans that were starting to unravel at the seams. Within ten minutes, he bolted out the door, hopped on his bike, and began peddling hard. He was riding his bike through the streets for only a few minutes when he looked at his watch. It read 2:51 pm.

"Damn it, I'll never get to the bar on time!" he hollered in frustration. "Well, I can cut my time in half if I use the ferry instead. It sure beats peddling another whole mile and crossing at the bridge."

Soon Bob came up to the side street that led to the ferry service, and then he steered his bike down its gravel texture. As he approached the ramp, he saw two individuals, a tall lanky man and a shorter, heavier one, standing by the water's edge.

"Thank God there's someone here," he uttered in a relieved tone. Bob got off his bike and walked over to the two gentlemen, glancing over at the ferryboat every so often.

"S'cuse me, sir. Are y'all still takin' the ferryboat outta here today?" he asked the tall man. "I'm runnin' late for work and was wonderin' if I might catch a ride over to the other side."

Mr. Ferr was standing with his back to Bob and looking up toward the sky when he spoke in a creepy, monotone voice, "I'm sorry, Mr. Earle, but I'm the owner of this piece of equipment, and I don't like to run the ferry when there's a chance of lightning."

"Please, sir," pleaded Bob. "Could ya maybe make an exception this one time? I'm runnin' very late t'day. I'm a desperate man!"

"Well, such a request is most unusual," Mr. Ferr curtly answered back while turning around. "We generally don't use the ferry for bicyclists. In fact, this would be the first time we transported anyone with a bike since we've been in this town."

"Really?" Bob responded, somewhat surprised. "For as busy as traffic has been around town lately, I was thinkin' y'all would get *many* different types of business goin' through here day after day."

"Oh," Mr. Ferr said with one raised eyebrow. "You think so, do you?"

"Yeah! In fact, I woulda thought *lots* of bicyclists would 'specially wanna take the ferry to the other side of town. At least, every so often anyway since it can save them some time and distance."

Mr. Ferr crossed his arms and sported a crooked grin. "Actually, we've only been up and running for a couple of weeks. Although we won the bid and got the 'okay' to set up business towards the middle of June, we did not actually open for business until after the fourth of July. But like I said before, we normally won't run the ferry when there's a chance of lightning. After all, I have to think about the safety of my employees, my equipment, and my passengers."

Bob looked up towards the blackened sky and then back down at his watch to check the time. He cringed because he realized that by turning around now, he would never make it to the bar by his usual time.

Just as he slowly wheeled his bike around and started to walk away, he decided to turn around one last time and ask, "So, there ain't no way I can get a ride over to the other side?"

Mr. Ferr gazed upon Bob with pity and scratched the whiskers on his chin as he thought for a moment. "Normally, I wouldn't break my own rules, but you look like an honest man with a good heart. I think we can work out some sort of an arrangement."

"Thank ya kindly, Mr. Ferr!" Bob uttered in a gratifying tone. "I can't even begin to tell ya how much I'm appreciatin' this! I promise

I'll find some way to repay ya for your hospitality. I ain't got much, but if there's anything I can do, please let me know."

"That's all right, Mr. Earle; there's no need to thank me. My assistant, Steve Jensen, will handle all the arrangements," said Mr. Ferr as he looked over at his would-be assistant with an eerie look upon his face and gave him a nod.

Mr. Jensen put on his raincoat and climbed onto the ferry while Bob and his bike followed behind him. "Hold on, sir, this could be a bit of a bumpy ride, and I *wouldn't* want you to fall overboard before I get you to your destination."

The ferry was actually fairly small, as far as ferries go. It had the capacity to transport only about seven cars, three on each side super structure (or pilot house), and one in the rear of the pilot house. The ferry was approximately 45' long and 30' wide. The super structure was roughly 20' long and 12' wide with an area for people to get out of their vehicles and go inside to sit down on the straight-back benches. The pilot house was located on the second deck of the super structure and above the seating area. It was about 12' long and 12' wide, made completely out of glass windows.

Strangely, the windows of the pilot house were of one-way glass reflection, and anyone within its confines could look out, but no passengers would be able to see inside. In addition, there were two yellow cats' eyes with black pupils painted on the front of the pilot house, giving the ferry a rather sinister appearance. The hull and main deck of the ferry was painted black with the super structure and pilot house painted crimson red.

Although its main structure was strong and secure, the ferry still appeared to look run down because the paint was chipping off the sides and the wood looked weathered. Aside from the one-way glass on the pilot house, the rest of the ferry was considerably out-of-date, and at times was referred to by passengers as a disgusting, rusted piece of machinery.

Mr. Ferr stood at the edge of the water bank and watched the ferry as it started to depart. "Take care, Bob!" he yelled out. Louis Ferr lowered his hand and his smile disappeared. "I'm sure we'll be seeing each other again…real soon." he stated in his odd monotone voice.

Bob sheepishly smiled back at Mr. Ferr as the ferry was pulling away. All of a sudden, a look of puzzlement came over Bob's face. He quickly turned his attention to Mr. Jensen and asked, "Hey, now how do ya reckon that old man knew my name?"

Mr. Jensen said nothing as the ferry left the dock, his eyes focused on the sky as the storm started to intensify. Dark clouds seemed to form completely around the ferry as the winds swirled with ferocious strength. Raindrops swelled into a monsoon-like bombardment punishing all that came in its way. As the rain pounded down, Bob heard a wild dog howl. All of a sudden, the murmur of hushed voices, like those of tortured souls, whispered in Bob's ear.

The sound of their discourse grew louder and louder in his head as they screeched in dismay, *"Beware of the ferryman! Get off now!"*

As the ferry was crossing the river, it approached a hair-raising, ominous looking fog—the type of fog that feels like a cold damp mist as it touches your skin and sends chills down your body. From the edge of the riverbanks, Mr. Ferr stood watching. He raised his arms above his head and began chanting an incantation that became increasingly thunderous until the sound was almost deafening.

"CALL THEE HERE NOW!" he roared. "Rise up, by ANU I summon Thee! Rise up, by ENLIL I summon Thee! Rise up, by ENKI I summon Thee! Cease to be the sleeper of EGURRA. Cease to lie unwaking beneath the mountains of KUR. Rise up, from the pits of ancient holocausts! In the Name of the Covenant, Come rise up before me!"

"What's goin' on around here?" Bob asked Jensen in a nervous tone. The sound of snarling made Bob's head turn, and an instant later, his body whipped quickly around. He reached over, grabbed Steve Jensen by his shirt, and roared, "What the hell is happening, take me back to shore this instant!"

"I'm sorry, Bob, but it's time to pay the *Ferryman*," Jensen answered in a raspy voice, "and what he wants is your soul!"

Bob pushed Jensen down to the ground and rushed up to the bow of the ferry. Suddenly, from the dense fog came an eerie, hair-raising sound. The noise was a low, piercing howl that carried an unusual, horrific note. On the old ferryboat, the encompassing sound was terrifying as it surrounded Bob from all sides, and yet, came from seemingly nothing.

Bob strained to see through the thick vapor but could not see the land on the other side of the river, which he so desperately sought. He debated whether or not to abandon his bike and jump overboard to take his chances in the whirling water. However, Bob's fear of the uncertainty as he gazed in the black water got the better of him, and ultimately he concluded that he would be safer onboard.

Inside the confines of the murky mist were ghoulish demons that hissed and snarled. However, even in the dense fog, Bob was able to distinguish a brief glimpse of the monsters' appearance. The demons had gruesomely mottled skin that appeared reptilian in nature, dagger fangs, and undulating horns that sprouted from the top of the head. Grunting echoed from their boar-shaped snouts and their hooves tramped along the old wooden deck boards.

Seconds seemed to pass as hours, and suddenly, Bob started to feel something from within the fog tearing at his clothes. Bob peered around fearfully with drops of sweat trickling down his face, and then he quickly darted over to his bike, grabbing his backpack off the handlebars. With his pouch in his hand, Bob sprinted over to the edge of the ferry and threw one leg over the side.

Bob paused for a moment and looked down at the water, taking a deep breath. Even though he was scared to death and tears were forming in his eyes, Bob was no swimmer and his decision was still hesitant as he cautiously contemplated jumping off the ferryboat.

All of a sudden, a powerful and pulverizing force knocked Bob backwards. Spinning downward, he dropped onto the deck hitting his head on the toolbox lying on the floor. Confused and woozy, Bob attempted to stand on his feet but could only muster enough strength to get to his knees. Suddenly, Bob heard a growling sound behind him. It was very close, so close in fact it seemed as if the demons were panting on his neck and nibbling on his ear.

Bob started to turn around slowly. The color drained from his face so much so that he appeared nearly as white as the shirt he was wearing. The fear in his eyes was apparent. His body started to shake fervently as he called out, "Oh, please Lord. Don't let this be happenin' to me."

When Bob shifted around, he came face to face with a pair of glowing red eyes staring back at him within the fog. The fog grew thicker and completely encompassed Bob. Now, those glowing red eyes were starting to emerge all around him, and within seconds he was surrounded by deranged demons. He knew there was nowhere to turn so he hung his head down, surrendering all hope of escaping this terror. In that instant, Bob started to sob.

He shut his eyes but was unable to shut his ears to the echoing screams. He cried unashamedly, the tears dripping down his cheeks and off his chin. He could only hope that the pain he was about to endure would not last for eternity.

Mr. Ferr continued to stand at the edge of the embankment, watching the events transpire on the ferry. Once again, Mr. Ferr raised his arms toward the sky and in a deep devilish voice he boomed, "Take him…*NOW*!!"

All at once, a horde of demons pounced upon Bob and began to tear at his body. In pain, Bob screamed as his skin and clothes were shredded like tissue paper.

Bob struggled in agony, flinching with each strike of the demons' deadly razor-sharp claws. Hopelessness was beginning to set in, when suddenly, a struggle ensued onboard the vessel. The tortured souls (the hushed voices that tried, in vain, to warn Bob of impending danger) attempted to intervene and free Bob from the demon's grip. Just as the beasts were about to sever Bob's limbs from the rest of his body and flay the flesh from the bones, there was a thumping noise on the deck—then a splashing sound in the river as something, or someone, tumbled into the water. A moment later, the splashing ceased; an unnerving calm followed.

In the distance, a man's heinous laughter could be plainly heard. A frightening laugh that echoed across town. Within minutes, the fog disappeared, and with it, the frightening sounds of a man's desperate cries for help were gone. No traces of demons or any wrongdoing remained to be found, and neither was Bob Earle.

Chapter 5:

Chaos at Night

That night, the sky became dark very early. By 8 pm the town was entirely encompassed in a pitch black blanket of supernatural obscurity. Darkness such as this was unheard of in the summer time…unless a big storm was coming.

It was about that time when Roger Fasick and Nellie Spencer pulled up outside Kitty's Bar and exited her Cancun-green colored 1995 Mitsubishi Mirage. Although they went to the tavern every Friday evening to meet with friends and have a few drinks, Nellie was the one who socialized and was very outgoing. On the other hand, Roger usually walked over, said "hello" to everyone, and was pleasantly polite; however, being a loner, Roger felt more comfortable being by himself. He'd stay close to the bar and chat with those who came up to him rather than going around and working the barroom.

Roger walked into the bar with Nellie coming in about two steps behind him. Even though it was a sultry night, Roger wore his usual blue jeans and a tight ivory colored T-shirt, which showed off his muscles. Nellie dressed more for the season and the temperature outside, wearing a light blue sundress and sandals that bared her bright red painted toenails, which matched her lipstick.

Nellie was a fiery red head with the temper to match. Despite those attributes, she had a tender side, which is what drew Roger to her in the first place. With short, curly hair and green eyes, Nellie was an exceedingly beautiful girl who always spoke her mind. It's an attitude she developed early in life because she felt people did not take her seriously about anything due to her small frame. She was a very short girl—merely five feet tall and 110 pounds. Nellie would've probably been mistaken for a teenager more often if it wasn't for the fact that she smoked cigarettes, had very large breasts, and displayed a tattoo of a sunflower on her right ankle.

As Roger and Nellie were standing in front of the tavern doorway, they saw their friends sitting over in the corner. When they glanced over at the bar, they were both surprised to see that the usual evening bartender, Bob Earle, was not working behind the bar. In his place was Holly Boliver, the afternoon bartender who just happened to be an ex-girlfriend of Roger's.

Holly had long, bright wavy blonde hair, which she wore down to the middle of her back like a character from the old *Charlie's Angels* television show. Her sparkling eyes were unnaturally blue, a shade of baby blue so bright, it was like looking at a high school swimming pool.

Although Holly was highly skilled at her job, she did not have the appearance of a typical bartender. She was just five feet three inches tall, weighed approximately one hundred ten pounds, and had the body of an aerobics instructor. Nevertheless, she was a very friendly woman with an upbeat personality, which all the customers loved and enjoyed. Those traits, along with her warm smile and her fondness to have a drink with the fellow patrons while listening to their problems, made Holly one of the most popular bartenders in town.

"What is *she* doing here?" Nellie questioned coldly. "Holly doesn't normally work this shift; she should've been gone hours ago."

"I don't know. It does seem strange," stated Roger. "Tell you what…you go over to the tables and find us a seat. I'll go up to the bar and have our drinks sent over."

"Why aren't you coming over with me?" Nellie asked.

"I'll be over in a moment. I want to find out why Bob isn't working tonight."

Nellie strolled over to the table where their friends were sitting while Roger approached the bar. In his eyes it was evident that he still carried a torch for Holly. His whole face seemed to light up as he made his way toward her. Although Roger and Nellie had been together nearly three years, Holly was Roger's high school sweetheart and, consequently, the special love of his life.

Holly was still dating Roger when his brother, Paul Fasick, disappeared. The loss of Paul struck Roger tremendously hard and dropped him into a deep depression that lasted an insurmountable amount of time. Holly didn't know how to comfort him, and with every attempt she made to try and get close to him, Roger would push her away. In the end, it became a wedge in their relationship that they couldn't overcome.

Roger stepped up to a bar stool and pulled out some money from his back pocket. "Hey, Holly," he said with an affectionate smile

Holly raised her eyes for a moment as she poured a Vodka Sour for a lady sitting at the bar, dressed as a clone of Princess Diana. "Hello, Roger. What'll it be?"

"Get me two drafts beers of whatever is on tap."

"Coming right up!" she hollered as she made a beeline for the freezer to get two frosty mugs.

"So, what are you doing working in here tonight?" Roger jokingly asked as she poured the beer. "Shouldn't you be on *this* side of the bar enjoying yourself?"

"Don't start with me Roger!" Holly snapped, banging the mugs down upon the bar. "I should've been out of here ages ago, and I'm *not* in a good mood. Bob didn't show up for work tonight, and he never even called in. Miss Kitty has been trying to call Bob for hours, but we still haven't been able to reach him."

Roger looked past Holly and through the doorway that led into the kitchen area. He noticed Miss Kitty was back there on the phone talking to someone. Although he could not hear the nature of their conversation, he could tell by the sour expression on her face that this was *not* a pleasant phone call. Her body language, and the fact that she shoved an entire pack of her nicotine chewing gum in her mouth, provided the evidence that she had a terrible day and seemed stressed from being short-handed on a Friday night.

Roger shifted his attention back over to Holly. With a puzzled look on his face, he said, "This doesn't make any sense. For as long as I've known Bob, he's never been late to work. I don't understand why he wouldn't call if he was going to be late or not show up."

"I don't know why either," Holly sighed. "I'm just as confused about the whole situation as anyone else." Holly put her hand on top of his, and her voice became gentler. "Anyway, I just want you to know that I'm sorry if I'm acting like a bitch tonight. It's been a long day and I just want to go home and relax. Trust me, hun. You're the last person I meant to snap at tonight."

"You don't have to apologize to me, Holly," Roger answered sympathetically. "I can understand why you would be upset. But on the other hand, I'm deeply concerned about Bob. Has anyone seen or heard from him at all today?"

Holly thought for a second and said, "Not that I know of, Roger, but I haven't left here all day either. I have spoken with some of the other customers who have come in tonight, and everyone seems to be just as surprised and surprised that Bob isn't here as you and I are. I think if someone had seen him, they probably would've mentioned it."

All of a sudden, a roaring bang was heard from the kitchen area as Miss Kitty slammed the telephone down while hanging it up. A few moments later, she came storming out from the kitchen and grabbed a shot glass and a bottle of tequila from behind the bar. She poured herself a shot of her favorite liquor, Bacardi Rum, and quickly gulped it down.

Then, she looked over at Holly as she poured herself another drink and said, "Well, on top of the problem I have with not being able to find Bob tonight, I can't locate a replacement for him either. The other two part-time bartenders that we have on staff for the summer are both busy and can't break their plans on such short notice. Holly, I realize that you've been here all day and you're probably tired, so if you want to go home, I'll understand."

Holly gave Miss Kitty a quick glance and grinned. "Thanks for the offer, Miss Kitty, but I wouldn't just leave you here all by yourself. I'm may be tired, but I'm not so tired that I'd up and leave someone who needed my help. And right now, it looks like we're going to be busy tonight."

"Are you sure?" asked Miss Kitty. "I don't want you to feel obligated to help if you don't want to. I'm sure there are far better things that you'd rather be doing tonight than to spend it tending bar."

"I'm completely sure," Holly answered back. "Besides, I could use the extra tips to help with my bills this month."

Nellie looked over from the table where she had been sitting and saw Roger still at the bar talking to Holly. She looked enraged and her face turned red. Nellie got up from the table, walked over to Roger, and forcibly yanked him away from the bar.

"Listen to me," she said furiously. "It's bad enough that you two used to date! Sure, you still come in here and drink while she's working, but do you have to stand up there and flirt with her while I'm with you? I'm going back over there to sit and talk with our friends. I want you over there with me this instant!"

Roger glared back at her and spoke in a stern voice. "Don't worry; I'll be over in a minute. I've got to make a phone call first."

"Now who are you calling?" Nellie questioned in an ardent voice.

"I'm going to call Bucky," he replied sharply.

His tone offended Nellie, and she slapped Roger in the face. "You bastard! How dare you treat me so cruel! You are *always* putting other people ahead of my needs and I'm sick of it. One of these days, Roger, you're going to push me too far, and I'll leave you!"

Roger looked at her with detest in his eyes and tried to hold his composure together as he said, "Go back and sit down, Nellie, before I say something that we'll both regret."

Roger turned away and walked over to the pay phone. He kept his head down and pulled out some change from his pocket, leaving Nellie standing there all alone.

Meanwhile, while Roger was at the bar trying to discover answers to Bob's disappearance, Bucky Morgan and Cristina Boyd had been at home in the middle of a heated discussion of their own.

Getting into arguments wasn't anything new for Cristina, especially when it came to the men in her life. She had been previously married to Glenn Boyd, a mill worker that she had dated in high school. Time and again, she constantly put her career over her marriage, and even though Glenn was content and very understanding, Cristina still felt as though their marriage was holding her back. Subsequently, those feeling led to resentment toward Glenn and she eventually filed for divorce.

Shortly thereafter, she became a bitter person toward all men once her divorce with Glenn was finalized. Deep down, her bitterness was only a façade, and ultimately, she regretted leaving him. Unfortunately, she realized too late that she really did love the man who loved her so much.

After several years of being along, Cristina decided to give 'love' another chance and began dating Bucky last year after the town's annual summer picnic. They have even been hinting around about getting married within the next year. Many of their friends and family feel this would be a match that was destined to happen, for Cristina could finally calm Bucky's rowdy behavior, while Bucky's compassionate heart could finally soften Cristina's bitter, cold attitude.

Cristina was standing in front of Bucky talking to him, almost yelling, as she said, "I don't know why you insist on poking your nose around where it doesn't belong. Every time you and Roger get together, the two of you always end up getting into trouble. Why is it that you have to be skeptical about everything? After all, not *every* person has a hidden agenda and not every situation needs to be put under a microscope and scrutinized."

Bucky said nothing while Cristina waited and listened for any sort of response. After a few moments, she thought of a topic that she felt would generate some type of reaction.

"I know we haven't discussed the whole fiasco regarding the town council vote of Mr. Ferr's ferry contract and why I voted against you on that issue, so maybe this would be a good time."

That seemed to be the words that caught Bucky's attention as his eyes lit up and he replied, "Actually, I was wondering about that, but I figured that you would bring it up when you were ready to talk about it."

"Okay then, let me explain myself," Cristina stated collectedly. "I think that this was, and still is, a great opportunity for our town to relieve the congestion of heavy traffic and procure a new business into Carthage for a reasonable cost. I envision this as the beginning of other companies approaching the Council—asking to establish their business in our town and stimulating the desolate economy in the upstate locality as well as possibly lowering the unemployment rate around this area."

Bucky nodded in agreement.

"After all," she continued, "our unemployment rate is the highest in the entire state, which is as serious a problem as it is embarrassing. But change needs to start somewhere, Bucky, and I think it should start now, with Louis Ferr and The Mephistis Pheles Ferry Service being the newest company to join our community."

"I think it's great that you care so much about our community," Bucky responded as if he comprehended her position for the first time. "Your ideas are fresh and optimistic, just what this community needs, but hiring a ferry service without a thorough background check is a risky venture."

Cristina rolled her eyes.

"I believe it would be in our best interest if I did a little checking on the validity of Mr. Ferr's company. If what I find out turns out to be acceptable, I will give him my complete support."

Cristina took a few steps back and glanced off to the side. The expression on her face appeared as if she was consumed in thought, as if she was trying to choose her words carefully for her next sentence.

"Bucky, let me say something that's been concerning me about you," she uttered in a serious manner. "I honestly believe that one day your poking around will lead you to *really* find something corrupt, and it could end up getting you hurt—or even worse. You are not a detective or a cop, and I wish that you would stop acting like you are. If anything was inauspicious in this town, I am confident that the police would find out and deal with it. So let the professionals do their jobs, and you need to stop taking so many risks!"

Bucky nodded his head. "I understand your concern, Cristina, but I have this intuition there is something unusual happening in this town that just doesn't seem right. I have no explanation or reason why I feel the way I do, but something keeps eating away at me indicating things aren't as perfect as they seem."

"Like what? You must have a hunch of some kind."

"I can't put the pieces of the puzzle together just yet, but it seems that things are oddly *too* perfect between Mayor Jordan, certain members of the town council, and the Police Department. Ever since Mr. Ferr arrived in town, the politicians and people with clout seem to have bent over backwards to make his stay and business a pleasurable, yet profitable one."

"Come on, Bucky," hollered Cristina, agitation evident in her voice. "This type of behavior isn't new with you. For as long as we've been together, you and Roger have gone out of the way to meddle in affairs that weren't any of your business, and I want to know *why* you would take so many risks all the time. Do you feel like you have something to prove to people, or do you have some sort of death wish that I'm just not aware of?"

For a second there was silence. Bucky stood with his head down and his eyes glued to the floor. All of a sudden, her voice turned softer and gentler as she moved closer to him, lifted up her arms, and touched his cheek.

"Listen to me, Bucky." she continued. "I know that you feel sorry for the guy after all he's been through, but this doesn't help him or you, and I just don't want to see anything happen to you."

Bucky walked over to the chair and sat down. He hunched over, placed his elbows on his knees, and cupped his face in his hands. As he gradually lifted his head up, his eyes were glossy from the teardrops starting to swell. He stared into nothingness with a look of sheer concentration, as if he was trying to remember something of importance.

"It's more than just feeling sorry for Roger, Cristina. I feel guilty as hell regarding happened to his brother, Paul. I don't know if you're aware of the fact that I was on spring break with Paul in Florida when he disappeared. I had no idea what happened to him. I couldn't help Paul, I couldn't help myself, and I couldn't even help the police with their investigation! It's a subject I do not talk with just anyone, and I still have nightmares regarding it."

"Are you referring to the horrendous nightmares that you've suffered on-and-off over the years?" questioned Cristina. "The same ones you don't like to talk about?"

"Yes." Bucky paused briefly, and then began again. "I keep going over that night in my mind. I can remember Paul telling me that he was going out to one of the night clubs across the bay where we were staying. He asked if I wanted to go, but I told him 'no' because I wanted to save some money for the rest of the trip. After he left the hotel that night, I never saw him again."

Bucky stood up and stepped around to the back of the chair. He placed his hands on the back of the chair and dug his fingers into the fabric. He lowered his head as he began to speak and suddenly his voice got all choked up as he said, "That's the only thing I remember about that night for some reason. The rest of it is a blur to me."

"I...I'm sorry," Cristina expressed in a voice slightly louder than a whisper. "You've never told me that story before, and I guess I can understand why. If that incident messed with your head as much as you just told me, then I can't even imagine what it must've done to Roger."

"I don't think anyone knows the answer to that." Bucky remarked. "Roger has become nearly devoid of all emotion since the disappearance of Paul. To look at him he appears normal, but there's something going through his mind, something that makes me nervous. I can spot it in his eyes."

"What do you mean?" Cristina asked.

"Whenever I catch him staring into nothingness, the expression on his face sends creepy chills down my body and makes the hair on the back of my neck stand straight up."

Cristina's eyes widened.

"I feel as if Roger has a lot of rage and anger inside of him just waiting to burst forth someday. I pity the person who happens to piss him off enough to send him into that type of frenzy."

At that moment, the telephone rang. Cristina and Bucky stared intensely at each other for a second, and then Bucky walked over and picked up the phone.

"Hello," Bucky said as though he was annoyed.

"Bucky, I'm glad I caught you at home!" Roger shouted hastily. "Nellie and I are down to Kitty's Bar and something strange has happened tonight."

"Is this urgent, Roger?" inquired Bucky. "I'm in the middle of a discussion right now. Can you call me back in about half an hour?"

"Hold on and listen to me, Bucky. It's really important that I talk to you. Bob Earle never showed up for work today, and from what I can gather, no one has seen him all day either." Roger voiced in an unsettled tone. "I was thinking that you might be willing to come down here tonight. The two of us could drive around town and possibly stop by his apartment. Maybe with our combined efforts, we can find out where Bob disappeared to."

Bucky sounded unsure, knowing that Cristina would be hurt if he left now. "I don't know, Roger. What about the police? Has anyone contacted them yet?"

"Miss Kitty called them earlier," Roger replied. "But the police won't even file a missing person's report for at least twenty-four hours, and both of us have known Bob long enough to recognize that something is not right."

Bucky hesitated for an instant. "Yeah, that's true. We can't wait around for the police to start an investigation when Bob could need help right now. Stay put at Kitty's Bar and I'll be over to pick you up just as soon as I can."

"Sounds like a plan; I'll see you in a while." Roger said as he hung up the phone.

Bucky moved slowly as he placed the phone back on the receiver. He knew that his friend was counting on him for his help and assistance. He also knew how much this talk with Cristina meant to their relationship and realized that this was going to be another night when things were left unsaid between them.

"Cristina, that was Roger." Bucky stated as he started walking over to the kitchen table to pick up his car keys. "He's at Kitty's Bar right now and wants me to come over there."

"For what!" she hollered with anxiety in her voice. "We were just getting somewhere in our conversation! I *thought* we were beginning to really understand one another."

"I know, hun." he said gently as he walked back over and touched her cheek. "But something disturbing has happened down at Kitty's Bar. Apparently, Bob Earle is missing, and from what Roger told me, no one has seen or heard from him all day. I told Roger that I'd come down and we could check it out together."

At first, Cristina did not say a word. She stood there for a moment and watched as Bucky sat down and started to put on his shoes. Then, Cristina smiled, realizing just how lucky she was to have such a special guy in her life that cared so much for other people.

"I'd be willing to come with you." she offered. "That is, if you want me to."

"No!" exclaimed Bucky. "I want you to stay here where I'll know you'll be safe. I may not know exactly what's going on, but if there's any foul play involved, I want you as far away from danger as possible."

He walked back over to her, put his hands on her shoulders, and looked into her sad, sullen eyes. "I'm just going down there to check it out. If there is *any* danger at all, I'll get the police. If everything turns out all right, I'll be back here in a couple of hours."

Bucky gave Cristina a passionate kiss and walked out the door.

As Cristina watched him leave, she thought about their life together and how she hoped that one day they would be married. However, deep down she wondered if that day would ever become a reality with the lifestyle he lived, and she worried about Bucky's safety each time he went out that door on another pursuit with Roger.

Chapter 6:

Searching for Clues

Bucky drifted off in thought as he was driving into town. He knew he should not have left Cristina, especially when they were at the point in their relationship where they had to make a decision whether to move forward or break it off completely. They were beginning to make some real progress during their conversation up until Roger called.

It appeared as if Bucky and Cristina were finally starting to appreciate one another and were coming to an understanding on why they act the way they do. Bucky could only hope that Cristina would understand why he left so abruptly; possibly she would forgive him. Although there hadn't been a crime problem in Carthage for some time, Bucky could not shake the feeling that something was terribly wrong with Bob. He knew, maybe more than anyone else in town, how much wickedness and evil lurks in the world—and perhaps, right in Carthage.

By the time Bucky reached Kitty's Bar, it was around 9:45 pm. As he was coming down Liberty Street, he noticed Roger standing outside on the street curb, so he decided to pull up next to him instead of trying to find a parking spot. When Bucky arrived next to him, he rolled down his window and asked, "What are you doing standing out here all by yourself? You could've waited for me inside."

Roger turned around and looked inside the bar for an instant; then he turned back to face Bucky and said, "Well, I would've, but Nellie and I got into an argument while I was in there. I thought it might be better if I waited for you outside where the air is clear."

"Alright then. Hop in my car and we'll go for a drive through town. Perhaps we'll come across a clue that'll provide us with something—*anything* that might lead to Bob's whereabouts. We can also stop by Bob's apartment and look around for any leads."

Roger strolled over to the other side of the car and slammed the door as he got in. "Alright, I'm ready. Let's get the hell away from here before Nellie comes outside and decides she's not through lecturing me."

Bucky looked around but saw nobody around. Then he pulled away from the curb and resumed his drive down the street. "You seem like you're in an irritable mood tonight. What were you two arguing about this time?"

"Still driving this jalopy around, huh?" asked Roger, pretending he didn't hear Bucky's question. "When are you going to get rid of this relic and get something new?"

"Now don't go changing the topic on me," Bucky replied. "Besides, this is a great car! This is a 1971 Mustang that I restored myself. It's a classic!"

"A classic piece of junk," mumbled Roger.

Bucky snapped his head around. "What was that?"

"Oh, nothing. I was just thinking that it *looks* like you restored it yourself," Roger said sarcastically. "By the way, did you paint it with a brush?" he laughed.

"I suppose you think that you could do better," Bucky responded, very irritated.

"Hey man, don't get upset," Roger voiced in an apologetic tone. "After all, I'm just joking around. You know that, deep down, I think this is a pretty cool car."

"Yeah, you're only saying that because I drive your ass all over town."

Roger shook his head and spoke with sincerity. "Not at all, Bucky. I appreciate when you give me a ride every time I need it. Luckily, you won't have to worry about driving me around too much longer; my car will be out of the garage tomorrow morning."

"I don't mind doing a favor for a friend." Bucky said with a grin. He paused for a moment, mulling over Roger's compliment. "So you think my car is pretty cool, huh?"

"Sure I do, but you have to admit, it's pretty unusual to see a guy who wears a three-piece suit to work every day driving around town in a magenta colored 1971 Mustang."

The two of them sat there for a moment reflecting on Roger's last statement. Then, they turned to look at each other and burst out in a roaring laughter.

Bucky was laughing so hard that teardrops began rolling down his cheeks as he said, "Well, it's not the most business-like looking car, is it?"

After that, things settled down. The men stopped laughing so they could concentrate their attention on watching the streets as they continued along, checking to see if Bob was anywhere to be found. Bucky and Roger drove up and down the streets for awhile with neither one of them speaking a word until Bucky broke the quietness and asked, "Well, are we going to sit in silence the whole ride or are you going to tell me what Nellie and you were arguing about?"

Roger looked out the passenger side window for several seconds before he spoke. "Alright," he answered back, still refusing to make eye contact or even turn in Bucky's direction. "Holly is working at the bar tonight, and Nellie was getting a little jealous. You would think after being together for a couple of years that she would be secure enough in our relationship that seeing an ex-girlfriend of mine wouldn't bother her. She gets so worked up over nothing at all."

"Does she?" Bucky asked as he looked over at Roger. "Or maybe Nellie realizes you still have strong feelings for Holly and that she'll always be second best in your heart. Y'know, women can pick up on these types of signals," he stated with a sympathetic grin.

Roger smiled back at Bucky but did not say a word. His silence made Bucky wonder if what he said had upset his friend, or if there was some truth in his words that Roger was not ready to acknowledge in his heart just yet.

"So you just left Nellie in there alone and stranded?" questioned Bucky.

"No!" answered Roger in a quick shout. "She is still inside and probably having a good time with *her* friends. I told Nellie I'd be back in a while and that I was going out with you to look for Bob."

"And she agreed to that?" Bucky asked confounded.

"Well, not exactly." said Roger. "She told me not to bother rushing back to Kitty's Bar because she will find a ride home. Nellie is a very selfish person, Bucky, and she can't understand what it's like to have good friends that you worry about,"

"I'm not a perfect person or a perfect friend either, Roger, but I at least try my best." stated Bucky. "As my dad once told me, you can never have too many friends, and the ones you have are pretty special. Friends don't do things expecting repayment, they do it because they are your friends and they want to."

"And as good friends to Bob, let's try to find him soon before neither one of us has a girlfriend anymore," exclaimed Roger.

"Y'know, you're absolutely right!" Bucky bellowed with exuberance. "Now, let's quit with all this kumbaya, man-hugging rhetoric and get to it!"

It was approaching 10:15 pm and Bucky and Roger still had no luck finding Bob. By now, both men were beginning to get restless and wanted to find some clue to Bob's whereabouts to prove to themselves that this search was justified and not in vain.

"Bucky, its quarter after ten, and we haven't seen him walking up or down on any streets," Roger said tiredly. "Where do you want to go next?"

Bucky exhaled a heavy sigh. "Since we've driven down every street on both sides of the town, I guess we only have one more option. We'll have to go to Bob's apartment to look around."

"I don't know about that idea, Bucky. After all, if Bob was there, he would've called someone by now. And without him there, there's no way to get inside. I'm sure you don't think we're going to do any breaking and entering. If it comes down to that, we'll just call the police and have them check things out."

"We're not going to be breaking any laws," Bucky stated nonchalantly. "I happen to know his neighbor very well. His name is Thomas Parker, and he has a key to Bob's house for emergencies and things. After Bob locked himself out of his apartment a few times, he decided it would be a good idea to leave a spare key with someone he could trust."

"Oh yeah, I know who old bird is." Roger said with a laugh. "Thomas has frequented the bar lots of times when I've been there; I've chatted with him and Bob on several occasions. Those two have some comical stories about when they were growing up together and all the trouble they got into at school."

The two friends pressed on down Champion Street until they reached the house of Thomas Parker, one of Bob's neighbors and his closest friend. Thomas was one of a kind; he had a keen sense of humor that was very sarcastic, like a true upstate New Yorker. Yet, much like Bob, he had a heart of gold. Bob and Thomas were about the same age, and had known each other since high school. They were best friends then and had remained best friends throughout the years.

Thomas lived in a small, yet modest home next door to Bob Earle, with his wife, Stacey, and their three children. It should be noted that this was Thomas' second marriage; he also had two other children, fraternal twins Trudy and Jefferson, with his first wife, Catherine, who he met while he was in the Air Force.

Catherine took the kids to raise after she and Thomas split up and, consequently, were now living in Sacramento, California. Thomas missed his children in California tremendously and saw them every summer and during the holidays. Even so, he still wished they were with him and his new wife.

Everyone teased Thomas about the number of children he had, but he would just laugh it off and say that the town doctor, Dr. William "Bill" Wiley, had fixed that problem with a pair of scissors, a needle, and some thread.

Thomas had lived in Carthage most of his life, except for the short four-year tour of duty he had in the United States Air Force and a few years that no one could account for. After that, he came back to Carthage a changed man. He may have never returned home at all, but he had been summoned back to Carthage several years ago when his father, Terry Parker, had a stroke, and Thomas was needed by his father's side. His father passed away shortly after Thomas' arrival, but he decided to remain in Carthage because he wanted to be closer to his father's resting place.

People speculated as to what may have caused the breakup with Thomas and his first wife. Some feel that it was the forced move back to Carthage that drove a wedge between him and Catherine. Others believed it may have had something to do with "The Lost Years" that Thomas refused to comment on. Whatever the reason was, it became a rift that would lead to their eventual split and Catherine's move to Sacramento.

When Roger and Bucky approached Thomas' home, they took a quick glance next door, noticing that Bob's bicycle was not parked in front of his apartment. Once they arrived at Thomas' front door, Bucky didn't even have a chance to ring the doorbell when Thomas opened the door.

"Come on in!" Thomas hollered. "Just as long as you're not here to sell me anymore friggin' Girl Scout cookies. Those damn kids have already been here three times tonight."

Thomas stopped and took a good look at the men on his doorstop. "Then again, you two don't look like twelve-year-old girls. It must be the facial hair and lack of a training bra that gives you away."

"Man, how'd you know we were here? You must be able to see through doors," Roger said jokingly to Thomas.

"Nah," Thomas replied as the two guests walked inside his house. He took a momentary glance over to Bob's apartment, and then he closed the door. "Actually, my kids saw your car pull up to the house."

Bucky glanced over the room but didn't notice anyone around. "Speaking of your family, Thomas, where is everyone?"

"Stacey is relaxing in the bathtub. She worked at the video store tonight, and her back is sore from being on her feet so long. My oldest son, Cliff, went to a lacrosse match in Watertown tonight; he won't be getting home until late. My two youngsters, Penny and Peter, are playing in their bedrooms and are supposed to be getting their pajamas on."

"Oh," Bucky said, checking the time on his wristwatch. "I realize it's late, Thomas. I hope we aren't disturbing you tonight."

"Not at all. To tell ya the truth, I was kinda expecting you."

"What do you mean by that?" Roger inquired, quite puzzled.

"Holly Boliver called me about a half-hour ago from Kitty's Bar and told me Bob never showed up for work." Thomas explained. "At first I was a little puzzled, but when she said that no one has seen or heard from him all day, I began to worry. She said that Miss Kitty and some of the other people at the bar were starting to get a little concerned and asked if I had seen him."

"Did you see him?" Roger blurted out in a rush.

"Well, if you let me finish what I was sayin' I'll tell ya!" countered Thomas. "Now then, what I was about to say before I was interrupted was...well, I'll just tell you guys the same thing I told Ms. Boliver. I haven't seen Bob since yesterday afternoon. She also told me that the two of you were out looking for him, so I figured you would eventually end up over here."

"Have you been over to his apartment yet?" asked Bucky.

"No," Thomas answered, sounding as if he were offended by the question. "I've been waiting for the two of you to show up so we could check things out together."

"That sounds like a good idea," Roger said as he turned around to open the door and head back outside. "Hopefully, we'll find something useful, or maybe Bob will turn up there soon."

Thomas reached for his keychain, dangling on a wooden pegboard that hung near the front door. "I am a little worried about Bob's sudden disappearance." he expressed in a concerned tone. "This certainly isn't like him at all."

The three men left Thomas' house and walked next door to Bob's apartment, somewhat hoping they *wouldn't* find him over there. Deep down, they knew that the worst-case scenario could be right behind his door. Bucky rang the doorbell, and after a few seconds of no response, he rang the doorbell a second time.

"Well, it appears no one is home," Roger said anxiously. "Maybe we should leave before someone thinks we're looters trying to rob the guy while he isn't home."

"Not just yet, Roger." uttered Bucky. "It's possible that he's inside his apartment and hurt or even unconscious."

Bucky turned his attention over to Mr. Parker. "Hey Thomas, do you still have a key to Bob's apartment?"

"Yeah, I do." he stated as he reached into his pocket, pulling out a ring of keys so large, it looked as if it might belong to a superintendent of an apartment housing complex. "I know it's somewhere on this keychain. Now then, let me see which one of these it is."

Bucky and Roger grew impatient as time dragged on, and Thomas was still having difficulty in the darkness locating the key.

"There!" Thomas shouted with enthusiasm. "That seems to be the right fit!"

As the lock was turned and the door was opened slowly, they noticed there weren't any lights on in the entire apartment, not even a nightlight. All three men walked cautiously into the deathly silent house and began to look around. Thomas reached over to the side wall next to the door and turned on the hallway light.

"That's better," said Thomas. "We don't need to be walking around in here tripping over things in the dark. Besides, if we break something in our little adventure over here, Bob would be pissed."

Bucky walked into the kitchen and turned on the light in there. "It looks like everything is in order. Nothing appears to be broken, stolen, or knocked over."

"Yeah," Roger stated as he stepped out of the living room. "I don't see any sign of foul play or any traces of blood on the floor. That takes away our theory that he might've fallen and hurt himself."

"It sure looks that way, doesn't it?" Bucky replied. "Hey, now where did Thomas go? Wasn't he right behind us?"

"Don't get your panties in a bunch!" Thomas shouted as he came from around the corner and into the kitchen. "I may have a bit of a limp, but I can still move around rather well. I was just checking his bedroom and the bathroom to see if there were any signs of Bob. Or, at the very least, some type of indication that would explain where he went."

"Did you find anything?" Roger asked.

"Yeah, I found Bob sitting on the toilet, and I asked if I could wipe his ass," Thomas said sarcastically. "Obviously, I didn't find anything or I would've hollered to you when I was looking around. Y'know, for a college boy, you don't ask the smartest questions."

Roger became slightly embarrassed and his face turned a little red. Unsure of what to say or how to take Thomas' eccentric sense of humor, he proceeded to put his hands in his pockets and remain silent.

Standing across the room was Bucky, who had a smirk on his face. He covered his mouth with his hand, trying not to laugh out loud at the way Thomas was giving Roger a hard time.

After he regained his composure, Bucky walked over to the refrigerator and leaned against it. He glanced over to the wall next to him and noticed a corkboard with numerous business cards and "post-it" notes tacked upon it. Next to the cork board there was a jumbo size calendar hanging upon a nail with a pen connected to it, dangling from a string.

"I can't believe it!" he exclaimed while glancing over the board. "There's not a single clue as to where he could be." Bucky stopped and looked over the calendar once again. "All I know is that there is no way he could have forgotten about work today and happened to take off somewhere."

Roger shot him a look and asked, "Why is that?"

"Well, my reason for assuming this is because he has his work schedule for the entire month written down on his calendar."

"That doesn't mean anything; he still could've gotten his days mixed up." Thomas replied in a non-believing tone of voice. "That sort of thing happens to me all the time. And knowing Bob for as long as I have, I'm positive it could happen to him, too."

"That's entirely possible," Bucky answered back. "But he has every day leading up to today crossed off on his calendar. So, in my opinion, he must've known that he had to work today...but something happened that prevented him from getting there. It's like he just disappeared into thin air."

Thomas shook his head and whispered to himself, "Disappeared without a trace."

"I don't like the sound of this discussion," Roger expressed in a weary voice. Then he turned his attention over to Bucky. "We've done some investigating on small problems around town in the past, but this is way out of our league. I'm not sure we should get involved in a situation where foul play could be involved."

Bucky stood silent for a moment before turning around to face the others. "You're probably right. There's nothing more that we can do here anyway. Thomas, I'm sorry that we dragged you over here tonight only to come up empty handed. I really thought that if we were going to find any leads, then this would be the place."

"Well, then it's probably time we take off and not waste any more of Mr. Parker's time," Roger said to Bucky, trying to hurry him along. "I think he has been more than generous with us tonight."

Quickly, Roger turned to face Thomas and said, "I realize how late it is, and I just want to say 'thank you' for your time and letting us into the apartment so that we could look around. We both really appreciate it."

"Hey, it was no problem at all. The two of you are probably the most level-headed people in town, and it was my pleasure to help you out. It shows a lot of compassion to be concerned over the welfare of someone and to take the time to go out and search for someone. Bob has some very remarkable friends, and you should be proud of yourselves."

The three men dimmed the lights in each room and made their way outside. So many emotions were running through their minds right then. Each of the men were perplexed at the sudden disappearance of their fellow friend as they walked away from the apartment with heavy hearts, wondering if they would ever see Bob again.

For Roger and Bucky, this situation seemed all too familiar to them, and Bucky began to question whether Roger could handle the emotional stress of another person disappearing—especially a person that Roger regarded as a good friend. Bucky noticed the distraught look upon Roger's face and thought it might be a good idea for Roger to return home before he relapsed into one of his deep, prolonged depressions.

As Thomas lingered behind to lock up Bob's apartment, Bucky and Roger strolled over to the Mustang. Bucky placed his hand on Roger's shoulder and asked, "Roger, are you all right? Do you want me to take you back to Kitty's Bar or over to your house?"

"No," Roger replied as he took a deep breath. "I'm all right. I'm ready to venture wherever you want to go next. Just point me in the right direction and we're off."

"Okay, as long as you're sure. But if you want to head back at any time, let me know and we'll leave. No questions asked."

Although Thomas' crippled hand made even the simplest tasks much more difficult, he finished locking the door and turned off the porch light without any assistance. He put the house key back in his pocket and waddled over to talk to Roger and Bucky.

"So, what are the two of you going to do now?" inquired Thomas. "Are you going to call it a night, go talk to the police, or look around a little more?"

Bucky glanced over and saw Roger issue him a nod to reassure him that he was fine and ready to recommence their search.

"We're going to check a few more streets before we head back to the bar," answered Bucky. "Maybe Bob was riding his bike and got into a wreck. For all we know, he could be laying on the side of the road somewhere with a broken leg or a concussion. I really don't want to go back into town until I've exhausted every possible notion."

Thomas nodded his head in agreement. "Okay, but if you discover something, promise me that you'll give me a call. I know I might be a little rough around the edges, and I sometimes have a sarcastic personality, but I am genuinely concerned about Bob. I've known him nearly twenty-five years, and he's been an especially close friend of mine during that time. I never had any siblings of my own so I've always considered Bob like a brother to me. I really don't know what I would do if I lost my best friend, and I'm not in any hurry to get to that point either."

"Believe me, I know how it feels," Roger expressed with sadness. "But if we unearth any answers, we will surely let you know. You can count on it!"

The men all shook hands, and then Roger and Bucky climbed into the car and drove off. Thomas stood out front of his house and watched as they drove away. He glanced over to Bob's apartment again and noticed how desolate, dark, and lonely it looked— resembling an old, abandoned home.

A single tear dripped from Thomas' eye and rolled down his cheek as he stood motionless, remembering the enjoyable times he experienced with his childhood friend. He let out a sigh of grief and wiped the tear away.

Thomas had a feeling something wasn't quite right, and deep down, he *knew* his dear old friend was gone, never to be seen again. With a heavy heart, he walked inside his house and gently closed the door.

Chapter 7:

An Eerie Encounter

Nearly half an hour had passed since Bucky and Roger left the house of Thomas Parker. Since then, the fellows had been driving up and down the streets of Carthage in their continuing search for Bob Earle. Their initial trek down the streets produced no answers to their questions, but after much frustration, and their visit to Bob's apartment came up empty, they decided to perform a more thorough inspection.

Cruising around in Bucky's magenta Mustang, they continued to roam around town into the early morning hours, searching for any hint that might unravel this mystery. Both men remained intently focused on the task at hand as the sounds of the Rolling Stones bellowed from the car radio. It had been a long and disappointing night for both gentlemen, and as the night dragged on, their optimism began to waver.

Roger rubbed his eyes as he tried to fight off fatigue. He yawned as if he had worked in a hay field all day, and then he lifted his arms up over his head as he stretched. After that, Roger leaned over to turn down the radio so that he could speak without having to yell.

"I know you wanted to keep the radio pretty loud so that it'd help keep us awake and alert, but I'm starting to get a pounding headache."

"What do you mean?" Bucky cried out. "*Sympathy for the Devil* is one of the best songs ever written by the Rolling Stones. It's a classic!"

"Maybe so, but right now I'm in the mood to listen to something a little more soothing to help calm my nerves. I don't like thinking about the possibilities of what might've happened to Bob, and I keep getting more and more frustrated with every street we turn down that ends up being another failure."

Bucky reached down and shut the radio completely off. "Alright, I'm open to ideas. What other places do you think we should check out?"

"Well, I don't think there's any more we can do around here." uttered Roger. "We've checked up and down these streets twice and haven't come up with anything. It's getting really late, and I don't know where else we can look. What do you think we should do?"

"Perhaps you're right." Bucky said reluctantly. "Let's call it a night and head back into town. We can still keep a look out on our way back through. Where do you want me to drop you off?"

"How about we have a few more drinks at Kitty's Bar before we go home." Roger suggested. "While we're there, we can determine if anyone has further news on Bob's whereabouts."

"Alright," agreed Bucky as he looked at his watch. "I don't have to hurry back to the house, and I don't have any other plans for the rest of the night. Just so you know, we'll probably only have time for one cold beer before last call. But then again, one beer is better than none, and after that I will drive you home."

Roger glanced at Bucky and smirked. "Thanks for the offer, but I don't need a ride home from you tonight."

"You don't?" said Bucky, surprised and confused. "Do you plan on sleeping at the bar, or are you walking home?"

"Hopefully neither." he replied. "Nellie is supposed to be leaving her car at the bar for me to drive back to the house. That's what I meant earlier when I said she'd get a ride home from one of her friends."

"Oh, I guess I didn't catch on to what you meant. I was under the impression you two had either taken a cab to the bar or got a ride from somebody else." Bucky paused. "Although, you have to admit, that *is* quite nice of her to leave the car there for you. After all, she could've been miserable about the whole situation and told you walk home. Is it safe to assume that the two of you are getting along better than you were when we talked at the bar a couple of days ago?"

"I guess, but after tonight's little argument at the bar, I'm sure that things will go back to being as tense between us as they have been lately. It seems like we've had more bad days than good over the past couple of months."

A moment of silence passed as Bucky reflected on Roger's words. Then his voice got serious as he said, "Let me ask you a question. Do you love her?"

"How do I know?" Roger asked.

"What do you mean 'How do I know?'" Bucky spoke in a baffled tone. "If you love her, you just know because you feel it in your heart."

"Well, I like having her around. I mean, it's great that Nellie lives with me, and I surely don't want her to leave. We have some good times together, and we have our share of problems too. Every couple has its share of ups and downs, but overall, I think I'd be lost without her."

"Whoa, hold on just a minute." Bucky countered sharply. "That's a bullshit answer and you know it! You have to be fair to her; don't play with her emotions. I think it's time you two had *the* talk. She loves you, Roger, and if you do not have the same feelings, then you've got to tell her so."

"I do love her." answered Roger quietly. "But sometimes I'm not so sure I'm *in love* with her."

Bucky's tone turned from an excitable rush to a much softer and slower manner. "I feel for you, I really do. But what good is it doing either one of you if you're in a relationship just because you're *content* with the way things are. If there isn't that bond of love and affection that every relationship needs to survive, then it will never work out. If you weren't ready for a serious commitment, then why'd ya ask her to move into your house with you?"

Roger pondered over Bucky's question, trying to come up with an answer that was truthful, while being honest with himself at the same time. "I guess, in my mind I felt I needed somebody there to help me with the commitment it takes to maintain a home. And what better person to have living with me than the person I'm dating?"

"I hope there's more to your story than that."

"Yeah, there is. You see, after Dad got his new job and my parents moved into their new place in Syracuse, I was nervous. They entrusted me to take over the family homestead when I've *never* owned a house of my own or even rented an apartment before. I've never been good with responsibility, and I was sure that I wouldn't be able to handle the upkeep of the house since I'm rarely ever there."

"Yeah, but as far as I can tell, you've done a fairly decent job of maintaining the house and making sure the yard work gets done. You haven't let the house deteriorate, you haven't had to do any major repairs on it, nor have you disappointed your parents or ruin their judgment of you."

"That's why it's great Nellie lives in my house with me. During the times when college is in session, I stay in a dorm room during the week. That way, I don't have to commute back and forth wasting my time, and I save money on gas. I make sure I get all my studies done during the week so I can come home on the weekends. Also, it makes me feel better knowing she's there and making sure that the house doesn't get robbed or catch on fire while I'm gone."

"Do you have a problem with your house catching on fire?" Bucky asked while laughing out loud.

"No, but....hold on!" Roger quickly shouted as he took a second peek out the passenger side window. "I think I see a light down by the ferry service."

"That's impossible!" Bucky voiced, quite surprised. "They close the ferry service at seven o'clock and everyone should've left there hours ago. I mean, I can't imagine Mr. Ferr would still be there this late since he arrives so early in the morning. After all, their hours are from 7 am to 7 pm, and everyone I've talked to says that he works the whole twelve-hour shift. All day, every day of the week."

"Well, I don't care what time they close or what time the owners and employees are *supposed* to go home. All I know is that I definitely saw a light glowing down there."

"Are you sure?" asked Bucky. "You're positive you saw a light through *all* those trees and hedges. You do realize that there is a lot of thick brush down there, and it has to be a good two or three hundred yards from here to the ferry service."

"Yes, I realize that! But I'm absolutely positive about what I saw." Roger replied earnestly. "I think we should drive down there and see if anyone is around. If so, we can ask whoever it is if they have seen Bob at all today."

"That sounds like a good idea," said Bucky. "Well, let's turn around before we go any further and check it out."

Bucky pulled into the next driveway he came across and turned around, heading back toward the ferry service. Within moments, they approached the large wooden sign that hung on a post by the corner of the road that led to the water. On the sign was a line with an arrow pointing toward the trees and read: The Mephistis Pheles Ferry Service. Slowly, they headed down the dead end road that led to the ferry service.

The road leading to the waterfront was a gravel road with three or four small dilapidated sheds along the way. The largest one, which was located down by the water, was being used as a place to keep tools and supplies. At the very end of the gravel road was a rundown shack that Mr. Ferr and his assistant had fixed up somewhat and were using as their office. Although these buildings were weathered, unkempt, and in need of a coat of paint, their structures were sound and had solid roofs on them, making the buildings usable.

Because the buildings were still considered usable, the town council was debating whether or not to charge rent for them, or whether to let the ferry service use them for free. Of course, the Council wouldn't have enforced any such charges until the ferry service was established in the community and started turning a profit. That was going to be a topic at the next council meeting on Monday, and Bucky was already dreading going to it. He knew that Becky Taylor was adamantly opposed to charging the ferry service for any additional rent or taxes, and if she got her way, the town would end up losing more potential revenue.

While proceeding along the gravel road, it struck Bucky as strange that no street lights led down to the ferry, making it horribly dark and eerie at night. In fact, the place was so desolate that it was giving him the chills right then.

How childish, Bucky thought. *I must have watched too many horror movies as a kid and now I've spooked myself.* Then he shrugged off his fears and turned his attention back towards the radiant light that was beaming from the direction of the ferry service office.

As they continued further down the road and approached the light, they observed the shape of a man in a long coat and wide-brimmed hat outside, standing on the steps of the porch that led into the office. Bucky's car pulled into the yard and came to a stop. The headlights shined on the buildings, which were throwing shadows, and making it difficult to distinguish much about the area, or the ferry that was now being used to transport traffic across the river.

By now, Bucky was close enough to see that the unseemly figure he had been watching from afar was Louis Ferr, standing on the porch steps alone. Ferr was staring intently out into the darkness and completely ignored the automobile that just pulled up in front of him. Roger and Bucky peered at each other for a brief moment, and without saying a word, proceeded to exit the car.

"Hello there," said Bucky as they strolled over to Mr. Ferr. "I hate to disturb you so late at night, but I was wondering if you might be able to help us."

Mr. Ferr finally turned his attention away from the empty darkness in front of him and scrutinized the two gentlemen. "I will most certainly try." he stated with a grin. "I'm always eager to assist my fellow patron whenever I can. Tell me, what seems to be your dilemma tonight, fellows?"

"Well, my name is Dave Morgan and..."

Mr. Ferr interrupted Bucky before he could utter the rest of his sentence. "Oh yes, Mr. Morgan, I remember you. We met when I first brought my proposal to the town council and then again at the ceremony when I was awarded the contract for my ferry service."

"Yeah, I remember that, too." Bucky stated with a hint of displeasure in his voice.

Mr. Ferr drew a deep breath and said, "Lately I've heard around town that you have a problem with the character of my company. Your hesitation seems to stem from the fact I haven't provided you with a piece of paper listing all of my company's credentials and previous contracts."

"I'm confident that your credentials are fine, but as a member of the town council I have to look out for the best interest of the people in my community. I find it most difficult to give my undivided support to a company that doesn't supply us with a work history and references for us to complete a background check. I get very suspicious of people like that because I always feel as if they're trying to hide something."

"Not to worry, Mr. Morgan. I assure you that everything is in order. In fact, I've been working on putting together a very detailed portfolio of my work history, credentials, and accomplishments for the town council to peruse and keep on file."

Bucky crossed his arms and his voice got all business-like. "One of the stipulations for awarding you the contract was that you would be hiring local individuals for your business."

"That's correct, Mr. Morgan."

"Well, I'm having a hard time understanding how your company plans to help those individuals that are currently unemployed in our community. Even after you've been open for a few weeks, there's still only you and Steve Jensen listed as employees on your company's records."

"How do you know that?" inquired Mr. Ferr, with his face beginning to taut and tighten up.

"We keep a file on all businesses in the community so that we can monitor their performance to make sure they are presenting themselves in a respectable manner as well as staying within the guidelines of our business codes."

"Huh, isn't that interesting." Mr. Ferr muttered, somewhat startled. "Well, to answer your previous question, Mr. Morgan, I am working on hiring some additional employees."

"Oh, yeah? When?" Bucky uttered as he rolled his eyes.

"Once I start turning a profit, I will be able to expand my business a little bit at a time. Eventually, I would like to purchase two more ferryboats, both of which would be nearly twice the size as the one I currently own. I would have to hire a six or seven-man crew to operate each of the ferryboats, and I'd also like to employ a few more individuals to assist Mr. Jensen on our present ferry while I devote more time in the office concentrating on paperwork."

Bucky let out a huff. "Is that all?"

"On the contrary, Mr. Morgan. As time goes on, I'd like to expand our hours of operation and hire a couple of people to conduct all my clerical work so that I can ease myself into a well-deserved retirement."

Bucky shook his head as though he was not pleased with Mr. Ferr's answer. "That's a noteworthy goal to work toward, but how is your long-term plan going to help the community at the present time?"

Mr. Ferr tensed up, visibly annoyed by Bucky's badgering. "You seem to expect a lot from me, don't you? After all, your idea for a second bridge was going to be a project that took at least a year or more to complete."

Bucky narrowed his eyes. "Do you got a point, Ferr?"

"Well, that's how long it will take before I can get my ferry service running at our fullest capability. In total, there will be between 25 to 30 part-time and full-time employees when everything is finalized. If I'm not mistaken, that's more than most of the retail stores have on their staff here in town."

Roger, who had been standing idly by as they conversed about town business, began to get antsy. Finally, his impatience got the best of him, and he stepped in-between Bucky and Mr. Ferr as he blurted out, "I don't mean to be rude, Mr. Ferr, but we have just a few questions that we'd like to ask. I know it's late, and you're probably anxious for us to leave, so if we could have a few moments of your time, I promise that we'll quickly be on our way."

"I'm sorry," apologized Mr. Ferr as his expression softened. "I didn't intend to sidetrack you from your mission. By the way, I don't think we have been properly introduced. My name is Louis Ferr. And you are?"

Roger extended his hand out to shake. "It's a pleasure to finally meet you, sir. I've heard many things about you. My name is Roger Fasick."

Mr. Ferr's eyes unexpectedly lit up when Roger stated his name. "Oh, the pleasure is all mine, indeed. So, what questions do you have that I might be able to help you with?"

Roger took a prolonged, deep breath as Bucky turned away. "We're looking for a friend of ours. His name is Bob Earle, and we were wondering if you might have seen him either this afternoon or sometime this evening."

"You think *I* may have spotted him?" Mr. Ferr inquired.

Roger shrugged. "We believe he might've been going through this part of town on his way to Kitty's Bar, which would've been around three o'clock or so."

Mr. Ferr spoke in an unconvincingly concerned tone of voice. "Does he have any distinguishing marks, or do you happen to know what clothes he had on?"

"Um, no." Roger mumbled. "We're not sure what he was wearing, but he would've been riding an old, dingy looking, blue mountain bike. He's in his late thirties, about five feet eight inches tall, and has a slim build with short brown hair that he keeps parted to the side."

Mr. Ferr raised his brow. "No, I can't say that I have. I have been here all day long and have not seen anyone that would fit that description. Do you perhaps have a photo of him that I can glance at?"

"No, unfortunately we don't have one of those, either." Roger answered.

As Roger was talking to Mr. Ferr, Bucky canvassed the area and saw the shed where Louis Ferr kept his supplies. Although it was very dark and difficult to make out objects, Bucky noticed Mr. Ferr's assistant was over there, pushing what appeared to be a bike.

Somewhat startled, Bucky squinted his eyes and tried to focus on what Steve Jensen was doing—attempting to determine what type of bicycle it was. Then, he cautiously watched as Mr. Jensen rolled the bike into the shed and firmly closed the door behind him.

"Is there something out there in the darkness that has struck your interest, Mr. Morgan?" asked Mr. Ferr, grabbing Bucky's shoulder.

Bucky turned his attention away from the shed and looked directly at Mr. Ferr. The pupils in his eyes expanded as his heart pounded in his chest. "No, not really I suppose. I thought I saw someone walking around one of your sheds. But whatever or whoever it was, I don't see it anymore."

"That must be Steve; he is probably putting the rest of the tools away for the night. We have been working on the office walls and fixing the place up ever since we closed earlier tonight. We have so little free time to work on the place, so we usually have to stay late every night and do a little bit here and there. It's starting to come along quite nicely."

Bucky directed his attention over to Roger and stuffed his hands in his pocket, fidgeting with the car keys. "Well, I think we've taken up enough of Mr. Ferr's time, Roger. I think we should leave now before we wear out our welcome."

"Um yeah, you're probably right." commented Roger. He veered to face Mr. Ferr and once again shook his hand. "Thank you for talking with us. We appreciate your time and gracious attitude. I'm sure you have another long day ahead of you tomorrow and eager to call it a night and go home yourself."

"It was no trouble at all. I wish I could have been of more help to you. I am *especially* pleased that I got to meet you, Mr. Fasick. I hope we can chat again sometime under more favorable circumstances."

Roger simply nodded and walked away, heading straight to the car. Bucky, whose heart continued to race in his chest, hurried past both men without saying a word. His hands shook slightly as he was fumbling the keys out of his pocket. He got in his car, never once looking back at the tool shed, fearing that Mr. Ferr would notice his bizarre demeanor and become suspicious.

Roger casually entered on the passenger side and barely had time to close his door before Bucky quickly drove out of the parking lot. Several minutes passed as they rode along and Bucky still had not uttered a sound. His eyes were focused straight ahead and his driving had become somewhat erratic.

"Is there something wrong?" Roger asked. "Ever since we left the ferry service, you haven't said a word to me. It's like you're spaced out on drugs or in a trance."

"I don't know," Bucky said with hesitation. "I thought I witnessed something when I looked over to Ferr's supply shed. Maybe it's nothing, but I could swear I saw the assistant, Steve Jensen, rolling a bicycle into their shed. The same type of bike that Bob rides to work all the time."

"What?" shouted Roger. "Are you sure?"

"No, I'm not sure. Nevertheless, it makes me uneasy thinking that it very well *could* have been Bob's bike I saw. I've got this incessant feeling that Mr. Ferr knows more than he's telling us."

"So what are you saying?" Roger asked swiftly. "Do you think we should go back there and ask him what's in his tool shed?"

Bucky shook his head in disagreement. "Ferr would never admit to anything we asked him, and I'm positive he wouldn't let us look inside his shed...even *if* he had nothing to hide!"

Roger nodded, knowing what Bucky meant. "You're right. It didn't look as if there was any love lost between the two of you. Your conversation was starting to get a little intense when I stepped in, and probably could've gotten out of hand. By the tone of his voice and his facial expressions, I don't think Ferr would go out of his way to help you out. We can't just ignore what you saw. So what do we do now?"

"We should just stay away for now so that he doesn't become wary of our behavior. There's nothing that we can really do, especially tonight. We can call the police in the morning and ask them to check it out. If there *is* something hidden in that shed, or anywhere else on the property, they'll find it."

The remainder of the ride back into town was quiet. Neither of the two men knew exactly what to say. Even though they had explored other mysteries before together, they were now charting into unfamiliar territory. The aftermath of their visit to the waterfront had left an unsettling feeling in their stomachs.

It had become so late that by the time they returned to Liberty Street, Kitty's Bar was closed. Exhaustion covered their faces and heavy eyelids hung over their bloodshot eyes. Bucky drove up beside Nellie's car, which was sitting in the parking lot, stopping to let Roger out.

Bucky leaned over and rolled down the passenger side window. "I'll call the police in the morning," he said. "Go home and get some rest. I'll get a hold of you in the afternoon and let you know what they say."

"Okay, but I don't know how much rest I'm going to get. Hopefully, Nellie will be asleep when I get home so we don't get in another argument. After the night we've had, all I want to do is collapse into my bed and unwind."

Roger unlocked the car and got in while Bucky drove away. Searching aimlessly through town for Bob, without finding so much as a single clue, had Bucky bewildered and worried.

Meanwhile, the similarities of the night's events dredged up memories of another friend of his that disappeared. Knowing how this situation could affect Roger, Bucky feared that it might put Roger into a relapse of acute depression and push his fragile psyche over the limit.

Chapter 8:

Old Memories

It was late at night when Bucky finally returned home from his adventure with Roger. He rested in bed, with Cristina snuggled closely next to him, and found it extremely difficult to sleep. Fear of the intangible had followed him into a restless slumber. The clock on the dresser read 2:43 am; however, the night was anything short of peaceful as he repeatedly tossed and turned. Every night for the past couple weeks he had problems sleeping. That's when the recurring nightmares would start.

For years after his trip to Florida, Bucky had horrible nightmares about what happened to Paul Fasick. Maybe it was guilt that triggered his nightmares, but then again, maybe it was a repressed memory or a warning of some type trying to enter his subconscious. Whatever it was, each time Bucky closed his eyes he could hear Paul calling out to him in pain. And each time, Bucky would be unable to locate and help him.

The incessant nightmares seemed to fade away about two years ago, which was the same time he and Cristina started dating. Bucky always believed that it was her affection that got him over his grief. He thought he had learned to cope with the events that happened and was able to move on with his life, keeping his past buried.

However, something had changed within the past few weeks. The nightmares were returning, but not like before. Now they were more intense, even more graphic than the actual events that transpired. It started the same way as all of the other nightmares. Bucky was in his hotel room in Florida reliving the events of the last night that he ever saw Paul alive.

Bucky relaxed on the hotel bed, reading an issue of MAD magazine. Next to him was Paul Fasick, a 5'11" hunk with crystal blue eyes and hair so blonde, it almost appeared white. Besides being Bucky's best friend and childhood neighbor, Paul also happened to be the person Bucky was sharing a hotel room with during their spring break in Florida.

Paul was rummaging through his suitcase, sorting out his clothes that he was going to wear out at the nightclub. "Are you sure you don't want to come with me tonight?" he asked, splashing some cologne on his neck and chest. "We only have three more days down here, and then it's back home to the cold weather."

"Yeah, I'm sure," Bucky replied. "We've been partying every night since we arrived here, and I'm running low on energy—and money. I'm going to take it easy tonight and unwind; maybe I'll go for a swim in the hotel pool or sit in the steam room for an hour or so."

Paul finished getting dressed and positioned his suitcase on the floor next to his bed. "If it's the money you're concerned about, Bucky, then don't worry. I'll pay for your drinks tonight. I just want ya to have a good time while we're on spring break."

"Yeah, yeah. Whatever." said Bucky.

"Seriously, bud. This might be the last time we get to go on vacation for a long time. After college, we'll be too busy with our jobs, dating women, and making money to pay off our college loans. We won't be able to even *think* about going somewhere like this for a quite a while!"

"I know, Paul, and trust me; I *am* having a good time down here." Bucky insisted. "I don't want you or anyone else to be spending any money on me. I'm not a charity case; I just want to save a little cash for the rest of the trip."

"For what?"

"I still have to pick up some souvenirs for my folks, and I'd like to play a round of golf on one these awesome courses before we go. I tell ya, we don't have any place back home that can even compare to the style or quality of golf courses down here."

"Alright, stay here, but it won't be the same without you," Paul expressed with disappointment. "How about I go out for a couple hours, and then I'll come back so we can hang out together?"

Bucky raised his brow. "Oh?"

"We'll go down to the hotel bar, have a few frosty beers, and shoot a couple games of darts. I just want to go check out that club we saw yesterday when we were on the other side of town."

"Okay, that's sounds fine." Bucky said, shaking his head in agreement. "But if you're going to that club, then how are you going to get there? Do you plan on taking a cab all the way to the other side of town? If you do, you'll spend half of your drinking money on the cab fare alone."

Paul slumped down on the bed and tied his shoes. When he finished, he walked over to the coat rack to grab his jacket and snatched a cigarette from the inside pocket, acting as though he was not paying attention to Bucky. "I'll just take the ferry over there," he stated casually. "It costs less anyways, and I don't have to leave the guy a tip."

"Just watch yourself. I got the feeling that old ferryman was kind of pissed at you for making fun of him the last time we were there. He might try to start an argument or maybe refuse to let you on the ferry altogether. That guy was *very* creepy looking and might even be dangerous."

"How do *you* know he was creepy looking?" questioned Paul. "He was wearing a broad-brimmed hat that was pulled down so low, you couldn't even see his face. I think the passengers on the ferry were creepier looking than he was. All they did was stare straight ahead with a blank expression on their faces. It looked as though the ferryman was transporting an entire group of drug addicts, since their skin was so pale and their eyes looked as though they hadn't slept in weeks."

A slow smile spread over Bucky's face. "Yeah, I remember the passengers on the ferry. You kept harassing them and saying how they all looked like zombies."

Paul chuckled. "Yeah, they sure did."

"That may be, but I think your rude comments about the passengers was beginning to annoy the ferryman. And if you decide to go back there, I would watch what you say around him. That old man warned you never to come back there, and then he said that someday your tongue would eventually get you into trouble."

"He was just acting irate because I was drunk and annoying," Paul responded as if unconcerned. "I'll go down there to talk to him and smooth everything over. After I work my charm on him, he will totally forget about the other night. Hell, I might even get a discount on my fare."

Bucky swung his feet off the bed and stood up. His smile disappeared as his expression and tone of voice turned somber. "Believe me, he looks like a man who means what he says. I think his whole demeanor seemed kinda peculiar and his presence gave me the chills. After all, his face was almost completely obscured by the shadow of his hat, and he was wearing a long black trench coat over his tall, slender frame. Even his raspy voice was unnerving."

"Don't worry, I'm not going to act like a jackass towards him or anyone else. I only get like that when I've been drinking a lot, and I don't plan on having too many drinks tonight. Maybe just four or five beers to go along with a couple Jack Daniels and colas."

"Yeah, it sure sounds like you plan on having an easy night," Bucky said sarcastically. "Most people would be staggering after that much alcohol!"

"Well, what can I say, I have a high tolerance." laughed Paul. "Besides, I learned my lesson the other night when we were bar-hopping. Do you remember what happened?"

"I most certainly do."

"I still cringe when I think about it," Paul said as his body shivered. "I ended up making-out with an awfully hideous-looking woman...and to add injury to insult, I shut my hand in the door as I was leaving the bar!"

"You're right! That was, without exception, the drunkest I've seen you since our high school graduation. Although, the girl I found you kissing at graduation was just as ugly, or worse, than the one at the bar. In fact, I think she even had more facial hair than you. If it weren't for the fact that she looked like a troll, your girlfriend would've probably dumped you!"

"Probably, but since Celeste was laughing nearly as hard as you were, I think she forgave me out of pity more than anything else."

Paul paused as he squirted some styling gel into the palm of his hand and began running his fingers through his hair.

"Alright, enough of bringing up my most embarrassing moments," he continued. "I'm heading into town, but I should be back in a couple hours. Just make sure you're ready to go down to the lobby for some brewskis by the time I return, okay? I am *not* walking down there with you if you're wearing your old, worn-out gray sweat pants again. Now, that's *my* definition of what is embarrassing."

"Fine, have it your way! But I'm not paying for the first round of beers this time. You still owe me for bailing you out of that mess with the ferry owner. If it weren't for me, you probably would've had to swim back to the hotel. I think that deserves a few beers on your part...and a free meal, too."

"Let's not over exaggerate the situation," Paul replied. "*Maybe* it's worth a few beers, but don't hold your breath about getting a free meal. I might be nice and buy you a bag of pretzels though."

Until recently, Bucky's dream had always progressed into the events that happened after Paul's disappearance, such as being questioned by the police and making the phone call to Paul's parents to tell them their son was missing. Those were the most grueling few weeks of his life, and on top of that, he had to come home to face everyone at the funeral and try to keep up with his studies for college.

Bucky always felt as if people looked down on him, or at least partially blamed him for the events that transpired. Those thoughts were the result of the negative gossip spread behind his back, and also because of his own insecurities about how he was unable to find Paul or help provide the police with any information in their search and investigation.

Lately, Bucky's nightmare had taken a new, strange twist. After Paul left their hotel room that evening, a bizarre and uneasy quietness overtook the room. Bucky stood alone in the room and the lights began to dim and flicker. An unusual fog started to seep into the room from underneath the outside door. He could hear what could only be described as chanting coming from outside as he felt his palms begin to sweat and his throat become dry.

Sounds of hissing and shrieking echoed all around Bucky as glowing red eyes surrounded him. A nauseous sensation made the room appear to spin around before his eyes. Scratching and pounding on the walls sounded like cannons in his ears and dropped Bucky to his knees with sharp pain.

Suddenly, an unusual voice of a man could be heard mumbling; a voice that sounded so close, the person could have been standing outside Bucky's hotel door. The voice muttered something so soft, it could barely be heard.

Step by step, Bucky gradually crept over and placed his ear to the door. For an instant, the man's voice seemed to fade away. However, as Bucky started to back up, the voice yelled in a booming, unnerving voice, "***You're Next!***"

Bucky's jaw dropped and the door burst open. An intensely bright light shone through, blinding Bucky while a loud, shrieking laugh came through the doorway.

"*AHHH*!!!" Bucky screamed as he woke up, breathing rapidly and drenched in sweat.

Bucky's scream awoke Cristina, who was sleeping next to him. "What's wrong, honey?" Cristina inquired as she turned on the lamp next to the bed and rolled over towards him. "Oh my god, you're shaking! Did you have another nightmare?"

Bucky sat up and wiped the sweat from his face. "Yeah, I did," he answered, catching his breath. "I'm sorry I woke you."

"I don't care about that." she voiced with worry. "I'm more concerned that you're alright. Was it the same dream as before?"

"Well, it started out the same as it always does. I was back in Florida with Paul, reenacting everything that happened the night he disappeared. But the dream ended different this time. There was chanting and all these red, glowing eyes surrounding me. It was as if something evil was trying to crash into my hotel room to take me. I heard scratching on the windows and a man laughing in a freakish voice outside my door. It was so strange, and yet, it all seemed so real."

"You should go see a medical doctor about these nightmares, or maybe a psychiatrist," Cristina suggested. "Someone must be able to help you get over these nightmares so you can get a peaceful sleep again. After all, it doesn't just affect you anymore. It affects me, too. Every night that you have these dreams, it wakes me up...and I get more and more worried about you."

"I don't need to see some shrink!" he roared defensively. "I'm *not* crazy. I don't know why these dreams have come back all of a sudden. Things have been excellent in my life, and I thought I was over the emotional guilt and pain which remained from Paul's disappearance."

Upset over Bucky's harsh tone of voice, Cristina threw off the covers and jumped out of bed. She paced back and forth while she glared at him and said, "Apparently you're *NOT* over the emotional guilt, or whatever it is, that keeps you up at night."

Bucky turned his head away.

"It's obvious to me you still have some issues to deal with, or you wouldn't be waking up at all hours of the night screaming over circumstances which happened many years ago."

"I may not know the reason for the reemergence of my nightmares, but I don't need to seek professional help to solve my problems," he snapped. "Maybe the stress from work has triggered some of my repressed memories."

Cristina let out a huff but did not speak.

"I don't mean to get all defensive," Bucky continued, "but when you mention a psychiatrist, it upsets me. I went to see one after I got back from Florida. I only did it for my parents' sake because they thought I was having a nervous breakdown. During the two months of sessions I had with the guy, all he did was make me feel inadequate around him."

"How so?"

"He had the audacity to insinuate that I wasn't really concerned about finding Paul while I was in Florida. His reasoning was that I looked like the typical college guy who only thought about partying and probably didn't have my friend's well-being on my list of priorities. I got pissed off and gave him a piece of my mind before I stormed out of his office. I swore I'd never go back to see him or any other psychiatrist again."

"I'm sorry," she whispered modestly. "I didn't know."

Bucky's voice mellowed. "I'm sorry, too. I've never told you that story before, and there's no way you could've known how I would react to your suggestion. I realize you mean well, and I shouldn't have jumped down your throat like that. I guess I should be more open to you about my past."

Cristina calmed down and hopped back into bed. She pulled the covers over her feet and legs and fluffed her pillow without saying a word.

After she got comfortable, she rolled back over so they were face to face and said, "I knew you shouldn't have gone with Roger tonight looking around for Bob. I'm sure that thinking about another missing friend probably brought back comparisons of how hard you searched for Paul. That's what might have triggered your nightmare tonight."

"You're probably right," admitted Bucky.

"I know you consider Bob a good friend of yours; one that you've known for a long time. I also know you don't want to go through the pain of losing someone by unexplainable circumstances all over again. That's the only reason why I brought up the topic of going to a psychiatrist. Trust me when I say that I do *not* think you're crazy. I love you and I only want to help in any way I can."

"You may be right," he agreed reluctantly. "Maybe it's time I admitted to myself that I need some help. I thought I could handle my problems all by myself, but I guess I was wrong."

Cristina put her hand on his head and stroked his hair. "You don't need to handle your problems by yourself; I'm here for you any time you want to talk. There's no longer a reason for you to feel as though you have to shut people out of your life or bottle up your emotions. I just wish you would open up more to me."

"That's something I plan to work on," smiled Bucky. "But right now, I'm tired and I'm not really in the mood to talk anymore tonight. I'm exhausted both physically and mentally. It was a long day at work, and it has been an even longer night. With searching all over town for Bob and having my nightmares creep back once again, I'm in no shape for a lengthy discussion right now. Let's just try to get some rest and talk about this in the morning."

Cristina gave Bucky a passionate kiss before she rolled back over on her side of the bed and turned off the light. Bucky laid silently still on his backside with his eyes open, staring up toward the ceiling. He knew he was too anxious and distressed to fall back to sleep. However, with the scare he had just experienced, he was also hesitant about whether or not he even *wanted* to try to get some rest. The images of his nightmares were too intense for him to endure, and he knew that if he closed his eyes, he was inviting those memories back to inflict more pain and heartache.

For the next several hours until daylight approached, Bucky's eyes did little more than blink. His eyes shifted back and forth, perusing the shadows of his room. Sweat remained on his brow as he listened to every tick of the wall clock, the creaks in the floorboards, and the tree branch that was scratching at his bedroom window.

Chapter 9:

Blind Judgment

Around nine o'clock the following morning, Bucky groggily sat up and threw his feet over the edge of his bed. Dark circles and heavy bags rested under his eyes and his feet were prickly with pain as he walked to his bedroom door. He lethargically stepped into his raggedy gray bunny slippers and wrapped himself in his tattered bathrobe.

As he staggered downstairs, Bucky observed that Cristina left the coffeemaker on with half a pot of coffee still brewing inside. He grabbed his favorite Scooby-Doo mug out of the cupboard and poured himself a cup. Minutes passed while he sipped his coffee, rubbing the sleep from his eyes and stretching the stiffness out of his limbs. Once he livened up a bit and had his bearings, Bucky decided to call the police station.

After three rings, a gruff voice answered the phone. "Carthage Police Department; this is Sergeant Kenneth Johnson speakin'. Whatta ya want?"

Bucky was appalled by Sergeant Johnson's candor and was apprehensive to say a word. For a moment Bucky debated whether or not he should just hang up the phone altogether, but inevitably, he decided to respond to Ken's blunt question instead.

"Hey, Ken," answered Bucky, hesitantly. "This is Bucky Morgan. I wanted…"

"Listen, *Dave*." interrupted Ken. "Just because you're a member of the town council doesn't mean you can call me 'Ken.' You refer to me as 'Sergeant Johnson,' just like everyone else."

"Alright, Sergeant Johnson." Bucky replied in a low, almost embarrassed tone. "Whatever you say."

Ken's voice mellowed somewhat. "That's better. Now then, what can I do ya for today, Bucky?"

"Well, to begin with, Roger Fasick and I searched the town last night looking for Bob Earle. He didn't show up for work yesterday, and there was no sign of him at his apartment."

"Yeah, we're aware of Bob Earle's disappearance." Ken paused for a moment. "By the way, how do you *know* there was no sign of Mr. Earle at his place? You didn't do any 'breaking and entering,' did you?"

"No, nothing like that." said Bucky, fumbling for words. "I, err, we talked to Bob's neighbor, Thomas Parker, and he mentioned that Bob hadn't been around."

Ken seemed suspicious of Bucky's answer but did not press the issue any further. "Yeah, well...maybe you're tellin' the truth, but from now on I suggest you let the police handle things and not get in the way of our investigation. I know how you and Roger like to stir up trouble."

"I wouldn't try to disrupt your investigation," stated Bucky. "In fact, I want to help you in any way that I can."

"Really? How can you do that?" Ken inquired. "Do ya got some crucial information to share?"

"Quite possibly. You see, while Roger and I were driving around, we saw a light down by the waterfront and made a quick stop by The Mephistis Pheles Ferry Service."

"And...?"

"We took a quick drive down there and saw an individual outside of the ferry office. It turned out to be Louis Ferr."

"So far, Bucky, I'm not impressed."

"I'm not finished, Ken. We then proceeded to go over to ask if he'd seen Bob Earle at anytime throughout the day. Although we only had a brief encounter with the ferry owner, I have reason to believe that Louis Ferr knows something about Bob's sudden vanishing."

"Is this a gut feeling," Ken said with a huff, "or did you call someone at the Psychic Friends Hotline?"

Bucky was flabbergasted, taken aback by Ken's sarcasm and rudeness. "Did I do something to offend you, Sergeant? Is there some reason why you have a bad attitude and are being condescending to me?"

"As a matter of fact there is," Ken stated. "You see, I received an anonymous call this morning and was tipped off that you might be inclined to harass Mr. Ferr. The caller also informed me that you harbor a strong dislike for Louis Ferr and would come up with *any* reason to have him investigated."

A numbing shock flowed through Bucky as Ken's accusations struck a nerve. "I don't know what you're trying to pull, Sergeant, but I did *NOT* harass anyone, and I don't make a habit of calling up the police department to make bogus allegations!"

Bucky's voice became insistent.

"You know as well as I do, Sergeant Johnson, that I have *never* done anything as malicious as try to get someone in trouble or arrested on false pretenses. The fact of the matter is that Roger and I were down to the ferry service for one reason and one reason only. That was to try to find our friend…nothing else."

"I figured you'd say that, Morgan," Sergeant Johnson grumbled, unmoved by Bucky's pleas. "That's why I took the liberty of calling Louis Ferr early this morning so I could get his side of the story. He mentioned that you were at the ferry service pretty late last night, and from what I understand, you engaged in a shouting match with the old ferryman. I guess you thought it'd be fun to put Mr. Ferr on the spot and play 'twenty-questions' about his business and his background, isn't that right?"

"That's not what happened at all! In fact, I'm calling because I want *you* to check *him* out!"

"Nice try, kid, but I'm just not buying it. I'm going to say this one time, Bucky. Stay away from the ferry service and leave the investigating to me!"

Bucky's face and ears were hot with anger but he remained silent.

"By the way, Bucky," continued Ken, "you many think you're someone 'special' in this town, but your menial accomplishments and accolades mean nothing to me. I don't care if you are on the town council, if I hear of any more complaints of harassment charged against you, I will personally pick you up and bring you to the station."

Sergeant Johnson slammed down his receiver, leaving Bucky with a sore eardrum and an annoying beeping in his ear.

After Bucky hung up the phone, his heart pounded in his chest with anger. A rush of adrenaline flowed though his body, and he was eager to get out of the house and blow off some steam. He took a quick shower, said goodbye to Cristina as he quickly snatched a granola bar from the kitchen, and took off for a drive in his Mustang to relieve some of his frustration.

For over an hour, Bucky blithely roamed the town streets, sorting out some thoughts. Then, as he was passing the Carthage Library, he slowed down and pulled over to the curb. Bucky felt the tension swelling inside himself and decided he needed to talk to someone he trusted and could confide in. Since Roger was working some overtime for his archaeology job on Fort Drum and unavailable for the day, Bucky opted to go inside the library and chat with Bryan Harsha.

Bryan was a small, rather meek individual who still lived at home with his mother even though he was almost thirty years old. Mr. Harsha was always immaculately dressed in formal business pants and freshly starched short-sleeved dress shirts with a neck tie, even in the middle of summer.

Bryan wore his hair parted on the side, just like he had always done since he was in elementary school, and he wore the same thick, bulky style of eyeglasses that he has sported since he was four years old. Always clean-shaven and neat in appearance, Bryan was often ignored by others because of his inability to fit in. On other occasions, he would be taken advantage of by his so-called friends because of his good nature and eagerness to please people.

It was evident from his conduct and shyness that Bryan had lived a sheltered life, which was probably due to growing up in a small town and being raised by only one parent—and an overprotective mother at that. While as a child, his mother rarely let him go outdoors to play with all the other little kids in town. And because he never developed social skills or learned how to interact with other children, when he got older, he found it difficult to intermingle with the rest of the crowd his age.

Although Bryan was considered the town nerd, he was also well liked and could be counted on and trusted with anything big or small. Bryan worked primarily as the town librarian, and he was unusually knowledgeable in the supernatural and folklore. He was also a research expert and knew exactly where to locate resources and find anything you needed to know. Little did anyone know, but Bryan's superb skills in these areas would payoff for the entire town in the near future.

Bryan was kneeling down in front of a large book shelf with a Snickers candy bar in hand and a small wooden cart sitting next to his side, full of literary works stacked upon it. Bucky made a beeline over to his pal and grabbed him by the shoulders, startling Bryan and making him jump nearly two feet in the air.

"Very funny, Bucky." Bryan said, not amused by Bucky's antics. "You almost made me knock over my cart of books, and I would've had to reorganize them again."

Bucky let out a chuckle. "I'm sorry, Bryan. I didn't mean to scare you." Bucky paused; his tone became solemn and his face became expressionless. "Hey, Bryan, I don't suppose you heard about Bob Earle? He's a bartender in town that vanished yesterday."

"Actually, yes I did. I overheard some of the people who came in today talking about it. I don't know him, personally, but it is truly a shame to hear of misfortunes such as that. I don't wish bad things and mishaps to happen to anybody."

"I agree; it really *is* a very sad situation." Just then, while glancing around at all the books, Bucky remembered telling Roger that he was going to do some research on the town's history. "Hey, Bryan, are there any archived news articles in this library that would give details to some of the strange events that have happened in Carthage?"

"Maybe." Bryan replied, hesitant and unsure. "Check the media center on the second floor. They have a small room towards the back called 'Local History' and it is filled with old articles on Carthage's past. Most of the old newspapers we held in reserve have been recently converted to microfilm."

"Great! I think I'll check it out right now and let you finish your work."

Bryan nodded his head to concur. "Okay. The last thing I have to do is finish putting these books back on the shelves by the time my shift ends at three o'clock. If you're not back by the time I finish, I'll come up and find you."

Bucky went upstairs and entered the media center. He made his way to the Local History room and sat down in front of the microfilm machine, turning on the screen as he sorted through a box of microfilm labeled '*Carthage Republican Tribune Archives.*' For two hours he went through one microfilm after another, going further and further back into Carthage's long history. Then, something caught his attention.

At approximately twelve minutes after three, Bryan finished his work downstairs and put his materials away before making his way to the break room. After Bryan put his nametag in his locker, he finished logging his hours on his timecard before heading up to the second floor to locate Bucky. He entered the Local History room in the media center and saw Bucky sitting in front of the microfilm machine, deep in concentration.

Bryan walked over, sat down next to him, and asked, "Have you found anything yet?"

Bucky pointed to the news article he printed off from the microfilm machine. "I found one account that detailed circumstances which could be categorized as 'weird.'"

"Really, what was that?"

Bucky started to skim the piece of paper once again. "It was dated from sometime in April of 1955," he explained to Bryan. "A reporter for the *Carthage Tribune* by the name of 'V. Dane' wrote an editorial that caught my attention. I'm lucky I found it at all. The article was buried in the bottom corner of the back page."

"Could it be categorized as strange?"

"Most definitely! His report speculated about a fire in Carthage where a Grim-Reaper-type individual was spotted."

"A Reaper, huh?" Bryan muttered, scratching his head. "That's eerie; I've never heard that story before."

"Neither have I." Bucky shrugged his shoulders and placed the paper down on the table. "Anyway, that was about the gist of the entire piece. There was no mention of any ferrymen, ferry services, or serial killers."

"Did you say that was the *only* article you found regarding strange happenings?"

"Yes it was. It appears as though there were more articles written by this guy—possibly about the mysterious fires Carthage has suffered, peculiar figures such as the Reaper, or other strange phenomena...but it seems that all of the other articles the reporter wrote during that time period have been removed."

Bucky pointed to the screen where a large, vacant white space remained. "Only the titles and the signature line at the bottom of the screen are left of those articles."

"I wonder who would've done that," Bryan thought aloud. "And for what reason, too."

Bucky didn't respond. Instead, he looked at his wristwatch, taking notice that it read 3:45 pm.

He turned his attention over to Bryan and said, "Hey Bryan, how about we clean up and get out of here? I want to find Roger and tell him about this article. I've never heard of this incident before, but maybe he has. It's possible that the strange events back then, as well as what's been going on lately, are somehow connected."

"I'll ride along with you; however, I doubt those two events are connected. The event in the 1950s had to do with a scorching, mysterious blaze in town and a Reaper-like individual that roamed the streets...*on land*. The person in question at present is a ferryman, and his peculiarity stems from the *water*."

"Yeah, maybe you're right. But I'd still like to tell Roger about it and ask him if he's discovered any additional information on 'The Mephistis Pheles Ferry Service' during his research. He told me he's heard of that name before and has stacks of college textbooks to thumb through to find anything he wants."

"He likes research, too, huh?" Bryan said, mulling over some thoughts. "Well, if he ever needs a hand, maybe I should offer my services."

"Well, you can tell him that when we find him."

"Good enough," Bryan stated with a smile. "So, where are we going?"

Bucky stood up, folded the article in half, and placed it in his back pocket. "Over to Kitty's Bar," he told Bryan. "I think Roger will probably be there; he usually stops for at least one beer after he gets out of work."

"Oh," said Bryan in an expressionless tone.

"Is there something wrong with that? You didn't sound very enthusiastic when I mentioned Kitty's Bar. Are you disappointed?"

"It's just that I've never been to that bar before." Bryan paused, looking down at the ground and shuffling his feet. "Actually, Bucky, I've never been inside *any* bar before. My mother doesn't hold those places in the highest regards...and I've never had any friends ask me to join them anyway."

Noticing Bryan's reluctance and anxiety, Bucky spoke in a comforting voice. "You don't have to go if you'll feel uncomfortable, Bryan. However, if you're interested, I'd really like you to come along."

Bryan pulled another chocolate bar from his back pocket and grinned. "Forget I said anything, Bucky. You can count me in."

Both men hurriedly picked up the material, gathered their belongings, and departed for Kitty's Bar. Bryan's eyes brightened up when they approached Bucky's car, and he was as giddy as a small child with a pocketful of candy once he entered the vehicle.

"This is awesome!" Bryan exclaimed, checking out Bucky's car.

Bucky was in awe, surprised by Bryan's reaction. "You really like my car?"

"You bet! My mom and grandmother are trying to restore one just like this in our garage. My mom even has this exact color in mind!"

Bucky rolled his eyes and exhaled profoundly. "Roger's right," he mumbled to himself. "Maybe I *should* repaint my car."

Bryan and Bucky traveled speedily through the residential streets until they approached Liberty Street. When the two men finally arrived at Kitty's Bar, Bucky parked his Mustang alongside the curb in front of the bar, but Bryan did not exit the car.

Bucky climbed out of the car, leaving the door open as he stretched his arms over his head and took a whiff of the lilacs that were growing on the nearby lawns.

Then, noticing that his passenger had not yet departed from the vehicle, Bucky bent down and asked, "Are you alright, Bryan?"

"Yeah," he answered, taking one deep breath after another. "Just give me a second to gather my thoughts...and courage."

Bucky smirked. "Take your time, pal. I'll wait for you."

Bryan closed his eyes and slowly stepped out of the car. He took a purple-colored handkerchief from his back pocket that appeared quite worn and wiped the beads of sweat off his forehead and palms before walking toward the entrance of Kitty's Bar.

Once the men were inside, they were instantly bombarded by the foul smell of stale beer, stale smoke, and sweaty clothes. It was the smell of any typical bar, but it was also a smell that Bryan was unfamiliar with...and the odor did not appear to agree with him. Bryan's face turned green and blue; his stomach suddenly became queasy.

After a quick perusal, they saw Miss Kitty and part-time bartender Tim Matthews behind the bar, restocking the liquor cabinet and beer fridge.

Unlike Bob Earle's sociable personality, Tim Matthews was a quiet individual who rarely chatted with the customers; for he was distant, standoffish, and kept mainly to himself. He had a slight resemblance to James Dean and looked the part of a wild handsome rebel. His hair had a golden hue, which he kept short and spiked up all over. A Marlboro cigarette always dangled from behind his left ear, and he sometimes held a matchstick in his mouth for a toothpick.

Tim had only moved to town a couple of months ago and very little was known about him, not even his age. Although he was friendly and polite, he tended to avoid answering questions when the topic of conversation involved him, his past, or his family.

After several seconds passed, Bucky stepped over to the bar and sat down on a stool; then he motioned for Bryan to join him. Bryan's stomach settled and, subsequently, the color in his face returned to normal.

Miss Kitty felt the presence of someone behind her and whirled around, directing her attention to the gentlemen who were now sitting in front of her.

"Hey, Miss Kitty," Bucky said in a solemn tone. "Have you heard any further news on Bob's disappearance?"

Miss Kitty shook her head and grimaced. "Nothing new, Bucky."

"I'm sorry to hear that, ma'am," Bryan butted in.

Miss Kitty shifted her attention to the gentleman sitting beside Bucky. She took one gander at Bryan Harsha and immediately became smitten with the scrawny man who wore thick eyeglasses and greased his hair to one side.

"Who's your friend, Bucky?" Miss Kitty asked, winking at Bryan and smiling from ear to ear.

Bucky chuckled slightly. "This is Bryan Harsha, Miss Kitty. We serve on the town council together."

Miss Kitty extended her hand to shake. "Pleased to meet you, Mr. Harsha." she said, blushing. "I'm Kitty Dunn, the owner of this place." Then she pointed to the man behind her. "This is Tim Matthews; he's one of the bartenders who work here."

Bryan's face became flushed, but he could not take his eyes off from Miss Kitty. Equally smitten with her, his heart began racing wildly. "It's good to meet the both of you, ma'am."

"Be gentle on him, Miss Kitty," Bucky voiced with a laugh. "He's never been in a bar before."

"You haven't?" Miss Kitty responded with surprise. She quickly took off her apron, came out from behind the bar, and took Bryan by the arm. "Here, let me show you around my humble little tavern."

Bryan looked at Bucky, not sure what to think or say. Bucky gave him a smile and nodded in approval as the two new acquaintances walked away. While Bryan was chatting with Miss Kitty next to the jukebox, Bucky moseyed over to the other end of the bar and plopped down on a stool.

Bucky placed a napkin in front of him and yelled out, "Hey, Tim. Do you have a second?"

"I suppose so," answered Tim, making his way over to Bucky's end of the bar. "What can I get for you?"

"I'd like a bottle of Budweiser if you don't mind."

"Coming right up!" Tim bellowed.

While Tim was reaching into the refrigerator, Bucky asked him, "By the way, I was wondering if Roger Fasick has been in here this afternoon."

"Nope, not while I've been here today. Why ya wanna know?"

"Oh, nothing. I wanted to discuss something with him regarding our venture through town last night."

Tim shook his head and the cheerfulness that had been in his voice was gone. "Oh, that's right. You and Roger went searching for Bob Earle last night. Did you find anything out of the ordinary?"

Bucky wavered before answering. "That depends. I don't want to jump to any conclusions just yet, but something at the ferry service didn't seem right."

"The ferry service?" inquired Tim. "Is that where the two of you went?"

"Not at first. We checked Bob's apartment, but didn't find anything there. But on the way back to the bar..." Bucky stopped in mid sentence, unsure of how much he should say. "Look, I don't want to go into specifics, but let's just say I believe some weird things have been occurring at The Mephistis Pheles Ferry Service."

Tim's eyes widened. "Really? Now that *is* interesting, isn't it?"

Bucky took a large gulp of his cold, frosty beer. Just then, Bryan came up and tapped Bucky on the shoulder. "Well, are you ready to go? I should be getting home soon. Mother will worry if I'm late for dinner."

"Alright, Bryan." Bucky said, taking another large swig from his bottle. "I'm finished here anyway."

Bucky stood up, placed a five-dollar bill on top of the bar, and headed towards the exit.

Tim Matthews smiled as the gentlemen left the bar. He cocked his head to one side and whispered, "So, there're strange things happenin' down at the ferry service, huh? I might have to check that out."

Chapter 10:

Questionable Intentions

Almost a week passed since Bob Earle's unexplainable vanishing. His disappearance was no longer a matter of front-page interest, but it remained a subject of discussion for Roger and Bucky. In fact, there were very few people around town that seemed remotely concerned about what happened to Bob, or the strange and abrupt way in which he became missing. Maybe it was because Bob Earle was not considered to be part of the upper crust in the small community, and nobody seemed to pay much attention to him anyway. On the other hand, maybe it was because so many folks in town had become unexplainably calloused to the feelings of others lately.

The police were not able to uncover any leads or potential scenarios to explain what could have transpired. They never did get a search warrant to look inside Mr. Ferr's tool shed either...not that Bucky was surprised all that much. In Bucky's opinion, it seemed as if the police department was deliberately turning a blind eye to whatever actions Mr. Ferr was doing—no matter how suspicious in nature they appeared to be.

After his conversation with Ken Johnson ended rather disastrously, Bucky became stunned and curious regarding why Sergeant Johnson and the rest of the police department had been so insistent that he stay away from Mr. Ferr. Bucky began to wonder what kind of power Louis Ferr had that made everyone in town defend him. And with each day that passed, it seemed as though Ferr's influence was stretching wider and growing more powerful.

Bucky decided he would continue his own investigation no matter what the police, or anyone else, thought about it. Although, now he realized that he would need to be more careful in the future.

It was a sweltering Thursday morning, with the temperature pushing 80 degrees and Bucky was sitting at his desk with a small, square-shaped desk fan blowing in his face. At only ten o'clock in the morning, Bucky already had a splitting headache, brought upon primarily from his lack of sleep over the past few weeks. A bottle of aspirin and a tall glass of ice cold water sat in front of him as he leaned back, rubbing his temples.

Becky Taylor walked hastily into Bucky's office and threw a large, accordion-style brown folder down on his desk. "Well, you can stop pestering Mr. Ferr about his lack of background information," she stated brusquely.

"What do you mean?" Bucky asked as he tipped forward in his chair and started to open the folder.

"There's his work history for the past ten years. Everything you *need* to know about him is in that folder. It contains all of his records of former employers, their addresses and phone numbers. He has also supplied a complete list of personal and professional references to describe his character, reputation, and work ethics."

Bucky flipped through a few of the front pages, appearing quite fascinated. "Wow, this portfolio really *is* quite detailed!" he remarked, very stunned. "I'm actually impressed that he took the time and effort to be so thorough."

Becky observed him thumb through the material closely, examining the expression on Bucky's face. "If you look toward the back of the folder, you will see that he even provided a listing of names of all the people that formerly worked for him and how much they were paid."

Several moments of silence went by as Bucky flipped carefully through the pages of the folder. Eventually, after several long minutes of silence, he lifted his head up and smiled at Becky. "I am very thankful you took the time to get this information for me, Becky. I know how busy you are and realize this must've been quite an inconvenience for you to obtain."

Bucky's compliments and courtesy softened Becky's demeanor along with the sour expression upon her face. "Well, I suppose it wasn't that much trouble," she answered modestly. "Besides, it pleases me to help rest assure your doubts, and I'm always willing to assist a fellow council member in any way that I can."

"I really appreciate it. I won't forget this either," Bucky uttered as he went back to looking through the pages.

Becky smiled, then peered down and glanced at her watch. Her eyes got wide and her face looked startled as she declared, "Oh my, would you look at the time! Now then, if you'll excuse me, I have some important paperwork sitting on my desk that's screaming for me to finish."

"Alright, thanks again for bringing this material over in person," hollered Bucky as she rushed out of his door.

Bucky swayed back and forth in his swivel chair, deep in thought. He inspected the papers sprawled across his desk, mulling over some thoughts that kept nagging on his mind. The intent of the file was clear, almost blatantly too clear. Louis Ferr was hoping this folder would get Bucky to stop snooping around, but Bucky was not fooled.

Not only did Mr. Ferr's plan backfire and arouse Bucky's curiosity more, it also got him thinking of an idea—an idea that could possibly catch Mr. Ferr with his guard down and shed some light on who Ferr really was. With that in mind, Bucky promptly stuffed all the papers neatly back into the folder, grabbed it from the desk, and headed out the door toward Scott Patterson's office.

Bucky enjoyed talking to Scott about circumstances that were out-of-the-ordinary since, like himself, Scott was a curious man. Though Scott had a character flaw of sometimes being a bit cowardly, he was very knowledgeable about all things bizarre because of his unusual hobby of researching old mysteries and unsolved crimes in his spare time.

Scott was also a very reputable man and was highly respected throughout the community; however, no one knew of the problems he had with alcohol. Like clockwork, Scott would arrive home, promptly at 5 pm, and before he would kiss his wife or say hello to his children, a tall cool 'Scotch on the Rocks' would be quickly devoured. Little did Scott know that his drinking problem would come back to haunt him very shortly.

When Bucky approached Scott's office, he peered through the door window and noticed that Scott was on the telephone. Bucky tapped gently on the glass to gain Scott's attention and was immediately motioned to enter the office.

Scott quickly, yet nonchalantly, put away a file on his desk that read: 'Hopkins.' Then, he readily finished his conversation and hung up the phone so he could converse with his colleague. "Bucky, you look horrible! What happened, did you have a few too many drinks last night?"

"No, nothing like that." he replied, rubbing his blood-shot eyes. "I've just been having some difficulty sleeping at night."

Scott pointed to one of the chairs in front of his desk. "Well, why don't you have a seat and take a load off. It looks like you could use a little rest. What can I do for you?"

Bucky sat down and let out a bellowing yawn. "I wanted to ask you a question that's been on my mind for several weeks. It's nothing serious, but it's been nagging away at me for some time."

"Well, if it's been nagging away at you, then by all means, ask me your question."

"Alright." Bucky said, clearing his throat. "Back when we were taking in bids for the ferry business, I was curious on why you voted in favor of Mephistis Pheles Ferry Service to represent our community as our new ferry service?"

"There's a question I wasn't anticipating," he voiced in a surprised tone. "I guess I hadn't really quite made up my mind on how I was going to vote at the time we received Louis Ferr's letter of intent. However, Becky delivered such a convincing argument on his behalf, which detailed why it would be beneficial for our community, that it won me over. She made some really solid points on why it would be profitable to hire Mr. Ferr and his company."

Bucky looked deep in thought as he tried to recall that meeting. "Yeah, I *also* remember how she really pushed for the council members to vote in his favor. At the time, I thought it was just a political and economic choice for her, but now I'm not so sure. I can't explain it, but there's a feeling in my gut that's telling me there's something wrong with that guy.

Something in Bucky's words caught Scott's curiosity and caused the hair on his neck to stand up. Scott watched with an attentive stare while Bucky rose from the chair and began to pace around the room.

"Maybe I've been somewhat overzealous about certain topics in the past," Bucky admitted.

Scott let out a sarcastic chuckle. "You can say that again."

"This time something is different, Scott! I really *do* want good things to happen to our town, but I fear Louis Ferr has an ulterior motive. For some unknown reason, I have a distinct and uncomfortable feeling he is hiding something, and I think Mr. Ferr knows I'm suspicious of him."

Scott took off his eyeglasses and reached inside his inner suit coat pocket, pulling out a gray handkerchief that had the letter "S" embroidered on it. He unfolded the handkerchief and began cleaning the lenses of his glasses with it.

"It sounds like you're fairly certain about your hunch," Scott said in a slow and restrained voice.

"You better believe it, Scott!"

"Listen to me, Bucky. I have known you and your family since you were just a little boy and have watched you become the man you are today. I know when your concerns are genuinely heartfelt and when you are just being paranoid. However, it sounds like your senses might be trying to warn you about something."

Bucky's face lit up. "Do you *really* believe I'm on to something, Scott?"

"Perhaps…just perhaps. Maybe I was a little hasty in giving Mr. Ferr my support for his ferry service when we knew almost nothing about him. I can't do anything about that now, but I can offer my help if you need anything or want me to look into some issues for you. If it makes you feel any better, Bucky, I suppose I can go down to the ferry service sometime and check it out for myself."

"Thanks, Scott," Bucky replied. "But whatever you do, don't tell Louis Ferr or Steve Jensen why you're there. I want Mr. Ferr to think that everything is fine. And that means you need to act as casual as you possibly can."

"I'm not exactly sure what you expect me to find out, Bucky, but if this will put your mind at ease, then I'll stop by there tonight on my way home."

Bucky's eyes lit up, and he breathed a huge sigh of relief. "Thank you, Scott. All I really want you to do is just to go down there and look around. Find out if there's anything that might be out of the ordinary, especially Mr. Ferr's behavior."

"I think I can handle that," Scott said with a smirk.

"Ask him about his background for starters. Becky loaned me a folder on Mr. Ferr that must be an inch thick. It supposedly contains all his former employers and work history, but I'm not convinced that all the information is accurate and reliable."

"Becky delivered the folder to you?" questioned Scott. "Not Louis Ferr?"

"No, I guess Mr. Ferr has Becky running his errands for him as well as being his biggest cheerleader in town."

Scott leaned back; his face looked as though he was deep in thought. "Considering all the weird behavior I've seen from her the last month or so, it doesn't really surprise me. Mr. Ferr and Becky seem exceptionally chummy whenever I see them together."

"Is that so?" Bucky remarked, raising his brow.

Scott paused, snapping out of his concentration as he glanced toward Bucky with a smile and a wink. "However, as for me being *discreet* and *alert* while I'm at the ferry service, you can consider it done my boy!"

Bucky departed Scott's office with a grin stretching from ear to ear. He was hopeful that Scott could get Mr. Ferr to slip up just once, even if it was as simple as one little detail. Something that might expose him for the fraud Bucky believed him to be.

"If there's one quality Scott excels in," he muttered to himself, "it's his exceptional way with words, always manipulating people to tell him the truth. If there is anything unscrupulous to be found, Scott can sucker Louis Ferr into revealing it."

Bucky let out a little snicker and laughed. "Now we'll see how clever Mr. Ferr truly is."

The hours rolled on throughout the day until it finally reached five o'clock. Scott looked at his watch and grinned as he let out a massive sigh. Before he left the office, he packed up his briefcase and made a quick phone call home to let his wife know he would be late for dinner. Although Scott told Bucky he would go to the ferry service after work, he decided to make a quick detour first.

Scott still planned on going to the ferry service. After all, he did give Bucky his word, and he considered that to be just as good as an official document. However, since he phoned his wife and already told her that he would be late, Scott saw this as a genuine opportunity to go to Kitty's Bar and have a few drinks.

Chapter 11:

There is Danger Ahead

Several hours went by until it was almost dusk, and Scott Patterson still had not been to the ferry service. He had become quite inebriated from several Scotch drinks and now sat at the counter of Kitty's Bar, peering into a near-empty glass and mumbling to himself.

"Hey Holly," Scott mumbled, still looking down. "I've almost dry to the bone over here. How about you serve me up another Scotch on the Rocks?"

Tim Matthews, the only bartender on-duty at Kitty's Bar, was kneeling behind the bar as he replaced the empty keg of draft beer with a full one. He stood up, looked at Scott with a puzzled expression, and pronounced, "Um, Holly went home about forty-five minutes ago. Don't you remember, Mr. Patterson? You gave her a ten-dollar tip and told her to have a good night."

"Oh yeah, now I remember!" replied Scott lightheartedly. "I guess I lost track of time. This liquor must be hitting me pretty hard tonight. Then again, I don't have to work tomorrow, so what harm will it do me to indulge myself a little tonight?"

"No harm at all! Just let me know when you've finished your drink and ready for another."

"Why? Are you bartending for the remainder of the night?"

"Yeah, I'll be here," Tim said with a shrug. "Another bartender that works during the summer, Jamie Gidney, is going to come in for a few hours as well."

"What the hell for?" Scott uttered loudly.

"Jamie has to relieve me for an hour so I can get a dinner break, and she is going to stay on for the rush of customers we usually get around nine o'clock."

"Alright, I'll keep that in mind." Scott mumbled as he chewed up some ice cubes.

Tim gave Scott a wink and a nod; then he went about his business.

Scott raised his glass as if to make a toast and proceeded to gulp down the remainder of his drink. "Fill me up another Scotch, Tim, and try not to give me too much ice for this one. It dilutes the taste."

As Tim opened the cabinet above the cash register to get the Scotch, Scott pointed over to Adam "Red" Richardson and John Sears, who were sitting three stools down from him. "While you're over there, Tim, get my friends a couple more beers."

"Anything you say, Mr. Patterson. It's your money!" Tim answered.

Adam and John grabbed their icy, cold beers from Tim and walked over to Scott. "Thanks for the beer, Mr. Patterson," said Adam.

"No problem, Red. It's my pleasure," he replied.

John pulled an ashtray over to him and lit up a cigarette. He tapped his beer with Scott's glass of Scotch and said, "We really appreciate it, Mr. Patterson. Next time we're all in here together, we'll return the favor."

Before Scott could reply to John's statement, Adam cut in-between them and butted in. "Not to be nosy, Mr. Patterson, but you sure have been throwing around quite a bit of money lately. If you don't mind, I was wondering how you can afford to buy so many drinks for people tonight?"

Scott let out a small chuckle. "No, I don't mind you asking," he replied, "and please, we've drank together many times, you can call me Scott."

"Alright then, 'Scott' it is!" hollered John.

"Anyway," continued Scott, "to get on with my story, I was at the casino in Vernon Downs last weekend and ran the blackjack table. Now, for the first time ever, I can afford to serve fresh fish to my dinner guests instead of fish sticks!"

The men all enjoyed a wholehearted laugh from Scott's cynical witticism. John and Adam thanked Scott once again for the beers, shook hands, and walked over to the foosball table.

Once Adam and John were gone, Tim Matthews walked over to talk to Scott.

"I have a question I'd like to ask you, Mr. Patterson." Tim set down a mug he had been cleaning and leaned over. Then, staring directly into Scott's eyes, he spoke in a curious manner as he asked, "Why do you, and everyone else in this town, drink so much?"

"Why?" bellowed Scott. "You *really* want to know why?" He slammed his glass upon the bar, spilling his ice all over the counter and onto the floor. "It's because this town sucks the life out of you a little more each day. It suffocates a person's hopes and dreams, replacing them with an endless state of depression. People who live here have to drink just to cope with their everyday life. It tends to numb the pain that runs through their body from being cloaked with failure for so long."

Tim snatched a towel and wiped up the mess that Scott caused from his obnoxious and inebriated condition. "It sounds like you're a bitter old man, Mr. Patterson. I'm sure life in this town isn't so bad. You just have a negative attitude and a poor outlook on life."

"What do you know?" Scott snapped back. "You're just a kid who hasn't been in this town long enough to even form an opinion!"

"Oh really?" Tim chuckled. "My family has been around this area a lot longer than you think. To be quite frank, I only recently moved nearer to town so I could be closer to all the fun and raise a little hell."

"You think this town is fun?" Scott asked, quite astonished. "Either you have lived a sheltered life or you are quite a strange individual."

An eerie-looking grin came across Tim's face as he sauntered over to the sink and rinsed out his drenched towel. "Strange?" he said softly. "Mr. Patterson, you have no idea."

At that instant, Bryan Harsha paraded through the door. He looked out of place compared to the other patrons who were sitting down and enjoying their drinks. His hair was slicked over to one side, and he had several noticeable nicks and cuts on his face—a result from shaving.

Wearing clean casual slacks, a nice pressed shirt, and reeking of cologne, Bryan looked as if he was a twelve-year-old boy ready to go on his first date. He stood nervously at the doorway for a moment before stepping up to the bar next to Scott.

"Now I *know* I've had too much liquor to drink!" Scott shouted. "I'm imagining that Bryan Harsha is in the bar and standing right next to me!"

"Hello, Scott, it's nice to see you, too," responded Bryan.

"Are you lost or something?" Scott asked curiously. "What brings you to a bar at this time of the night, or any time for that matter?"

Bryan appeared embarrassed to be there and talked in a quiet voice. "Um, actually I'm here to see Miss Kitty."

Scott wiped his mouth with the back of his hand. "For what? Are you looking for another part-time job?"

The butterflies in Bryan's stomach, along with Scott's continual questions, kept him feeling nervous, queasy, and uneasy. "No, we sort of have dinner plans this evening."

Scott's eyes lit up from shock and enthusiasm. "You do? Well, you sly little fox! How the hell did that all come about?"

"We met last week when I was in here with Bucky. He was trying to find Roger, and we knew that this is his favorite hangout. Miss Kitty was here, and we got to talking about business and other things. We really hit it off and she asked me if I'd like to have dinner with her sometime—tonight became 'sometime.'"

"Well, congratulations, old buddy!" expressed Scott with enthusiasm. "I am very happy for you...and very proud of you, too."

Tim Matthews walked over to where the two men were positioned and tapped Bryan on the shoulder. "Miss Kitty has been expecting you, Mr. Harsha." Then he turned and pointed to the door beside them. "She's in the kitchen finishing some formalities if you would like to go back there and see her."

"Thank you; I think I will." Bryan took out his purple handkerchief, wiped the nervous sweat off his forehead, and gave Scott a pat on the back before entering the kitchen. "You have yourself a good night, Scott. Please be careful if you plan to drive anywhere tonight. I don't want to read about you getting a DWI in tomorrow's newspaper."

Scott shook his head, took another sip from his drink, and nonchalantly glanced up at the wall clock. "Oh my god!" he yelled. "It's almost eight o'clock! I better hurry up and get to the ferry service before they close up the place for the night."

Tim's attention quickly shifted toward Scott. "Where did you say you were going, Mr. Patterson?"

"The ferry service," he answered. "It's 'bout time I find out if there's any funny business goin' on down there."

He hurriedly pulled out his wallet and threw a fifty-dollar bill on the counter. Then Scott guzzled down the remainder of his Scotch, slammed the glass down on the counter, and wiped the dribble off his chin with a napkin.

"This should be more than enough to cover my bill for tonight," he stated to Tim. "Put the remainder in your tip jar, and have yourself a good night."

"Thanks, and you have a good night too, Mr. Patterson!" Tim yelled to Scott as he was making his way out the door.

Scott staggered out of the bar and fumbled with his car keys as he headed toward his dark-red 1997 Ford Escort. It was not the dream car he always thought he would own as an adult, but then again, he always felt as though his life had been one big continuous disappointment after another.

"Huh, I guess I stayed at the bar a little longer than I intended to," he sighed, talking to himself. "Oh, well, it's Thursday night; and, for me, the weekend has officially begun! I would've liked a few more drinks to quench my thirst, but I gotta keep my word to Bucky. Good thing I still have my spare bottle of Scotch in the glove compartment!"

After several near misses and potential accidents, Scott Patterson arrived to The Mephistis Pheles Ferry Service sometime around 8:20 pm. He parked his car so abruptly that he scraped his bumper against a huge rock and spilled his drink in his lap. Then, before he shut off the engine, he took one more huge gulp from his bottle of Scotch and stuffed it back into the glove compartment.

As Scott opened his car door, he stumbled out and tumbled down, landing face first upon the gravel driveway. Luckily for him, the only ones who witnessed Scott's graceless antics were a couple wolves in the nearby woods.

Scott rose to his feet, brushed himself off, and looked around in embarrassment. "I hope no one saw that sorry excuse for a swan dive," he stated with a smile. "I suppose I should try to be a little more careful from now on."

Scott wandered along as the evening turned increasingly dark, guided only by the lights of the ferry office. When he walked up to Mr. Ferr's office, he noticed that the door was slightly ajar so he pushed it forward. Mr. Ferr was sitting with his back to the door and talking on the phone.

"Do you think he believed you?" Scott overheard Mr. Ferr say. "Do you think we can expect any additional problems from him?"

Just then, Mr. Ferr turned and spotted Scott from out of the corner of his eye. "I have to let you go, I have a visitor in my office," he mumbled quietly into the phone. "I'll call you again soon."

Caught completely off guard by Scott's unexpected presence, Mr. Ferr's demeanor suddenly turned peculiar as he quickly hung up the phone. "Mr. Patterson, what an unexpected surprise! What brings you down here tonight?"

"I was passin' through on my way home and figured I'd drop in for a visit. I haven't had a chance to come down here since you opened up and wanted to see how the town's newest business is doing."

"Really?" Mr. Ferr uttered in a disbelieving tone. "And you thought that tonight of all nights would be the best time to come here, even though we closed over an hour ago?"

"Um, well...that is..." said Scott, fumbling his words.

"Mr. Ferr stood up and walked over to Scott, instantly smelling the liquor on his breath. "Mr. Patterson, I notice you have been drinking. Can I assume your insatiable love of Scotch is what prompted this sudden visit of yours?"

Scott got defensive from Mr. Ferr's allegation. "Hey, I might've had one or two, but I'm *not* drunk if that's what you're implying. I just wanted to make sure everything was going alright and that your ferry is running safely."

"I see," said Mr. Ferr, rubbing his chin. "There seems to be a lot of concern about the safeness of my ferry lately. I don't suppose Bucky Morgan had anything to do with you stopping by here tonight?"

"No, not at all." Scott replied, somewhat jittery. "This is purely a social visit. But while I'm here, we can discuss any questions or concerns you might have regarding our town politics?"

Still unsure of the true nature of Scott's visit, Mr. Ferr was apprehensive about what to say. "No, there aren't any major concerns I can think of. Just certain members of the community who keep looking over my shoulder...but that's simply trivial and of no concern to you."

Scott swallowed hard.

"As for my ferry, it's in rather excellent working order and runs quite safely. Would you be interested in a quick ride to witness its efficiency for yourself?"

"Oh, I don't think so. I've never used any kind of ferry service before; I'm kinda fearful of open water. In fact, the only swimming I do is from one bottle of Scotch to another," laughed Scott, loudly and somewhat over the top.

Mr. Ferr let out a small chuckle. "I assure you my ferry is entirely safe. There is no need to be nervous. If it would make you feel any better, why don't you let my assistant take you for a trip across the river and back. After all, he is much better with the controls than I am. Then you will be able to make a substantiated observation for yourself."

"Well, I ain't no chicken if that's what ya think!" Scott roared back. "I suppose I have time for a short trip around the river."

"That's fantastic!" Mr. Ferr hollered excitedly. "Trust me; it will take no time at all. You will be gone and back before you know it, and just as safe and secure as you are now I might add. Now then, if you will follow me, I'll take you down to the ferry."

Mr. Ferr led them down the platform as they made their way to the ferry. He carried an old-fashioned lantern with him instead of a modern flashlight. The lantern was fashioned in the shape of a cage, with Scott thinking to himself how he had never seen anything like it before. He marveled at its contour and was awestruck at how strange and peculiar it looked.

The detail of the lantern was very intricate and looked like something ferrymen used hundreds of years ago. The handle was twisted in the form of a snake and the top piece was crafted to resemble the head of a wild boar.

When the two men approached the assistant, Steve Jensen, they saw that Steve was busily coiling rope on the deck of the ferry. Mr. Jensen had recently finished scrubbing down the deck and neatly coiled the mooring ropes, placing them out of the way.

For as mysterious as Steve Jensen appeared to be, it was evident he was an unusually hard worker. He always kept the ferry neat and clean and was very proficient when it came to any mechanical repairs that needed attention. However, by the look upon Steve's face, it was apparent he was exhausted from working all day, and he didn't appear happy to see the two gentlemen approaching him.

"Try not to get overly relaxed, Jensen," Mr. Ferr uttered. "There is one more task I need you to do for me tonight."

Mr. Jensen straightened as he waited for his instructions. "Yes, sir?"

"I would like you to take Mr. Patterson for a quick tour around the river. And while you're out there, take a quick stop at the dock on the other side to make sure nothing was left behind."

"My pleasure, sir." he uttered gingerly, trying to force himself to smile. Steve turned toward Scott and waved him over. "Right this way, Mr. Patterson. It'll only take me a few minutes to get ready and we'll be on our way.

The two men boarded the ferry. A few minutes later, as the vessel pulled away from the dock, they began to enter the same sort of eerie, thick fog that emerged the night Bob Earle disappeared. The approaching fog puzzled Scott since there was a clear evening sky before he boarded the ferry.

However, Scott was unable to concern himself with this conundrum because the alcohol in his body, and the rocking of the ferry, was making him nauseous. His stomach took an unexpected turn for the worse and sent Scott running for the side of the boat, vomiting over the side.

Scott reached for the handkerchief he kept in his back pocket and wiped his mouth clean. "I hope Mr. Jensen wasn't watching me just now," he whispered to himself. "That would be very humiliating."

As he was putting the handkerchief away, an eerie howling spooked Scott, and his heartbeat began to quicken. Taken aback, Scott stood motionless, fixated on the piercing noise that punctured his ears. His attention was so consumed on the noise that he was unaware when his cloth slipped from his hand and fell in-between a wooden crate and a large, heavy toolbox.

All of a sudden, Scott began to notice how silent and still everything abruptly had become. As he grew more cautious, a twinge of panic and confusion coursed through his body.

The street noise could no longer be heard, nor could the traffic on the bridge. Scott looked up toward the pilot house where Mr. Jensen was and yelled out to him, "S'cuse me, Jensen! Can I have a word with you?"

Mr. Jensen stuck his head out the pilot house and hollered to Scott, "What can I do for you, sir? Is there some kind of problem?"

"Do ya know what's goin' on 'round here?" Scott asked agitatedly. "Somethin' doesn't seem right...and I feel an odd stillness in the air. In particular, I'm curious why everythin' has gone deathly quiet so suddenly?"

"I do not know, sir." answered Mr. Jensen, apathetic to Scott's concerns. "I was completely unaware anything was amiss. However, I'm sure that if something was indeed wrong, Mr. Ferr would undoubtedly know about it. After all, he *is* keeping an eye on our tour from the mainland."

Jensen extended his hand and pointed over to the shore from where they departed.

"Why don't you take a look for yourself?" he remarked.

Scott focused his attention across the river and strained to see through the fog as he glanced over toward the ferry office. He took notice that Louis Ferr was still idly standing on the edge of the riverbank, and wondered why Ferr had not moved at all since the ferry pulled away from shore.

"What the hell is he doin' over there?" Scott inquired, curious and nervous, both at the same time.

Mr. Ferr was observing the events on the ferry with a look of deep concentration until the ferry and its occupants got a little further distance between themselves and the shoreline. At that time, Ferr rose up his arms and began chanting the incantation that he recited when Bob Earle was a passenger onboard. His eyes burned a reddish glow and his voice turned raspy as, once again, his chanting roared louder and louder until the sound of his words became all but earsplitting.

"CALL THEE HERE NOW!" Mr. Ferr howled. "Rise up, by ANU I summon Thee! Rise up, by ENLIL I summon Thee! Rise up, by ENKI I summon Thee! Cease to be the sleeper of EGURRA. Cease to lie unwaking beneath the mountains of KUR. Rise up, from the pits of ancient holocausts! In the Name of the Covenant, Come rise up before me!"

A hissing sound, like that of a rabid animal, pierced through the fog. Jensen stepped down from the pilot house and walked over to where Scott was standing.

Before he could even say a word, Scott reached over, grabbed Mr. Jensen by his shirt, and sneered, "What the hell is happenin'; where are those sounds coming from? I want some answers from ya, and I want 'em now!"

"Unfortunately, Scott, there's nothing I can do to help you. You never should have come here tonight," he expressionlessly stated.

"This was only intended to be a one-way trip for you, and my boss requires I obtain your payment before we reach the other side!"

By now, half frantic from helplessness, Scott was clutching onto Jensen's shirt so tight that his knuckles were beginning to turn white. "My payment?" he said, noticeably perplexed. "What kind of payment do you mean?"

Jensen simply smiled and lowered his head as if to look down towards the deck. Only a brief moment passed, but when he lifted his head back up, Jensen's eyes had become as red and glowing as those that had begun to circle around Scott. He smiled once again, showing his teeth, which had become sharp and jagged, like those of some deranged beast.

With a snarl and a groan, he bellowed out to Scott, "We want your soul!"

A look of intense fright flowed over Scott's face, and he released his grip from Jensen's shirt, taking a few steps backwards. At that moment, a gray reptilian-like arm with long thin fingers and razor-sharp fingernails reached out and ripped the sleeve off Scott's shirt. Scott gasped in fright as glowing red eyes peered all around him while a hideous snout with a mouthful of dagger fangs snarled within inches of his face.

Scott let out a small whimper before he was pounced upon by the demons within the dense fog. He screamed as the wretched devils tore him apart limb from limb and carried his soul down to Hell.

While saliva dripped from his tongue, Jensen's eyes looked like that of a madman as he bellowed with glee. Jensen stood and watched as demons fed upon Scott's flesh, and listened as Scott screamed in tortured agony.

As blood was being splattered and body parts were torn apart, Jensen leaned down to grab a portion of flesh that had landed by his feet. He picked it up, licked the blood off his fingers, and sniffed the mangled hunk of meat before he proceeded to munch on it.

"Another satisfied customer," Jensen said with a smirk.

By the time the ferry reached the opposite side of the river, the fog had all but disappeared just as mysteriously as it formed. Immediately after the fog cleared, an unnatural silence settled over the river, and only the sound of the ferry striking the dock could be heard.

Mr. Jensen moved in slow motion, checking over his shoulders and glancing around the tree line to see if anyone was watching. Once he deemed no one was around, he grabbed a mop and a bucket of water and commenced cleaning the bloody remains off the deck.

After he finished disposing of Scott's remains, Jensen stepped off the ferry and began to whistle as he reached for a broom to sweep the trash and leaves from the dock. He acted nonchalantly while picking up debris around the dock and behaved as if nothing out of the ordinary had happened. Unfortunately, Jensen's whistling prevented him from hearing a twig snap in the nearby woods and the footsteps walking in the opposite direction from the riverbank.

Shortly thereafter, Steve Jensen fired up the engine and proceeded back to the ferry office. The ferry casually puttered along, moving in a nonchalant sort of way, and showing no signs of any strange behavior that would draw attention to it.

No one would ever suspect a heinous incident had occurred there, and Carthage's appearance of being a 'tranquil community' remained intact. However, appearances can be deceiving, for although nothing peculiar seemed to have transpired, the reality was that Scott Patterson was no longer a passenger aboard the ferry with no traces left behind to show that he ever was.

PART TWO:
Raising Unholy Hell

Chapter 12:

The Mystery Heightens

It was six o'clock the following morning and Bucky was at home sleeping. Friday mornings were his favorite time of the week because he did not have to be at work until noon. Also, after Cristina would leave the house at 6:30 am, he always got to sleep in for a couple more hours and hog the pillows and blankets all to himself.

As he laid peacefully in his bed, the phone rang and abruptly awoke him. "Who the hell is calling me so damn early?" he grumbled.

Bucky slowly picked up the phone as he tried to get his bearings. He dropped the telephone a few times and fumbled around with it before eventually putting the receiver up to his ear. "Hello," he mumbled into the phone.

A female voice greeted him back. "Hello? Bucky, is that you? This is Barbara Patterson…Scott's wife."

"Hello, Mrs. Patterson," he said with a yawn. Then he grabbed his alarm clock off his nightstand to check the time. "I haven't talked to you in a long time. What can I do for you at 7:02 in the morning?"

"I'm sorry to be calling so early, but I'm trying to get in touch with all the members of the town council to find out if they saw Scott last night."

"Why?" he asked, startled and confused. "Is there something wrong?"

Bucky listened carefully and noticed that Mrs. Patterson's voice was hoarse and unsteady.

"Scott didn't come home last night and I'm very worried," she sobbed. "He called me at five o'clock and mentioned that he had an errand to do right after work. He said it wouldn't take very long and he'd be home shortly after he finished the task. That was the last time I heard from him. I don't know what to do or what to think. Nothing like this has ever happened before. I'm a nervous wreck and was awake all night crying."

Her words hit like a freight train as Bucky nearly fell out of bed while trying to get to his feet. His heart raced and pounded heavily in his chest. "Have you been in touch with the police yet?"

"Yes," she sighed. "I phoned the police department a few times last night. I had the displeasure of talking to a very sullen and rude man. He was not sympathetic to my feelings or to Scott's vanishing."

"Who did you speak to, Mrs. Patterson?" inquired Bucky.

"His name was Sergeant Ken Johnson. Do you know him?"

"Yeah, I've also had the displeasure of chatting with Sergeant Johnson before." Bucky paused momentarily as curiosity entered his thoughts. "Mrs. Patterson, did the Sergeant tell you why he was hesitant to look into Scott's disappearance?"

Mrs. Patterson mentally reviewed her conversation with Ken Johnson in her thoughts. "No, but when I called again first thing this morning and talked to Sergeant Johnson, I finally got some headway with him. Apparently, he was on the tail end of a twelve-hour shift and was too exhausted to argue. His voice sounded tired, and I believe he would've said or done anything to get me off the phone."

"Well..." Bucky prodded. "What did he say?"

"It seems that after calling him six times throughout the night, he's finally going to send an officer over to ask me some questions about what Scott likes to do and the places where he hangs out the most. They also want to know what he was wearing yesterday and to obtain a picture of him to put in their file. I just thought that maybe one of the other council members saw Scott in his office or somewhere else last night and could give me any information at all to his whereabouts."

Even though Bucky had an ill feeling in his stomach and felt somewhat responsible for Scott's sudden disappearance, he could not bring himself to tell Mrs. Patterson the nature of his conversation with her husband.

"I saw him earlier in the day," he said collectedly. "It must've been sometime close to 10:30 am because shortly after that, I went home with a terrible headache. Although, I do seem to recall him telling me that he was going to stop by The Mephistis Pheles Ferry Service on the way home."

"The ferry service?" she said, very confused. "Why would he stop by the ferry service? Scott always takes the bridge home from work because he feels that it's safer, and also because he's been afraid of open water since he nearly drowned when he was a child. He can't swim *at all* and won't even get in the pool we have out back of our house."

"I, I don't know." Bucky stuttered. His face turned flaming red from the guilty feeling nagging away at him. He was also angry at himself for not being completely honest with Mrs. Patterson.

"Well, if you think of anything, will you *please* call me?" Barbara's sobs became louder as she started to ramble. "I'm so worried about him, Bucky. I can't stop crying and my legs feel weak. I realize we don't have a perfect marriage, but honestly, who does? I love Scott dearly, and I don't know what I'd do if I had to live the rest of my life without him."

"I completely understand, Mrs. Patterson. You have every right to act and feel the way you do. If I hear of any news or remember anything, I promise I'll give you a call."

Bucky could barely say goodbye as he hung up the phone, finding it hard to swallow from the lump in his throat. For the next several minutes, he remained silent while Mrs. Patterson's words kept echoing over and over in his mind.

Nearly twenty minutes passed after Bucky's conversation with Mrs. Patterson before he moved from his chair or changed his facial expression. Eventually, Bucky found the will to get ready for work but remained preoccupied by his telephone conversation that morning and his chat with Scott the day before. The severity of the issue kept nagging in the back of his mind, and he felt an undeniable inclination to divulge the topic with the one person he trusted...Roger.

It was 11:15 am when Bucky was driving by Roger's house while on his way to work. He noticed Roger's car in the driveway and decided to stop. As soon as he got out of his car, Bucky heard screeching music booming from around back of the house as he began to stroll in that direction. When he reached the back yard, he observed Roger sitting outside in a lawn chair, wearing nothing but a pair of Hawaiian shorts and Rayban sunglasses while he relaxed under the sun.

Bucky walked up beside him and stood so that he was blocking the sun. "Hey buddy, you're lookin' very comfortable this morning," Bucky said in a lackadaisical tone.

"I was," Roger replied disdainfully. "What're you doin' here at this time of the day? After all, I'm sure this *isn't* strictly a social visit."

"I was on my way to the office and driving in this direction so I thought I'd drop by. I figured I'd take a chance that you might be home, even though I wasn't expecting to see your car in the driveway. Aren't you supposed to be working on Fort Drum today? I heard they were starting a huge archaeological dig this weekend."

"Not to change the topic, Bucky," Roger said, without twitching a muscle or acknowledging Bucky's question, "but it's kind of difficult to get a tan when you're blocking the sun."

"Let me cut to the point then," Bucky stated in a more serious tone. "We need to talk."

Roger turned toward Bucky and lifted up his shades. "About what?" he asked. "This had better be important, Bucky. I called in sick today specifically so I could lounge around and relax in the sun."

Bucky grabbed one of the other lawn chairs sitting beside Roger and sat down. His body was hunched over with his head looking down at the ground. "Trust me, it's *very* important."

Roger detected the solemnity in Bucky's tone and twisted sideways, sitting up straight in his chair to face him. "Alright, you have my full attention. What is so imperative that we absolutely need to discuss it right now?"

"I received a phone call from Mrs. Patterson this morning," he stated. "She was upset because Scott did not return home last night. There's a strong chance that, like Bob Earle, Scott's gone missing. Her voice sounded so distraught, and I'm feeling awfully guilty about the whole thing. This situation is bad for sure, but what's even worse is that *I* may have been the one who sent him into a situation that he was unprepared for?"

Roger was surprised and baffled by Bucky's unconventional statement. "I don't understand. Why do you think that?"

"I don't think it, I know it!" Bucky cried out. "Scott and I were talking in his office yesterday, and I told him about my apprehension with Mr. Ferr and his questionable company. Scott was very understanding to my uncertainties and mentioned he would go down to the ferry service after work last night to speak with Mr. Ferr himself. And now, apparently, no one has seen or heard from him since."

"So you feel that Mr. Ferr may have something to do with Scott's sudden disappearance? What are you intending to do? I know you were warned to stay away from Mr. Ferr, but have you called the police department yet and told them what you just divulged to me?"

"No, and I'm not even going to bother, either." stated Bucky. "Somehow, Mr. Ferr has the police department wrapped completely around his little finger. Sergeant Johnson has already informed me that if I call him again with another complaint about Louis Ferr, he's likely to place me in jail for harassment."

"So what are you going to do?" Roger asked heatedly. "Just disregard the fact that you might possibly know of Scott's last whereabouts? Or ignore the possibility that Scott may have come across the same danger that occurred to Bob!"

"Not at all!" Bucky answered in a defensive tone. "I plan on doing some checking around myself. I'm just not sure when I'll get a chance to do it. I want to go down to the ferry service this afternoon, but I have to go to dinner with Cristina and her parents tonight. We're all supposed to meet at the house around three-thirty this afternoon, and I still have to run to the office to finish some paperwork."

"So...make a quick ride over there when you're done with your job," suggested Roger.

"I won't have time after work to go to the ferry service and get back in time to go to dinner. Cristina would be pissed if I was late, and having an argument in front of her folks is *not* how I want to start off the evening."

Roger picked up his wristwatch off the ground and checked the time. "Well, I'm going to dinner with Nellie tonight as well, but that's not until five o'clock. If you'd like, I can always swing by and talk to Mr. Ferr before I go to the restaurant. After all, you just want to know is if he mentions whether or not Scott was *definitely* there last night...am I right?"

"Yeah, of course that's all I want to find out. I'm not asking anyone to stick their neck on the line when it comes to dealing with a possible psychotic. However, I would definitely appreciate any assistance you're willing to lend!" Bucky said exuberantly. "That is, if you don't mind."

"Nah, I don't mind," replied Roger. "I'm still very curious about that bike you saw the last time we were there. Maybe I can get Mr. Ferr to give me a tour of the place, possibly even get a peek in the old shed out back."

Bucky laughed and smiled at Roger's facetious remark. "I wouldn't hold your breath waiting for that to happen." Then he reached over and put his hand on Roger's shoulder. "Thanks for helping out old buddy; this really means a lot to me. I have been stressed out thinking about Scott's disappearance and I can't stop wondering if he actually made his way to the ferry service last night, if he got in an accident along the way, or if something else happened to him."

Bucky's voice became solemn once again as he turned his head so that he was not looking directly at Roger anymore. "To be perfectly honest, there's more to my curiosity than just asking Mr. Ferr if he saw Scott or not."

Something in Bucky's tone of voice disturbed Roger and sent goose bumps up and down his arms. "What do you mean?" he asked.

"Well, I have some information that's a little disturbing to hear. I didn't say anything to you before because I'm not sure what to make of it myself. Last week I got a few calls from some of the people who live near The Mephistis Pheles Ferry Service. All of them pretty much stated they witnessed Bob riding his bike at about three o'clock on the day he disappeared. They also said he turned down toward the ferry instead of taking his normal route to the bar."

Roger was stunned by this latest news and stuttered as he attempted to speak. "But if that's true, it means Mr. Ferr was lying to us when we asked him if Bob was there."

"Exactly!" Bucky yelled. "That also means it could very well have been Bob's bike I saw Steve Jensen rolling into their tool shed."

"There's something about that old ferryman, as well as this whole scenario, just makes me nervous. It seems to me that Louis Ferr is keeping important information from us."

"That's why I'm so eager to get down there. I want to see if I can rile Louis Ferr up a little bit and find out why he lied to us." Bucky stopped to think. "Now, I'm wondering what other lies this mystery man has been feeding us and what his connection to these disappearances is. If he..."

Roger grabbed Bucky by the arm to interrupt him. "Hold on a moment! I don't quite understand something. Why would these people just call you out of the blue? Haven't they already been in contact with the police?"

"Yes, they have," Bucky responded. "However, before these residents could tell their story, they got the same brush off from the police officers as I did. The people who contacted the police prefer to remain anonymous, but they called me because it's well-known around town how good friends Bob and I are. I suppose they figured that since I'm on the town council, I might have more influence with the cops and could get an update on their search."

"So, are you going to relay their statements to Ken Johnson or anyone else on the police squad?"

"I want you to understand something, Roger. I believe that the information those people passed on to me is very intriguing, and much too valuable for me to just hand over to the cops. Especially considering how disinterested the police have been acting while conducting this whole investigation. With information as important as this is, a person would assume the police would go over to the ferry service in an instant."

Perplexed, Roger stared at Bucky in confusion. "Don't you think the cops would do anything?"

"I'm not so sure. With the strong influence that Mr. Ferr has had over the police in town, I wouldn't be surprised if the cops simply mention it to Louis Ferr and accept his flimsy excuse…or disregard the people's accounts altogether." Bucky annunciated his words, trying to get his point across. "That's why I don't want to tell the police anything further!"

Roger stood up, grabbed his towel, and put his flip-flops on while he wiped the suntan lotion and sweat from his body. "Well, you can always count on me whenever you need assistance—and you know that!"

Bucky nodded. "Yeah, I know that."

"As soon as I shower up and get some decent threads on, I'll venture over to the ferry service…probably this afternoon. I have to do some odds and ends around the house today, but that shouldn't take me more than a couple hours."

"That sounds fantastic!" shouted Bucky enthusiastically. "I probably won't get a chance to talk to you tonight, so I'll stop back in the morning to see if you find out anything."

Bucky turned and started toward his vehicle. After a few steps, he veered around and asked, "Oh, before I forget, did you discover anything in your textbooks regarding the name of the ferry service?"

"No, but I really haven't done a lot of researching thus far," Roger answered back. "To be honest, I forgot all about it. How about you; have you found anything of significance during your exploration?"

Bucky shrugged his shoulders. "About a week ago, I went to the library and looked up various newspaper articles about Carthage and the neighboring towns, but I didn't find much."

"What does 'not much' mean?" questioned Roger. "Either you found something or you didn't."

"I went through the library's periodicals dating back almost fifty years and could only find one news account that would fit into the category of a paranormal occurrence."

"Only one? Well, that's what you get for using the library as your only source of information." Roger paused and then asked curiously, "So, what was it that you found?"

Bucky shook his head. "Nothing of importance, I suppose. It was just a small newspaper article about someone who thought he saw the figure of a Reaper-like individual in the vicinity at one of the town's mysterious fires. However, the clipping was dated back to the mid-1950s, and it was more of an urban legend story than a fact-based article anyway. After all, as eerie as Louis Ferr may seem, he would *never* be mistaken for looking like the Grim Reaper."

Roger accompanied Bucky as the two men walked slowly out to the front of the house and over to Bucky's car. As Bucky opened the door and started to enter the automobile, Roger said, "Don't concern yourself about the ferry service tonight, old buddy. Go out and have a great time with Cristina and her family. If I discover something I believe is significant, I will call you tonight when I get home."

The two friends shook hands; then, Bucky pulled out his keys and closed the car door. He started the engine, rolled down his window, and hollered out as Roger was walking away.

"Remember that I'll be stopping over in the morning. Therefore, try not to get overly intoxicated tonight, okay? After all, I would hate to come over tomorrow and have to roll your ass out of bed!"

Roger scoffed at Bucky's comments but did not say a word. He simply grinned and waved as Bucky backed out of the driveway and drove off to work.

Several hours later, Roger arrived at the ferry service. He checked his wristwatch to ascertain he had plenty of time to spare before his dinner with Nellie; it read 4:25 pm. Roger stopped his car on the gravel road about thirty yards short of the main parking area and decided to walk the rest of the way.

While walking toward the ferry office, Roger carefully glanced around, trying to spot if there were any abandoned cars in the vicinity or any other clues that might indicate whether Scott was in the surrounding area last night. Although there was no hard evidence to be discovered and nothing substantial grabbed his attention, Roger did happen to come across a large rock in the front parking area that had slight traces of red paint on it.

"I wonder if this paint splotch was made from a vehicle," he whispered to himself. "Then again, I don't know what kind of car Scott drives or what color it is, so it's pretty much a moot point anyway."

After another quick perusal around the area, Roger conceded that nothing was amiss and continued over to the ferry office where he walked up the steps and opened the door. Mr. Ferr heard the footsteps and readily looked up to see Roger standing in the doorway.

"Mr. Fasick, what a pleasure it is to see you again! I didn't hear anyone pull up in a vehicle; have you been waiting long?"

"No, I just arrived a few moments ago," Roger replied. "I parked up the road a little ways because I know the traffic gets hectic around here this time of day. I also wanted to walk around a bit and check out what this place looks like in the daytime."

"Well, I hope you weren't too disappointed by our humble little company. We're still fixing up the place a little bit at a time."

Roger stepped inside the office and became immediately awed with the many strange, morbid-themed paintings that hung on the dark-colored walls. About the only thing in the room that didn't seem morose was an old, hand carved ferryboat. The object was as small as cigar box and sat upon a rickety shelf behind Mr. Ferr's desk.

"Yeah, I see that you've made some real headway with all these run-down buildings. They've sat here so long without any upkeep that I figured they'd eventually be torn down. But somehow you've managed to bring them back from the dead."

"Thank you for the compliment, Mr. Fasick. I guess I seem to have a knack for bringing things back 'from the dead' so to speak. I take great pleasure whenever someone notices the hard work I put into a project, and this one is quite laborious." Mr. Ferr shuffled some papers on his desk, trying to appear busy. "So, what can I do for you this afternoon? I hope that this visit is a more favorable one than the last time you were here."

Roger shook his head. "Unfortunately, Mr. Ferr, it's not. I know this may seem like an odd question, but can you tell me if Scott Patterson stopped by here last night?"

Mr. Ferr jerked backwards in his chair and rubbed his chin, pretending to be deep in thought. "I cannot be certain whether he did or not. Nonetheless, even if he *did* stop by here, I would not know about it anyway. I left early yesterday because I was not feeling well and returned to my abode to rest. Is there any particular reason why you are asking?"

"Scott disappeared last night and nobody has a clue as to what might've happened to him. Scott's wife has been frantically calling all over town inquiring if anyone knows where he might be or where he might've gone to. I figured I'd help out and swing by some of the local businesses to see if he stopped anywhere on his way home."

"Another person has disappeared? Oh dear, that's such a shame to hear," Mr. Ferr said sympathetically. "Mr. Patterson is one of the many people who've acted kind and friendly towards me since I've arrived in town. He is courteous, polite, and in my humble opinion, a credit to this community. It's just too bad that he has such a serious problem with alcohol."

"What do you mean by that?" Roger inquired.

Mr. Ferr looked at Roger with a peculiar grin. "Oh nothing. All I mean is that he's a very personable guy. Although, in my opinion, I believe he drinks entirely too much. A person like that is bound to get himself into trouble someday. Alcohol can make a person say and do things they would generally refrain from when they are sober. I only hope that is not true in his circumstance."

Roger stood motionless for a moment, completely baffled by Mr. Ferr's bizarre response. "Yes, well that may be, but a very reliable source told me Scott was on his way over here to meet with you last night."

"A reliable source, huh? Well, I don't know where these people get their information, but they are most definitely mistaken. My assistant, Steve, took over for me, and ran the ferry by himself after I left. If Scott Patterson was here yesterday, my assistant would be the one for you to ask."

Roger glanced from side to side. "Is your assistant around so I can talk to him?"

"Unfortunately, Steve is busy running the ferry back and forth right now and is unavailable to chat. I suppose if you would like to stay around and wait for awhile, I can ask him when the traffic lets up a little bit. It shouldn't be more than an hour or two at most."

Roger took a momentary look at his watch and noticed it was 4:45 pm. "No, that's fine. Thanks for the offer, but I really gotta get movin' along. I'm supposed to be at the Superior Restaurant in the next fifteen minutes. I have a dinner date with my girlfriend, and if I know what's good for me, I won't be late."

"You're absolutely right!" Mr. Ferr laughed. "A gentleman should *never* keep a lady waiting. It's just not proper manners."

Roger stopped as he was walking out the door and veered around. "By the way, you don't happen to remember anything new or have any pertinent information about the night Bob Earle disappeared, do you?"

"Unfortunately, I do not have any new facts to update you. Everything I know about your friend's disappearance was already relayed to you the night Mr. Morgan and you stopped by. However, I'd be grateful if *you* would keep *me* informed. I'm very intrigued by this whole situation myself."

"Um, okay," Roger said as though he had doubts about Mr. Ferr's sincerity. Then he paused and spoke again softly. "Well, thanks anyway. Have a good day Mr. Ferr."

"And a good day to you, too." Mr. Ferr stated with utmost courtesy. "Our conversation may not have been very helpful; however, I do hope that we will be able to chat sometime when the circumstances do not concern a dreadful situation."

Roger smiled and continued out the door. As he started to walk back to his car, he gave the area a quick perusal to see if he could locate Steve Jensen. Although Jensen was nowhere to be found, Roger's eyes *did* wander across the old tool shed that Bucky had seen a bicycle being rolled into. His curiosity got the best of him, and he was struck with an impulsive urge to peek inside. Roger glanced around to check the territory once again, but this time it was to see if anyone was around or watching him.

While Roger inched closer to the shed, the fierce wind began to gain more strength with every step he took. Strange noises filled the air as Roger listened to the trees and leaves rustle ferociously. He twirled around several times as his heart began to quicken. A distinct whisper could be heard, that of a man's voice seemingly chanting words. Of which, Roger was unable to understand.

Suddenly, there was a loud cracking noise as one of the limps snapped off a tree that was close to Roger. It dropped so quickly that he could not get out of the way as it came crashing down upon the top of his head, knocking him unconscious as he tumbled to the ground.

Sometime later, Roger regained consciousness and slowly rolled to his side. He pulled himself up and brushed off the dirt, leaves, and twigs that were covering his body. His head and neck ached, but Roger was more concerned about the scarlet-colored blood drops that were trickling down his face. And if things couldn't seem to get any worse, his eyes were also giving him problems as he found it hard to put objects into focus.

He rubbed his ailing neck with one hand and reached up to touch the top of his head with the other. "Ouch!" he yelped. He pulled his hand off his head and dazedly looked at the blood on his fingers. "Just great! I can feel a gash up there, and I bet I need stitches, too."

Slowly, Roger's eyes began to put objects back in focus. He checked his other body parts to make sure nothing was broken and inspected the seriousness of the cuts and bruises he acquired.

After Roger inferred that he was alright to move without medical treatment, Roger stood up and began to walk back to his car, checking the time on his wristwatch along the way. Just then, he cringed in shame and embarrassment as he noticed that the watch read 6:35 pm, and now he was over an hour and a half late to meet Nellie.

"Damn it!" he yelled furiously. "I missed our dinner reservations again!"

Chapter 13:

Night of New Beginnings

As Roger drove up to his house, he noticed that the lights were on inside. He also saw Nellie's car was still parked in the driveway, so he knew she was there. Of course, whether or not she would listen and understand what happened to him, he did not know.

Roger parked his car next to the curb in front of the house and slowly walked up to the house. As Roger was approaching the door, Nellie came storming outside with a small suitcase in one hand and her car keys in the other. She glanced over at Roger, who was standing in the middle of the yard, shook her head disapprovingly, and then continued on to her car.

"Wait a minute, Nellie!" Roger shouted in desperation. "I need to talk to you!"

Nellie stopped in her tracks and turned around to face Roger. She gave him a dirty look and glared at him so fiercely that Roger could see the rage in her eyes.

She shouted angrily, "You have some nerve showing up now! You're *only* two hours late for the dinner plans we made tonight!"

"I know, and I'm sorry," he said apologetically. "I feel terrible about letting you down, and I'd really like to make it up to you. If you still want to go out to dinner, I would be *more* than happy to take you. Anywhere you want to go, babe, the choice is yours."

"Forget it; I'm not in the mood anymore!" Nellie hissed furiously. Then she paused for a second, noticing the cut on Roger's forehead and how dirty his clothes were. "What the hell happened to you?" she asked in a sarcastic tone.

Roger exhaled as if breathing a sigh of relief. He hoped that if Nellie would turn her attention to his wounds, then perhaps she would calm down enough to listen and understand why he was late.

He took another deep breath and started to walk towards her. "It is a long story..."

Before he could say anything more, Nellie turned her back around and strutted toward her car while shouting to Roger, "Well, tell it to someone who cares, because I'm just not interested in hearing it."

Roger was flabbergasted by her callous remark but did not say a word to refute. Although his feelings were hurt, he felt that Nellie's attitude was somewhat justified. He also knew if he was to act defensively towards her right then, it could potentially set her off again.

When Nellie reached the car, she opened the driver's side door and leaned inside. She placed her suitcase on the passenger side seat and sat down on the driver's seat with one hand on the steering wheel and her other on the door handle.

"By the way, Roger, I'm going to spend some time at my folks' house," she uttered with watery eyes. "I thought you might've asked me *why* I was carrying a suitcase with me, but I can see now you didn't even take the time to notice—or care."

"That's not true!" Roger blurted out.

"I think we could both use some time apart right now, and I'm going to stay in Syracuse with them for the week. I've already called my work and made arrangements to take next week off."

"A whole week?" Roger remarked in shock.

"Yes, that way we'll have plenty of time to think and decide if we really want to continue this relationship. I'll call you tomorrow to let you know when I'll be back, but more than likely it'll be next Sunday."

The culmination of all the discouraging incidents that have plagued Roger and Nellie's relationship recently had finally hit hard, and a rush of emotions rose to the surface. Tears of sadness and frustration began to form in his eyes, and his throat became dry as sandpaper, making it difficult to swallow.

"Don't you want to talk about this first before you just take off?" he asked with a shaky voice.

"I'm done talking," she responded coldly. Then she slammed the vehicle's door and drove away.

As Roger returned to his car, he was hurt, discouraged, and confused over the events that occurred over the duration of just a couple hours. It was just too much for him to handle. He decided he needed a strong drink, maybe several, in order to de-stress and relax.

Roger slunk back into his car and turned the automobile around. He squealed the tires as he headed for Kitty's Bar, the only place he felt would supply any pleasure at all. Maybe there he could drink enough to forget about his disastrous afternoon and numb his body of everything.

When Roger arrived at Liberty Street and entered Kitty's Bar, he noticed there weren't many people in the establishment. Although it was still early and the crowds didn't usually start rolling in until about nine o'clock or so, it still seemed somewhat slow. He only saw a total of three or four people who were gathered around the billiards table, a couple more playing darts, and about four others standing at the juke box.

The first thing Roger did once he stepped inside the bar was go to the men's room and splash his face with cold water. The cool refreshing sensation helped clear his head since he was still feeling slightly dazed from his escapade at the ferry service. Next, he proceeded to wipe the dried blood from his forehead and tried to clean himself up a little before he went back out to the bar.

Holly Boliver was tending bar and reading a romance novel between serving drinks. She was so engulfed in her book that she didn't notice Roger had entered the tavern until he sat down at the bar and cleared his throat to attract her attention—so he could order a drink.

As Holly looked up and saw Roger, she exclaimed, "You look like hell, Roger! What happened to you?"

Roger turned his head so that he wasn't looking directly at her.

"To tell you the truth, Holly, I'm not quite sure," he groaned. "All I know is that it has been a horrible day, and right now, I could definitely use a drink."

Holly poured him a double shot of Jim Beam Whiskey and a draft beer to chase it down. She was sure he needed something strong from the looks of him.

"Here you go, hun," she said softly. "This one is on me. Do you wanna talk about what happened, or should I wait until you've had a few drinks to get the story out of you?"

"I'm not really in the mood to talk tonight," Roger uttered impassively.

"Okay, you don't have to talk if you don't want to. But it's going to get quite lonely—and boring—sitting over here without talking to anyone."

"Well, I'll take my chances," he grumbled before gulping down his whiskey.

After several more drinks, as well as trying to avoid Holly's persistent questions, Roger decided he'd better go home and call Nellie's parents to see if she arrived safely to their house. Hopefully, he could make amends and smooth things over with her.

As Roger started to stand up from his stool, he staggered and nearly fell down. The realization that he was tipsy was beginning to register, and Roger knew he had succeeded in drowning all the sorrows he came to the bar to drown.

Holly noticed Roger's wobbly condition and put down her book. She walked to the end of the bar and placed her hand on his back, rubbing his neck as she spoke in a soft feminine voice.

"Hold on there, big fella. You're not driving anywhere in your condition. Would you like me to call Nellie for you? Maybe she can come pick you up."

"Don't bother," he said, hunched over and garbling his words. "There's nobody at my house to answer the phone anyway. There probably won't be anyone in my life to worry about me *ever* again."

By the negative attitude and his surly tone of voice, Holly realized that Nellie was at least part of the problem which was bothering Roger.

She leaned over the bar, and in a soothing voice, she whispered, "All right, I won't call anyone if you don't want me to. Wait right here for a minute, would you please?"

Holly stepped out from behind the bar, walked beyond the billiards table and went directly to Tim Matthews, who just happened to be off-duty that night. "Hey, Tim, would you do me a favor?"

"Like what?"

"Will you take over for me while I get Roger out of here? He's had too much to drink and is in no condition to drive himself home. Apparently, he has no one to pick him up right now either."

"Too much to drink?" Tim hollered out, quite astonished. "How can that *possibly* be? He's only been here a little over an hour—and he's one the regulars who drink here!"

"Well, he's had five double shots of Jim Beam whiskey and four beers."

"In an hour!" exclaimed Tim. "What the hell is he trying to do? Drink himself into a coma?"

"I guess he's had a really bad day, and he doesn't want to talk about what's bothering him...not even with me. And we're supposed to be close friends!"

Tim's tone turned sarcastic and he pointed towards Roger. "Well, I've had plenty of bad days too, but I think I handle them a little better than he does. Doesn't he realize what he's doing to his body when he does shit like that?"

"Apparently not."

"He needs to be more responsible. Too many nights like tonight and he'll be drinking himself into an early grave."

"I don't think he really cares what you think, Tim, but I'll let him know you're *really* concerned about his welfare." Holly replied, somewhat snippy. "So, will you cover for me or not?"

"Yeah, I'll do it," he mumbled. "I can use the extra couple hours anyway. Besides, the tips will come in handy this weekend when I'm in New York City, watching the Yankees baseball game."

"You're a Yankees fan, huh?"

"Definitely! They're playing the Montreal Expos in an Inter-league baseball game, and I'd like to purchase some souvenirs while I'm there. I've also heard rumors that the Expos will be leaving the city of Montreal soon, and I want to stock up on the team's paraphernalia while I can."

"Whatever you say," Holly expressed in a tedious voice. "I've never understood the fascination of watching a baseball game. I've always been a football fan myself and would rather drive the extra miles to watch a Baltimore Ravens game over the Yankees any day."

"Oh really? Well...good for you!" Tim countered, slightly peeved. "Is there anything else you came over here to talk about?"

"Nope, that's all I wanted. Thanks for taking over for me tonight; I owe you one," she said, smiling. Then, Holly turned around and walked back toward the bar.

Even though they had not dated in several years, there was still a part of Holly that felt as though it was her responsibility to take care of Roger. She knew that Tim was right about Roger and he definitely *did* drink too much. But she also knew that Roger was with another woman now, and it was not her place to tell him how he should live his own life. It saddened her to watch him act this way because he still held a special place in her heart...and she felt guilty about having those feelings.

She approached Roger and put her hands on his shoulders. Then Holly leaned down and spoke gently in his ear. "Alright Roger, I'm back. How are you feeling now?"

Roger was still hunched over in his chair; his face appeared pale. "I ain't feelin' so good, Holly. I think I'm gonna be sick."

"I had a feeling you might say that," she stated as she placed his arm over her shoulder and helped him to his feet. "Why don't you come with me outside, and we'll get some fresh air."

As Holly tried to help Roger up, she realized she wasn't going to be able to take him very far because he was much too heavy and very unstable. Holly lived directly above Kitty's Bar and had a private entrance to her apartment out front, near the corner of the building. Since her place was so close to the tavern, she decided to escort him up to her apartment and let him sleep it off on her sofa.

While she was assisting Roger up the stairs to her apartment, Holly became aware of his muscular build and how much more mature-looking he had become since the days when they were a couple. She always thought Roger was attractive, but for some reason that she could not explain, he just seemed to be even *more* handsome than ever before. However, he didn't look so 'appealing' once his face became gray. Roger abruptly stopped, leaned over, and then puked; splashing regurgitated liquor and pretzels all over Holly's stairs and shoes.

Roger was so drunk that he was nearly as helpless as a child and totally dependent on her. With each step, it was getting increasingly harder to make it up the stairs to her apartment—especially since she was wearing a tight, short skirt and jet black pumps with a three-inch heel, which were now covered in vomit.

When they finally got to the top of the stairs, Holly guided Roger into her apartment and onto the recliner across the living room. She kicked off her shoes, turned on the miniature lamp sitting in the middle of the coffee table, and moved over toward the couch.

She began removing the scattered newspapers off from the cushions and spoke in a hushed voice. "Just sit there for a moment, Roger, while I get the couch cleared off. You can rest here for awhile until you feel better. Or at least until you're able to drive."

When she lifted up the pizza box that was sitting on the couch, she noticed that the grease had leaked through the box and all over the cushions and pillows.

"Damn it! I knew I shouldn't have left that box sitting there all day." She sighed and said, "Well, I guess you can't lie down on the couch. It's going to take me awhile to clean up this mess and wipe the upholstery clean. Oh well, I'll just put you in my bedroom for now and you can rest in there."

Before she went over to get Roger, Holly walked over to the compact disc tower beside the couch and took a CD off the rack. Roger's eyes were half open as he watched her remove the disc from its case, insert it into the stereo that sat on the top shelf of her TV entertainment center, and push the PLAY button.

"That's one of my favorite songs," he said, slurring his words. "*The Lady in Red* was our song when we were a couple. Do you remember that, Holly?"

"Yeah, I still remember," she replied as she helped him back up to his feet. "I just bought Chris DeBurgh's Greatest Hits the other day when I was at the mall."

"I'm surprised stores still keep his music in stock," Roger commented.

"Me too!" Holly admitted. "When I saw the CD, I knew I just had to get it. I remember how I'd listen to his songs when I was stressed out as a method to calm me down."

"Yeah, it soothes me too."

"I wasn't even thinking about *our* past when I put it in the stereo, Roger. I was just in the mood to listen to it. He has a pleasant voice...and after dealing with customers all day, I need something to relax me."

With a big yawn, Roger said, "I can't think of it right now, but I know DeBurgh had another hit song—aside from *Lady in Red*."

"Your right. Something about a ferryman, I think."

Roger put his hand over his eyes and grimaced. "Ugh. I can't concentrate on anything right now with your room spinning around so much. Do you have any Aspirin or some other type of pain reliever?"

"Don't worry, hun. Everything's going to be all right," Holly whispered as she approached him. "I'll help you lie down and then look for something to ease your headache."

Holly took Roger by the arm as she escorted him into the bedroom and laid him down on her bed so he could rest. She was staggering as she carried him along and felt as if her legs were going to give out beneath her.

By the time she finally had Roger situated on her bed so he wouldn't fall off, she was nearly out of breath. Holly was exhausted by his weight leaning against her, and also from trying to haul him up the stairs to her apartment.

She laid down on the bed next to him to get her breath, and once again became aware of Roger's muscular arms and chest. With a smile on her face, she eased over to Roger, nuzzled up close to him, and rested her head on his shoulder and her hand upon his chest.

Nearly forty-five minutes passed while they relaxed in the darkness, silent and still. She remained alongside him the entire time, listening to him breathe as he slept.

Shortly thereafter, Roger opened his eyes, and for the first time, began to be aware of his surroundings and Holly lying beside him. He could feel her warm breath on his neck and smell her alluring perfume. It was called *Navy*, he remembered. The same kind of perfume she had worn ever since he bought her a bottle the night they went to the prom together, some years ago.

As Holly shifted closer to Roger, he could hear the swish of her nylon stockings as she crossed her legs. He started to realize that Holly was stroking and rubbing his chest and abdomen in a stimulating manner. By now, her hand had wandered down near the top of Roger's jeans as he was now becoming more aroused, and he was all-too certain Holly was aware of it.

Roger lifted his hand up and began stroking her hair and rubbing the small of her back. He maneuvered his hand under her shirt, touching her bare back. His hand inched upward to the middle of her back and unhooked her bra with the speed and ease of an expert.

Holly jerked her body and glanced up at Roger, staring him in the eyes without saying a word.

"I'm sorry," he said. "I shouldn't have done that."

"Shh..." she whispered. Then she lifted her head up towards his and began kissing him on the cheek and lips.

They kissed, with a slight tenderness at first, but then became more aggressive and passionate. It invoked memories of the past but felt as new and pure as the first kiss they ever shared. Holly slid her hand from his chest to his face, feeling the hard lines of his body and tasting the intoxicating heat of his mouth.

His arms wrapped around her, and he pulled her close to his body. Holly remembered how his touch had always made her feel safe and secure, and at that moment, she couldn't help but think how 'right' it felt to be in his arms again. His electrifying kisses made her swoon with desire and his touch made her body quiver. As she fell deeper into his seduction, Holly knew she was exactly where she wanted to be.

Roger could no longer resist the urges he felt, and in one swift movement, he rolled over and had his muscular frame above Holly, looking into her eyes. In the dimness of the room, her eyes didn't appear blue at all; they seemed a more subtle shade of green.

For a moment, Roger was confused, not knowing why she looked so different. He took a quick glimpse over and saw her eyeglasses lying upon her bedside table and a contact lens case sitting beside them. Roger glanced back and smiled, adoring the amazing color of her eyes.

He kissed her hard, and in an instant, they were frantically pulling at each other's clothing and undressing each other. As they continued to grab at each other with an animalistic ferocity, their breathing got heavier. Within a matter of seconds they had all their garments off, thrown on the floor and were making love.

Holly arched her back and thrust her hips into Roger, making his body burn with lust for her. They rolled over again, and he rested his head back down on the pillow while she positioned herself on top of him. Her legs were straddled along his sides, and she let out a massive moan while she tensed her body.

With her body heating up, Holly leaned downward to kiss his neck and chest for a moment, but her body was completely overwhelmed with passion so she quickly sat up, pulling his hands up to her chest. Roger stroked her smooth and soft skin, affectionately caressing her supple bosoms. Holly threw her head back and tossed her golden locks from side to side as her moaning got progressively louder.

They made love for what seemed like hours until Roger finally rolled over and collapsed. He and Holly gasped for breath as they lounged next to each other, regaining their composure. They laid in the dark silence and embraced, covered only in their own perspiration and breathing heavily.

With exhaustion setting in, and with feeling a type of closeness that they had not shared in a long time, the two former lovers held onto one another until they drifted off asleep.

Chapter 14:

Frightening Phantasm

As Roger woke up the next morning, he suffered from an excruciating pain in his head while his mouth felt as if it was stuffed with cotton. He sat up and looked around the room, remembering that he stayed at Holly's apartment, even though she was no longer next to him. He heard the sound of water running in the bathroom and listened as Holly was singing *The Lady in Red* in the shower.

Roger tossed the covers off and sat on the edge of the bed, moaning in discomfort. It was a self-induced throbbing, which was the result from all the liquor he drank, leaving behind the severe hangover he suffered from. His stomach grumbled from hunger, but he was more concerned about the dry, crusty blood on top of his head and the lump on the back of his neck he received at the ferry service. He swallowed some aspirin Holly had left for him on the nightstand and rubbed his temples to try to get some relief.

"It sounds like you're finally awake," yelled Holly from inside the shower. "Did you have a nice rest, 'Sleeping Beauty'?"

"Yeah, I suppose." Roger moaned tiredly.

Holly's tone of voice was very cheerful and vivacious. She was bursting with enthusiasm and sounded like a woman who had just won the lottery. "Hey, babe!" she hollered out to him. "Can you do a huge favor for me and check what time it is?"

Roger slowly reached over to the nightstand and grabbed her alarm clock. "Its 10:30," he said, quite surprised. "Wow! I can't believe I slept as long as I did. I apologize if I've kept you from any plans you might have. I'll hurry up and get dressed so you can get to wherever you have to go."

Holly turned off the shower and grabbed a towel. "No, don't be silly. You're not in the way at all. There isn't any place I really need to be at right now. I plan to go to the supermarket today, but I can do that anytime." She wrapped the towel around herself as she opened the bathroom door and walked into the bedroom, still soaking wet. "I was just wondering if you wanted to go to the Superior Restaurant and get something to eat. I know it's a little late for breakfast, but I'll treat you to lunch if you'd like."

Roger, who was bent over and rubbing his neck, lifted his head up to look at Holly. His heart began to ache when he saw the smile upon her face.

"Listen, hun," he uttered soberly. "Can you sit down for a minute? I think we should talk."

She flopped down on the bed next to him, snuggling up close. "Okay," she said, still looking joyful. "What do you want to talk about?"

Roger's heart pounded swiftly in his chest, and his palms began to sweat, knowing what he was about to say. "I think that maybe it wouldn't be such a good idea if we went out for lunch today."

His statement perplexed Holly. She also noticed the stiffness in his actions and a quiver in his voice as he spoke, which made her feel quite uncomfortable.

"Why not?" she inquired as her hands began to fidget and her tone turned weary.

Roger fumbled his words and began to stutter, appearing almost embarrassed, as he tried to find the right terms to express his emotions. "I appreciate all you did for me, and I can't thank you enough for letting me stay here. Last night was great," he quietly stated. "It was everything I wanted and needed it to be. You were there when I needed you most, just like you've always been. But I don't want to give you the wrong impression about what happened between us last night."

Holly sat speechless for a moment. She felt as though someone had knocked the wind out of her, and she was unable to say a word. Finally, after several agonizing seconds of dead air, she was finally able to muster, "So what is it you're trying to tell me?"

Roger took a long, deep breath before he told her the words that were almost too painful for him to say. "What I did was wrong. I'm still with Nellie and even though our relationship isn't perfect, I'm not ready to throw everything we have together away...not yet anyway."

These were the words Holly may have been expecting Roger to say, but not hoping to hear. Her once exuberant voice had turned silent, and she remained perfectly still as Roger reached for her hand, trying to hold back tears of his own.

"I am *so* sorry if I've misled you in any way. I don't want to hurt you, Holly. In fact, under different circumstances, I would love to be holding you in my arms again. Believe me, my decision is not meant to belittle you...or what happened between us last night."

Holly bit her lip but remained silent.

Roger closed his eyes tightly while squeezing Holly's hand; his stomach ached, and he felt as if he was going to be physically ill. "I've always cared about you, and deep down I know I'm still in love with you."

Tears swelled in Holly's eyes. She lowered her head and stared at the floor so Roger could not see her face. "Okay," she mumbled in a shaky voice. "If that's the way you feel, then I'm fine with it, too."

Roger stood up and began gathering his belongings while Holly sat on the bed in silence. She bit her lip again and fought to hold back her tears. She desperately wanted to burst out crying but was making an attempt to hold off an emotional breakdown until Roger left. She realized that Roger's words were truthful, and this was not the way, nor the time, to begin a relationship. As much as it pained her, Holly knew she had to let him go.

After Roger finished getting dressed, he sat back down on the bed to put on his shoes. Then he leaned over next to Holly, gave her a kiss on the cheek and said, "I just want you to know how truly sorry I am. Hurting you is the last thing I ever meant to do."

Holly grabbed a tissue off the nightstand and wiped away the tear running down her cheek. "There's nothing to be sorry for. It's not like I thought we were getting back together or anything."

Roger opened the bedroom door but was unable to leave. With his back turned away from her and his body halfway out her room, he suddenly stopped and stood motionless. He wanted to turn around and say something to her, but nothing appropriate came to his mind. Instead, for fear of saying something unfitting and risk upsetting her more, he decided to remain silent and continue out the door.

While driving home, Roger thought about whether or not he should call Nellie, and if so, what would he say. He wondered if he should tell her over the phone what happened last night or wait until she came back. The one thing he was sure about, however, was that he had to be honest with her and hope for the best.

As Roger pulled up to his house, he noticed a magenta-colored Mustang parked alongside the street curb and Bucky standing in the driveway. He pulled up behind Bucky's car, and before he could even turn off the engine, Bucky ran over to Roger's car and opened the door.

"Where were you last night?" Bucky yelled, hurriedly and with impatience in his voice. "I tried calling you about twenty times! I realize it's the weekend, and you also like to have a few drinks, but you were *supposed* to get in touch with me after you talked to Louis Ferr. I started getting really worried that something happened to you and Nellie."

Roger pushed Bucky aside and stepped out of his car. "I didn't come home last night because I spent the night at Holly's apartment."

Bucky's mouth dropped to the floor in shock. "You did what?" he shouted. "How the hell did that happen?"

"It was a mistake brought upon by a combination of poor judgment and too much self-pity. Last night, after I went to the Mephistis Pheles Ferry Service, I came home and Nellie was completely pissed off because I missed our dinner plans."

"Can you blame her?"

"Not funny, Bucky. Nellie had a suitcase in her hands and drove to her parents' house in Syracuse. I was feeling awfully low after she took off and needed a drink to relax me."

"Any you went to Kitty's Bar next?"

"Yeah, but I ended up having a few too many and had to be escorted out of the bar by Holly, who let me stay at her place for the night."

Bucky calmed down and put his hand on Roger's shoulder. "Listen, if you need a place to stay for the night or need someone to talk to, you can come to my house. For god's sake, don't be hanging out with your ex-girlfriend at a time when you're having relationship problems and are vulnerable! Do you actually think Nellie would be all right with the fact you were at Holly's last night? That kind of news would absolutely crush her and you know it!"

"I realize what I did was wrong. And I'm in total agreement with you. I feel absolutely horrible about the entire situation—about destroying Nellie's faith and trust in me, and also about what happened between Holly and me."

"I don't know what to say, bud." Bucky said, shaking his head. "I wish I had some words of wisdom for you, but nothing comes to mind."

Roger sighed. "I was so upset after Nellie stormed off and I lost control of my drinking. I let it impair my judgment and ended up hurting two very important women. I don't know what I'm going to say to Nellie just yet, but I already told Holly that spending last night with her was a mistake. She looked so sad when I left her place, and I feel like an asshole for leading her on. She was practically in tears when I left her place."

Roger's eyes began to swell with tears, and his voice drifted off to the point where it resembled a whisper when he said, "And so was I."

Bucky noticed the sorrow in Roger's face and decided to change the topic and lighten things up a little. "Hey, are you hungry? Have you eaten anything yet today?"

"No, I haven't," Roger replied. "Holly wanted to take me out for breakfast, but I declined because I thought it would be too awkward."

"Oh, I can understand that. How about I take you out for a late brunch at the Chatterbox Diner? It's close by and they have great food, too."

Roger nodded. "Sounds good, but I ain't got any money."

"I'll pay for both of our meals and leave the tip this time. Putting some food in your stomach will probably help you feel better, and it'll give us a chance to talk. I have so many questions and I don't know where to begin!"

"Sure, you can ask me all the questions you want. Let's just hurry up so we can get to the diner. I haven't had anything to eat since yesterday afternoon, and I'm starving!"

Bucky chuckled to himself as he walked to the other side of the vehicle. "Okay, hop in my car and we'll go." He reached in his glove compartment and pulled out a granola bar, then handed it to Roger. "Here...munch on this until we get there. Hey, if you don't mind, I'd like to go the back roads so we have some time to talk. Besides, we can drive past the ferry service and see if Scott's car is anywhere near there."

Roger swiftly tore the wrapper off, tilted his head back, and stuffed his face with the entire granola bar. With his mouth full and his voice muffled, he said, "I don't care, it's only a few minutes out of the way, and I wouldn't mind checking that road again. Maybe I'll see something that'll jog my memory."

After traveling only a few hundred yards down the road, Bucky's curiosity got the best of him and he asked, "So, Roger, did you and Holly sleep in the same bed last night?"

Roger felt uncomfortable answering his question and was not sure of what to say. Finally, he blurted out the first thing that came to his mind. "Bucky, if it's all the same to you, I'd prefer to change the subject. I really don't want to think about that topic right now."

"Fine," Bucky said as though he was insulted. "If you don't want to talk about it, I'm not going to pry the information out of you." He paused for a moment before asking, "By the way, did you find anything suspicious while you were at the ferry service?"

"Not really. There were a couple things Mr. Ferr said that seemed peculiar, but nothing so far out of the ordinary that it'd lead someone to believe he had something to do with Scott's disappearance."

Roger stopped and hesitated for a second. "The place seemed pretty quiet to me. The only thing I was able to get a good look at and check out was a large rock in the main parking lot that had some red paint scuffed on it. If I were to make an assumption, I'd say it looked as though it could've come from a vehicle of some sort, but I can't be sure of that either. Besides, I don't know how long the paint has been there, what caused it, or who did it."

Bucky's expression turned into a complete blank, emotionless stare as he inquired, "What color did you say the paint was?"

Roger took a deep breath as he tried to concentrate even harder on the previous night's events. "It was a reddish tint. Actually, I think it was more of a dark red."

"The same color as Scott's car," Bucky replied, his face starting to turn white.

Suddenly, a chill ran down Roger's spine, and his voice became emotional. "Really? What do you think we should do?"

"I know Sergeant Johnson warned me to stay away from Mr. Ferr, but right now I don't care if he throws me in jail or not. I'm going down there, take a look at this rock, and maybe ruffle some feathers at the same time."

"Alright," Roger stated reluctantly, "but I don't think this is such a good idea. Mr. Ferr might call the police the moment we pull up to his office."

Bucky's behavior turned irregular, as though he was a person obsessed with an objective. "Maybe so, but I absolutely *have* to see if the paint matches Scott's car, and I'm not leaving there until I do. Do you remember any other details? Or how about your conversation when you asked Louis Ferr about Scott Patterson?"

"He didn't say too much about Scott either; although, I don't remember a lot about our discussion. My memory is still a little foggy from all the alcohol I drank last night, and my head is throbbing from getting whacked by a huge tree branch. The damn thing rendered me unconscious for more than two hours, and I still have a large goose egg on top of my head."

"A tree branch?" Bucky said, curious and confused. "How the hell did that happen?"

"Well, let me see if I can sort this out," Roger responded. "I remember that I had just finished talking to Mr. Ferr and was on my way to meet Nellie at the Superior Restaurant. As I was heading back to my car, I saw the old tool shed out back of the office and remembered how you thought there was a bicycle inside. I wanted to see if it was Bob's bike, so I started to walk over towards the shed to have a peek inside."

Bucky jerked in astonishment. "The tool shed! Don't you realize how much of a risk you were taking? For one thing, I can't believe you were trying to sneak in there during daylight hours. Did anyone see you snooping around?"

"I didn't think so; although, I can't be sure. I glanced around to see if anyone was watching me, but saw no one. I figured that would be my best chance to get inside the shed without having to ask or be escorted. But as I got closer, the wind started to pick up, and just as I was about to open the door, I heard a loud cracking noise before everything went black."

"Well, isn't that just convenient for Mr. Ferr that you got injured," Bucky uttered sarcastically. "The luck this guy has is uncanny!"

"Why do you say that?" questioned Roger. "It's not like he could've had anything to do with the tree branch hitting me in the head."

"Yeah, I guess you're right," Bucky stated reluctantly. Then he took his eyes off the road for a moment, staring directly at Roger. "However, I gotta say, it sure seems like anything that *could* go in Mr. Ferr's favor, usually does."

As Bucky was talking, Roger glanced at the road and saw a ghostly, almost zombie-like figure standing in the middle of the road with no intention of moving out of the way. Roger's eyes widened and Bucky shifted his attention back to the road.

"Bucky, look out!" he screamed at the top of his lungs.

Bucky yanked the wheel hard to the right so that he missed the figure in the road. The car veered off the side, and the tires screeched while it went out of control. Mud mixed with gravel splashed up on the hood and windshield, and a loud thud was heard as the car landed forcefully into the ditch.

"What the hell was that?" Roger hollered. "There was some freaky looking person just standing in the middle of the road!"

Bucky checked himself over for any injuries before answering. He peered out his dust covered window and said, "I saw him too, but I don't know who it was."

Bucky paused, and after determining that his view was too obscured to see clearly, he went on to say, "I seem to be all right; I can't find any bruises anyway." He turned his attention to his passenger. "How about you, Roger? Did you get hurt at all, or are you okay?"

"No, I suppose I'll be fine." replied Roger, starting to calm down. "I guess that's just one of the risks you take when you get in an accident with a car that has no airbags."

"I see your inane sense of humor is still intact," Bucky responded. "Make sure all your body parts are in working order; I'm going to see if that person is still in the road and examine how much damage I just did to my car."

Bucky opened his car door and climbed out. He walked around the car and shook his head at the damage done. "Well, it appears that going over to the ferry service is out of the question, and unfortunately, so is going to the Chatterbox Diner to get some food."

"Why?" Roger asked as he opened his door to get out. "What happened?"

"For starters, I blew a tire on the front passenger side when I threw my car into the ditch. I also busted a headlight and scraped up the side fender. Other than that, I don't know if the frame is bent, and there might be additional damage to the engine or other parts under the hood."

As Roger walked over to the fender and inspected the damage, Bucky reached into his sport coat and grabbed his cell phone. "Roger, look in the road to see if there's any sign of anyone around! While you do that, I'll try and get a hold of a tow company or a mechanic."

Roger stepped out of the ditch and stood in the middle of the road, looking for any possible footprints. He searched for any sign of tracks and kept looking up and down the street hoping to catch a glimpse of whoever had been in the road.

Roger walked up and down both sides of the road, checking the ditches and surrounding area for the ghostly person. After a few minutes of unsuccessful investigating, Bucky walked up to him and said, "Well, I just called the tow service."

Roger let out a sigh of relief. "That's good. I'd rather not be stranded out here all day. What did they tell you?"

"Well, I gave them our location ran down a general overview of the damage. They said an employee of theirs is in the vicinity, and he's driving a truck big enough to handle the job. He should be here in about 15 to 20 minutes."

Just then, John Sears and Adam "Red" Richardson came running down the road, screaming at Roger and Bucky to get their attention. They were wearing knee-high rubber boots, carrying fishing poles, and lugging around large tackle boxes as they lumbered their way over to the car.

Adam rushed up to Bucky, huffing and puffing as he tried to catch his breath. "Hey, dudes…you two alright?"

"Yeah, Red, we're fine." Bucky answered. He jerked his head around and pointed to his vehicle. "My car, on the other hand, took her fair share of dents and scrapes." Then Bucky shifted his attention back to John and Adam. "Hey, where'd you guys come from anyway?"

"We were over the hill doin' some fishing, and we heard your tires squealing," John responded.

"Ahh, I see," said Roger.

John walked over to inspect the damage of the car, pulling a flashlight out of his tackle box. He leaned down on one knee and pulled several chunks of mud away from the tires. Then he got down on all fours, sweeping the beam of the flashlight back and forth beneath the undercarriage of the car.

Roger followed John over to the ditch as Adam continued to talk to Bucky.

"I'm glad to hear you're okay, cuz." Adam said with a relieved sigh. "I was just about to put a worm on my hook when I saw a vehicle fishtailin' off the road. I recognized your car, and my eyes nearly jumped out of my head. That's when John and I high-tailed it over here to make sure you were okay. I gotta look out for my family, y'know."

"Thanks, Red. I appreciate the concern."

At that moment, Roger and John came back over. John placed his fishing pole and tackle box on the ground next to where Adam had placed his.

"Now that we're all together," Bucky announced, "did any of you see the person who was standing in the road as we were going into the ditch?"

John and Adam looked at each other and shrugged their shoulders.

"Nah, I didn't see anybody," Adam replied.

"Nope. Neither did I," John answered.

Their answer perplexed Bucky and left him in a state of awe. "That is so strange," he stated while shaking his head. "I wonder how that person disappeared so fast without the two of you noticing him."

Bucky paused to think for a brief moment before he asked, "How about you, Roger? You told me that you saw someone. Are you sure you didn't see the person's face, or recognize who it was standing in the middle of the road?"

"Actually I did," Roger answered cautiously. "But I still can't believe my eyes. I mean, it can't be who I think it was. It just can't be! However, if I was to make a guess, I'd say it looked as if the person was Bob Earle."

"Yes, that's what I thought, too," Bucky concurred. "I'm *not* positive it was Bob, but whoever it was appeared to be very pale. He was just standing in the middle of the road, looking like a zombie and wearing nothing but a ripped-up pair of pants."

Bucky paused once again as if he was not sure if he wanted to say anything more. Finally, he built up enough nerve but could only speak in an uneasy voice. "Did anyone see his chest?" he asked the guys.

"Yeah," replied Roger wearily. "It seemed as if something was written in blood, but I didn't get a good enough look to see what it was. I was too busy grabbing onto the dashboard and bracing myself for the impact."

Bucky leaned in close and peered over his shoulders, perusing the area one more time. He turned back to the men standing before him and spoke in a somber, almost monotone voice. "Well, I *did* get a good enough glance," he said. "There was definitely *something* on his chest, but I don't think it was written. He got pretty close to my car as we were veering off the road, and his eyes..." Bucky stopped.

"What about his eyes?" inquired Adam.

"They seemed so black, so empty," mumbled Bucky. "I swear...it appeared as if he had no pupils."

All four men were silent.

"As for the rest of his appearance..." Bucky continued. "With the ragged clothes, the pasty white skin, and the blank stare upon his face...he looked like death itself. And because of the jaggedness of the letters on his chest, I would be willing to believe the writing was carved with a knife or some other kind of sharp object."

Adam and John faced each other with confused looks upon their faces. They remained quiet as neither one of them knew what to make of this situation.

Roger, on the other hand, was as curious as he was astounded. His heart raced with excitement and fear, and he felt his throat go dry;

however, he somehow managed to find the courage to ask, "Did you see what it said?"

"Yes I did," Bucky stated solemnly. "It was a warning of some sort. It said...*Beware.*"

Chapter 15:

Revelations

The following week went by with relative ease, with no strange instances or more disappearances occurring. By the time Sunday approached, Roger was able to set aside some free time for himself. Instead of relaxing in the sun or going to the beach, he was at home during the afternoon, sitting in front of his desk with a stack of old textbooks in front of him.

Roger leaned back in his wooden chair to stretch and looked at the clock, noticing it was 4:20 pm. Since so much commotion had been occurring around town lately, he hadn't been able research the name "Mephistis Pheles" like he discussed with Bucky at Kitty's Bar several weeks ago.

Over on the couch thumbing through books of his own, and munching on a Hershey's candy bar, was Bryan Harsha. Because of Bryan's vast knowledge of folklore, Roger telephoned him and asked if he could come over, thinking he might be able to help. Not only was Bryan a good friend of Roger's, but he was also someone he trusted. And with all the peculiar events that transpired in town as of late, trust was a highly valuable asset.

Roger had been reading one book after another, trying to dig up information for the past few hours. He was having little to no luck at all, and then Bryan arrived at his doorstep not more than thirty minutes ago with a stack of texts of his own. Now, both men sat without speaking, deep in concentration, when all of a sudden Roger broke away from his train of thought and turned his attention over to his partner.

"Thanks for coming over today and helping me examine all this material," Roger said. "I have so many books; it would've taken me several days to look through them all."

"No problem," Bryan responded courteously. "I'm just sorry I showed up so late. I would've been here two hours ago, but I had to finish some paperwork Becky Taylor dropped off in my office."

"She still workin' ya like a horse, huh?"

"Yeah, she has. I've been trying to keep up with my duties at the library and stay on top of my work for the town council, but I'm starting to feel worn out."

"I know how busy you are, and I appreciate the fact you took time out of your hectic schedule to come over here and give me a hand. By the way, thanks for bringing some of those old books on mythology and folklore from the library."

Bryan just smirked and said, "Hey, if there's anything you need for literature, I can pretty much get it for you. That is, if it's not already checked out by someone else."

"You certainly are my 'go-to' guy for information, buddy."

With a long sigh, Bryan uttered, "And by the way, I know it's my fault we got such a late start today…which must be kind of an inconvenience for you. So, if you have other things to do this afternoon, I won't hold you up."

Roger shrugged. "Actually, I made sure I didn't have anything planned for my day. I wanted to keep my afternoon open so I could devote all my attention to this little project. I told Bucky I'd research the name of the ferry service almost three weeks ago, but lately I haven't been focused on much of anything other than the disappearances of Bob Earle and Scott Patterson."

"That's understandable. The disappearances have kept *all* of us preoccupied."

"Bucky seems more preoccupied than anyone else," stated Roger. "Now that he *completely* believes Mr. Ferr is somehow responsible for the strange happenings, I figured it was high time I kept my word to him and found out if there's a hidden meaning to the name of Ferr's curious company."

"Great!" Bryan yelled exuberantly. "I have no pressing engagements of my own, either. If you want, we can spend as much time as we need going through all these texts."

"Well, I'm supposed to meet Nellie at the Superior Restaurant for a late dinner," Roger replied. "She's coming back from being at her parents' house in Syracuse all this week so I thought it would be a nice gesture on my part to take her out for an elegant meal."

"What time are your dinner plans?"

"Nellie's supposed to be back in town around six o'clock, but she called earlier and said she probably wouldn't come back to my house before dinner. I guess she has to go to the drug store and do some other little errands first."

"So, what time do you have to leave?"

"I told her I'd make the reservations for us at the Superior Restaurant, and I'd meet her there by seven o'clock. We still have a couple of hours left before I have to go."

"That's fine. I'm certain we'll be worn out from reading and ready to call it quits by that time anyway. Besides, if we're lucky, we might find what we're searching for before then and won't have to go through each of these books with a fine-toothed comb."

Roger looked down at his watch to check the time, and then shifted his attention towards Bryan. "Can you do me a favor, Bryan?"

"Possibly. What is it?"

"When it gets close to seven o'clock, remind me about my dinner with Nellie or I'll probably forget. As unsteady as our relationship is right now, I don't need to do something foolish, which would make her hot-tempered and unpleasant toward me again."

"Are you and Nellie having some problems?" Bryan asked with concern. "Is there something going on you'd like to talk about?"

"I'm not really sure what's going on in our relationship anymore," Roger answered in a bewildered tone. "The only thing I'm absolutely sure of is that I don't want to lead her on about anything, and I want to be totally honest with her."

Bryan raised a brow. "Honest about what?"

"I've made plenty of stupid blunders and asinine mistakes since we've been together, and I want to find out if our relationship is strong enough to survive them."

Roger's voice became very soft, drifting increasingly quiet to the point where his words were barely louder than a whisper as he said, "Some more serious than others."

"So this isn't just any ordinary night out on the town for the two of you?" questioned Bryan. "This dinner has an actual purpose to it?"

Roger stared into emptiness with a look of intense concentration upon his face. "This dinner is very important to me...and to our relationship. Tonight we're going to have a deep meaningful talk about our future. A real heart-to-heart talk, just the two of us."

"That's terrific, Roger. I've never been in a relationship before, so I don't really know what that's like."

"Relationships are hard work, Bryan. Tonight's little talk is something we should've done a long time ago, but I've been putting it off until now. I'm going to be up-front about my feelings, and I *need* to be completely honest and truthful with everything that's happened recently."

After a second, he snapped out of his daze and glanced at Bryan. "Well, I have to quit rambling and get some research done before I leave. Just do me that favor and inform me of the time every so often, okay?"

"No problem," Bryan said with a grin, trying to lighten the mood. "I wouldn't want to be the reason you get into any trouble tonight."

Forty minutes passed by with barely a word being uttered between the two friends. Each man kept basically to himself, concentrating on reading books and taking down notes.

The daunting silence finally collapsed when Roger got up out of his chair and a loud squeak echoed through the room. He walked to the middle of the living room where he had compiled a stack of old textbooks and research guides, setting aside the ones he already looked at. Roger grabbed a couple more off the unread pile, carried them over to the desk, and placed them down.

"Have you found anything yet?" Bryan asked.

"Not much," replied Roger. "I've found some bizarre stories of strange, ghostly ferry services and ferrymen in a North American folklore literature book. One urban legend tells of a ferryman from a small town in Louisiana called Strangeville."

"That's an odd name for a town," Bryan remarked.

"You ain't kiddin'. The description of the ferryman in that story is similar to Mr. Ferr's physique and appearance. However, that story was written by someone over sixty years ago, and there was no mention of Mephistis Pheles at all."

Bryan removed his eyeglasses and cleaned them with a purple handkerchief before he went back to his reading. Barely a minute passed by when he came across something exceedingly peculiar that grabbed his attention.

Bryan could hardly contain his enthusiasm as he yelled over to Roger, "Come here and take a look at this! I found something in this old dictionary from the library!"

"What is it?" asked Roger as he stood up and walked over to the couch.

Bryan set the dictionary down on the coffee table and pointed to the word 'Mephistopheles.'

"I couldn't find anything on Mephistis Pheles either, but look at how similar *this* word is. I knew I'd find something in this dictionary!" Bryan replied eagerly. "This book is so old, I figured there'd *have* to be words in here that are odd or not used in common speech anymore."

Roger ran his finger down the page until it reached the word Bryan pointed out to him. "This is kind of eerie…" Roger began. "The word is actually a name for a person in the diabolical world. This leaves me guessing why anyone would name their ferry service after someone evil."

Bryan scratched his head. "I wonder what kind of wacky individual Mr. Ferr *really* is. I may not know him very well, but there's just something about that guy which sends chills down my spine and out my feet!"

Roger turned his attention back to Bryan, who was now holding the book in his hands. "Is there any more information on that term in the book," Roger asked, "or is there any other texts lying around here that might elaborate more on the name?"

"Yes, actually there's an entire article on the following page," Bryan uttered as he grabbed the book, turned the page, and began to paraphrase. "It says that Mephistopheles first appeared in 1587 in a German book dealing with Doctor Faustus. He was an evil spirit to whom, for the enjoyment of this world, Faustus had sold his soul. Mephistopheles was then portrayed as a vicious itinerant magician who, by devilish art, created mischief wherever he went."

Bryan and Roger stared at each other, not knowing what to make of the information.

Then, Bryan, seemingly disturbed by what he had read, continued to say, "It was through the use of the legend in great dramas that the medieval legendary figure of Mephistopheles gained world fame. It did so in such large measure that, for many years, Mephistopheles shared the status, if not actually took the place, of Satan."

"Satan?" Roger mumbled curiously. "What link could there possibly be between Louis Ferr and Satan? I wonder if he's into the occult or devil worshiping. And if he is, then why would he want to come to Carthage."

Bryan quickly snatched his pencil from behind his right ear and grabbed a piece of paper. Before Roger could ask him what he was doing, Bryan was already consumed in thought and began scribbling on the paper.

"Did something I say get your attention?" Roger asked. "What's that you're writing down over there?"

Bryan wrote out the name 'Louis Charles Ferr' at the top of his page.

"I had a thought!" Bryan stated enthusiastically. "If you take Mr. Ferr's name and begin to narrow it down by eliminating some of the letters and shortening the name in the appropriate areas, you start to come up with a clue to the identity of our mystery man."

Roger crossed his arms and appeared skeptical of Bryan's theory. "Okay, now I'm confused. What're you referring to, and what clues are we *supposed* to be looking for?"

Bryan peered down at his piece of paper for an instant, wrote a few more words, and then looked back up at Roger. He turned the piece of paper around so it was facing Roger and able to be read.

Roger's eyes got as large as ping-pong balls, and his face appeared horror-struck. He stared at the paper with utmost concern and attentiveness as the name was written to form a single word. No longer did the name Louis Charles Ferr cover the sheet of the paper. Now it read Lou C. Ferr, or as Bryan wrote beneath it, **Lucifer**.

"I don't think he worships the Devil, Roger. I think he *IS* the Devil."

Roger gasped. "What could all of this possibly mean?" he said as if talking to himself.

"I don't know, maybe it means nothing at all. After all, this is just a theory that popped into my head. I don't have any proof or anything. But at the very least, it sure is a bizarre coincidence, don't you think?"

Roger hastily bolted out of his chair and dashed over to the desk. In one swift motion, he snatched his car keys, his wallet, and headed for the door.

Bryan stood up and grabbed Roger's arm as he was walking by him. "Where are you going in such a rush?"

"I'm going to pay a visit to Mr. Ferr!" hollered Roger. "I have some questions to ask him, and I might do some looking around while I'm there, too. I've had my skepticism about him and so has Bucky. If this guy actually believes he's the Devil, then who knows what he's capable of doing. Maybe he *did* have something to do with the disappearances around here. Now it's time to find out!"

"Don't you think we should talk about this for a minute?" Bryan asked as he tried to calm Roger down. "At least sit down so we can get our composure together."

"Why?"

"I don't think it'd be a good idea to go off half-cocked about circumstances we don't know a lot about."

"What more do I need to know, Bryan?"

"This man could be dangerous, Roger. Very dangerous! I think we should call Bucky, calmly sit down, and talk this over with him. After that, we can make a decision on how we want to handle things."

"I understand your concern, Bryan, and I appreciate what you're trying to do, but I just don't have the time to make any phone calls right now. I wouldn't be able to forgive myself if I waited to pursue my instincts and something happened to a person I care about just because I didn't have any evidence."

"But...but..."

"Listen, if it makes you feel any better, you can call Bucky. Tell him where I'm going and what we've uncovered. If he feels there's any danger involved, he'll either get in contact with the police or meet me out at the ferry service himself. You can stay here as long as you wish, Bryan, but do me a favor and lock the door when you leave."

As fast as lightning, Roger charged out of the house and drove off in his car like a man possessed. Bryan stood at the door and yelled out to him, "What about your dinner date with Nellie!?"

Bryan's words went unheard as a cloud of dust arose from the road, and he watched Roger drive off, worried that something harmful might happen to his friend.

While Roger and Bryan were digging for clues, Bucky was at home. He was sitting in his recliner, completely absorbed in a Stephen King mystery novel, when the phone rang.

"Yeah...hello," Bucky grumbled into the phone, annoyed by the interruption.

"Hi, can I speak with Dave Morgan please?" uttered a voice from what sounded to be an elderly man.

Bucky hesitated for a moment before he spoke. He tried to see if he recognized the voice, but was unable to identify it. Then, he ran his fingers through his hair and scratched his head before saying, "Yes, this is Dave Morgan."

"Good afternoon, sir. How're ya today?" replied the gentleman. "My name is..."

Before the person on the other end of the line could finish his sentence, Bucky interrupted. "Look, if you're one of those telemarketers, I'm not interested in whatever you're selling. Besides, I don't have the time, or the desire, to talk on the phone right now anyways."

"Nah, I ain't sellin' anything, Mr. Morgan. In fact, I might be able to help you."

"Who *is* this?" Bucky's words were more of a statement than a question. "And what makes you think I need help with something?"

"My name is Jim Draven. I'm a retired police officer from Chicago. I used to work in the homicide department."

"Yeah...and?"

"I've been keeping my eye on the events happening in your town for the past couple of weeks, and I thought maybe we should talk. The circumstances occurring in Carthage remind me of an incident that happened in Chicago when I was a young man."

"I don't mean to be rude, but how could a retired detective from another state help me?" inquired Bucky.

"Oh, I don't live there anymore," Mr. Draven stated. "I moved back to New York about twelve years ago—right after I retired. Now, I live in a small hamlet by the name of Natural Bridge. Do you know where that is, Mr. Morgan?"

"Yes, I'm familiar with Natural Bridge. It's a town about thirty miles Northeast of Carthage. But I still don't see how something that transpired in Chicago could have any bearing on what's been going on around Carthage lately."

"Well, let me tell you," Mr. Draven responded in a serious manner. "I was assigned to a 'missing persons' case about forty-five years ago, back when I was just starting out with the force. I had, however, previously worked on cases with several of the other officers during my first few months as I strived to gain experience and techniques, but *that* was my first big assignment."

Jim stopped and breathed heavily before continuing on. "And what makes your town's dilemma so intriguing is...the things that went on back in Chicago during the 1950s are similar to the events happening around your town lately."

Mr. Draven's words captured Bucky's attention. He sat in his chair and focused all his attention on what the former detective was saying.

"Alright, I'm listening. What's the information you have that you believe is important to me?"

"Well, I'd rather not get into the specifics over the phone, Mr. Morgan. Is there any way you could meet me at my house? I'd go to you, but it's hard for me to go anywhere these days. I'm seventy-one years old and move around with the speed and energy of a garden gnome."

Bucky laughed at Mr. Draven's joke. "Sure, no problem. I can be there in about forty-five minutes. All I need are the directions...and by the way, please call me Bucky."

Bucky grabbed a pen and paper and wrote down the directions as Mr. Draven told him how to get to his house. He believed this old man—this stranger—could supply him with the big break he had been searching for to link Louis Ferr and the strange disappearances around town together.

Bucky was in such a hurry to meet Mr. Draven that he forgot all about calling Roger to tell him about his impending meeting with the enigmatic Jim Draven. As he got in his car to drive away, a phone call by Bryan Harsha arrived only too late to inform his fellow colleague of the rash actions that their friend, Roger, had taken and the potential consequences that could incur.

Chapter 16:

A New Companion

Within an hour of their phone call, Bucky pulled into Jim Draven's driveway. Jim's home was located at the far end of the Rogers Crossing road, just outside the village limits of Natural Bridge. It was an older looking two-story house, painted in a dark green color, which was starting to chip and peel off the sides. To the left of the house stood a small barn, which probably had not been used in many years and was starting to collapse from the many years of neglect.

Bucky sat in his car looking around for any sign of an old man and hesitated for a moment before shutting off the engine. Still feeling uncertain, he stepped outside his car only to be greeted with an unsettling silence from the house that sat alone in this wooded nearby town. Bucky started to walk toward the house when he heard a crashing sound bellow from the barn.

"Hello? Is...is anyone there?" Bucky asked cautiously. "Mr. Draven...its Dave Morgan. We talked on the phone just a short while ago."

The wind picked up and blew through the surrounding trees, shaking the branches back and forth. Aside from the rustling of the leaves, however, Bucky did not hear a response.

Ever so slowly, Bucky began to walk over to the barn with extreme caution to find out where the noise came from. The hair on his neck stood up, and he felt the goose bumps on his arms.

"I don't like the looks of this so far," he whispered under his breath. "Okay, Bucky, what have you gotten yourself into. I can't believe I agreed to come all the way out to Natural Bridge to meet with someone I've never seen before…and when I get here, all I find is a run-down, deserted house with a spooky old barn."

As Bucky inched closer, he remained silent to try to hear anything from inside the barn. His hands became clammy as they always did when he got nervous, and a lump formed in his throat. He slowly moved his hand down to the door latch and was about to open the barn door when he heard someone speak from behind him.

"Well, I guess ya didn't have any trouble findin' my house," a man's voice said.

Bucky jumped up in the air and spun around quickly, losing his balance. He stumbled backwards for a few steps and eventually fell on his behind. Squinting as he looked up, Bucky saw an elderly man bending down with his hand stretched out to help him back on his feet.

"Sorry 'bout that, fella. I didn't mean to startle you. My name is Jim Draven. I saw you pull in the driveway from my living room window, but it took me a few moments to get out of my chair and out the front door. These old bones don't move as fast as they used to."

Jim paused as he observed his guest. "You must be Dave Morgan, the man I spoke to earlier on the phone."

Bucky stood up and brushed the dust off his pants. "Yeah, but you can call me Bucky. You have quite an interesting house out here."

"Thanks. It ain't much but it's been in the family for years. Hard to part with it, y'know."

"I thought I heard a noise coming from inside your barn," Bucky said. "I called out to whoever is in there but got no response. I was thinking maybe you were in there and might've fallen down, so I decided to check things out."

"Oh, that was probably my cat," Jim said with a laugh. "His name is Jinx; he catches all the mice that've taken up residence in my barn. Jinx snares enough of those rodents to earn his keep around here, but he always makes a damn mess in the barn. I constantly have to clean up after him."

Bucky exhaled deeply. "Ah, I see."

"Anyway, enough about my cat. Follow me to my house so we can go inside, sit down, and talk for a while."

Jim led the way up to his house while Bucky walked about a step or two behind him. Jim Draven was a thin old man of average height with long gray hair that ran down to the middle of his back, which he kept in a ponytail. His dust-covered cowboy boots were nearly worn out and splitting near the heels, but he still had his riding spurs on them (although it looked like there hadn't been any horses on the farm to ride for quite some time).

Dressed in faded blue jeans and a white T-shirt with a brown leather vest, Jim looked more like a country singer than a retired police officer. He had a scruffy looking beard that made him resemble Willie Nelson and wore a bandana of the American Flag around his head.

After walking a few yards, Bucky broke the awkward silence and asked, "So what made you decide to move to Natural Bridge, Jim? This place must seem kinda boring after working for the police department in Chicago."

"Yeah, I can see why you'd think that," Jim said with a snort. "I came out here after I retired to get away from the hectic city life and all the crazy people that pollute it. My family is originally from this town, and I knew the surrounding area quite well. I figured this was a good place to tap back into my family roots and get closer to nature all at the same time. I can't think of anything better than spending the rest of my life relaxing in the majestic beauty of the wilderness and do whatever I want to do, whenever I want to do it."

"You have relatives in the North Country, Mr. Draven?" Bucky inquired.

"No, not anymore. All of my kin have moved away or passed on a long time ago. Hell, I wouldn't even have come back to Natural Bridge if I hadn't someplace to come back to. You see, this house was bequeathed to me when my grandfather died many years ago."

Jim paused to smile, as if recalling a happier time in his life. "I have fond memories playing hide-and-go-seek with my cousin, Vance, when we were just kids. I wanted to come back here and be close to those memories once again."

"Do many of your neighbors ever stop by to listen to all your stories as a former police detective?"

Jim shook his head. "Nobody ever bothers me out here, and nobody knows about my days as a police detective when I lived in Chicago. I had a lot of difficult times back there and almost went crazy on a few occasions trying to solve some of my cases."

"Was the job very stressful?"

"At times, it could be. Y'see, in order to catch a criminal, you have to start to think like them—to get inside their mind so you can understand what makes them tick. It's when you're at *that* point of instability when you get to see how truly sick in the head some people really are. Anyway, I guess I put myself into that frame of mind a few too many times and ended up with a nervous breakdown and an early retirement as my only rewards."

"I'm sorry to hear that," Bucky said in a low voice.

"Oh, it wasn't all bad," replied Jim with a half-hearted laugh. "I got a nice wristwatch from the police department as a going away gift."

The two men made their way to the porch and walked inside the house. Jim removed his bandana and hung it up on his coat rack as if it were an ordinary baseball cap. They talked briefly about themselves to get acquainted as they continued their way into the house and down the hallway.

Eventually they reached the living room, and Jim motioned for Bucky to sit down on the couch as he said, "So, Bucky, I'm sure you're wonderin' why some stranger would call out-of-the-blue and ask you to come to such a secluded place as Natural Bridge, especially just to talk about a case file from the Chicago Police Department that happened over forty-five years ago."

"The thought has crossed my mind a few times."

"Have a seat and listen up, Mr. Morgan. I'm sure you'll be quite interested in what I have to say."

Bucky settled down on the couch as Jim strolled over to the chair sitting across the way. Jim pulled a snot rag from his back pocket, blew his nose a couple times, and cleared his throat with some mouthwash he had sitting beside his recliner. He sat down and took a few breaths, preparing himself to tell his guest of the experience he had with a similar case back in Chicago.

"I remember it all as if it happened recently," Jim began, holding a cigarette in one hand and trying to light a wooden match with the other. "A person just doesn't forget somethin' as horrific as that, do you catch my drift?"

Bucky nodded his head.

"It was the most baffling mystery I ever encountered during my stint on the police force," said Jim, his eyes lost in thought. "For eight months—from the Fall of 1954 to the Spring of 1955—I ate, drank, and slept that case. A series of disappearances and grisly murders plagued the waterfront area in Chicago."

"Really, what did you do?"

"My partner, Mac, and I interviewed dozens of beach bums, dock workers, and joggers, but no one saw anything. At least, no one was talking to the police anyway. In order to make a living on the shipping

169

docks, you had to do everything you can…but that did *not* include being in cohorts with the cops."

"Why is that?"

"There was a seedy bunch of thugs always around, each tryin' to eke out a livin' any way they could. Y'see, down on the waterfront in Chicago, people are always biting off more than they can chew. Sure, it's tough on the wind pipe, but you never go hungry."

"Doesn't sound like a great place for nice people to hang out," commented Bucky."

"You're right, Bucky. The waterfront in Chicago is a 'eat or be eaten' kind of place. You're either high on your toes or flat on your back, if you know what I mean."

"Yes, sir. I know exactly what you mean."

Jim leaned back and continued with his story. "Mac and I worked the waterfront for a long time, trying to find a shred of evidence that would explain what was happenin'. Finally, after months of dead-ends, we finally got a lead."

"Like what? Did it blow the case wide open?"

"I got a tip from a guy—I think his name was Timmons. He told me he saw one of the murdered victims boarding a boat near the shipping docks on the night he disappeared."

"Wow!" Bucky blurted out. "An eyewitness to one of the disappearances! What was the victim's name?"

Jim was caught off-guard by Bucky's question. "I don't remember, son. It was Steven Jettison…or something like that, I think. Sorry to say, but that's all the information Timmons gave me. He said a thick fog formed afterward, and he never saw the victim, or the boat, the rest of the night."

"Remarkable!" Bucky uttered, hanging on to every word Jim said.

"Shortly thereafter, Mac and I ended up crossing paths with an older guy, probably in his late sixties at the time, who ran a small ferry service near the shipping docks."

"A ferryman?"

"Yeah, he carried passengers back and forth…some kind of 'lovers rendezvous' kind-of-thing. At the time, I didn't believe the old man had anything to do with the disappearances…but Mac did. Over the next few days, I followed other leads along the waterfront while Mac intently pursued that ferryman. Then, one night while we were on patrol, Mac disappeared."

Bucky's heart began thumping in his chest.

"I searched for hours until I found him—his lifeless body lying next to graffiti-covered concrete wall at the waterfront. His chest and neck were torn to shreds by some sort of animal."

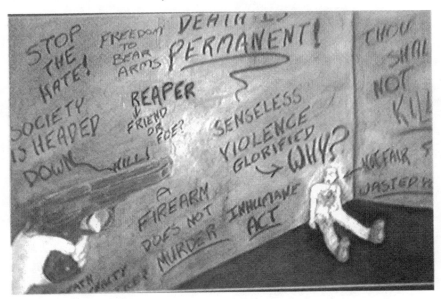

Bucky stared at Mr. Draven intently, trying to concentrate and listen as close as he possibly could. His eyes were big and glossy as he became increasingly more immersed in the old man's tale.

Maybe something in the old man's words will help me unravel the mystery plaguing my small town, Bucky thought.

Jim talked for nearly a half hour, describing the mystery in full detail to Bucky. He explained how the events that occurred along the riverbanks in Chicago all those years ago baffled him to no end. Jim also mentioned the circumstances which eventually led him to believe that the ferry owner he questioned on the shipping docks was probably the same person Timmons allegedly viewed and contacted Jim about.

After investigating the waterfront area for a few more weeks, Jim was able to piece a few clues together. The result made Jim began to think that the mysterious ferryman had *actually* been responsible for the disappearance of the victim Timmons saw on that foggy night. And quite possibly, the death of his partner, Mac, and all the other disappearances that occurred around the same time period.

After Mr. Draven finished his story, Bucky sat in awe and did not speak for several seconds.

"So, do you have anything to say?" Jim asked.

"That's an amazing story!" shouted Bucky. "I can't believe you pieced together the clues to find out that everyone who disappeared were all people who didn't own a personal vehicle. And that's what led you to discover the only thing the victims had in common was they were all using the same ferry service to get back and forth to work every day."

"That's correct," stated Jim.

"Wow!" Bucky looked astonished. "You must've been excited about having the opportunity to work on such a challenging case file."

"It may have been challenging, Bucky, but I'd hardly call any of the circumstances exciting. It was an utterly difficult, as well as very disturbing, mystery."

Bucky glanced at the old detective, who had frozen for a moment and fallen deep in thought. "Jim, did the case ever get to you? Did you ever think about giving up?"

"Sure I did," Jim answered. "Right when I was in the thick of it all, I received a phone call from my cousin. Vance still lived around this area and he phoned me to say our grandfather had passed away. I was devastated at the time...I was very close to my grandpa. After I heard the news, I was tempted to drop the case completely, quit the force, and move back permanently."

"What stopped you?"

"My grandfather didn't teach me to be a quitter. As much as I wanted to leave Chicago, I just couldn't bring myself to give up...no matter how bad things got."

Leaning back on the couch, Bucky mentioned, "So, Jim, you never did tell me how the case ended."

"Well, the murders eventually stopped but the mystery was never cleared up," Jim replied as he stood up and grabbed a scrapbook from the bookshelf. He shuffled back to his chair and handed the book to Bucky. "Here's a collection of clippings from the *Chicago Tribune*. They detailed all the events that were going on at that time."

Bucky set the book down on his lap and proceeded to open it up, glancing over the articles.

"The similarities are eerily too familiar" he uttered in disbelief. "You're telling me that no one was ever prosecuted for these crimes?"

"That's right, Bucky." Jim answered. "The ferry owner disappeared into thin air, and we had no way to track him down. With no other suspects and no other leads to follow, the case was left unsolved."

"Do you think it's possible the same person could be in Carthage and *also* be responsible for the disappearances that've occurred lately?"

Jim took his glasses off and cleaned them with his handkerchief before he responded. "Oh, I don't think so. At best, it might be a crazed lunatic trying to copycat the actions of a crime that was never brought to justice."

"Why don't you think it's the same person?"

"The incident in Chicago happened over forty-five years ago, Bucky, and the ferryman who was our prime suspect back then was easily in his sixties. He'd be over a hundred years old if he were still alive today."

"Do you remember any specifics about the suspect you were after?" questioned Bucky.

"Oh sure," Jim replied. "I told you before, I remember it all like it was yesterday. He was from Hungary I think. Or maybe it was Russia. I don't know for sure, but that's what I believe anyway."

Bucky shook his head. "You don't sound so certain, Jim."

"I remember the ferryman definitely spoke with a European accent, and he even had one of those weird foreign names. That old man gave me chills down my spine. His hollow eyes and evil stare haunted my dreams for months afterwards. I never got over that case, and I'll never forget that man's face for as long as I live."

Bucky pulled a clipping from the *Carthage Republican Tribune* newspaper out of his pocket, which showed Louis Ferr shaking hands with Mayor Pat Jordan as he accepted the contract for Carthage's new ferry service.

He handed the clipping to Jim and asked, "Did he look anything like this guy?"

"This is impossible!" Jim exclaimed. "The person in this picture looks *exactly* like the old ferryman I tracked down in Chicago."

"Don't you mean that it looks *similar* to the guy you were after. After all, there's no way it can be the same person you pursued. You said that yourself."

Jim kept staring at the photo with his mouth hung open.

"Maybe it's a relative of his with a remarkable resemblance, Jim. A family member who's taking over where his grandpa left off. That sounds more feasible and realistic, don't you think?"

"No!" Jim yelled impatiently. "I meant what I said! The guy in this picture looks *exactly* like the suspect I was chasing after. But it can't be! He was an old man when I was on the case over forty-five years ago. By all accounts, he *should* be dead by now!"

Bucky got a confused look on his face from Jim's contradictory statements and fumbled his words as he tried to speak.

"I'm having a hard time following you, Jim. Are you saying you believe this is the same man you were chasing when you were a young man?"

"That's what I'm sayin', Bucky."

"You actually think Louis Ferr is the *same* ferryman who was believed to be responsible for eleven disappearances in Chicago?"

"Yes, I do," Jim concurred in a somber voice."

Bucky seemed puzzled by Jim's words. "Didn't you just tell me the suspect you chased back then should have died from old age many years ago?"

"I realize that...but there's no mistake about it. That man in your picture is the same person I pursued in Chicago in 1955," Jim stated emphatically. "He went by a different name back then, but I think your so-called Louis Ferr is actually my old nemesis—Liv Edeht."

Jim stroked the whiskers on his chin and said to himself aloud, "So what he said to me at our last encounter must be true."

Bucky started to feel uneasy as he heard Jim's words, but he was so mesmerized by his intriguing story that he felt compelled to inquire about it some more.

"Tell me, Jim...what happened at your last encounter with the ferryman?"

Jim rubbed his hands nervously. "It was the strangest, most spine-tingling thing anyone has ever said to me. I remember his words as if they were tattooed on my tongue. The image of the ferryman's face as he glared at me with those red eyes will live with me till the day I die. His bellowing voice had a distinct shrill to it, and he told me I hadn't heard the last from him."

Jim stopped. His lip started to tremble.

"It's okay, Jim. You don't have to talk about it if you don't want to."

"No...I'll go on," Jim responded, noticeably shaken. "The ferryman said that one day our paths would cross again, and when that happens, no amount of prayer would save me from his wrath."

The pupils in Bucky's eyes expanded. "Whoa! Pretty frightening words, huh?"

"Yeah, then, he said that while I grew older, he would become more powerful...and with every sin committed in the world, he was one step closer to bringing Hell on Earth."

"Whew! That just sent a cold chill down my spine," Bucky blurted out.

"Don't you see?" shouted Jim. "He must be back to keep his word! The ferryman wants to carry out his plans and then hunt me down like I did to him all those years ago."

"Um, maybe you should take a breather and calm down for a second," Bucky suggested. "I mean, that's a good theory and all, but highly unlikely. After all, you just sat there and told me the man you hunted down should be *dead* by now."

"I know what I said, damn it!"

"I think your first assumption about a copycat killer was more practical and accurate. It's also likely what we're dealing with is a guy who *may* be a relation of the person who was a suspect in your old case, and now he's following in the same footsteps as his past relative."

"Maybe, just maybe, you are right," Jim said as his voice calmed down. "Although, I wouldn't be taking any chances if I were you. If you take a person of his caliber too lightly, you might wind up dead. The person I chased after was a cold-blooded killer who was never brought to justice." Jim exhaled heavily and grinned at his companion. "Whoever this Louis Ferr is, you already have an edge on him."

"What do you mean by that?"

"Well, you have me as an ally, and I can share with you all the notes from my old case files to see if this man is *really* trying to copycat those crimes of forty-five years ago."

"That's a good point," uttered Bucky.

After a brief yawn, Bucky said, "Oh, and by the way, I don't want you to think I don't have any manners."

"What do you mean?"

"I'd like to say 'thanks' for contacting me and tell you how much I appreciate the information you've shared."

"I'm glad I could be of some help to you!" Jim expressed, smiling broadly.

"It's frightening to think about the events in those newspaper clippings in your scrapbook. It's bizarre how similar the two incidents are. Those articles could've been written about the recent disappearances that've occurred around Carthage."

"That's true," stated Jim. "And if you need anything else, just give me a call or stop by sometime. We can go over the characteristics of the occurrences in your town and compare them to the ones from the Chicago clippings and files I have to see how the events unfold. Then, we can determine if there is a pattern emerging."

"I'd really like that, Jim."

"Until then, I'd be more than happy to go over any thoughts or ideas that are on your mind. Hell, maybe we can come up with some definite answers to the vanishings if we work together on it."

"That sounds great!" Bucky yelled, feeling as though a burden had been lifted off his shoulders. "Actually, I would appreciate it if you could do me one more favor."

"Ahh, I might be able to accommodate ya. What is it?"

"Can you write the name of the Chicago ferryman down on a piece of paper for me?"

"You want me to write it down?"

"I'm sure I'll either forget it or mess up the spelling by the time I get a chance to research this guy from the computer in the Carthage Library. That'd be my best chance to find out where the ferryman went after he left Chicago. It has the Internet hooked into it with software that supposedly is able to track information regarding a person who has owned or operated a business within the past fifty years. He definitely falls into that category."

Jim shook his head in amazement. "Christ, what will they come up with next?"

Bucky nodded his agreement. "I know what you mean, Jim. It's funny, but that computer and all its software is the most modern piece of equipment in the whole town."

Jim went over to his desk and pulled out a pen and a pad. His hand shook from his arthritis as he scribbled letters on the paper. A moment later, he tore off the sheet and walked back over to his chair.

He handed over the paper to Bucky as he sat down and said, "I hope you can read it. Since I've been diagnosed with Parkinson's disease, my handwriting isn't what it used to be. Nowadays, I can barely write my name to sign for my retirement checks."

Bucky looked at the paper and replied, "No problem; I've seen a lot worse from men who are half your age. The only discrepancy I see is that your E's are written backwards."

"Oops, sorry 'bout that. I have a mild case of dyslexia. Sometimes I write letters, and entire words, backwards."

"Oh...ah...um, it's not a problem at all," Bucky stuttered, visibly embarrassed. "It's still very readable and all. I mean, I wasn't trying to make fun of you or anything. I'm sorry I even brought it up."

Jim sat up straight and uttered in a directing tone, "There's nothin' to be sorry for, Bucky. Hell, there ain't no way you could've known 'bout my situation. Besides, I ain't one of those overly sensitive, politically correct type-of-people who gets upset whenever someone mentions a handicap I have. I like to take a light-hearted approach to life while I'm still around to enjoy it. So, there ain't no need for ya to feel awkward or embarrassed."

Bucky breathed a heavy sigh of relief. "Thanks, I'm glad you feel that way. I was feeling a little uncomfortable about what I said. I didn't mean to point out any handicap or offend you by my statements, but I'm glad you know that it wasn't meant to be intentional or malicious."

Jim laughed loudly. "I told ya, I worked as a police officer for a long time. That means I've heard practically every kind of offensive remark ever spoken. There's nothin' you could say that someone I arrested, or even someone I worked with, hasn't called me before. The cops I worked with had some of the foulest mouths I've ever encountered."

Bucky smiled and laughed as he reached into his pocket to grab his keys.

"Well, I suppose I should head back into town. I want to share this information with a friend of mine and tell him all about you."

"Is your friend someone to be trusted?"

"Absolutely! His name is Roger Fasick, and he's practically the only person in the village who believes there's a crisis going on in our community. I'm sure after I talk to him, he'll want to meet you for himself."

"Alright, I think we can set something up."

"I'll be in touch within a couple of days, Jim, to find out when would be a good time for all three of us to get together. I'll see if I can dig up any information on Louis Ferr, as well as Liv Edeht, between now and then and bring it with me."

"Well, now you know the way here, and you should still have my phone number. So, if anything comes up and you need to talk, I'll be around."

Bucky shook Jim's hand and headed for the door. On the way out of the living room, he passed a full-length mirror in the hallway and glanced at it for a brief second. Nevertheless, that was all the time he needed to stop him dead in his tracks. Something he saw was so alarming that it got his attention and made his face pale.

"Jim, you'd better come here and take a look at this."

Jim got out of his chair and made his way over to Bucky. "What is it? Do you see something wrong?"

Bucky held the torn off sheet of paper in front of the mirror so it could be seen backwards by both men.

"Stand beside me, Jim, and take a look at what your piece of paper reads as I hold it in front of the mirror. With the letters that you've written backwards, you just uncovered a strange and unsettling discovery."

Both men looked in the mirror and stood silent. Jim's jaw dropped and his hands started to shake as he saw, for the first time, the *real* name of his old nemesis and the haunting realization of his true identity.

"It..it says…th..the Devil!" Jim stuttered.

Jim's legs became weak and began to buckle beneath him. Bucky took him by the arm and led him back into the living room.

"Take it easy, Jim. Just sit down in your chair for a minute and regain your composure. Do you want me to get you a glass of water?"

"No, no. Thanks anyway, but I'll be fine."

After a brief moment, the old detective was able to catch his breath and the shakes seemed to go away.

"I can't believe it," Jim muttered soberly. "All this time it was right there, staring at me in the face, and I couldn't see it. Some detective I was. That homicidal monster put the clues right in front of me, and I still couldn't put the pieces together. He must've been laughing at me behind my back the whole time."

"Don't be so hard on yourself. I'm sure the thought of an evil being, especially one that's supposed to be mythological and fictitious, causing those disappearances never even crossed your mind."

"But still…" Jim started to say.

"People are always trying to figure out a logical explanation for things," Bucky said reassuringly. "It's just the way humans think. Besides, even if you did find this out back then, there's probably not much you could've done about it."

"That's not entirely true. Maybe I missed my chance to defeat the ferryman back then, but I have something that just might turn the tables in your favor this time around."

Jim walked over to his desk and opened the top drawer. He pulled out an object that was wrapped in an old black cloth with strange markings on it. He laid the object down upon the desk and unwrapped it to show an ancient dagger with a curvaceous blade that was about six inches long.

"You'd better take this with you," Jim insisted, handing the dagger to Bucky. "I'm thinkin' you're going to need it."

Bucky took the weapon into his hands and looked it over. "Thanks, Jim…but I have just one question. What exactly *is* this thing?"

"I got this from a priest back in Chicago the day after I had my last run-in with Mr. Edeht. It's one of the seven deadly daggers of Megiddo; they're instruments to destroy the Anti-Christ. He said this is the *only* weapon that would help me defeat my enemy."

Bucky scoffed in disbelief. "Isn't it a little farfetched to believe that this little dagger is the only thing that could kill someone?"

"Do not judge this weapon too lightly, Mr. Morgan. The dagger has incredible power!"

"Why do you believe I'll need this dagger to confront Louis Ferr?"

"If the ferryman in Carthage turns out to be the same person I knew from Chicago, then I think it's entirely possible he really *is* the Devil."

"And if he is…?" Bucky prodded.

"And if he is, there ain't no amount of bullets you fill him with that'll be able to bring him down. This weapon will be more for your protection than anything else!"

"I don't understand. If bullets aren't going to stop somebody like him, then how is this dagger going to protect me?"

Jim's eyes widened with anxiety. "Let's get something clear; you can't kill the Devil or even render him powerless, but if you stab him with this dagger, it *will* destroy his mortal form and send him back to Hell. You must act quickly before anyone else disappears. But whatever you do, Bucky, don't go after that maniac alone. Too many men have failed before."

Bucky paced nervously as his mind raced with ideas. "Don't you think we should sit down with my friend and discuss a strategy?"

"Why?"

"Because something of this importance shouldn't be taken lightly. It may take some time to develop a plan that's safe and effective enough so no one gets hurt or even killed."

"There is no time for useless banter!" Jim scowled. "The priest I talked to told me once the Devil gets his fill of souls, then he'll move on to the next town and do it all over again. At first, I didn't believe the priest's words, but now things are starting to make sense."

Bucky looked on, unsure what to think and believe.

"Don't you see?" Jim continued, his voice sounding desperate. "You must stop him before he continues his carnage. The next person he takes might be someone close to you."

"Okay, I get your point. But I also don't have any proof yet, either."

"We don't have time for proof!"

Bucky put his hand on Jim's shoulder in an attempt to calm him down.

"I appreciate your eagerness, Jim, but I can't go marching into Ferr's office with a flurry of accusations without any basis. If we're wrong, I'll be thrown in jail for sure."

Jim shook his head and breathed deeply.

"I'll call Roger when I get home tonight so we can get together and plan what direction we want to take," Bucky stated in a calm tone.

"And then what?"

"After I talk to him, I'll call you in the morning and tell you everything we discussed and the conclusions we come up with. Obviously, this is *not* a topic to be taken lightly. I want to make sure we're absolutely certain in our assumptions, and our choice of action is sound before we confront this guy."

"I suppose that's a wise, and probably the best, decision, Bucky. I look forward to your call and meeting your friend. I'm sorry you had to get involved in this mess; I should've finished my business with the ferryman years ago."

"You can't blame yourself for this mess, Jim."

"Maybe...but I *know* that if I would've had many allies and believers when I first met this madman, I could've stopped him then and there, preventing all of this from happening."

Bucky nodded in agreement and headed toward the door. He rushed over to his car and drove away, leaving only a cloud of dust behind him.

Meanwhile, inside Jim's house, the former police detective sat in his chair and shook as he stared at the picture of Mr. Ferr that Bucky brought with him. It was not known whether his shakes were brought on from fear, his arthritis, or the onset of another nervous breakdown.

As Jim sat there thinking, images of his last encounter with the ferryman flashed before his eyes, as if he was reliving the events, and he got an ill feeling in his stomach.

Jim looked away from the picture with tears in his eyes and said, "Oh god, it's happening again."

Chapter 17:

And One Will Fall

As Roger drove toward the ferry service in his 1987 Pontiac Bonneville, which he nicknamed 'The Silver Bullet,' a million thoughts raced around in his head. He kept going over the things that he and Bryan talked about, trying to make sense of it all. Was this Louis Ferr a 'mad man' who really thought he was the Devil, or was there more to the story than Roger could really comprehend? In any event, his curiosity got the better of him, and as unprepared as he was to go to the ferry service alone, Roger was determined to get to the bottom of this horrible mystery—with whatever means it took.

In the back of his mind, Roger kept thinking maybe he should have waited and discussed the situation with Bucky or elicited some help, but he had to get some answers—NOW! Between the disappearances of Bob Earle and Scott Patterson, and the strange connection to Louis Ferr, the whole situation was driving him crazy. Roger couldn't wait any longer; he had to discover what was happening before any more people came up missing—or before he completely lost his mind.

Roger arrived at the road that led to the ferry service at around 5:30 pm. He stopped just short of the wooden sign and studied it for a moment before he slowly turned down the road to the sound of gravel crunching beneath the tires.

Roger had a lump in his throat as he drove nervously down the path. A few seconds later, he pulled in behind an exceptionally large pine tree, which was about a hundred yards from the ferry office and waterfront. This was a good spot to regain his composure, he figured, and decided it would also be better to walk the rest of the way. Roger was confident from the size of the tree and the thick brush surrounding it, no one would be able to spot his car. With his vehicle camouflaged and out of sight, Roger felt this was his best opportunity to snoop around the surrounding area without being caught.

Although Roger felt secure about the location of his car, his nerves were anything but calm as his heartbeat quickened and his palms sweat. Nearly fifteen minutes went by before he gathered enough courage to get out of his vehicle and venture down into unfamiliar territory. Although Roger tried not to think about it, he knew his impatience and reckless behavior might end up having serious consequences.

Slowly he crept down the road, compassing his surroundings and glancing over his shoulder from time to time. He stopped as he got to the edge of the tree line, which led to the parking area and the ferry office. Roger hid behind one of the towering oak trees and looked around the waterfront area to see if anybody was walking around or if anyone might be standing outside the ferry office.

Several minutes passed before he felt comfortable enough that the coast was clear. Once he determined that it was safe to proceed, he focused all his attention on the old shed located between the parking lot and the tree line. The same shed, consequently, that Bucky saw Steve Jensen wheel a bicycle into.

Whether or not the bike belonged to his friend, Bob Earle, he was not sure. However, Roger was so filled with curiosity that he was willing to risk potential danger in order to find out.

Roger crept over to the shed; only to be seen by a few wolves in the woods. Ever so carefully, he eased the door open just enough so that he could squeeze himself inside and look around. As he was searching throughout the piles of old machine parts, he noticed an object of some kind covered by a canvas tarp. Curious, he walked over to the tarp and pulled it off. Roger's face turned white and his mouth dropped open as he discovered that the object under the canvas was unmistakably Bob Earle's bicycle.

Roger stood motionless as if he were unable to move. Every thought and every emotion was fixated on the bike that stood before him. Trying to make out the significance of what this discovery meant, he suddenly felt sick to his stomach at the thought of what possibly happened to his friend.

Suddenly, a shadow formed from behind Roger's back and seemed to swallow up his whole body within its form. Roger became startled by the expanding shape and quickly whirled around. In shock, he stumbled backwards and landed on his tail when he became aware that the shadow which had been behind him belonged to Louis Ferr.

"Y'know," Ferr said to Roger, "you shouldn't be sticking your nose into business that doesn't concern you. But, then again, isn't that what your brother always told you?"

"P..P..Paul?!" Roger stuttered and gasped. "What do you know about Paul?" he asked as his voice started to quiver.

Mr. Ferr smiled from ear to ear, baring his yellow stained teeth and looking like a crazed madman. His eyes widened and his pupils changed from black to red as he stared at Roger with an evil stare.

"I know that if you don't watch yourself, you're going to end up with the same fate that befell your brother, as well as your friends Scott Patterson and Bob Earle."

Even though the shock was starting to overwhelm Roger and his body was stiffening, he still managed to sputter out, "Are you responsible for what happened to my brother?"

"I'm afraid so, my dear Roger," Ferr said mockingly. "I reaped his soul and left his body a hallowed shell. I then called upon my beasts to finish the task. My demons take the remains of my victims to a place called 'The Dimension of Pain'. That's where those unfortunate souls remain until I decide what I'm going to do with them."

Roger's face turned from a pasty white to deep red as anger began flowing through his body. Rage overtook the fear that was in his body and he lunged at Mr. Ferr to lash out at him. But before he could get to him, Mr. Ferr grabbed Roger by the throat with lightning speed. He lifted Roger off the floor with one hand as the color of Roger's cheeks began to turn purple, and he started to choke.

Unable to get loose and still gasping for breath he sputtered out, "Who in god's name are you?"

"God has nothing to do with it, and even your God can't save you now. Look into my eyes!" Mr. Ferr bellowed in a diabolic tone. "I am the one you fear the most. I am the reason your brother is gone and your world crumbled around you. You see me in your nightmares, and I follow you in the dark...You can call me *Satan*!"

While still holding on to him with one hand, Mr. Ferr flung Roger through the air with such ease that you would think he was tossing an old rag doll out of the way. His strength was so enormous that he flung Roger across to the other side of the shed, crashing into the shelves hanging on the walls. Roger hit the wall with such force that it broke the shelves, and he landed on the floor as the debris of tools, and some spare parts, piled on top of him.

"You weren't the one that I wanted, Roger," continued Ferr, "but now you've left me no other choice. I have to deal with you now and get you out of the way before you can cause me any trouble."

Roger was lost in the rubble, bleeding badly from the head and gasping for air from Mr. Ferr's crushing grip on his throat. Pain ran down Roger's back and into his legs. He felt helpless and unprotected laying there but was too dazed and confused to do anything about his situation.

"Mr. Jensen!" Ferr yelled to his lackey, who was standing outside the shed door. "Come in here and tie this man up!"

Mr. Jensen walked in the shed and said, "My pleasure, Master."

"I've got some matters to tend to, and I don't want Mr. Fasick getting in our way."

"Would you like me to take the young punk for a ride on the ferry and toss his body into the river, sir?" Jensen suggested.

Ferr mulled over the idea for a moment before responding. "I'm not sure what I want to do with him just yet, Jensen, but I have a few ideas in my mind. Maybe I will summon the demons and let them consume his human body while I devour his immortal soul. Then again, he may come in *more* handy if he is alive."

"Alive, sir?"

Suddenly, Ferr's eyes lit up. "Yes…especially if Dave Morgan comes poking around looking for him. Oh, what fun we would have then. Just thinking about the possibilities makes me as giddy as a choir boy at a Sunday concert," he expressed with excitement. "And we both know how tastefully sweet a choir boy's soul is!"

An evil smile once again appeared on Mr. Ferr's face, and his eyes became a reddish glow. He then walked out of the shed and looked around for any onlookers as he shut the door.

While Mr. Ferr was walking away, Jensen grabbed some rope from one of the few shelves that still hung on the wall and began to walk toward Roger. Just as he was getting close to the incapacitated man on the floor, Roger rose abruptly and lunged forward. Roger tapped every ounce of energy he had remaining in his body and punched Steve Jensen in the stomach. Jensen keeled over in pain, howling like an injured beast.

With Roger still on his knees, he punched Jensen square in the jaw, sending his enemy to the floor and landing hard against his back. Roger mustered all his strength and adrenaline in one last effort to get up off the ground. Surprisingly, Roger managed to stand, even though his legs were wobbly, and began kicking Mr. Jensen in the face and chest.

Roger's face looked like that of a madman who had lost complete control of his sanity. All reason and compassion left his eyes, which now appeared hollow and empty. Every bit of rage and frustration Roger had been harboring inside himself over the years finally erupted. *This* was the anger Bucky feared would be unleashed one day on somebody. Unfortunately for Steve Jensen, he was getting the brunt of Roger's fury.

"I'm not giving up that easy you son of a bitch!" Roger screamed furiously. "If this is my last stand, I'm *not* going out without a fight!"

Mr. Ferr, unaware of the events that were transpiring, walked back into the shed and asked, "What's going on in here, Jensen! I heard a commotion and...Oh my!"

A stunned look came upon his face, as if he wasn't expecting Roger to fight back or even have enough energy left to stand up on his own.

"You have certainly amazed me, boy. I will give you credit for that. You are much stronger than your brother. My demons tore him apart limb from limb while I feasted upon his soul, and he screamed for help the whole time. He even cried like a baby, which is something I assume you won't be doing, will you?"

"You arrogant bastard!" Roger hollered. "If it's the last thing I do, I'm going to wipe that friggin' smile off your face!"

Roger grabbed the first thing he found on the shelf beside him and threw it at Mr. Ferr in order to distract him. As Mr. Ferr was momentarily diverted, Roger ran toward him and attacked in a blind fury, throwing punch after punch into his mid-section.

While Mr. Ferr was stunned by the blows, Roger leaned back for a brief moment, thrust his himself forward using the weight of his body, and gave Mr. Ferr an uppercut to his chin, sending him to the floor. Roger shifted his attention away briefly and glanced over to see the steel pipe that was used to hold the door open. It stood there, leaning against the wall, and he reached over for it so that he could use it as a weapon.

While Roger seized the pipe, Mr. Ferr rolled to his side, touched his lip with his hand, and looked down to see blood on his fingers.

"You insignificant fool!" hollered Ferr. "No human has dared lay a hand on me knowing that I can destroy them in an instant. With the blood that drips from my flesh, you have sealed your fate."

Roger moved as fast as he could, but before he could twist back around and swing the pipe, Mr. Ferr jumped to his feet. Ferr snatched the pipe in mid-air with one hand and Roger's throat with the other.

"Prepare to be broken," Mr. Ferr stated in a serious manner.

Ferr ripped the pipe forcibly out of Roger's hand and threw it on the ground. Then he slapped Roger in the face several times with the back of his hand. Roger was smacked so hard that blood from his nose and mouth splattered on the walls.

In Louis Ferr's grip, Roger's body hung lifeless off the ground, and his head wavered limply as he swayed in and out of consciousness. Mr. Ferr spat in Roger's face and tossed him aside so effortlessly that it looked as if he were flinging a bag of dirty laundry.

Roger fell about ten feet away and landed face first in a messy pile of garbage and soiled rags. Mr. Ferr gazed at his motionless body for an instant, and then walked over to Steve Jensen, who remained on the ground during the entire commotion. He looked down, shaking his head in disapproval and nudged Jensen with his boot.

"Get up Jensen. That is, if the boy didn't beat you up too badly," Mr. Ferr said mockingly. "You have disappointed me Jensen; don't let it happen again. I would hate for you to lose your usefulness to me. Let yourself be warned, my servant, it would not be in your favor to get on my bad side. Do you understand?"

"Yes, my Master. I understand completely." Jensen responded in a humble tone.

After making his way up onto his knees, Jensen took in a breath and released a grunt as he stood up. Two of Mr. Jensen's front teeth remained on the shed floor from Roger kicking him in the mouth, and he coughed while spitting blood out of his mouth.

Trying to get his poise, Jensen pulled a gray handkerchief out of his back pocket that had an 'S' embroidered on it. Painfully, he wiped the dirt off his forehead and the blood from his nose. Jensen had a split lip and his left eye was severely bruised and swollen. He grabbed his mid-section and winced in pain, as if he might have had a few ribs broken.

Then, Jensen hobbled over to where Roger was laying and asked, "What do you want me to do with him, sir?"

"Bind him up if he's still breathing," Ferr responded in an unemotional tone. "Then tie a rag around his mouth so he won't be able to yell for help. Most importantly, make sure you do *not* take him out of this shed."

"Why, sir?" questioned Jensen.

"Spectators might be around the area, and we don't want to draw any attention to ourselves, especially when I am *so* close to getting what I came here for. Do you think you can handle this little task?"

"Certainly, sir. I will get on it with the utmost urgency. And may I inquire what would you like me to do with the young man's car?"

"Car?" Mr. Ferr voiced in a cautious tone.

"Yes, sir, I assume that he must've driven some type of vehicle here. And if so, then it should be nearby. We can't very well just leave it out in the open. If people see it, they will want to question you."

"Hmm, that's a good point," said Mr. Ferr, musing over his options. "I suppose you should look around and see if you can locate it. Find it quickly and roll it into the river. I don't want the police here poking around, and I don't have the patience or the time to deal with them anyways."

Mr. Ferr walked over to the office and stood on the porch with his hands behind his back. He peered over toward the dark water and stared out into an empty nothingness, smiling to himself the whole time.

His eyes changed from black to a glowing red as he uttered only a single word—"Soon."

Chapter 18:

The Search is On

Bucky returned to town at around 8:30 pm from his meeting with Jim Draven. So many thoughts were racing through his mind and he was having trouble sorting everything out. About the only thing he was certain of was that he needed someone to talk to, and he knew who that person was...Roger. Bucky was sure that if he could talk to him, they might come up with some answers that made sense of it all. He and Roger always had a unique connection when it came to brainstorming and usually had great success.

A strange feeling was stirring in Bucky's gut to go along with a desperate need to tell Roger about his conversation with Jim. Every time Bucky thought about Jim's story and what they discovered about Mr. Draven's past nemesis, he became lightheaded and disoriented. Bucky had never dealt with so much confusion and obscurity; it made him think his mind was overloaded with uncontrollable circumstances.

Nellie's car was in the driveway as Bucky drove up to Roger's house. Although Roger's car was nowhere to be seen, Bucky still decided to pull into the driveway to find out if he was home. After all, with as many problems Roger had experienced with his car recently, it could very well have been in the shop while he was just sitting inside his house.

Bucky hurriedly got out of his car, briskly walked up to the porch steps, and knocked forcibly on the door. His hands were slightly shaking, and he appeared to be somewhat edgy.

"God, I hope he's here," Bucky whispered.

"Come on in!" he heard Nellie yell from inside.

Bucky entered the house and saw Nellie standing in front room. "Hi, Nellie," he said cordially. "I was hoping I could talk to Roger. I realize his car isn't in the driveway, but I was wondering if he is here anyway."

"No," she stated rudely. "He was supposed to meet me at the Superior Restaurant at seven o'clock for a late dinner, but he never showed up. I waited over forty-five minutes for him to arrive...or at least call the restaurant to say he would be late. However, like always, he doesn't give me the common courtesy that I deserve!"

"I'm, uh, sorry to hear that." replied Bucky, stunned by Nellie's unfriendliness. "Then again, I'm sure there's a good explanation for his actions."

"Oh, I'm sure there is," she countered sarcastically. "He always has *plenty* of excuses and explanations for any circumstance." She stopped what she was doing and paused to think for a moment. "Actually, I have no idea what he's been doing all day. I haven't spoken to him since we talked on the phone this morning; I was on my way to work."

"Did he say anything that sticks out in your mind?"

"Um...I called him on my cell phone as I was driving down Route 81, coming from Syracuse. The only thing he said to me was he was going to stay home and do some research, and after that, we would meet at the Superior Restaurant for dinner."

"So, you haven't seen or talked to Roger since then? You two haven't been in contact all day *and* all evening?"

Nellie's tone of voice turned from sarcastic to hostile. "Not only haven't I seen him, but I don't care if I do either!"

Her thoughtless response made Bucky feel uncomfortable and left him speechless. He decided not to remark on her comment and pretended as though he did not hear her.

"I tried phoning here about an hour ago when I was on my way back to town," he said. "I was coming back from an important visit in Natural Bridge and wanted to talk to Roger. There's some significant information I wanted to share. Even though I didn't get very good reception on my cell phone, I still got no answer. Your answering machine didn't pick up, either. I guess you must've still been at the restaurant at that time."

"Yeah, I suppose I was. And by the way, Bucky, the answering machine doesn't work very well. Roger has to take it apart and fix it *again*...instead of just buying a new one."

Nellie walked past Bucky and listened to his concerns without batting an eye. She went over to the desk in the living room and began writing something on the notepad.

Then, without even looking up, she uttered in an apathetic voice, "Maybe he's with Holly. That's the first place I'd look for him, and if he isn't with her, I'm *sure* she knows where he is. Don't you think it's just so uncanny how she's with Roger whenever he's late—or the fact she knows *exactly* where to find him?"

Nellie's voice had a distinctly bitter sound every time she mentioned Holly's name. Although this disturbed Bucky, he did not have enough time to defend Roger, his friendship with Holly, or do any fence mending between Nellie and Roger.

"Actually, I called over to the bar, and Holly was the person who answered the phone," Bucky responded. "Holly told me she'd been working all afternoon, and Roger hasn't been in there either."

Nellie shrugged her shoulders. "Oh well, then."

"I even tried to call his folks in Syracuse, but all I got was their answering machine, which said they were out of town for the weekend. It seems as if nobody has seen Roger all day, and I'm getting worried about him."

"So, he wasn't at the bar, huh?" Nellie said, slightly shocked. "I would've thought that'd be the first place he'd go tonight, especially if Holly is working. Y'know, I was under the impression she *doesn't* work the late shift."

"Normally Holly doesn't," Bucky answered back. "I guess the new guy, Tim Matthews, called in tonight and stuck her for the evening shift. She wasn't very talkative on the phone, but she didn't seem overly thrilled about it either."

For a brief moment, Nellie raised her head up to look Bucky in the face and spoke in a polite manner. "About the only thing I can tell you is that when I got home, there were books lying all over the place with a piece of paper on the floor."

"Paper?" inquired Bucky.

"Yeah, I think it said Lucifer on it or something strange like that. I wasn't exactly paying close attention, and I can't really remember right now. I was *so* mad; I threw his books out the back door and the paper in the garbage."

The name 'Lucifer' struck a nerve and sent a chill down Bucky's spine. He was curious why that would be written on a piece of paper and wondered if it was connected to Roger's abrupt absence, but he kept his thoughts and emotions to himself.

"As erratic and immature as Roger's behavior has sometimes been in the past, it's still unlike him to be gone with nobody knowing where he is."

Bucky paused for a moment and stared out the window, deep in thought. He began to mutter softly, almost as if he was talking to himself. "His disappearance concerns me," he continued. "I'm afraid Roger might have become another victim of these strange disappearances happening around Carthage."

Nellie finished what she was writing, ripped the piece of paper off the notepad, and clenched the note tightly in her hand. She put the notepad and pen back in the drawer, slamming it shut.

"Well, let someone else worry about him from now on!" she snapped. "I've got better things to do with my time."

Bucky did not comprehend the extent of her hostility and anger until he looked over toward the door and noticed several large suitcases sitting on the floor. "What's going on here, Nellie? Is there something you're not telling me?"

Still holding the note in her hands, she lowered her head and began to sob. "I'm leaving him, Bucky. I just can't take it anymore."

A look of shock rushed over Bucky's face, and his jaw dropped to the floor. "Where are you going to go?" he inquired, utterly befuddled.

Nellie grabbed an envelope from the desk and stuffed the note inside. She walked over to the wooden corner stand in the hallway and set the letter upon it. "I'm going to stay at my mother's house in Syracuse for awhile and sort some things out. After that...I don't know."

Bucky was flabbergasted by what he heard. "You're not even going to stay long enough to talk this over with Roger!" he exclaimed. "Or even to say good-bye?"

Nellie stopped to think for a moment. She stepped back over to the corner stand in the hallway, grabbed the letter, and clasped it tightly in her hands. Her palms became sweaty, and she took a few deep breaths as she prepared herself to march out the door.

She extended her hand out and gave the letter to Bucky. "When you see him, will you give him this for me please?"

Bucky gazed at the envelope in his hands and said nothing. He looked up and saw tears in Nellie's eyes and the sorrowful emotion upon her face.

"Yes, of course I will," he replied softly to her.

Nellie wiped her eyes and let out a phony laugh. She took a deep breath, gave Bucky a hug, and walked over to her suitcases. "I don't know why I'm crying. There's no need for me to get emotional. After all, this development has been a long time coming."

Another instance of uncomfortable silence went by with neither one knowing what to say next. Nellie snatched a tissue from her purse while Bucky searched his pants pockets for his cell phone.

"I know this may seem out of place, Nellie, but do you mind if I use your telephone? I must've left my cell phone in the car and would like to call Cristina…just to tell her where I am. I swear, I'll only be a minute."

"Go ahead! Make all the calls you want!" she answered back with coolness in her tone. "As of right now, I don't live here anymore and could care less what happens to Roger or this house."

Nellie picked up her two suitcases and stormed out of the house, slamming the door behind her.

Bucky watched in sadness as Nellie loaded up her car and drove away. He grimaced for a moment while shaking his head in despair. However, as uncaring as it may seem, he could not concern himself with Nellie and Roger's quarrel. First and foremost, he had to call Cristina and let her know what was going on, and then he had to continue his search for his friend.

As Bucky picked up the phone to call Cristina, hoping she would be there, several questions began to rush through his mind. He wondered if his friend was safe and if Roger had tried to contact him. What's more, he was also unsure what he would tell Cristina without upsetting her or scaring the hell out of her. But most of all, Bucky wondered why there was a piece of paper at Roger's house with the name Lucifer written on it and what exactly Roger had stumbled upon. Just so many questions and still no answers.

"Hello," said Cristina as she picked up the phone.

"Cristina, this is Bucky!" he stated hurriedly. "I have something to tell you."

"Bucky!" she cried out before he could get out another word. "Where have you been? You weren't here when I got home, and there wasn't a note stating where you had gone. I was starting to get really worried."

"I don't have time to explain where I've been or what I was doing, but you're going to have to trust me. I have something very important to tell you." He took a deep breath and regained his composure so he could speak in a rational tone of voice. "There has been another disappearance and..."

Cristina interrupted Bucky in the middle of his sentence. "Let me guess. You and Roger are going to play detective again and try to find this person. You know something, Bucky, I'm getting *awfully* sick of this."

There was a long pause before Bucky broke the silence and answered, "It's Roger who has disappeared."

"Oh my god, I am *so* sorry," she said sympathetically. "You must be a nervous wreck about this, especially since its Roger, and being as close of friends as you two are. If there's anything I can do, just let me know. I'm here for you."

Bucky fought through his emotions so he could keep his calm, or at least pretend long enough until he was off the phone with Cristina.

"It's tearing me apart inside," he mumbled in a solemn tone. "I want you to pack up some clothes and go to your folks' house for a couple of days. I think it'd be the best thing for you to do…that is, while all this mayhem is happening around here."

"Why?" Cristina asked inquisitively. "What reason could you possibly have for wanting me to leave? Don't you think I can fend for myself, or is there something *else* you're not telling me?"

"No, it's nothing like that. I simply don't think it's safe to be here right now. There are too many unexplained disappearances around town, and I just don't want anything to happen to you. I think going to your parents' house for a little while is for the best. At least, until we've found out what happened to Roger."

"Well…"

Bucky butted in. "Please do not argue with me on this, Cris! It will put my mind at ease knowing that you're far away from here and out of whatever danger is lurking around Carthage."

"And what are *you* going to do while I'm gone?"

"I don't know, Cristina. Actually, I haven't thought that far ahead."

"I hope you're not considering going to the ferry service or roaming the streets to try to find him all by yourself."

Bucky was silent.

"Bucky, his disappearance is a *POLICE* matter. That means they will find Roger because that's what they are trained to do."

"But…"

"No 'buts' about it. They are professionals in their field of work, so let them do their jobs and don't get in the way. Please don't do something stupid that might put Roger at more risk than he already is."

"Trust me," he uttered reassuringly, "I won't do anything crazy like trying to find him by myself, I promise. I'm going to let the police handle this, hun. Right now, all I want is to make sure you will be safe. With so much chaos going on in Carthage, the best thing for you to do is to leave town until all of this mess blows over"

Cristina was still hesitant in her decision. "I understand you're upset, but what about my obligations to the council and the other town functions?"

"I'm sure we can manage a few days without you," Bucky told her, trying to sound as though everything that had been going on was just an inconvenience so as not to upset Cristina more. "Besides, the council isn't due to convene again for another almost three weeks from now. I'm certain everything will be straightened out by then."

"Alright, I'll pack a few things and go stay with my parents for a few days. Just promise me you'll keep me informed on how things are going," Cristina responded insistently.

"Okay."

"I love you, Bucky, and I don't want to see you getting hurt by acting foolishly."

As Bucky pondered his next move, his mind was drowning out Cristina's words. He tried to keep his mind focused on the problem at hand and getting Cristina to safety, but it was getting increasingly difficult to concentrate. Two nagging questions kept coming up in his mind…Was Roger still alive, and if so, where was he?

"There's nothing to get overzealous about." Bucky stated, cutting her off while she spoke. "All I am going to do is drive by the basketball court to see if he's been there and then maybe stop by Kitty's Bar. If I find out anything pertinent, I'll go straight to the police station and let them handle it."

"Good. That makes me feel a lot better about leaving. I'll call you tonight when I get there to let you know I arrived safely and to see if you have discovered anything new about Roger's situation. Just remember what I said about being careful."

"I know…and I will. Have a safe trip, hun. I'll see you soon." Before she hung up, he said, "By the way, Cristina, I love you too."

Bucky slowly set the phone down on the receiver; his heart hung heavily in his chest. In a quiet whisper, Bucky said, "Sorry, Cris, but Roger's the closest thing I have to a brother, and I'm not going to lose him. With you safely out of harm's way, I can concentrate on finding him and getting to the bottom of the strange occurrences going on around here."

Already he was thinking more clearly, and he had a better idea of what he needed to do. A sickening feeling churned in the pit of his stomach as he thought of what may have happened and what he might find.

As Bucky started to turn and head towards the door to leave, he looked down into the wastebasket beside the corner stand and saw a receipt with the local pharmacy's logo on top. Curious as to what it could be, he reached down and picked it up to glance it over. In sheer astonishment, he noticed that on the receipt there was but only one purchase itemized. A $9.99 purchase for an at-home pregnancy test.

Chapter 19:

Mission of Improbable Success

By the time Bucky arrived home, Cristina had already packed her travel bag and departed. As he approached his driveway, Bucky observed that Bryan Harsha's automobile was parked in front of his garage, and Bryan himself, was sitting on Bucky's porch steps.

Bucky was startled by Bryan's unexpected presence, and very curious as to the nature of the visit. Not only was Bryan's visit uncommon, the truth is, he had *never* stopped by Bucky's house before.

"Bryan, what are you doing here?" he asked while walking up to the front door.

Bryan stood up and wiped the sweat away from his forehead. Although Bucky was preoccupied and his thoughts seemed elsewhere, he still sensed that Bryan was troubled.

"I stopped by to see if you've heard anything more about Scott's case," said Bryan, "and when I arrived, Cristina was on her way out the door. She was carrying a small blue suitcase—or something like that. I spoke with her briefly before she drove off. Cristina mentioned that she was going to stay at her parents' house for a few days, and then she told me about Roger."

Bucky did not respond.

"Bucky, she's concerned you might start some trouble by trying to pin Roger's disappearance, as well as all the others that have happened recently, on Louis Ferr. Do you think they're all connected?"

"Yes I do, Bryan," Bucky stated. "Unfortunately, I haven't got time to explain it all at this moment. I wish I had more time to talk, but there are more important matters I've to tend to right now."

After searching several pockets, Bucky finally found the key to open his front door and walked in.

Bryan followed behind him saying, "Bucky, I was with Roger this afternoon, and I know where he is. At least, I knew where he was heading to when he left his house."

Bucky stopped in his tracks and turned around to face Bryan. "What's going on, Bryan? Where did he go and what do you know about his disappearance?"

"I don't know what he was thinking," Bryan stammered.

Pausing for a moment, Bryan strolled along as if in a daze while he made his way to the couch. Bucky was puzzled by his actions and sat in the recliner across from him.

"We were at Roger's house researching the name of the ferry service," continued Bryan. "Y'know, just like you wanted him to do."

Bucky leaned closer to Bryan, hanging on every word he said. "Yeah, I'm listening. Then what happened?"

Bryan was almost incoherent as he spoke barely above a whisper. "It all happened so fast. I never should've let him leave. I was playing around with the letters of Louis Ferr's name when everything just fell into place. I couldn't believe what they spelled at first but as I stared at them, I realized they formed the name Lucifer!"

A chill ran down Bucky's spine as Bryan's words sank in. "Oh my god!" he exclaimed, his voice noticeably shaken. "Where did Roger go after he left his house, Bryan? Don't tell me that he went down to Mephistis Pheles Ferry Service by himself!"

Bryan continued to stare off and acted as though he was in shock. "Roger fully believes Louis Ferr is the Devil and is convinced that Ferr is responsible for the disappearances in town."

After a moment of silence, Bucky shook Bryan's shoulder, snapping him out of his stupor.

"I'm...I'm sorry, Bucky." he sputtered, regaining his bearings. "This whole situation has me stressed out to the max. Roger was acting insanely irrational and stormed off in such a hurry that I didn't have time to reason with him or calm him down. Before he left, Roger said he was going to confront Mr. Ferr, and I'm worried he might have done something foolish."

Bucky leaped out of the recliner and anxiously paced back and forth. "He doesn't know what kind of trouble he's getting himself into! This time, Roger is in *way* over his head!"

"I think you may be right," admitted Bryan.

Bucky stopped pacing momentarily and said, "Listen, Bryan. This afternoon, I received a phone call from a gentleman who is also interested in this case. I went to his place in Natural Bridge, and while I was there, he and I came up with the same conclusion about Mr. Ferr. The more I thought of it, I was sure it was a big mistake. But now, with your findings, it seems to connect the whole thing together."

"What are we going to do?" Bryan asked with a profound urgency in his voice.

"I don't know…I wasn't expecting to be handling this situation so soon." Bucky rubbed his throbbing temples to alleviate some stress. "I hadn't even thought of developing a strategy on how I was going to deal with Ferr. But whatever plan I come up with, I know I'll have to go down to the ferry service and get Roger *soon*…no matter what the risks are."

Bryan swallowed hard, trying to muster all the courage he had in his body. "Whatever you decide, I want to come along when you leave for the ferry service. Roger is my friend, too, and if Louis Ferr is who we *think* he is, then I can't just leave Roger out there to suffer the same fate that happened to Bob and Scott."

Bucky took a deep breath to calm down and clear his mind. He sat back down and began thinking of ways to get them to the ferry service unnoticed in order to search for Roger. He pulled a pen from his back pocket and started drawing up a plan without any hesitation—for he knew what needed to be done. Bucky just hoped that he would be quick enough.

With so much on the line, Bucky did not even consider the possibility he might be throwing himself into danger or risking his own life. In fact, he moved with such assuredness that one would never know the severity of the danger he would have to confront. But then again, that's just the type of behavior one would one expect from Dave "Bucky" Morgan.

Bucky reached into his front pocket and pulled out Jim Draven's phone number. "The gentleman I talked to earlier is a retired police detective from Chicago. His name is Jim Draven, and he's someone we can trust."

"How can he help?" Bryan asked.

Bucky picked up the phone and began to dial; then he looked back at Bryan. "Jim believes the disappearances in town are related to similar instances that happened in Chicago over forty-five years ago. Trust me; I think we're going to need his help."

After many rings, Jim answered his phone and yawned into the receiver. "Hello?" he said tiredly. "Who is this?"

"Jim, it's Bucky Morgan," he responded hurriedly.

"Bucky? I wasn't expectin' to hear from you so soon. Damn, it's only been a few hours since you left my house. Is something wrong?"

"A close friend of mine has suddenly become missing. Would it be possible for you to come to Carthage right now?"

"Hold on a second," Jim replied. "Calm down and tell me exactly what's going on."

Bucky paused for a moment and took a deep breath. "It's my friend...Roger Fasick. The one I mentioned when I was at your house. He went down to talk to Mr. Ferr today and no one has seen him since. Like us, Roger also figured out Ferr's identity, and he stormed down to the ferry service to confront him. I think he may be in trouble, and I'm afraid if I don't get to him soon, Roger might end up dead."

"You have good reason to be concerned. I can get ready and be in Carthage in less than an hour. Where do you want me to meet you?"

After a short breather, Bucky asked, "Do you know where the town council conducts its business? We're located on the second floor of the City Hall building."

"Yeah, of course I do," Jim stated. "I've driven by there many times when I've traveled into Carthage. Do you wanna meet out front, around the back, or somewhere inside the building?"

"It might be better if we meet out back," answered Bucky. "We have to be careful; we don't want to draw attention to ourselves. I'll be waiting for you by the back door. Another friend of mine will be joining us."

"Oh? What *kind* of friend are ya havin' tag along with us?" Jim inquired.

"His name is Bryan Harsha. Don't worry, Jim, he's a member of the council like myself, and he happens to be one of only a few people that I trust."

After he hung up the phone, Bucky rummaged around his house and grabbed a few things such as some flashlights, his cell phone, and the most important item of all—the dagger of Megiddo. He stuffed his gear into an old duffle bag that he pulled from his bedroom closet and quickly bolted out the door with Bryan following closely behind him. Within seconds, they were in Bucky's Mustang and speeding down the road.

Time seemed to stand still as Bucky and Bryan waited for Jim to arrive. It had been forty-five minutes since they left Bucky's house, but for the gentlemen that kept pacing back and forth on the back steps of City Hall, it seemed like an eternity.

Just as Bucky's impatience was beginning to get the best of him, Jim Draven arrived in his rusty, orange-colored Nissan pickup truck. He stepped out of his vehicle, dressed in black dungarees, a black tank top and, of course, his old western boots. As Jim stuffed a pistol in a holster on his side, Bucky noticed Jim was wearing his old detective shield on a string around his neck; a gesture for luck more than anything.

"I brought my gun with me, just in case!" Jim yelled out. "It's not as potent a weapon as the dagger, but it might still come in handy."

"We'll take whatever we can get," Bucky uttered with a heavy sigh.

When they were all standing next to each other, Bucky introduced Bryan and Jim to each other as he picked the duffle bag up off the ground and pulled out his keys.

"Let's take my Mustang," announced Bucky. "We can get to the ferry service faster, and we're going to need the extra backseat room if we find Roger there."

The men all agreed and climbed into the sports car as Bucky revved up the engine and headed toward the ferry service. Bucky rushed through the streets of Carthage, breaking just about every speed limit. With a lunatic on the loose and Roger missing, it seemed as though everything was chaotic.

On the way, the men exchanged stories with each other so that everyone was up to speed on the perilous situation. During their conversation, the song *Die Young* by the classic rock band Black Sabbath came on the radio. The song suddenly and unexpectedly upset Bryan, seemingly striking an uncontrollable fear in him.

"Quick! Turn that song off!" Bryan cried out.

Bucky and Jim turned around, looking at Bryan as though he was crazy.

"What the hell are you jabberin' about?" asked Jim.

"I'm sorry for getting so worked up, but I get freaked out whenever I hear it," Bryan explained. "There's an urban legend that states a person dies whenever that particular song is played on the radio. It's a bad omen I tell you."

Bucky took a quick glance over his shoulder toward Bryan. "I've heard of that urban legend before, too; although, I was told a different version of the tale. There's nothing to worry about, Bryan. It's purely superstition However, if it will make you feel better, I'll turn it off."

"Thank you, I'd like that a lot," sighed Bryan.

For the remainder of the ride, the men sat in silence, a sense of fear and uncertainty weighing on their minds. Bucky turned onto the gravel road that led to the ferry service, shut off his headlights, and parked ten yards down the road. He veered off to the side so his car was would be obscured by the small trees and bushes.

"Alright we're here," Bucky mumbled in a low, quiet voice. "I'll park here. This should give us some distance and a lesser chance of being noticed."

The men exited the car and scoped out the surroundings. Due to the combination of humidity and nervous perspiration, their clothes were sticking to them. The smell of dead fish and rotting vegetation was so intense along the river they could taste it. Bryan looked down the road leading to the ferry service, staring into the foggy unknown that awaited them.

Bucky grabbed his duffle bag from the back seat and walked to the front of the car. He set his bag on the hood of the car and began pulling out the contents, spreading them out across the hood as Jim loaded his pistol with bullets.

"Remember, this is a *rescue* mission." Bucky stated, stressing his point. "Don't try to be a hero and think you can take on Louis Ferr by yourselves. Our main priority here is to locate Roger, and then get the hell out of here."

Jim spoke up and said, "How will I know if I find Roger? I don't even know what he looks like."

"Good question, Jim," Bucky replied. "Roger has dark-blonde hair, a goatee, and always wears a metal bracelet on his wrist with the letters WWTJD inscribed on it."

Jim nodded. "That'll do. I've located people on less information than that before."

"Okay, then. If there aren't any more questions, everyone grab a flashlight—but only use it if *absolutely* necessary. I realize it's a bit foggy around this area, but there's a full moon out tonight, so hopefully it won't be too dark, and we'll be able to see where we're going. The less we use the flashlights, the smaller the risk will be that we draw any attention to ourselves."

Bryan looked at Jim and Bucky as they inspected their own weapons. He felt troubled without anything to protect himself and grabbed Bucky's arm to get his attention. "So, you have a dagger and

Jim brought a gun. What do I get? You don't expect me to go down there unarmed, do you?"

"No, of course not," Bucky said reassuringly. "I have a wooden baseball bat in the trunk of the car. You can carry that if you'd like."

Bryan was hoping for something bigger or more lethal, but accepted the baseball bat saying, "I suppose it's better than nothing at all."

It was a long, winding trail leading to the ferry service. Aside from the occasional vehicle driving down Main Street and the sound of crickets chirping in the woods, there was nothing. Footsteps walking ever so slowly on the crunchy gravel and idly drifting fog were the only two constants as they traveled down the road. Staying within arm's reach of each other, the men flocked toward the center of the desolate road, where their forms seemed like haunted shapes beneath the light of the large, pale moon that shined high above them.

Suddenly, Bryan's head spun to his left side and looked intently into the woods, gripping the baseball bat tight. "What was that noise?" he whispered nervously.

"I didn't hear anything," answered Bucky.

"Me neither," Jim added. "It is probably just your nerves working overtime."

"No!" Bryan exclaimed, refusing to take his eyes off the dark emptiness that stared back at him. "I'm sure I heard something. It sounded like someone or something was walking in the woods."

Bucky gave Bryan a reassuring pat on the back. "Well, there is plenty of wildlife out here. After all, this *is* the North Country. I wouldn't be overly concerned about it. All you'll do is get yourself worked up and scared. Just keep alert; remember to stay out in the open and away from the shadows."

As they inched closer to the ferry service, nothing else moved. It was if all the wildlife in the surrounding woods had suddenly become silent. When they got within a few yards of the main parking lot, Bucky stopped and scanned the area to make sure no one was around.

"Is something wrong?" asked Jim.

"I think we should split up," Bucky announced to his companions. "That way, we can cover a larger area in a shorter amount of time." Pointing to the tool shed where Bob's bike was hidden, Bucky said, "Jim, you go look in the tool shed over there. Bryan, I would like you to inspect the ferry, and I will go check Louis Ferr's office."

The men ventured out to their designated areas. The wind picked up as Bucky walked to the ferry office. The rocking chair on the porch moved back and forth in the breeze, but when Bucky looked over at it, the chair abruptly stopped. The hair stood up on the back of his neck, encouraging Bucky to pick up the pace as he stepped onto the office porch.

As Bucky entered the darkened building, he scanned the room with his flashlight. Next, he walked over and opened the door to the stock room where extra supplies were kept for Mr. Ferr's business.

"Damn it," Bucky whispered. "There's no one here."

Bucky exited the office and started to walk over toward the ferry. As he got close, he saw Bryan was about to board the deserted-looking ferry. Bucky decided that, just to be on the safe side, he wanted Bryan to wait so they could check it out together. However, before he could get to his friend or holler out to him, *someone* or *something*, clubbed Bucky from behind…knocking him out cold.

Chapter 20:

Confrontation with the Beast

While Bucky was out cold on the ground, Bryan sneaked onto the ferry and began looking around. The fog was much thicker by the water, making the objects in front of him indiscernible and he needed his flashlight to see.

Bryan observed an object on the deck boards. It was no bigger than a rat and barely caught his attention. He wandered over, leaned down, and reached to pick it up. When Bryan held it in his hand, he noticed that it was a gray handkerchief with the letter "S" stitched in the cloth.

"This belonged to Scott Patterson!" Bryan gasped. "I'm positive of it!" Bryan's heart beat heavily in his chest; he started to hyperventilate. "Oh my god, Scott *did* make it to the ferry service on the night he disappeared…Bucky was right all along!"

An ill feeling began to form in Bryan's stomach.

"Scott must've dropped his handkerchief on the ferry before he…"

Just then, Bryan heard the creak of a loose deck board. Approximately ten yards in front of him, he saw the body of a person. As Bryan walked closer, he swept the beam of his flashlight upon the figure, noticing that the individual was Mr. Ferr's assistant, Steve Jensen. He appeared to be hurt and in pain as his body was hunched over and shaking wildly.

"Mr. Jensen, is there something wrong? Do you feel all right?" he asked with unease.

When Jensen lifted his head, he had glowing red eyes and was growling like some kind of animal. His face was terribly distorted. Bryan looked upon him in sheer terror, unable to move a muscle.

Jensen lunged toward Bryan and tackled him to the ground, knocking the baseball bat out of Bryan's hands. His razor-sharp claws dug deep into Bryan's chest and abdomen, shredding his skin as if it were tissue paper. Bryan tried to defend himself but to no avail, as Jensen attacked with the ferocity of a rabid beast. Luckily, Bryan was able to remain focused long enough to muster a sufficient amount strength to kick Jensen off and send him over the railing, plummeting to the ground.

Bleeding badly, Bryan attempted to get up and run away, but the steady loss of blood was making him dizzy. The gouges in his chest were so deep, it seemed as though he was mauled by a grizzly bear. He managed to pull himself up and stagger off the ferryboat, but once Bryan stepped onto the shore, he was tackled once again by Jensen.

The two men rolled on the ground a number of times until Jensen was able to maneuver his body so that he was on top of Bryan. He swiftly sank his pointed fingernails into Bryan's throat, ripping his flesh to shreds. Jensen was crazed with blood and tearing at Bryan's body long after the librarian had stopped moving.

After several motionless minutes, Bucky slowly rolled onto his side and gazed over to the ferry. His vision was blurry and his body ached, but a sudden fear chilled his spine, and he quickly reached for his back. Only when he checked his sheath and was reassured that he still had the dagger with him did he finally allow himself to breathe.

Gradually, Bucky made his way to his feet. His legs were weak and wobbly. As he tried to walk, he found it difficult to maintain his balance. Although curious as to who hit him from behind, and for what reason he was attacked, Bucky disregarded his concerns about the ambush for a much more distressing situation, which was happening before his eyes.

Bucky saw a figure of a person by the water, but he was unable to make out a clear identification. However, even though his eyes had not yet fully adjusted themselves, he was sure the individual was choking the life out of Bryan Harsha.

Fighting through pain, Bucky ran over to the ferry as fast as he could. By the time he got within twenty yards of the individuals, his vision improved enough for him to see that Bryan was in the clutches of Steve Jensen. The attacker grunted like pig and raised his head high, letting out a thunderous yowl before reaching, once again, for the throat of the bleeding and motionless Bryan Harsha.

"Stop!" Bucky screamed in desperation. "Hold it right there, Jensen! Let go of him or I'll put you down myself...permanently!"

Even though Bucky's words may have been meaningless to the monster once known as Steve Jensen, the tone was all too clear. A tone that got the beast's attention.

"Whatever you say...Hero," he growled.

Jensen turned around so that Bucky could see his face. In his horror, Bucky watched as Jensen squeezed Bryan in his grasp. However, as Bucky looked closer, he saw that Jensen was *not* choking Bryan, he was feeding on him. Where Bryan's face used to be was now a mangled hunk of flesh.

Jensen wiped the blood off his chin with the back of his hand; then he licked his fingers clean. His eyes met with Bucky's.

"And now," Jensen screeched, "it's your turn!"

Enraged and slightly traumatized, Bucky charged toward Jensen at a full run. The two warriors collided, engaged in a fierce confrontation, both knowing that only one would survive. Jensen swung violently with his claw-like hands and tore the midsection of Bucky's shirt, leaving minor gashes in his skin. Wincing in pain, Bucky managed to shove Jensen backwards a few feet; just far enough for Bucky to leap forward and tackle the crazed man.

The two men fell to the ground. As they were rolling around, each trying to gain the edge over the other, Bucky was able to free his hand—the one holding the dagger. With as much strength as he could muster, Bucky flung Jensen on to his back, raised the weapon, and struck downward with a mighty blow. Jensen wriggled free from Bucky's grip as the dagger narrowly missed his face by inches.

Jensen seemed distracted by the close call and his hesitation hurt him, for Bucky's next try was successful. As the two men made their way back to their feet, Bucky sprang toward his opponent and swung wildly. The sound of steel cutting through bone echoed in the sky as the dagger went deep into Jensen's upper body.

Trembling, Bucky released the dagger and took a few steps backwards. Then, he watched in horrified fascination as Jensen looked down to see the handle of the dagger protruding out of his chest. The blade was lodged in the madman's ribcage, embedded to the hilt. Jensen's eyes were as big as golf balls, and his face twisted with pain and disbelief.

Now, Jensen's clothes were soaked in the blood of two people. The first being his victim, Bryan Harsha, and the latest crimson to drench his shirt was his own. He collapsed and fell to his knees, groveling on all fours for several agonizing seconds as he let out an inhuman scream. His body twitched and quivered, then dropped forward as his face hit the dirt.

For a moment Bucky stared at Jensen, waiting to see if there was any movement, and then slowly turned him over. He briefly looked upon the hideous creature and shuttered before he drew a deep breath, pulled the dagger with both hands from Jensen's chest, and looked up at Bryan's motionless body.

Bucky rushed over to Bryan, who was lying motionless on his back. One look said it all; there was no need to check for a pulse, but he did anyway. Tears fell from his eyes as no pulse could be found and he lifted Bryan off the ground, holding him in his arms. Bryan's body was already getting cold to the touch.

While everyone else had been busy searching by the ferryboat, Jim Draven made his way over to the tool shed. He carefully opened the door and examined the interior with his flashlight before entering. As the flashlight moved around the room, the light came to a rest on a figure lying on the floor.

Jim stared hard at the object for a couple of seconds and then realized it was a man. Jim shined his flashlight over the person as he inched closer, and although the man had his back to Jim, he was still able to notice the ash-blonde hair. A closer inspection found that the person was wearing a metal bracelet on his left wrist with the letters WWTJD engraved on it. Jim smiled as he exhaled, relieved that he had found Roger at last.

Roger's hands were bound behind his back. His clothes were tattered and torn, there were several contusions over the body, and his head was severely bruised with his left eye being swelled shut.

"Are you conscious?" Jim inquired.

"Yeah...who are you?" Roger asked groggily.

Jim shook his head in disbelief and disgust over the way Mr. Ferr and Steve Jensen had beaten him. He kneeled down and leaned forward to untie Roger's hands.

"I'm a friend, and I'm going to get you out of here. That's all you need to know for now."

"No!" Roger stated abruptly. "I'm not going anywhere with you until I know who you are! You could be one of Ferr's lackeys for all I know."

"My name is Jim Draven. You don't know me, but I'm a friend of Bucky Morgan's. We thought you might be in trouble, so we came down here to rescue you. Look, you can ask me all the questions you want once we get out of here, but right now, I don't know how much time we have until we're noticed."

As Jim untied Roger and was about to help him to his feet, a shadow appeared. Jim noticed the shadow creeping up behind him and spun around quickly as he stood up, coming face to face with Louis Ferr.

Ferr's eyes widened with surprise; and then an unexpected grin appeared on his face. "Well, well, if it isn't my old pal Jim Draven."

Jim's jaw hung open but otherwise remained silent.

"It has been a long time since our days in Chicago together."

Jim's eyes narrowed and flashed. "Y...You!" he stuttered, overwhelmed and visibly startled. "I knew it was *you*, Liv!"

Mr. Ferr looked him up and down, sizing up his foe. "That's right, Jim. But I must say, the years have *not* been kind to you. The last time we crossed paths, you were in your prime. Now, you look like a feeble old man."

"And you still look like a walking corpse who just entered a candy store."

"Ah, Jim, how I've missed your quirky witticisms."

Mr. Ferr glanced at Roger lying on the floor. He sneered and spat on him.

"I'm quite surprised you are here, Jim," Ferr continued. "I certainly didn't expect to see you here tonight. Is this a social visit, or are you here to finish what we started many years ago?" he asked with an evil laugh.

Jim paused as he stared in bewilderment at his enemy, feeling as if he had entered a living nightmare.

"So, you're going by the name Louis Ferr now," Jim's lips trembled as he spoke.

Ferr nodded his head.

"Not that it really matters; it doesn't make any difference whether your name is Ferr, Liv Edeht, or whatever else you want to call yourself. I know *what* you really are...Pure Evil."

Mr. Ferr cocked his head slightly and grinned; Jim's hands began to shake.

"I don't know how it can be possible that you're standing in front of me or why you're still alive after all these years. It's not logical— you should have died long ago!"

"I could say the same for you, old man," Ferr countered.

Jim took a few steps backwards. In the back of his mind, a realization set in that without the dagger he gave to Bucky, he was completely defenseless against Louis Ferr. Although Jim had his pistol with him, he knew that it would do little more than slow Ferr down and buy him only a few seconds of time.

In the most crucial time in Jim Draven's life, he began to understand just how costly his mistake would be. For he was not as young as the first time he and Mr. Ferr encountered each other, and without his precious dagger or the virility of his youth to aide him, he had become a sitting duck to his most powerful enemy.

As Mr. Ferr took a few steps into the shed, Jim decided he had no other option but to pull out his gun, and pointed it in Mr. Ferr's face.

"Don't take another step!" roared Jim as he cocked his gun.

Mr. Ferr let out a bellowing, shrieking laugh. "You know as well as I do that your little toy can't hurt me. Where is your dagger, Jim? I know you have one of the seven daggers of Megiddo. After all, I saw it in your hands the last time we encountered each other."

Jim continued to point his gun at the ferryman's face but said nothing.

"Don't tell me you've lost it, Jim," Ferr continued. "That would be a most fatal mistake on your part."

A creepy grin swept across Mr. Ferr's face, stretching from ear to ear. His boldness carried him a few steps closer; then Jim's trigger finger began to twitch and he swallowed hard.

Jim's upper lip curled up into a snarl as he glared at Mr. Ferr and aimed his gun. "I said 'don't take another step!'"

With almost lightning speed, Mr. Ferr slapped Jim's pistol out of his hand, catching him totally off guard. As the pistol landed in a pile of old paint cans, Ferr stepped forward and shoved Jim backward against the wall, knocking the breath out of him.

Roger somehow managed to muster enough strength to swing his leg around, knocking Mr. Ferr's legs out from beneath him and sending the ferryman face first onto the ground.

"Quick!" Roger yelled to Jim. "Find your gun before he gets up!"

Jim seized the opportunity and kicked Ferr in the side of the head a few times with his steel toed boots before running past the old ferryman. Jim frantically pawed through the pile of empty paint cans, looking for his gun but unable to find it. After abandoning his search for the pistol, Jim's eyes searched frantically for *any* object to use as a weapon, finally coming across a pipe that was leaning against the wall.

As Jim reached for the pipe, Roger cried out, "Hurry up, Jim! Hit him or…"

But before Roger could get out the rest of his sentenee or Jim could even raise his weapon, Mr. Ferr was already back on his feet. He backhanded Jim in the mouth, sending him to the knees.

"Ugh!" groaned Jim. "You dirty, rotten son of a..."

Before Jim could finish, Ferr delivered a devastating blow to the back of Jim's neck. He struck with such force that it immediately broke Jim's neck and sent him crashing to the floor. Mr. Ferr grabbed Jim's limp body and hurled him into the boxes and crates that were stacked against the wall, bringing them down upon Jim's lifeless body.

Mr. Ferr walked over to Roger and kicked him in the ribs a few times; then he leaned down to pick up the metal bar. "That wasn't very nice, Roger, tripping me like that. I'm afraid you're going to have to be punished—and I must warn you, this is going to hurt you *a lot* more than me."

Roger laid helpless as Mr. Ferr hovered over him like a vulture stalking his prey. The ferryman hissed and snickered at his victim, taunting him to try and fight. Roger tried to stand, but his legs were too weak and bruised to hold his body weight. He managed to get to his knees before falling to the ground once again and didn't have enough energy to make another attempt.

Mr. Ferr shook his head in disgust and said, "You're not even worth my time, boy. I suppose I'll have to go find someone else to play with; maybe your friend Dave Morgan is around here someplace."

Before Mr. Ferr walked out the door, he stopped dead in his tracks and turned around. He ran over and slammed the metal bar down upon Roger, striking his back and legs as Roger screamed in anguish. Roger tried to shield himself against the blows, raising his arms high above his head, but Ferr kept swinging with a ferocity that Roger had never experienced before. With one last whack, the unnerving sound of bone cracking filled the room, and Roger's metal bracelet flew across the shed.

Roger's agonizing screams echoed loudly through the night sky, signaling Bucky's attention. He quickly seized the dagger and stuffed it in his sheath before running off toward the parking lot to try to get a fix on where Roger's screams were coming from.

Meanwhile, as the commotion by the waterfront culminated, a shadowy figure in a black cloak appeared from out of the woods and made its way through the fog to the backside of the ferry office. The night shrouded the figure in so much darkness that it was impossible to discern the person's face or even recognize the type of build it had in order to identify if it was a man or a woman. Slowly, yet gracefully, the individual moved through the shadows of the night, trying to keep itself from being noticed.

The figure stood close against the building and made its way across to the back door. Leaning down and glancing around, a square-like package, roughly the size of a child's lunchbox, surfaced from underneath its cloak. The mysterious stranger in black set the package at the foot of the back door of the ferry service and then headed back toward the cover of the trees, disappearing just as mysteriously as the entity emerged.

Chapter 21:

The Grand Finale

When Bucky arrived at the tool shed, he was almost too afraid to open the door, fearing what he might find on the other side. He kept telling himself not to think about it, hoping deep down that, like the office where he had inspected earlier, there would be no one inside. However, a terrible uneasiness lingered in his thoughts and kept his stomach in knots.

He opened the door and was immediately shocked by the image before him. Roger laid motionless on the shed floor, and Bucky rushed over to his side. He took in the whole situation, noticing how dangerously critical Roger looked. Even in the darkness Bucky was aware of the crumbled legs, the swollen eyes, and the bleeding gashes.

Bucky leaned down to check for a pulse.

"He's still breathing," he said with a sigh of relief.

"Bucky...that you?" asked Roger weakly.

"Yeah, bud. It's me. Just relax and save your strength. I'm gettin' you outta here right now," Bucky uttered in a determined tone.

"No, wait," Roger sputtered. "Check that other guy first."

Bucky thought Roger was going into shock and possibly hallucinating. "Who are you talking about?"

"In the corner," replied Roger.

Bucky looked over his shoulder and saw a human leg sticking out from under a pile of junk, tools, and other debris.

"Oh, please no!" he said, his heart racing with worry.

As fast as he could, Bucky moved over to the pile of rubble, pulling the wooden crates off from Jim's broken and battered body.

Laboriously, Bucky turned the body over and gazed into the face of Jim Draven. The look of fear was permanently tattooed onto his face. The very same look Bucky saw when he told Jim that his old nemesis was still alive...only worse. A grotesque face set in shock stared back, the eyes sightless, rolled back in their sockets and showed only white. Jim's mouth hung open with a trickle of blood running down his chin.

Bucky thought of his conversation with Jim in Natural Bridge. Initially, he believed the whole idea of Ferr being a supernatural entity seemed preposterous, but the events of this night were making a believer out of him.

Could it be true? Is Mr. Ferr really Satan? he wondered.

Bucky didn't know if it was true, and he really didn't care anymore. He only wanted to get Roger out of there.

As Roger laid feebly upon the floor, almost completely unconscious, Bucky rushed back to his side. He scooped Roger up off the floor quickly and opened the door to the shack.

As Bucky stepped out into the parking lot with Roger in his arms, he glanced around, searching the area to be sure all was safe. He turned to look back at the shed and a flood of fear raced through him as he noticed a dark figure standing several yards away in front of the tool shed entrance.

When the figure stepped out of the shadows, Bucky was able to see that the individual was Louis Ferr. Trying not to show fear in his voice, Bucky spoke in a loud determined tone as he said, "Who are you *really*—and what do you want?"

Mr. Ferr stared at Bucky with wide eyes and a creepy grin that stretched from one ear to the other. "Take a look at my face and try to concentrate. Are you sure I don't look familiar? Perhaps we have met someplace else, before I came to Carthage."

A look of complete confusion covered Bucky's face. "No, I've never seen your ugly mug before this whole fiasco. What're you getting' at?"

"Well, I guess that's understandable," he said with a sinister smirk and a haunting stare. "After all, it *has* been quite a few years since we last crossed paths. Besides, I was wearing a long coat and my face was covered by a large hat the night I gave you and Paul Fasick a ride back to your hotel room on my ferry."

Bucky's face became pale.

"You do remember Florida, don't you?" Ferr inquired.

"Who are you and what do you want?" asked Bucky again, this time in a shaky voice.

"Come on, let's not be coy. I'm sure you've figured out who I am by now. I certainly don't think it's a coincidence that you and my old enemy, Jim Draven, just happened to show up here at the same time."

Bucky remained silent.

"I am the one who haunts your dreams and the one you fear the most," continued Ferr. "Actually, I'm surprised you figured it out as fast as you did. You are very clever; I like that about you. That's just one of *many* things that fascinate me about you, which leads me to answer your other question. As for what I want, well that's simple. You eluded me back in Florida—but your friend did not. Now that I've found you, I want your heroic soul!"

Bucky found his voice and said, "If you wanted my soul so badly, why didn't you just take it when you first got to town?"

"Contrary to what you might believe, Mr. Morgan...I am *not* all-powerful. Even the Devil is bound by certain rules and restrictions."

"What makes my soul so special, Ferr?" Bucky asked as his hand slowly reached behind his back.

"Long have I craved a soul such as yours to add to my realm. Not tainted, and yet, you are not exactly pure of heart, either. Your soul is very powerful, and quite a rare find, indeed."

"I hate to be the bearer of bad news, Ferr, but my soul is *not* going with you—not today, not ever!" Bucky screamed as he jerked his arm forward and pulled out the dagger Jim had given him.

The emergence of the weapon startled Mr. Ferr, and his once smug expression became much more serious. "So, I see you have one of the seven daggers of Megiddo in your possession. I suppose Jim gave that to you in order to give you a better chance to defeat me."

Bucky nodded as his eyes narrowed into an incensed stare.

"Well, I'm not as helpless as you think I am. You may have killed my assistant, Jensen, and it's true I *must* fear your weapon, but I do have a surprise of my own. There is another person who is willing to sacrifice everything to ensure my safety, thus ensuring my ultimate goal...retrieving your soul! I think you know my *other* assistant whose been helping me all along quite well."

Becky Taylor stepped out from behind Louis Ferr with Jim Draven's pistol in her hand. Bucky's expression changed to shock, and his jaw dropped in horror. Mr. Ferr watched the confusion in Bucky's eyes and smiled proudly.

"Ms. Taylor has proven to be very resourceful, and she is willing to give up her life for me, Mr. Morgan." Ferr threw his head back and laughed, utterly amused at the look of terror upon Bucky's face.

"I think I'm going to enjoy watching her kill you even better than if I did it myself," Ferr gloated. "Just think of it…a young and dashing would-be hero taken down in the line of battle by a puny, old woman." Mr. Ferr paused and began to laugh. "It has a sense of dramatic irony, don't you think?"

Bucky stared in surprise. "Becky, what are you doing here?"

She gazed at him without uttering a word, having little more than a blank expression upon her face. Seeing Becky standing there with Jim's pistol in her hands, Bucky was in complete bewilderment.

He then turned his attention back over toward Mr. Ferr and asked, "What's wrong with her, Ferr? What have you done to make her act this way?"

Louis Ferr laughed his evil laugh. "Your friend is weak, and she is a very easy creature to control. Actually, she doesn't even possess a soul worth taking, but she does come in handy occasionally."

Another outburst of putrid laughter bellowed from the ferryman as the fog grew thicker and the hissing from the nearby demons became louder. Bucky grew more uneasy, and his heart began pounding in his chest.

"Try and fight the control he has on you!" pleaded Bucky. "Becky, listen to me! You're a good person, and I know you don't really want to hurt anyone."

"You're wasting your breath and what little time you have left, Mr. Morgan," Louis Ferr said mockingly. "She is *with* me now."

Bucky looked over and glared at him.

"That's right," Ferr continued. "Like many others who've served me over the years, Ms. Taylor is with me in body and soul. She has become an apostle of mine."

"Never!" Bucky roared back, his jaw clenched in anger. Bucky focused his attention back toward Becky, raising his arms as though to surrender and talking softly to her. "Roger is hurt, Becky. He may die if we don't get him out of here soon. I don't know what's happened to you, but we can end this without any more people getting injured. But first you have to put down the gun and let me get Roger to a hospital."

"No!" screamed Becky hysterically. "There is no reason for me to fight against his power. Resistance is futile, Bucky. I live only to serve him, and right now, the master commands that I kill you. Only then will I receive his unconditional love."

There was no more rationalizing with her. Becky was so engrossed by Mr. Ferr's grip that no words or actions could change her mind or convince her to put down the gun.

"Please, Becky." Bucky pleaded, trying to circumvent Ferr's influence and reason with Becky by appealing to her compassionate side. "As a friend, I beg you."

Unexpectedly, Becky's hand began to shake and she dropped her head down to cry as she started to lower the gun. "I...I can't help myself, Bucky," she said, sobbing. "I can't stop. His control is too strong."

Bucky took a few more steps forward, but his actions were too quick, too soon. When he got within a few feet away, she lifted her head up and pointed the gun directly between his eyes. Her emotionless expression stared him in the eyes, and her voice became cold once again. Bucky stopped as if he had walked into a wall, his face white with shock and anger.

"I'm sorry, Bucky; this is the way it has to be. Please forgive me," she uttered in a monotone voice, her finger trembling as it rested upon the trigger.

Bucky turned his head and closed his eyes as if to shut out the sight of her. It was much too painful for him to watch as Becky, his longtime friend, had become a hostile, sneering stranger. And now, the realization was hitting him that in a few short moments, she was going to gun him down in cold blood.

All of a sudden, a shot rang out and Becky fell backwards onto the ground. Bucky opened his eyes and swerved around, noticing an unfamiliar figure standing in the fog. Although he could not make out their face, Bucky definitely noticed the barrel of a gun protruding through the haze as the figure began to walk forward.

In an instant, Bucky's expression changed from uncertainty to perplexity as Thomas Parker stepped out from the fog. He had his trusty shotgun raised high up in the air and aimed at Louis Ferr's face.

"Don't worry, Bucky," Thomas stated, "you're safe." He looked over at Becky's body with tears mounting in his eyes. "I wish it didn't have to come to that."

Then Thomas switched his attention over to Mr. Ferr. "I don't know who or what you *really* are, but we don't take too kindly to strangers around here," he voiced in his best John Wayne impression. "And strictly speaking, I think you've worn out your welcome."

"Thomas, I don't mean to sound ungrateful, but what are you doing here?" asked Bucky in a relieved tone.

"Your old lady called me," he replied.

"Cristina called you?"

"Yup," Thomas answered. "Cris said Roger was missin' and was worried you might come down here lookin' for him. She also mentioned you think this maniac is responsible for Bob's and Scott's disappearances."

"Yeah, and I'm sorry," Bucky said apologetically. "I didn't tell you because I didn't have any proof to back up my hunch about the connection of the disappearances...and I wasn't *absolutely certain* Ferr was to blame for the whole mess anyway."

"I guess I can understand that part," Thomas retorted, "but why didn't you let me know Roger had vanished?"

"I just found out Roger was missing a couple hours ago myself. Bryan Harsha showed up at my doorstep and told me Roger had taken off in a huff to confront Mr. Ferr. In all the commotion, there wasn't enough time to call you. Besides, I didn't want to put anymore lives in danger."

"Roger and Bob are my friends, too!" Thomas exclaimed to Bucky. "And if somethin' devious is going on down here at the ferry service, or if they're in some kind of trouble, then I owe it to my friends to be here to help. Besides, from some of the weird stuff I've just seen here tonight, I'd say you definitely needed it."

While Bucky and Thomas were talking, Louis Ferr stood over Becky's body. "What a waste of perfectly good help." he whispered. "Well, it looks like today just wasn't a good day to be one of my assistants."

Standing up, Mr. Ferr looked upon the men and rolled his eyes as he laughed condescendingly. His snicker redirected Bucky's attention towards him.

"Hold it right there, Ferr!" commanded Bucky. "I came here tonight to save my friend. It wasn't my intention to get into a tangle with you. But now, you've made it impossible for me to just walk away. My purpose is to take you down and stop you from ever inflicting pain on anyone ever again."

Ferr chuckled. "Oh, really?"

"I ain't ever kicked an old man's ass before," Thomas said, "but tonight I'm willin' to make an exception! Let's rumble, you son of a bitch!"

"Do you two even realize how ridiculously foolish you sound? Even without any aide, neither of you are a match for me. You stand here before me, cocky and thoughtlessly optimistic, talking about how you're going to take me down and destroy me. It's such a tired cliché, really. I've heard it all before by people who were smarter and stronger than either of you. And each one of them failed, too. Just as you are going to fail now!"

Bucky gripped the dagger firmly, glaring at Ferr and gritting his teeth. "Even if you are somehow immortal, you aren't indestructible. I think my partner can hold you off long enough with that shotgun of his for me to stab you with the dagger." Bucky's voice became more serious and even somewhat cocky. "And if you *are* who you claim to be, then I expect this dagger should do the job it was meant for."

Shockingly, for the first time in quite a long time, a spot of panic seeped into Mr. Ferr's consciousness. Initially, he laughed at their false bravado when he noticed their presence at the ferry service—the blind confidence they had in their meager numbers, carrying their petty weapons.

Just then, Mr. Ferr was stricken with relentless fear as a vision of his own dispatch was driven into his head. A vision of Bucky somehow managing to get close enough to pierce his skin with the dagger and sending him on a one-way ticket back to Hell.

"You two are just stupid enough to try something risky, especially if there was a chance you could pierce me with the dagger of Megiddo," Mr. Ferr said, a drop of sweat trickling down his temple. "Even if it meant certain death to one or both of you."

"Ya got that right, asshole!" hollered Thomas.

"Although you might be willing to take such a risk, I am not. Savor your victory while you can, Dave Morgan. I assure you there will not be another. You'll eventually pay for all you have cost me, but it shall be at a time and place of my choosing. Farewell, Bucky. You *will* be seeing me in your nightmares."

Mr. Ferr turned around and raced towards his office. Bucky paid no attention to Ferr's retreat and headed over to Roger as Thomas began to run after Ferr. Thomas stopped when he noticed Bucky was not following him.

"Shouldn't we go after him?" shouted Thomas. "After everything he's done, there's no way we can just let Ferr go! He's gotta pay for his crimes—with *extreme* prejudice. If ya know what I mean!"

"I'm not sure if he is fleeing, or if he is trying to lure us to follow him," insisted Bucky. "Besides, I don't have time to go chasing after him right now. I've gotta get Roger to a hospital as soon as possible. If you wanna chase after him into the ferry office, go ahead, but you'll be on your own."

Thomas shifted his attention back around and watched Ferr sprint up the stairs to his office. "Damn it! The bastard's gettin' away!"

Just as Mr. Ferr stepped into his shack, an explosion with a deafening boom rang loudly. Pieces of wood and metal scattered over the ground, and the remnants of the building began to burst into flames.

The explosion startled the men, and Bucky quickly transferred his gaze to the office, not knowing what to think. However, even as the ferry office went up in a glowing inferno, Mr. Ferr's crazed ranting echoed through the air one last time. Roger was too groggy to look at the blaze despite his relief that their nightmare was over.

Bucky stared in awe at the burning building, wondering what or who caused such an explosion. And as he heard Louis Ferr's echoing laugh, a deep, disturbing chill came over him once again.

Everything looked hazy to Bucky, and it was not because of the flames that scalded his face, nor the smoke which blinded him; it was the tears that filled his misty eyes. He was overcome with emotions, praying the nightmare was finally and truly over. As he watched the flames, Bucky hoped he could eventually learn to accept the fact that in the fire, the enigmatic past which has haunted him, and its secrets, may have been lost forever.

Thomas glanced over to the tree line behind the ferry office and noticed the silhouette of someone or something fleeing into the woods. "What the hell was that?" he said in a panicky whisper.

Bucky lifted Roger off the ground and supported him while they made their way back to the car. "Come on, buddy, I'm getting you out of here."

Roger groaned in pain as he feebly put his arm around Bucky's neck.

After taking a few steps, Bucky turned around and saw Thomas staring carefully into the woods. "What's the matter, Thomas? Do you see something?"

Without turning his head or taking his eyes off the trees, Thomas replied, "I thought I saw something running by the ferry office right after it exploded."

"Was it Louis Ferr?" Bucky asked.

"I don't know. I didn't get a good look at whatever it was. It may have been an animal, or maybe even another person. I only saw a shadow of something as it was dashing through the trees."

In the woods surrounding the ferry service, there were many walking trails for patrons to use for exercise, but there were also several other trails that led straight down to the waterfront. It was on one of these particular trails that John Sears and Adam "Red" Richardson were walking home from another unsuccessful night of fishing.

John tripped and spilt the contents out of his fishing tackle box. "Damn it!" he grumbled. Then he handed his fishing pole to Adam and said, "Hold my pole for me while I pick this shit up."

"No problem, dude," Adam belched as he finished off the last of his can of beer.

While John was kneeling over to gather up his lures and hooks, a cloaked individual raced past Adam. The figure moved unnaturally quick and without a sound. A shiver shot down Adam's spine and goose bumps on his arms

"Hey, did ya see that?" he asked John. "Someone just ran by us."

John tilted his head and looked at Adam as though he was dumbfounded. "Huh? You high on reefer, Red?" laughed John. "How many bong hits did you have tonight?"

"No man," replied Adam, "I'm serious. I just saw a cloaked individual with a skull face. I think it was the face of death!"

"You mean like the Grim Reaper?" John said jokingly.

Adam veered around and peered into the woods, listening attentively for any sign of footsteps. He whipped the beam of his flashlight back and forth through the trees and bushes, taking deep breaths to get his heartbeat to slow down.

"Yeah, John," he stated in a serious tone. "That's exactly what I mean."

Chapter 22:

With the End, Comes Goodbye

In the weeks following the death and destruction at the ferry service, people attempted to move on with their lives. They tried getting past the events that transpired by finding tedious activities to occupy their time as well as keep their minds off the loss of so many of their fellow patrons. The horror in the sleepy little town had shaken up the community and left residents searching for answers to help give some type of explanation for the tragedy and help ease their pain. Unfortunately, the answers they sought would never come.

Sergeant Kenneth Johnson concluded his investigation by determining the explosion was intentional, and it most certainly *was* a bomb which destroyed the ferry office. Even so, no one was brought in for questioning or officially charged with the crime. All Sergeant Johnson found were fragments of the bomb scattered over the area, but with no fingerprints or eyewitnesses, he was unable to determine who the perpetrator was.

When Bucky heard of the findings, he automatically assumed it must've been Thomas Parker who placed the bomb at the ferry service. But regardless of whether or not Thomas was responsible, Bucky had no intention of divulging his theory to the police *or* to Thomas. Ironically, Thomas fostered the same suspicions toward Bucky. Yet, like Bucky, he also felt there was no point in saying anything to the police. In Thomas' eyes, what happened was over, and he saw no reason to point fingers at anyone for doing a deed that improved the lives of everyone in the entire community.

Along with the mystery of the explosion, no remains of either Mr. Ferr's or Steve Jensen's bodies were ever recovered. These were questions that still ran through Bucky's mind, but he did not care if they ever got answered. For the first time in many years, he was happy with his life.

Bucky finally uncovered the truth about Paul Fasick's disappearance, and he had learned to come to terms with all the guilt he had been harboring over the last few years. His painful nightmares vanished once again, and this time, Bucky hoped, they would be gone for good. Furthermore, while in the process of confronting the person who was behind his pain and torment, Bucky was able to save his best friend's life and watch his enemy's dwelling burn to the ground.

On a sunny afternoon in August, a large crowd gathered down at the riverbank where Father Eugene O'Donnell was presiding over a mass funeral, in memory or those who died during the altercation with Louis Ferr.

The waterfront area that once was the site for The Mephistis Pheles Ferry Service was now nothing more than burned-out buildings and debris strewn about. The vicinity where the ferry office stood was still off-limits to the public, and police tape still surrounded the burned remains.

Within days of the ferry office explosion, a petition circulated through town asking for support to clean up and preserve the area that'd been the site of one of Carthage's worst tragedies. The petition was approved by Mayor Pat Jordan, and eventually the Community Planning Board intended to tear down the remainder of the buildings that consisted of the ferry service and build a memorial park in its place.

A dedicatory spire was commissioned by the Mayor—and the remaining members of the town council—to be built and positioned at the entrance to the new Waterfront Memorial Park. However, construction wouldn't begin for several weeks. Until then, a substitute stone was being used at the memorial service as the people of the town congregated on this particular afternoon to pay their respects and say their final farewells to those who perished.

There had never been a gathering of patrons quite like this in Carthage. Yet, that is only fitting, for there had never been an incident so atrocious in this town before. An incident that claimed the lives of several upstanding members of the society. These were not just any other people; they were friends to some, family to others, and considered heroes by all. But one thing connected them all; they were all taken from this world much too early, and they would be sadly missed.

The eulogies had all been said. The somber realization that they were indeed gone was yet to fully come, but in a few short minutes, they would be buried.

Thomas Parker, his wife, Stacey, and their three children were at the service. Thomas stood straight and tall; a single tear stained his cheek as he mourned a man who was like a brother to him...and more. Bob Earle's life was empty after his wife died of cancer many years ago; now he could join her...in peace.

Bryan Harsha lived a sheltered life, and just when it seemed that he was on the verge of breaking out of his shell, he was gone. He had never been married or even had a steady relationship, but with him and Kitty Dunn beginning to get close, it seemed as though all that was about to change. Now, Miss Kitty stood by herself at the memorial service, mourning a relationship that might have been.

Even though Becky Taylor had fallen from grace, she had still been a good person and dedicated a majority of her life to helping the town. Bucky decided it would be better if no one knew the details of her affiliation with Louis Ferr, for he felt that Becky's intentions toward the village were completely sincere, all the way to the end. Unfortunately, her over-trusting personality caused her to be led astray by Mr. Ferr's brainwashing. An ill-fated partnership was formed which eventually led down the path to her eventual demise.

The life Scott Patterson lived was not considered idyllic by any stretch of the definition. Known as an alcoholic and someone who often neglected his family, his good natured personality rarely got to stand out.

Scott was a firm believer that in order to have friends, you had to be one. He was always the first to lend a hand or make one laugh whenever someone needed a lift. However, these traits often went unnoticed, and sadly, Scott will be remembered by most people for his flaws. Today, two of his drinking buddies, Adam "Red" Richardson and John Sears, attended the funeral on his behalf. They had come to the service in order to honor their friend and place a flask, which had been engraved with Scott's initials, upon his casket.

Although Jim Draven was not well known in the community, his participation was extremely instrumental in the success of defeating Louis Ferr. He supplied Bucky with the background and knowledge of his longtime enemy, as well as giving Bucky the tool that would destroy Mr. Ferr. Even though neither Jim nor Bucky were able to use the dagger of Megiddo on Louis Ferr, its presence was enough to frighten the ferryman and send him fleeing toward what would become a fiery death.

When Jim was a cop, he always believed he would never be able to retire. He figured his dangerous lifestyle would eventually catch up to him and that he'd probably die in the line of duty. Jim did manage to survive the crime-infested streets of Chicago for many years; and even though he hadn't worked for the police or solved any cases in a long time, his final moments consisted of aiding a helpless stranger and confronting his greatest enemy. So, in some aspects, it can be said that Jim actually did fulfill his prophecy.

Roger Fasick luckily survived the beating he suffered and the wounds he sustained from his encounter with Mr. Ferr. Multiple fractures in his legs would keep him in a wheelchair for the next couple months with endless hours of therapy to follow. The doctors needed over 120 stitches to sew up the numerous lacerations he sustained, and his four broken ribs made breathing a painful chore for awhile.

When Roger finally regained consciousness at the hospital, he kept calling out for Nellie. After several failed attempts by Bucky to reach her in Syracuse, he was forced to inform Roger that she was gone and not coming back. He gave Roger the note Nellie wrote before she left; however, with all the injuries Roger suffered and the emotional disappointment he now faced, Bucky decided not to mention the receipt to the home pregnancy test he found.

Standing behind Miss Kitty was Celeste Braxton, Paul Fasick's longtime girlfriend. Celeste was the 'girl next door' sort of woman every man spends his life looking for. She was tall and slim with that cover-girl type of look to her, with ivory pale skin as soft as rose petals. Her chestnut colored hair was streaked with blonde highlights, and she had beautiful dark brown eyes that sparkled whenever she spoke.

The warm summer's breeze blew against Celeste's flushed cheeks, which were speckled with just a hint of freckles. Wearing a tight-fitting black dress that ended just above the knee, her natural beauty and poise made her look as though she just stepped out of a fashion catalog.

Around Celeste's neck was a string of pearls given to her by Paul back in June of 1991 for their one-year anniversary of going steady. She became so emotionally devastated when Paul disappeared in Florida that she moved to New York City shortly after his funeral. It was there she felt that she could come to terms with her loss and possibly develop into a serious artist. Lately, however, she had been content writing a weekly column for the *New York Times*.

As she glanced over her shoulder, Celeste saw Roger out of the corner of her eye. She tilted her head and smiled caringly; then she walked over to him. She went unnoticed from Roger's perception until she leaned toward him and gave him a kiss on the cheek.

When Roger looked up and saw her face, he gasped in astonishment from such a pleasant, but unexpected surprise.

"Celeste!" he yelled enthusiastically. "It's great to see you again; it has been such a long time. What are you doing in Carthage? Are you still living in New York City?"

"Yes, I am!" she said, noticeably amazed. "I'm shocked you remembered after all this time. I haven't seen you in years, and in my opinion, it has been much too long. I think the last time we chatted was during the *other* funeral we attended together."

Roger nodded his head. He knew she was referring to Paul's funeral, though neither one of them would mention him by name.

"We have got to stop meeting at such depressing events," he said with a half-hearted smile. "What brings you here today?"

"Miss Kitty called the other day and told me what's been happening around here. I've known Bob Earle for years, ever since we used to work together at Kitty's Bar. I filled in as a part-time bartender in-between semesters for a couple years. I considered him a friend and owed it to him to be here today."

"That's very kind of you, Celeste."

"Miss Kitty also told me *you* were almost killed by the same homicidal maniac. I had to come here in person and make sure you were okay."

Roger nodded his head and smiled. "Still acting like my big sister, huh?"

She kneeled down and placed her hand upon his cheek. "I guess some things never change," she said softly. "It's funny how life is a constant series of changes. Last time we talked, you were developing into a severe alcoholic with a brazen attitude. You've certainly mellowed with the years."

"You're right, and I'm sorry about that. I didn't like who I was back then. It took awhile, but I figured it was time I started acting like an adult and cleaned myself up."

Roger and Celeste chatted for several minutes to get caught up on each other's lives and talk about their families. After they said their goodbyes, Roger wheeled his way over to Bucky and Cristina.

Holly Boliver was standing beside them as they all conversed and commented about the funeral. "That was a beautiful service," she said to Bucky. "It's nice to see so many of the townspeople actually showed up today."

"Yes, I'm surprised myself," Bucky commented. "Too bad it took a tragedy and the loss of so many friends to bring the town together once again."

Roger nodded his head in agreement as he interrupted the conversation. "It's hard to imagine how one person could inflict so much pain and suffering. Louis Ferr was insane, there is no denying that, but I wonder if there's any truth to his claim that he was Satan." Then he looked Bucky directly in the eyes and spoke in a profound tone. "Do you think he really was the Devil?"

I'm not sure," Bucky replied. "Although, I don't think he was human either. Of course, it doesn't really matter what I believe he was. All I know is that in his mind, he *believed* himself to be the Devil."

"That's true," Roger concurred.

Bucky went on to say, "Nevertheless, whatever or whoever Louis Ferr was, he definitely had incredible power—the power of persuasion, to manipulate a person's actions, and defy the elements of age & time. Quite honestly, when I was face to face with him, I was never more scared in all my life."

"I still have a hard time believing that story," voiced Holly. "Who would've guessed it was Mr. Ferr who was behind the disappearances the entire time?"

"Don't forget that Ferr was also the driving influence behind the townspeople's strange attitude." Cristina added.

"It just doesn't make sense," continued Holly. "The man looked so old and frail; I never would've presumed *he* causing all the fear and panic throughout the community."

Roger reached for Holly's hand as he said, "I don't think anyone would've believed it. He was a clever con man who had the whole town completely fooled until it was too late. I'm very thankful to have a friend like Bucky who was brave enough to come rescue me. And I definitely needed rescuing from that nut. I'm lucky to be here today!"

Seeing how Roger's words left everyone with sad faces and glum sentiments, Bucky changed the topic of conversation in an attempt to lighten up the atmosphere. "Hey, Roger, do you and Holly have any plans after we leave here? Cristina and I were wondering if the two of you want to go to the Chatterbox Diner and get some coffee, or maybe a bite to eat."

"Sorry, Bucky," Roger said apologetically, "I'm gonna have to decline your invitation. As appealing as that offer sounds, I've gotta head on home to get some rest. Also, I need to take some more medication for my pain, and Holly has offered to drive me. That way, you and Cristina can go do whatever you want without having to chauffeur me and my gawky wheelchair around."

"Nonsense, Roger. You aren't a burden at all!" Cristina blurted out.

"We wish you'd reconsider, but we understand you need your rest," Bucky added. "Besides, you've certainly earned it, buddy."

Cristina put her hand on Roger's shoulder and smiled kindly. "I'm sure you will be in good hands with Holly. Nevertheless, regardless of what you think, you will be missed, and next time, we won't take 'no' for an answer."

Holly turned Roger around and wheeled him over to her car. As Bucky watched them leave, he glanced to his left side and spotted Thomas Parker standing alone by Bob Earle's casket. He nudged Cristina to gain her attention, and then pointed his finger in Thomas' direction. "Excuse me for a minute, Cris. I want to go over and speak with Thomas for a moment before we leave."

A smile appeared on Cristina's face. She realized how distraught Thomas must feel over his loss and knew how important it was for Bucky to comfort and support him in his time of need.

She leaned over to give him a kiss on the cheek and said, "Go ahead, hun. I'm in no hurry to leave; I'll meet you back at the car in a little while."

Bucky walked over to Thomas and tapped him on the arm. Thomas twitched as he snapped out of his daze and turned around to face him.

"It's good to see you here, Thomas," Bucky said in a pleasant, consoling voice. "I'm glad you could make it."

Thomas had tears in his eyes, and his voice was choked up. "I wasn't sure if I could be here for this. Bob was my best friend and I'm going to miss him." Then he paused and started to reminisce. "We met on the first day of school during our freshman year in high school. He said I was the funniest guy he ever met, and I thought he was the strongest kid in the whole school. He watched out for me like a big brother although we were almost the same age."

It sounded as though Thomas had a huge lump in his throat as his words started to break up and his voice drifted off. Bucky moved closer and stood next to him, putting his arm over Thomas's shoulders, trying to console him.

"It'll be alright, Thomas. If you ever need a friend to talk to, I'll be around. I know what's it's like to lose a best friend, and I understand the pain you're going through at this time."

"For twenty-five years, Bob was my friend and the one person I could count on to always be there for me." Thomas said, trying to maintain his composure. "Bob was closer to me than if I had a brother of my own, although I never got a chance to tell him that."

Bucky hung his head low and let out a sigh.

"I guess I thought there'd always be another day ahead of us. I understand now that, sometimes, tomorrow never comes—a simple realization that's come at a time when he's no longer here to listen. I only wish there was a way we could sit down and talk one last time. Maybe then I could tell him all those things I thought were insignificant."

As Thomas talked, Bucky remembered how he fostered the same feelings of guilt and regret after he lost his own best friend—Paul Fasick. Not only could Bucky offer advice and comfort to Thomas; most importantly, he was genuinely sincere in his devotion because he was able to relate to such heavy, powerful grief.

"I'm sure he knows how much you are grieving," Bucky said sympathetically.

The wind blew gently through the trees, and Thomas watched the sun sparkle upon the river. A large maple tree with a small, grassy area underneath stood alone by the water and caught his attention.

As he began to walk toward it, Bucky yelled out to him and asked, "Hey Thomas, where are you going?"

Thomas wiped his eyes and nose with a tear-drenched handkerchief and cleared his throat.

"I'm not ready to leave just yet. It's a beautiful day and I think I'm going to stay a little longer," he said with a grin. "I feel like being alone for awhile; perhaps I'll sit down by the riverbank to relax. Hell, I might even lie down on the grass and take a nap."

Book 2

Don't Fear the Reaper

Original Concept design of the Reaper
By Clay Dumaw—July 2004

The Reaper

From the heavens above comes the sound of a deafening boom.
It bellows ferociously for an instant, then all goes quiet like a tomb.
Tonight the thunder god has beckoned repeatedly to the sky.
But the fear you feel is caused from the Reaper who waits outside.

He hides in the shadows, masked in the darkness of the midnight.
Close enough to feel his presence, but always out of sight.
He will follow wherever you hide and any place you try to flee,
And take you to the places where it is *not* safe to be.

With a ghastly appearance, he strikes fear in both poor and wealthy,
Stalking his victims from rooftops and purging the streets of those he deems unworthy.
Disguised in a black cloak, the glowing red eyes highlight an already chilling skull face.
His victims are swallowed into darkness…
    Whereabouts unknown and empty clues leave no trace.

(over)

Nightly strolls become nerve-wracking chores as shadows become
enemies of light.
They hide the evil and inflict panic to those who dare enter the night.
When suddenly, there is breathing on your neck; a chill races
down the spine.
The hushed, raspy voice whispers in your ear: "Now you are mine."

From under the hood of his cloak, he hides the face of death.
You find yourself running so fast it's difficult to catch your breath.
He was long believed to be an Urban Legend, something that could
never be true.
However, myth has crossed over into reality…
     And now the Reaper is coming for you.

By: Marcus J. Mastin
Stalked and terrorized by the Reaper
February 3, 2003

And I looked, and behold a pale horse: and his name that sat on him was Death, and Hell followed with him.

—*REVELATION* VI, 8

Prologue

It has been a time of sorrow and transition for the residents of Carthage since the waterfront incident. As bizarre as the occurrence at the ferry service was, Carthage had no doubt made its way onto the tourist map of the North Country region in upstate New York. It is too bad the town's new fame came at such a terrible expense.

Five years have passed since Louis Ferr terrorized this little town. During that time, Dave "Bucky" Morgan has risen in the town ranks and is now Mayor of Carthage. At thirty-two years of age, Bucky is the youngest person elected to that position in Carthage's long history. Bucky won the mayoral election by a very narrow margin over the older and more experienced Edgar Polansky. This contest led to some strained feelings between the two candidates with Edgar even hinting that members of Bucky's campaign committee might've attempted to fix the election results.

The mayoral position became vacant about nine months ago when the previous mayor, Patrick Jordan, was killed during one of the town's mysterious fires. Although the town coroner, Harry Moon, had determined the cause of death was from smoke inhalation, it remained a mystery how Mayor Jordan received burn marks solely on the back of his neck.

Bucky and Cristina Boyd were married one month after the ferryboat ordeal with Mr. Ferr, and by Christmas of that year, she was pregnant. Their son, who they named Michael Jeffery Morgan (and nicknamed Mikey), was born on the following Labor Day weekend in 2001. At four years old, he has already developed Cristina's intense personality and inherited Bucky's impatient curiosity.

Shortly after Mikey's birth, Cristina stepped down from the Carthage Town Council so she could stay home and raise her son. However, after Mikey reached the age of three and learned how to do things by himself, she started to become disenchanted with the idea of staying home. Last year, she began doing some medical transcription work for the local hospital to occupy her free time and make her feel as though she was doing something constructive with her life.

Following a semester off to recover from injuries sustained with his confrontation with Louis Ferr, Roger Fasick graduated from Syracuse University with a Bachelor's Degree in Anthropology; and two years later, Roger finished his Master's in Criminology. After graduation, he quit his job as an Archaeologist Research Assistant on Fort Drum and began searching for his true calling.

After contemplating many career propositions, including an offer from renowned investigator Dakota T. Stevens to work at his private detective agency in Manhattan, Roger ultimately decided to remain close to his hometown. In the end, he eventually accepted a position with a local law firm as an investigator for cases involving fraud and missing persons. Nowadays, he confers with a local reporter on a regular basis, seeking advice and techniques to help develop his investigative skills. His intrigue for mystery has even rubbed off on his live-in girlfriend, Holly Boliver, as they often discuss unsolved cases, research information, and investigate clues together.

In Holly's arms, Roger found the solace to comfort him after Nellie Spencer left Carthage. It was a consoling feeling that he didn't experience when his brother, Paul Fasick, disappeared. This time around, they have decided to move forward in their relationship slowly. Even though Holly stopped by Roger's house everyday to visit and help him while he was recuperating, she did not move in with him for almost a year and a half. It took nearly two more years before they even mentioned the word 'marriage', and they still have not sat down together and had a serious discussion about when, or if, they want to establish a definite wedding date.

Holly still works as a bartender at Kitty's Bar, and now she has added taking night classes at the local community college in Watertown a few times per week to her already hectic schedule. Over the past couple years, Holly has enrolled in many business courses with aspirations to be an entrepreneur, and she hopes to eventually open up her own business. She has many years of customer service under her belt and knows a majority of her customers at the bar on a first-name basis. It is because of these traits and her impeccable reputation in town that makes her feels as though her business would be a huge success.

Celeste Braxton, who still resides in Manhattan's East Side, quit her job for the *New York Times* and is now an aspiring author with three successful novels under her belt. She has made a sufficient amount of money from her novels and is able to support herself from her royalties. This has freed up much of her time so that she can visit her family and friends in Carthage on a regular basis. Celeste finds the area to be relaxing and draws on the picturesque upstate countryside for inspiration. For her next book, Celeste plans on writing a fictional story, loosely based on the enigmatic Mr. Louis Ferr and chronicle the events of the ferry service trauma that transpired in Carthage five years ago.

Dramatic changes have occurred in Carthage in the past five years. Since the nation's War on Terrorism began, the country has increased its position on homeland security; therefore, the state politicians voted to expand the size of Fort Drum extensively. In all, another 5,000 army troops were added to the local military base along with their families. With Fort Drum expanding, Carthage has also grown.

Carthage was once a small town that tried to keep up with the neighboring town of Watertown, but not anymore. Within the past five years, Carthage has eclipsed Watertown in size as far as population and incoming businesses, and it is now considered an urban region (though it is still considered small compared to other, larger cities such as Syracuse) with the prospect of constructing a shopping mall in the area. Some of the new businesses to the North Country include a full-service Super Wal-Mart and a high-tech Internet Service call center, which were built on the outskirts of Carthage. These companies have done wonders to reduce the unemployment rate of the area; however, most of their employees consist of military spouses, and the rate of pay is barely more than minimum wage.

In contrast to the new developments, the local paper mill that once employed over seven hundred people closed its doors due to foreign competition. The closing of the mill has had a trickle down effect in the whole community. People couldn't afford to pay mortgages, and subsequently, lost their homes. Other residents moved away, and without their economic support, some local businesses could not compete with the bigger companies and were forced to close their doors. Military personnel and their families have been supplied with their own shops on Fort Drum, which offer better prices, and, therefore, most of the military never shop at the local stores. Because of the major layoffs in the community and the tougher competition in the job market due to the Fort Drum expansion, Carthage has seen, for the first time in its history, homeless people living on its streets.

Since the majority of the businesses in Carthage have several floors of apartments above them, recent years have seen the rooftops become a hot spot for teenagers to hang out and throw parties. After that fad died off and teenagers were no longer spending time up there, the rooftops have now become a place for the homeless to stay during the warm months. They climb the fire escapes after it is dark and sleep on the rooftops at night. However, this summer has seen very few homeless people wanting to go up there at all.

Fear and panic have spread through the small homeless community. A rumor has surfaced that a mysterious, cloaked figure with a skull face, looking like the Grim Reaper himself, has been prowling through the streets and rooftops at night.

Years ago, back in the 1950s, there was a story of a Reaper-like figure that stalked the streets of Carthage. After awhile, the sightings of the Reaper dropped off and it seemed as though the cloaked figure had disappeared or moved on to another place. In time, the rumors became myths and the story became nothing more than an urban legend of the upstate region.

The previous mayor, Pat Jordan, had been curious about the rumors that were circulating around town regarding this cloaked individual and remembered the old fairy-tale from the 1950s about a Grim Reaper figure who appeared at mysterious fires. Some townspeople believe that Mayor Jordan had started to keep a secretive file on the Reaper and accumulated some intriguing information. Supposedly, the Mayor was about to reveal his findings to the Police Chief, but Mayor Jordan died in a village fire before he ever had a chance to hand the information over. When his office was cleaned out after the funeral, the alleged file was never found.

Autumn has returned in the North Country, and in addition to the strange individual roaming the streets, an evil from long ago has also crept back into the thoughts and fears of the residents. Mysterious fires, like those that have plagued this town throughout its history, have come roaring back.

Mr. Joshua Roberts, the top reporter for the *Carthage Republican Tribune*, has been investigating the mysterious fires as well as the reports of the so-called Reaper. The journalist has attempted to link a connection between the two enigmas but so far has been unsuccessful. After a tell-all article he wrote about corruption in the Carthage police force, Mr. Roberts received a cold shoulder from all officers, with Kenneth Johnson being his biggest critic. Ken is one of the officers that Josh singled out in his article and even revealed Ken's alleged extramarital affairs. In questioning Ken's integrity, Roberts also insinuated that Ken might have taken kickbacks early in his career.

The police have been vigorously and furtively compiling a file of potential perpetrators who might be involved in the town's fires, making a list of motives and tracking their whereabouts. One name in particular on their list is Thomas Parker, a personal friend and drinking buddy of Bucky Morgan, whose odd behavior as of late (plus his involvement with the waterfront incident years ago) has signaled a huge red flag for the police.

Being the town Mayor and close friend of several officers, Bucky is aware of the police's suspicions about Thomas, but he has been trying to deter them from making Thomas their prime suspect. However, with more fires spreading through town and the panic that is mounting, the police are anxious to put an end to this terror, and Bucky doesn't know how long he can protect his friend.

PART ONE:
Panic and Disarray

Chapter 23:

The Sighting from the Past

It was ten o'clock on Friday morning, April 11, in the year 1955. Vance Dane was sitting on the corner barstool inside Dunn's Pub, sipping on his coffee and writing some ideas down in his notepad. Vance was a reporter for the *Carthage Republican Tribune* and was occasionally hired to do some private investigative work throughout the upstate area in northern New York during his spare time.

Vance was making pretty good money between his two jobs and was thinking of leaving his job at the *Tribune* so he could focus all his attention on his own P.I. business. In fact, Vance's income was so good that he even hired an assistant, Grace Marcell, to help him with all his paperwork and manage his appointments.

Vance was a handsome twenty-eight-year-old with a quick wit and good sense of humor, which made him very popular with the ladies throughout the North Country. Although he had a pack-a-day cigarette habit, he still enjoyed a good cigar occasionally while sipping a good Irish whiskey. By 1950s standards, Vance was considered a tall man at just over 5'10", and he was also a slender man in that he only weighed about one-hundred and seventy pounds. He was solidly well-built in spite of his slender frame due to all the rigorous work he performed growing up on a dairy farm. It had been many years since he worked on his family's farm; however, he still had wide, muscular shoulders and large, powerful hands that looked like a slab of ham at the end of each arm.

Unlike his usual unkempt appearance, the typical look of an overworked P.I. with a two-day growth of whiskers and a three-piece suit that looked like he slept in it, he appeared at Dunn's Pub clean shaven and wearing a swanky, pressed suit.

Standing on the other side of the bar was Alton Dunn, the owner of the bar. Al was a forty-year-old Irishman who was born and raised in Ireland. In spite of living in the United States for the past twelve years, he still spoke with a thick Irish accent. Al was a rather big man at nearly six-feet-tall and two-hundred-twenty pounds. He earned the money needed to come to America by performing as an amateur boxer in Ireland. Al kept his dark-blonde hair slicked back (like most men did in the 1950s) and his face was tattooed with many nasty scars from his boxing career.

"Top of the mornin' to ya, Vance," Al said with a smile upon his face. "How're things goin' t'day?"

Vance stared off in silence.

"I'm more than a tad surprised to see ya in m'bar this mornin', laddie. Don't ya usually stop by Durkee's Bakery to get yer coffee and doughnuts?"

Again, Vance said nothing.

"Hmmm...y'know laddie, yer lookin' down in the dumps and could use a wee bit of my sweet Irish whiskey to cheer you up."

Al pulled out a half-empty ceramic jug and set it on the counter. Inside the gray, old jug was some of Al's homemade whiskey—a recipe he learned while still living in Ireland. Vance raised an eyebrow as he glanced at the moonshine, but he decided to keep still and remain silent.

"Hey, Vance, is there somethin' botherin' ya?" Alton asked, snapping his fingers in front of Vance's face.

Vance broke out of his daze and turned to face Al. "Things are going alright, I suppose."

"Are ya sure, laddie? You seem lost in a daze t'day. Is there money problems on yer mind and you'd like to chat 'bout it?"

"Nah, money isn't stressin' me out right now, Al. I'm making enough dough now so I don't need to be robbin' any graves for cigarette money."

Al let out a bellowing laugh.

"How 'bout you, Al? How's life treating ya these days?"

"You know me, laddie. I can't complain. My son, Andy, will be graduating from high school in a few months and then he plans on joining the Navy. Also, the tavern business has been good for me lately, and I'm startin' to get preparations ready for my anniversary party, which is comin' up in a few weeks. It should be a blast."

"That's right! I forgot you were throwing a celebration to commemorate the bar being open for three years. I'll be sure to come, Al, and I'll have my dancing shoes on, too!" Vance chuckled.

"So, Vance, why're ya all dressed up t'day? Those aren't the normal digs you wear to work at the newspaper. Do ya got yourself a hot lunch date t'day?"

"Nah, it's nothing like that, Al. I had to go to the lawyer's office today."

"What for? You get into some trouble doin' that investigative work of yours?"

Vance laughed and shook his head. "That would've been more exciting than my actual reason for seeing the attorney. Today was the reading of my grandfather's last will and testament."

"Sorry to hear that, laddie." Al expressed solemnly. "Your grandfather was a nice man."

"You knew him, Al?"

"Sure, laddie. Ol' Luke Dane would come in here from time to time on a lazy afternoon and we'd exchange stories. I'd tell him about life in Ireland, and Luke told me about growing up with his sister in the prairies of Nebraska."

Vance grinned. "Yeah, gramps was never short on tales of the wild west. My favorite story was the time he had to rescue his sister."

"Rescue?" inquired Al.

"My great-aunt, Clara, was kidnapped when she was nine years old. Grandpa Luke tracked down her abductors and saved Clara from a tribe of angry Indians."

"Well ain't that somethin' crazy!" Al said with genuine surprise. "Luke never told me about that adventure before."

Vance's grin faded. "Gramps didn't talk about it too often, Al. His father was killed by those same Indians...died tryin' to protect his daughter."

"That's a damn shame," Al replied with a heavy sigh. After a slight pause, he asked, "Did there happen t'be a very large estate to settle, Vance?"

"Nope. He gave most of his stuff away years ago. To be quite honest, I was kinda hoping Gramps would've left me the old farm house he owned in Natural Bridge. It's been in my father's family for several generations."

"Natural Bridge, huh? Hey, I've been up that way many times. Whereabouts is the house located?"

"Well, it's actually on the outskirts of Natural Bridge. It's the big green house on the Rogers Crossing road with a large red barn just off the driveway."

"I know just where that is!" Alton remarked. "So what happened, Vance? Didn't yer grandfather leave the house to ya in his will?"

Leaning back on his barstool, Vance crossed his arms and made a sour expression as he let out a sigh. "Nope, it was bequeathed to my cousin, Jim Draven, who lives in Chicago." Vance sighed. "I should've known that'd happen. Jim's mom and gramps were pretty close; the farm house was bound to go to Aunt Laura or someone from that side of the family."

Al raised a brow. "Oh, I see. And your father...?"

"He had a falling out with my grandfather many years ago and they never repaired the rift in their relationship." Vance groaned and rubbed his whiskers once more. "If there's one think Jake Dane is...it's a stubborn man. Believe me; growing up with the man wasn't easy!"

"I've got a feelin' your father will live to regret his actions one day. In fact, he may not tell ya, but it's probably botherin' him right now. Losin' a parent can affect a person very deeply, Vance."

"Y'know what bothers me *most* about today, Al? It's that my cousin didn't even have the decency to show up today. When I called him a couple days ago to tell him about gramps' death, Jim told me he was involved in a very important case but would try his best to make it up here for today's funeral. Then, he called me early this morning and said he couldn't pull himself away right now." Vance exhaled deeply and said, "I guess family doesn't mean as much to some people."

Al nodded his head to concur. "I don't know much 'bout police business, but I can't imagine *ANY* type of job that'd be more important than attendin' my grand-pappy's funeral. Even if he lived hundreds of miles away!"

"Well, I don't know all the specifics about Jim's situation in Chicago," Vance answered back, "but he said he's workin' on a case involving a string of murders and disappearances along the riverbanks."

Al raised an eyebrow but remained silent. Then he reached behind, grabbed the Proctor-Silex coffee pot off the burner, and filled their cups to the rim while Vance went back to writing in his notepad.

"By the way, Vance, how's work at the *Tribune* coming along? I heard through the grapevine that ya had a fallin' out with yer editor recently and you were thinkin' of resigning."

244

Vance looked at Al with a surprised expression upon his face. "You certainly have your connections, Al! I swear you know more about what's goin' on in this town than the Mayor himself."

Vance took a sip of his coffee and said, "Well, once my P.I. agency gets off the ground and I'm able to take on more clients, I'll definitely be quitting my job at the *Tribune* and be a full-time gumshoe from that day on. Until then, I'll have to put up with all the crap from that meatball editor. But I suppose I can handle it a little while longer."

"Sorry t'hear things are so strained between the two of you, laddie. I've known Jared Andrews for several years now, and in my opinion, he sure has become quite the arrogant jerk since taking over operations as editor of the *Tribune*." Al paused to sigh, and then he inquired, "If you don't mind me askin', what was yer argument 'bout?"

Vance took a deep breath and leaned back on his stool. "We had a squabble about a month ago. It was in regard to the fire at the empty law office on South Clinton Street back in mid-February. The same one that local dentist & town realtor, Jacob Gordon, died in. It was my belief that maybe Jacob's death was a homicide, which was deliberately set up to look like an accident."

Al looked confused over Vance's remarks. "But I thought he died tryin' to save the woman workin' in the insurance office on one of the upper floors?"

"Well, that's the story we ended up printing in the paper. The truth is that the police *assumed* Mr. Gordon was in the building to rescue that woman because so many people heard her screaming for help. But because of my instincts and some of the clues I've found, I think that maybe Mr. Gordon was dead, or possibly unconscious, before the fire started, and the woman was just an innocent victim who got caught up in the middle of it all."

"Wow, what an interestin' thought! So what did yer editor say to ya when you went to him with yer ideas?"

"To put it mildly, Mr. Andrews thought I was nuts. He told me that it was a dumb idea and axed my entire story. And he has been burying all of my other stories in the back of the paper or cutting them out completely ever since."

Just then, the town fire alarm began to sound off. Vance rushed over to the door and peered out a window.

Alton, who was still standing behind the bar asked, "What's goin' on? Can you see what all the commotion is about, Vance?"

Vance opened up the door and took a few steps outside to look down the street. Then he walked back inside the bar, took out his wallet, and pulled out a few dollar bills.

"All I see is a lot of smoke coming from the old movie theater. You stay here, Al, and I'll go check it out. Put two pieces of your homemade Johnnycake in a bag and fix up two cups of black coffee for me. I'll pick them up when I come back and then I'll tell you what's going on down there."

"What? Why do ya want two of everything?" asked Al. "I thought you weren't workin' at the *Tribune* today."

"I'm not," Vance replied, continuing to look out the window. "But I have to do some cleaning in the building I'm renting for my new 'Vance Dane-Private Inquiry' office and Grace is gonna to be there to help."

"Ahh, I see. Don't worry, laddie. I'll have everythin' ready to go by the time you get back!" Al yelled out as Vance was running out the door and towards the fire.

Thick, black smoke began to encompass the sky. Within a few moments, Vance arrived at the theater, bent over and gasping to catch his breath. He perused the area and his eyes became fixated as he glanced into the vacant lot next to the burning building. Approximately 100 feet away from the movie house was a snow fort with fresh footprints leading up to it and a shovel leaning against the snowy structure.

Inside the snow fort, three 8 year-old kids were playing along, unaware of the danger that lurked nearby. Little Tammy Gordon and Becky Taylor were sitting on a snow-carved bench and playing the card game Old Maid while Darren Fasick was on the other side of the fort, trying to fashion a compartment made of twigs so that he could keep his toy cars and trucks parked when they weren't being used.

"Ah-choo!" sneezed Tammy.

"Bless you, Tammy," said Becky. Then she shifted her attention toward Darren. "Hey, whatta doin' over there?"

"Building a garage for my cars," Darren replied. "Why do ya wanna know?"

"No reason, bud. Look, Amy's getting cold. Let her wear your girlie jacket so she doesn't get sick."

Darren, who was layered with several sweatshirts under his coat, took off his jacket and handed it to Tammy.

Tammy gazed at him adoringly with her big blue eyes. "Thank you, Darren...my sweetie."

Darren cringed and his face became the color of a ripe tomato. "Uh, you're welcome, Tammy." He turned around to face Becky and said, "Listen Becky, for the last time…my jacket's red! *Not* pink!"

Becky rolled her eyes and uttered, "Whatever you say, bud. *I'm* not the one who's colorblind."

"Shut up, Becky! Stop making fun of me or I won't play with you anymore!"

Vance trampled through the snow in the vacant lot and quickly made his way over to the snow fort. Vance heard voices of children as he got closer and leaned over to stick his head in the entrance.

"Hey!" yelled Vance. "What're you kids doin' here? Didn't ya hear the fire alarm goin' off?"

"Yes, we heard it," Becky said. "And we also heard the fire trucks too."

"Why do you ask, mister?" Darren asked, wiping the snot from his nose with the sleeve of his sweatshirt. "Is the fire getting' close?"

"Yes!" Vance exclaimed in a panicky voice. "The old movie theater is on fire! You kids need to leave, and do it quickly! The flames are startin' to come out the back side of the building." He took a fleeting peek in the fire's direction and said, "The flames are less than a hundred feet from your little fort!"

"See, I told you, Darren!" Tammy screamed at him. "I told you the fire was close by, but you said we were just being stupid! You *always* think girls are stupid, but this time, *you* are the one who's wrong!"

"I'm sorry, mister," Darren replied in a quiet tone. "I just figured we were okay. We play here all the time, and nothin' has ever happened before."

As the flames began to intensify and the sound of crackling wood became louder, Vance knocked a hole in the wall of the snow fort and began to make a path so the children could get out.

"Well, it doesn't matter who was right or wrong," Vance said calmly. "Let's just get you kids out of here in a hurry."

Vance looked up to see the smoke and flames rising up into the sky as the children climbed out of the snow fort and began to run off. He shifted his attention over to the building across the street and saw a cloaked individual, with what appeared to be either a scythe or a torch in his hand, standing on the rooftop.

For a brief moment, Vance glanced away make sure all the kids were away from the building and out of harm's way. When he was sure the kids were safe, he ran across the street, climbed the fire escape, and gave chase to the ghastly figure.

Vance moved swiftly, thinking that the individual may have had something to do with the fire. Within minutes, he had reached the top of the fire escape and began to pursue the mysterious man across the rooftop. To Vance's surprise, when the man reached the end of the roof, he leaped from the rooftop to the next building; a span too far apart for Vance to follow.

At that moment, the cloaked man turned and looked directly at Vance, exposing his skeletal image. The reporter stopped dead in his tracks as the sight of the stranger's face sent chills down Vance's spine.

Is this man wearing a mask to cover his identity, Vance wondered, *or am I looking at the face of Death?*

They stared at each other for a brief moment before the stranger turned and fled away. Vance stood in shock, unable to move a muscle or utter a word. Several seconds passed before Vance was able to move, and as he started to walk away, he whispered softly, "What the hell was that?"

Chapter 24:

A New Danger; It's happening Again

Night had just fallen over the town of Carthage, and the 2005 Labor Day festivities were beginning to wind down. It had been a relatively quiet Labor Day; that is, until the town fire alarm began to bellow angrily throughout the sky.

An outbreak of several mysterious fires had been occurring within the past few months and left everyone in town wondering why it was happening. It was no secret that Carthage has endured many fires over the years, some very suspicious and mysterious in nature, but never had so many erupted in such a short period of time. Nearly all of the historic buildings in Carthage had gone up in smoke over the last two centuries, a phenomenon which kept the residents on edge for many years. The occurrences of the fires had been sporadic during such time, which also left the residents to wonder when and where the next devastation would happen.

Fire trucks raced to the old opera house; one of the abandoned buildings where the homeless slept at night. In its heyday, the opera house was a beautiful building and even hosted well known entertainers and prominent acts in the late 1800s and early 1900s. Even after it was no longer being used as a theater, the building was the site of popular car shows during the 1940s and 1950s. However, over the last twenty years the opera house had fallen on hard times. Other than a brief period in which the building was being used by a beer bottling company, it had been neglected by its owners and left to decay.

When the firefighters finally reached the opera house and were able to witness the fire up close, they began to fully understand the magnitude of what they were about to encounter. The fire was spectacular, with orange and yellow flames pouring out every window of the three story building and reaching heights of twenty to thirty feet above the roof. Some of the windows that flames were coming from exhibited a hint of deep blue color, which probably meant there was plastic or some petroleum product in the area.

Thick black smoke rapidly began bellowing from the windows, obscuring the light of the full moon and giving the night sky an eerie look. The smoke was so thick that it was hard for the numerous spectators to breathe and caused their eyes to water profusely, encouraging people in the vicinity to move further away from the scene. And to make matters worse, the heat from the flames was so intense that windows in nearby buildings were beginning to crack.

Officer Kenneth Johnson stepped out of his patrol car and looked up towards the roof of the burning building and the other surrounding buildings. Although he was not expecting to see anything or anyone in particular, he was not dismissing the possibility that the person or persons responsible for the fire might still be in the vicinity. Biting down on his Winchester cigar, he glared at the shadows with a scowl upon his face. His dark-brown trench coat flapped in the wind and appeared like a boat sail as it tried to cover his mountainous physique.

Ken was in his mid-forties and was a hulk of a man, with an overly large frame and a head that seemed too small for the rest of his body. His thick, black beard was beginning to show traces of gray, and his appearance was more like a bum than a police officer. He usually wore a wrinkled dark brown trench coat and a wide-brimmed Stetson hat. His tie and food stained shirts gave him a slobbish appearance, and he usually reeked of cheap cigars.

Officer Johnson glanced around at all the fire trucks and police cars in the area. As Ken walked up and down the street in front of the burning building, he began to work the crowd; a term police detectives used to describe how they scan the faces and actions of the spectators at the fire. He had been to many crime scenes in his career, and he found that examining the crowd would sometimes reveal clues to who may have been responsible for the crime simply by someone's demeanor.

After several more minutes, Officer Johnson finished scrutinizing the spectators in the area and conferred with his other officers. Then he turned his attention toward a person standing off to the side of the commotion. "Christ!" he grumbled to himself. "It's Roberts."

Joshua Roberts was walking around the area and jotting down some notes for the article he was transcribing for the *Carthage Republican Tribune*. Ken Johnson had a deep dislike for Josh, partly because of an unflattering article he wrote about the Carthage Police Department and also because the two men were complete opposite personalities.

Josh was a slight man, only about 5'6" tall, and a well groomed individual. He wore neat, pressed suits and shined shoes. He kept his hair perfectly styled, he was always clean-shaven, and at times, Josh would be mistaken for a lawyer or a politician instead of a newspaper reporter. However, what probably irritated Ken the most was Josh's cocky attitude and the smug grin he always wore.

Josh stopped while in mid-stride. Slowly he walked over to the shadows of a near alleyway, standing off to the side of the commotion. With his pad and pen still in his hand, Josh began interviewing a bearded homeless man, Sam Cushman, who claimed to have seen the person that set the fire.

Sam wasn't always a homeless soul and at one time he was an upper-middle class contributing member of society. There are times when Sam has managed to shower and shave, and for a moment, a person can sense that Sam was probably a handsome man in his earlier years. Unfortunately, it was hard living on the streets and Sam's complexion always seemed as if he were sunburned—with skin like leather from being out in all types of weather every day, and his light-brown hair was beginning to turn white on the sides.

Although he stood nearly six feet tall, Sam appeared shorter than he actually was due to arthritis in his back, which made him walk slightly bent over. His teeth were decayed from many years of neglect, and the crows' feet lines around his eyes were probably caused from excessive squinting due to poor eyesight and going without his much-needed glasses.

Sam had a smelly body odor that was almost unbearable, and his worn clothes appeared to be nothing more than Salvation Army rejects. He wore a wrinkled blue overcoat with a stained Buffalo Bills sweatshirt underneath, a dirty pair of Dickies work pants, and very tattered tennis sneakers that he wore with no socks.

While Josh was writing, his words began to appear fainter on his paper as his favorite ballpoint pen started to run out of black ink. In frustration, he threw his pen to the ground and kicked it away. As Josh reached into his jacket pocket to pull out another pen, Sam took out a bottle of liquor from under his coat and began to gulp it down.

"Hey, before you go and get yourself too drunk, can I get a description of the person you saw do this?" Josh asked.

"I saw something that *almost* made me give up drinking." the homeless man replied. "I saw the face of Death; I saw the Grim Reaper!" Then he pulled out a hunting knife with an eight-inch blade. "I carry this with me at all times since this whole fiasco has been happening. Don't know how much good it will do me, but I gotta give myself a fighting chance in case he comes after me next."

Josh shook his head, figuring that he wasn't going to get any useful information from Sam. Although Josh had spoken with several of the residents in the homeless community over the course of the past year, and they had all mentioned a strange entity prowling the rooftops, Josh was yet to find any shred of evidence to support their claims.

Just for the sake of humoring the homeless man, Josh decided to ask him, "So, Sam, did you get a good look of him this time?"

"I sure as hell did!" the homeless man exclaimed. "I was sleepin' not more than twenty feet away from the edge of a building as a dark figure went running by me. The Reaper was jumpin' from rooftop to rooftop, wearin' a long black coat, or maybe a cloak. The black attire went down to his feet and covered most of his face. But I got a good look at 'im as he ran by me, and this time I saw his face!"

Josh's eyes lit up as he grinned a crooked grin. "Go on, Sam. You've got my attention!"

"Well, his face looked like a frightening skull, and his eyes were black as coal. I watched as he was sneakin' into the opera house and waited t'see what he was goin' to do. A few minutes later I saw smoke and flames coming from the building, but I didn't see the Reaper come back out."

"Thanks, I appreciate the information." Josh said, writing down the description on his pad. Then he handed the homeless man a twenty-dollar bill. "Here you go, Sam; get yourself some food."

Officer Johnson hurried over as the homeless man walked away and tapped Josh on the shoulder. "What are you doing here, Roberts?" he said in his usual deep, throaty voice. "You're contaminating my crime scene! Pick your damn pen up off the ground before I give you a ticket for littering."

Josh spun around quickly, unaware Ken was behind him. "Oh, hello, Officer Johnson. I hear we just had ourselves another alleged Reaper sighting. I think that's five sightings in just under three months, isn't it? And that amounts to eleven sightings altogether if you go back to last year."

Ken stared and clenched his teeth together, but did not remark.

"We've had as many fires in town during the same time period; including the deaths of Shelby Webster and Patrick Jordan. Do you have any comment?" taunted Josh.

"Shelby who?" Ken smirked, attempting to look puzzled. "I must've forgotten all about that incident. Was she someone of importance?"

"How could you forget her?" Josh retorted in an astonished voice. "She was the homeless woman who died during the fire that demolished the Youth Center. The coroner told me it appeared as though parts of her clothing were doused in some type of fire accelerant such as gasoline or kerosene."

"The coroner told you that?" Ken shouted as he rolled his eyes. "Harry Moon is the biggest wacko the hospital has on its payroll. He'll always be a hippie in my eyes; a former deadhead whose skills are inept and whose medical opinions are worthless."

"Harry is a good man, Ken, and he happens to be a friend of mine."

Ken let out a huff.

"Besides, regardless of whether or not I believe anything Dr. Moon has to say, I'm also looking to get an opinion from someone who works on the police squad. Do you think the attack on Ms. Webster was an intentional act committed by the Reaper or some other unknown assailant?"

Officer Johnson squinted his eyes at Josh. "There is no Reaper," he remarked. "If there were, we would find him; we would arrest him. It's just some young reporter's wild and wishful imagination. This is the newspaper's way of explaining the sudden surge of fires around here lately and exploiting it as a method of selling a lot of papers."

Josh just grinned and tried to ignore Ken's comments. Then he put a tape recorder up to Ken's mouth and said, "I hear the Mayor's office is now searching frantically for the lost file Pat Jordan was supposedly working on before he died; the file which is supposed to contain information about the Reaper. Is that true?"

"You must have selective hearing." Ken remarked coldly. "Like I've told you many times before, I don't believe in ghosts, devils, or reapers."

Josh just stared at Ken as though he was dumbfounded. "In light of what happened in this town five years ago at the ferry service, how can you believe that another catastrophe like that couldn't happen again, or even worse?"

Officer Johnson glared intently at Josh and threw his cigar towards him. The cigar struck Josh's trench coat as sparks and ashes fell to the ground.

"You asshole!" bellowed Josh, brushing the hot ashes off his coat.

"Don't be writing this stuff in the *Tribune*, Roberts. It will ruin your already useless career. You don't want to be known as a 'has-been' reporter before the age of thirty-five, do you?"

"Thanks for the advice, Ken. But I'm the reporter, and you, you are just a beat cop now." Josh stood toe to toe with Ken and said in a very cocky voice, "So why don't you go away and act like a beat cop."

"Am I supposed to thank you for that?" Ken said rudely.

Josh scoffed and took several steps backwards. "Are you still pissed off at me for writing that article on crooked cops in our town?" he asked with sarcasm in his voice.

"Your little column of lies nearly cost me my job and my marriage! How dare you put in your article that I've had several love affairs with other women! It's none of your business what I do in my personal life. And furthermore, you have no evidence to prove that I ever accepted a bribe from a felon—past or present!"

"A word to the wise...watch your damn mouth," countered Josh, glaring back at Ken. "Remember," he continued, "our conversation is definitely *not* 'off the record.' If you don't watch yourself, you're going to end up working a school crosswalk."

By now, Ken's temper had reached its breaking point. "You smug bastard! You cost me more than just my dignity. I was about to be promoted to Detective before your editorial came out. And if that wasn't bad enough, my wife was raving mad after she read your expose and even considered a divorce!" screamed Ken.

"Really? I guess she would've been really upset if I mentioned the *name* of the piece of ass that you've been screwing behind her back."

Ken pulled his fist back as though he was going to take a swing at Josh. "You Son of a Bitch! I should kick the shit out of you right here, right now!"

"Calm down, Ken," Josh expressed in an arrogant tone. "I wouldn't want to see you get suspended, or possibly lose your job, for not being able to control your temper."

Ken put his arm down and gave Josh a look of disgust. "You're not worth my time, and you're certainly not worth losing my job over."

Josh decided to ease the tension and change the topic of conversation. "Look, we may not like each other, but the circumstances that are happening around town are starting to get serious. There are too many fires in town and too many sightings of what is being described as the Grim Reaper to be just a coincidence."

Ken curled his lip and rolled his eyes.

"Don't give me a patronizing look!" roared Josh. "All I'm trying to do is get some answers to these two mysteries just like you are. Nearly everyone in town is afraid to leave their homes at night. Every delinquent that peddles the streets is now shaking in their boots. Those who reportedly have seen the Reaper say he can walk through walls and that he cannot die. They also say…"

Officer Johnson cut him off in the middle of his sentence and said, "I say you're full of shit." Ken started to walk away while Josh stared at him in disbelief. Then Ken turned around and stated, "By the way, Roberts, you can quote me on that!"

As Officer Johnson walked back to the squad car, Josh yelled to him, "That's not a denial, you know!"

Josh veered his attention toward the fire once again, shaking his head in sadness. "The devastation of the fire will undoubtedly leave the three-story brick building a hallow shell that will certainly have to be torn down," he said in a low whisper. "And with it, another piece of Carthage's history will be gone forever.

Meanwhile, perched on a rooftop several buildings away and high above the haunts of man, a grotesque and gawky figure in a black cloak sat. His every sense was attuned to the commotion below as he watched the firefighters fight feverishly against the flames.

This tragedy seemed to have little effect on the stranger as he just sat there with no emotion at all upon his skull-like face. A moment later, the eerie individual was gone, lost in the endless night.

Chapter 25:

Igniting the curiosity of a past Hero

The next morning, Holly Boliver made her way downstairs to the kitchen wearing one of her boyfriend's old T-shirts. The length of the shirt was just short enough to expose her shapely legs, and it was thin enough to reveal the contour of her firm breasts, which obviously needed no support.

Over the past couple years that Holly and Roger Fasick had been together, she had put on slightly more weight, but mostly in the form of muscle; especially since she started accompanying Roger to the gym. Holly also changed her hair; cutting off her long, wavy blond locks to a short, bobbed style with red highlights. At twenty-eight years old she was still a striking young lady, but she was neither vain nor prudish about her looks.

"Boy, I could definitely use a couple more hours of sleep," she said with a yawn. As she sat down, Holly rubbed the sleep from her eyes and looked over at the counter where Roger was making a fresh pot of coffee. "Oh god that aroma smells good! How long before it's done?"

"It'll be ready in a few minutes," Roger replied.

Roger's appearance had also changed considerably in the past five years. Due to the company he currently worked for, he was required to wear his ash-blonde hair short and tapered; with no sideburns and no facial hair. This gave Roger a more business-like appearance; however, he still refused to wear a necktie to work, and he vowed to his friends that someday he would have his own investigative firm and would dress any damn way he pleased. But until then, he had to look and dress like a Wall Street broker.

As Roger was getting some coffee cups from the cupboard, he looked over to Holly and said, "You must be pretty exhausted from last night."

"I sure am. That's the third 14-hour shift I've done in the past month. I can't believe Tim called in and stuck me with his shift again. His irresponsibility is starting to affect his job, and he's treading on thin ice with Miss Kitty; she's even threatened to replace him."

Roger jellied some bagels and brought them over to the table. "Firing Tim wouldn't solve your overtime issue," he remarked, licking the apple jelly off his fingers. "If she does, then you'll have to put in more grueling hours than you've already been until she can get someone hired and trained."

"Yeah, and I don't want to work more late night shifts than I absolutely have to. Not to mention that it really would be sad if he got fired." Holly stood up and yawned as she stretched her arms over her head. "Tim really is a sweet guy and I like him, but sometimes he does act a little peculiar."

"Peculiar? Are you sure we're talking about the same Tim Matthews; don't you mean he's down right weird?"

"Roger, don't make fun of Tim like that!" she snapped. "He's been at Kitty's Bar quite a few years now, and he knows how to do the job well. Not to mention, he always makes the town's Fourth of July party an exciting time for everyone, too."

Holly paused to take a bite of her bagel.

"Did you know that Tim makes his own fireworks? His are even better than the ones the Department of Public Works buys for the town."

"Yeah, I think you've mentioned that before," Roger answered in a somewhat jealous tone.

When the coffee was brewed and ready, Holly poured herself a full cup and stepped outside to get the morning paper. She walked back inside and started to skim the articles while sipping her hot, dark mocha coffee. As she flipped the paper over, she glanced at an article on the bottom of the back page, and her eyes suddenly began to bulge.

"Roger, take a look at this!" she yelled to him. "There was another fire last night. This time it was on the other side of town!"

Roger went into the living room and Holly handed him the paper. He went over to the recliner, sat down with the paper, and began to read the article.

After he finished, he shifted his attention back to Holly and said, "Well, it is an interesting story, but it contains a hell of a lot of information and background about some homeless man who witnessed the fire and not a lot of details about the fire itself." Then he paused for a moment before continuing. "I think I'm gonna go downtown for a little while after breakfast and do some checking around."

"Where are you going to go?" she asked. "Over to Bucky's house to talk about last night's fire?"

"No, he really doesn't have time for just sitting around and solving all the world's problems like we used to. Now that he's taken on the responsibilities of being the Mayor, I think he's beginning to realize just how much work is actually involved. Instead of trying to hunt him down, I was thinking of heading over to the *Tribune* office."

"Oh, you're going to see Josh then."

"That's right," he replied, winking. Then he noticed her demeanor and how distracted she seemed. "Is there something wrong?"

"No, not with that. I was just thinking to myself." She turned and looked him in the eyes with vigor, seemingly coming to some sort of conclusion. "Y'know something, even though Josh and I are *very* distant cousins, this is still a small-town community and we aren't even remotely close. Don't you find that a little strange?"

"Not really. I'm not close to many of my relatives either; and besides, you and Josh are like third or fourth cousins anyway. Not to mention, there's a six-year age difference between the two of you."

"Well, I suppose," Holly replied. She took a deep breath, exhaled slowly, and changed the topic. "Take as much time as you want hanging out with Josh. There are plenty of things I'd like to do around the house today anyway. And it always seems like I can't get anything accomplished when you're here."

Roger got a petrified look upon his face. "What do you want to do around here?"

"Oh, I thought I might mow the lawn today. It's starting to look a little shabby compared to all our neighbor's yards."

"Um, that's a really sweet idea, Hun, but I'd rather you didn't."

"Why not?" asked Holly.

"Well, you don't have a good track record when it comes to mowing the lawn. You've broken five lawnmowers in three years, and quite honestly, every time you mow the lawn, it ends up costing me money in one way or another."

Holly rolled her eyes.

"Holly, I know you have good intentions, but you would be doing me *more* of a favor if you just overlooked the mowing or any other yard work today."

"Fine, I won't touch any of your damn machines!" she said in a huff as she walked briskly out of the room.

During the mad streak of fires in recent months, Roger had been privately researching the fires for any connection or pattern with the blazes. Lately, Roger was spending a hefty portion of his free time at the *Carthage Republican Tribune*, comparing notes and opinions about the fires with Josh Roberts.

Roger had questions about the most recent fire, so he decided to go over to Josh's office to get some answers. Even though he and Josh have focused the majority of their attention on the fires, Roger now planned on asking him some probing questions regarding the enigmatic Reaper.

It was just after noon when he arrived at Josh's office. As he was walking inside, Roger overheard Josh talking into the telephone and saying, "There is no Reaper? Then who lit the homeless woman on fire? Suicide! Let me get that on tape. Hello? Hello? Damn it! He hung up on me!"

Josh suddenly became aware that Roger was in his office.

"Sorry, Roger, I didn't notice you come in. I was having a provoking conversation with our chief of police."

"Really?" said Roger as he raised a brow. "And what did Captain Zimmerman have to say?"

"Actually, he was pretty vague in his answers. I tried to get some information about the cloaked individual people have seen around town, but the Chief was giving me the runaround instead."

Josh pulled his yellow-colored lighter from his shirt pocket, lit up a cigarette, and opened a window to let the smoke out. "So, Roger, what brings you to my office so early in the morning?"

"Oh, not much. I read your article about last night's fire in the newspaper and thought I'd stop by to see if there was any new information. After all, the story didn't give very many details."

Roger noticed Josh's oversized cup of coffee and his bloodshot eyes with black circles underneath them. "Wow, you look like hell, Josh! Are you feeling a little sluggish today?"

Josh grinned and nodded as he took another sip from his enormous cup. "I was at the fire scene last night, and then I stayed up most of the night working on my article to make sure it went in this morning's edition. I'm running on about two hours sleep and nine cups of coffee."

At that moment, a grumbling Ty Harris came rushing into Josh's office. "What the hell is the meaning of your ridiculous article?" he yelled as his chubby cheeks vibrated. "You better have a good explanation for this one, Roberts!"

"What's wrong with it, Chief?" Josh asked, surprised by Ty's demeanor. "I think I was objective and informative in my analysis."

"Is this all the information you got?" exclaimed the editor, holding up a copy of Josh's story. "I wanted a column. You bring me back a couple of sticks! You were there to get the story on the fire, not to give me some crap tale about an out-of-work bum. Nobody in town cares about his background; the readers want details about how the blaze started."

"There really wasn't much to tell about the fire. The origin of the fire was still undetermined at the time, and the information I gathered about the Reaper was purely speculation. Instead of writing some bland story, I thought I'd give the readers a taste of some creative writing."

"You call this writing?" Ty asked as he gritted his teeth, and his face began to turn scarlet red. "A brain-damaged cocker-spaniel could do better. Your material has gone to hell lately, Josh, and your job is hanging by a thin thread. I better start seeing better news stories soon, or you can start looking for another job!" Ty took a few steps toward the door; then he turned back around. "And didn't I tell you not to smoke your filthy cigarettes in this office anymore?"

Ty stormed out of Josh's office and slammed the door on his way out. Josh stood still, keeping his opinion of his asshole editor to himself while Roger was trying to think of something to say to break the uncomfortable silence. After a long period of dead air, Roger blurted out the first idea that came to his mind.

"So, who is this homeless guy that Ty was talking about?" Roger asked in a lighthearted tone. "He must be very interesting, or a pretty good friend of yours, for you to write such an elaborate piece on him and give his background equal billing in your article about the fire?"

"His name is Sam Cushman; he's just a guy I've chatted with a couple of times at some of the fire scenes," Josh explained. "He usually has some very useful news, but this time I didn't really get much information regarding the specifics of the fire so I thought I'd give a brief background about him. Besides, he allegedly saw the Reaper, and I wanted to build up Sam's reputation before I mentioned that he was my sole eye witness. Another reason for writing the article was to focus attention on the plight of Sam and others like him in Carthage. It's a damn shame that no one seems to care anymore!"

Roger grabbed the paper off Josh's desk and perused the article in question one more time. "Maybe Ty doesn't understand your reasoning why you wrote the article. One thing I have learned about him is that although Ty is concerned about what goes on around town, he is only interested in the trials of people's lives if it will sell papers. And he probably doesn't think this guy is fascinating enough to be considered reading material."

"Yeah, when you put it that way, I can see your point. However, I feel sorry for Sam, and I wanted to do something nice for him. I thought that by telling his story, I could generate some sympathy for Sam and others like him. Maybe with enough exposure, we can get *our* politicians to do something about the growing homeless population in *our* town."

Josh slammed the door shut on his file cabinet. "Sam is a good man," he continued. "He's had some hard times the past few years, and he deserves better. He worked as a foreman at the paper mill for twenty years before it closed down and laid off over 700 workers. Sam's luck went downhill from there. Businesses wouldn't hire him because of his advancing age, and right before the bank foreclosed on his house, his wife left him for another man. That string of bad luck was just too much for him to cope with. Sam took to drinking heavily, that is, until his unemployment ran out. After that, he was left to beg for handouts and live on the streets."

"Well, if it's any consolation to you, I thought it was a good article," Roger stated as he put down the paper. "I mean, I don't know much about the newspaper business, but it seems that Ty came down on you pretty hard for something so trivial. After all, I wouldn't have believed much about what some homeless guy told you until I got to know something about him and realized that he wasn't some run of the mill bum on the street."

"Don't worry about it," Josh muttered, shrugging his shoulders. "Ty has been on everybody's case lately; he's just letting off some steam."

"Why? What's his problem?"

"Ever since he and Mr. McGary broke up, he has been in a bitchy mood."

Roger stared at him with a befuddled look upon his face. "Are you talking about Eric McGary; the former co-editor of the *Tribune*? The same guy who just moved away to become editor of the *Times*? The *Tribune's* most hated rival from Watertown!"

"Yep, that's the one," Josh answered back. "Ty and Eric got into an argument about a month or so ago, and Eric moved out of their apartment. Shortly after that, Eric put in his resignation. Then he..." Josh stopped in mid sentence when he saw Roger's shocked expression and began to chuckle. "Don't tell me you didn't know they were a couple; they've been together for years. Christ, they dress alike and everything. Is it really that hard to figure out?"

Roger's face got red with embarrassment. He shifted his attention to the paper Ty had thrown on Josh's desk and said, "So, this homeless guy saw the Reaper, huh? His sightings are really starting to accumulate."

"You got that right!" Josh announced. "I was going over my notes last night and discovered that there have been five Reaper sightings to go along with five fires in town, all in the last three months. Before that, there were six other sightings earlier in the year and six other mysterious fires."

Roger sat silently still and listened attentively to Josh's words.

"It seems like whenever this guy shows up, disaster is not far behind," Josh stated, shaking his hands in the air. "Even though there have been an equal number of both fires and sightings, last night was the first time the Reaper was spotted *AT* a fire scene. And that makes him a suspect at possibly even starting the blaze. At least, in my book it does."

"Equal number of sightings and fires, huh?" repeated Roger. "That's a little strange, don't you think? What do you think the Reaper's capable of?" he asked. "That is, if he even exists at all. Do you really believe this so-called Reaper, or ghost, or whatever he is, could be the one actually setting all these fires?"

"Given his reputation, the whispered, fearful urban legends said about him throughout town, anything is possible. At one time, I didn't believe in such nonsense tales such as ghosts and goblins, but after the strange things that have happened in this town, I don't rule anything out anymore."

At that moment, Josh's phone rang. "Hold on a second, Roger." Josh picked up the receiver. "Hello," he grumbled into the phone. "This better be important; I'm in the middle of typing up an editorial."

He paused for a moment and then said, "Jason! How the hell are ya, bro? I haven't talked to you in nearly two months! Are you taking good care of my nephew, or do I have to come down there and do it for you? You need to watch kids like a hawk in order to keep them safe, y'know."

Josh turned toward Roger and raised a finger, letting him know he would be on the phone for a while. While Josh was immersed in his phone conversation, Roger glanced at all the newspaper clippings and post-it notes scattered across the walls and covering his filing cabinets.

Either this guy is extremely unorganized or Josh is obsessively devoted to his work, Roger thought.

After a few minutes, Josh hung up the phone. Roger veered his attention back to the reporter.

"Sorry about the interruption, Roger. That was my brother, Jason. He was having a crisis at his house and needed someone to talk to."

"I hope it wasn't anything serious."

"No, not really. He was just ranting about some bizarre spoon he found in his silverware drawer. Jason is an intelligent guy, but he overreacts way too much and is very pig-headed. I just hope our little chat helped calm him down."

"Calm?" inquired Roger. "He was that upset, huh?"

"Jason is an at-home dad and doesn't get much interaction with other adults. His mind tends to wander—probably from all the isolation he has to deal with."

"I can't even imagine what that must be like."

"Exactly! For instance, Jason thinks Polansky's business partner, Stanley Spillanski is flirting with his wife just because he found a spoon with the letter *S* in his utensil drawer. Crazy, I know! But don't worry; I *think* my words got through that thick, stubborn head of his."

Roger nodded as his thoughts suddenly turned to memories of his brother, Paul, and the heart-to-heart talks they used to have.

"Okay," Josh announced, "where was I? Oh, that's right…we were discussing the Reaper." There was another moment of uncomfortable silence before the reporter said, "I heard there was a phantom file on the Reaper. Supposedly it was started by former mayor, Pat Jordan, but no one was able to locate the papers after he died. However, I believe it really *does* exist and that it is being kept in Mayor Morgan's office."

Josh stopped to think for a moment.

"Hey, Roger, I've got an idea. You and Mayor Morgan are supposed to be good buddies, right?"

"Yeah, he's as close to family as I have in this town."

"Good! How about you get in contact with Bucky and see if you can get some more information about that mysterious Reaper file?"

Roger laughed. "Trust me, there *is* no file. If there were, Bucky would've told me about it a long time ago."

"Really," said Josh with hesitation in his voice. "How close are the two of you *these* days?"

"What're you gettin' at?"

"Being the mayor, I'm sure he has to make some difficult decisions. Sometimes, a politician has to keep quiet about certain issues."

"Stop beating around the bush, Josh."

"Okay...Roger, do you really think Bucky tells you *everything* that goes on in the Mayor's office?"

Chapter 26:

Choose your enemies Carefully

Meanwhile, as Roger and Josh were conversing at the *Tribune*, Mayor Bucky Morgan was pacing back and forth in his office at Carthage City Hall. The building that was being used as City Hall was one of the oldest in town.

Originally, the building was a large boarding house in the early 1900s but closed down years ago when tourism had started to decline, and the building was eventually sold back to the town at a fraction of what the structure was actually worth. When the City Hall renovations were finally completed, the Town Council and Mayor's offices were located on the second floor, and the Police Station was on the first floor with the jail cells in the basement of the building.

Bucky was preoccupied with disturbing thoughts, and he was starting to feel rather restless. His mind was a rattled mess as he continued to dwell upon the peculiar events happening in Carthage as of late. After pacing around his office for nearly an hour, Bucky decided to step out of his office and go for a walk to get some fresh air and hopefully think more clearly.

The last few years had not been very kind to Bucky. He seemed to show his age more these days, with a touch of gray streaking his hair at the temples and signs of slightly thinning on top. At the corner of his eyes, the faint signs of wrinkles added to his older appearance. Although he was still in fairly good physical shape, he had lost some of the muscle tone he once showed off. With his job as Mayor taking up enormous amounts of his time, he rarely had the opportunity to exercise at the gym anymore.

With the little "free" time he did manage to set aside, he liked to spend it with his wife, Cristina, and their son, Michael, who enjoyed going everywhere with his Dad.

Probably due to the many late nights he worked at the office and spending so much time in front of the computer, Bucky now required reading glasses. This unanticipated nuisance was something Bucky was not very happy about and avoided wearing them as much as possible, especially when there were people around. Call it vain if you will, but he detested wearing them and felt uncomfortable being seen with them on.

When Bucky made his way down to the first floor, he strolled over to the police department side of the building and was standing in the doorway of Chief of Police Bernard Zimmerman's office.

Chief Zimmerman was a tall, lanky man who was rather thin with nearly all white hair and a gray moustache. At 6'1" tall, he did look rather distinguished, and he usually wore black dress slacks and a white dress shirt with a black tie. This was the Chief's usual look, even when he was Police Chief in Watertown, New York, a neighboring city, where he had retired from three years ago.

At Bucky's request, Bernard Zimmerman accepted the position of Police Chief of Carthage about six months ago, mainly because he was bored with retirement. He felt Carthage was a quieter lifestyle than what he was used to in the city of Watertown…or so he thought.

The Chief had lost his wife to leukemia a few years ago and had one daughter, Maureen, who still lived in Watertown and worked for the Social Services Department. Maureen was a quiet mother of two who was married to what else…a police officer.

Chief Zimmerman, or C.Z. as his men sometimes called him, lived in a modest apartment above Intorcia's Doughnut Shop with his frisky cat, Dirty Harry. It seemed surprising that the Chief stayed as slim as he did despite the amount of time he spent downstairs in the doughnut shop.

There wasn't much furniture in the Chief's tiny apartment. He preferred to keep the setting of his residence as simple as possible, which is exactly how he liked to live his life. However, aside from the blandness of the décor, C.Z. did have several frames of medals, awards and accommodations, and a letter of thanks from the Watertown Mayor and City Council. This correspondence was his most cherished possession and had significant meaning because it was written in appreciation for solving an extremely difficult criminal case.

Bernard's reputation was well-known throughout the upstate area, which was the main reason why Bucky chose him to take over as Chief of Police in Carthage.

After a few moments of waiting, Bucky knocked on the door window and asked, "Captain Zimmerman? Do you have a moment?"

The old Captain waived him in. Bucky closed the door behind him and sat down.

"I seem to have nothing but moments, Mayor Morgan. Irritating, inconclusive, puzzling moments that just don't fit into a suitable chain of logic."

Bucky leaned back in the chair and crossed his arms. "Are you saying there are no clues in the arsonist case or in the Reaper sightings? Nothing at all?"

"Nothing," the captain stated. "A signature for an arsonist would be a particular target or a set of targets, but *our* perpetrator doesn't seem to have any. So, that aspect doesn't' give us any leads."

"Do you have anything concrete—any facts that are known?"

"Sure, we have facts," Zimmerman divulged. Let me tell you *all* the facts we have. There's been five sightings of the Reaper within the past three months and over a dozen sightings in total if you go all the way back to last year. During the same period, there have been nearly as many fires. I know the two are connected, and yet, I might as well be chasing a ghost. Whoever is doing this leaves absolutely no clues."

"None?" Bucky asked once again.

"None whatsoever, Mr. Morgan."

"So what are you going to do?" asked Bucky.

The Chief rubbed his forehead and grimaced. "I know you've asked me to stay away from investigating Thomas Parker as a personal favor to you, but with no other leads materializing, I might have to take a closer look at his background and activities."

"What for?" exclaimed Bucky. "Based on some strange behavior and a mysterious past? If I'm not mistaken, the last time I brought up concerns to the Police Department about having someone checked out because of a mysterious past, the police captain told me I shouldn't be so paranoid. He also stated it would be best to keep my nose out of other people's business."

"If you're referring to the ferryman case a few years ago, that was a case which was handled by a *different* police captain. Jared Monaghan was, at best, a mediocre Police Chief. I don't intend on letting the town's problems escalate to out-of-hand proportions before I take the initiative on resolving them. I think you know by now that the distinctions between me and the previous person who held this post are as different as night and day."

"So, what if you are? I still don't see why you think Thomas's past, or his unique personality, make him any more of a suspect than some of the other peculiar individuals living in this area. After all, this *is* the North Country!"

Captain Zimmerman just shook his head. "That's not the only reason Mr. Parker is being looked at. Did you know that the last place Patrick Jordan was seen alive was at Kitty's Bar?"

"Yes, I remember when Officer Streeter interviewed Tim Matthews at Kitty's Bar. Tim stated he saw Pat having a few beers in there."

"Well, do you also know that the only other customer who was there drinking that night was Thomas Parker?"

Bucky sat silent, not knowing what to say.

"His name just keeps popping all over!" the Chief continued.

"I don't buy that at all!" Bucky's voice became loud and forceful. "I'm fed up with excuses, Zimmerman! I want this rampant arson stopped...and I don't mean by Christmas! I suggest you create a special squad to bring in this Reaper individual. I want results, and I want to be kept up-to-date on every little detail, too."

Zimmerman leaned forward, his hands gripped tightly on the edge of his desk and his teeth clenched. "I'm doing the best I can do with the limited resources I have. You're just going to have to deal with that fact!"

Bucky tensed up. "I'd hate to have to go outside our community to get some assistance on this situation."

"What do you mean by that?" asked the Chief in an irate tone.

"Well, I'm sure Lloyd Mordal and the rest of the State Troopers would love to get their abhorrent paws on this case. Chief Mordal can be here with a carload of troopers in less than twenty minutes!"

C.Z. inhaled deeply and bellowed, "With all due respect, Bucky...Mordal is an idiot! Besides, we don't need any troopers from Pulaski butting their nose in Carthage's affairs."

"I don't *need* to get in touch with the State Troopers for any assistance, C.Z." Bucky rebutted. "I have other contacts as well."

Zimmerman scoffed. "Like who?"

"Colonel Mark Gaines has called me recently from his office on Fort Drum. He expressed his concerns about the recent fires occurring in town and inquired whether or not there was any truth to the Reaper persona. He informed me that he's more than willing to lend any support I need. After all, many of his soldiers live in this town with their families, and he doesn't want to see any of his Army people getting hurt in this mess."

"Is that all he's worried about?" questioned C.Z.

Bucky looked C.Z. straight in the eyes and stated, "Colonel Gaines also told me that he needed this town, and the surrounding areas, to be secured because our 'Commander-in-Chief' is coming for a visit soon."

"Really?" C.Z. said an apathetic sigh. "And I wonder what Ol' George Bush hopes to gain by making an appearance up here in the North Country."

"Watch your mouth!" Bucky snapped back. "You address him with respect. Call him President Bush; or in your case, you may refer to him as Mr. President!"

The police chief knew well enough that it's not wise to discuss politics with a politician, and he quickly dropped the subject.

Bernard Zimmerman was an old-fashioned man, maybe a bit too old-fashioned for the times. He stroked his bushy, gray moustache and spit chewing tobacco in the wastebasket as he said, "I beg your pardon, Mayor Morgan, but when you hired me, I got stuck with a police department where half of the squad has a questionable integrity and the other half is as green as grass. You want to talk about a group of individuals who are inexperienced and wet behind the ears? Some of the cases they are involved in are way out of their league. Until I can effectively monitor my own department and get these men trained properly, how in heaven's name can I police this town?"

While the two men were exchanging words, in what was becoming a heated debate, one-time Mayoral hopeful Edgar Polansky arrived at the police station to file a complaint against his neighbor's dog.

Now we all know it's not appropriate to make fun of people; however, Edgar Polansky has got to be an exception. Edgar was a burly bear of a man at 6'4" and weighing approximately three hundred pounds. If he were to wear a brown suit to the zoo, he would probably have been mistaken for a bear. With his dark, thick bushy eyebrows, round face, and bulbous nose, he had no problem sticking out in a crowd. It could be said that his looks were directly attributed to his Turkish/Russian heritage.

Even though he was known by people in town as a whiner, a complainer, and a sore loser, Edgar was basically a nice guy. Last year he ran for Mayor against Bucky, thinking he had the people's best interest at heart; however, with his whining and sniveling, he alienated most of the voters in town and probably some of the nonvoters too.

Although Edgar lost the election, he took over as leader of the Town Council and still spent as much time at City Hall as Bucky did, usually making complaints of one kind or another and making a nuisance of himself.

Edgar smugly walked up to the counter where the receptionist, LaTesha Prince, was directing patrons to the various departments in City Hall. He carried himself with a swaggering confidence, as though he was someone of importance; however, when he approached the counter, the receptionist simply ignored him and pretended that no one was there.

Ms. Prince was not just window dressing at City Hall, she was a very intelligent receptionist. On the other hand, when people (mostly the men) stopped to ask her advice or questions, they had a hard time keeping their mind on the business at hand and often tended to forget what their reason for being there was.

LaTesha, at 5'7", was a very striking Latino woman with a Dolly Parton figure, narrow waist, wide hips, and large breasts. She often wore flower printed cotton dresses with the hem line so high that it left little to the imagination. Being above average height compared to other upstate New York girls, LaTesha looked even taller with her stiletto shoes that sported a four-inch heel, which made her seem *very* tall indeed.

LaTesha's long, flowing dark hair cascaded over her shoulders, and her dark inviting eyes could make any man uneasy in her presence. Having been married twice and divorced twice, she was not shy with men, and having served four years in the Army herself, she could out run, out drink, and out swear most of the men in the area.

During her stint in the Army, LaTesha worked in the Personnel Department. It was there she acquired some outstanding people skills and became proficient at managing records, just some of the reasons why Bucky thought she would be a great addition to City Hall.

For awhile now, LaTesha had been serving two administrative positions; she was the Mayor's secretary during the morning, and she was also the receptionist for the police department during the afternoon and some evening hours. Because of a lack of qualified help in the area, she had to endure the strenuous workload, constantly hoping that a replacement or an assistant would be found soon.

Despite her keen abilities and excellent skills, LaTesha seemed bored with her post and didn't appear too concerned about any patrons that entered the building or with anything else that was going on around her. She continued to file her nails while smacking her gum as Edgar stood patiently by the counter. After a few seconds, she directed her attention to Edgar.

"Hey Edgar, whatta ya doin' here today? Did some little girl go and steal your newspaper again?" she asked in a condescending voice.

"No," he responded in a blasé tone. "If you must know, my neighbor has a problem keeping his dog in his own backyard. It seems his mongrel would rather relieve itself in *my* flower bed instead of its own yard."

"I see," LaTesha said, trying to appear concerned. "Well, you know the drill. Take your complaint down the hall, and one of the officers will be happy to help you."

"Thank you as always, LaTesha," said Edgar in a fairly sarcastic tone. "You've been a great help."

"Your welcome, Mr. Polansky," she responded with a half-hearted grin. "Have a good day."

Once Edgar walked away, she pulled out her crossword puzzle book and went back to work on her nails.

"I'll say whatever it takes to get you away from my counter, you fat freak," she whispered to herself.

As Edgar was making his way down the hall, he heard loud voices coming from the Chief's office. Curious to what was going on, he decided to get up close to the door and eavesdrop on their conversation. Right away, Edgar recognized Bucky Morgan's voice. After all the debates and mud-slinging during the Mayoral election, it would not be a voice that Edgar would soon forget.

Back in Chief Zimmerman's office, the discussion between the two men had taken a turn in a disturbing direction.

Bucky's face was flushed with anger as he said, "I'm not sure I can accept such a defeatist attitude, Zimmerman. Do you know how hard it is to convince an entire town that there is no Reaper and that it's just some urban legend made up by either a few kids or some of the homeless population? I don't like lying to the community, but I can't take a chance on stirring up panic and chaos in our town. If word got out that this character was real, some locals may think they can do better than the police force and go after him themselves. And I sure as hell don't want a bunch of hillbilly vigilantes raising an uproar and creating more chaos and mayhem in our community than there already is!"

"I don't think you have to worry about that, Mayor. If that's what is troubling you, then maybe we should at least post a town curfew or put out a warning to anyone who happens to be out on the streets at night."

"Listen carefully," Bucky said, loosening his tie. "This town is looking at a major Real Estate boom once the mall project has been approved and gets underway. The last thing we need is a psychopathic arsonist stirring up trouble, or people fleeing town because they are afraid."

The old police captain was taken aback by Bucky's rudeness and became defensive. "For starters, we have no proof that the Reaper actually exists except for some alleged eyewitness accounts, and none of those have been by *credible* eyewitnesses. Secondly, we still don't have any evidence linking this spectre with the surge in fires."

Then the Captain stood up and started to put some papers away in his file cabinet as Bucky began to walk out of the office.

Captain Zimmerman turned around before Bucky exited and said, "I will keep you informed as long as it doesn't interfere with my investigation, Mayor. Once it becomes a problem or a distraction, I will handle things my own way...and that includes investigating Thomas Parker if I think it's necessary."

On the other side of the door where Edgar had been listening with earnest, he heard footsteps heading towards the door and quickly scampered away.

Bucky stepped out of the office and slammed the door behind him. He stood there for a moment, trying to calm himself down, and suddenly he looked over at Ken Johnson's desk. Ken glanced up from his paperwork and nodded to Bucky, who in turn, smiled back.

Bucky continued to walk toward the stairs leading to the second floor as he whispered, "If you won't give me the information I need, Captain Zimmerman, I'll get it from someone else."

As Bucky was leaving, Edgar Polansky reemerged from around the corner and stared as he watched his nemesis walk away. He watched Bucky with daggers in his eyes, his anger seething with each step Bucky took until he exited from view. A sneer appeared on Edgar's face as he shook his head in displeasure.

"So, Mr. Morgan," he uttered in a voice barely louder than a whisper, "it seems you have some skeletons in your closet after all. Keeping vital information from the town will ultimately be your downfall. I'll think of a way to get you, and when I do, I'll expose you for the liar and fraud you really are."

Chapter 27:

Be cautious of your Allies

Several days had gone by and Roger could not get Josh's words out of his mind. The idea that Bucky might have been keeping vital information from him was nagging in his thoughts. Bucky was Roger's best friend and he knew Bucky had always been completely honest with him in the past. Actually, Bucky was the most trustworthy person Roger knew. However, Roger also realized that Bucky's attitude had changed since he became Mayor, and for the first time, he conceded to the possibility that Bucky might not be the honest and trustworthy friend Roger had known for so many years.

Then, on Monday, September 12, just after 6 pm, Roger went over to Bucky's house knowing that Bucky would surely be home from work. Bucky always set aside Monday nights for 'family night,' and because they never went anywhere on 'family night,' Roger would be able to talk to him in private.

Roger remained deep in concentration during the drive to Bucky's house. He kept the radio off so he could think about his profound thoughts, and he was *still* debating what he was going to convey to his friend when he arrived and knocked on Bucky's front entrance, waiting for someone to answer the door.

After a few seconds, the doorknob slowly turned and Roger looked down to see a little boy answer the door.

"Hey Mikey!" he bellowed excitedly.

"Uncle Roger!" Mikey leaped into Roger's arms and gave him a welcoming hug.

Roger was surprised how big Mikey had become. Now at four years old, Mikey, with his mother's black hair and brown eyes, was quite tall for his age. Roger hadn't been over to Bucky's house since Bucky took over as Mayor nearly a year ago; he had only seen Mikey sporadically since then. That was a point which made Roger feel somewhat guilty about, especially since Roger is Mikey's godfather.

"Wow, Mikey!" Roger said, kneeling down. "You're getting nearly as big as your dad," he joked, "and you're probably almost as strong as him, too!"

Mikey smiled and laughed. "Nooo...but I am getting to be a big boy now. My mommy told me so. She showed me how to tie the laces to the new sneakers I got."

"That's great!" Roger's excitement suddenly subsided as he remembered that Mikey's birthday was last week. "I'm sorry I missed your birthday, bud. I had to...um."

Mikey interrupted Roger, possibly noticing him stumble his words as he searched for an excuse to say. "That's alright, Uncle Roger. I wish you could've been here, but I know how busy you've been. Thank you for the baseball glove you got me; I love it! I can't wait to play catch with my dad!"

Mikey was fairly smart for a four-year-old. He was very astute for his age, and he had such a way with words for a child not even in kindergarten yet. *He probably gets all that intelligence from his mother*, Roger mused to himself.

Roger stood up and rubbed Mikey's head, messing up his hair. "Oh, that's good. I wasn't sure if you would get it by the time of your party."

"Sure did!" yelled Mikey. "Aunt Holly dropped off my present before my party started. She couldn't stay though; she was on her way to work."

A big smile came across Roger's face. He was glad that Holly was in his life and she was always remembering the important events that Roger frequently seemed to forget.

"Well, buddy, if you ever want to learn how to throw a great curve ball, just ask your Uncle Roger. I used to be one of the best baseball pitchers at old Carthage High, and I can still strike out your dad every time we play...to this very day!"

Mikey giggled. "My dad told me you would say something like that."

Roger puffed out his chest and winked. "He did, did he? Well, speaking of your old man, is he here tonight?"

"Yeah, but I don't know where he is. You can ask my momma if you want. She's doing something in the kitchen."

"Thanks, little man. I think I will."

Roger stepped into the kitchen and Cristina was standing on a stool fumbling around with some Tupperware. As Roger watched Cristina putting dishes away, he thought how little Cristina had changed over the years. Her raven colored hair had no hint of gray (unlike her husband Bucky). The only noticeable change was that Cristina had kept some of the weight she had gained while pregnant for Mikey. She had a small belly as a reminder of the pregnancy; however, even with the little extra weight, she still had a near perfect body with flawlessly shaped legs.

The years had mellowed Cristina; becoming a wife and mother probably had contributed to that. Over time she had gone from being the "town bitch," as she was known around City Hall when she was on the city council, to being recognized as a devoted mother and a caring individual.

At one time, Roger had really disliked Cristina because of her attitude, but that was another aspect that had changed over the years. She and Roger had become good friends, and Cristina had become the one woman in town, other than Holly, he confided in whenever he needed someone to talk to, especially if he needed advice on what types of gifts to get Holly for holidays. However, Cristina still would get a little upset with Roger when he and Bucky would occasionally leave on one of their so-called investigative searches, or if the boys were out too late at Kitty's Bar.

Roger stood by the refrigerator for nearly three minutes before Cristina noticed that he was there. "Roger!" she said with enthusiasm. "This is a pleasant surprise! What brings you over here tonight?"

"Oh, nothing in particular. Holly is up to the college for a few hours. She has class tonight, and I had some spare time so I thought I'd stop by to say "hello" and see if Bucky was around." He glanced over to the stove, noticing the pots and pans next to the burners. "Um, I hope I'm not disrupting your dinner plans."

"No, we already finished eating," Cristina replied. "I'm just washing the dishes and putting them away."

Mikey hopped like a frog into the kitchen and stopped when he got beside Roger. Just then, Bucky opened up the back door near the kitchen table, coming in from taking out the garbage. He wiped his boots and immediately became aware of Roger standing in the middle of his kitchen. A smile, accompanied by a look of confusion, covered Bucky's face.

"Hey man, what are you doing here?" Bucky asked.

"I came to visit my godson," Roger answered, looking down at Mikey. Then he turned his attention to Bucky and said, "And I was wondering if you had a free moment to chat."

Bucky looked over at Cristina who simply shrugged her shoulders. "Sure, I have no plans," he answered.

"Um, do you mind if we talk in private?"

Bucky wasn't certain, but by the look in his eyes, he perceived that something was bothering Roger. "Okay, come with me."

Roger followed Bucky to the back end of the house where he had built an addition that was being used as a den. As Roger scoped out the room, his first impression was that it seemed more like a trophy room for all of Bucky's awards and achievements, rather than a den.

Instead of shelves filled with books and magazines, the room was wall papered with newspaper clippings that pertained to Bucky. The room even had its own fireplace, with a hand carved oak mantle and sports trophies lined all the way across it. However, resting upon the center of the mantle, there was a long wooden box, with strange markings etched across its side, which had white and gold striped candles placed on each side.

"What's in the box?" Roger asked, pointing to the mantle.

Bucky looked over to the mantle for a brief moment then diverted his eyes down upon his handcrafted mahogany desk.

"It's the dagger I got from Jim Draven when we had to go..." he paused for a moment. "When we had that incident at the waterfront a few years ago."

Roger nodded, knowing what Bucky meant; then he opened the box and looked. Inside was the dagger with its six-inch triangular steel blade. It had an ivory hilt, fashioned in the shape of a crucifix with the body of Christ wrapped around the end.

"You still have one of the daggers of Meggido?" he questioned. "What are you still holding onto that for? Do you need a memento from that night?"

"I keep it in case we ever need it again."

"Oh, I see." Roger closed the box. "What's with all those symbols on the box?"

"Those aren't symbols," Bucky answered, shuffling papers on his desk and trying to get off such a sensitive issue. "It's Latin. It says: 'Dispel the Dark Death; Go and Slay the Beast.' Well, that's what the antique dealer I bought it from told me."

A shiver flowed down Roger's spine and out his toes. After a moment of silence, he opted to change the topic. "So anyway, I came here to ask you what you know about this Reaper fellow. Or maybe I should ask you what it is that you are *allowed* to tell me." Roger laughed. "After all, I know how cryptic politicians can *really* be."

"There is nothing to say," Bucky stated in a matter-of-fact tone of voice.

There was something in the way Bucky quickly dismissed his question that bothered Roger. "You wouldn't be hiding anything from me, would you?" he prodded.

Bucky gasped, offended by the accusations. "How can you even ask me something like that?" he exclaimed. "You're the closest thing I've got to a brother, and I have always been straight with you!"

"I'd really like to believe that; really I would. But Bucky, you've changed since you've took over as Mayor. It seems to me that you are beginning to act evasive and calculating, just like most other politicians I've known."

"Have you gone mad?" Bucky screamed, slamming his hands upon his desk and quickly standing up. "You come here and ask me about some mythical urban legend and then you have the gall to question my integrity?"

The room suddenly became deathly quiet. Roger felt slightly embarrassed.

Bucky took a few deep breaths, hesitated, and continued. "What the hell have I ever done to get the third degree from you, huh? When have I ever been dishonest with you before?"

"You're right," Roger answered, lowering his head. "I don't have any right to come in here and start making insinuating accusations." Then a thought came to Roger's mind. "Let's just forget about it and talk about something else."

"Okay," said Bucky, sitting back down. "What *else* do you want to talk about?"

"Well, there is something else that I have always wanted to know the answer to but never had the nerve to ask you. However, since we're alone, and you have nothing to hide, would you like to tell me the truth about what happened during the election? There were many nasty rumors circling around that you were attempting to fix the election. Is there any truth to that?"

"No," Bucky stated bluntly. "It was just some vicious rumor started by Edgar Polansky's friends to try and ruin my reputation."

"Well, I guess it was good for you that no one took it seriously," commented Roger.

"Yeah, I suppose. Listen Roger, if I were you, I'd forget all about this Reaper nonsense," Bucky replied, changing the subject.

"Really, is that so?" he retorted with coolness in his tone. "Is that just some brotherly advice or an order from the Mayor?"

"Look, there's no need to get defensive, all I'm saying is…"

Roger cut him off in mid-sentence. "I'll take your suggestion under advisement, Bucky, but I don't think I can *forget* about it. You know how much I like a challenge!"

Bucky was taken aback and tried to smooth things out. "Hey, I didn't mean to come across as brusque or negative, I just think you should be more concerned with that pretty lady of yours. You'd be better off concentrating your time on getting that wedding you've been putting off planned and finally starting a family."

"Excuse me?" Roger remarked.

"C'mon, Rog. I really don't see a need to overreact and start investigating something as preposterous as a Reaper," Bucky said lightheartedly.

Roger's faced became flushed with anger and frustration. "You can't tell me what to do with my life, old friend. My father once told me that 'every man goes his own way.' If you're not going to help me investigate, make sure you don't interfere with *my* investigation and don't try to put obstacles in my way either!"

Bucky watched as Roger turned and walked out the den, slamming the door behind him. He sat in bewilderment, unsure of what just happened and wondering what Roger meant by that crack.

Shortly after Roger left Bucky's house, Bucky called the police department to see if there had been any new leads to the Reaper case, the town's fires, or Pat Jordan's mysterious file. When he eventually got through, LaTesha Prince answered the phone.

"Yeah, hello?" she yelled into the phone.

Bucky remained silent. For a moment, he thought he'd avoid her temper and simply hang up the phone.

"I'm sorry," LaTesha said in a calmer, more soothing voice. "This is the Carthage Police Department. How can I help you?"

"It sounds like you're having a bad day, LaTesha. Is everything alright?"

"Mayor Morgan!" she responded quickly, surprised and humiliated. "I am *SO* sorry about the way I answered the phone. Edgar Polansky was here again, and he was very rude!"

"Polansky was there again? What did he want?"

"I'm not sure what his dilemma was this time," she answered, her voice flustered. "All he said was that he wanted to talk to the Police Chief. When I told him Chief Zimmerman went home for the night, he immediately became irate and starting screaming at me. Edgar kept saying he wasn't going to leave here until he spoke to the Chief." LaTesha paused momentarily. "I'm not positive, but I think his tirade might've had something to do with you, sir."

"Oh, really? Well, what did you do?" Bucky asked in a troubled and curious tone.

"Nothing. Luckily, Ken Johnson came over before the situation escalated out of hand and escorted Edgar out of the building."

"Hmmm. That's quite interesting. Speaking of Officer Johnson, is he still there?"

"Yes he is, Mayor. He's back at his desk right now. Hold on and I'll transfer you over to his phone."

"Thank you, LaTesha."

A few seconds later, Ken picked up his phone. "Officer Johnson here. What can I do for ya?"

"Hello, Ken. It's Bucky. How are things going tonight? I heard you had a little commotion at the station earlier."

"Nothing I couldn't handle," he answered gruffly. "So, what do I owe for a phone call this time of night, Mr. Mayor?"

"I was wondering if you had any information for me."

"No, we still haven't found anything," Ken stated.

"Well, if you find *anything*, call me immediately. Remember, I told you it would be very beneficial on your part if you help me locate Pat Jordan's file. You just *may* get that promotion to Detective yet."

"Look Bucky, I'm grateful you talked to Chief Zimmerman on my behalf, and I'm not trying to tell you how to do your job; however, I don't understand why you're so anxious to find some alleged missing file. Maybe it would be better if you concentrated your efforts on something with a little more substance."

Bucky scratched his head. "I don't follow what you're hinting at."

"What I mean is, why look for some papers regarding an imaginary being when we already suspect that Thomas Parker is the likely arsonist?"

"Don't make accusations unless you have proof to back them up, Ken!" snapped Bucky. "If you were doing a more thorough job of investigating, you wouldn't have only *one* alleged suspect. What I'd really like to see is you get off your fat ass and broaden your search a little bit! And I would also like to get a little more cooperation on this matter, Ken," he uttered in a rather demanding tone.

"Don't tell me how to do my god damn job!" Ken shouted angrily. "Just remember, *Mayor*, you still owe me!"

"I do?" Bucky replied, sounding surprised. "For what?"

"Have you forgotten that I was the one who covered up that little fiasco for you during the election?"

Bucky said nothing.

"Oh, come on, Bucky. I'm sure you remember the scandal that you barely averted when certain members of your campaign committee got caught trying to fix some of the votes."

"Well, I appreciate your help," he answered back sarcastically, "but it was a moot point anyway. I already had enough votes to win the election by simply being the better candidate. Furthermore, I fired those individuals responsible for the ballot tampering the moment I found out what they were doing."

"Yeah, well, it still wouldn't look too good in the eyes of taxpayers and potential voters if they were to ever discover the truth about how it all went down."

"It would be wise to watch who you blackmail or threaten," said Bucky sternly. "I am not usually a violent person, but don't get me angry, Ken. You wouldn't like to be around me when I'm angry." Then there was a moment of silence. "Just get me the information I want, okay?"

"Yes sir, Mr. Mayor," Ken said condescendingly.

Bucky hung up the phone. He sat for a moment and waited for his heart and pulse to calm down. When his anger finally subsided, he got up and started to leave, but before he reached the door, the phone began to ring.

He rushed back over to his desk. "Boy, that was fast!" he said as he answered the phone.

"Um, excuse me," a woman's voice said. "I may have the wrong number. Is this Bucky Morgan?"

"Yes," Bucky said hesitantly, "this is Bucky. May I ask who this is?"

"This is Stacey Parker." Her voice sounded soft and distraught.

"Hello Stacey! Sorry about the way I answered the phone; I thought it was someone else calling me. A business call in fact."

"That's alright, Bucky. I've had people answer with a worse greeting than that before."

"I didn't recognize your voice; I haven't heard from you in a long time. I must say, this is quite unexpected, but then again, this sure has been a day full of unexpected surprises. Is there something you called for in particular, Stacey, or were you just calling to see how everything has been?"

"I'm sorry to be calling like this, but I didn't know who else to turn to," she said hurriedly. "I think there might be something wrong with Thomas."

Her words got Bucky's attention and he sat back down in his chair. "Take it easy, Stacey. Slow down and tell me what's going on."

"He has been acting very strange lately. I think it might be due to a letter that he received in the mail."

Bucky's curiosity began to grow. "A letter? What kind of letter, Stacey? What were the contents about?"

"I'm not exactly sure; he won't let me or anyone else look at it."

"He hasn't told you anything about it? Nothing at all?"

"The only thing he would tell me is that it has something to do with his time spent in Louisiana." Her words trailed off for a moment. "But I'd rather have him tell you more about the letter himself. That is really a part of Thomas's life I know nothing about, and I'm still a little shaky about this whole situation. Since that letter arrived in the mail, he has acted like a completely different individual."

Stacey let out a sigh. "I'm hoping if *you* talk to him, Thomas will voluntarily offer an explanation concerning this letter."

"Okay, Stacey, I'll come down sometime tomorrow," he said reassuringly. "Don't worry yourself too much about it; I'll talk to him and see what's wrong."

Stacey sounded relieved. "Thank you, Bucky. I knew I could count on you. You've been a real friend to Thomas over the years, and I know that he trusts you. If there is something bothering him, he may feel more comfortable talking to you about it than me."

Bucky hung up the phone and remained in his chair for a long time as he sat in silence. A plethora of thoughts flooded his mind and he mulled over them for quite a while. However, the one item that kept popping up over and over again was the letter Thomas received regarding the time he spent in Louisiana, the place of origin of the mysterious period in his life called "The Lost Years."

Chapter 28:

The "Lost Years" Revealed

The next morning, Bucky went to work a couple hours late. On his way to the office, Bucky stopped over to see the Parker family. Thomas sold his place on Bender Avenue shortly after the waterfront incident and now lived on the Baker Road, which was located on the West side of town. His current house was much older and smaller than his previous one; however, it was situated nicely along the Black River and was nearly a quarter-mile away from his closest neighbor. Most of all, it was far away from the sight of Bob Earle's old apartment and the constant reminder of the loss of his best friend.

As Bucky approached the house, he took an initial glance around the yard only to notice that nothing seemed out of the ordinary. The house stood in the drowsiness of a glum early morning, with dew glistening on the grass and the autumn sunlight pouring like molten gold over the weather-beaten cedar shingles of which the house had been built. A few songbirds splashed and chirped as they swam in the ceramic birdbath that stood in the middle of the front yard, and along the side of the house a few yellow butterflies drifted in the morning haze.

After knocking on the door several times, Stacey Parker, Thomas's wife, opened the door in her nightgown and bathrobe. She did not seem embarrassed at all about the fact that her nightgown was somewhat see-through and very revealing.

"Um, hello Stacey," Bucky uttered, trying not to stare. "Is Thomas here today?"

Stacey yawned and pointed behind her. "Thomas is outback in the tool shed doing some woodworking. Would you like to come and talk inside?"

"Uh, sure," he said with slight hesitation. "I'm sorry. What I meant to say was 'I'd love to come in.'"

Stacey turned and walked towards the couch as Bucky let himself in and closed the door behind him. He followed her into the living room, unable to keep himself from staring at her butt as her hips swayed in her translucent gown.

Stacey was a tall brunette with blue eyes, and her high cheekbones gave her the appearance that she may be of Native American heritage even though she was of German and French ancestry. At 5'9" she was quite taller than most women in town, and with an hourglass figure, she looked good in anything she wore. Her long well-formed legs, wide hips, and narrow waist contributed to her model-like features. In fact, one time in Kitty's Bar, Thomas had remarked that Stacey had done some modeling when she was a teenager.

Stacey was working as an exotic female dancer in a swinging nightclub in Syracuse when Thomas had met her. He spent many nights there trying to forget the pain of his divorce and the struggle he was going through to get custody of his kids. Stacey was in college at the time and working as an exotic dancer to help pay for her tuition. However, she had not been working there very long and she was getting tired of the depressing and nauseating atmosphere.

The late nights were affecting Stacey's grades and she was always nervous that another drunken idiot would try to grope and maul her, which in her opinion, seemed to happen much too frequently. Every night she would have to cope with the suffocating smell of raunchy cigars and cigarettes, a smell so rancid that it seemed to linger in her hair and clothes for weeks.

The life of an exotic dancer seemed exciting at first, but Stacey became disenchanted with the seedy bar scene after a couple years. She was happy, thrilled, and relieved when she met Thomas. Her whole life seemed to change for the better from then on. Nowadays she was content on living a much simpler life, staying at home during the day and taking care of their three children while working part-time at the local video store during the evening hours.

Bucky walked in and plopped down on one side of the oversized couch. Stacey moved the newspaper to the coffee table and sat on the opposite side of the sofa.

"I'm sorry I haven't been here in a long time," he uttered, his mouth feeling as though it was stuffed with cotton. "The job has been keeping me busy from morning 'til night."

"That's alright. It's been kind of hectic around here anyway, but now that things have calmed down, I am ready for visitors like you to stop by."

Bucky laughed uneasily. "So, how have the kids been?"

Stacey noticed how Bucky was trying to change the topic. She sat up straight, pulling her silk robe back over her shoulder. "They're doing fine. We just took Thomas's other kids to the airport a few weeks so they could go back home."

"Trudy and Jefferson were here from California?"

"Yup, they spent their whole summer vacation here and didn't leave until the end of August. They ended up missing the first few days of college, but they had a terrific time here, and I don't think they minded missing those couple of days all that much."

There was a long pause as Stacey stared coyly at Bucky, and Bucky feverishly trying to think of something to say. "So Stacey, you seemed very upset on the phone last night. Do you want to tell me what's going on?"

"It's Thomas." Her voice changed to a much more serious tone, and she sounded genuinely concerned. "He has been acting as if his mind is preoccupied ever since he got that letter in the mail. I don't know what it is that he keeps thinking about all the time, but whenever I or any of the kids ask him about his behavior, he just cuts us off and tells us there is nothing wrong. I'm getting so worried about him and what this strain may do to our relationship as well as his relationship with the kids."

"When did he receive the letter?" Bucky inquired.

"About two months ago," she answered, "but he would never show me what it said. I came across the letter yesterday when I was doing laundry; it was stuffed in his pants' pocket. I recognized it from the letterhead I saw when it arrived a couple of months ago. The way I figure it, if Thomas is still carrying it around after all this time, it may be the reason for his strange behavior. I wanted to open it and read what it said, but he has the entire envelope wrapped in scotch tape and I knew he would notice if I tried to look inside."

Bucky could only think about the fact that two months ago (when Thomas's letter arrived) was the same time frame when the latest outbreak of fires started. Then he remembered the night of the ferry incident five years ago and how Thomas conveniently showed up right before Mr. Ferr's office exploded. In his thoughts, Bucky began to wonder if Thomas really *was* capable of arson, and possibly murder.

After several more minutes of uncomfortable chit-chat, Bucky stepped outside and continued on to the back yard to talk to Thomas. So many questions began to arise in his mind, but most of all he wanted to ask Thomas about the period in his life he called "The Lost Years," a subject that Thomas never mentioned, and about the strange letter that he had been keeping to himself. Bucky was nervous when he approached the workshop. He did not know how to bring up either topic, and he wasn't sure how Thomas would react to his questions.

As Bucky got closer, he could hear Thomas hammering on something inside. On the outside, it looked like an ordinary shed, except the two tiny windows which seemed to be covered with some kind of canvas material to prevent anyone from looking inside. While crossing the yard, he noticed that Thomas's grass needed mowing. It was quite tall and thick, and with the heavy morning dew, Bucky's shoes were becoming damp.

Thomas was sitting on his stool and tinkering around with something on the workbench. Although his crippled hand was more mobile now than it had been in years, it still gave him problems. On the other hand, Thomas had endured several operations over the past couple of years to fix his hip and now was able to walk without a limp.

Since the night of the ferry service incident, Thomas's actions had become increasingly peculiar. Everyone knew that Thomas would be affected emotionally from the loss of his friend, Bob Earle, and his encounter with Mr. Ferr, but no one knew just how much. Although Thomas had held several jobs over the years since that happened, he was unable to keep any of them for very long. If it weren't for the trust fund his father left him after his death, Thomas would also be among the ranks of the homeless.

Over the past few years in particular, he had become more withdrawn from his friends and family. Thomas barely had any contact with Stacey in months and his reclusive attitude was frightening his children. He would spend long hours, late into the evening, in his workshop, and sometimes he would go for long walks that would last from late at night into the early hours of the morning. Lately, there had been many times when Stacey would wake up in the middle of the night only to find that Thomas was not lying beside her. She would look out the window and see the light on in Thomas's workshop, or in other instances, she didn't know where he was at all.

Bucky had butterflies in his stomach as he tapped gently on the glass of the workshop door.

"I see you out there!" Thomas yelled out, looking through the cracks in the wall. "Come on in, Bucky!"

Bucky stepped in and stood close to the doorway. As he entered the dimly lit wooden shed, he was a little overwhelmed at the condition of Thomas's shop. It was more than just a little cluttered and in disarray, or more to the point, a complete mess. Bucky gave a quick perusal around the area and was somewhat surprised at the bizarre newspaper clippings on the walls. There were also several books about the occults, black magic, witchcraft, and other strange titles mixed in with his shop manuals and construction building books—just the type of reading material the Unabomber would be proud of.

He wanted to ask Thomas about his strange collection of books and news clippings about disasters, local fires, and articles depicting people missing over the past several years, but he was there on other business. In particular, the letter Stacey was so worried about and why Thomas had been behaving so peculiar lately.

After several moments of silence, Thomas was beginning to get annoyed. "Christ," he moaned. "Don't just stand there, have a seat!"

Bucky's knees almost buckled as he made his way over to the stool. Bucky kept his eyes focused entirely on Thomas, watching as he just sat and tinkered with a used motor, which had its parts sprawled out across the workbench.

"Interesting shop you have here, Thomas," Bucky began. "You must spend hours out here. I see you have several projects started," he said as he glanced around, noticing more than a few half finished items.

When Bucky took a closer look, he saw several pairs of black high-top leather boots and a long, black overcoat hanging on a nail in the corner.

Strange thing to have in a workshop, Bucky thought.

"What brings you out here today, Bucky?" Thomas asked blithely, not lifting his eyes off the greasy machine parts.

"Oh, not much. I haven't been here in a while, and I thought I'd see what you've been up to."

Thomas lifted his head and took off his safety glasses. "Cut through the shit, Bucky. I may have been born at night, but it wasn't last night. We both know you could go to Kitty's Bar if you wanted to hang out with me. However, when you stop by my house early in the morning on your way to work, then I know you have a purpose."

"You're right," Bucky stated, his face becoming red with embarrassment. "I've forgotten how you can always tell when something's on my mind."

Thomas chuckled to himself. "Now that we've cleared the air, why don't you tell me what's really going on."

Bucky took several deep breaths, loosened his tie, and unbuttoned the top button on his shirt. "Okay, Thomas, I don't know any other way to bring it up, so here it is. Last night I got a call from Stacey."

Thomas interrupted him and his voice became firm. "What the hell is my wife calling you for?"

"She's worried about you, Thomas. We all are."

"Worried? What for?"

"Your behavior has been, well, less than normal. I know you've gone through some rough spots; we all have. But if you're having a difficult time handling a problem, then you should talk to someone about it."

Thomas's brow curled down and he looked as though he was extremely perturbed. "Get on with it, Bucky. What are you hinting around to?"

"Well, Stacey mentioned that you received a letter recently. A letter you wouldn't share with anyone in your house. She thinks this letter might be the reason for your recent preoccupation."

"So, my wife told you about my letter?" he said angrily. "That's none of her business!"

"As I already told you, Thomas, she's worried about you and the way you've been behaving lately. Listen to me; I know she only has your best intentions in mind. If there's something bothering you, you can talk to her, or you can always come to me about it. We're supposed to be good friends, and yet, there is so much of your past that you won't talk about. Maybe this would be a good time for us to be open and honest with each other, don't you think?"

Thomas set his tools down and sat on his work stool. "Alright," he paused and sighed. "That letter you're referring to is from a Southern mental hospital where I used to be a patient many years ago. They were just doing a checkup to see how I've been doing lately."

"A mental hospital?" Bucky stated in a confused tone. "I didn't know you were ever in a mental hospital. Why were you there?"

Thomas turned and looked away before he spoke. "I'm sorry, Bucky. I just can't talk about it. I don't want to rehash old memories about the worst time in my life."

"Does this have something to do with that period of time you call 'The Lost Years'?"

"Yeah, it does," he answered solemnly. Then Thomas got off his stool and began to pace around the room. "That was two years of a living hell that's better off staying in the past."

"Why won't you talk about it?" questioned Bucky. "All I know is that it was during that time period when you crippled your hand and the reason why you walked with a limp for so many years."

"Yeah," Thomas hesitated, staring off in a daze. "I had permanent damage to the ligaments in my hand, and my leg was broken in three places. It never did heal correctly. It's taken many years and many operations just to be able to walk without a limp anymore."

Bucky decided to move closer. He walked slowly over to the stool on the other side of the workbench and sat down.

"What happened to you, Thomas?" Bucky prodded.

"It has to do with a house I was renting in Louisiana," remarked Thomas. "I moved there right after I got out of the Air Force, and my first wife, Catherine, was still in California, taking care of the twins. Trudy and Jefferson were only a couple of months old at the time and they couldn't come to Louisiana until the house was ready for us to move into it. I'd gone to the house early so I could clean it from top to bottom before they arrived, and Catherine stayed behind to take care of all the final arrangements. She wanted to remain there so she could pack all of our stuff, back at our government housing in Sacramento, instead of having the moving company do it. She was always nitpicky about other people touching her belongings—especially her personal 'womanly' belongings."

"Okay, so what happened at the house?" Bucky inquired.

"Something I've never shared with anyone before. At least, no one other than the doctors at the mental hospital."

"C'mon, Thomas," Bucky spoke in a reassuring tone. "Please tell me."

Thomas nodded and rubbed the scar on his crippled hand as he spoke. "It's difficult to say just when I realized there was somethin' different about the house—somethin' evil. Certainly, the presence was there before I ever went inside or opened the shuttered windows. My dog, Socks, which was a golden retriever, refused to enter to place. When I finally dragged him in by his collar, he broke into a furious snarling and barking. His back constantly bristled with rage."

"How long was it before he calmed down?"

"He never did," Thomas responded. "This behavior happened on an almost endless basis. As the days went on, Socks continued to act strangely, as if terrified by something in the house. About a week after

I was there, I let him out so he could do his business, and Socks *never* came back."

Thomas stopped and took several deep breaths.

"Alright, so something in the house probably spooked your dog," Bucky said, sounding skeptical. "You're not the first person to have a pet run away. Besides, what you've just told me doesn't explain anything about what happened to you or why you think your house was haunted."

"Oh, believe me, Bucky, there's *much* more to my story," Thomas continued. "It seemed like such a peaceful, comfortable old place to raise a family, or so I thought. That is, except for one of the bedrooms upstairs. A few days after I was there, I was shaving at the mirror in my bedroom when I heard *it* for the first time."

Bucky's eyes narrowed. "It?"

"From somewhere within that room, from a few feet behind me, I heard a loud, shuddering sigh. Yet, when I glanced around, there was nobody there. However, when I turned back to continue shaving, there was a face I didn't recognize staring back at me. I figured I must've been hallucinating so I splashed cold water on my face, and when I looked again, I saw my own reflection."

"What did you do after that happened?" asked Bucky, his tone somewhat doubting.

Thomas stood and began pacing back and forth around the room. "Initially, nothing at all. I thought my overworked imagination was playing tricks on me. But then, on the night before my wife and the twins were to come join me, something happened; something that'd change my life from that point on."

Bucky remained silent, listening attentively to Thomas's astounding story.

"It was just after midnight. I was tossing and turning in bed, and suddenly I heard a piercing noise. I quickly sat up and saw something in the doorway to my bedroom. A spirit was there and it sort of swayed as if it didn't know what to do—then it just faded out. I hurriedly leaped out of bed and stood motionless in the middle of the room. I waited for a while, and when I didn't hear any more noises, I went over and shut the door. After a few more seconds of silence, I climbed back into bed. I was sweating and trembling all over, but I thought I'd be able to see it through."

Bucky's eyes were wide with curiosity. "And then what?"

"It wasn't long before I heard the ghost start up again. I sat straight up at stared intently at the door. Then the knob slowly turned, and the door opened wide. The ghost came right across the room, straight toward me, and grabbed at my flannel shirt."

"Are you saying the spirit actually *touched* you?"

"It sure as hell did, Bucky. I recognized it from the vision of the face I saw in the mirror. It looked like an old Indian man about sixty years old. His hair was torn and tangled, and the flesh was drooping off his face so I could see the bones and part of his teeth. He had no eyeballs and his nose looked like it had been ripped off his face."

Thomas's forehead began to sweat and he took several long, deep breaths before continuing his story. "My body was beginning to stiffen and I could barely breathe. I fell out of bed, trying to evade its touch, and quickly rose to my feet."

"Did the ghost disappear after that?" Bucky asked as he teetered on the edge of his seat.

"No. As a matter of fact, the ghost began to approach me. As fear and confusion took control, I began backing up to distance myself from the eerie sight. Without realizing what was happening or where I was going, I backed into the window. When the ghost reached towards me, I tripped and fell backwards through the glass panes and landed onto my car. I smashed through the windshield and messed up my body pretty bad."

"Holy damn, Thomas! It's a wonder you survived at all!"

"Yeah, I realize that, but while I was in the hospital, I told them about what I witnessed, and they put me in a mental hospital so I could 'come to terms with reality' as they put it. When I was released from the psych ward, I attempted to act normal and live an ordinary life. Unfortunately, I couldn't open up to my wife, and I became very distant toward her and the kids."

"Considering your mental state at the time, I'm surprised your wife would consider another move so soon."

Thomas grinned. "She had the best of intentions. You see, when we came back here to Carthage, Catherine was initially ecstatic. She thought that coming home would get me out of my slump; however, my father died of complications from his stroke shortly after I got here. I suffered from deep-seeded depression and withdrew from my family and friends even further. My behavior drove an even *deeper* wedge between Catherine and I until she couldn't take it anymore and left me."

Bucky began to empathize with Thomas and his voice became quieter as he spoke. "That must've left you completely devastated."

"Yeah, you could say that. I definitely hit rock bottom at that point. Ironically, instead of going over the edge, I motivated myself to move forward and do something with my life."

"Speaking of your father, Thomas, I'm kind of curious about something," Bucky said. "How'd people get in touch with you in Louisiana after your dad had a stroke?"

Thomas sat back down and tapped his finger on the workbench as he thought.

"Some of Dad's friends took the initiative to go through his address book and find my last known address. Then they contacted the Air Force base I was stationed at prior to my release from active duty. I had to give a forwarding address to the Air Force before I was discharged. That way, I'd still be able to receive correspondence from them and get my monthly disability checks."

"Disability?" Bucky inquired.

"I was in a truck accident while in the service," Thomas began to clarify, "and I suffered a head injury that left me with severe migraine headaches. Ever since then, I receive a thirty-percent disability pension."

"Thomas, I'd like to change the topic for a moment. There's something I need to ask you."

"Okay, I'm listening," Thomas retorted.

"Were you hanging out with Patrick Jordan on the night he died?"

Thomas was taken aback by Bucky's question. "I was at Kitty's Bar during the same time he was, but I wouldn't say we were 'hanging out' together. Why do ya ask?"

Bucky stared at Thomas, waiting to see what type of reaction Thomas would have to his comments. "I was informed by Chief Zimmerman that you may have been the last person to be seen with him before he died."

"Hey, I wasn't the last person to see him alive or even to talk to him. I know that for a fact. After I left the bar, I saw him standin' on the other side of the street talkin' to one of those homeless people. It was the same guy that reporter did a story on a short while ago."

"You mean Sam Cushman?"

"Yeah!" Thomas exclaimed. "That's his name. I saw Mayor Jordan talking to him, and then Pat handed the bum a package of some sort."

Bucky leaned closer. "What happened next?"

"Nothin'. Jordan just walked away."

"Well, what was in Jordan's hand?" Bucky asked. "Did you get a good view of the object he was holding?"

"Well, they were standing under a streetlight so I did get a good look at the shape and size of the package. It was thin and square-shaped, like he had a book wrapped up or something. It had writing on the outside that I couldn't see, but I did overhear Mayor Jordan tell the other man where the packet was to go."

"Oh yeah, and where was that?"

"He said it was to be sent out to Watertown. That was the last thing I heard."

Bucky became confused and paused for a moment to think. "Why would Patrick Jordan have asked a homeless man to mail a package for him that late at night?"

"I don't know," Thomas answered back, "but old man Jordan seemed pretty nervous when he left the bar. I don't know what happened to him, either. He seemed normal when he came in, but by the time he left, he seemed petrified."

"Petrified?" inquired Bucky.

Thomas's eyes lit up as if a light bulb went on in his head. "I wonder if that package was the supposed file Jordan was working on about the Reaper sightings."

"Don't know," replied Bucky nonchalantly. "It's never been confirmed to be more than a myth anyway. But I read in today's newspaper that the alleged file is rumored to be in the Carthage Library—that is, if it even exists."

A look of surprise covered Thomas's face. "The Carthage Library, huh?"

"That's what the writer of the article thinks anyway."

"That's a pretty bold assumption," Thomas replied, shaking his head. "I wonder what they hope to achieve by printing such nonsense."

Bucky began to wonder if he should've mentioned that little tidbit to Thomas and quickly changed the topic.

"Look, Thomas, thank you for confiding in me about your past. I know that couldn't have been easy for you."

"No, it certainly wasn't. But those memories have been haunting me for a long time, and truthfully, I probably needed to get that story off my chest."

An uncomfortable tension overtook the room as neither man knew what to say next.

Bucky, looking down at his feet and kicking some sawdust around, suddenly became aware of the time on his wristwatch.

"Damn it!" he exclaimed. "I've got to get going or I'm gonna be late. I hate to be rude and just leave, especially at a moment like this, but I've got the *only* set of keys to the building today. So, until I give LaTesha's set back to her, she doesn't have any way into our office."

"Oh, it's alright. It was good to take a trip down memory lane and all," Thomas said sarcastically, "but I kinda think I'm all tapped out on that topic for awhile."

As Bucky left, he felt sorry for Thomas and the suffering his friend had went through. However, Bucky wondered if all the stress and trauma Thomas endured over the years had damaged his psyche. Because he might not be stable, Bucky thought perhaps Thomas just *might* be behind the fires. Bucky also wondered if what Thomas told him about Patrick Jordan was the truth, or if he was telling him something to get Bucky off his back.

Chapter 29:

When your lies catch up to you

The long days passed into long nights, and in what seemed like an eternity, the horrible week was finally over. By Friday, Roger's guilt about his behavior at Bucky's house was beginning to get the best of him. On top of that, Holly was telling Roger for days that he should go back over there and apologize to Bucky. In his heart, Roger knew she was right; however, his pride would have to be swallowed for him to attempt an apology, and that had never been an easy task for him to do.

After many hours of debate, Roger decided to stop by Bucky's office after work to talk to him before he went home for the night. Roger was hoping he could apologize quickly and leave, and, therefore, he could relax and enjoy the weekend instead of being riddled with guilt.

On the other side of town, Josh Roberts was having an equally atrocious week. He hit a dead end on every lead he hunted down for his story, and his editor at the *Tribune* was on his case to come up with some earth-shaking material for the paper, which was nearly impossible in a small town like Carthage. Furthermore, Josh was already preoccupied with the Reaper piece he'd been working on, even though it seemed everyone else wanted to sweep the story under the rug and ignore it.

While Josh sat with his arms upon his desk and pulling at his hair, the *Tribune* editor, Ty Harris, had calmly waltzed into his office with a notepad in his hand.

"Sit up and look lively, Roberts. I've got some fascinating news to tell you!" bellowed Harris.

"What do you want, Ty?" Josh asked as he flopped backwards in his chair, looking like a beaten down man. "I'm not in the mood to argue with you right now. If you've got a gripe with me, hold it till tomorrow, okay?"

"I'm not here to criticize, Josh. I wanted to let you know that I just got off the phone with Edgar Polansky, and he told me quite an interesting story. It seems that he was at the Mayor's office earlier in the week and overheard Mayor Morgan and Police Chief Zimmerman talking."

Josh lifted his head in wonder. "Yeah, what did he overhear? How much of a pain in the ass they think Edgar really is?"

"You're just full of humor today, aren't you, smart ass?" Ty snapped back. "Actually, it had something to do with the existence of the Reaper and trying to cover it up so the town council can preserve their precious real estate project. As you well know, if this project goes through, there will be big bucks to be made by many people, not to mention feathers in some people's caps. Not everyone is aware the mall project might possibly be coming to town, but we need more information before we can print a word."

Ty realized that he had gone off on a tangent and opted to get back on track. "Well, anyway, back to the scuttlebutt we got from Edgar. Now get this, Edgar didn't know what to do with the information he found out, so he called the newspaper and told *me* what it was he overheard Bucky and the Police Chief talking about. I figured this was a big story, and I'd come over to your office and tell you that I'd like *you* to get on the story."

Josh looked puzzled. "Why me? After all, you are always criticizing my work."

"Even though I may not agree with your topics and perspective all the time, you are still the best writer on staff. You have a comprehensive understanding with words these other slackers just don't possess."

A slight smile came across Josh's face as Ty pulled out a notepad and his reading glasses.

"So, do you want to hear what I have or not?" Ty asked.

"Sure," Josh responded, pushing his chair away from the desk and leaning back with his feet upon the desk. "Let's hear it."

"Very well then." Ty opened up his reporter's notepad and began going over his comments. "Edgar said that he tried to talk to Chief Zimmerman earlier in the week. He was going to confront the Chief about the conversation he overheard between him and the Mayor discussing the whereabouts of Patrick Jordan's missing file.

Unfortunately, when Edgar got to the police station, the receptionist wouldn't let him through. After repeated calls to the Chief throughout the week that went nowhere, Edgar decided to call the *Tribune* instead and tell *me* the story."

"There is no story," Josh butted in. "I've already talked to one of my connections, and he just happens to be close friends with the Mayor. My contact told me he's discussed the topic with Mayor Morgan and was informed there is positively *no* file."

"That may be, but that's not the only piece of information Edgar told me."

"Oh yeah? There's more, huh? Coming from a crackpot like Polansky, it doesn't surprise me all that much."

"Apparently, he also overheard them mention that the police suspect Thomas Parker is the Reaper, or at the very least, responsible for setting the fires. That's something they haven't released to the press or the public. I want to know why they have been keeping that a secret."

"All this sounds interesting, it really does. However, I don't see where there's anything *really* substantial to get excited over. Polansky has provided us with tips in the past that have turned out to be less than useful before, and I don't plan on being duped again."

Ty ripped the pages from his notepad, slamming them down on top of Josh's desk. "Look, you need this one, Josh. Take my word on it. Your work has been a little lacking lately. You haven't hit the front pages in months, and this, this is front page material!"

Josh snatched the papers off his desk and held them out in front of him.

"This is a waste of my time, that's what it is!" he stated in a brusque tone.

"Don't give me any attitude on this, Roberts. I'm still getting heat from the police department about your last infamous story. You know which one I'm referring to; that nice little ditty about the corruption within the police ranks. That story was the last time you hit the front page; let's hope it won't be the *very* last."

"What's that supposed to mean?"

"The bottom line is…" Ty took a deep breath. "If you don't start producing some quality work in the next thirty days, you're outta here!"

Meanwhile, Bucky was in his office at City Hall. His face looked tired, his soft blue eyes bloodshot behind his glasses, as though he had been staring at a computer screen for hours without a break. The stress of the job was really getting the best of him lately, sapping his energy and weakening his optimism.

Roger walked into City Hall and waved to LaTesha before heading up the stairs. Slowly, he edged into Bucky's office, looking shamefaced. Then, watching Bucky's tense, robotic motion, he began to feel pity.

"Bucky?" He gave him a tense, worried smile. "Are you all right, Bucky?"

Bucky took off his glasses and rubbed his eyes. "Hey Roger!" he said, hopping out of his chair and tucking in his shirt to try to make himself look more respectable. "This is an unexpected visit. What brings you down here tonight?"

"Well, I felt really bad about how we ended our conversation the other night. I said some things..." He shook his head. "It isn't that I don't trust you anymore..."

"You don't need to say anything, bud. It's all water under the bridge."

Roger's gaze shifted to the floor, trying not to make eye contact with Bucky. "Well, I'm glad you didn't take my comments to heart, but I still feel is though I should apologize for my rude behavior."

Back at the *Tribune*, Josh was alone in his office once again, but unlike before when he sat in quiet, this time he was going over the information that Ty had laid out in front of him. After staring at the pages until his eyes began to hurt, Josh suddenly had an urge to call Roger on his cell phone to tell him everything that Ty had said.

While Roger and Bucky were talking, a loud ringing abruptly came out of Roger's rear end. "Excuse me for a second, Bucky. I better answer my cell phone."

"Take your time," Bucky answered, shuffling papers and other miscellaneous items into a desk drawer. "It'll give me a few moments to clean some of this clutter off my desk."

Roger reached into his back pocket and pulled out his phone. "Hello," he answered in a jovial tone. "Roger here!"

"Roger!" Josh screamed into the phone. "I'm glad I could reach you! Listen, I got some information from my editor about your friend the Mayor and the Chief of Police," he said hastily. "I'd like to get together to talk to you; I think your pal might be keeping some things from you."

"Really?" Roger said in a hushed voice. "Like what?"

"Did you know that our good ol' Mayor and Police Chief were overheard to be discussing the Reaper case in detail and even named Thomas Parker as a suspect?"

Roger turned away and whispered softly so Bucky could not hear his conversation. "I can't really discuss that at this moment. I'm with Bucky right now."

"That's great! Can you talk to him and see what, if any, of the information Ty just told me is true. I've tried to set up an appointment several times in the past to get a private interview with the Mayor, but his secretary keeps ignoring my requests."

Roger looked over at Bucky; suddenly his heart and mind were filled with doubt. Then he remembered something his brother, Paul, once told him, 'The seeds of doubt grow bitter fruit.'

"Hey!" Josh yelled into the phone, regaining Roger's attention. "You didn't answer me. Will you talk to him and see if he *really* knows something about the Reaper?"

"I'll see what I can do, but how do I get him on the subject of the Reaper?" asked Roger.

"I don't know. You're clever enough to be resourceful, why don't you create some fictitious story about the Reaper." Josh suggested. "Tell him that he has struck again and then ask him if he has any thoughts."

"All right, Josh," Roger reluctantly agreed. "I'll see what I can do. If he's hiding something, I can get it out of him."

Josh knew he had chosen well when he had picked Roger Fasick for a partner. For the young man was serious, yet affable; friendly, yet discreet.

Roger hung up the phone, placed it back in his pocket, and walked over to Bucky.

"Is everything okay?" Bucky asked. "It seemed like an important call."

"Actually, I just got some intriguing news." Roger stopped. His eyes moved rapidly around the room as he quickly pondered something to say. Finally, his eyes abruptly stopped as he saw a distant barn silo from outside the office window. Suddenly, he had an idea.

"That call was from a friend of mine from work. He stated that there was another fire at a farm near his house—just outside of town. One of his neighbors seems to think they saw the Reaper hanging around there before the farmhouse and barn went up in flames."

"Really!" Bucky said, genuinely surprised. "When was that?"

"Um...I think my friend said the fire occurred around eleven o'clock this morning," Roger answered.

Bucky turned around so that his backside was to Roger. "So, it couldn't have been Thomas. At least, I don't think so," Bucky said in a whisper, as if speaking to himself. "I'm almost positive Stacey said Thomas was home with her when I called their house earlier today."

"Thomas?" Roger said. "What are you talking about?"

Bucky snapped out of his thoughts and turned toward Roger. "Uh...yeah."

Bucky inhaled deep and let out a sigh. His head and shoulders seemed to droop as well.

"I've been collaborating with some of the officers in the police department. We've been looking for the file our former Mayor kept on the Reaper sightings and the town's fires." Bucky's voice was getting progressively softer. "I had a meeting with Chief Zimmerman recently and he believes Thomas Parker is a likely suspect in all of this."

"What?" Roger asked with agitation in his voice. "You told me there is no file and the Reaper was just an Urban Legend!" Roger bit hard and said, "Don't tell me you're working with Ken Johnson—he has a history of being the most crooked cop in the entire department!"

After a prolonged silence, Bucky answered, "I didn't feel like I had any other option than to seek help from inside the department. And Ken may have a questionable reputation, but his skills are the best I've seen."

"No other option?" hollered Roger. "Are you serious? You could've asked for help from me—after all, I *do* work for a private investigative agency! And if that wasn't good enough, your cousin, Grant, works for the police department in Watertown!"

Bucky decided to come clean since he knew he was caught in a lie. "I'm sorry I lied to you, but I was only doing it for your own good."

Roger's once shameful expression was nothing more than a memory. Now, his cheeks burned with intense anger and his stone-faced expression showed anything but guilt or compassion.

"I stood up for you, Bucky!" he roared. "How could you lie to me?"

Bucky became demoralized and tried pleading with his friend. "Roger, you don't understand...I had to keep this a secret! There's more at stake here than just my reputation, your feelings, or acknowledging some unsubstantiated sightings of someone running around dressed for Halloween and allegedly setting fires."

Bucky's voice became more desperate as he tried to convince Roger. His longtime friend stood silent with his arms crossed.

"First of all, no one has proven any of this; not the existence of the so-called 'Reaper File,' or the existence of the Reaper himself. And most importantly, I had to think about the panic it would cause and how it might drive people and businesses away from town. I can't emphasize enough the need to keep this under wraps until we prove the existence of a Reaper or catch the person that is responsible for the fires."

Roger let out a huff but did not utter a word.

Bucky leaned forward and placed his hand gently on Roger's shoulder. "You've got to trust me, Roger. I know what I'm doing."

"Like hell you do!" Roger hollered. "You're just covering your ass so that the mall project will get underway!" Roger grabbed Bucky by the collar and glared directly into his eyes. "What other things have you kept hidden from me over the years?" he grumbled; his jaw clenched in anger. "How many other times have you lied to me?"

In an abrupt rush of memories, Bucky suddenly remembered the time he found the sales receipt for a home-pregnancy test when Roger's ex-girlfriend, Nellie Spencer, walked out and left town several years ago. However, Bucky quickly decided that even though he *did* keep that from Roger in the past, it was still a topic that should be brought up at a later date and time.

"There's nothing else," mumbled Bucky, unable to look Roger in the eyes.

Roger noticed the slight hesitation before Bucky's response. "I don't believe you!" he snarled.

Then he pulled his arm straight back and thrust forward, punching Bucky in the mouth and sending him downward to the ground. Bucky landed hard on the side of his face, smacking his head against a filing cabinet in the process. The hard surface provided no cushion against his cheekbone, and his lip split against the tiled floor.

"Just for the record," continued Roger as he started to walk towards the exit. "I made the whole story up about the farm fire and the Reaper. I received a tip that you might know more about the Reaper case than you were telling me, and I had to find out for myself if that were true."

Dazed and unsteady, Bucky managed to roll onto his side and wipe the dripping blood from his lip as he tried to regain his composure. Although his jaw was in severe pain, he still attempted to blurt out a few words as Roger was walking away. Unfortunately,

Bucky's voice was so garbled that Roger didn't hear a single word he was trying to say.

Roger stopped halfway outside the door and turned around. "Since you've become Mayor, I don't even know you anymore, Bucky. What has happened to my *best friend*? All I see now is just some petty excuse for a man."

After Roger left, Bucky made his way to his desk chair and plopped down, rubbing his chin and neck. He remained there for a while, thinking to himself and contemplating what just happened between him and his longtime friend.

As he turned to glance out his office window, he saw Roger's automobile headlights pull away from the parking lot. In that brief flash, the headlights washed over the old barn that stood out back and the trees beyond it.

It was there, behind the barn and not far away from the trees, that the lights momentarily illuminated a lone figure, a man who stood near one of the nature trails. Bucky wasn't positive, but the person appeared to be that of Tim Matthews, walking by the riverbank and carrying a duffel bag. However, the hour was getting dark and the fog had started to roll in, making it quite difficult for Bucky to make out shapes—especially faces.

Roger was driving home, feeling confused and raged all at the same time. He was uncertain what had just taken place with his oldest friend, Bucky. All Roger knew for sure was he definitely wasn't in *any* condition to discuss it with anyone right then.

Just as he was accelerating down one of Carthage's back streets, his cell phone rang. "What do you want?" he asked, speaking forcibly into the phone.

"Whoa! Calm down, bud. This is Josh; I just wanted to hear how your conversation with Bucky went. Did you learn anything new?"

"Yeah, I guess you could say that," he groaned.

"Great! Like what?"

"For starters, I learned my best friend is a liar!"

"Uh, sorry to hear that, Rog...but what did he say about the Reaper and the fires?"

"Look, Josh, I don't mean to be rude, but things didn't go very well and I'm not in any mood to chat right now. If you want some information from *your* Mayor, you're going to have to ask him yourself. I don't want anything to do with him. And besides, anything I tell you would be pure hearsay. You couldn't print any of this speculation without a chance of being sued. I'm sorry; I just can't help you."

"Okay, Roger. I can tell you're too upset to talk about this right now," Josh said in a quieter tone of voice, not wanting to distress Roger any further or put any unwanted pressure on him to reveal what had happened. "Maybe later you'll feel up to talking. Why don't you call me when you calm down?" he suggested. "You know the number to my cell; I'll be at my office until late."

"I can't promise anything," Roger answered back. "I'll see." Then he shut off his cell phone and stared blankly ahead, a million thoughts on his mind.

Once he arrived home, Roger hastily pulled into the driveway. He was so stressed that he slammed the car door and threw his prized cell phone to the ground, breaking it into several pieces. He stared at it for a few seconds; then he grumbled some obscenities as he walked into the house.

"What's wrong, Hun?" asked Holly.

"Sorry, babe, but I don't feel very talkative right now."

Holly moved over to give Roger an affectionate hug. "I don't like seeing you like this." She brought her arms up and over his shoulders, and then she gave him a passionate peck on the right cheek. "Didn't you go talk to Bucky tonight?"

"Yeah, I went to see Bucky all right!" Roger said, raising his voice and pulling back from her embrace.

"Oh, I take it you didn't apologize to Bucky for your ugly attitude the other day."

Roger began pacing back and forth. "On the contrary, I went there and apologized for being sarcastic and accusing him of withholding information…only to discover I was right all along!"

"I'm sorry you're in such a wicked mood," she said in a voice barely higher than a whisper. "Do you want me to help you feel better?"

Roger let out some air and started to calm down. "How are you going to do that?"

Holly walked seductively up to him and put her arms back around his shoulders. "I thought I'd make your favorite dinner tonight, and then I'd run some water in the tub so we can take a hot prolonged bath while I read you '*The Cat in the Hat.*'"

"Very funny," chuckled Roger. "Thanks for the offer, but I think I've already read that book before."

Holly playfully stared him in the eyes. "I don't think you've seen my adaptation yet."

He walked over to her, wrapping his arms around her tight waist, and with a kiss, she mellowed his anger. He relaxed into her, and for a brief moment, she pulled back to gaze into his eyes. She reached down and squeezed his hand hard, and then without saying a word, they journeyed upstairs, closing the bedroom door behind them.

Keeping her hand tightly in his, Roger tugged her into his chest. There, he reached up under her shirt and unhooked her black, lace bra. Still holding her close to his body with a warm grasp on her lower back, Roger lifted Holly off her feet and carried her over to the edge of the bed. She sank onto the plush mattress with a sigh. After removing his shirt, Roger laid upon the bed, relaxing into her arms and letting the quietness in the air settle him, too.

"Make love to me," Holly whispered into his ear.

Roger turned and gazed deeply into her eyes. "With all my heart."

He nibbled on her lip and pulled her shirt over her head. Leaning forward, Roger kissed her, gently at first, and then a little harder as he filled her mouth with his tongue. The way his hot breath felt upon her skin, and the way his mouth teased her breasts made her crave him more.

Roger made love to her, keeping his eyes open to watch their bodies come together. Roger's hard, rough body was a direct contrast to Holly's smooth, delicate one, but they joined as one just the same. He plunged into her, thrusting himself hard and fast until the wild passion inside of him had been satisfied.

As if to prolong the moment, Roger held Holly's body close and still against his, remaining motionless himself. Finally, exhaustion made them relax their grasp upon each other, and they rested in a cuddling embrace.

They laid in bed and caressed for nearly an hour. On the nightstand, a copy of 'The Cat in the Hat' rested under a red and white striped Dr. Seuss hat made out of felt. A smile appeared on Roger's face, a look of complete content. He was happy. A short time ago, he was so angry that he was having difficulty breathing, but all that changed with Holly's touch. She could always soothe him when he needed it, and as Roger looked down upon his chest, he knew that he wanted her in his life forever.

"Holly…" Roger began.

"Yeah, babe," she said, smiling.

"I love you," he stated.

"Well, that's good," she answered with a sarcastic laugh. "I'd hate to think this was a one-way relationship."

"No, I mean it. I *really* love you, and I always want to have you in my life. You're the best thing that's ever happened to me."

Turning to face Roger, Holly's expression became much more serious like. "Hey, Hun, I feel the same way. I *really* do love you, with all my heart." Then she gave him a half-grin and said, "What's with all the sentiment anyway? You're not setting me up for some bad news, are you?"

"No, nothing like that." Roger grabbed her hand and stroked her fingers. "I guess what I'm trying to say is, 'Holly, will you marry me?'"

Holly jumped out of bed, screaming in excitement and hopping around like a little kid at the circus. "Are you serious?" It was more of a statement rather than a question. "I would love to marry you! Whenever you are ready to pick a wedding date, it's perfectly fine with me. I've been hoping for this moment for a long time. I want this to be the most perfect day for *both* of us!"

"I'm sure it will, babe. You can trust me on that. I'll make it perfect. However, I think it would be very special if *you* were to pick the date. I'll walk down that church aisle tomorrow if you'd like!" he bellowed.

"Um, well, I'm glad you're so eager, Mr. McBeaver. But that's not how a wedding works. There's a lot of preparation that's involved." She saw the confused look on Roger's face. "Never mind, I won't even begin to tell you how much work it is, just trust me."

Holly went over to the calendar on the wall and began flipping through the months. She stopped on a page and pointed.

"Here!" she stated proudly. "Next summer on Sunday, August 20. That seems like a perfect fit."

Then she hopped back into bed and snuggled up close to Roger, gazing into his eyes. "Maybe we should start practicing for the honeymoon," she said slyly.

Roger smiled back and reached over to turn off the lamp.

Chapter 30:

Consequence of Rashness

The following month went by without any major catastrophes, and, as the days stretched into October, it seemed as though maybe the worst of times for Carthage had finally subsided. Bucky was still feeling angry with himself for deceiving his old friend, Roger.

Bucky wished he could think of some way to make amends for lying to him, and an old saying his grandfather used to say came to mind, 'When you tell the truth, you never have to remember what you said.' The more Bucky dwelled on the whole jumbled mess, the more he realized that it could have all been avoided if he had only been straight with his closest friend. He knew Roger could be discreet and keep whatever he was told confidential.

Bucky was hoping his long friendship with Roger would overcome the bad feelings between them after their last meeting. It did bother Bucky, however, that Roger hadn't returned any of the telephone calls he'd made in an attempt to apologize. Bucky hoped it was just because Roger was busy, not because he was still provoked with him.

It was the weekend before Halloween, and Bucky was at home with Cristina and Mikey. They had an early dinner that night, and Bucky finished putting the dishes away from dinner. After that task was completed, Bucky began getting ready to go into town to get them some snack foods to munch on because they were planning a relaxing night on the couch, huddling close under a blanket while watching a movie. Cristina had some transcription work left to finish; therefore,

Bucky was nominated to run to the store to get the snacks and pick out a movie.

Cristina was sitting on the ottoman sorting out some coupons on the coffee table and naming off some grocery items for Bucky to purchase; all the while, he was making his own list of things to get and not really paying attention to what she was saying. Then, Cristina said something that got his attention.

"Bucky, do you know if Celeste is still in town visiting her folks?"

"I don't know," he replied, somewhat surprised by her question. "I remember she told us what her plans were when the three of us went to dinner the other night, but I'm not sure if she said she was going to be in town for one week or two. Why do you ask?"

"Well, I was thinking of calling her up and asking if she'd like to go shopping tomorrow." Then she paused and turned toward Bucky. "Y'know, it's too bad Celeste doesn't have someone special in her life."

"What's going through that pretty little head of yours?"

"Well, if she did, we could invite them over for drinks and conversation, take in a dinner together sometime, or even go on one of those couples getaway weekends—just the four of us. Wouldn't that be great?"

"Yeah, that's just what guys wanna do on their weekends off from work," Bucky responded, rather sarcastically.

Bucky continued to write his list for the store. After a few moments, he put down his pen and looked up at Cristina. "Now that I think about it, I remember Celeste telling me earlier this summer that she's gone on some dates over the past few years but hasn't had a serious relationship since Paul died."

"Do you mean Paul Fasick?" she questioned.

"Of course," Bucky stated bluntly. "What other Paul would I be talking about?"

Cristina shrugged her shoulders. "I'm just surprised that's all. I mean, that was over ten years ago."

"Well, Paul was her first love. It's hard to get over such a traumatizing event."

"Hmm," she mused to herself. "Perhaps I can help introduce Celeste to a man. In fact, maybe we'll go to lunch at the Superior Restaurant. If I remember correctly, the Superior is particularly busy on the weekends, and I'm sure there'll be plenty of men hanging around there for her to check out."

"Is that the only reason you want to go to lunch?" inquired Bucky. "So you can find her a date?"

"No, that's not the only reason for going to the Superior. I haven't been there in a few weeks and I really like their Sunday specials. Besides, I enjoy Celeste's company, and little Mikey sure likes her a lot."

"Well, I'm not sure I like your methods, but overall, that sounds like a great idea. That would give me some alone time to put all of the lawn ornaments in the shed before the weather changes."

"And while you're outside, I would like you to put the picnic tables away, take down the screen tent, remove the gutters from the house, and put the sitting bench inside the garage."

Bucky's eyes got big and his expression turned to shock. "Whoa, you're compiling quite the long list of 'hunny-do' chores for me, don't you think?"

"No," Cristina chuckled, "but I'm sure I'll think of some more later."

Bucky walked over to the coat rack and grabbed his jacket. "I'll be right back," he grunted as he slipped on his sneakers, "I'm going to go start the Blazer and let the engine warm up for a few moments."

Mikey, who was playing on the floor, put down his toys that he was playing with in the living room and made his way over to his mom. She put down her coupons, stood up, and picked Mikey up in her arms. Mikey smiled and gave her a hug, squeezing tightly. Then, still holding on to him, they went to the window and watched as Bucky pulled his tan-colored Chevy Blazer from the garage, picked up some of Mikey's toys off the ground, and placed them off to the side of the house.

As they were watching Bucky through the window, Cristina turned and put her face close to Mikey's, rubbing his nose with hers.

Cris gave him a kiss on the forehead and said, "Hey Mikey, I have to do some transcription for awhile, but when I'm done, we can do anything you'd like. How about you color me some of your famous pictures while I work, okay? By the time you finish, I should be finished too!"

"Okay, Mommy. I'll get started right away. They'll be really good, you'll see!"

Mikey got down and ran over to turn off the television before departing to his room. Cristina went into her bedroom, sat down at the computer and put her headset on to begin some transcription work.

Bucky entered from the front door and his body jerked as a cold chill ran down his back. While the door leading outside was still partially open, and Bucky was busy taking off his coat, the family cat, a large white longhaired Himalayan named Zack, slipped outside. Unfortunately, the cat went by unnoticed and Bucky closed the door behind him.

After grabbing his shopping list off the table, Bucky walked into Mikey's bedroom. "Hey, bud, I'm leaving now. What are you going to do while I'm gone?"

"I'm going to color some pictures until momma gets done typing. Then we're going to play together."

"Well, you can come with me if you want. Then you won't have to stay in your room by yourself the whole time. We can even stop and see if the doughnut shop is open if you want. Would you like that, sport?"

Mikey perked up and he smiled wide. "Yeah! Let's go!"

Mikey jumped up off the floor and sprung onto his dad's back. Bucky took him to the coat rack to put Mikey's sneakers and jacket on him.

When they both finished getting their gear on, Bucky yelled to Cristina, "I'm leaving now, Hun."

"Okay," she replied, not listening carefully. "Have fun."

"By the way, I'm taking Mikey with me," Bucky added. "That way, neither of us will be distracting you. I'll rent an extra movie for him to watch and probably pick up a large bag of popcorn while I'm there, too. We'll be back in a couple hours."

Mikey finished zipping up his jacket and opened up the door, hopping down on the steps. Before Bucky left the house, he yelled out, "And try not to forget about the beef roast simmering in the oven! I'm going to make a stew with it later on this evening; that's supposed to be our dinner for tomorrow night!" Then he looked down at Mikey. "That is, if Daddy can get this new recipe I got from work to taste good."

Cristina, who was busy concentrating on her transcription, heard nothing more than a muffled voice as she tried to focus on the task at hand. In truth, with her headphones on, it was extremely difficult for Cristina to hear *anything* very clearly.

"Uh huh." she answered, continuing to type away on the keyboard and not paying attention to what he said or what she was agreeing to.

In the early 1950s, during the Korean conflict, Carthage had around thirty bars, saloons, and hotels; unusual for a community of only 3500 residents—which led to the town being nicknamed "Sin Town." Back then, patrons could stagger out of one bar and fall down in another.

Over the years, most of the taverns have since closed down, and all of the hotels have left the area also, leaving Carthage with little of its history and heritage in tact.

Nowadays, only four bars remained in town, with Liberty Street hosting two: '*Kitty's Bar*,' which was owned by Kitty Dunn, and across the street was '*Wally's Pub*,' owned by Wally Turck. Kitty's Bar was the most popular because it catered more to the likes of the younger crowd, whereas Wally's was geared more for the over forty age group and the town's blue-collar workers who wanted to relax after a hard night on the job.

On this particular afternoon, however, the bars seemed to swell with customers early on. By four o'clock, Kitty's Bar was packed to near capacity with individuals who just got of work and wanted a drink to celebrate the weekend.

It was around a quarter after five when the phone rang at Kitty's Bar and Miss Kitty answered the phone from her office in the back of the kitchen.

"Hello, Kitty's Bar," she said. "How can I help you?"

"Um, Miss Kitty," a low voice said. "This is Tim."

"Tim!" she screamed. "Where are you? Your shift starts in fifteen minutes, and you know that you're supposed to come a few minutes early to check your supplies. Please tell me you're on your way right now!"

"Well, actually, I'm feeling kind of sick tonight, and I won't be coming in for my shift at five-thirty."

This was *not* what Miss Kitty wanted to hear after the hectic day she had, and in a strained tone, she said, "Tim, this is the second time this week and the fifth time this month. Tell me, Tim, don't you like your job here?"

Tim answered shyly. "Yes, of course I like my job, and I *need* my job too. It's just that I haven't been feeling well lately, but I'll try to make it up to you and Holly. I promise."

In a little less agitated response, Miss Kitty answered, "Okay, Tim, but I want you here for your shift when you're scheduled to be, and I want less excuses from now on. And for God's sake, go to the doctor's office and get a thorough check-up. You're too young to be having all these medical problems."

Miss Kitty hung up the phone and went over to Holly. "I have some bad news," she said in a glum voice. "Can you guess what it is?"

Holly put her hands on her hips and took a deep breath. "Don't tell me Tim called in again!"

"Yeah, I'm sorry, Hun. This might mean you'll have to work a double, or at least until I can find a replacement."

"That's alright, Miss Kitty. Besides, I usually work till six o'clock anyway and it will give me a few extra hours of pay and tips."

Miss Kitty looked at Holly and gave her a sympathetic smile. "Thanks, Holly! You're a gem! Do you need anything?"

"Just give me a few minutes to get away so I can call my house to let Roger know what's going on. May I use your office, Miss Kitty?"

"No problem, Holly."

Within five minutes, Holly had returned from Miss Kitty's desk. Unfortunately, her look of disappointment didn't give Miss Kitty a promising feeling that things went well.

"Well, I can't reach Roger to let him know that I might be late tonight," Holly said in a depressed tone.

"Why not?" asked Miss Kitty. "Are our phones out of order again?"

"No, it's not that. Roger's not home right now, and our answering machine is broke so I can't leave him a message either. I also needed to get my professor's phone number so I can call her to let her know that I probably won't be in class tonight. Class starts at six-thirty, and there's no way I'll be able to get there by then."

"Well, what time does Roger normally work till?" Miss Kitty asked.

"He got off work at four o'clock. I think he said something about going over to the Cellular Communications store to buy another cell phone for us. That way, we could avoid situations like this one." Then she sighed. "Oh well, I suppose I'll try him again in a little while."

Several moments passed by as Miss Kitty and Holly leaned over and rested their arms upon the bar without saying a word to each other.

"I think I missed my true calling in life," Holly said, staring out at all the customers.

"Really," Miss Kitty responded. "And what is your true calling?"

Holly shifted her attention to Miss Kitty and smiled. "I don't know, but I'd hate to think I was born to be a barmaid for my entire life."

As Bucky and Mikey were driving to the video store, Bucky saw Intorcia's Doughnut Shop ahead and began to think to himself. *Cristina would love some fresh doughnuts; they will be great to munch on while watching a movie.*

And with that thought in mind, he pulled over to the curb in front of the doughnut shop. He unbuckled Mikey's car seat to let him out and held his hand as they walked inside. When they entered the shop, a friendly smile from Bill Intorcia, the store's owner, greeted them.

Bill owned the doughnut shop for nearly forty years and had known Bucky's family nearly as long. Although Bill was getting up there in age, he still enjoyed getting up at two-thirty each morning to prepare fresh doughnuts for his customers. Bill's doughnuts were famous around the North Country, and were so tasty that he single-handedly closed down other doughnut shop competition, even well-known establishments such as Dunkin' Doughnuts and Krispy Kreme.

"Hi, Bucky!" Bill said with a thick Italian accent. "How's everything tonight?"

"Things are going well, Bill. Thanks for asking."

Bill looked down at Bucky's side. "Who is that big fella you've got there with you?" he said with a wink and a grin.

Mikey smiled and pulled on his dad's hand, acting unnaturally shy. "This is Mikey," Bucky answered, "I guess it has been awhile since you've seen him."

"Oh yes, now I remember!" Bill leaned down and looked directly at the boy. "My, you're getting big! What can I get for you today?" he asked.

Mikey's eyes got big and his mouth began to salivate. "What do you have, Mr. Intorcia?"

"Hmmm…let's see. I have doughnuts, and even more doughnuts!" laughed Bill. "So what shall it be?"

"I'll take that one!" Mikey said, pointing to a glazed doughnut.

"I think that's a good choice, little man! And how about for your daddy, eh Bucky?"

"Well, I guess I'll get a dozen of your crème-filled éclairs, but put them in a bag to-go, would you please? Mikey can eat his here."

Bucky and Mikey sat down at the counter as Bill snatched a sheet of wax paper and reached down to grab a glazed doughnut.

"Better make that one cup of coffee and a tall glass of milk, too," Bucky added.

"Coming right up!" Bill placed the doughnut on a napkin in front of Mikey and shifted his attention over to Bucky. "By the way, Bucky, what's been keeping you so busy that you haven't had time to stop by?"

Lowering his head and sagging down in his chair, Bucky said, "I've been under a lot of pressure because of all the recent fires in town and people claiming to be seeing ghosts, or something like that, hovering from the rooftops. I'm sure you've read about it in the paper."

Bill's demeanor suddenly became solemn. "Yes, I've read about it, and everyone in town is nervous about the whole thing. Have you got any leads at all?"

Bucky's voice was nearly as quiet as a whisper. "Bill, we don't have squat. The police think they have a possible suspect, but that's about as paper thin as it gets."

Bill shook his head, and then turned to grab two cups off the shelf. "So, Bucky, how has your family been?" he asked, changing the subject.

"They're doing great, Bill. Cristina is continuing her transcription work for the hospital, and as far as I know, my folks are vacationing in Europe for a few months."

"What do you mean?" asked the old doughnut maker. "Haven't you talked to your dad lately?"

"I don't see my mom or dad all that much anymore since they both retired; it seems as if they're always traveling somewhere. I've tried calling them on their cell phone a few times, but my calls go straight to voicemail. And they haven't called me back in weeks." Bucky reached for his wallet and pulled out some cash. "Speaking of my family, Bill. Last night I was thinking about something my grandfather once told me when I was just a little kid."

Bill finished pouring the milk and set the carton back in the refrigerator. He placed the cup of milk in front of Mikey and poured the last of the hot coffee into the other.

Then he turned back toward Bucky and asked, "Oh yeah, what was that?"

Bucky leaned forward. "Let me ask you something, Bill. What can you tell me about the old underground coal tunnels that run the on both sides of State Street?"

Bill let out a hearty laugh. "Why are you asking about those old death-traps?"

"I was just curious, that's all," he replied, taking a sip of his coffee.

"Come on, Bucky. You just don't come in here and ask a question like that without some substance to it. What's your real interest in the coal tunnels?"

"I wanted to get some information on them and find out if they were still usable...just in case the person setting the fires is really a man instead of something supernatural."

Bill's tone suddenly became serious. "Oh, I see." he said, stroking his thick, bushy moustache and twisting it at the ends. "Well, first of all, those coal tunnels don't run just the length of State Street. There are other side streets that have some tunnels too. There were many stores in town back when the tunnels were built, and years ago, *ALL* the businesses in town used coal to heat their places."

"Really? I did not know that."

"Yeah, the tunnels were constructed in the 1920s and used by the businesses to store coal for many years. Nowadays, they are full of junk and trash that people tossed in there to fill them up."

"Fill them up?" questioned Bucky.

"Sure. After the businesses quit heating with coal and went to fuel oil, most of the store owners stuffed them with debris and boarded up the openings so no hoodlums could get into their cellars."

Bucky sat in silence for a moment to think while Mikey nibbled on his glazed doughnut. Then, an idea popped in Bucky's thoughts.

"Hey Bill, would it be possible for someone to walk or crawl through the tunnels, or hide in them if they needed to?"

Bill nodded. "Well, I suppose it'd be possible to do that...if someone moved all the junk around to open a path. But I don't know how they'd get in there to it."

"Is it a challenge to get inside?"

"Yeah, there's no outside entrance to them, and the only way someone could get in there would be to enter through one of the buildings that has a tunnel connected to it. You would have to check nearly every store in town in order to find out where the person was entering from."

"You know, Bill, I think that might be just the break we've been looking for. I'm going to talk to Chief Zimmerman first thing Monday morning and mention it to him. It might be another dead end, or those underground tunnels may possibly lead us straight to whoever is setting these fires."

Just then, Josh Roberts walked into the doughnut shop and overheard the tail end of their conversation. He simply nodded to the other gentleman and proceeded to walk past them. He sat down at one of the booths close by, listening attentively but remaining silent.

"Underground tunnels?" he whispered under his breath. "What nonsense are they discussing now?"

Around that time, Cristina, who was still at home working on her transcribing, abruptly decided to take a break as she smelled smoke, and a whiff of burning meat, coming from the kitchen.

"Damn it," she exclaimed, "the roast is still in the oven!"

She jumped out of her chair and rushed to the kitchen to shut the stove off. Her heart was beating rapidly and she was feeling a little ashamed of herself for not keeping an eye on the roast cooking in the oven.

Cristina sat down at the kitchen table to catch her breath after her near disaster when she suddenly noticed the house seemed unusually quiet. After a moment, Cristina decided she had better check in on Mikey because she knew when he was *that* quiet, it usually meant he was into some type of mischief.

"Mikey, where are you?" she said, peering around the corner into his room.

After searching the house from top to bottom, Cristina realized that neither Mikey nor the family cat were in the house. Then, remembering how much trouble they have had trying to keep the cat from running off, she began to get worried and wondered if Mikey went outside to look for Zack. She tore a piece of paper off the notepad near the phone, grabbed a pen, and took them over to the kitchen table. Cristina quickly jotted something on the paper, and then grabbed her jacket as she bolted out the door.

After searching around the yard without any success, she then decided to take a quick walk around the block to see if Mikey had wandered off somewhere.

Cristina began to pick up the pace as she was hurrying along the sidewalk, and soon, she was starting to panic. As she became more unnerved, she began to run up and down the street calling out for Mikey. Tears began to swell in her eyes and her mind was running wild with fear.

Dusk had started to shed darkness into the bushes and tress, making it hard to see objects as she squinted to peruse the area. Suddenly she bolted into the middle of the road, throwing caution to the wind and praying that the glow of the streetlights would be enough to illuminate the area and spot Mikey.

In a tree not far away, an abrupt fluttering sound came from a branch near the top. Although Cristina was oblivious to the noise, a huge raven had swooped in, staring at her with piercing, wicked eyes.

Just then, she heard the faint sound of a cat meowing, and she quickly turned around to try to get a bearing on where the sound came from. Cristina took a few steps forward and saw the silhouette of a cat in the dim shadows on the other side of the street. She called out Mikey's name thinking the cat was theirs and that Mikey might be nearby. All that greeted her back was dead silence.

Several seconds passed.

And then there was a frightening sound, the sound of a loud engine. In the distance, a large black 1975 van with tinted windows was coming down the street. Coming like a freight train.

Cristina turned her head to the noise, but only for a brief second. Her priority was finding Mikey; tears were now streaming down her face and impairing her vision. The raven watched and followed Cristina with its eyes.

When the van veered around the curve, it was coming much faster than it ought to on a residential street. It struck Cristina, throwing her several feet into the air and nearly fifteen yards in distance. As her body dropped on the pavement, Cristina laid there barely conscious in a broken, bleeding heap.

With blood seeping from the back of her skull, she struggled to breathe and her eyes failed to put objects into focus. Cristina knew that she was seriously hurt, but she was still thinking about Mikey and tilted her head so she could look towards the curb.

Through half-glazed eyes, Cristina saw the dark form of a person get out of the van and walk over. He was dressed in a long, black overcoat with the collar turned up about his ears and a wide, broad-brimmed hat was pulled down over his eyes, hiding most of his facial features.

Standing over her, the figure raised a hand, covered in a gray, leather glove, and placed a finger up to his lips.

"Shh..." he said in a hushed murmur.

Even though blood was beginning to fill her throat, Cristina somehow managed to speak. "Please..." she uttered weakly. "Please help me."

Just then, headlights from an oncoming car shone briefly on the stranger as it rounded the corner, illuminating the features of the dark figure. Her eyes widened as she caught her breath and her heart began to beat fast and hard.

The last thing Cristina said before she slipped out of consciousness was, "It can't be...it just can't be!"

315

Chapter 31:

An unforeseen tragedy

Shortly after six-thirty, Holly was in the back room at Kitty's Bar getting several cases of beer to restock the refrigerator. For some reason, she was feeling unusually tired and sweat began to form on her upper lip and brow. A feeling of nausea started to creep up on her, but she tried not to think about it and continued to gather her stock.

Miss Kitty, on the other hand, was just getting off the phone near the cash register. "Has anyone seen Holly?" she asked, addressing the patrons sitting in front of her. "I want to tell her I've found someone to relieve her tonight."

John Sears, who was sitting at the bar with his pal and fellow "Deadhead," Adam "Red" Richardson, lifted his head. "Yeah, I saw her." he said, pushing his long, greasy black hair over his ears and smiling a crooked grin, exposing is yellow, rotted teeth. "I think she's still in the back getting some more booze."

"Yo, Miss Kitty," interrupted Adam, raising his multi-colored Jamaican Tam hat high on his forehead so he could see. "Who'd you get to come in tonight?"

"Oh, it's Gary Wolff. I'm not sure if you remember him, but he worked here during the summer and is home this weekend from college. He said he had nothing else planned and could cover Holly's shift tonight."

The bar suddenly became silent as the sound of glass breaking was heard from the backroom.

Adam's smile suddenly faded away, replaced by a look of curiosity. He whipped his head around in the direction of the noise, his long brown dreadlocks smacking ol' John in the face.

316

"What was that?" Adam asked.

A concerned and confused look came across Miss Kitty's face. "I don't know. I'd better go back and check it out."

Pushing through the door leading to the kitchen, Miss Kitty entered the stock area to see what the noise was. Her jaw dropped when she saw that Holly was stricken and down on one knee, and a bottle of liquor was smashed to pieces beside her.

"Oh my!" gasped Miss Kitty. "Holly, are you okay?"

"Yeah," Holly answered wearily. "I don't know what came over me. I felt faint and everything seemed like it was spinning."

Miss Kitty helped Holly into a chair. "Stay here for a moment," she insisted. "I'll be right back."

Miss Kitty went over to the sink and turned on the faucet. She grabbed a cup from the dish rack, filled it up with cold water and took it back over to Holly.

"Here, drink this. You look terribly pale, Hun."

When she was sure that Holly was all right, Miss Kitty went back to the front area.

"Listen up everyone," she hollered, addressing the entire bar. "Holly isn't feeling well and needs to be taken to the hospital. I have to stay here until another bartender arrives, so I was wondering if anyone would be willing to take her."

John Sears raised his hand. "I'll do it!"

"I don't think so!" Miss Kitty snapped. "Just look at yourself, John. Your eyes are half-shut! You aren't taking anyone anywhere." She shook her head in a disapproving manner. "Tell me, John, why do you feel like you need to get wasted all the time?"

John turned and looked at her through half-open, glazed-over eyes. "I've had a hard life," John replied sarcastically. "I'm just a left-handed man in a right-handed world, and there's not a damn thing I can do about it."

"Yeah," Adam butted in, lifting his fingers to his mouth as if pretending to smoke a joint. "That's why he only smokes those lefty cigarettes."

"Lefty?" inquired Miss Kitty."

"Also known as wacko-tobacco," laughed Adam.

"Never mind those two jokers, Miss Kitty," Thomas Parker spoke up. "I'll take Holly to the hospital for you."

Miss Kitty smiled and breathed a sigh of relief. "Okay, Thomas. I'll let her know. Are you sure you're in good enough shape to drive?"

"Hell yeah! I just got here about thirty minutes ago. I haven't even had two beers yet! I'm willing to wager I'm in better condition to drive than anyone else in here."

A reassured grin appeared on Miss Kitty's somber face, and then she strolled back to the supply area where Holly was. Still sitting in the chair, Holly grasped her drink in both hands as her arms rested upon her legs. Her head hung low between her legs and she was taking slow, deep breaths.

"Holly, Thomas Parker is going to take you to the hospital."

Holly put down her drink and shook her head. "Miss Kitty, I don't need to go to the hospital. I just need to rest for a moment and then I'll be fine."

"Well, just to be on the safe side, I'd still like you to go. It will put my mind at ease."

"Okay, Miss Kitty," she reluctantly agreed. "But who'll take my spot?"

"Don't worry; I've already contacted Gary Wolff. He's in town for the weekend and willing to come in for tonight." Then Miss Kitty walked over to get Holly's coat off the rack near the rear exit. "I want you to call the bar when you are finished and let me know if everything is fine. You know I'll worry the whole time you're gone! And if you can't reach Roger or find a ride, let me know, and I'll have someone go to the hospital and pick you up."

After Bucky and Mikey left the doughnut shop, they quickly went to the grocery store and picked up their goodies. When they got to the video store, Bucky parked in front of the building. He noticed a figure walking along the street, wearing a black short-sleeved T-shirt and dark pants, heading in their direction. He squinted to get a better look at the figure, and as he came into view from the light of the store window, Bucky recognized the person as Tim Matthews.

Tim hadn't changed much over the years. He still kept to himself, had few close friends, and lived alone. Even though Tim had lived in Carthage several years now, people still knew little about him.

After they got out of the Blazer, Bucky leaned down to young Mikey and said, "Go on in, son. Go up to the counter and talk to Mr. Parker's wife, Stacey, for a few minutes. I'll be inside in just a moment."

"Okay, Dad," Mikey replied as he walked toward the store entrance, "but hurry up before all the good videos are taken."

Bucky gave him a grin and a wink, and then he sped off in Tim's direction.

Tim's appearance was not as clean cut as it once was. He dressed in a gothic style of clothing, and he kept his hair longer nowadays, sometimes even in a ponytail. He still had his handsome James Dean looks to him, and he came across as a bit of a rebel with his standoffish behavior. In fact, the only time he would interact with the community members was during the annual Fourth of July festivities.

Tim enjoyed making his homemade fireworks and setting them off from atop of Kitty's Bar. He said all those bright, beautiful colors reminded him of better times in his life when he would sit around a campfire and tell eerie ghost stories as a youngster.

When Tim got directly under the street light in front of the store, Bucky noticed that Tim was sporting a couple of tattoos these days, something Tim didn't have in the past. On his right forearm was what appeared to be a dagger, and he had another tattoo on his left arm that Bucky could not recognize.

"Hey Tim!" Bucky called out, trying to catch up to Tim. "What are you doing on the streets of Carthage at this time of night?"

Tim stopped and peered over his shoulder. He seemed preoccupied and startled; he obviously did not expect anyone to approach him.

"Oh...uh, nothing really," he uttered. "I haven't been feeling well. I thought maybe some fresh air might do me some good."

"I see. Hey, Tim, I thought I saw you out back of my office, by the riverbank last week. I think it was Thursday evening, around five o'clock."

"No," Tim responded bluntly. "It wasn't me." His voice was as impersonal as ever and his face equally expressionless.

"Oh, sorry. I guess my eyes must've been playing tricks on me." Then Bucky changed the topic. "Anyway, aren't you supposed to be working at Kitty's tonight? Friday nights are your regular shift, right?"

"Um, well I'm supposed to be, but I'm too sick tonight to be behind a bar counter and breathing in second-hand cigarette smoke all night."

"Yeah, I know that feeling. Sometimes I walk out of the bar smelling like I've just inhaled an entire pack of cigarettes. And I'm not even a smoker!"

"Exactly! I've been feeling light-headed and nauseous; it's either from the smoke or I have a touch of the flu. I'm just going to walk down to the grocery store and buy some cough syrup and a can of soup. Besides, I'm not sure if I like working Friday nights anymore; I might talk to Miss Kitty about changing that."

"I'm surprised you'd be out tonight in just a T-shirt. It's beginning to get pretty chilly tonight. I think the thermometer read fifty degrees at my house before I left. And with you not feeling well, I would've thought you'd be wearing a jacket tonight if you were going outside."

"Actually, I've been feeling hot all day. I think I might have a fever. This cool air really feels nice right now."

Bucky simply shrugged off Tim's ridiculous logic and his poor judgment not to wear a coat. He put his hands in his pockets and looked down at Tim's side.

"Do you always go to the market with a duffel bag?"

Bucky's comment stirred a nervous shuffle from Tim as he fumbled for an explanation. "Oh, this old thing. It's just some garbage I've decided to throw in the dumpster on the way. I can't be a pack rat anymore and save every little item forever. My apartment is getting cluttered, and I needed to clear some space."

"I can relate to that," Bucky said with a laugh. "I need to clean out the mess that has taken over my garage!" Then he checked the time on his wristwatch. "Well, I better go find my son before he runs off on me. Have a good night, Tim. I hope you feel better."

Tim just nodded and continued down the street, occasionally looking over his shoulder to see if Bucky was watching him.

Josh Roberts had left Intorcia's Doughnut Shop and made his way to the video store by the time Bucky and Mikey arrived. He was in the Horror section, searching for a movie to watch, when he saw Bucky enter the building. Excited about the chance to talk to the Mayor, Josh decided to walk over and converse with him.

"Hello, Mayor Morgan. I'm Josh Roberts. We've met a couple of times before, but I'm sure you don't remember me. I'm a reporter for the *Carthage Tribune*."

"Oh, yeah, I remember you, Mr. Roberts," Bucky responded, glancing over to the checkout counter to make sure Mikey was there. "I understand we have a mutual friend. Roger Fasick has frequently mentioned you. It seems you've made quite an impression on him."

Josh looked uncomfortable and swallowed hard. "I hope it's all been good," he replied.

Feeling a little nervous, Josh popped a stick of nicotine gum in his mouth to calm his nerves.

"I haven't known him as long as you, Mayor Morgan, but Roger has become a very good friend of mine. He's a bright young man with an eagerness to learn and a quick wit. I suspect he's got a bright future ahead of him."

"I couldn't agree more," Bucky replied, smiling. "And Josh, please call me Bucky."

"Okay…Bucky."

After a moment of hesitation, Bucky asked, "So, you're the *Tribune* reporter who writes about urban legends?"

"Yeah, among other things. Speaking of urban legends, I was wondering if we might be able to talk sometime about all these Reaper sightings by our town's homeless community. And maybe we can discuss the missing file that Pat Jordan was compiling regarding all these strange occurrences."

Bucky's smile faded away. "Mr. Roberts, I'm with my son tonight and don't have the time or the interest to talk right now. Besides, just so there is no confusion, I don't believe there actually is a Reaper in our town. Furthermore, there is nothing to prove that he, or the file you are referring to, even exists."

Josh reached into his jacket pocket and pulled out a pencil and his notepad. "Well, if you're sure that it's not this Reaper person setting the fires, do you think it could be Bud Hopkins back in town? After all, he is out of prison now. You do remember him, don't you? Bud was the person who set several fires around Jefferson County back in the early 1980s. When they caught Bud, he was put in prison for awhile and later he was institutionalized in a mental hospital for many years. I read somewhere that he was released about a year ago…maybe longer."

Bucky looked down at Josh's notepad, appalled at his lack of consideration. Then he stepped forward and got face to face with Josh, glaring intently as their eyeballs locked into a stare.

"No, I don't think Hopkins is responsible for these fires." Bucky said, his voice becoming hostile. "He has to wear an electronic bracelet on his ankle until *next* September that monitors everywhere he goes. I'm way ahead of you on this, Mr. Roberts. I checked into that possibility very thoroughly." After pausing for a moment to take a deep breath, Bucky went on to say, "Now, if you will excuse me, sir, my son and I have things to take care of. Good-bye."

Josh put his notepad away as Bucky brushed by him in a huff. "Thanks for your time, Mr. Mayor," he said, watching Bucky walk away. "I'm sure we'll speak again."

Twenty-two minutes later, at the Carthage Area Hospital, Dr. William Wiley, the town's oldest and most respected doctor, was finishing up his medical tests on Holly.

William "Bill" Wiley was a tall, distinguished looking man in his mid-sixties with white hair and a great sense of humor. He was well liked around town and delivered a good number of the local children.

Dr. Wiley was rarely seen without his white lab coat and stethoscope hanging around his neck. His opening statement to every patient was, "You need to stop smoking." He said this whether or not the person smoked cigarettes, or *ever* did smoke; however, it was something of a trademark saying of his that his patients had grown to appreciate and expect.

The elderly doctor looked at his clipboard for several silent minutes before shifting his attention back to his patient. "Well, Holly, I'm sorry it's so busy around here tonight. I'll send your urine sample and blood work over to the lab immediately; however, I won't have the results available to you until tomorrow or the next day."

Holly rubbed her temples and groaned. "Should I call you tomorrow to see if the results are in?" she asked.

Noticing her discomfort, Dr. Wiley grabbed his pad and began writing. "That won't be necessary. Either my receptionist or I will call you when we know something." Then he tore off the piece of paper he was writing on and handed it to Holly. "Take this prescription over to the pharmacy at the Kinney Drugs store."

Holly looked at the scribbles on the paper but could not discern what it said.

"What is it for?" she inquired.

"It's just something that will help with your nausea," he replied casually. "I want you to take it easy for the rest of the night." Dr. Wiley noticed her unsteadiness as she tried to stand. "Even though you don't need to stay at the hospital tonight, I would rather you not drive yourself home. Do you have someone who can pick you up?"

"Yeah, I can call my boyfriend, and if he's not home yet, someone from work will come and get me."

"Good, and if you can't get someone, we can make arrangements for you with one of the ambulance drivers to chauffeur you home."

Holly gathered her belongings and left the exam room. On her way out, she walked up to the receptionist at the counter.

"May I use your phone?" she asked.

The receptionist seemed uninterested and didn't even attempt to make eye contact. "Sorry, but I have to keep this line open for incoming emergency calls."

"Oh, okay," Holly said in a soft, somewhat disappointed tone. "Do you have a pay phone nearby so I can call for a ride?"

"Sure we do. The closest one is right outside that door," the receptionist answered, pointing to the exit doors.

Holly dug into her purse for some change and went outside. Holly, glad to be out of the hospital, took in a deep breath of fresh night air, and then she started over to the phone booth. In mid-stride, Holly stopped and changed direction.

"I'll call Roger in a little bit," she said to herself. "I'd better hurry up and get over to Kinney Drugs before the pharmacy closes."

While on her way to the drug store, she witnessed a peculiar individual walking on the other side of the street. It appeared as though he was purposely trying to stay within the shadows as he walked, so as not to be noticed by anyone.

There were not many persons on the street. The district was dreary and forlorn. But the few who passed—among them some homeless— paid no attention to the man walking in the shadows, trying not to draw any attention to himself.

The hood of his black cloak was pulled up over his head despite the fact that the night air was no more than cool. His purpose evidently was to avoid observation without exciting suspicion.

Holly stood behind a telephone pole and watched with earnest, keeping herself from being noticed as she observed him. In the middle of the block, the stranger slowed his pace and almost came to a stop in the doorway of a darkened furniture store. His head turned quickly as he glanced around in both directions; then he moved swiftly across the street and slipped into the shadowy alley between the public library and Widrick's Laundromat.

The behavior of the stranger stirred Holly's curiosity, and she decided to follow him into the alleyway, trying to sneak up close so she could see his face. In Holly's opinion, she figured that if Roger could do investigating, then she could too. However, in the back of her mind, she wished that Roger were there with her; he would know exactly what to do.

Even though she was more than a little frightened, Holly decided if she left to go for help, this person would get away and still no one would know who was sneaking around, entering the buildings that were supposed to be closed for the night.

Staying in the shadows herself, Holly tried to avoid being seen by the stranger she was following. Even with her hands sweaty and shaking, the whole idea of this cloak and dagger stuff was immensely exciting to her.

When she got to the edge of the laundromat, she glanced around the corner and saw the stranger crawl in through an open window in the library. Holly's curiosity began to intensify, and after a few seconds, she followed down the alleyway.

After Holly was certain she could sneak into the library unnoticed, she pulled herself onto the garbage dumpster below the window and kneeled down on the windowsill to peek inside. Something was moving inside the library; moving silently, invisibly. The mysterious presence was roaming around and Holly opted to obtain a better view.

While crawling in the window, the bottom of her right pant leg caught on a nail protruding out from the siding. Holly lost her balance as she attempted to shake her pants free and fell down, landing hard against the floor and knocking the wind out of her. As she was falling, her left foot bumped the stick that held the window open, making it come banging down behind her. The sound of the window slamming shut alerted the attention of the stranger, who was in the adjoining room.

Once she was able to catch her breath, Holly sat up and brushed off some dirt and lint from her chest and hands. When she looked down at her right leg, she saw that her pants were torn. When she tried to move, Holly found that her ankle was twisted and she was now incapable of standing up on her own.

Lying there in pain and completely defenseless, a strange, terrifying laugh suddenly pierced the room. Holly closed her eyes, unable to move. When she reopened them, the Reaper was standing above her, his black eyes meeting with hers.

Panic stricken, Holly stared into those cold black eyes, and then she stuttered as she spoke. "Who...who are you? *What* are you? What're you going to do?"

The stranger continued to stare but did not answer. Then he leaned down over her and raised the skull mask from his face.

"Oh my god," she shrieked. "It can't be...it just can't be! It's you!?"

The Reaper lowered his dark mask before letting out another terrifying laugh. Holly panicked and struggled to get away, but the pain in her leg made it impossible to move more than a few inches. The Reaper then reached into his cloak, pulling out a stun gun.

The instrument was eight inches long and black; when the Reaper turned it on, the stun gun sparked and made a low buzzing noise. Holly attempted to speak but could only make a minor whimpering sound.

At that moment, the Reaper extended his hand close to Holly's face, lifted his stun gun up to her forehead, and zapped her. The last thing Holly saw was a bright flash of light, and then only blackness.

The Reaper turned and walked away, leaving Holly's limp and unconscious body lying on the library floor. He disappeared into the next room, and in minutes, the acrid smell of smoke filled the library along with the crackling sound of wood burning and flames illuminating the darkened rooms.

Chapter 32:

Chaos and Agony Collide

Not long after, Bucky arrived home from the video store with Mikey. Once they entered the house and removed their shoes and coats, they noticed there was no sign of Cristina. Her cell phone and her purse were still on the coffee table. Bucky strolled over to a window and peered outside into the garage, noticing that her silver colored Ford Escort was still in its stall, and yet, there was no sign of Cristina anywhere. Then he proceeded into the kitchen and spotted a note on the kitchen table.

> *Bucky,*
> *I've gone to look for Mikey. I think he followed the cat*
> *outside. I'm sorry for not keeping a better eye on him!*
> > *Love,*
> > *Cristina*

"What the hell is this?" he whispered.

Mikey walked in from the living room with a sad look upon his face. "Dad, where's Mommy? I can't find her anywhere."

"I don't know, son. Her car and cell phone are here, but I found a note stating she went to search for you because she thinks you're outside with Zack. Unfortunately, it doesn't explain *where* she ended up or *why* she thought you were still here. I told her you were coming with me before we left."

Bucky thought how odd the whole situation was. Not just because of the strange note Cristina left behind, but because she always took her cell phone with her, even if she went down the road to the convenient store to buy some gas or simply purchase the daily newspaper.

"Mikey, check and see if the outside light is on in the back yard. If so, take a look out by the patio and clothes lines; while you're doing that, I'll look upstairs and check down cellar."

"Okay, Dad!" Mikey hollered exuberantly, running toward the back door.

The little boy quickly opened the door and ran outside. Bucky gripped the note tightly in his hands and went from room to room, searching for any sign of Cristina. After a few minutes without any success, he came back to the kitchen and sat down, staring at the note she had written.

Mikey flung open the back door and strutted inside, holding the family cat. "I didn't see her, Dad, but I found Zack wandering around in the yard."

"Huh, that's weird. I searched every room, and she's not inside the house either," Bucky said, scratching his head. "I wonder where she went."

Just then, the telephone rang.

"Maybe that's her calling now!" Mikey yelled out.

Bucky hurried over to the phone. "Hello?" he said in a rather strained voice.

Officer Johnson was on the other end of the phone. "Bucky, it's Ken Johnson. I'm so glad I could reach you! Your wife has been involved in a hit-and-run accident. Can you come down to the hospital right away?"

In an instant, Bucky's heartbeat began to quicken. "What? What happened? Is Cristina okay?"

"There's no easy way to say this, Bucky," he said solemnly. "I'm afraid your wife's condition is critical."

An uneasiness began to form in Bucky's gut, and he felt as if he was going to be sick. "Is she at the hospital right now?"

"Yes, the ambulance driver should have her there by now. I've already called the hospital and informed Dr. Wiley the ambulance is on its way."

Bucky hung up the phone; fear, anxiety, and a million other thoughts suddenly bombarded his mind. Trying to remain calm, he picked up the phone once again and called Celeste Braxton at her folk's place.

"Celeste! Thank god you're still in town," he said, his voice extremely agitated and unsteady.

"Yes Bucky, I'll be here until tomorrow night," she answered in an upbeat manner. "By the way, I was going to call tonight to thank you and Cristina for a great time the other evening."

"That's great, but…"

Celeste continued to say, "Of course, I always have a fabulous time with the two of you when I come to Carthage for a visit. I enjoyed the delicious dinner at the Superior Restaurant, and I appreciate your talking about the waterfront scenario. Your perspective will give me some great information for the plot of my book."

Bucky cut her off as she was talking. "Celeste, I hate to be rude, but I have to tell you something."

"Okay," she said with caution. "Is something wrong, Bucky? You seem awfully upset."

"Cristina has been in an accident," Bucky blurted out, nearly in tears. "I need to get down to the hospital right away!"

"Oh my god! Is she alright?" Celeste asked in a very worried voice.

"I don't know. An officer called me, but he did not know the extent of her injuries. He told me that her condition was critical and she was on her way to the hospital. I was wondering if you could come by and look after Mikey so I can go to the hospital."

"Yes, of course," she assured him. "I can be there in less than ten minutes."

A short time later, Roger arrived home; a little confused, mad, and exhausted after everything that had happened throughout the day. First, nothing went right at work, and after that, he got into a heated argument with the salesperson at Radio Shack about the cost of replacing his cell phone.

Roger unlocked his front door, entered, and plopped down in his overstuffed chair. Taking deep breaths and trying to relax, Roger closed his eyes. His thoughts focused on his "not so great day" briefly, and then he tried to clear his mind of all his troubles.

Roger had been sitting for a couple minutes when the phone rang. He rolled his eyes and groaned before answering the phone.

"Hello," a female voice said. "Can I speak with Holly Boliver please?"

"She's not here right now," Roger answered in a blasé tone. "May I take a message for her?"

"Well, this is Angela Barns. I'm the instructor for her Business Communications class."

"Oh, hi Ms. Barns!" Roger said in a more cheerful tone. "I've heard a lot about you; Holly talks about you all the time." Then a strange feeling came over Roger. "Excuse me for asking, Ms. Barns, but why are you calling for Holly?"

"I was curious whether Holly is feeling alright."

"Yeah, as far as I know," he said. "Why do you ask?"

"Well, she wasn't in class tonight, and it's the first class she has missed. I know how much she wanted to have perfect attendance so I thought maybe she was sick or something."

Roger sat up straight in his chair. "Wait a minute. Did you say that Holly *wasn't* in class?"

"Yes, were you not aware of this?"

"No, ma'am," Roger replied promptly. "I'm just as surprised as you are! She's not here, and I haven't spoken with her all day."

Ms. Barns's voice suddenly became soft and strained, as though she was sincerely worried about Holly. "Oh, okay. Well, if you do happen to talk to her, will you *please* tell her I called and that I'm *very* concerned about her?"

"I sure will, Ms. Barns. I'll make sure she gives you a call when she gets home."

Concerned over the disturbing news, Roger decided to call Kitty's Bar as soon as he hung up with Ms. Barns.

The phone rang seven times and still no one had picked up the phone at Kitty's Bar. Roger was getting uneasy and feelings of dread began to form in the pit of his gut. Just as he was about to call it quits and hang up, someone finally answered the phone.

"Kitty's Bar," Miss Kitty said. "How may I help you?"

"Hey, Miss Kitty, this is Roger Fasick," he said with an exhausting sigh, as though he was somehow relieved that someone, *anyone* had answered the phone. "Is Holly there by any chance?"

"No, she isn't, Roger. Didn't anyone call you?"

"Call me about what?" he asked, slightly unnerved.

"Oh, dear," she said despairingly. "Well, tonight has not gone very well at all. First of all, Tim called in sick, which meant that Holly had to work an extra few hours. Then, somewhere between seven and seven-thirty, she fainted when restocking some supplies and was taken to the emergency room."

"She fainted!?" Roger said with a gasp.

"Yes," Miss Kitty continued. "We tried to reach you several times, but your answering machine was not working. I called the hospital to tell them what had happened, and the hospital receptionist said she would try to call you, too."

A trickle of nervous sweat appeared on Roger's temple. "No, the only person I talked to was Holly's college professor, but then, I just got home a few minutes ago." He felt a lump begin to form in his throat as he asked, "Miss Kitty, can you tell me if she's alright?"

"She seemed much better by the time she left the bar, but I wanted her to go to the hospital anyways. Just in case something was seriously wrong. You can never be too cautious, y'know?"

Roger felt slightly relieved by Miss Kitty's answer; however, he was still concerned about Holly's well-being and butterflies were still buzzing in his stomach.

"Hasn't she called you since she arrived to the hospital?" he asked, looking at the clock on the wall.

"Actually, no she hasn't. The last I knew, she was supposed to call the bar when she was ready for a ride and someone would go pick her up."

Roger shook his head and his stomach got queasy. "Well, I'm going to call the hospital and see if she is still there. If she isn't, then I'm going to go look for her." Roger wiped the sweat away with the back of his hand. "Miss Kitty, would you do me a favor?"

"Sure, Roger. What is it?"

"If you should hear from Holly, please give me a call at 555-0820. This is my new cell phone number."

Miss Kitty grabbed a pen off the counter and wrote the number down on a napkin.

"Okay, Roger. If I find out anything… anything at all. I'll call you."

Roger hung up the phone and dialed the hospital, shaking slightly as he dialed. A woman answered the phone. "Carthage Area Hospital," she said in a tedious, uninterested voice. "How can I direct your call?"

"Yes, hello, ma'am. Can you tell me if Holly Boliver is still there? She was taken to the hospital about an hour or two ago for a fainting incident."

"Let me check, hold please," the receptionist answered in her blasé tone.

While on hold, Roger's attention shifted to the television. His eyes became fixated as a news bulletin came across the bottom of the screen showing breaking news that the Carthage Library had caught fire.

"Christ!" Roger exclaimed, his eyes getting wide. "The library is only a few blocks from the hospital!"

A few seconds later, a woman came back on the line and said, "Sir, my name is Lori Lyndaker...I'm Dr. Wiley's personal nurse. The receptionist said you were asking about Ms. Boliver?"

"Yes, that's correct, ma'am."

"Well, I'm not certain, but I think she left the Emergency Room area about thirty minutes ago, and as far as I know, no one has seen her walking around the lobby or anywhere outside since that time."

Roger hung up the phone, very worried. "I don't like the sounds of this," he said, pacing tensely around the room. "I should drive down there to make sure she is alright."

As Roger was about to leave, the phone rang again. Roger thought about not answering it, but then changed his mind on the off chance it could be Holly trying to reach him.

"Holly?" he said as he picked up the phone.

"No, Roger. This is Celeste."

"Celeste, this is an unexpected call. Hey, can I call you back? I have to go into town for a little while. It's really important."

Celeste broke in. "Roger, I thought you should know that Bucky called me and asked if I would watch Mikey for him."

"Why? Did *Mr. Mayor* suddenly have an important errand that he had to attend to?" Roger said derisively.

"No, it's much more serious than that. Bucky got a call from the police saying that Cristina was in a hit-and-run accident. She was rushed immediately to the hospital."

"Oh damn, I am so sorry," he uttered in a quiet voice, feeling like an ass for his smart remark. "Look, Celeste, I'm on my way over to the hospital anyway," he stated. "While I'm there, I'll see if I can locate Bucky and get an update on Cristina's condition."

"Why do you have to go to the hospital?" Celeste asked. "Is something wrong?"

Roger's tone seemed evasive. "Well, apparently Holly fainted while she was at work and had to be taken to the emergency room."

"Oh no!" she said with a gasp. "Is she alright?"

"I don't know. I called the hospital but didn't get much information. All they told me was that Holly had already been released over half an hour ago, and as of right now, no one knows where she is. I'm going to drive over to the hospital anyway to try and find her. Maybe she is sitting in the lobby waiting for someone to give her a ride. While I'm there, maybe I can get Bucky to help me look for her. That is, if everything is okay with Cristina."

Celeste sighed. "This sure has been a horrible night. I'm going to worry myself sick until I know everything is okay."

331

After a moment of dead air passed and he was sure that Celeste was finished talking, Roger spoke up and announced, "Well, I don't mean to be rude, but I'm kind of in a hurry to get to the hospital. Thank you for calling me, Celeste; I really appreciate it. And don't worry, I promise that I'll call you as soon as I hear any news about either of them."

Roger raced out to his car and drove speedily towards the hospital. His mind was just a blur, not knowing what to think, with Holly on his thoughts and, now, with the terrible news of Cristina.

Bucky arrived as the paramedics were wheeling Cristina out of the Emergency Room corridor and into her own private room. He quickly ran up to the people wheeling her bed, grabbing one of the nurses by the shoulder and twisting her around.

"Excuse me, Nurse..." Bucky looked down at her name tag, "Lyndaker."

"Yes, can I help you?"

"Is she alright? How bad is she hurt? How did it happen?" asked Bucky in a flurry of questions.

"Are you the husband?" Nurse Lyndaker asked.

"Yes," Bucky answered.

"Well, you need to back up out of our way so we can get her into the room and get her hooked up to a monitor and insert an I.V. Then you can see her."

Bucky stopped just short of the door leading to her room. He watched from the window as the doctors and nurses checked her vital signs and inspected her bandages.

Cristina's head was wrapped in white gauze, which also covered nearly all of the right side of her face. Her left eye was swollen and had been blackened by the accident; bloodied scrapes dug deep on her chin and cheeks.

Nurse Lyndaker checked the dressing on her forearms and hands, which were also wrapped in gauze and left only the tips of the fingers showing. Once the nurse finished getting Cristina situated, Bucky walked into her room and stood at the foot of the bed.

She looks so weak; so helpless, he thought. *Cristina is my life! I love her with every fiber of my being. I can't lose her now; I just can't.*

Minutes later, a doctor stepped into Cristina's room. Bucky wiped the tears from his eyes and turned to face him.

A tall, rather dark-skinned man, probably of Middle Eastern origin, stood before Bucky with a kind smile. "Hello, Mr. Morgan. My name is Dr. Hiam Abyss."

Bucky noticed that the doctor spoke with a slight accent and that he was wearing an extraordinarily expensive business suit under his lab coat. A little unusual for such a young doctor who was just starting his own medical practice.

"I am the doctor on-duty this evening," continued the doctor. "I am filling in for Dr. Wiley tonight."

"I'm sorry," Bucky replied, extending his hand to shake. "I don't believe I know you, doctor."

"That's understandable, sir. Tonight is my first night on the job."

"But I thought Dr. Wiley was working tonight? The officer I spoke with said he called Dr. Wiley to let him know the ambulance was coming."

"Well, he was here earlier, but the doctor got an emergency phone call about a half-hour ago and had to leave. I believe it was a personal matter."

"Oh, that's too bad." Bucky took out a tissue from his pocket and wiped his nose. He wished Dr. Wiley were there; especially for a situation as grave as the one at hand. For many years, Wiley had been their regular family doctor and always knew what to do and the right things to say to his patients in emergencies and bad times.

As Roger was pulling his automobile up to the hospital, he saw fire trucks and police cars down the street at the public library. Not knowing where Holly was located, he debated whether to go to the fire or to stop by the hospital first, wondering where he would have better success. Ultimately, he relied on his heart and disregarded the commotion at the library as he rushed into the hospital, hoping and praying Holly was still there.

Roger flew through the hospital entrance doors and hurried to the counter to speak with the receptionist.

"Excuse me, can you tell me if Holly Boliver is here?" he said, short of breath.

The receptionist promptly grabbed an admission's chart and glanced it over to confirm that Holly was there. "Yes, Ms. Boliver was here tonight, but she was released over an hour ago, and I believe she has already left the hospital."

"Would you happen to know where she went, or if she left with anyone?"

"I'm sorry, sir. We've had such a busy evening, I really couldn't say for sure."

"I understand," Roger replied. "Thanks anyway." Roger was about to leave when he turned back and asked, "Sorry to bother you again, ma'am, but can you tell me which room Cristina Morgan is in?"

Once again, the receptionist reached for her chart that listed all the patients that had been looked at or admitted for the day. "Mrs. Morgan is in Room 117."

Roger rambled up to Cristina's room and stopped just outside the doorway when he heard voices coming from inside. He overheard Bucky and the doctor talking.

Roger listened carefully and heard Bucky ask, "Is she..." Bucky stopped, trying to hold himself together. "Is she going to be okay?"

"We'll do everything we can, Mr. Morgan," Dr. Abyss told him. "However, you need to be aware that your wife has been involved in an *extremely* bad accident. Cristina has suffered major trauma and has massive internal bleeding. Her condition has stabilized, but she is far from being out of the woods yet. Do you understand, sir?"

"Yes," Bucky uttered. "Just promise me you'll do the best you can."

Roger inched a little closer and peered into the window leading into Cristina's room. The blinds were partially drawn, but he could still see Bucky sitting at her bedside. Watching her through the window, Roger realized the seriousness of Cristina's condition and decided not to enter the room after all.

Roger knew Bucky needed to be there with his wife and thought, *It would be best if I look for Holly alone.*

As he started to step away, Roger turned around once more and whispered, "Take care, ol' buddy. We'll catch up another time."

Chapter 33:

When the unimaginable becomes reality

Roger slowly walked out of the hospital and sat on a bench outside of the main entrance. Even though Roger hadn't smoked in years, the news about Holly and Cristina was decidedly disturbing to him, and he dug into his hiding place (the crease of his wallet) where he always kept an emergency cigarette. They were his "relaxers" he called them, a way to cope with times of extreme stress and anxiety; and right then, he couldn't think of a time when he needed them more.

He reached into his pants pocket, took out his lighter (an aqua colored Zippo which was a gift from Holly and carried everywhere with him), and fired up a Winston cigarette as Sam Cushman walked over to approach him.

"Hey there, young man," Sam said in a strange, muffled voice. "You're Roger Fasick, right?"

"Yeah," Roger replied, not paying any attention to the stranger next to him. "And who are you?"

"The name's Sam Cushman."

"Oh yeah, you're the famous homeless guy I've read about in the paper," Roger said casually, continuing to stare straight ahead.

Sam chuckled. "Yeah, I'm the poorest celebrity I know. Maybe now I can date a supermodel, too. Wouldn't that be nice?" Then his tone got all serious-like. "Do you know what I saw tonight?"

Finally, Roger turned to face him. Roger's eyes looked distant and he had an unnerving grin. "Let me ask you something, Sam. Are you familiar with Abbott and Costello?"

Sam cocked his head in confusion. "Um, yeah, they did the 'Who's on first?' comedy skit. That's one of my all-time favorites."

"Exactly! Now, do you remember the name of the guy who played shortstop?"

"Um, I don't know."

"Nope, *'I don't know'* was on third base. The shortstop was *'I don't give a shit!'*"

Sam shook his head and his face became flushed. "If my memory serves me correctly, I think his name was 'I don't give a *darn.*'"

"Same difference," Roger replied, blowing smoke in Sam's face. "Now go bother someone else."

For a moment, Sam stood speechless; he was caught completely off guard from Roger's response. "Hey, you date that pretty bartender over at Kitty's Bar." Sam scratched his temple as he thought. "Let's see, what's her name? It's Holly, isn't it?"

Roger was not in a talkative mood and let it be known as he stood up and began to walk away.

"I don't see where that's any of your business, old man." Roger uttered in an apathetic tone.

"Maybe not, but I saw her tonight just in case you're wonderin' where she is."

The old man's words caught Roger's attention and caused him to stop dead in his tracks. "What did you say?" Roger said, spinning around. "Where did she go?"

"She was following someone down the alley behind the library; I think it was that Reaper individual."

Roger's eyes widened. "Did you say the *Reaper*?"

"Yeah," Sam replied. "Anyway, shortly after the stranger disappeared into the shadows, she came sneaking along behind him. I saw her climb in a window just before the library went up in flames."

With his heart pounding in his chest, Roger grabbed Sam forcibly by the collar of his coat.

"Where'd she go after that?" he yelled. "Tell me now, or so help me..." Roger stopped, appalled by his own actions. He calmed down and released his grip on Sam.

"I, I don't know," Sam stuttered. "She didn't come back out, but neither did the Reaper."

Roger quickly shifted his attention to the fire down the street and watched as the flames towered even higher toward the sky.

"Oh, please no!" he screamed.

Roger dashed off as rapidly as he could, running so hard that his lungs felt like they were on fire.

While Roger was rushing to the fire trucks, Cristina Morgan regained consciousness back at the hospital. Doctor Abyss came out of her room and told Bucky that Cristina was asking for him. Bucky removed a tissue from his pocket and wiped the tears from his eyes and blew his nose, trying to make himself appear a little less worried and a little more calm and collected.

Then Bucky took a long deep breath to calm his nerves and went inside her room, standing at her bedside. He became aware of how weak and pale she looked, obviously from the amount of blood she lost. She opened her eyes and lifted her hand up, stretching it out as she reached for Bucky.

"Bucky, where's Mikey? Is he alright?" she said, grimacing in pain.

Bucky sat down in the chair next to her bed and gently caressed her hand. "Yes, Mikey's fine. He was with me, Hun; we were getting a movie. Why did you think he went after the cat? I yelled out to you before we left that he wanted to come along, and I thought you heard me."

"Those damn headphones," she groaned. "I can't hear anything when I'm using those transcription tapes."

"Don't worry yourself, babe," smiled Bucky, wiping his nose with a tissue. "Do you remember anything about the accident?"

Cristina shook her head. "No, I can't remember anything that happened."

While Bucky sat next to her bed, holding onto her hand and stroking her fingers, a raven flew up beside her window. Cristina saw a flutter of wings and glanced over, noticing the large bird that was pecking at her window.

The raven stared viciously into Cristina's eyes, and suddenly, she remembered what had happened. She gasped in fright as her heart pounded heavily in her chest. At that moment, she abruptly went into cardiac arrest, and the monitor hooked up to Cristina began to blare a loud, piercing sound.

Bucky stood up and began to panic. He heard a voice over the loud speaker yell, "Code Blue! Bring the Crash Cart to Room 117! STAT!"

A nurse came running and pushed Bucky right out the door without saying a word to him. Several doctors and nurses rushed into the room and began preparing the shock paddles in an attempt to stabilize Cristina's heart. Bucky remained close by, gazing through the windows to her room.

After a moment, Bucky opened the door and walked back in, frantic with concern. "What's going on?" he asked, his heart racing like a freight train.

Dr. Abyss placed his hand on Bucky's chest, stopping him in his tracks as he entered the room. "Mr. Morgan, you can't be in here right now! Please leave the room so we can work on your wife!"

Bucky looked frightened and felt helpless; unsure what was happening or how he could help her. "What's wrong with her?" he asked in a crackly voice. "She was fine just a moment ago."

Dr. Abyss turned to face him, his features were stern and his voice became more strict. "Please, Mr. Morgan, wait outside for now! We will do everything that we can to save her, but we can't have you in her right now!"

As Bucky left the room, his body was shaking hysterically and tears flowed down his face.

Roger ran up to the police barricade and began yelling Holly's name over and over. Josh Roberts was also there, talking to several spectators at the fire scene when he noticed Roger running up to the building from out of the corner of his eye. Roger's behavior seemed unusually erratic to Josh and roused his curiosity. He swiftly put his notepad back in his pocket, and he rushed over to Roger to find out what was going on.

"What's the matter, Roger?" questioned Josh. "You seem distraught."

"Holly's in there!" he hollered in a panicky voice. "I've got to go find her!"

As Roger started to walk around the barricade, Ken Johnson came over and stopped him. "Roger, get back!" he roared. "It's too dangerous for you to be near here! GET BACK!"

"Please!" Roger begged. "I have to get in there!"

"What the hell is so important, Fasick?" shouted Ken. "Are you trying to get yourself killed?"

Josh stepped in-between the two men and glared at Ken. "It's Holly!" he said forcibly. "There's a possibility she might be in that building!"

Inside the blazing library, Holly slowly began to awaken. Flames were engulfed around her, and she was choking on the black smoke. She called out for Roger, but no one could hear her.

She moaned as she rolled to her side and called out for Roger once again. She heard a crackling noise above her and pieces of the charred beams began to fall. She looked up for a brief moment before everything came down upon her and all went black.

Just then, the entire ceiling collapsed on the library, and the whole place went up in flames. Roger's face turned to utter shock and horror as he watched his love, his life, perish in the flames.

"Oh no!" he cried out. "Oh my god, no! Holly!"

Roger could not bear to look. He closed his eyes and turned away, trying to block out the sights and sounds around him. A moment later, he lifted his head and looked up towards the sky, noticing someone on a rooftop nearby. Although he couldn't make out who it was through his teary eyes, he could tell that whoever was up there, they were dressed completely in black attire.

After using the sleeve of his jacket to wipe the teardrops away, Roger squinted to get a better look, and then gasped in horror as the stranger peered down directly at him and they locked eyes. Just then, a fire truck went zooming by, sounding its horn and briefly diverting Roger's attention for a brief moment. He veered his head over to the fire trucks and the commotion down the street, and when Roger glanced back over to the building, the figure was gone.

Meanwhile, back at the hospital, the doctors had wheeled Cristina into the operating room and were frantically trying to get her condition stabilized. The doctors had used the shock paddles several times to get a normal rhythm to Cristina's heart, and just when the shock treatment seemed to be working, she opened her eyes and began crying and yelling, "I saw him! It can't be...He's dead! It just can't be!"

She yelled that over and over again as the paramedics tried to sedate Cristina, but the excitement was just too much for her. And with a long gasp, Cristina stopped breathing.

The emergency personnel and the E.R. doctor, Hiam Abyss, tried vigorously to revive her with CPR and electric shock with no success. Finally, after what seemed like an eternity, the doctor said, "Okay, time of death 9:57 pm."

The E.R. nurse walked over and gazed into Cristina's lifeless eyes.

"So sad," she remarked, placing her hand upon Cristina's face and closing her eyelids. "She was so young with her whole life ahead of her." As she began preparing Cristina's body to be removed to the morgue for an autopsy, Nurse Lyndaker turned to Dr. Abyss and asked, "What did she mean when she shouted 'I saw him, it can't be! He's dead?'"

Dr. Abyss shrugged his shoulders and replied nonchalantly. "I don't know, Nurse Lyndaker. It was probably just the hallucinations of a dying person. She was simply ranting and raving; I doubt it was anything at all."

The puzzled nurse looked at the young doctor unconvinced. "Well, I'll write it down on her charts just in case it does have some significance. Someone may know what she was talking about."

"Okay," Dr. Abyss said after a slight hesitation. "And...uh, when you're done with her file, put it in my office on top of my desk," he insisted.

With his head hanging low, Dr. Abyss came out of the operating room. He saw Bucky sitting nervously in a chair, rubbing his hands as they shook.

Bucky stood up as the doctor came toward him. "We did everything we could," said Dr. Abyss sadly.

Bucky fell silent, his knees buckled, and he sagged against the hospital wall. His posture began to droop downward as he raised a trembling hand to wipe flowing tears from his cheeks and eyes. Perspiration began to accumulate on his brow and stream toward his temples.

"Her injuries were just too severe," continued the doctor. "We were unable to arrest the internal bleeding and get her heart stabilized."

Bucky turned away and started down the hallway, never uttering a word. He stepped out of the hospital and strolled somberly to a bench outside the hospital door. He hung his head down and began to sob uncontrollably. Slowly, after many minutes, he began to get himself under control, and as he did, his active mind became flooded with heartbreaking thoughts and upcoming decisions.

He had to ask Celeste if she could stick around and watch Mikey while he made funeral arrangements. Bucky also had to notify Cristina's family of the unfortunate news and, oh god, Mikey. How was he ever going to tell that little boy what happened to his beloved Mom and that she would never be coming home to him again? Bucky began to cry again. All these racing thoughts were overwhelming him and he began to tremble as he sobbed.

After a few seconds passed, Bucky tried to pull himself together once again and determined it would be best if he went home. He felt drained, exhausted, and still shaky; but he understood he had a funeral and a burial to plan and he was the only one to get it done.

As he was crossing the parking lot, he noticed a black van with tinted windows parked near his Blazer. The engine was still running;

however, Bucky could not see if there was an occupant inside through the vehicle's tinted glass. Even though he thought it was rather odd that someone would leave their automobile on in the hospital parking lot, he passed by the van without giving it another thought.

While Bucky continued on to his vehicle, the dark and shadowy figure of someone wearing a broad-brimmed hat was watching him from inside the van, hidden behind the tinted windows and the shadows of the night. The same inexplicable shape that nearly scared Cristina to death as she laid on the street. Sitting motionless in the van, his eyes remained fixated on Bucky as he got in his Blazer and pulled out of the parking lot. Bucky drove away, and the stranger kept watching long after the lights of the departing automobile disappeared into the distance.

After a long intense battle with the blaze, things were finally beginning to be brought under control at the library. The fire was nearly extinguished, but there was still quite a bit of smoke bellowing from the ruins. Already the Fire Department's special fire investigators were beginning to sift through the rubble to try and determine the exact cause of the fire and also to look for any victims, not knowing as of yet that Holly had gone into the building before the fire started. As far as the firemen knew, there weren't supposed to be any individuals in the building at that time of the evening and everything was believed to be locked up for the night; therefore, the fire officials didn't expect to find any bodies or other wounded victims.

All of a sudden, someone began shouting from somewhere in the thick smoke and darkness.

"Over here!" one of the officers yelled. "Quick! I've found something; I think it's a woman!"

"Bring more lights!" another frantic and alarmed voice screamed out.

As more men with flashlights raced to where the shouting was coming from, Holly's body was discovered under a large pile of timbers and stone from the wall that had crashed down. Surprisingly, the body was not charred; however, it was badly bruised and battered from the weight of the ceiling and walls that collapsed on top of her.

The firemen began the painstaking task of removing the rubble that was covering Holly. Although it took only a few minutes, it seemed like an eternity until they were able to free her broken, motionless body. As they cautiously carried her out of the smoke-filled establishment, Roger and Josh could only watch in anguish and despair, unable to move or even think coherently.

The firemen carried Holly's body onto a stretcher and placed it into the back of the waiting ambulance where three paramedics immediately began checking for any signs of life. Unfortunately, their attempts were made in vain.

Roger stood next to the ambulance, trying to see and hear what was going on inside. Then, after a few minutes, one of the paramedics who had been administering CPR on Holly shook his head and grimaced as he emphatically exclaimed, "Time of death approximately..."

Roger never heard the paramedic's last words. He dropped to his knees and began to weep hysterically. Josh Roberts attempted to console his friend the best he could, not really knowing what to say or do for Roger in his time of sorrow.

Josh eventually convinced Roger to let him drive Roger back home, even though Roger protested that he wanted to stay at the library. Josh explained there really wasn't anything Roger could do at that point, and he would be able to get a handle on things and function better if he went home and rested for awhile.

Reluctantly, Roger gave in and rode home with Josh, remaining silent for the entire ride. Once they arrived at Roger's house, Roger got out of the car and walked into his house without saying a word to Josh. He dropped onto the couch, completely in shock and drained. Even though he tried to fight off his fatigue, within minutes he passed out on the couch, too tired to even move.

The Carthage firemen remained at the fire scene for the next several hours. They completed their search through the rubble and did not find anything or anyone else among the ruins. However, the scent of gas in the air, accelerant residue left over on some of the wooden bookcases, and other key factors led the investigators to determine that the fire was intentionally set—and it was now considered another case of arson and murder.

The ambulance had left long ago, and with it had taken the battered body of Holly Boliver to the hospital. An hour later, Holly's body was wheeled downstairs to the morgue where Harry Moon, the town coroner, and Anthony Durgo (Harry's young, impetuous assistant) had begun to prepare an autopsy to determine the exact cause of death...a procedure which had already been performed on Cristina Morgan a short time earlier.

As the coroner and his assistant began their gruesome task, Harry noted there were some unusual impressions, similar to burn marks, on Holly's forehead. After spending a lengthy period of time inspecting the abrasions with delicate scrutiny, Harry was unable to determine the exact cause of the blemishes. Once frustration set in and Harry ultimately decided to give up trying to classify the marks, he recorded them in Holly's chart as 'unidentifiable signs' because he was not familiar with markings left by a stun gun.

Chapter 34:

Mourning the Losses

The next few days seemed to drag on forever. The entire town was in shock over the events that happened. The destruction of Carthage's town library would have been enough to damper the spirits of most of the residents, but the untimely added deaths of Holly Boliver and Cristina Morgan made the black cloud which hung over the town seem that much darker.

On a sad autumn day, during the joint funeral at the cemetery, a town stood silent as the pastor spoke. The combined funeral service was agreed upon by Roger and Bucky to avoid prolonging the grief and pain of the families and all others concerned. As unbelievable as it seems, it took a tragedy of enormous magnitude in order to get the two friends talking to each other again.

Bucky and Roger stood in silence across from each other. Neither man glanced at one another, and yet, both men were aware of the others' pain. They were not so alike as some of the townspeople might believe. And they were not so different that they both didn't feel the anguish of two lives lost before their time.

After the pastor finished talking and the funeral service had ended, people began to leave the cemetery. As folks were heading back to their vehicles, Roger and Bucky were still standing at the gravesite with a 'far-off' distant look on their faces and a vast emptiness inside.

The priest that was overseeing the funeral, Father Bruce Emerson, was a new Priest in town. He was a tall man, of courtly appearance. His hair was slick and gray; his face was clean-shaven with stern features. Outside of church functions, Father Emerson kept mostly to himself and not much was known about this stoic clergyman. His most peculiar characteristic was he had shifty eyes, which left members of the congregation feeling somewhat suspicious of him. Aside from that, he was otherwise normal in appearance; however, his behavior did come across as slightly brusque.

All the while Father Emerson was conducting the service, Tim Matthews gazed directly at the priest. Tim continued to watch the clergyman with an intent stare long after the memorial service was over. His facial expression appeared as though he recognized him; however, Tim neither approached the clergyman nor said anything that would attract the priest's attention.

Just then, Thomas Parker came up and gripped Tim's shoulder. "Hey there, Bud. How're ya doin'? I know you and Holly were close and worked together for several years."

Tim's body jerked as he snapped out of his daze, he whirled his head around and turned to face Thomas. "Yeah, I'm still in shock like everyone else."

Thomas nodded his head.

"Death is such a terrible thing." Tim said unexpectedly. "My mother passed away when I was a teenager. I didn't even have a chance to say goodbye. I wasn't with her when she died; I don't think I ever got over that."

"Sorry to hear that, kid," Thomas uttered in a consoling tone. "That must've been very traumatic for you and your father."

"Actually, I didn't really know my father that well," Tim continued, staring ahead and appearing lost in his thoughts. "My parents split when I was very young and my mom took me to live with relatives out of state. I never really saw my father after that."

"Jesus, man. You've had your share of bad luck, too." Thomas paused, feeling slightly uncomfortable. "It's too bad that you and your dad didn't remain close. Did the two of you ever talk again?"

"Oh sure. I found my dad right before he died. He suffered from an extended bout of cirrhosis of the liver, but before he passed away, we sat down and had a long talk. He told me interesting facts about my family's history. I knew virtually nothing up until then."

Thomas grinned as he pulled out a cigarette. "I swear, that's the most I've ever heard you talk about your family."

Tim realized he was getting a little too sentimental and revealing more about his secretive past than he intended. He thought it would be best to move on to another topic of conversation.

"Hey, Thomas, that's a really sharp-looking lighter," Tim exclaimed "I've never seen a lighter quite like that before."

Thomas lit his cigarette, caressing the lighter in his fingers. He handed Tim the lighter and he held it in his hand, marveling over the unique design. The lighter had a dull copper finish with a black flip top. It was a classic Zippo design with a unique raised pentagon pattern affixed in the center. The pentagon had a golden hue to it with the initials T.P. engraved in the center and the inscription 'Thomas Parker' on the opposite side.

"I don't think I've ever come across a design like this in my life; it looks very historic," Tim said, very intrigued. "Where did you get it?"

"I spotted it at a country flea market when I was living in Louisiana. The merchant engraved my name on it for free."

"So, you spent some time in Louisiana, huh?"

"Yeah," Thomas stated. "It's something I don't wish to talk about."

Standing in the trees behind the mourners at the gravesite, Josh Roberts noticed Ken Johnson strolling toward him.

"What the hell are you doing here, Roberts? Did you come to get some *facts* for your next article?"

"Go to Hell," Josh replied. Then the news reporter wiped the tears from his moist eyes and turned to confront Ken. "We both know there's no love lost between us, but can we put aside our differences and leave out the snide remarks for just one afternoon?"

Ken could see how distraught Josh was by the teardrops in his eyes. Ken became somewhat embarrassed by his rudeness and spoke, "I'm sorry, Roberts. You're right; this isn't the time or the place. Please forgive me."

Josh nodded in appreciation.

"I'm here to pay my final respects to a friend, Ken. To be completely honest, Holly was much *more* than a friend; she was a distant relative of mine. Her mother's maiden name was Clark, and so was my grandmother's."

"That's something I didn't know about you," replied Ken.

"You're not really from around here, Ken. At least not born and raised. You'd be surprised how many of us are related to one another in some way," Josh added, now feeling surprisingly at ease conversing with Ken.

As the two men conversed by the trees, a tall, clean-cut young Carthage police officer in a finely pressed uniform approached Roger as he started to saunter back to his car.

"Excuse me, Mr. Fasick. My name is Officer Rick Streeter; may I speak with you for a moment, sir? I just have a few questions that I'd like to ask you."

Roger continued walking in utter silence.

"Please, Mr. Fasick. I know this is a bad time, but it won't take long, sir."

Roger stopped and nodded. "Yeah, I guess so."

"Thank you," the young officer responded, pulling out a pen and pad of paper. "First thing is, do you have any idea why Ms. Boliver would've been inside the library at the time of the fire?"

"I believe that Holly was in the library because she possibly saw the Reaper, or whoever it was that ignited the fire, and followed him in there," he said in a low, monotone voice. "I also suspect that she must have been noticed, or possibly even captured and then murdered."

"Well, it is possible that someone had done her in," the officer thoughtlessly remarked, continuing to write notes on his pad. "That would explain those marks on her forehead."

"Marks?" Roger uttered. "What kind of marks? You don't mean like the ones Pat Jordan had on his neck after he died, do you?"

"Yup, same type as his. I paid a visit to the coroner's office a few days ago. While I was there, Harry Moon showed the marks to me himself."

Roger stood in sheer astonishment. *Old man Cushman was right!* he thought. *Holly must've tried to go after the Reaper by herself.*

"Now then," Officer Streeter continued, "I was wondering, what leads you to believe that she saw the Reaper, or anyone else?"

"That's what someone mentioned. That homeless gentleman was featured in the newspaper over a month ago."

"Are you referring to Sam Cushman?" asked the officer.

"Yeah, do you know him?"

"We're familiar with him, sir. He conveniently seems to *always* be around at these recurring disasters." A moment of silence passed. "Anyway, I think I got everything I need to know. Thank you for the information, Mr. Fasick. We'll be in touch if we find anything."

Roger didn't say anything as the police officer turned and stepped away, he simply stood and mulled over the officer's last sentence.

Shortly after Officer Streeter had left, Josh Roberts came up to Roger. "I saw a policeman talking to you," he said to his friend. "What did he want?"

"Nothing much," Roger stated. "He just needed to ask me some questions."

"Oh," Josh replied, stuffing his hands in his pockets. After a few seconds of uncomfortable silence, Josh took a deep breath and cleared his throat. "Hey, I don't really know what to say in a moment like this." he said in a low, glum voice.

"It's okay, Josh. I understand."

"Y'know, even though Holly and I were related, I didn't know her too well. But I *do* know how happy she made you and..." His voice trailed off. After another brief moment, Josh continued. "Every time I saw her she always had a smile on her face, and her bright blue eyes could light up any room she walked in to."

"They were green," Roger stated in a monotone voice, his lip trembling as he continued looking straight ahead.

"What was that?" Josh asked, as though he was surprised by Roger's comment.

"Holly's eyes were actually green, but she never liked the way they looked. Although she only needed glasses to read with, she decided to buy some blue contacts lenses. She liked to show them off everywhere she went; there were only a few times she went out of the house not wearing them."

Josh decided to change the subject and ask Roger a question. "I've been meaning to ask you something."

Roger coughed to clear his throat. "What is it?"

"The other night, at the fire, how did you *know* that Holly was inside the library?"

"Your slipshod homeless buddy, Sam Cushman, told me, Roger said with a tinge of hostility."

"Sam? Sam was there that night?" I didn't see him anywhere. Are you sure it was him?" Josh asked, genuinely surprised at learning the news.

"Oh, I'm sure it was Sam alright. That was pretty convenient though, don't you think?"

"What do you mean?"

"Your pal, Sam, seems to show up at nearly all the fires that the Reaper has supposedly started. Maybe there's more than just a coincidence there, that's all."

"Are you joking? Or are you just trying to point fingers at the first name that pops into your head?" Josh remarked with a hint of anger in his voice. "Listen Roger, the guy is homeless! Sam has nothing to do but wander around Carthage, and frankly, I don't see where he even has a motive."

"Yeah, and maybe he *really is* the Reaper, and you've let your sympathy for the guy get in the way of your once-superb objective opinion!" Roger fired back.

"Look, you're angry and confused right now. Why don't you give me a call when you're thinking level-headed again?" Josh said, trying to soften the situation.

Roger rolled his eyes and huffed in frustration. "Yeah, we'll see."

Josh shook his head in disbelief as he rambled away. Roger felt a little ashamed about what transpired, but at the moment, he was in no mood to make excuses for his actions or apologize for his behavior.

Bucky and Celeste remained standing near the graves after the crowd had dispersed. The Mayor of Carthage look humbled and worn out, as if he hadn't ate or slept in many days. Celeste's bloodshot eyes stood out against her pale freckled face, and she took the barrettes out of her chestnut hair so that it could dangle about her cheeks and hide the tears that were falling. Even in despair, she looked radiant in her knee-high charcoal colored skirt and black blouse.

Bucky hung his head low and Celeste held Mikey tightly in her arms. Mikey was dressed formally in a black suit and tie, looking like a little gentleman. However, his actions were that of a normal four-year old boy as he grasped securely onto Celeste and sobbed, burying his face into her shoulder.

Bucky looked at Roger, who was still at his car. He was leaning with his back against the passenger side door and his head hanging down. "Celeste, can you take care of Mikey for me while I speak with Roger?"

"Sure," she answered soothingly, "and tell him I'd like to chat with him before he leaves."

A whirlwind of emotions was going through Bucky's mind. He was attempting to put on a strong front for Mikey's sake, even though he was hurting inside. He knew that people were going to go to him for guidance, but he didn't know what he was going to say or do. There was a multitude of questions and much heartache in town; the residents needed someone to turn to. But right now, the only thing the Mayor of Carthage wanted to do was comfort his friend and lean on one another for mutual support.

Bucky walked slowly up to Roger and put his hand upon his shoulder.

"How are you holding up?" he inquired.

Roger lifted his head upward. "I'm doing the best I can do," he replied. "How 'bout yourself?"

"I'm hanging in there...barely. Honestly, I have to be strong for Mikey's sake. It wouldn't do any good if both of us were falling to pieces at a moment like this."

"Yeah, I feel so sad for that little boy. He's got to be hurting so bad right now. I can't even imagine what thoughts are festering through his mind. No kid should have to lose a parent at such a young age. It's just not fair."

Bucky nodded. "Look Roger, I don't want to argue with you anymore."

"Neither do I, my friend. You're all I have left now," Roger responded, slightly choked up.

Bucky smiled, his eyes began to swell with teardrops, and his voice was muffled. "I want to say how sorry I am for everything that has happened and apologize to you for my behavior lately."

Wiping tears from his eyes with a white handkerchief from his pocket, Roger tried to regain his composure. "It's alright, Bucky. I also acted in a way I regret. Hopefully we can get past all those hurt feelings and move on."

"I'd really like that," Bucky said with a slight smile.

Roger suddenly turned to Bucky with a serious, determined look. "I know you've had your doubts about the Reaper, Bucky, but I saw him. He looked right at me and our eyes locked."

"I do believe you, Roger; I'm not in denial any longer. And we *are* going to do everything we can in this town to find him! You can trust me on that."

Both men stood in silence, not sure of exactly what to say to the other, as neither man was accustomed to apologizing for his behavior or actions.

Struggling to make eye contact, Bucky went on to say, "I just want you to know that this whole nonsense regarding the Reaper and Pat Jordan's file *really* was the first time I ever lied to you."

Becoming increasingly uneasy, Bucky's tone suddenly became lower and more serious-like.

"However, there is something else that I've held back. Partly because I didn't think it was any of my business and also because I didn't know how to bring it up in conversation. But since I'd like to start things anew with a clean slate, this seems like as good of place as any."

"What, Bucky? What are you saying?" questioned Roger.

"Several years ago, right before Nellie left town for good..."

Bucky paused and began to fidget as he swallowed hard.

"Yeah," Roger said, quite interested in what he had to say.

"Well, it was the night everything happened at the ferry service with Louis Ferr, and I had stopped at your house to look for you." He swallowed hard once again as his heart raced. "Anyway, that's where she gave me the letter to pass on to you, the one stating that she was not coming back to Carthage. After she took her suitcases and left, I remained there to make a phone call to Cristina, but as I was leaving, I looked down and saw something in your waste basket."

Roger stared curiously at Bucky, listening attentively to his story. "Uh-huh."

"I picked a piece of paper out of the basket and discovered that it was a receipt for a home-pregnancy test. Now, I never saw the actual test lying around anywhere, and I didn't talk to Nellie about it either. For all I know, you could've already known about it or it might not have even been Nellie's."

For a while, Roger said nothing at all. Then he cocked his head to the left as he mulled over his puzzled thoughts.

"I don't know what to say," Roger uttered in a quiet voice similar to a whisper. "I respect that you told me, Bucky, but I think I need to be alone right now."

"Whatever you need, bud. I'm always here if you need anything," Bucky announced, trying to comfort Roger. "Celeste wanted to talk before you leave, but I'm sure she'll understand. We'll all catch up later."

Roger slowly entered his car and drove away, leaving Bucky standing all by himself as Roger's car kicked up a cloud of dust and the wind carried it across the open field surrounding the cemetery.

Once Roger was gone, John Sears approached Bucky from behind and tapped the mayor on the shoulder to attract his attention. Dressed in nontraditional funeral attire, John was wearing a faded, wrinkled, black t-shirt and black work pants; and he did not look like the rest of the funeral crowd.

John had become immersed in his Indian heritage, covering his body with tribal tattoos, which he showed off with his short-sleeved shirt. John's long hair was braided downward past his shoulders. He also wore a traditional Indian headband with tribal markings as well as high buckskin boots, which extended up to his knees and had fringes along the top and sides.

"Hey John, I appreciate you and Adam could come here today. I know the two of you have been doing roofing work in Baltimore lately."

"Don't mention it, Bucky. It's the least we could do," John said with sincerity.

351

"John, you've known Adam a fairly long time, haven't you?" Bucky inquired.

"Yeah, dude, we were both harassed by the same friggin' bullies back in high school." John spit out a wad of chewing tobacco and said, "And because we were culturally different, it was only natural us 'misfits' would band together and become close friends."

Bucky raised a brow. "*You* were bullied, John?"

"Yeah, but those bastards didn't bother me anymore after I threw flaming paper bags with dog shit through their family's windows," laughed John.

Bucky ignored John's last comment and said, "Let me ask ya something that probably only you'd know."

"Okay, whatta ya wanna know."

"Is there something wrong with Adam? He seems very distant and preoccupied today. Almost like his mind is on something *other* than the funeral."

John let out a deep sigh and spoke in a near whisper. "Well, to be honest, he's kinda spooked about what's been going on at night around this area."

"I don't think I follow what you're getting at."

"The Reaper sightings," he explained. "It's dredgin' up some painful memories for the guy."

"What kind of memories?"

"Red and I were fishing on the riverbank five years ago. It was the same night all the horrible shit went down at the ferry service. Y'know...the incident with Mr. Ferr."

"*Really*? So, what happened when you guys were down at the waterfront?" questioned Bucky, his curiosity now fully aroused.

"Well, while we were walkin' back to my truck, Adam believes he saw the Reaper runnin' through the woods. He was comin' from the direction of the ferry service."

"This is news to me!" Bucky said in a raised voice as his face became serious.

"Red don't like talkin' about it," John answered. "He gets all freaked out whenever the topic gets brought up." John looked over his shoulder and saw Adam, who was gazing at them while Bucky and John talked. "Well, I better go. Don't say a thing to Red about what I told ya, okay?"

"No problem, John. But thank you for letting me know."

Hours later, Roger arrived home from the funeral and went to the refrigerator to get a cold, frosty beer. His feet dragged as he somberly made his way to his living room and plunked down in his armchair. He stared into nothingness for awhile before opening his beer and guzzled half of it down in one swig. As he sat alone in the silence, the phone began to ring, shattering the noiseless room of its eerie stillness.

Roger slowly made his way over to the telephone. "Hello?" he wearily asked.

The docile voice of an elderly gentleman greeted him back. "Hello, this is Dr. William Wiley. I've been trying to call all day."

"You have?"

"I'm sorry for the delay, Mr. Fascik, but I had an unexpected emergency out of town, and I just got back to Carthage today. There's a pile of papers and files on my desk; I've been sorting through them all day and calling my patients one by one."

Dr. Wiley's phone call puzzled Roger, and he shook his head in confusion. "Um, I'm sorry to hear about your emergency, Doc, but what is it you're calling about today?"

"Oh, I'm sorry if I've been rambling on," Dr. Wiley retorted. "Is Holly Boliver there? I got the blood work back from our lab."

"Blood work?" Roger said curiously. "What are you talking about?"

"Holly had some blood work done after her fainting spell. We ran several tests, one of those was to determine if she is pregnant, and I'm happy to say that she is."

Roger gasped and dropped the phone; the line went silent.

"Hello?" the Doctor said. "Is there anyone there?"

Carthage Chronicles Volume I

PART TWO:
To Catch a Killer

Chapter 35:

Time Marches On

Many things happened during the next ten months. Finally, the Carthage police admitted to the public that there really was a Reaper terrorizing the town, and the Town Council instituted a curfew for all residents of the community. For those that were homeless, the night had become an exceptionally frightening experience. Whether the quaint town was quiet and peaceful, or if there were times in which remnants of destruction reared its ugly head, a subtle uneasiness had slowly settled into the residents' thoughts, and the dark cloud of fear and trepidation had blanketed itself over the tormented community.

Roger's sanity teetered on the edge after his phone call from Dr. Wiley. He was a mess but managed to get through. After all, he was starting to become accustomed to unfortunate things happening in his life. It began with his brother, Paul Fasick, who died eleven years ago. Since then, he had suffered from bouts of depression and struggled with alcoholism. He confronted the Devil and faced death, then cheated it, and now he had to come to terms that his beloved fiancée was gone. Murdered by the Reaper.

A lesser man would have crumbled under the strain, but not Roger Fasick. He'd been to the edge, fought his way back, and vowed never to take that journey again. This was not to say that he was numb to the pain of his loss. Holly was the love of his life, and every day was another agonizing step to getting his life back on track.

Bucky didn't report to work for nearly two weeks after Cristina's death, trying to assist the police in tracking down the hit-and-run driver in the black van. Unfortunately, the combination of no solid clues and the lack of any eye witnesses made their attempts to find the motorist impossible, and the driver remained at large.

After learning of Cristina's accident and the chaos that followed, Bucky all but forgot about his conversation with Bill Intorcia, and never ended up telling Chief Zimmerman his theory on the antiquated underground tunnels. So, for the time being at least, the tunnels would go unchecked.

In actuality, Bucky rarely went anywhere or talked to anyone after the night Cristina died. His routine consisted of going to the office, putting in his time, and going directly home to spend time with Mikey. Sometimes he didn't even have the motivation to do that after having one of his 'tough' down-in-the-dump days, when his thoughts consisted only on Cristina and the depression that was getting him down. In times like those, Bucky would ring up Celeste and invite her over to watch Mikey while he secluded himself.

Celeste decided to put her next novel on the back burner for awhile and opted to stay in Carthage to assist Bucky with Mikey. When she wasn't with them, she was working part-time at Kitty's Bar to help out Miss Kitty, who needed another barmaid since Holly's demise.

Tim Matthews was now the only full-time bartender Miss Kitty had, and he was not known as the most reliable. Celeste also got her old job back at the *New York Times*, writing her own weekly column in the newspaper that she e-mailed to her Manhattan editor each Friday.

Celeste was experiencing a feeling of closeness and tenderness toward Bucky, a feeling she did not expect nor encourage. Even so, as time went on, those feelings became stronger until she could ignore them no longer. However, she knew how distraught Bucky had been with his wife's passing and how inappropriate it would be to make her emotions known at that time. She did not want to risk being rejected and possibly lose a long-time friend; therefore, she decided to keep her feelings to herself.

Once again, Thomas Parker could not come up with an alibi to where he was when the library fire occurred. He contended that after he dropped Holly off at the hospital, he decided to go home for the night and got a flat tire on the way home. A story that no one could vouch for. He was still the police department's number one suspect, but despite everything that happened, the department felt as though there wasn't enough evidence to charge him with anything. Therefore, for the moment anyway, Thomas Parker remained a free man.

The police were beginning to keep tabs on Thomas's whereabouts, yet trying not to alarm his curiosity in the process. Nevertheless, every time he left his house, Thomas always had a nagging suspicion in the back of his mind, as though he were being followed or watched. This unnerving feeling deterred him from going out in public; consequently, Thomas spent most of his time cooped up in his workshop behind his house.

Josh Roberts continued in his pursuit to locate the Reaper, and sometimes, he would get a tip from Ken Johnson. Since the funeral, they hadn't necessarily set their differences aside, but the men came to a mutual understanding. Josh felt a portion of his stress had been relieved since he and Ken were on civil speaking terms; however, Josh wasn't sure he wanted to become good friends with Ken just yet. There had been plenty of mistrust and bad blood between the two for some time, but Josh liked the cordial relationship he and Ken were experiencing at the moment.

This new truce had been beneficial to Josh. He had received tips, information, and even some cold case files from Ken. All this was helping Josh piece the parts of the Reaper case together, even though he knew he had a long way to go before he got to the bottom of it all. All the same, Josh's main interest was the sensational news story, and what it might do for his journalism career; Ken could have the credit for bringing down the Reaper as far as Josh was concerned.

On a warm summer's morning in mid-August, Roger sat on one of his kitchen table chairs next to the refrigerator and stared at the calendar on the wall while holding a photo of Holly in his hands. His eyes were bloodshot, as if he had not slept in several days.

"I have a real problem, Holly," he said, holding the picture close against his chest and closing his eyes. "It seems like my life has turned into a real mess. Everything is spinning out of control so fast...I don't know if I'm coming or going. You've been gone for such a long time that I've almost forgotten what your voice sounded like. Even when you were alive it seemed as if we never spent enough time together."

Roger lowered her picture back into his lap and turned his attention back to the calendar at his side.

"Well, Hun, I see we're coming up close on what was supposed to be our wedding day. Right now, we should be finalizing our plans for our honeymoon. Instead, I'm sitting here alone and missing you."

There was a knock on the front door and Bucky entered. He took a few steps inside the darkened, silent house. Then, standing in the hallway, Bucky yelled out, "Hey, Roger! Are you here?"

Roger stared blankly forward. "Yeah, I'm in here."

Bucky then walked into the kitchen where he saw Roger sitting at the table, staring at Holly's picture. How pathetic Roger looked, Bucky thought. He was only a shell of his former self. Roger just didn't look like the man Bucky had called his 'best friend' for so many years, and it really disturbed Bucky to see his old friend in this condition.

As he got closer to the table, Bucky noticed the large dark circles under Roger's eyes. "How are you doing lately?" he asked in a fretful tone. "Have you gotten any sleep?"

Moments went by without Roger saying a word. "Roger?" Bucky said. "Are you okay?"

Roger twitched and snapped out of his daze. "Oh, I'm sorry, Bucky. You said something about sleeping. No, I'm not sleeping any better. Thanks for asking. It's been a long time since I dreamed of anything....other than the way things were. I still see her in my dreams."

Bucky nodded in agreement, knowing the same feeling of restless nights and agonizing dreams.

"You know, it's funny all the small things you miss. Like, the way she flipped her hair back, or the way..." Roger's voice trailed off.

Bucky twisted away so Roger could not see the anguish in his face. "I understand what you're going through," he said, his voice hoarse and his eyes watery, "but I'm also very worried about you."

"Worried?" Roger exclaimed. Bucky detected a hysterical edge to Roger's voice, but now wasn't the time to bring that to his attention. "But why, Bucky? I'm getting by just fine and doing all right, don't you see?"

"You're *not* all right," snapped Bucky, "and it's not healthy for you to be living like this either!"

With a long sigh and a shake of the head, Roger said, "I know you're right, Bucky. Who am I trying to kid here? I guess just myself. Y'know something, I almost didn't make it back from my last severe depression. This time I don't even have the desire to help myself."

Bucky became upset over Roger's behavior, and soon, his concern turned to frustration. "You really need to stop feeling sorry for yourself," Bucky said in a stern voice. "You're not the only one who lost a loved one; or are you too immersed in your own self-pity to remember that Cristina died?"

Roger hung his head low.

"But unlike you, Roger, I don't have the luxury of wallowing in old memories and living in an endless depression. I have a young son to raise who misses his mother and needs me to be his pillar of strength. Don't you think I've wanted to fall to pieces every time Cristina has crossed my mind?"

"No, I know you must've gone through Hell, too, and you are probably still hurting inside. However, you have Mikey to help get you through the rough times and the two of you can lean on each other for support. Celeste has also been around to help you, too, hasn't she?"

Bucky nodded in agreement. "You're right. Celeste has been great through all of this. Most days it feels like my heart is hanging by a thread, but Celeste has been an overwhelming comfort to me, and she is the reason why I can even get up each morning." Bucky paused as his thoughts turned to Celeste and he smiled. "She has also helped me in taking care of Mikey, and we have been getting closer ourselves."

"So what are you saying, Bucky? Is there a relationship developing between you and Celeste?"

"Listen to me, Roger. I know you're the type of person that sees everything as black and white. There are a lot of grays in every situation. We may not like them; it's just part of life. And my relationship with Celeste is, at best, gray." Bucky paused for a moment. "I think she might want something more than just a friendship, but I'm not ready to move on and commit to anyone. It's just too soon."

Roger turned and looked at Bucky, staring him in the eyes. "But at least you're in a position to make a decision like that. I have no one in my life. All I do is sit around here day after day, surrounded by everything that reminds me of Holly. I can't forget about the way she died and about our last conversation together."

Roger's words triggered Bucky's curiosity. "What do you mean? Did the two of you have a fight?"

"Never mind, forget I said anything."

"Why does it feel like you're shutting me, and everyone else, out of your life?"

He glanced at Bucky and said in a somber tone, "You don't really want to know, Bucky, so why do you ask?"

"But I *do* want to know," insisted Bucky. "Did you two get into a heated argument? If so, and you're having guilty feelings about it?"

"Something like that. The day before Holly died she told me that she wasn't feeling well, and she wanted to take a pregnancy test. I told her that I hoped she wasn't pregnant because I didn't feel as though I was ready to have any kids. She didn't say anything, but I could tell by her facial expression that she was upset."

"She was pregnant?" Bucky asked in a hushed voice.

"Yeah," he finally admitted.

"Oh my god," Bucky said, sitting down in a chair next to Roger. "I didn't know."

"No, no one did. Not even me. I found out right after the funeral, but I decided to keep it to myself. The only people who know besides me are Dr. Wiley and my folks."

"You told your parents, but not me?"

"Not exactly," Roger declared. "I didn't *plan* on telling anyone. However, my parents stopped by my place after the funeral and found me curled up in a ball on the floor. I broke down in tears and cried like a child as I told them."

Bucky's eyes became misty.

Roger glanced at the calendar. "Her due date would have been sometime last month, maybe even on Holly's own birthday. But I guess I'll never know for sure."

Roger stood up and paced around the room as Bucky sat silently.

Teardrops formed in Roger's eyes and began to trickle down his cheek. "To say that my actions were the biggest mistake of my life would diminish the severity of my wrong. I just wish I could tell her how truly sorry I am for saying what I did."

"You need to let this go, Roger. It's not healthy."

"What I *need* to do is kill that maniac," Roger said hastily. "I want to ensure that what happened to me will never happen to anyone else again. I will have my revenge!"

"Listen to me Roger, I'm your friend and…"

Roger cut Bucky off in the middle of his sentence. "I don't need a *friend* right now, Bucky. I need a *partner*. The Reaper has got to pay for what he's done, and I need someone who will help me track him down."

Bucky paused for a moment and reflected upon Roger's words. "Have you talked to your folks lately?"

"No I haven't," Roger responded, confused by Bucky's question. "Why do you ask?"

"Maybe you should go to Syracuse and visit them. Maybe they can give you the guidance and comfort that I cannot."

Roger pondered over Bucky's suggestion and then remembered that his father still owned a pistol. "That's a good idea, Bucky. I think I'll go down there today."

"Great!" Bucky yelled, standing up and clasping his hands together. "Get out of Carthage and get yourself some rest and relaxation. A different view and some time away might do you some good."

After Bucky left Roger's house, Roger mustered enough energy and motivation to stand up and walk to the refrigerator. He stood with the door open, peering inside but not really looking for anything. Roger slammed the door shut and a piece of paper fell off the top of the refrigerator and landed at his feet. He picked it up and walked into the living room as he began reading it to himself.

> *Dear Roger,*
>
> *I will be late getting home tonight so go ahead and fix yourself some dinner without me. If you get some free time, I would like you to do a favor for me and call Bucky.*
>
> *I know that you two aren't talking right now, but life is too short to hold a grudge and a true friend will always be by your side when you're in need. Please try and make amends with him. It would make me happy.*
>
> *Love ya,*
> *Holly*

Roger crumbled up the letter in his hands and tossed it in the trash can next to the couch. Then he slumped down, put his hands to his face, and wept.

Later that afternoon, Roger motored to Syracuse to visit his mother and father, Darren and Tammy Fasick. Roger was distracted, and it showed while driving down the highway. His car swerved back and forth in the lanes several times and his speed kept fluctuating from very slow to dangerously fast. He narrowly avoided several potential accidents on his way to his folks' place and nearly broadsided a black van with dark tinted windows while veering to the off-ramp exit.

Roger continued his erratic driving all the way to his folks' home, almost crashing into their mailbox as he pulled into the driveway. When he entered the house, the smell of French Vanilla coffee and Old Spice cologne lingered in the air. It was a comforting aroma that reminded him of his childhood.

"Roger!" his mother cried out. "What a pleasant surprise!" She ran over and gave him a huge hug. "To what do we owe this delightful and unexpected visit?"

"I needed to get out of the house and out of town for awhile. I was hoping to talk to you and Dad."

"Sure thing, Hun. We're always here for you." Then she pointed into the next room. "Your father is in the living room. Go on in and visit with him while I go get us some drinks."

"Thank you, Mom," Roger said with a smile.

Mrs. Fasick disappeared into the kitchen while Roger continued on to the living room where his father was relaxing on the couch with a crossword puzzle in his hands, in deep concentration. He had been stuck for nearly half an hour as he diligently tried to come up with a ten-letter word that was synonymous with 'Exceptional' and began with a 'P.'

"Hey son, it's good to see you!" Mr. Fasick said, putting down his book and taking off his glasses. Then he motioned toward the chair on the opposite side of the couch. "Sit down and take a load off your feet."

He sat in the recliner, across from his father on the couch. His mother returned from the kitchen with a serving tray in her hands and placed it on the coffee table. Then she handed a cup to Roger and sat on the couch next to her husband.

After he took a sip of water and found his nerve, Roger got up the courage to say, "I need to ask a favor of you, Dad."

His father looked at him with concern. "What is it, son?"

"I need to ask you for your revolver."

Mr. Fasick was taken aback, shocked by his son's request. "What for, Roger? Don't do anything you will regret, Roger. There's nothing you can do to bring Holly back."

"That maniac murdered my fiancée and my unborn child. As for doing something I'll regret, I live with regret everyday of my life, Dad. Things I wish I'd said to Holly. Our future is all gone now, and I plan to make the Reaper suffer as much pain as he has caused."

"I know you're hurting, son," he said sympathetically. "But I think you're making a grave mistake. Maybe you should speak to someone, a professional, who can help you sort all of this out; possibly a therapist. Trust me when I say that if you don't let your demons out, they may eventually consume you."

"I don't need to see a therapist!" Roger roared in anger. "I don't need someone asking me what's on my mind; I already know what's on my mind. All I can think about every second of the day is getting the Reaper. He took my whole life." Then he paused and began to walk back and forth around the living room. "I have these dreams, night after night, that I have my hands around the Reaper's neck, squeezing the life out of him…and with his death, all the pain went away. Do you follow what I'm saying?"

"Believe me…I most certainly do, son," Darren Fasick answered back.

Roger grinned and his eyes lit up. "Good, because you've got to lend me your gun, Dad. I'm gonna track the Reaper down, and when I finally catch up to him, I'm going to kill that son of a bitch!"

"So, it has come down to this," Mr. Fasick said in a serious tone. "My son is willing to commit murder and take a life in cold blood?"

"As long as it's the Reaper!" Roger snapped back. "I would gladly do so!"

"And then what?" asked Mr. Fasick. "What happens after you kill him?"

"I don't know," Roger whispered softly. "I haven't really thought about *after* that. But at least I'll be able to watch the expression on the Reaper's face, knowing it was *me* who killed him."

"You're not thinking about the long term effects, son. I will tell you what will happen after you kill him," his father remarked. "You kill the Reaper, thinking your stress and heartache will be alleviated. But, unfortunately, your pain and despair doesn't end when you kill the Reaper; it grows. So you start another fight to find another person that will help you get past your anguish—when that fails, you will search for another, and then another! And along the way, you might end up making a victim out of an innocent person."

Roger kept his head down as he listened to his father's words.

"You will keep up your rampage until one terrible morning you wake up, take a good look at yourself in the mirror, and realize that revenge has consumed your whole life, and you don't know how to stop it."

"You can't understand, Dad, you haven't had a loved one killed by *that* evil maniac. You don't know what the Reaper is capable of doing!"

Roger's mother stepped in and gently caressed his shoulder. "We do understand, Hun, and yes, I have had a loved one killed by *that* maniac."

"What do you mean?"

Tammy hesitated, preparing herself for what she was going to say. "Son, my father, your grandfather, was murdered in Carthage back in the fifties."

"But I thought Grandpa Jake's death was an accident; that's what the newspaper said…and what I've always believed to be true."

Mrs. Fasick nodded. "Yes, I know. That's what the final police report stated. However, a local reporter saw someone who looked like the Grim Reaper at a fire scene that your father and I were at when we were just little kids."

"The Reaper? In Carthage in the 1950s? I think I've heard that rumor before. But, Mom, I don't see how this is connected to grandpa's death?"

"The reporter wrote a few news articles about the incident, thinking the strange individual he saw might've been responsible for that fire, and possibly some of the others, which occurred in town during that time. One of which was the fire my dad died in."

"I don't understand," Roger said, shaking his head. "All my life I was told that Grandpa Jake died trying to save some woman he never even knew. The whole town thought of him as a hero. How come you never told me this story before?"

"Nothing was ever confirmed," she answered back. Tammy glanced over at Darren, who had a nervous look on his face. She gently took Roger's hand and sat him down on the sofa, and then she continued. "One night, when I was a youngster, I awoke to the sound of loud voices. I hopped out of bed and walked to the top of the stairway where I saw my mom talking to a man in a long trench coat, a shabby-looking suit, and a two-day growth of whiskers."

Mrs. Fasick sat back down as she lost herself in thought.

"As I stayed there and listened, I overheard that same reporter tell my mother there was strong evidence the Reaper was responsible for my father's death and then tried to make it look like a rescue attempt. I had completely forgotten about that discussion until I read the *Tribune* reports that mentioned the Reaper was back in town."

"Then help me avenge their deaths," pleaded Roger.

"We can't," his father answered adamantly.

"Why not?" Roger asked in a troubling voice.

Tammy's voice was choked up and tears dripped from her eyes. "The Reaper killed my father; now he's also killed Holly, who was like a daughter to me. I couldn't bear the thought of losing you to that maniac, too. Our family has already lost one son. My heart couldn't take the strain of losing another. Please, Roger, you need to let this go."

Roger lowered his head and his shoulders relaxed. For the moment, he appeared as though he was going to concede to their wishes. "I'll do my best, Mom. That's the best I can promise you."

As Roger left his parent's home, his father said to his mother, "Why did you tell him about your father? Roger's still a young man with his whole life ahead of him. And your story probably encouraged him more."

"You're right about one thing, Darren," Tammy replied. "He *is* a young man. And young men with a mind for revenge need very little encouragement…what he *really* needs right now is our love and guidance."

Roger stopped at a gas station on his way out of Syracuse to fill up and grab a snack for the ride home. While pumping the gas, he glanced around and saw a small red-haired boy standing by the corner of the building. The little boy was all alone and kept staring at Roger with a smile upon his face. Roger thought the boy looked familiar although he was certain he'd never seen him before.

I know I've never laid eyes on that boy previous to now, but for some reason it seems as though I recognize him from somewhere, Roger thought.

Roger took a closer look at the boy's features. In a way, he sort of resembles my old girlfriend, Nellie Spencer. Wow! With as many thoughts going through my mind right now, I wonder what made me think of her after all these years.

Roger turned briefly in order to shut the pump off, and when he veered back around to look at the building, the boy had vanished.

Late that night, in the gloom of the midnight hour, Sam Cushman stood in the shadows of the Carthage streetlights behind the old Durkee's Bakery, which was now empty and used as a warehouse. Sam was looking across the Mighty Black, as some people referred to the Black River, and lit a half smoked cigarette butt he found along the road.

Suddenly, a shiver ran down Sam's spine, and he became very tense. Then, without warning, someone grabbed Sam around the neck. Sam felt the arm tighten, choking off his air. Instinctively, Sam dropped down on one knee, grabbed the assailant's arm, and threw the attacker over his shoulder to the ground; a fighting technique that Sam had learned while serving in the Army many years ago.

In the blink of an eye, both Sam and his attacker were on their feet face to face. Sam froze as he stared into what looked like the face of a skeleton, shrouded under a dark hood. As Sam stood as still as a stone statue, the dark cloaked stranger dashed into the night, leaving Sam surmising that he had just been in a horrifying nightmare.

Chapter 36:

Advice & Secrets

At Kitty's Bar a couple of days later, Celeste was behind the bar leaning against the cash register while Tim was washing dishes back in the kitchen area. Being that it was Saturday, Miss Kitty had expected an unusually busy day and had scheduled two bartenders to come in, but it turned out to be a decidedly slow day. Sam Cushman had been one of only a handful of customers which stopped by during the course of the day, with his afternoon being a little out of the ordinary. The twist was that Celeste, the bartender, was telling the customer her problems instead of the other way around.

Sam sat pie-eyed and dazed while Celeste was revealing her story of how she was developing some deep feelings for Bucky and was asking Sam's opinion of what she should do. She reasoned she had to tell someone what was really bothering her, and Sam seemed like a good listener.

"I have *very* strong feelings for him," she announced, sounding desperate for advice, "and I dislike the fact I have to conceal them, but I don't want to push Bucky away."

Sam looked her in the eyes and nodded understandingly. "Has Bucky given you *any* inclination that he might have the same feeling as you do?"

Celeste pulled back her chestnut hair and pointed to her ears, showing off a pair of princess-cut, diamond studded earrings. "Well, he gave me these as a birthday present back in June. He didn't give me a birthday card or tell me he loves me, but these earrings have to mean *something*, don't they?"

Sam noticed a crack in her voice as he leaned forward to get a better view of the quarter-carat diamonds. "I realize my opinion may not matter," he told her, "but if I were you, I'd tell Bucky how you feel 'bout him. Ya can't keep this bottled up inside of you forever."

Tim came through the door from the back area, wiping his hands dry with a dish towel. After hearing Sam's last sentence, Tim decided to jump into the conversation and put in his two cents. "Yeah, you *should* tell Bucky how you feel. But if he doesn't feel the same way, I think it would be a good idea if you moved on with your life. Stop pining for someone who doesn't return your affection. You'll only get yourself hurt in the end."

"I know you're right," she concurred, "but sometimes it seems that he doesn't want *anyone* close to him. He's always so wrapped up in work, and he spends endless hours in his den investigating the Reaper case. He's in there until all hours of the morning." Celeste stopped to sigh and then began again. "There are times when it feels like Bucky is in his own little world and keeping his feelings, or maybe some secrets, from me."

"I wouldn't hold that against him," Sam said with a slight grin. "I think it's very commendable we got ourselves a Mayor who's so concerned about the well-being of the community. And as for his privacy, we all have our own little secrets. Hell, even I have some that'd surprise ya."

Sam's last statement took Celeste by surprise. She paused and peered at him for a moment, and then she glanced at the bottle of whiskey he was drinking from. Celeste stopped dwelling on her own problems and realized, quite unexpectedly, that Sam had finished off half of the bottle of whiskey and was now sitting in front of her three sheets to the wind.

"Um, Sam," Celeste said, not sure of what to say, "I've noticed that you've been drinking quite heavily since you've come in here tonight. You've already had seven glasses of straight whiskey and you've only been in here a little more than three hours!"

Sam looked at the bottle with a half-glazed look. "Damn!" he yelled. "I guess I did! I hope I have enough money to cover my tab."

Celeste took some cash from the tip jar and placed it down next to Sam. "Don't worry about that. I'll cover for you if you can't afford it. I'm just concerned about your behavior tonight. Is there something wrong, Sam?" she asked caringly. "I know it's none of my business, but you're drinking the whiskey like it's going out of style."

"You don't have to be concerned about me, pretty lady. I'm just trying to numb my body and forget about the dangers in life."

"I don't understand, Sam. What dangers are you talking about?"

"Well, I think there's a strong possibility that I might be next on the Reaper's list of victims," Sam said, half joking and half serious.

Celeste leaned closer, completely attuned to Sam's mumblings. "Why would you think that?"

"Because…" Sam began as he took another sip of whiskey. "He's already attacked me once—a few nights ago when I was behind the old Durkee's Bakery building."

"Oh my god, Sam!" gasped Celeste. "What happened? Did you get hurt?"

"I'm alright; I think I showed that psycho I ain't no pushover. However, I'm suspectin' he knows my secret; that's why the Reaper has been after me."

Tim, who had previously been uninterested in anything Sam was saying, abruptly turned around.

"What hidden secrets would you possess that the Reaper would be interested in?" he questioned. "Maybe he's just trying to purge the streets of the homeless people like I've been reading in the newspaper."

"Tim, don't start," Celeste interjected, putting her hand on his arm.

"Well, it's true. As far as I can tell, there's no other link between *any* of the people who've been attacked."

"I didn't realize you were so knowledgeable about the case. You must do a lot of research on it," Sam said in an aggravated tone. "Sounds like one heck of a hobby you've got there, Tim. If that's all it is."

"Just what are you implying, old man?" Tim answered through clenched teeth.

"Alright!" Celeste butted in. "The testosterone is so thick in here you can cut it with a knife."

The two men looked away from each other.

"Tim, why don't you go home for the night?" suggested Celeste. "We're dead in here tonight, and I can lock up myself. Go get a good night's sleep and loosen up a little. You've been real cranky lately, and *I don't like it very much!*" she stated in a stern voice.

"Yes ma'am," said Tim, smiling. "I'll be sure to work very hard on my mannerisms."

The two bartenders stared at each other and laughed. Tim gave her a hug and a kiss on the cheek; then he gave her a wink and proceeded out of the bar.

Shortly thereafter, Miss Kitty stopped at the bar to relieve Celeste for her dinner break. It had started to rain, and all of the remaining customers had left the bar, including Sam, in anticipation of a bad storm coming. Since she knew Miss Kitty wouldn't mind, Celeste opted to leave the building for her break. She decided to take Sam and Tim's advice and hopped in her car to go talk to Bucky. She just couldn't keep her feelings bottled up inside any longer.

On the way to Bucky's house, the rain smacked her windshield forcibly as the thunder bellowed ferociously around her. Celeste paid no attention to the storm as rehearsed what she was going to say over and over in her mind, trying to come up with the perfect words to express herself. Butterflies were aflutter in her stomach, making her nervous; but more importantly, she was eager to get everything off her chest.

There was a lull in the storm by the time Bucky arrived home. He was in his own little world as he parked his car in the driveway, not noticing Celeste's vehicle parked along the curbside. He sat in the silent car for a few moments, thinking back on the events in his life. After wiping a teardrop from his cheek and exhaling a sorrowful sigh, Bucky reached over and picked up his suit coat off the passenger side seat, only to notice that his wallet was not in the side pocket.

"Great! Where the hell did my wallet go?" he mumbled in an annoyed tone.

After searching the floor of the vehicle and the glove compartment, Bucky started to get concerned. His pulse quickened as he looked frantically for it, not because of the money or the credit cards, but because it contained the picture of him and Cristina from their first date. They had it taken together in a photo booth at a mall in Watertown many years ago, and Bucky loved the way she looked in it. He always carried it in his wallet, and he was not willing to part with it, not now.

"Come on," he pleaded, "I need to find it. Please, my pictures are the *only* thing I want."

Then, like an answer to his call, his wallet appeared, underneath the passenger seat and completely intact.

"Thank you," Bucky said, kissing his wallet.

Bucky lumbered out of his Blazer like an old man. Just as he slipped his coat on, the downpour started once again and he hurriedly ran from his vehicle to the house, keeping the collar of his jacket turned up to block some of the rain. After fumbling with his keys, he walked in the door to his house and leaned against it, breathing a heavy sigh.

It had been another stressful day, catching up on some paperwork in the office on his day off, and now he was ready to relax. Mikey was spending the weekend with one of his friends from school, and Bucky had the whole house to himself for the night...or so he thought. When he walked into the living room and plopped down in his favorite recliner, he saw Celeste standing in the shadows near his bookshelf.

Bucky quickly sat up and turned on the lamp next to him. "Celeste?" he said, astonished by her unexpected visit. "What are doing here in the dark? Aren't you supposed to be tending bar tonight?

"I am...I mean, I was..." she sputtered out. "Miss Kitty is covering for me right now; I'm on my dinner break."

"Oh, I see," Bucky said, hesitantly. "But that doesn't explain what you're doing *here*."

Celeste stepped forward and positioned herself on the couch, her hands trembling nervously in her lap. "Bucky, I have a lot of things on my mind and I need to talk to you."

"Well, if it couldn't wait till tomorrow, it must be important. What's on your mind tonight?"

After several deep breaths, she gathered the courage to tell him what she came over to say. "I have developed some strong feelings for you," she admitted. "I understand that it is very soon since Cristina died, but I want to determine where I stand with you." She paused for a second. "I want to know if there is a future for us."

He was silent for a moment, but she could almost sense his racing thoughts.

"I can wait as long as you need me to," she continued, hoping for some sort of reaction from Bucky. "That is, if you think there might be a chance for us."

"I can't..." Bucky said at last, his voice little more than a whisper. "Not now."

"If not now, how about sometime in the future?"

"I'm not sure, Celeste," he mumbled, shaking his head. "There's a part of me that thinks maybe we *can't* be together."

"Why do you say that? Please, tell me."

Celeste watched his face, saw from his expression that he had an answer. She could see just as clearly that he was struggling to formulate it in words she could understand—he could understand.

After more than a minute, he shrugged and said, "I'm just a confused guy who's trying to put his life back together."

"And I'm here to help you any way I can," she said, encouragingly.

"Look," he retorted in firm voice. "I can't consider anything right now because my mind is still so messed up, and every time you are around, the way you smell makes it so I can't think straight."

Bucky walked around to the backside of his recliner, digging his fingers into the cushion of the chair.

"Christ, I'm so screwed up, Celeste. You shouldn't waste your time with me."

Celeste gazed at him caringly and smiled. "There's no one else I'd rather *waste* my time with."

"I'm glad you're ready to move past your relationship with Paul, but maybe you should search for someone who has less emotional baggage than I have right now." He hesitated before beginning again. "Sometimes I think that maybe it would be best if I was alone…away from everyone. I don't know how long I'll feel this way, and I don't want to ask you to wait for me either. As much as I *do* care for you, Celeste, I can't promise you anything right now."

Celeste's sensitive feelings were hurt, but she tried not to let it show. She had to accept what he was saying, but that didn't make her feel any better. With a long sigh, she turned away from Bucky and bowed her head. Then she grabbed her belongings, and started to walk out.

Before leaving, she turned back around with tears in her eyes and said, "I'm sorry for being such a problem for you, Bucky. I won't come around anymore."

Bucky stood still for a moment, and then he took off after her. He ran into the dark, trying to see which direction she went in, but found it difficult to locate her. It was raining, the visibility poor, and he was about to give up when he spotted Celeste walking down the street.

"Celeste wait!" he called out. "That's not what I meant!" But she was too far gone and the sound of the pounding rain was very loud, making it so she couldn't hear Bucky yelling to her.

For the past four years, Sam Cushman had blithely roamed the streets of Carthage. Though homeless and jobless, he maintained his eternal optimism, his zest for life. Sam never once surrendered to despair…until this particular night.

Hours after leaving Kitty's Bar, Sam was on the street. His clothes were drenched from the downpour a short time earlier, and he was searching for a dry place to stay for the night, preferably one with a roof over top.

While he was walking along, a strong sense of nervousness overwhelmed him as he was suddenly stricken with suspicions of being followed. The continuous feeling of being "on edge" had taken its toll on Sam's nerves and had wearied him more than the long nights without sufficient sleep. He constantly looked over his shoulder and scanned the rooftops for signs of movement as he passed along.

Sam stopped when he reached the end of the block; exhaustion was beginning to set in and he let out an uncontrollable yawn. He rubbed at his paining eyes and felt their puffiness.

I don't know how long I can stay awake, he thought. *I need to get someplace safe so I can rest.*

"Like I'd tell anyone about my secret," Sam said to himself as he continued across the intersection. "If it got around that I knew where Patrick Jordan's missing file was, my life would be in more danger than it already is. I sure hope the person who has it can put the clues together fast, so we can bring this nutcase in. I know Mr. Jordan gave me a number to call if I ever needed help, but up until now I've done a pretty good job of keeping myself out of harm's way."

Sam dug deep into his pants pockets, trying to find some money. He pulled out his hand and smiled as he looked in his palm and counted about seventy-five cents in loose change and a wrinkled piece of scrap paper with faded numbers written on it.

"I hope this is enough to call Watertown," he said, clutching the coins tightly.

Sam turned his head from side to side, and then he went straight to a coin-operated pay phone and dialed up a number.

"Hello?" a female voice said.

"Hello, I'm sorry for calling so late. My name is Sam Cushman. I got this number from Patrick Jordan before he died. I'm the one who sent the package to you, and Mr. Jordan told me that if I ever needed help, or if I needed to get out of town, then I should telephone you."

"You've called the right place," the woman replied. "I can help you, Mr. Cushman. What do you need?"

"Can you get me out of Carthage tonight?" Sam asked, constantly looking over his shoulder. "I think my life is in danger."

"It might take me an hour or longer to get there, but I can come get you. Tell me where you want me to pick you up."

"Do you know where the Carthage Athletic Field is?"

"Yes, Mr. Cushman."

"I'll be at the back entrance. It's on North Washington Street."

"I know the place you're talking about," the woman stated. "I'll be there as soon as I can."

"Thank you," Sam said as he breathed a heavy sigh of relief. "If something should happen, and I don't make it, get in contact with

Bucky Morgan. He's the new Mayor in Carthage and probably the one person in town that you can trust."

"Thank you for the tip, Sam. I'll see you soon. Oh, and by the way, I'll be driving a powder-blue 1985 Plymouth Reliant," said the voice on the other end of the phone.

Sam left the phone booth and began to walk away fast. He rambled down to the end of State Street and turned left down the road to the Carthage Athletic Field. He stayed on the narrow road close to the light posts as the path wound around the two ball fields and headed out toward North Washington Street.

About two hundred yards into his jaunt, Sam stopped as he heard a branch snap.

Is there a stray animal in the woods, he thought, *or something I'd rather not think about, which sends chills up my spine?*

He shrugged off his fear and quickly picked up the pace, but after only a few steps, he slowed once again as he began to hear noises. When he stopped to gaze around the area, he saw a shadowy figure standing in the far away bushes.

Fear and panic overtook Sam's emotions, and he stumbled as he tried to pick up the pace. He turned off the paved road and ran hastily through the ball field and passed the tennis court to the walking trail at the edge of the tree line which led to the old Carthage Water Tower. Sam had spent dozens of nights up at the top of the water tower as a kid, and he knew the path very well, probably better than most. He perceived that if he could somehow make it to the tower, then he might have a chance to climb up the tower to safety.

Sam ran faster than he had in years and arrived safely at the water tower in one piece. He leaned against one of the posts, huffing and puffing, trying to get some air to his lungs.

A bellowing, sinister laugh echoed from a few feet behind Sam, and he spun around quickly as he pulled out a hunting knife. There in the ominous shadows was a figure of someone in a long, black hooded cloak.

Sam stood motionless and quivered as the stranger began to walk closer. Petrified and speechless, Sam's body began to shake as the Reaper pointed at him and spoke.

"I know you've spoken to the police and to that reporter, Roberts, on several occasions," the Reaper stated in a grisly voice. "I believe you know a great deal about me. And even if you don't, I think you're in a position to be a danger...or pose a threat to me."

Although he was almost too frightened to move, Sam knew he would have to battle if he was to have any chance of survival.

Sam was tough. Gasping for breath, he raised his hunting knife above his head, wobbling into a military fighter's en garde. He knew his skills were rusty from inactivity and his form was ragged, hardly dangerous. The Reaper settled into a guard as well, his left hand kept at his side and curled into a fist. Unseen by his opponent, the Reaper's right hand reached slightly behind his back. Eight inches of a black stun gun slid from its hip sheath.

They stood, each assessing his strategy. The Reaper shifted slightly and Sam decided to take his chance. He whipped around his hunting knife, cutting a wild arc. However, the Reaper's maneuver had been a trick. He stepped away from the incoming blow, spinning inside Sam's reach as he was lunging towards him.

The Reaper's right arm flashed up, and he extended the stun gun towards Sam's face. Sam regrouped and straightened himself a second before the stun gun made contact. He moved swiftly and ducked as the Reaper swung, delivering an elbow to the back of the Reaper's head and making the cloaked one lose his balance as he tumbled down into the dirt.

Sam saw the stun gun flicker as it hit the ground, and he wondered what other weapons the Reaper was carrying with him. Realizing how unprepared he was to fight such a shrewd opponent, Sam determined that he was no match for his foe, and decided to retreat.

While the Reaper remained on the ground, Sam whirled around and quickly began climbing the ladder on the side of the water tower as fast as he could. When he reached the top of the tower, he stepped onto the tower platform, nearly collapsing from anxiety, exhaustion, and fear.

"I made it!" he said, sucking in air and exhaling nosily. "Thank heavens, I made it!"

Sam bent over, wheezing and coughing and then slowly stood up. He rotated around and looked down the ladder to see if he had been followed up the tower. Unfortunately, Sam did not realize that the Reaper had been behind him the entire time and made his way straight up the tower while Sam was catching his breath.

As Sam squinted into the night, he didn't see anyone on the ladder and let out a small sigh of relief. He figured with only one way to the top of the tower, that being the ladder, he could defend himself much better.

While watching the ladder, Sam tried to focus his eyes to the darkness only to hear a spine-tingling noxious laugh behind him. The hairs on the back of Sam's neck stood on end and Sam sat straight up. Just as he was about to turn around, Sam was grabbed around the throat.

"Urgh…" Sam cried out as the Reaper tightened a forceful grip around his neck.

Sam struggled to kneel down far enough so that he could reach his hunting knife, which was still lying next to his feet. Despite his misfortunes, Sam was still a strong man with a quick wit, and within a few seconds, he had maneuvered himself so that his hand was within a few inches of the knife. However, just as he was about to grab it, the Reaper reached into his cloak with his free hand and pulled out his stun gun.

The Reaper leaned in close and muttered into Sam's ear, "Now it is time to die, Sam."

The last thing Sam heard was a faint clicking noise before he lost consciousness from the sting of the notorious stun gun.

As Sam's body went limp, the dark figure picked Sam up and threw him downward from the top of the tower. Sam's twisted body laid upon the ground with his lifeless eyes staring up toward the sky. The Reaper laughed his evil laugh again, thinking his deed would look like an accident or possibly a suicide.

Chapter 37:

A Killer among Us

It was Friday, August 18, around 9 pm. There was the low buzz of various voices at Kitty's Bar all chattering at the same time and the clinking of glasses as the customers drank. The prime topic was Sam Cushman's death a couple days ago, and it seemed everyone had more questions about the incident than answers even though Sam's grim death was officially ruled a suicide.

Adam "Red" Richardson was standing in front of the jukebox as the other patrons sat at the bar drinking their beers. As Adam finished choosing his song selections and sauntered back to his table, a Frank Sinatra song abruptly came over the speakers. Everyone at the bar stopped their conversations, glanced over to the jukebox with a look of surprised confusion, and then turned their attention to Adam.

"What the hell is that?" Thomas Parker yelled out.

"What's the matter?" Adam answered back, his face beginning to become flushed. "Can't a person listen to some variety?"

John Sears, who was sitting next to Adam, gave him a nudge and said, "Boy, you sure can pick 'em!"

"Yeah, I guess so," Adam responded, shrugging his shoulders. "Actually, I goofed and pressed the wrong numbers, but I don't really care what the friggin' jukebox plays anyway."

Irritated over Adam's remark, John said, "Jesus, man, are ya gonna sit here and sulk all night?"

"No," Adam stated. "Y'know something, sitting here tonight gets me thinking about Scott Patterson. Its times like these I wish he were around so we all could have a couple beers and shoot the breeze. He was a good guy and a great drinking buddy."

John sighed. "It's a damn shame what that old ferryman did to him, Red. But I'm thinkin' it'd be best to drop the subject. There ain't no sense in gettin' yerself any more depressed than ya already are."

A few seconds later, Adam said, "Do you remember the mythology course we took together at Canton College?"

"The one with Professor Moody?"

Adam's eyes lit up like a light bulb went off in his head. "Yeah, that's right! Professor Kyle Moody. When we started talking about Greek mythology, he mentioned a tale of a ferryman who transported the dead over the Styx River."

John nodded. "Oh yeah, I remember now. The ferryman's name was Charon."

"And do you remember the poem he read aloud to the class? The one titled 'The Ferryman'?"

"Vaguely," John said uncertainly, peeling the label off his bottle of beer. "What're ya gettin' at, Red?"

"Well, Professor Moody said it was written by one of his close friends. Supposedly, it was based on a real-life occurrence. Thinkin' back on it now, I should've made the connection and got in contact with our old professor back when all those strange incidents started happening at the ferry service."

At that instant, Roger Fasick came in the door. He was there to meet with Josh Roberts, who was already at the bar and sipping on a tall Tequila Sunrise. On his way over to the bar stools, Roger stopped when he noticed John and Adam sitting at one of the tables. He gave them a grin and a nod, and then he walked over to them.

"Hey guys!" Roger bellowed, pulling up a chair. "How's it going tonight?"

Adam just shrugged his shoulders while John turned to face Roger. "I'm doin' alright," John answered. "But our buddy, Red, is feelin' a bit on the depressed side tonight."

"What's bothering you, Red?" Roger prodded.

"Oh, nothing much," he responded dully. "Just thinking about life and things. My girlfriend, Jamie, and I broke up yesterday. I guess you could say I'm having a hard time getting over it. My life has been a constant whirlwind of good and bad experiences for so long now...why can't things be like old times? Everything in town, and my life, seemed to be great."

John leaned over toward Roger and spoke in a hushed voice. "Red was really whipped on that girl," he stated. "I remember he once told her he'd change his last name to hers if they ever got married."

Roger looked at Adam, who was still staring straight ahead and sipping his beer. "Is that true, Red?"

"Yeah," he replied solemnly.

"And what is her last name?" Roger inquired with a grin. "That is, if you don't mind me asking."

"It's Gidney," Adam replied. Then he ran his fingers through his hair and let out a sigh. "Her name is Jamie Gidney."

"Hmmm…why does that name sound familiar?" Roger wondered aloud.

"You've probably seen her before," John remarked. "Hell, she probably served ya a few beers as well. Jamie used to be a barmaid here during the summer of 2000."

Roger's eyes lit up. "Oh, yeah! I remember her; she was a very cute girl…but awfully quiet, too." Roger veered his attention back to Red and stared at him with a strange look upon his face. "So, if you two got married, you would've gone by the name Adam Gidney?"

"Yeah, I suppose so. But that's sort of a moot point now."

Roger put his hand on Adam's shoulder. "Now, it's just my opinion, but I think it may have been for the best. I don't think 'Adam Gidney' has a good ring to it. If you were to change your last name, we would've had to change your nickname, too."

"Why is that?" Adam asked.

"Well, if you think about it, Adam 'Red' Richardson sounds a hell of a lot better than Adam 'Red' Gidney. Hell, the next thing you'll tell me is that John wants to change his name from Sears to Bears."

John mulled over the idea while rubbing the stubble on his chin. "Hmmm…John Bears, huh? I think I like the sound of that. It sounds more tribal than the last name I have now."

Adam looked over at Roger and tried not to laugh, but within seconds, all three men were chuckling over John's words.

"Anyways," Roger continued, shifting his attention back to Adam. "I'm sure that someone with your abilities will be back on the horse again in no time."

"What abilities?" Adam replied. "The only abilities I have are fly-fishing and falling for the wrong women."

Roger looked upon Adam with pity and said, "Want a little advice, Red?"

"Not really."

"Well you're going to get it anyway," Roger countered. "Stop wallowing in self-pity; stop living in yesterday and appreciate what you've got *here and now*. There's nothing that you or anyone else can do to change the past, and you need to accept that. All we can do is keep remembering the good times we shared and learn from the lessons our loved ones have taught us."

Roger walked away, continuing on to the barstools and leaving the two men to sit at the table in silence. *Was I talking to Adam?* Roger thought. *Or were those words directed towards myself? Both of us, I suppose. The one thing I know for sure is that I'm not going to end up on a barstool somewhere, several years from now, still crying over what might have been.*

After a few moments, Adam turned to John and asked, "So, anyway, what are you doing tonight?"

"I think I'm goin' over to the church."

"Say what?" Adam exclaimed.

John chuckled. "I mean, I'm gonna do some midnight fishin' along the Black River—probably somewhere near the Episcopalian church on Water Street."

"Hey, I have nothing going on and I haven't been fishing in over a month. Mind if I join you?"

John looked nervous and began to stutter. "Um…nah, that's alright. Thanks dude, but I'll probably only stay there a short while. Shit, it's not even worth your time. We'll get together and do some serious fishin' together soon, okay?"

Meanwhile, over on the other side of the bar, Celeste and Tim were engaging in a playful conversation of their own as Tim was getting ready to leave for the night.

"So, Celeste, what are you doing the last weekend of the month?"

"This month?"

"Yeah."

"Nothing I can think of, Tim. Why do you ask?"

"Yesterday, I received a gift certificate to the Renaissance Restaurant from my landlord. I did some maintenance work around the building for him and that old cheapskate wouldn't pay me in actual cash. Anyway, I was wondering if you'd like to go with me."

"That's very sweet, Tim. I suppose it all depends on what shift Miss Kitty has me scheduled to work."

"I checked the schedule in the break room, and Gary Wolff is supposed to work Saturday night. And after that, Miss Kitty is training some guy named Travis Kull on Sunday to be our newest 'call-in' bartender. That means neither of us are scheduled for a night shift the whole weekend."

Celeste's eyes lit up.

"The Renaissance, huh? I've *always* wanted to go there to eat," she said enthusiastically. "I heard they have the best steak dinner in the upstate area."

"So…is that a 'yes'?"

"Well, I have a meeting with my publisher in Syracuse, during the morning hours, on that Saturday. However, as for the rest of the weekend, I'm free every night after work. So, yes, I would definitely like to go with you."

Tim smiled, beaming from ear to ear. "Great! We'll plan on going Sunday night."

Then she blushed and spoke softly. "Thank you for asking me, Tim."

"The pleasure is all mine," he replied. "So, does this meeting with your publisher have anything to do with that novel you've been working on?"

"Yeah, the on-again, off-again novel about the ferry incident six years ago. I finally have a working title for it; and since I've had plenty of free time on my hands lately, I've been getting an enormous amount of writing done!"

Tim gave her a little pat on the back.

"Good for you! I feel privileged to be working with such an intellectual person," he joked. "So what's the name of the novel going to be?"

"I think I'm going with 'Beware of the Ferryman,' but it still might change."

An approving grin appeared across Tim's face. "I like it. In fact, I wouldn't change a thing."

As Celeste and Tim were chatting, Josh and Roger were sitting at the bar talking. Josh had switched from hard liquor to beer and had bought one for his friend. With a long, deep exhale, Josh leaned back in his stool and took two, four-inch cigars out of his inner coat pocket, handing one to Roger.

Josh pulled out his Zippo, lit up their cigars, and sipped on a Molson Golden. "I need to shake off the lethargy I've been experiencing lately, and buckle down on the Reaper story again."

"I've noticed that you haven't put out any editorials about the Reaper sightings in awhile," Roger commented.

Josh nodded. "I've been in a rut lately, and it's only gotten worse since Sam's death."

"What's wrong?" inquired Roger. "Is it 'writer's block', or are you having a problem at work?"

"A little of both I suppose," admitted Josh. "But tensions at work *sure* have been mounting lately. Ty's been on my ass for several weeks."

At the mention of Ty's name, Roger rolled his eyes and asked, "What's his gripe *this* time?"

"He's threatening to take me off the Reaper story."

Roger's eyes widened. "You can't be serious!"

"I *wish* I was joking. Ty told me that if I don't produce some gripping material soon, he's going to assign the story to someone else."

"He can't do that!" exclaimed Roger. "You've been handling the Reaper story since the very beginning. Besides, who would he get to write editorials as good as yours?"

After a short pause, Josh gritted his teeth in annoyance and replied, "There's a new reporter on staff, Roger. A young girl fresh out of college—I believe her name is Jennifer Louise. She's a little wet behind the ears when it comes to tracking down a story, but I've heard she's one hell of a good writer."

"Sorry to hear that, Josh. You know I'm pulling for ya."

Josh let out a sigh and raised his bottle. "Enough about my problems at work. Right now I'd like to propose a toast to the memory of my good buddy and informant—Sam Cushman."

Roger raised his glass as well and swallowed a large gulp of beer. Then, he took a deep puff on his Winchester and said, "I just can't believe Sam killed himself. I feel bad about the way I treated him when I first met him, and about accusing him of being the Reaper when you approached me at the funeral."

"Don't take it to heart, bud. There's no way you could've known what would happen." There was a brief pause. "Besides, Sam didn't kill himself," Josh said, squinting at Roger through a cloud of cigar smoke. "He was murdered."

"How can you be so sure, Josh? Ken Johnson told me that Sam jumped off the water tower. He said it straight to my face when I was visiting Bucky at City Hall yesterday."

"Well, it definitely *appeared* to be a suicide, but I paid a special visit to the coroner's office, and Harry found two burn marks on the back of Sam's skull. The same type of marks that Pat Jordan and..." Josh stopped in mid-sentence, catching himself before he mentioned Holly's name. "Well, the same kind that Jordan had when his body was found."

"That's strange," Roger replied. "The police never released that information about Sam to the public."

"They were probably unaware of it. The marks were under Sam's hair. That's why no one noticed them. The way his body was all twisted when they found him, there was no doubt that the fall had killed him. However, those burn marks prove that something happened to him *before* he fell. I guarantee it!"

After a minute of mulling over some ideas, Roger let out a groan. "It's too bad that Bucky couldn't make it out tonight. The three of us could have discussed all of this."

"Yeah," Josh agreed. "I'm glad everyone's working *together* now on this whole thing."

Roger tipped up his bottle and finished the last of his beer. "Then again, maybe it's a good thing he didn't show up here tonight after all."

Josh was confused. "Huh? Why do you think that?"

"Take a look over there," Roger said, pointing towards the two bartenders.

Josh turned and shrugged his shoulders. "Yeah, what about it? It's just some friendly flirting between them."

"That's Celeste Braxton," Roger said in a quiet voice. "The woman who was helping Bucky take care of Mikey after his wife died. They were starting to get really close, and she even told Bucky she had feelings for him. Bucky said something like he didn't feel the same way and they haven't talked since. Nevertheless, I doubt he would like seeing her flirt with Tim Matthews."

"Hey, it's like you said, he doesn't feel the same towards her. I'm almost positive he wouldn't care."

"Maybe, but I'm not so sure. I don't think Bucky knows what he feels about anything anymore," Roger said in a weary tone. "Hey, I wonder if I should tell Bucky about this."

"Tell him?" Josh exclaimed. "What good would that do? If you're interested in finding out if he would be jealous, I assure you, you're making a poor decision. Their relationship, or lack of one, may be a topic he does not care to discuss. Take my advice; don't go sticking your nose in other people's relationships. No good ever comes of it."

Roger was about to reply when he noticed that Celeste had ended her chat with Tim and walked over to grab a couple of beer bottles from the fridge. She moseyed over to the gentlemen and handed Roger a beer, then pushed another across the bar to Josh.

"Roger, can I ask you something?" Celeste asked.

"Sure, Celeste, I always have time for you."

Celeste took a deep breath. "Do you know why Bucky pushed me away?"

"Pushed you away? What do you mean? Did you and Bucky have a talk?" Roger asked, pretending as though he didn't already know.

"Yes, I told him I was starting to develop some deep, intimate feelings for him."

Roger glanced over at Josh, but he just looked away and acted as though he was not paying attention to their conversation. Then Roger shifted his attention back to Celeste.

"And what did he say to that?" he asked.

"Nothing," she said emphatically. "Just what I mean to him."

Roger was thrown back by her pessimistic statement, completely surprised and not sure of what to say next. "That's not true, Celeste. You know Bucky is still going through a difficult time. His job is stressing him out, especially with all the eerie things that have happened in town. On top of that, Bucky has to take care of Mikey and help his son adjust to Cristina's death."

"I am aware of all those things, and I would never try to take the place of Mikey's mom; however, I *do* care for that little boy and I try to help Bucky look after him as much as I can. I just feel as though there's more to Bucky's behavior than just stress and other preoccupations."

Roger put his hand on top of hers and caressed it gently. "In my opinion, I believe that deep down in Bucky's heart he has genuine feelings for you, but he thinks that starting a relationship with you would betray the memory of Cristina."

Celeste bowed her head and spoke softly. "I guess I just feel like if I stay around him long enough, he'll eventually decide to open up to me and want me in his life as much as I desire him."

"Don't give up on him, Celeste!" Roger insisted. "He's a good man and a good friend. It's just going to take some time for him to get past all the pain and guilt he's experiencing right now."

Celeste nodded and tried her best to smile. She leaned forward and gave Roger a kiss on the cheek and walked away.

Another moment of silence passed as the two gentlemen sipped on their beers. Then, Roger lowered his legs off the footrest, stood up, and ground out his cigar in an ashtray. "Excuse me for a minute, Josh. I'll be right back; I've got to hit the 'Men's Room.'"

Roger started to walk toward the rest room. When he got to the other end of the bar, Thomas Parker stopped him. Thomas was drunk and his breath reeked of booze. His eyes were somewhat bloodshot, and he was swaying when he spoke.

Aside from his apparent drunkenness, Thomas's clothes were badly wrinkled and his shirt was hanging half out of the top of his pants, which was unusually sloppy for Thomas. He was wearing heavy twill pants and black high top boots, another aspect that seemed out of the ordinary since Thomas was dressed in rather warm attire for the hot, humid August weather.

"Hey there, Roger," Thomas mumbled. "I haven't seen you in months. How's everything been?"

"Oh, I'm hanging in there. Doing the best I can do. Thanks for asking, Thomas."

"I'm glad to see you're doing better. You were a complete mess when I saw you at the memorial service."

Thomas's words struck a nerve. "Um, yeah. I suppose," Roger responded in a quiet, half-hearted tone. "That was a tough time for me."

"I know it was," Thomas said, patting Roger on the arm. "It was a nice funeral though, all except for that damn Father Emerson."

Roger was curious and confused. "Excuse me? What do you mean by that?"

"Oh nothing," Thomas replied, tipping his glass for another swig of whiskey. "Quite honestly, I was surprised to see him at the funeral; I didn't think he would be the officiating priest."

Roger ignored Thomas's statement. "Are you feeling okay, Thomas?"

The inebriated, stoop-shouldered Mr. Parker looked at him dully.

"Yeah, I'm sorry to say something negative about the funeral and all, but I just don't like Father Emerson very much. In fact, I have half a mind to go down there and give Father Emerson a piece of my mind."

"With as much alcohol as you've had, half a mind is about all you have functioning right now."

"Yeah, I reckon you're right. Never mind me; I'm just a drunken old man."

"Drunk, yes; however, I'd hardly consider you old."

"Thanks, but sometimes I sure feel like I am."

Thomas finished off the last of his beer and laid some more money on the bar. Then he gave Roger a slap on the back and stumbled over to the exit, nearly falling out the door.

"Hey Tim," Roger said, turning around towards the bar. "What's Thomas's beef tonight?"

Tim was putting on his jacket and divvying up the money in the tip jar. "What do you mean?" he answered back.

"It's just not like him to be in here getting plastered; and it kind of threw me for a loop when he was talking about how he doesn't like Father Emerson. Did he say something to you?"

Tim stood silent and glared at the exit thinking to himself.

"Tim?" Roger prodded. "Are you listening?"

"Oh, I'm sorry," Tim said as he snapped out of his daze. "No, Roger. Thomas didn't say anything at all about his problems...or about Father Emerson, either. It's all new information to me."

Chapter 38:

Danger in the Dark

By the time John Sears arrived at Water Street, it was barely after 11 pm. He walked down the trail that led to the Black River carrying his flashlight, a bucket with some worms, and his fishing pole.

The night air was heavy and humid, with layers of fog rising from the river. The moon kept sliding in and out from behind the clouds, and the only sounds that could be heard were the ripples on the water, crickets chirping in the brush, and frogs croaking as they leaped from one lily pad to another.

John was hypnotized by the peacefulness of the night and he stopped in mid-stride to look around and take a deep breath. He could smell the scent of vegetation and damp soil on the night air as he approached the riverbank. The damp air made John's clothes cling to his skin, and he had to frequently wipe the sweat from his brow.

"This looks like a nice spot to fish, Brutus," John said to his dog.

After a few minutes, because his flashlight was not throwing off enough light for him to see, John decided to start a fire. As he was gathering some twigs, he heard a quiet noise on the river. He shut off his flashlight and walked back toward the riverbank. Choosing a secluded spot beneath a tree, John sat down and listened. A few minutes went by; he began to be doubtful. Then he was sure that he had heard a splashing noise on the river.

He listened, and the sound occurred again. It seemed as though someone was paddling on the river, but John could see no lantern or flashlight. Suddenly, he could see an image coming from out of the fog. It was someone heading towards the shore in a canoe about eighty yards away. Despite the paddler's care and painstaking attempt to remain unnoticed, slight ripples had been made by the splashes.

The sound had not been repeated, and the fog began to grow thicker. For a moment John thought he might've been imagining the whole thing. Then came a grating sound, not more than twenty or thirty yards further up the riverbank. The canoe had beached on the pebbled water front, but it was invisible in the darkness and fog.

John waited expectantly. At last he detected a slight footfall; and in another moment, a figure was silhouetted against the clearing toward the shoreline. Just then, Brutus became aware of the stranger nearby and began to growl.

"Shh! Sit down and be quiet," John whispered in a forceful tone.

Brutus bowed his head and whimpered as he laid down and covered his head with his paws. John gave Brutus a stern look and then turned his attention back toward the clearing, but before he had time to observe the stranger carefully, the person was gone.

Not far from John's fishing spot was Carthage's Episcopalian church. Although it seemed dark and abandoned, Father Bruce Emerson was inside and sitting at his desk in the church den writing his sermon for Sunday's mass.

As the priest sat, he stopped recording for a moment and tipped back in his chair to rest his tired, old eyes. He took a deep breath as his mind began to drift, remembering his shady days as a young priest down South.

Many years ago, Father Emerson was once a priest in Louisiana. It was during that time, approximately twenty-two years ago, in which he was accused of a scandal that involved a young boy and sexual misconduct. As a young priest, he fought his urges...his desires of flesh from a child. It had been an intense struggle that he wrestled with and ultimately gave into, but only once. He was sickened with himself and even had thoughts of suicide. Instead, he repented his sins, finally coming down on the right side of the fence and begging the Lord for mercy.

To avoid any further embarrassment to the church, the scandal had to be dealt with—meaning the boy who accused Father Emerson would have to be silenced. The child was labeled a liar, and was hauled off to an institution.

After the boy was sent away and his mother mysteriously disappeared from the Louisiana town, the church covered up the fishy details. Once this deed was taken care of, Father Emerson went about his normal church business. That was, until six years ago. Another scandal surfaced, and this time, it was a much more public affair. Father Emerson was briefly transferred to another Episcopalian church in Ohio. Once he wore out his welcome there, he was transferred from one church to another. However, tonight in Carthage, his past was finally about to catch up with him.

While Father Emerson was relaxing, he turned his head and peered though his half-drawn shades, gazing at the river. Just then, from out of the blue, he heard what he could only describe as a loud thud. Even though it didn't sound like anything fell over or broke, he still thought that a noise came from the bathroom.

Ever since the time he received death threats years ago, stemming from an incident that happened in his past, he's been nervous about sleeping alone in the church. Every night he ended up investigating some odd noise or other; and every night he found nothing but the creatures that lean between the bookends of his own overzealous imagination...that is, until this particular evening arose.

As Father Emerson stepped out from behind his desk, one of his legs buckled, stiff from sitting so long, and he almost tumbled. It was completely dark now, and as he limped from room to room with a flashlight, the dimness made it extremely difficult to see.

"I know that I didn't handle my recent encounter with Thomas Parker very well," he said to himself, trying to settle his nerves. "I hope he's not here again, wanting to engage in another argument."

He perused the place until he came upon an open window with an open shudder. Father Emerson walked over, glanced outside at the yard and trees, and closed the window, locking it tight.

"I know I should be more tolerant and easy-going to the people around here if I'm to make a fresh start in this town," the priest said, quivering as he walked away. "The last thing I need is to have another controversy hanging over my head."

After he was satisfied with his search, he returned to his den and closed the door behind him. Without hesitation or concern, he turned around and strolled over to raise the window shades even further so he could watch the moonlight on the Black River as he finished his sermon. Then, he apparently changed his mind, for he stopped short, and whirled around as he got to his desk.

He looked at the opposite wall of the room and was immediately taken aback as he observed a curious figure moving near his bookcase. He gasped in fright and dropped his flashlight onto the ground, breaking the glass and bulb.

Just then, there appeared a haunting figure, clad entirely in a black cloak, its face white as a ghost and eyes as scarlet as blood.

The figure became immobile. Father Emerson stared in astonishment.

The Reaper moved away from the bookcase, and stood motionless. He was a strange, swarthy figure. His presence seemed so surreal, leaving the priest limp with fear and his mouth gaped open.

Father Emerson tried to speak, but he could muster no sound from his lips. This Angel of Death in front of him, that seemed to come from the depths of Hell, and yet appear out of nothingness, transfixed his gaze.

The Father's body trembled and the hairs on the back of his neck began to tingle as the Reaper moved slowly forward. The priest's eyes significantly enlarged as the being came up and stood before him.

"Why are you here?" Father Emerson questioned. "Who are you and what—?"

"I am the Reaper!"

The low, hissing voice was more terrifying than the ghostly form itself. Father Emerson felt faint and began to sway; then he gripped the edge of the desk to steady himself.

"Close the blinds," the intruder ordered.

Father Emerson walked over and obeyed the Reaper's command.

"Sit down."

The long, sleek arm of a black wool cloak extended in the direction of a worn-out armchair. Father Emerson could not ignore the demand. Instinctively, he reached for the chair, but his eyes were still fixated upon the eerie individual standing before him.

The Reaper appeared to glide gracefully across the floor. His hand reached the light switch near the doorway and flicked it off; the ceiling light went dark.

Father Emerson squinted; he could no longer see the man in black. Then he choked and coughed while gasping for air as the Reaper suddenly switched on the desk lamp. Just then, the stranger walked over and appeared directly above the priest—hunched over and hovering like a monstrous creature of death.

The man in the armchair looked up. Below the hood of the cloak, Father Emerson could see two ghastly eyes that gleamed like living coals. Dark, burning eyes, which seemed to pry into the deep, dark secrets of Father Emerson's rattled mind.

A voice spoke through the shadows of the cloak. It was a weird, chilling voice—scarcely more than a whisper, yet clear and penetrating.

"What is your name?"

The Reaper's words were not meant to be an inquiry. Rather, it was a command for the humbled priest to speak.

"Bruce Emerson," replied the man who sat trembling in his chair. "What do you want? I am a holy man; a man of the cloth."

"I know the type of person you are. You preach of the holy but indulge yourself in the practices of sin. You ask for donations from the townspeople and act like a pauper in need; however, I know it's just a thin veil that covers a misconception and hides all your greed."

"I have done nothing to you!" Father Emerson screamed angrily.

"You molested a boy."

The Reaper's hissed words were a statement—not a question.

"Answer me!" the intruder roared. "You molested a boy!"

Father Emerson nodded. "How could you know that? Unless..." The color suddenly drained from Father Emerson, leaving his face deathly pale. "Oh no, you can't be!"

"You physically abused a child, and when the boy finally got the courage to tell someone what happened, you told everyone he was crazy. The judge who presided over the case sent the boy off to a state mental hospital for five years, stripped him away from his mother."

Father Emerson hung his head shamefully and said nothing.

"Look at me!" instructed the Reaper.

Father Emerson's head snapped up at the command. He stared at the Reaper with eyes as dreary and fearful as a harsh winter storm.

The cloaked individual leaned back and laughed with satisfaction. "You lied about the boy," he said strictly. "Answer me!"

"Yes," he uttered in a small voice. Father Emerson's shoulders drooped in despair as he sobbed. "I'm sorry. I was a young man when it happened. I was weak and have repented many times over."

The Reaper stood erect and pointed his finger in the priest's face. "Are the bones of your sins sharp enough to cut through your excuses?"

Tears were flowing down Father Emerson's cheeks. "What are you saying? Are you going to kill me?"

"You'll find out soon enough," the Reaper roared.

As the Reaper wheeled around, Father Emerson quickly stood up and ran across the room. He grabbed a Louisville Slugger baseball bat from beside his file cabinet and charged his assailant. The Reaper turned back around, holding forth his stun gun, and reached out to touch Father Emerson's upper torso, zapping him in the middle of his chest. The priest dropped the baseball bat and fell to his knees.

"You display a courage I never knew you had, Preacher. I applaud that." Then the Reaper put the stun gun up to the Father's neck and pronounced, "Your technique needs some work, however." Then the Reaper zapped him again.

The Reaper grabbed Father Emerson's motionless body by his ankles and dragged him out of the office, down the hallway, and onto one of the wooden pews. Then he returned to the priest's den and grabbed a jug of gasoline that was sitting next to Father Emerson's Briggs & Stratton Power Generator.

The Reaper popped the top off the jug and splashed around some gas upon the pastor's cabinets and papers. Before he exited the doorway, the Reaper pulled out a copper colored lighter and lit a crumpled up piece of newspaper that was lying on the floor. He tossed the paper upon the gas drenched desk and watched as the structure started to go up in flames.

A short distance away, a beam from a flashlight was bouncing around on the winding trail to the Black River. John Sears was trudging along, walking back from his fishing excursion with his black lab, Brutus.

"I didn't want to be rude back there at the bar," John said to his dog, "but Adam is a horrible fisherman, and he always makes so much noise that he scares the fish away." Then he held up an 18" Northern Pike fish in front of Brutus's face. "I never would've been able to hook one of these beauties with Adam around."

John continued down the trail, banging his flashlight on his leg from time to time as the batteries started to weaken. As he went along, he started moving slower and taking smaller steps as it was getting more difficult to see. A full moon hung in the sky; nevertheless, it was overshadowed by the dense fog that swallowed the night.

The cool breeze shifted directions, and John abruptly stopped, dead in his tracks. The hair on the back of his neck was tingling, and his ears became attuned to every sound in the vicinity. This rarely occurred; it was his body's way of alarming him of danger, traits he had acquired from his Indian ancestry. John closed his eyes and smelled the air around him; the slight scent of burning wood broke through the fog and startled him.

John opened his eyes and said, "I smell smoke." He squinted as he peered through the thick shrubbery. "But where is it coming from?"

He looked around and saw that approximately three hundred yards off in the distance, the church was on fire. Alarmed, John quickly grabbed his cell phone from his back pocket and dialed the 911 emergency hotline.

While the phone was ringing, John remained fixated on the burning building while Brutus had made his way over to John's side. He bent down to pat the dog, who remained looking at the thick brush with very alert, intelligent eyes.

Finally, someone picked up the telephone. "Hello, 911, what is your emergency?" a lady inquired.

"Yes, this is John Sears. I'm down on Water Street, near the Black River, and the Episcopalian Church is on fire!"

"Please stay on the line, sir," the operator said in an indifferent tone. "I'll be back in a moment."

As John continued waiting on the phone, something abruptly caught Brutus's attention. The dog sniffed danger in the air before hearing anything and the antennae of his whiskers quivered in the murky darkness. Brutus's eyes became narrow, his tail wagging slowly at the air. His upper lip curled, revealing his sharp yellow fangs as he took a few steps toward the shrubbery.

As Brutus approached a particular section of the bushes, he let out a slight growl, with pointed ears and his thin rope of a tail perked up. He pawed at the ground with his front feet and then started to crouch down low to the ground.

Suddenly, Brutus began barking ferociously at the hedges along the left side of the trail. "Calm down, Brutus. I'm on the phone." However, when John looked at him again, he realized that something was seriously bothering his dog. "What's the matter boy; what are you barking at?"

At that moment, the operator came back on the line. "Okay, sir, I have notified the fire department," she informed him. "The firefighters should arrive within a few minutes."

"Thank you, ma'am," John replied. "I'll be on the lookout for them!"

Just then, Brutus let out a loud yelp. John looked over toward the hedges, but his dog was nowhere to be seen. Carefully, he hung up the phone and slowly walked closer to the spot where his dog was just standing.

"Brutus? Are you alright?"

The hedge was a scraggly, ill-kept mass of shrubbery. John discovered an opening in it, and peered through. As he pushed aside the brush with one hand, John kept his flashlight in the other so he could look for his dog.

John tried to whistle, but he was too jittery and his lips were too dry. Then John saw a dark form about ten feet away, lying on the ground. "Brutus…" he said in a shaky whisper, "is that you?"

As John kneeled down, frozen with fear and concern for his dog, he began to push aside more branches and leaves until his body was completely engulfed in the brush. He shined his flashlight in the bushes once again, sweeping the beam from side to side and squinting to make out the darkened objects in front of him.

Unfortunately, John failed to witness another dark figure which was standing off to his side.

The Reaper lunged forward and John let out a bone-chilling scream. Unfortunately, in the woods, there was no one to hear John scream.

With one swift motion, the cloaked creature struck John in the head with his stun gun, rendering him unconscious. Then, the Reaper picked up John's cataleptic body and heaved him over his shoulder. Next, he grabbed Brutus's neck collar and began to drag the dog's unmoving corpse as he carried John to the riverbank and dumped him at the edge of the water. The Reaper stared at them for a brief moment, watching as they laid unmoving before him. Then, one after the other, he tossed the two bodies into the river.

The Reaper laughed loudly as he walked away. It was a long, mocking laugh; a type of laugh that would chill a person's heart—even those who had never known fear before.

Chapter 39:

Hints and Suggestions

In the early hours of the next morning, the fire scene was crawling with police officers and firemen, sifting through the remains of the church. Police were able to put out the church fire before it reached Father Emerson's body; but when they found him, he was already dead. Burn marks caused by the stun gun covered his face, neck, and chest; the air reeked of burned hair.

Ken Johnson was there searching through the rubble and attempting to formulate a scenario. He had concluded that the person who did this knew this part of town quite well due to the ease the suspect maneuvered inside the church and was able to disappear from the vicinity so suddenly. The killer also had to be strong in order to haul the unconscious body of the priest such a considerable distance. Because of the clues he had found so far, the circumstances indicated that the killer was a male of medium height, who weighed between one hundred and sixty to one hundred seventy-five pounds.

With such an early tip about the fire and being able to extinguish the blaze quickly, the police had expected to find many clues, considering the quick get-away of the murderer. Unfortunately, there were very few pieces of evidence at all. There were no fingerprints anywhere to be found, and the fire investigators didn't notice any footprints either entering or leaving the church.

Just then, one of Ken's men called out to him. "Sir, you'd better come over here! I think we've found something!"

Ken hurriedly stumbled through the charred remains on his way over to the officer.

"I found this near the area where the priest's body was discovered," the young officer said, pointing to a small metal with his long, retractable pointer. The object was discretely placed next to a half-burned pew.

Ken looked down and said, "Oh, hell. You'd better wrap it in plastic and tag it. Then get me the Chief on the radio; we're going to need a search warrant for Thomas Parker's house."

Just then, the voice of another officer came over Ken's radio. "This is Officer Streeter."

"Go ahead, Rick," Ken said, speaking into his radio.

"Sir, I'm down at river edge and there is something floating in the river. I think you had better come take a look at this!"

Ken lumbered over to where the officer was and witnessed two bodies floating face down near the water's edge. One was that of a human, although they couldn't tell if it were a man or woman. The other was that of an animal, a large dog to be precise.

"Get those bodies out of the water!" Ken said hastily. "I mean NOW!"

Several officers plunged into the water and pulled the two bodies to shore. When they turned over the body of the person, they discovered that it was the dead body of John Sears, and the other was his pet dog, Brutus. A closer inspection by the officers revealed that John had stun gun marks on his forehead.

Around 8 am, three police cars pulled into Thomas Parker's driveway. Thomas gazed out his living room window in sheer nervousness and his heartbeat began to quicken.

Ken Johnson got out of his patrol car and browsed around the area as he approached the front door.

Thomas Parker met them at the door. "What're all of you doin' here?"

"We have a search warrant, Thomas," Ken stated.

Thomas looked confused and placed his coffee mug down on the stand next to the door. "What the hell is this nonsense about a search warrant?"

Ken took a few steps inside and confronted the man. He held out the search warrant and said, "We'd like to inspect the inside of your house and your workshop out back."

Thomas bent down and squinted at the search warrant. He straightened and rubbed his chin. There was a raspy sound of whiskers. "That little piece of paper you got don't cut no shit around here."

"The hell it doesn't!" snapped Ken. "Now, I want inside that workshop of yours, and if you don't cooperate, I'll have the boys knock the door off its hinges! I had hoped to avoid trouble for you, Thomas, but don't push me! Do you understand?"

Thomas stared at Ken with enraged eyes and nodded.

Ken put the search warrant back in his jacket pocket and said, "Alright then, I'm glad you see it my way." He turned to face the officers behind him. "Come with me, men."

Ken and a couple other officers walked inside and began looking around, sifting through Thomas's personal belongings. Ken remained close to Thomas, keeping an eye on his movements.

"What's this all about?" demanded Thomas.

Ken got up in Thomas's face and asked, "Why don't you start by telling me where you were last night?"

"I was at Kitty's Bar having a few drinks," he answered rudely. "After that, I came home and spent the rest of the night in my workshop. What business is it of yours?"

"We already *know* you were drinking at the bar; there are several witnesses that can attest to that. We also heard you were even saying threatening things about Father Emerson."

Thomas shook his head in confusion. "Father Emerson? What're ya gettin' at?"

"There was a destructive fire at the Episcopalian Church last night, and Father Emerson was murdered. We also found John Sears's body floating in the river near the church. We have reason to believe you had something to do with those incidents. Do you have anything to say?"

"Hold on, ya fat bastard! I didn't do anything! I don't know what kind of a monster you think I am, but I'm *not* a murderer! I've *never* killed anyone, and I certainly wouldn't leave someone to die in a burning building!"

Ken curled his lip as he listened to Thomas ramble on. "Well, perhaps I misspoke myself," he interjected. "Father Emerson didn't die because of the fire."

Thomas cocked his head in confusion. "If Father Emerson didn't die in the fire, then how *did* he die?"

"Well, it's just speculation right now, but it looks as if Father Emerson had the same type of burn marks on his neck that Patrick Jordan and Holly Boliver had when their bodies were examined. We believe Father Emerson had a heart attack—looks like from being shocked so many times by a stun gun."

Thomas sat down to regroup. Ken stared at him to try and read his body signals. "So you don't know anything about what happened last night?" Ken asked hesitantly.

"No, I honestly don't."

"And you weren't upset with Father Emerson either, I suppose."

"Yeah, I was angry with Father Emerson. But I wasn't mad enough to kill him. I may have said some derogatory statements about that crooked piece of shit, but it was only because I felt he swindled my wife out of some money."

"Can you elaborate on that, Mr. Parker? But first, I must inform you of your rights and ask if you want to speak to an attorney before you say anything further. After all, anything you say can be used against you."

"I don't need a damn lawyer!" Thomas shouted. "I haven't done anything wrong. Listen, I'll tell you why I've had issues with our *esteemed* Priest. My wife went to church last Sunday and put a check in the donation plate. However, the check she put in was the wrong one. Apparently, she was talking to one of her friends when the donation plate came around, and because she was distracted, she placed her paycheck, which she had already endorsed, on the tray instead of the twenty dollar check she'd written out."

Ken continued writing down Thomas's statement. Without lifting his head up, he asked, "And what was the amount of the check she gave the church instead."

"It was *four hundred dollars*!" he exclaimed. "She only gets paid every other week and she worked extra hours that pay period just so we'd be caught up on our bills."

"So, it's safe to say that money was important to you," Ken remarked.

"Yeah, you moron! We couldn't afford to lose that much cash! It was a terrible mistake, and we desperately needed the money back. I went over to see Father Emerson the next day and tried to explain the mix up to him. I asked him for the check back, but he said he already deposited it, and there was nothing he could do."

Then Officer Johnson pulled out a plastic bag with a Zippo lighter inside. "Can you explain this?" Ken handed Thomas the plastic bag to inspect. "We found your lighter beside Father Emerson's body," Ken continued.

Thomas took the bag and inspected the lighter with the dull copper finish. "My lighter? Yeah, that's mine, but I haven't seen it in months."

Thomas was confused. He stood up and began pacing around the room. An officer walked up to Ken.

"What do you think, sir?" the young cop said to Ken.

"I think he's got motive and a flimsy alibi, too. I think we should haul him in for more questioning."

Thomas kept murmuring to himself, staying out of earshot of the officers in the room. "That's so odd," he whispered. "How did my lighter get there?" An idea popped into his head, and Thomas went to over to his roll-top desk, grabbing for something in the bottom drawer.

"Hold it," one officer commanded. "I don't want you grabbing anything—like a weapon!"

"What the hell are ya jabberin' about?" Thomas said. "I'm just getting my journal. I made an entry the day I lost my lighter. I've had that lighter a long time, and it had a lot of sentimental value."

Thomas reached again into his drawer, and the officer's face turned rigid with anger as he seized his gun.

"Put your hands up!" said the cop, straightening. His pistol was pointed at Thomas's chest.

"Alright!" Ken shouted out. "Let's run this guy in!"

It was almost quitting time on the following day, and Roger was at his desk rushing through his paperwork and eager to leave. He and Bucky had plans to meet at Kitty's Bar after work so they could discuss Father Emerson's murder, the burn marks that covered his dead body, and Thomas Parker's connection to it all.

Roger was already inside when Bucky pulled up to the bar. He tossed his sport coat in the back seat of his Blazer and was on his way into the bar when Celeste came out of the coffee shop next door. In her left hand was a double mocha latte with cream and hint of cinnamon. As she stepped along the sidewalk, she kept her head down while searching for some item in her purse with her free hand.

"Hello, Celeste," Bucky said as she went past him.

She lifted her head up and turned around. "Oh, hi Bucky. I almost didn't see you."

Bucky grinned and spoke in a soft voice. "I missed you at Mikey's soccer game the other night."

"I know and I'm sorry. I just had some things to work out. I wasn't trying to avoid you."

"It's okay. I don't need an explanation. That's not why I brought it up. I just wanted to let you know that you were missed, that's all."

There was a long pause.

"Well, I better go now, Bucky. I have some errands to run before it gets too late."

"Yeah, I should get going inside myself," Bucky said, pointing behind him toward the bar.

"Take care of yourself, Bucky," she said, crossing the street.

Bucky stared as she walked away, feeling disappointed over the way things were between them. "You too," he answered.

After a few moments, Bucky stepped inside and approached the counter bar, sitting down next to Roger.

"Hey, Bucky," Roger voiced. "Anything new goin' on with you?"

"Not much, bud."

"Well, I'm sure you heard Thomas Parker was arrested for suspicion of arson and murder," Roger said to his friend. "They think he might be the Reaper."

"Yeah, but it's still difficult for me to believe it. Something about it all just doesn't seem right."

Roger glanced at his wristwatch to check the time. "Well, do you want to buy a pitcher of beer and analyze some of the facts in the case?"

"Sure, I don't have anything else to do tonight. Why don't you go get us a table and I'll order up a pitcher of draft beer and get a couple of frosty mugs."

Roger located a table in the far corner of the bar, away from the noise of the jukebox. Meanwhile, Bucky held up two fingers as he yelled out to get Tim Matthews's attention. When Tim came over, Bucky placed his order, and within minutes, came over to Roger's table with an overflowing pitcher of beer in one hand and two frosted mugs in the other.

"Is it okay if you're out late tonight?" Roger asked. "I mean, Celeste isn't going to be upset is she?"

Bucky hesitated before answering Roger. "Actually, we just passed each other on the sidewalk, and no, Celeste isn't watching Mikey for me tonight. He's spending the night at one of his friend's house. Celeste hasn't watched him for me in several days...I thought I told you that."

"No, the only thing you mentioned to me was the two of you had an argument; I figured that spat would've been resolved by now. I can't believe she doesn't even watch Mikey for you anymore," Roger said, shaking his head disapprovingly. "Maybe you two should get together, sit down, and talk things over."

"Actually, we haven't spent *any* time together since we had our last little 'talk' last week and she bolted out of my house. She barely even said ten words to me when we were outside a few moments ago."

"That's ridiculous! You need to get over the awkwardness and talk to her. She's a good friend of ours, and she cares for you very much. You two can't just ignore each other forever!"

"I know, but I think she wants some space right now. After all, I told her that she should move on and find someone else. I can't even imagine what that did to her feelings. She'll probably end up accepting a date from the first guy who asks her."

After a moment of silence, Roger said, "Really, well that would clear up a few things then."

"Like what?"

"Well, I saw Celeste in the bar the other night. She and Tim Matthews were acting pretty chummy together. Then I heard him ask her out on a date. I know it's none of my business, but I thought you should know."

"That's none of my business, either. She's a young, single woman."

"Oh, alright. Well then, let's change the topic," Roger suggested.

"Good idea," Bucky responded.

Roger filled their mugs to the top with beer and asked, "So, what do we know about this Reaper so far?"

Bucky got situated in his seat and started to concentrate. "Well, we know that he prowls around at night and wears a dark-colored cloak to shroud his body and face. And his weapon of choice seems to be an electrical device, possibly a stun gun."

Roger leaned back in his chair and thought. "You know, Louis Ferr used to wear a long, black *coat*. To be honest, when these fires first began, I thought Mr. Ferr might've come back to town."

"That's impossible!" Bucky butted in. "I saw Ferr run into an exploding building. There's no way that psycho survived such a blast."

"That's true; Mr. Ferr *did* go into the building right before it exploded. But bear in mind, his body was never found." A thought suddenly popped into Roger's mind. "Bucky, do you remember that old, news article you found in the library a few years ago?"

"Do you mean the one that mentioned the Grim Reaper at one of the town's fires?"

"Yeah, that's the one! What year was that article from?"

"Sometime in 1955, I think," Bucky answered, scratching his temple. "What relevance does that have?"

"I was wondering…do you think Mr. Ferr could've been in Carthage more than just once? I mean, if Ferr is who he said he is."

"You mean—*the Devil*?"

"Yes. If Louis Ferr really *is* Satan, then he could have been responsible for setting those fires here all those years ago." Roger paused for a moment and then asked, "How about you? Do you think he was here in '55, returned in 2000, and now he's back again?"

"Well, 1955 is the same time period he claimed to be 'recruiting souls,' whatever he meant by that," Bucky said, shrugging his shoulders. "Even so, we both know that Ferr was in Chicago fifty years ago, having a go-around with Jim Draven. Besides, creating fires really isn't his method of murder and mayhem."

"So you believe I'm crazy for thinking such a thing?"

"Hell no, Roger! There's been at least a half-dozen times where I've had serious thoughts that Louis Ferr could have survived the explosion and returned to town; however, I really don't believe it's him. I think we're dealing with a different individual."

"Why?"

"For starters, it's not Ferr's style—being secretive like that. This is not the way he would get to us. I encountered him both here and in Florida, and this situation is completely different than either of those." Bucky stopped, his eyes lit up as though he had come to a realization. "Then again, maybe it's someone who wants us to think it could be Louis Ferr."

"Maybe you're right," Roger said. "Alright, lets move on to something else. How about we take a look at this case from a different approach?"

"Okay, what do you have in mind?"

"Didn't John Sears tell you that Adam saw a ghost in the woods the night of the waterfront incident?"

"Yeah, where are you going with this?"

"If it wasn't Mr. Ferr that caused the fire at the waterfront, do you think it might've been the Reaper who was responsible for the explosion?"

"I suppose it's possible, but Thomas was at that place too. I can only hope it was someone else, and not him, who was behind it."

Roger's voice became low and serious. "I know you don't want to think about it, Bucky, but do you *now* believe that Thomas *could* actually be the Reaper?"

"Well, now that he has had surgery on his leg, and he gets around really well, he has the means to do it and not have his limp to hinder him or make him noticed. Also, the police *did* find his lighter at the crime scene, and several people, other than just you, overheard him making some offensive remarks about Father Emerson the night the priest died. Not to mention that Thomas's background does have ties to Louisiana, the same as Father Emerson."

"How do you know that Father Emerson had ties to Louisiana?"

Bucky grinned. "I'm the Mayor of this town, Roger. I made sure the Town Council did a thorough check on his previous whereabouts. Although, now I'm wondering if they did as thorough a job as I wanted them to do. I thought these people would've learned from the ferry incident about the importance of investigating someone's credentials!"

Roger nodded in agreement. "So, Bucky, what are you saying about Thomas? Does it appear to you as if the evidence is stacked against him?"

"I guess so, but it still doesn't explain the sighting of the Reaper in the 1950s. After all, Thomas wasn't born yet. Maybe we should take a ride to the Police Station and have a talk with Thomas," suggested Bucky.

"I don't know if it would be a good idea for me to go. My head is spinning from mixed emotions right now. I don't want to believe Thomas is the Reaper, but if he is, I don't know what I would do if I found out he was responsible for Holly's death."

"I realize that it could be very emotional for you," Bucky said in a soft voice. "You don't have to come if you don't want to."

Roger felt a sudden push against his bladder. "Excuse me, bud. It seems I have to make a trip to the rest room and release some bodily fluids. I'll be right back."

"That's a little more information than I needed to hear," Bucky jokingly replied.

When Roger rose and went to the restroom, Bucky proceeded to go get another pitcher of beer. As he stepped up to the bar, he engaged in conversation with Tim Matthews.

"So, Tim, I've heard through the grapevine you and Celeste have become fairly close."

"I'd like to think we're getting *very* close," Tim replied as he refilled the empty pitcher. A sly grin appeared upon his face.

"Well, I think you should back off for a while," insisted Bucky.

"She's a big girl, Bucky. *I* think she can make her own decisions and…"

"You don't understand, Tim," Bucky cut in. "She's just confused right now, and if you try to make a move on her, you'll be taking advantage of a very vulnerable person. I don't want to see Celeste get hurt and I don't want her to end up being just another notch on your belt."

Tim squinted at Bucky and spoke snidely. "From what I understand, *you're* the reason for her feelings getting hurt in the first place."

Bucky snatched the pitcher off the bar. "Just watch yourself, asshole," he said angrily.

At that moment, Adam "Red" Richardson came strolling in the bar. Bucky veered his attention toward the doorway as Tim made his way to the other end of the counter bar.

Adam smiled when he noticed Bucky and strolled over.

Bucky looked at him with concern. "How are you holding up, Red?" he asked.

Adam soberly shrugged his shoulders. "I'm doing as well as can be expected, I guess. I still can't believe John's gone. It's going to take some time for the shock to wear off and everything to sink in. That's why I'm here, so that maybe I can drown everything out and forget about life for a little while."

Roger came out of the bathroom and walked up behind Adam, putting his hand on Adam's shoulder. "Hey, Red, I'm sorry about John."

Adam turned and nodded in acknowledgment. "Thanks, Roger." He shifted himself so that he was facing both men. "I don't mean to sound rude, but I'm pretty bummed out and don't want to talk about anything that has to do with John right now."

"I understand," Roger said sympathetically. Then he turned to Bucky. "Are you ready to go?"

"Ready? What about the pitcher of beer I just bought?"

"We don't have time right now," Roger insisted. "Not if you want to drive down to the police station."

"Okay," Bucky replied. "But we won't be able to take the beer with us."

"Just give the pitcher to Adam," suggested Roger.

Bucky reluctantly places the pitcher of been in Red's hands, unhappy about wasting beer and money.

"There!" Roger shouted. "Are you ready to go now?"

"Yeah, I'm ready," he answered back. Bucky finally shifted his attention off the beer and back to Adam. "It was good to see you, Red. If you need someone to talk to, don't hesitate to give me a call. It doesn't have to be about John, it can be anything at all. We can get together for a beer, talk, hang out, or just shoot some hoop together. Remember, we're family."

"Okay, Bucky," he said, trying to smile. "You two have a good night."

Bucky and Roger walked out of the bar, one behind the other. As Bucky was about to exit, he stopped and turned around, staring angrily at Tim.

Roger and Bucky made their way over to the jail to talk to Thomas. Roger opted to wait out in the vehicle while Bucky went inside the police station. This was mutually agreed upon for the simple reason that if Thomas was discovered to be the Reaper, Roger thought it would be best if he wasn't near him. Roger was hopeful that his friend was innocent; however, on the chance that he was wrong about Thomas, Roger was afraid of what he might do—especially since he had thoughts of wrapping his hands tightly around the Reaper's neck.

Downstairs at the police station, Bucky tapped on the cell bars to get the attention of Thomas, who was reclining on the cot with his back facing the door.

"Thomas," Bucky said. "Are you up for talking?"

"Bucky!" hollered Thomas as he turned around and sat up. A smile appeared across his stubbled face. "Boy, I sure am glad to see a friendly face."

"How are you doing, Thomas? Have the officers been treating you alright?"

"Yes, I'm fine. This has all been a huge mistake! You have to get me out of here, Bucky!"

Bucky gaped into Thomas's eyes with total concentration. "Thomas, I want to help you. But you need to tell me the truth. Did you kill Father Emerson?"

"No, Bucky! You have to believe me! As much as I would've liked to give him a piece of my mind, I didn't kill him. I don't miss the guy, but I shouldn't take the rap for someone else's actions."

"Okay, Thomas. Just tell me what happened."

Thomas explained his side of the story about Father Emerson's refusal to return his wife's check or give back at least a portion of the money. He talked constantly, sometimes incoherently, barely stopping to take a breath every now and then. And yet, in all of Thomas's rambling, he did not seem distraught over the priest's death and his words were uncharacteristically derisive and harsh. He compared Father Emerson to a swindler and couldn't believe how a religious man could take advantage of someone who had so little.

While Bucky listened, his mind kept reverting to a single thought—the indifference that Thomas had expressed regarding Father Emerson's death.

Bucky asked Thomas several times whether he and Father Emerson had argued that night or any night previously; yet Thomas had sidestepped this matter entirely. Even though this type of evasive action was inconsistent with Thomas's regular method of behavior, Bucky still had a feeling that Thomas was *not* the killer.

After the men finished talking, Bucky left the police department and returned to the parking lot, reflecting on the discussion he just had with Thomas. When Bucky opened the door to the Blazer and got inside, Roger asked, "So, do you think he's the killer?"

"Don't you mean to ask if he's the Reaper?"

"Yeah, I just didn't want to word it that way."

"I don't know." Bucky replied. "I honestly can't say one way or the other. But I have this nagging feeling in the back of my mind that he's innocent."

"So what now?"

"Well, if I *am* right about Thomas…that means someone went to a lot of trouble to make it look like Thomas is guilty."

"Just great, Mr. Mayor!" Roger said brusquely. "Now we're back to square one."

Chapter 40:

Clues to the Past

In the days since Thomas was arrested, the police had attempted to check his whereabouts during specific dates, making a conscientious effort to match him with the places of the other fires in town as well as the Reaper sightings. However, they were still checking other leads and not trying to focus *all* the attention on him. Unfortunately, in spite of efforts to distance Thomas as a suspect, it began to look questionable for Thomas because of the sudden halt of fires and Reaper sightings in town since he had been arrested. Another strike against him was that the police were having trouble verifying any of Thomas's alibis.

Late at night, on the last Saturday of the month in August, Bucky and Roger were at Bucky's house. It was pouring outside and the lightning was making the lights flicker every so often, which was a slight annoyance as they tried to read over their notes regarding the Reaper case.

As they were pondering over the papers they had sprawled out over the coffee table and half of the living room floor, a little old woman, yet full of energy, knocked on Bucky's door.

Bucky was not expecting any company and cautiously stood, then walked quietly to answer the door. He slowly turned the knob and opened, peering around the corner as the door was still only half open. What he saw was an elderly woman, probably in her late sixties or early seventies, who was about five feet nothing in height and wearing a wide-brimmed rain hat, carrying a brown umbrella, and covered up in an old, khaki rain coat.

The lady had a pug nose, a wrinkly face, and her long, wet gray hair fell past her shoulders and clung to her coat. The woman was clutching a hand bag in her arms tightly, as if she would have done anything to prevent it from being taken from her. Bucky eyed the mystery woman, completely perplexed.

"Can I help you, ma'am?" he asked.

"My name is Grace Marcell," the elderly woman replied. I have something I'd like to discuss with you, Mr. Morgan. May I come inside?"

Bucky was hesitant to let her inside, but he did not want to have an open conversation on his front porch either. After a few seconds of careful thought, combined with the fact that raindrops were beginning to splash him on the face, Bucky opened up the door completely and waved her in.

"Sure, won't you come in out of the rain? We can talk inside."

Bucky turned and motioned for her to follow him down the hallway.

Grace shook off her rain-drenched coat and cleaned off her glasses with a silk pink handkerchief as she followed behind him. She was wearing a plaid skirt with tan stockings and an embroidered beige cotton blouse.

Despite her gray hair and slight build, Grace was quite attractive for her age. Bucky was studying her characteristics, noticing that she was wearing a gold wedding band and had a rather professional attitude about her. Most importantly, her insistence on speaking to him had Bucky more than a little confused.

When they entered the living room, Bucky gestured towards the couch and said, "Please, have a seat. Is there anything I can get you?"

"No, thank you," she said with a polite smile. "I can't stay long."

Bucky pointed to Roger. "Roger, this is Grace Marcell. Ms. Marcell, this is a good friend of mine, Roger Fasick."

"Nice to meet you, Roger."

"Likewise, Ms. Marcell," answered Roger with a grin.

Grace looked around the room, taking in her surroundings. She gazed out to the kitchen and then glanced over to the stairway.

"Are you alone or is your boy home, too?"

"No, it's just me. My son is visiting some relatives on my wife's side of the family for the weekend." Bucky paused. "And may I ask you how you know so much about me and my family? Have we ever met?"

"No, we haven't met personally. But I do read the newspapers, Mayor Morgan," Grace remarked with a fairly serious look on her face. "And although I live in Watertown, I keep tabs on the happenings around Carthage for personal reasons." Grace paused and breathed deeply. "Right now I need your undivided attention. What I have in my hands is the one piece of information that you and the whole police department have been searching for."

Bucky appeared wary. "What information are you referring to?"

"I have Pat Jordan's missing file."

Both men looked at Ms. Marcell in astonishment. They were completely floored by the news, wondering if it were real or all a big hoax.

"Did you say you have the file?" Bucky questioned. "How do we know you're telling us the truth?"

"Fair enough, Mr. Morgan," Grace replied. "I can understand how apprehensive you must feel right now; a strange woman showing up unexpectedly and unannounced at your door step. But I can assure you, sir, this is no joke. I was told by someone named Sam Cushman that you can be trusted. He also knew of Pat Jordan's file and told me that if anything was to happen to him than I should contact you."

A reassured grin appeared on Bucky's face. "Thank you for clearing that up, Ms. Marcell. Now, about that file you were speaking of…is it fully intact and does it contain information about the Reaper?"

Grace pulled out a large manila folder from her handbag. "Yes, it is in one piece, and yes, it contains vital information about the Reaper, both old and new."

"Excuse me for asking," interrupted Roger, "but how is it that you have the file?"

"I received it in the mail."

"It was *sent* to you?" questioned Roger.

"Yes, I was helping Pat Jordan with his research, and the file was mailed to me right before he died. He contacted me because I have some knowledge about the chaos and fires during the 1950s. Initially, I was a little hesitant, but after the fires and sightings began to mount, I decided to help Mr. Jordan compile information as best as I could."

Bucky seemed hesitant of her story. "How is it that you have knowledge of the fires in the 1950s?"

"I used to work for a news reporter who moonlighted as a private investigator. I was just twenty years old and newly married when I got the job as his assistant, but I kept my ears open and eyes sharp. After he left the upstate area, I protected his old notebooks in case they were ever needed again. I guess it's a good thing I did save them."

"Why would your boss keep records about an urban legend?" Roger butted in.

"You see, years ago, my employer, Vance Dane, worked for the *Carthage Republican Tribune* and wrote a story about a Reaper-like individual that was stalking the streets of Carthage. It was perceived as nonsense and got very little recognition. Shortly after the fires subsided, so did the rumors of the Reaper. When the sudden surge of fires returned recently, Pat Jordan listened to the rumors of the homeless."

"Pat always was an intuitive person," Bucky uttered.

"That he was, Mr. Morgan. A few of the homeless folk mentioned a skeletal figure prowling on the rooftops and Pat remembered the old fairy tale from the 1950s. He pulled the old case file on the events back then, but he discovered most of the information was missing. He did plenty of research on his own and then contacted me for additional help. The last thing Pat told me before he died was he was getting his hands on old photographs of many of the potential suspects from 1955. After that, I never heard from him again."

Bucky sat and stared at Grace for a few seconds, lost in bafflement. Then he asked, "Grace, what is your interest in all this? Why have you been following this case for such a long time?"

Grace looked down at her hands, rubbing her wedding ring between her fingers. In a quiet voice she soberly stated, "My dear husband, Evan, came to Carthage about two years ago to deliver some information to Pat Jordan and was killed in one of the unexplained fires in town."

"I'm sorry about your loss," Bucky said somberly. "Do you know if your husband's death was accidental or did someone intentionally murder him?"

"The newspaper reported that a dark cloaked man was seen running from the scene. No one was caught or punished for Evan's death so I've made it my 'quest' you might say to help in any way I can to capture the person or persons responsible for all these fires and deaths."

Bucky sensed Grace's voice getting a little shaky as she continued.

"I believe if Mr. Jordan had lived, he would have gotten to the bottom of this. But now, I guess the task has been passed to you, Mr. Morgan," she said, wiping her teary eyes with her handkerchief.

Ms. Marcell stood up and cautiously passed a sealed legal-size package to the Mayor.

Both men ogled the package in astonishment; Bucky was too dumbfounded to speak. A few moments of silence passed and Grace spoke up saying, "Well, gentlemen, I will be leaving now." She reached into her hand bag and handed Bucky a card with her name, phone number, and other contact information on it. "If there's anything more I can do for you, feel free to contact me at this number."

Bucky also stood and proceeded to walk her to the door. "Thank you for bringing me the folder, Ms. Marcell. You don't know how much I appreciate it."

"I know it's in safe hands now," she said, smiling.

Bucky smiled back. "Don't worry; I'll give this matter my utmost attention. I'll keep in touch and let you know of any new developments."

After she had gone, Bucky took the file to his den, his mind a baffled mixture of disbelief and curiosity. Roger followed behind, a silent spectator who was deeply bewildered and engrossed with thoughts of his own.

Pat Jordan's notes, thorough as they were, showed nothing unusual. There were in-depth reports about the fires over the past several years as well as the sporadic Reaper sightings; that is, up until the time of Pat's death. The most important item in the package Grace gave them was the journal written by Vance Dane. Inside there was a list of victims who died from the previous fires as well as a list of names the police suspected might be involved.

On the inside flap of the leather journal there was one more piece of paper. It was Vance Dane's own private list of whom he thought the Reaper was, back in the 1950s, along with a brief background on each individual. Unfortunately, he neglected to write in his journal exactly *why* these people were listed as suspects.

In the file, Pat Jordan wrote a notation which stated that the Reaper prowling through the streets today is using a weapon similar to the original one used back in the fifties. It was a device that inflicted an electric shock to its victims. Originally, it was probably a cattle prod, and now possibly a stun gun. Pat had inscribed in the margins that maybe this Reaper got the idea from the original guy.

There was a single sheet of paper clipped to the back of the folder. It was a wrinkled piece of paper that appeared to name the individual who Pat Jordan thought might be dressing as the Reaper and responsible for the fires. However, the paper was worn and had been exposed to water; therefore, the handwriting was illegible. The only part they could make out was the first letter of the person's given name, and it began with a 'T.'

"Could he have been spelling out Thomas's name?" Roger asked.

"Maybe."

Roger looked closely at Bucky to see his reaction. After observing Bucky's puzzlement, Roger asked in a cautious tone, "Are you beginning to think that Thomas *really is* the Reaper?"

"I don't know, Roger," Bucky replied, thinking to himself about Thomas's background. "But it sure would explain some things, wouldn't it? Like his strange behavior for starters."

Roger nodded silently and continued browsing through Vance Dane's journal. After a few moments, he looked at one particular page of notes and shook his head.

"Wow! Take a look at this," he said, passing the journal over to Bucky.

Bucky looked it over and began paraphrasing as he read aloud. "It says that there was a sighting of a peculiar spectator during the last major fire of 1955. He was a tall, gangly mysterious man who had a white beard and wore a long black slicker with a wide-brimmed hat. The stranger looked out of place alongside the other town's residents. Apparently, he showed no emotion as he stood there and watched the blaze and he disappeared into thin air before the police arrived."

Roger pulled the journal out of Bucky's hands so he could see for himself. "I know you don't want to believe that Louis Ferr could be behind all of this, but that description of a tall, mystery man with a white beard in Carthage sounds an awful lot like Mr. Ferr. Don't you think it's even possible that it could be...?" Roger's words trailed off.

"Do I think it's possible it could have been Ferr back then and doing it now, too? Well, I suppose *anything* is possible; but for some reason, something in my gut...I *still* don't believe Mr. Ferr is behind all of this," Bucky maintained.

Bucky took the journal from Roger once again and began pacing back and forth as he read it. After continuing to examine Vance Dane's journal further, he discovered on the list of victims the names of Jacob Gordon and Frank Timmons. Mr. Timmons was documented as an acquaintance of Jacob Gordon, and coincidently, he was also on the list of people suspected of starting the blazes in Carthage.

On the following page, one particular note written by Vance Dane caught Bucky's eye. "Look here, Roger!" said Bucky, pointing to a section of scribbled words. "There's an entry that mentions Terry Parker, Thomas's father, as one of the suspects in the fires of 1955;

and at one time, Terry was listed as the prime suspect in Jacob Gordon's death!"

"Move your finger!" Roger yelled as he ran up and stood close to Bucky's side. "Let me see that!"

"Jacob Gordon?" Bucky uttered, mulling over some thoughts. "I know that I've heard that name before. But how can he be a *victim*? If my memory serves me correctly, Jacob Gordon was killed trying to save someone; he wasn't murdered."

"Gordon is my mother's maiden name," Roger spoke up. "Jacob was my grandfather."

"Really?" Bucky said in a surprised tone. "Do you know anything about the events of his death?"

"Not much. Just recently my mother told me it was suspected that the Reaper had something to do with her father's death, but she never mentioned the circumstances regarding Terry Parker or some guy named Frank Timmons."

Bucky leaned back and began to rub the whiskers on his face, just like he always did when his mind began to race with ideas. "Hmmm… Do you think maybe she knows who Frank Timmons is?"

"I'm not sure. I suppose I could take a trip to Syracuse tomorrow and see what I can find out."

"That sounds like a good idea," Bucky said. "You know, Roger, this case gets crazier and more complicated the more we dig into it. Do you think we are a little out of our league on this one?"

Roger was thrown aback by Bucky's cynicism. "What kind of talk is that? You've *never* thought any case was 'out of our league' before."

"I was just wondering if you think we should get some professional help on this case," Bucky asked, sounding a little desperate.

"No, definitely not! Ken Johnson hasn't come up with anything but hearsay and circumstantial garbage; and now, the one person I confide in other than you, Josh Roberts, has been hanging out with Ken more and more. Believe me; I think we're on our own on this one. Just like old times."

"You're right, Roger. Forget I said anything."

Roger exhaled a moan. "Look at it this way, Bucky. Who knows more about this case than you and I?"

"Probably no one."

"And who has been any more touched by what has happened than you and I?" Roger stood up and began pacing around, shaking his head. "If we brought in outsiders, they would dismiss half of the evidence as rumors, tall tales, urban legend, or superstition. And we both know better than that!" he said adamantly.

"I realize what you're saying is correct, Roger. It's just that it gets so frustrating sometimes."

"I could think of a few other words to describe it," Roger joked, "but that pretty much sums it up. Look at it this way, if we get too deep in over our heads, we can always call Grant for help. You're cousin may work for a different police department, but he's never let us down before."

"Good point," Bucky concurred.

Both men let out a large sigh, and then, after deciding that it had been an exhausting day, began to gather the notes and papers from the table and floor.

"Let's call it a night," Roger said with a yawn. "I've got a long drive to Syracuse tomorrow, and I want to get some rest, if that's possible after all we found out tonight."

Bucky rubbed his tired eyes. "Yeah, a little rest sounds like a good idea."

The two men stood up and Bucky walked with Roger as he headed to the front door. Both of them were mentally drained and needed some time to process all the news they received.

"One of these days, Roger, we've got to take some time off and just go fishing, or at least take an extended vacation and go someplace where they don't have frequent fires, spooky Reapers, and crazy old ferrymen running loose."

Roger laughed and slapped his good friend on the back. "You're on, old friend."

As Bucky watched Roger walk out to his car, he noticed it had stopped raining. He grinned and thought to himself how lucky he was to have a friend like Roger.

Chapter 41:

Revealing skeletons in the family closet

The following morning, Roger hopped into his car and sped off towards his parents' house. His mind was not on his safety or the safety of the other cars around him, and it showed. He was driving erratically, and occasionally swerving back and forth, as questions about his grandfather kept buzzing through his head. He was beginning to realize the severity of his distraction, and thus, made his main objective to try and get to Syracuse as quickly as he could. Roger would look down at the speedometer occasionally and catch himself creeping up over the speed limit. A few times he would find the needle hitting ninety miles per hour, and Roger would immediately back off on the accelerator and curse out loud, angry with himself for not keeping his mind on his driving.

There were so many questions Roger wanted to ask his mother; he just hoped he could remember them all when he got to his folks' place. As he drove, he kept pondering how little he really knew about his family heritage, and he felt that he had better make a concentrated effort to find out more about the family history before his parents passed on and all their knowledge of the ancestors would be lost.

When Roger arrived in Syracuse at his parents' house, his mom dashed out the front door to greet him with a welcoming smile.

"Roger! I'm so glad to see you! We've missed you, son!" she said excitedly. "Come inside and let me fix you something to eat."

This was his mom's answer to everything—"*food.*" A person couldn't go to Mrs. Fasick's house and come away without eating to the point of nearly exploding, or at the very least, eating a slice of one of her tasty homemade pies.

"Dad will be back shortly," she continued to say as they stepped inside the house and into the kitchen. "He went to the hardware store to get some grass seed, but you know how he is when he gets in a store with tools."

As Roger sat at the kitchen table, his mom brought him a heaping plateful of cold cuts and vegetables to eat. Roger's stomach growled, so he grabbed a slice of honey ham and stuffed it into his mouth. While he was chewing, Roger decided to get to the point and ask his mom some questions while they were still fresh on his mind.

"Hey, Mom," Roger mumbled, swallowing his food. "Do you remember when we were talking about Grandpa Jake a couple of weeks ago?"

"Um, yes," Mrs. Fasick answered. Her facial expression appeared as though she would rather not discuss the topic. "I believe I remember that conversation."

"What was the name of the person who told Grandma that Grandpa's death might *not* have been an accident?"

Tammy stopped what she was doing and focused on his question. "Oh, gee. It was so long ago. I believe he was a reporter for the local newspaper. I can't be certain, but I think his name was Vance Dane."

Roger's eyes got wide. "I know that name! I met his former assistant, Grace Marcell, at Bucky's house last night. I read some notes from an old journal of his. He was the guy who investigated the previous Reaper sightings. Do you know if he is still around the upstate area? Is there a way I can get in touch with him?"

"Roger, didn't his assistant tell you what happened to him?"

"No. She really didn't say too much about Mr. Dane."

"Well, all I know is that Mr. Dane moved out of Carthage shortly after the fires stopped. I know that he spent some time in Watertown and started his own detective agency, but he departed from the upstate area many years ago."

"Why did he leave the North Country?"

"Although I don't know all the details, I know that there were some unfortunate circumstances that occurred while he was living in Watertown, which forced him to leave the area. He never came back to the North Country as far as I recall, and I don't know what happened to him after that."

Mrs. Fasick stopped to recollect some old memories. "What I remember most about Mr. Dane is that people looked up to him and thought he was a great man, a brilliant man. He was known as a most respectable fellow around this community who dedicated his life to always uncovering the truth." Then she took a deep breath and frowned. "That's pretty much all I know about him. If you want any more information, I suggest you contact the woman who told you she was Mr. Dane's former assistant."

"Hmm," Roger was concentrating on his thoughts, taking in all the information his mother was relating to him. "Well, it looks like I'll have to go a different route then." Then he turned and asked, "Mom, can you tell me why Thomas Parker's dad was a suspect in Grandpa's death?"

"Well, the newspaper reported that several witnesses who saw the blaze told the Police they had seen Terry Parker walking around the vacant Law Office right before grandpa entered the building. Shortly thereafter, the building went up in flames."

Roger shook his head, flabbergasted over the news. "What did Terry say when the police questioned him?"

"Terry's story was that he had spotted the Reaper and was tailing him; however, the police didn't believe his story so they locked him up in the Carthage jail for awhile. Eventually they found no proof that Terry was connected to the fire, and all they had left was a weak motive."

"Motive?" Roger questioned. "What kind of motive?"

"Terry Parker took over Frank Timmons's place at the real estate office, and although Terry was a hard worker, he and your grandfather tended to butt heads from time to time. I know that they had an argument over a piece of property the day before my dad died. The officers on the case tried to link those two events together but were unsuccessful. When the final police report came out, they stated that the fire was an accident and grandpa died trying to save the woman on the upper floor."

"In your opinion, do you think it was Terry Parker acting as the Reaper back then, and now it's Thomas?"

"I don't know if it's Thomas or not; however, I seriously doubt that it could've been Terry."

"You sound pretty sure, Mom."

"Terry was a sweetheart; he wouldn't have hurt anyone. If I was a betting person, I would say my dad's killer was his old business partner, Frank Timmons."

"Really? Why do you think that?"

"Originally, Frank was also a suspect for my father's death. That was, until they classified it as an accident. Frank was a friend of Dad's who worked for Grandpa Jake as a real estate broker for many years. Then one day, they had a falling out and my dad fired him."

"What were Grandpa's reasons to fire Frank Timmons?"

"I don't know. Grandpa died before I could ask him. I don't think my mother knew either. All she said was that he was wrestling with a decision of whether to tell something to the cops." Tammy paused as she recalled the events of long ago. "Maybe Frank was stealing from the company and Dad found out about it. That's all I can think of."

"So, do you have any idea who could be copying the Reaper persona now?"

"Hmmm. Well, it couldn't be Frank because he died in a fire many years ago—during an enormous blaze in Carthage which consumed three buildings back in 1955. Some believe he was murdered, but others say that Frank was responsible for the fire and his death was suicide."

"Suicide?" Roger said in shock. "Why would he commit suicide?"

"Frank lost everything after Grandpa fired him. He couldn't find another job, and he was virtually poor and bankrupt by the time he died in a fire himself. As far as I know, he didn't leave his family anything except a huge pile of bills to pay after his death."

"He had a family?" Roger inquired.

"Yes, Frank Timmons left behind a wife and a son."

"He had a son!" Roger exclaimed to his mother. "What was his name?"

"It was Russell. Russell M. Timmons and I remember him very well. He was a strange kid who was always getting into trouble. Russell was roughly the same age as I am, but we weren't close friends or anything. Actually, both Russell and his father gave me the creeps."

"Do you know what happened to him?"

"All I know is that Russell and his mom moved away many, many years ago," Tammy answered.

"Do you think he could be back in Carthage and setting the fires?"

"I don't know. He was pretty upset over the way the community shunned him and his mother after his father died." She let out a sigh and mulled over her thoughts as she said firmly, "Even if his father really was the Reaper, it still wasn't right to treat a seven-year-old boy the way they did."

Roger disregarded his mom's last statement and fixated on his own thoughts. "Do you have a picture of this Frank guy or his son?"

"I don't think I have one of Russell, but I'm certain I have a picture of Frank somewhere. He and dad used to be very close before their split, and he came by our house for dinner several times."

Tammy walked over to one of her many photo albums and took it off the book shelf. She sat down on the couch and began thumbing through the pages. Then, she stopped on a page that had several aged, black and white photos. After scanning the page for a moment, she took one picture out of its holder and handed it to Roger.

Roger took the photograph and held it under a bright table lamp, inspecting the picture very closely. "The face looks sort of familiar, but it is definitely no one I've seen before," he said with disappointment.

Mrs. Fasick noticed the preoccupied look on her son's face as he studied the photograph. "Are you okay, Roger?" she inquired.

"Yeah, I'm fine," he said, handing the photo back to his mother. Then he shrugged his shoulders and exhaled loudly. "Well, thanks for your help, Mom. I wish I could stay longer but I have to get back to Carthage and see Bucky. I'll have him get on his computer and do a background check on this Timmons guy when I get back."

"I hope you're not thinking of doing anything rash, son," she said sternly. "What are the two of you planning?"

Roger shook his head. "Nothing...yet." Then he smiled and gave his mother a peck on the cheek. "Don't worry yourself, Mom."

"Easy for you to say, Roger."

"I won't do anything stupid or dangerous."

"Why don't I believe you, son?"

"Look, if I had more time, I'd tell you everything. But right now, I *need* to get to Carthage. Just do me a favor and tell Dad I'm sorry I had to leave so soon and that I'll call him sometime tomorrow."

On his way back to Carthage, Roger decided to return to the same gas station he was at a couple of weeks ago. He needed to fill up the gas tank and thought he'd get a cappuccino for the ride home. As Roger was pumping gasoline, he saw a handsome young boy by the corner of the gas station. The same little red-haired boy he came across the last time he was there. The mysterious boy was standing alone, staring at Roger with a grin upon his face.

"Hi there little man," Roger spoke loudly. "What's your name?"

The little boy turned and ran around the corner. "Hey wait!" Roger yelled out. "I didn't mean to scare you!"

Roger quickly put the nozzle back on the pump and closed the gas cap. He dashed to the edge of the building where the little boy was standing, glanced around, and scampered around the corner to try and find him.

When he arrived at the back of the gas station, he saw a sporting goods store about thirty yards away. Roger stopped dead in his tracks and his facial expression changed from tenacity to unbelievable shock.

He spotted the boy up ahead of him at the storefront, and he was huddled to the side of a petite, redheaded woman who was sitting at the picnic table doing some paperwork...a woman he knew all too well.

"Oh my god," he said in a voice barely more than a whisper. "That's Nellie Spencer sitting at the table."

Nellie sat at the table lost in thought, wearing a long, orchid-colored sundress that hung down to her ankles, nearly covering her brown leather sandals. She had one arm up on the table with her head resting upon it while she was crunching numbers into a business calculator that spit out a printout after each entry.

Roger remained still for a moment, watching the sun shine down on Nellie's hair, giving it an almost strawberry-blonde appearance. Her cheeks looked blushed from the warmth of the sun's rays, and Roger smiled as she wiped a bead of sweat from her upper lip. Roger stepped over to the picnic table at a very slow pace and kept his eyes on the little boy, staring at him with an odd grin. The boy smiled back at Roger and climbed on top of his mother's back.

"Mama, mama," the boy said. "There's someone comin' this way."

Nellie looked up from her stack of papers and immediately became shocked with excitement. She began to smile for an instant, and then she turned away so Roger would not notice her emotions.

"Nellie!" he said with both shock and delight in his voice. "What're you doing here?"

"Oh my god, Roger! What an unexpected surprise!" She smiled nervously, trying to disguise the awkwardness she felt. "I was just taking a break and having a bite to eat." She pointed towards the store behind her. "I work here. Actually, I'm running this place as a favor to my brothers for a couple of months while they are out of town for awhile."

"Which brothers would those be? Are you talking about Joel and Toby?"

Nellie grinned; thrilled that Roger remembered their names. "Yeah, they're just like the rest of the Spencer boys in my family. They're always going on some kind of adventure and traveling a lot."

Roger laughed. Then he turned his attention to the boy. "And who is this little guy?"

"This is my son..." Nellie started to say.

"Wow!" Roger blurted out excitedly. "Nellie, I can't believe you're a mom! When did this happen? How old is your son?"

Nellie fidgeted around, seemingly uncomfortable about the topic of conversation. "He's five years old now. He just had a birthday a few months ago, on April 20."

Roger paused. Something had caught his attention. "That's the same month as mine."

"Yes, I know," Nellie responded.

"And what about his father? Are the two of you together?"

Nellie hesitated. Then she swallowed hard and cleared her throat as she said, "You are his father."

Roger gasped, feeling as if he had been punched hard in the chest. Nellie paused and watched, waiting for Roger to say something, anything.

Roger was pale and visibly shaken.

"Well?" questioned Nellie.

Roger stared straight ahead with a confused look, remaining speechless. His heart pounded heavily in his chest, and he had difficulty breathing.

"Well?" she questioned, slightly nervous by his silence. "Do you have anything to say?"

"Why didn't you tell me?" Roger sputtered out.

"Please, let me explain. I know that we didn't end our relationship on good terms. I also know how much I was acting like a big bitch before we broke up." She paused and her voice became softer. "I'm sure it must've seemed like nothing you did or said was right. I apologize for that; I was very stressed and anxious because my period was late. Then I found out I was pregnant, and I didn't handle it very well. I guess I was just unprepared for the news."

"You still should've told me. We could have gone through this together."

"I know; you're absolutely right. I'm sorry about it all," she pleaded. "I *really* am!"

Roger glanced down at the boy, his baby blues staring back at him. Then Roger took a deep breath and looked Nellie in the face. "I wish I could be angry at you, but I can't. I'm just so surprised to find out that I'm a father."

"So, you don't hate me?"

"No, I may be disappointed and confused, but I don't hate you." Roger turned his attention back to the little boy who was still clinging to Nellie's leg. "What's his name?" he asked faintly, his voice slightly choked up.

"His name is Alexander Paul Fasick. But everyone just calls him Alex."

"You gave him my last name?" he said, quite surprised.

"I decided it was the right thing to do since you are his father; I wanted him to have a part of you in his life. Since we are not together, I thought giving him your last name would be the best way."

Roger kneeled down and gazed into his son's eyes with extreme emotion. "Alexander, I'm your daddy," he said softly. Then he lifted his head to look at Nellie once again. "I can't believe you gave him that name. That's the name I told you I always wanted to name my child if I ever had a son."

Tears of joy began trickling down her cheeks. "I know; that's why I used it." She took a tissue from her purse and wiped her face. "That way, I could tell Alex his daddy gave him his name."

"I can't believe you did that. After everything that happened between us."

"You need to understand something, Roger. There was never a question of whether or not I loved you, but maybe we weren't ready to make the commitment for a mature, lasting relationship. I've been raising Alex by myself, and I've found that raising a child is hard work and can be very stressful at times. Quite honestly, I don't know if our relationship could've lasted through that kind of strenuous tension."

"Maybe—but you should've let *me* make that decision for myself," Roger declared.

Nellie closed her eyes and breathed deeply. "You're right, Roger; I know now I should've told you. There were so many times I wanted to call you, to tell you about him. But I didn't want to interfere with your life."

"Why would you be interfering?"

"When I finally found out about what happened to you during the ferry service incident, Holly had already moved in and was taking care of you. I knew there would be no place for me and a new baby."

Roger took a deep breath and looked down at the ground as his expression turned from joy to sadness. "Yeah, Holly was there to help me through a very difficult time, but she's gone now."

"Yes, I know. I'm sorry about what happened to Holly, I truly am."

"Thank you, Nellie. That means a lot to me."

"That was a horrible tragedy. Becoming a mother and giving life has shown me how precious life really is. It's too short to hold grudges or carry petty jealousies in our hearts. I still think about you often and have wanted to contact you a thousand times to express my condolences, but no time ever felt like the right time."

Roger turned his attention back to Nellie and gave her an approving smile. "You have really matured as a person, Nellie. I'm very impressed."

Roger and Nellie stared intently at each other for a few moments until Nellie broke the silence. "By the way, I ran into Celeste Braxton at the diner by my apartment a few months ago."

"Oh?"

"Yeah, she said things were getting better for Bucky and Mikey and that she and Bucky are getting closer. Celeste mentioned she was thinking about getting a place in Syracuse and came here to price some houses. She was hoping she could convince Bucky to move down here with her."

"Really?" Roger said surprised. "I didn't realize you knew Celeste. I'm fairly certain she moved away from Carthage before we started dating."

"Y'know, Roger, I did have my own friends and knew other people in town *before* we got together. In fact, Celeste used to baby-sit me and my younger sister, Sarah, when we were just kids. My parents didn't think any of my three older brothers were mature enough to watch over us. Joel and Toby always had their head in the clouds, and Lee always had his head up his ass."

Roger chuckled as he shrugged his shoulders. "Oh, I didn't know that Celeste ever did any baby-sitting—that's all. Anyway, as far as Celeste and Bucky moving down here, I don't think that is going to happen any time soon."

"Why?" asked Nellie. "She seemed so happy about the idea."

"She was asking for a commitment from Bucky, and he said it was too soon since Cristina died and he couldn't commit to another person right now. She felt and hurt and embarrassed, and then she walked out of his life."

Nellie sighed. "That's tragic. Has anything been resolved between them?"

"I don't think they've talked to each other in weeks. I hear she's been hanging out with Tim Matthews, the bartender from Kitty's Bar. Do you remember him, Nellie?"

"Yes, I remember him. I wouldn't have expected those two to date. I don't see where they have anything in common." Nellie paused for a moment. "Hey Roger, I was wondering...can I ask you something personal?"

"Sure," he answered nonchalantly.

Nellie's voice became soft and she appeared as though she was about to cry. "Are you happy?"

Whatever question Roger had expected, that certainly wasn't it. He looked closely at Nellie, not sure of what she meant. Then he gave a slight nod and said guardedly, "What do you mean?"

"With your life," she remarked. "Are you happy with the way things are?"

Roger looked down at the little boy clinging to Nellie's leg and smiled. "I'm reminded of something I read, Nellie. Happiness doesn't come easy. If it did, hell, we'd all be smiling."

"Ain't that the truth," Nellie added.

Roger took a deep breath and thought for a moment before he spoke again. "Maybe we can never have *exactly* what we want in life, Nellie. Perhaps happiness just isn't in the cards for a man like me. I've learned to live with that. I'm content. That's more than some people have."

Nellie nodded, understanding what he meant. "I don't suppose I ever cross your mind anymore?" she prodded.

Roger looked Nellie directly in the eyes. "Actually darlin', the fact is you still do."

Nellie blushed and turned away. "Really, I still think of you, too," she said. "At least once every day," she whispered to herself.

There was a moment of silence that passed between them. "I'm now on my way back to Carthage," Roger stated, "but I was thinking, and hoping, that maybe you could make a trip up there sometime soon. I'd enjoy seeing you again, and I'd like to get to know Alex." He looked down at the boy again. "We have a lot of catching up to do."

Nellie smiled and a tear began to form in her eye. "I'd like that, Roger. I mean, *we'd* like that a lot. As a matter of fact, I have to come up there in about two weeks for my ten-year high school reunion. I'll bring Alex along with me and give you a call. Is your number still the same?"

Roger grinned. "It sure is; you can call me anytime."

"Thank you, Roger. It's very nice of you to ask us to come visit. I had almost forgotten there's still some kindness left in this world."

Staring deeply into Nellie's eyes, Roger spoke in a tender voice. "And I had almost forgotten there was still some beauty in it."

Although hesitant, Roger bent forward and gave Nellie a peck on the cheek. She did not pull away. In fact, Nellie leaned in and gave Roger a hug with one arm. He looked down at the boy near his leg and gazed at him affectionately.

"Would it be asking too much for a hug?" he asked the little boy.

"Sure!" Alex replied exuberantly.

Roger kneeled down and grasped onto the child, squeezing him tightly. A tear came to his eye as he released, and he wiped it away before standing up.

"Thank you, buddy," Roger said with a frog in his throat. "You take care of yourself, and I'll be seeing you and your mama real soon."

Alex jumped up and down and waved. "Bye-bye!"

"Take care, Roger," Nellie commented in a gentle voice. "I'll be in touch."

The feeling of butterflies in his stomach and a heartbeat racing a million beats per second made his hands tremble, and he was unable to utter a word. With one last look, Roger turned and headed back toward his car.

Chapter 42:

Unraveling tangled Clues

While Roger Fasick was returning from his parents' house in Syracuse, other events were unfolding at the Carthage City Hall.

Adam "Red" Richardson had made his way to the town building and walked inside to the first floor where the police department was. He wanted to question Thomas Parker. Adam knew it was a long shot that the officers would let him down into the holding cell area, but if there were a chance at all, he wanted to talk to Thomas. He needed to. It was the only way he would be able to ease his mind.

Adam took a deep breath and walked right up to Ken Johnson's desk. He looked Ken square in the eyes and uttered in a confident tone, "I'd appreciate it if you'd let me talk to Thomas Parker, please."

Ken was taken aback, surprised Adam would have the gall to ask him a question like that. Then Ken shook his head and told him, "No, absolutely not!"

"Why?" Adam asked.

Ken's eyes widened. "Because your emotions are getting the best of you, and I don't think it'd be a wise decision. You might do somethin' you'd end up regrettin' and maybe you'll spend some time in a jail cell yourself."

Adam scowled and turned around, pretending he was leaving the station. As he was walking away, Adam switched directions and snuck downstairs to where the cells were. Quietly, he opened up the door to the prisoner's area and walked over to the cell where Thomas was being held.

Adam banged on the bars to wake Thomas up. "Rise and shine, Parker! I've got some serious questions to ask you."

Thomas sat up on his jail cell bunk, rubbed his eyes, and looked at Adam groggily. After a couple of seconds, he focused on Adam and answered, "What the hell do you want, Richardson? Can't you see I'm trying to get a little rest around here?" He twisted his body around so that his front was facing the cell wall and laid his head back down on the pillow. "Besides, I ain't in the mood to answer any questions right now."

Adam's face looked enraged, and he started interrogating Thomas, yelling at him in a ferocious tone. "I don't care if you're 'in the mood' or not! I want to know something right now! Were you at the waterfront six years ago?"

Thomas was perplexed. "What are you—? Was I where?"

"At the waterfront! Were you there...back when the ferry office exploded?"

Thomas hopped up off his bunk and came within a few inches of the cell bars. He did not like Adam's tone and Thomas became defensive.

"You know I was there!" he roared back. "I helped Bucky and Roger get outta there alive!"

"That's not what I meant!" snapped Adam. "What I mean is, was it *you* who dressed up as the Reaper and planted the bomb?"

"No," Thomas stated. "It wasn't me, Red. I was just as surprised as everyone else!"

"You'd better not be lyin' to me, Thomas. John Sears and I were also near the ferry service that night. I saw the Reaper running on the fishing trail into the woods! He passed right in front of me and couldn't have been more than a few feet away from my face. If it was you..."

Thomas cut him off, frustrated by the grilling Adam was giving him. "Listen to my words, Richardson. I'm tellin' ya it wasn't me. I'm an innocent man!"

Adam glared at Thomas with daggers for eyes, unconvinced by Thomas's declaration. "If you're such an innocent man, then tell me how *your* cigarette lighter got inside the Episcopalian Church the night Father Emerson and John were killed."

Thomas thought as he spoke. "I don't know. I mean, the last time I saw it was..." Thomas paused and his eyes lit up. "Hold on a minute! I finally remember when I last saw that lighter!" He started pacing around from excitement. "You'd better get one of them officers down here, Red. I have something to say!"

Before Adam could turn around, Ken Johnson came bustling downstairs. Thomas began to tell Ken about the lighter and Adam was complaining to Ken that he needed a few more moments alone to question Thomas. Each of the men was talking so fast that Ken couldn't understand a word either one was saying.

After a few seconds of their rambling, Ken cut them off and yelled, "Both of you shut up right now!"

"Sorry, Officer Johnson," both men stated in low voices.

Ken stared meanly at Adam and said, "You don't listen very well, boy! I told you NOT to come down here!"

"It's alright," Thomas answered back. "I don't mind. In fact, while we were talking, I remembered some information I'm sure you'll be interested in."

Ken stuck a toothpick in his mouth and said harshly, "Yeah, what is it?"

"I remember the last time I saw my lighter!" shouted Thomas. "It was at Holly and Cristina's funeral last year. I was standing near Tim Matthews, and we got to talking to one another right after the service ended. I let him look at the lighter because he liked the design, but people kept coming over to talk to me. I got distracted and forgot to ask him to return it."

Ken appeared unimpressed. "Ya got a point, Parker?"

"Damn straight, fat man! I'm *positive* Tim didn't give it back!" Thomas paused to catch his breath before continuing. "Tim was tending bar the night I was complaining about Father Emersion; I'm sure he overheard everything I said. Maybe he had something to do with the fire and left the lighter in the church. Why don't you go talk to him?"

Ken looked at him, sizing him up and down. "I'll look into it, Parker. You better pray I find something." He veered towards Adam. "Until then, I want you out of here, Adam."

"Yes sir!" Adam answered in an irritated tone, upset because his interrogation had been interrupted so soon.

Adam turned and grumbled to himself as he huffed back upstairs. His emotions were running high, and he craved a quick fix to numb the exasperation he was feeling. Adam reached into his pocket and pulled out a twenty dollar bill. He raised his brow in delight of his unexpected surprise, and then he proceeded over to Kitty's Bar to drown out his problems for a while.

Shortly before dusk, Roger arrived back in Carthage and headed straight for Bucky's home. His mind was flooded with thoughts and he was struggling to sort them out. He wondered how to handle the situation with Nellie and the realization that he was a father to a five-year-old boy.

Initially, Roger thought he would share his news with Bucky. And yet, until he knew how to handle it himself, he decided to keep it quiet and focus on relaying the information that he had been down to Syracuse to find out—information regarding the names of those listed as suspects in Vance Dane's journal, and most importantly, the enigmatic Reaper.

Roger walked into Bucky's house without knocking, not really realizing he had done it. Bucky was just finishing up washing some dirty dishes that had been piling up for over a week when he looked over his shoulder. His heart skipped a beat as he became aware of Roger's presence.

"Christ!" he bellowed. "Don't ever sneak up on me like that again."

Roger jumped back, snapping out of his daze. "Oh, sorry. I wasn't paying attention," he smirked slyly. "I forgot how weak your heart is."

"Very funny, wise guy," Bucky said flippantly. "So, were you able to talk to your mom?"

"Yeah, we chatted for awhile."

"What did you find out?" inquired Bucky.

"My mom said that Terry Parker was the kind of person who wouldn't hurt anyone. She went on to say that Frank Timmons was a co-worker of my grandfather's. From what I understand, Frank was quite a strange character. She also mentioned that Frank had a wife and a son; I think she said the son's name was Russell."

"Did she mention anything that was *really* out of the ordinary?"

"Nope, not really. She did, however, show me a picture of that Frank Timmons guy. His face looked slightly familiar, but he's definitely *not* anyone I could say I've ever seen before. On the other hand, I was thinking you could check out Russell Timmons's background on the Internet; maybe we'll get a break and find something we can use. You have the capability to do that, right?"

"Yes, I can probably do that," Bucky said, walking off towards his den. "Let's give it a shot."

Bucky sat down at his desk and logged onto his computer. Once connected to the Internet, he checked several search engines in an attempt to obtain any and all information on Frank's son, Russell Timmons. After about ten minutes of surfing through the web pages, he finally hit pay dirt and located a site relating to 'ancestry' which listed his name.

Although optimistic at first, their hopes dimmed after clicking on his name and reading the diminutive biography which had been written about him.

"There isn't much information on the guy," sighed Bucky. "About the only significant piece of information on here says that Russell died about twelve years ago. The cause of death was liver failure."

Roger was hovering over Bucky's shoulder, reading the material. He pointed to an object in the lower right-hand side of the screen and said, "Bucky, there's an icon that says 'Known Relatives.' Click on that!"

When Bucky clicked on it, they were transferred to another web page, one that had an alphabetical list of all known relatives of Russell Timmons and their respective date of births. On that list, one item in particular stood out. Bucky and Roger's gaze both fixated on the part of the screen which stated Russell had a child of his own, a son named Matt.

Roger scratched his head as he thought. "Well, I'm willing to bet there's not gonna be much information for this Matt guy on this website. Let's check out Classmates.com to see if we can find anything. I've heard from some buddies how in-depth that site is; it's supposed to be one of the best."

"Fine by me. I'll try anything right now."

Once they arrived at the Classmates.com website, they turned their efforts to researching Matt Timmons. After only a minute of surfing from one piece of information to another, Bucky smiled as though he hit the jackpot.

"Here we go! You were right, Roger! This web page has everything we need. It lists his hometown, a brief bio, and there's a link where we can even download his senior picture."

"Hey, this is weird," Roger whispered solemnly, continuing to read over Bucky's shoulder.

Bucky looked up at him, as though he was annoyed. "Here, let me move over." He shifted his chair over a few inches for Roger to stand next to him. "Now then, what piece of information are you looking at?"

"I'm reading his bio," answered Roger. "This guy was raised in Louisiana, and he lived in the same town Father Emerson told you he came from."

Bucky turned his attention to that part of the screen. "Oh shit," he said with an uneasy feeling in his stomach. "And look here, in his 'former places of residence.' It looks as if Matt Timmons lived in Louisiana during the time Thomas would've been residing there. I'm beginning to worry there might be more than just a coincidence to all of this."

"Um, I think we should go straight to the picture to see if we've come across this guy before."

Within seconds, Bucky's computer downloaded the 1993 high school senior picture of Matt Timmons. Simultaneously, their faces turned into shock as they realized that it was a picture of the bartender from Kitty's Bar—Tim Matthews.

Bucky stood up, his heart pounding wildly. Roger remained staring at the screen in awe, not moving a muscle. Dashing to the phone, Bucky quickly dialed the police station but only got a busy signal.

Meanwhile, Josh Roberts was at home sitting on the couch and looking at some old maps of Carthage he had sprawled out on his coffee table. Off to his left side, he had some blueprints of the historical buildings and businesses in town. After perusing the maps for some time, Josh suddenly spotted something interesting on one of the old maps and abruptly got up.

"Well, I'll be damned!" Josh yelled out. "Bucky and old man Intorcia were right! There really *are* tunnels that run underneath the town!"

He rushed to the phone to call Roger's house, but all he got was the answering machine. Unfortunately, he couldn't remember where he put the piece of paper that had Roger's cell number on it.

Josh began pacing around the room as he continued talking to himself. He grabbed the map off his coffee table and spread it out in front of him. "I can't believe how many tunnels there are!" he cried out. "Several streets have them, in fact, and every building that's been torched has one of those tunnels connected to it."

Josh stopped and grabbed the phone once again. He decided to try the one place Roger and Bucky always frequented—Kitty's Bar.

Tim Matthews was at Kitty's Bar to pick up Celeste for their date. While he was there, the phone began to ring. Celeste and Miss Kitty were both in the back, and Tim answered the phone.

"Thank you for calling Kitty's Bar. This is Tim speaking. How can I help you?"

"Hey, this is Josh Roberts. I'm looking for Roger Fasick or Bucky Morgan. Are either of them there?"

Tim gave a quick glance around the bar and said, "I'm sorry, Mr. Roberts. Neither Bucky nor Roger is here tonight."

Josh rubbed his forehead, completely stressed and out of ideas. "Well, can you do me a favor?"

"I can't guarantee anything," laughed Tim. "But what is it anyway?"

"If you see either one of them come in, please let them know I have some thoughts about the Reaper case. I'm on my way to the police station tonight to talk to Ken Johnson and ask Thomas Parker some questions."

Tim paused and his jovial expression disappeared. "Um, sure. Anything you want, Mr. Roberts."

Without hesitation, Josh placed the phone back on the hook and hurried over to his desk, snatching his briefcase and car keys.

"I'd better get down to the police station; I should show this to Ken!" he said as he sprinted out the door.

Tim hung up the phone just as Celeste was returning from the back area. She grabbed her purse from behind the bar and retrieved her tips from the jar, placing them in her pocket.

"I'm ready whenever you are!" she said exuberantly.

Tim looked nervous and distracted, as though something was troubling him. He turned, looked her in the eyes, and said, "I'm sorry, but I'm not here to pick you up."

Celeste looked dumbfounded. "You're not? Then what *are* you doing here?"

"Well, I just remembered there is something I have to take care of first and I'm going to be a little late for our date."

The frown on her face showed that she was let down.

Tim gave her a comforting grin and said, "Hey, don't worry. I'm not canceling on you. Tell you what, I'll meet you at my place in two hours, and I'll cook you a homemade meal instead."

Celeste was slightly confused and somewhat disappointed. "Oh, alright," she uttered in a quiet voice. "I'll see you then."

Celeste turned and walked back into the kitchen area. Tim did not smile or express any other emotion when she left. He just stared into nothingness, the handsome man with a looks of a movie star...and the gaze of a rabid beast.

Miss Kitty, who was sitting at her desk, looked up and asked, "Is Tim still here?"

Celeste shrugged her shoulders. "Nope, not anymore. He just left."

Curiosity set in and Miss Kitty placed her paperwork down and removed her eyeglasses, focusing all her attention on Celeste. "Why didn't you go with him?" she asked. "I thought the two of you were going on a date tonight."

"Oh, we're still going out," Celeste said, setting her purse on the coat rack. "Tim's got a last minute errand to take care of, and after that, we're having dinner at his place." She paused before saying, "I don't know what's so important, but he said it shouldn't take too long."

"Tim? Late for something? What a surprise!" Miss Kitty said sarcastically.

Celeste let out a little chuckle. "Miss Kitty, I know my date doesn't start until later, but do ya mind if I leave now? I'd like to get freshened up and change my outfit."

"Of course, Hun. Go ahead," she answered with a nod. "It's kinda slow in here right now. I think I can handle it myself. If things get too busy, I'll call Gary Wolff to come in and give me a hand."

Celeste left Kitty's Bar and walked to her apartment to change her clothes, take a long hot shower, and apply some deodorant and perfume. She took her time, debating which outfit she wanted to wear, and when she was finally ready, Celeste hailed a cab to take her to Tim's apartment because her car was in the shop for repairs.

A mud splattered cab, which had as much rust on it as it had yellow paint, pulled up to the curb and Celeste stepped inside. The blond-haired cabbie turned his head around and said, "Good evening, ma'am. My name's Ben and I'll be your driver. Where can I take ya tonight?"

"Drive me to the Buckley Building, please," she replied with a warm smile.

"Sure thing. I, uh, hope we don't get lost getting there."

Celeste cocked her head. "Excuse me?"

"Y'see, ma'am, I'm not from around here. Tonight's my first night on the job. In fact, you're my first customer!"

"Well, if you need any help, Mr..."

"Reilly. Benjamin Reilly."

"Okay, Mr. Reilly. Since you're a newbie in town, I'll show you how to get there."

Ben smiled back. "Thanks. I'd appreciate that."

As the cab drove to the Buckley Building, Celeste began to wonder if she was doing the right thing going out with Tim. After all, she still cared deeply for Bucky, but she rationalized that tonight was only a date and nothing serious; therefore, she may as well just enjoy herself for the evening.

Chapter 43:

In the face of adversity

Josh packed his car and rushed to the police station. Lying on the passenger-side seat was a large accordion-style folder which held his town maps, store blueprints, and pieces of scrap paper with jotted lines of his own personal annotations. On the way, he pulled out his cell phone and tried over and over again to reach someone at the police station. Unfortunately, every attempt was accompanied by the buzzing sound of a busy line.

When Josh finally arrived at City Hall, he hastily pulled up to the curb, his tires screeching as they came to a stop. He grabbed his belongings from the car as quickly as he could and took off to find Ken Johnson. Although the two men had their differences in the past, Josh was beginning to realize how much of an asset Ken could be on this case, and that by sharing valuable information, they possibly could solve the mystery together.

Josh hurried into City Hall and rushed over to the receptionist area leading to the police station. Then, noticing that LaTesha Prince was not at her post, he continued on down the hallway to the officer's area, clutching his folder tightly.

Ken was at his desk, reviewing some documents that were sprawled out in front of him. Josh stood for a moment, in silence; then, realizing time was extremely precious, he coughed to attract Ken's attention. A little startled, Officer Johnson looked up.

Noticing the disgruntled expression upon Ken's face, Josh said, "Boy, Ken, you look as though you've had one hell of a day." Josh smiled a small, crooked grin as he walked closer. "And now you're looking at me as if I'm the icing on the cake."

"Can I help ya with somethin', Roberts?" Ken asked with an annoyed expression.

"Yeah, you can keep an open line to this place from time to time. I've tried calling here at least twenty times over the past hour, and the line has been busy!"

"There's a reason for that. LaTesha is out sick today and the phones are down. None of the other officers knows what she does to fix them."

"Yup, there's my hard earned tax dollars being put to good use I see."

"Very funny, Roberts. Whatta ya want, anyway?" Ken asked rather brusquely. "I'm busy and don't have time to waste chatting, especially with you."

Josh pulled out his folder and set it upon Ken's desk. "Trust me; this definitely won't be a *waste* of your time. I have some information in my folder that you might be interested in!"

"Really? Is this life saving?" Ken remarked sarcastically. "Because if not, I'm kinda occupied with another matter right now, and I *really* don't have time to chit-chat."

"I think Thomas Parker was set up to look like the killer," Josh said in a hurried voice."

"Ya got any proof for that theory?"

"Remember how the fire at the church was set in the back side of the building?"

"Yeah, so?"

"I think the Reaper knew the fire wouldn't have time to spread before the fire department put it out. Therefore, he wanted the lighter to be found near the front pews and make everyone think that Thomas had dropped it."

Ken leaned back in his chair and crossed his arms. "It's funny you should say that. Thomas just told me he lent his lighter out to someone at the funeral for the Boliver girl and the Mayor's wife. He also mentioned the lighter was *never* returned to him."

Josh looked surprised. "Who'd Thomas say he gave his lighter to?" he asked.

"Tim Matthews," Ken answered in a hesitant tone.

"The bartender?" inquired Josh. "What would his motive be for placing the lighter at the church fire?"

"I don't know—just yet."

Just then, Officer Rick Streeter approached Ken with a file in his hands. "I got the information you requested, sir."

Josh and Ken stared at the young officer as he stood in silence.

"Well, do you want me to hold a séance while you give me the information by telepathy?" Ken asked gruffly and with irritation in his voice.

The officer's face became red with embarrassment. "Oh, sorry. I just did a thorough background check and discovered Tim Matthews didn't even exist before he came to Carthage."

"What?" Josh and Ken said at the same time.

Ken stood up and got in the officer's face. "That doesn't make any sense!" he yelled at the young man. "How could he not exist, Streeter?"

"Look, I'm telling you," Rick replied, standing his ground, "Tim Matthews doesn't have a history before he came to Carthage. The only shred of information I could find on the guy was he previously lived in Louisiana."

"How do you know that?" Josh butted in.

The officer glanced over at Josh and rolled his eyes. "Because he listed it as a previous residence when he applied for his driver's license."

"Was there anything else?" Ken asked.

"Everything I found is in the file, sir."

"Alright then, Rick. That'll be all."

Officer Streeter started to turn, then stopped, and shifted his attention back to Ken. "You sure are grumpy tonight, sir."

"Don't worry about how I am and get back to work!" snarled Ken.

As the officer walked away, Josh sat down in a chair by Ken's desk, perplexed by this new and shocking information. Ken followed suit behind him.

"What about Tim's birth certificate or a Social Security card?" Josh asked. "He would've had to show those items to the people at the DMV before they'd even consider issuing him a license."

Ken opened up the file and glanced at it for a moment and then said, "Yeah, apparently Officer Streeter checked those documents too. It says here all his identification documents were forgeries."

Josh's head was spinning with puzzlement. "That *is* strange, but it still doesn't explain why he'd kill Father Emerson and frame Thomas Parker for the murder."

Ken began coming up with a possible scenario. "Well, I know that Thomas once lived in Louisiana years ago. And if Tim Matthews really *does* have ties to Louisiana like his bio states, then maybe there's a connection between him and Parker." He paused for a second. "I just wish I knew how the priest fit into all of this. I mean, why would anyone have a grudge against a holy man?"

Josh snapped his fingers as a thought popped into his head. "That makes me curious about something I discovered just recently?"

"About what?"

"Well, ever since Father Emerson died, I've *also* wondered who would've had such a bloodthirsty grudge against him. Then, a few nights ago, I was doing some research on my computer and discovered Father Emerson lived in Louisiana years ago, too."

Ken raised a brow as the mere mention of Louisiana triggered his interest.

"It seems that our esteemed priest was involved in a sexual misconduct charge about twenty years ago, but for some unknown reason the case never went to trial, and he was acquitted of all charges. Maybe Tim knew of Father Emerson back then and harbored some ill feelings about him regarding that ordeal."

Ken mulled over some thoughts and spoke aloud. "That does make sense. It's possible he could've killed the priest and set Thomas up to take the fall. They've talked together at the bar many times, and I'd be willing to bet Tim knew Thomas once lived in Louisiana—and the police would discover the connection! That, along with the argument between Thomas and the priest, would put the spotlight solely on Thomas and we wouldn't look for anyone else."

They sat in silence as Josh thought about Ken's last statement. "If all this is true, then Thomas's life is in great danger!"

"Why do you say that?" Ken asked. "Thomas is already in jail for the crime."

Josh looked uneasy, as though he had just made a horrible mistake. "Well, I just happened to call Kitty's Bar before I came over here. I thought maybe Mayor Morgan or Roger Fasick was there."

"Why do I get the impression I'm not going to like what you say next?"

"Tim Matthews answered the phone and said they weren't at the bar, but I was impetuous about my discovery and told him I'd found some important information about the case. I even told him I was coming down here tonight to talk to you and Thomas about it!" Josh was becoming more excited as he talked. "If Tim actually *is* the Reaper, he's going to want to silence Thomas soon before he can clear his name!"

"Okay," rebutted Ken. "Take a breather and calm down." Ken also took a long, deep breath to settle his nerves. "There is a point to what you say about the possibility of Tim being the killer; however, this doesn't explain how Tim would be able to enter buildings, set them on fire, and manage to exit without being seen or caught."

Ken paused briefly to think.

"Didn't some of the homeless people you interviewed tell you the Reaper can walk through walls and that's how he gets out of those buildings? No human man I know of can do that. And I'm fairly sure Tim is human!"

Josh pulled out his blue prints of the town. "I think I figured out how this 'would-be' Reaper accomplishes that 'disappearing act' of his."

Ken's eyebrows rose slightly. "Really? Well, let's hear it; I'm all ears."

"There are underground tunnels that run beneath the town streets," Josh responded.

Ken and Josh exchanged a horror-struck glance, Ken completely at a loss.

"Bear with me for just a moment," continued Josh, pointing to a dotted line drawn under some of the streets on the map. "Almost every business on the east side of Carthage has these tunnels underneath them, and they all connect to one another. That's where the store owners, and even some home owners, previously stocked their coal when these buildings used it as their fuel source years ago."

Ken looked at Josh with a doubting expression. "How would Tim or the Reaper even get into these underground tunnels?"

"I don't know. It seems to me he'd have to find an entrance other than one of the established businesses. After all, he'd run too much of a risk being seen or caught."

Ken leaned forward, placing his elbow on his desk and stroking the whiskers on his chin as he stared off in thought. "But other than the stores, what other areas of town do the tunnels run under?

Josh inspected the tunnel lines on the map. "I don't see many opportunities; however, there's an entrance to the coal tunnels near the old smokestack on Tannery Island Boulevard."

"A what? Let me see the area you're talkin' about," Ken said. "Uh oh, that's also near the Buckley Building."

"So? What's so special about that?" Josh asked.

"The Buckley Building is where Tim Matthews lives."

Josh shook his head. "Oh, damn...this doesn't sound good at all!"

At that moment, it finally hit them; the feeling of sudden, frightful clarity. They knew they were right, but instead of a racing heartbeat, joyous in victory; there was a sickness in the pit of their stomachs, and Josh had thoughts of being physically ill.

Josh and Ken perused the map again. This time, they scrutinized all the buildings where the tunnels ran underneath. "Hey, Ken, this map shows there's even a portion of the tunnel that connects here in the police basement."

"We don't have a basement," Ken responded. "This building is just an old house that's been renovated, expanded, and converted into our Police Headquarters. Our so-called basement you mention is actually our holding cell for the prisoners."

"Well, look for yourself. There's a dotted line that connects the tunnels to *this* very building."

"Hmmm," Ken mused. "Maybe you're right. There *is* a section of wall down there that'd been covered up with insulation board and sheetrock. I suppose it's possible that area could've connected to the coal tunnels at one time."

"Not bad for a 'has-been' reporter, huh?" Josh smiled slyly. "I know you probably weren't thrilled when I walked in here, but I'll bet you're thankful to see me after all."

Ken nodded, and a little smirk appeared on his face. "Yeah, I suppose."

Josh knew that was all the thanks he would ever get from Ken. But it was plenty, better than cliché words that were meaningless, and yet, so easy to say. For the first time he felt Ken was accepting him, maybe not as his equal, but at least as a comrade.

Josh nodded back, allowing the silence to speak for itself.

At that moment a loud boom, like the sound of a wall exploding, rang through the building. The windows rattled and books fell off shelves. Several officers fell to the ground as the floor shook beneath them.

Ken yelled over to some of the officers on the opposite side of the room. "You two make sure everyone in the building is alright! I'll go down to the cell area and see if I can find out what caused that sound!"

"I'm coming with you!" Josh insisted.

"Alright, but I won't be held accountable if something happens to ya, Roberts!"

On the other side of town, Celeste stood knocking on Tim's apartment door. Tim did not answer, and after waiting for ten minutes on his doorstep, she decided to quit waiting in the hallway and let herself inside.

Let's see, she thought. *Where does Tim keep his spare key? I remember seeing where he put his key when I stopped by before the town's festivities last month.*

She looked at the top of his doorway and noticed that part of the molding was different than the rest.

That's right! He keeps a spare key lodged behind that odd-shaped piece of molding."

Celeste unlocked the door, immediately becoming stunned. Tim's apartment was not what she had expected. She glanced over the dainty and drab surroundings with astonishment as she made her way inside.

To Celeste, stepping into Tim's apartment was like stepping into a Salvation Army thrift shop. Although she had visited once before, on July 4th to be exact, she hadn't stepped foot inside until tonight. Back then, she'd given Tim a ride to his apartment, but she waited in the hallway while he went in and grabbed the box of fireworks for the festivities. Now, she saw everything in its whole entirety.

The room in which she stood alone in could hardly have been termed a living room, yet that appeared to be what it was intended for. There were no curtains on the windows—only blinds which were kept closed. Celeste also realized there were no pictures on the gray, dingy sheetrock walls. The living room had very little furniture as well; and the unvarnished coffee table and lamp stands were plain and of shabby construction. There was a raggedy couch and a dingy looking recliner.

Once the shock and awe had worn off, Celeste walked over and set her purse on his couch. Then she continued on to the bathroom. When she came out, she glanced into his bedroom and saw his footlocker at the end of the bed. Tim had neglected to lock it up, and the top was left half open. Her female curiosity overwhelmed her, and she just had to peek inside.

Maybe this is my chance to find out more about Tim, she thought. *After all, no one in town really knows him very well, and there could possibly be some items in there that'll shed some light on Mr. Tall, dark, and mysterious.*

Chapter 44:

Creeping Death

When Josh and Ken reached the jail cells, they saw that the Reaper was there. Smoke from the explosion and dust particles from the sheetrock walls lingered in the air. The Reaper was standing over Thomas's body like an inauspicious form, with a stun gun in one hand and a hunting knife in the other, waiting to deliver a death strike. Thomas was face down in the rubble, barely moving. Blood was seeping onto the floor from a knife wound in his shoulder, and Thomas was fluctuating in-and-out of consciousness.

Ken pulled out his gun. "Hold it right there, asshole! Don't move another muscle or I'll put a slug in the middle of that ugly head of yours!"

With cat-like speed and reflexes, the Reaper spun around and hurled his knife in the direction of Ken's body, creating an opening as the Reaper came rushing toward the two men. Ken's eyes widened and he hesitated for a split second before finally dodging away from the knife's path. That was all the time the Reaper needed. He lunged at Ken and slapped the gun loose from Ken's tight grip, plummeting it to the floor. The force of the Reaper's body crashing into Ken thrust him backwards into the wall, knocking him down to his knees.

Before Josh could react or catch his breath, the Reaper veered around and zapped him in the chest with his stun gun. Hurriedly, the Reaper picked up Ken's gun and pointed it at Josh. Josh's face went pale, and suddenly, everything moved in slow motion. Just as the Reaper pulled the trigger, Ken leaped in front of the oncoming bullet, taking it squarely in the chest.

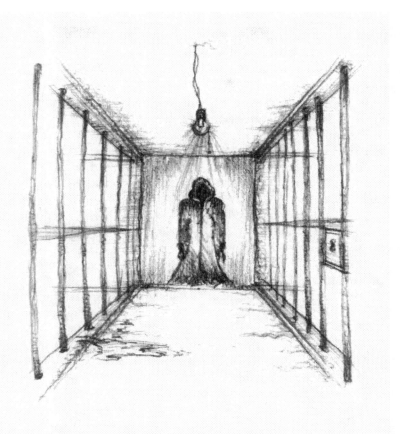

Ken dropped and landed on the cement floor, coming down hard against his face.

The Reaper slithered a few feet to his left side. He reached down, retrieved his knife off the floor, and placed it back in his hip sheath. He shifted his attention over at Ken and said, "Courage…it couldn't have come at a worst time, eh, Ken?"

Josh struggled to rise, pain surging through his body. "You're through, pal! We know who you are, and I'm going to stop you once and for all!" he shouted at the masked man.

"I wouldn't advise it, Roberts," the Reaper announced firmly, pointing Ken's pistol at Josh's chest. "As your friend, Ken Johnson, has already learned to his sorrow…life is too short," he stated with a strange, evil laugh.

At that moment, the Reaper heard footsteps and people running down the stairs, toward the jail cells. He knew he had to leave quickly.

"I hate to maim and run," the Reaper said, stepping backwards, "but I'm late. I'm late for a *very* important date." The Reaper let out a strange chuckle. "And much like the White Rabbit, I better I better cut my losses and get out of here as fast as possible before any of the other officers get down here."

In a flash, the masked man disappeared into the darkness of the tunnel hidden behind the basement wall.

Josh hobbled over to Ken as the Reaper ran away. He covered his hand over Ken's wound and applied firm pressure. "Easy, Ken, its Josh. Just stay still. Help should be here any second."

Blood began to trickle out of Ken's mouth, and his breathing got slower.

Josh looked at Ken as though he was in disbelief. "Why'd you do it, Ken? Huh? After the way I've treated you over the years...why? Why sacrifice yourself for me?"

"Felt like...I hadda do at least *one* good thing in m'life," Ken struggled to say.

"But I'm sure you've accomplished lots of great things in your life," said Josh, applying more pressure on Ken's chest to try to get the bleeding under control. "After all, buddy, you're a cop."

"No, I haven't," Ken countered. "I've been an asshole to everyone my whole life, especially to my wife. Even after all those years she put up with me and my flaws, I still didn't appreciate her...now...now it's too late to ever tell her how much I love her."

"Don't talk like that, Ken. You're going to be fine, you just hang in there."

Ken began to cough. "You were right about me, Roberts. I was just a bastard."

"No, Ken! I was *wrong* about you! I never would've thought you'd do something so heroic. You've made a believer out of me."

A gurgling sound erupted as Ken's throat began to fill with blood, and he started choking.

"Ken! Hang on, Ken!" Josh veered his head and yelled toward the door. "Somebody! Get down here! There's an officer down!"

Ken's body went into convulsions for a few seconds and then suddenly stopped. He stared into Josh's eyes for a moment as a blue gauze curtain seemed to pass over him. Ken inhaled with a shallow gasp and then closed his eyes as he exhaled. After that, two things never happened again; Ken didn't open his eyes and he didn't take another breath.

Josh sadly hung his head down; his one-time adversary turned friend had died in his arms.

Across town, Bucky and Roger were still at Bucky's house. "I've tried calling the Police Station for over an hour," Bucky said in a frustrated tone, "and the line is still busy!"

"Hey, why don't you see if Tim is working tonight?" suggested Roger. "Remember…he doesn't know we found out who he *really* is! We could always confront him and find out what he says, or how he'll react to the information we've uncovered."

"That's a good idea," Bucky replied, reaching for the phone. "Even if Tim's not there, I need to warn Celeste. If anything ever happened to her…" Bucky stopped in mid-sentence and thought about what he was going to say. "Oh my god," he continued, speaking mainly to himself. "I can't believe I'm just noticing this now."

"Is there some news you'd like to share?" Roger prodded.

"I'm referring to my feelings toward Celeste. I don't know why it always takes a crisis in my life in order to realize what's important to me. All this time I've pushed her away because I thought I'd be cheating Cristina's memory, but now I know that she's exactly what I *need*."

Bucky quickly dialed up Kitty's Bar to get in touch with Celeste. When Miss Kitty answered the phone, Bucky began speaking hastily.

"Hello? Miss Kitty, this is Bucky. I need to speak to Celeste! It's extremely important!"

"Hello, Bucky!" Miss Kitty answered in an upbeat tone. "She's not here tonight, but would you like to leave her a message."

Bucky let out a sigh of relief. "No, that's okay. I'll try to get in touch with her at her apartment later on. By the way, is Tim working tonight?"

"No," Miss Kitty replied. "He, uh, had some…um…" her voice trailed off.

"Hello? Miss Kitty, are you still there?"

"Plans!" Miss Kitty erupted. "Tim has some important plans, and I'm training a new bartender tonight—a college kid by the name of Travis Kull. Do you know him?"

"No, I don't. So, uh, you don't have any idea what he's doing tonight."

Miss Kitty fumbled her words. "Actually, Bucky, he's cooking dinner for…um, his date."

"A date!" Bucky shouted. "Look, Miss Kitty, I don't want to worry you, but there's a chance Tim could be dangerous."

"Please, I've known Tim for years," she scoffed. "He's perfectly fine."

"No! He's *not* fine. He's been lying to everyone in town about who he really is!"

"C'mon, Bucky. Is this a joke?"

"No, Miss Kitty; I'm dead serious. Tim's real name is Matt Timmons; and right now, there's a strong inclination he might be a killer."

"A killer?"

"Yeah, and I think he's responsible for setting the fires all over Carthage!"

"Oh no!" Miss Kitty gasped in shock.

Bucky cut in before she could say another word. "Miss Kitty, do you have any idea where Tim is right now? It's extremely important we get to him before anything happens! We really don't know how dangerous he *actually* is."

Miss Kitty was silent for a moment. "Um, yes I do. He's at his place right now." She swallowed hard as she said, "Bucky…Celeste is out on a date with Tim."

Bucky's voice became almost inaudible and his chest felt as though it had just been stepped on. "Oh no," he murmured. "Oh, please…not Celeste."

Back at Tim's apartment, Celeste had made her way into his bedroom and was staring at the open lock hanging on the hasp of Tim's footlocker. Curious to learn what could be inside, she walked over, looked around to make sure Tim had not arrived yet, and opened up the box.

Inside, she found two skull-like masks, both made from some type of foam-like material that could pass for rubber. One of the ominous masks was fitted with black contact lenses over the eyes, and the other had red lenses covering its optical area. There were also numerous hand guns, knives, and several stun guns of different sizes and shapes.

Looking at the contents in Tim's footlocker…she stared at the arsenal in wonder, recognizing the black cloak and masks. Suddenly now, it was all clear.

These are the belongings of the Reaper! she thought.

Celeste pawed through the footlocker and came across a large, red leather-backed scrapbook. She pulled the book out and sat it upon her lap, gathering the courage to look inside. When she opened it, she discovered clippings of newspaper articles pertaining to the town's fires. Some of the articles dated back to late 1800s.

Celeste began inspecting the old photos of the fires and reading the editorials that accompanied them. She was completely engrossed on this startling discovery and was deep in concentration.

When Celeste first walked into Tim's apartment, she didn't notice the living room window was left open. Just like she probably didn't hear Tim's feet hit the windowsill as he reentered the apartment from the fire escape.

As her attention remained fixated on the contents of the footlocker, Tim slowly made his way into the bedroom. The last thing Celeste heard was a crackling noise next to her ear from his stun gun, and then everything went black.

Across town, at the Morgan residence, Roger was talking to Bucky as they were plotting their next move. "It all makes sense now!" Roger said, coming to a realization.

"What does?" Bucky asked.

"Tim's homemade fireworks for the Fourth of July! I should've made the connection that he'd have *some* knowledge of timers and explosives."

Bucky came to a conclusion of his own. "Tim must've placed the bomb at the Mephistis Pheles Ferry Service six years ago and Adam probably seen him dressed as the Reaper while running on the trails in the woods." He snapped his fingers and said, "I'm going down to the Buckley Building to find him."

"And I'm coming with you!" Roger exclaimed.

"The hell you are!" hollered Bucky.

Roger stared at him with a look of confusion.

"You can't keep me from going, Bucky. I'm a part of this whether you like it or not."

"Maybe so, Roger, but I can't ask you to put yourself in that type of danger again," Bucky continued. "The last time you tried to stop a psychopath, Roger, you nearly *died*. Do you remember that?"

Roger nodded but remained silent.

"When we got you to the hospital after our altercation with Louis Ferr, your heart gave out twice! The doctors had to do CPR on you for twenty minutes." Bucky's voice calmed down. "You had an experience very few people live to talk about, not to mention that most people wouldn't want to relive that kind of horrific situation ever again."

"I said, I'm coming with you, Bucky," stated Roger, not backing down. "It's my choice, not yours."

Bucky knew he was not going to be able to leave without Roger coming along. He decided not to quarrel any longer and try to put their efforts together. "Okay, but we do things my way. Got it?"

"Anything you say, bud," Roger replied, nodding his head in agreement.

Bucky walked over and took Jim Draven's pistol out of his desk drawer. "We'll need this if we are to be successful. It wouldn't be wise for us to walk into a hostile situation unprepared. After all, we don't know whether Tim is armed, if he's suicidal, or if he's so desperate to achieve his goal that he's willing to take the life of others with him."

"Okay then, let's go!" Roger yelled.

Both men hustled out of the house toward the garage. Bucky lifted up the garage door to the stall furthest from the house, exposing his classic 1971 magenta colored Mustang.

"I think we're going to need her speed for this mission. She's got more pickup than my Blazer."

"Good thinking," Roger concurred.

Bucky and Roger raced to get inside the car. While grabbing for the door handle, Bucky slipped on a small oil puddle by the driver's side door and his feet went out from under him. Bucky fell and landed hard on the garage floor, hitting his upper back and head against the concrete.

"Are you alright?" Roger asked.

Bucky blinked his eyes, trying to get everything back into focus. "I hurt, but I'll live. Now let's get in and go."

The two men took off in Bucky's car and were beginning to pick up some speed as they traveled through town. A severe throbbing was starting to set into Bucky's neck, and he winced every time he twisted from side to side. With one hand on the wheel, he used the other to massage the back of his neck, trying to fight off the pain.

Roger was a bundle of nerves and bouncing all over the car seat as he rode beside Bucky, talking to him and waving his hands about. However, in Bucky's anxious state, he hardly caught a word Roger was saying.

A thousand thoughts raced through Bucky's mind—not only what was happening at the moment, but also past events which he thought had been put behind him. It had been six years since Carthage was terrorized by Louis Ferr and his ghoul, Steve Jensen. And now, Tim Matthews was ushering in another wave of evil and crime as the Reaper.

Bucky speculated if there was a connection between Tim Matthews and Louis Ferr, and what Tim's motive was for blowing up the ferry service office. Bucky couldn't help wondering if this horrifying chaos would ever end, and if Carthage would ever be allowed to live in peace again. Even though Bucky was trying to remain optimistic, in the pit of his stomach, he feared the citizens of Carthage would surely endure more death and destruction before things improved.

Then, breaking his silence, Bucky said, "My stomach's all in knots." A large lump formed in his throat. "I hope Celeste is all right; I don't know how I'd react if something should happen to her."

"Don't worry, Bucky. We'll find her."

"I'm such a fool, Roger. I can't believe I let her run into Tim's arms. If only I'd been more open and honest with her..." he said in a desperate voice as his words drifted off.

Roger became tense; a sickening feeling flowed over him at the idea Celeste could have already become Tim's next victim.

What will Bucky do if Celeste is dead? he wondered.

As Roger began to dwell on his own thoughts, his breathing became heavier and his eyes flashed. The rage Roger had inside of him, the anger he believed he had under control, was now rekindled and Roger was becoming so tense he could hardly contain himself. The notion of getting his hands on Holly's killer was eating Roger up inside and he knew he had to focus on something else, or the anxiety would drive him over the edge.

"I'm feeling uneasy myself," Roger admitted, turning the topic away from Celeste. "I can't quite explain it. There's fear in the back of my mind—fear that I don't know what I'm going to do when I come face to face with Tim. I've relived the events in my mind over and over again about what would happen when I found out who the Reaper was and what I'd do to that person. But now that it's really happening, I can't stop shaking."

Bucky nodded as though he understood. "Fear is a strange thing. Sometimes it starts with doubts, with vague suspicions. Then, suddenly it's there!"

The meaning of Bucky's words went over Roger's head as he sat in confusion. "Yeah, okay. That may be true, but it doesn't help me all that much. When it comes right down to it, I can't promise you I won't kill him," Roger stated.

"A man's got to go his own way," Bucky responded. "A good friend of mine once told me that piece of advice."

Roger grinned the best he could and extended his hand. "I'm not just any good friend…" Bucky reached out and shook Roger's hand. "I'm your *best* friend, Bucky, and I will *always* stand by your side," Roger continued.

After that, neither Bucky nor Roger said anything. The tension and apprehension they were experiencing was clearly evident by the expression on their faces. Neither of the two men dared to mention Celeste's name again, although she remained in their hearts and minds. The two friends sat in quietness, silently praying that Celeste was safe, and most importantly, still alive.

Chapter 45:

Sins of my Father

Once upon a time, the old Buckley Building was known as Carthage's First National Bank, and it had its own share of history and scandal. When it was built in 1886, it was the most attractive building in town. Located at the corner of State and Mechanic streets, the five-story stone and red brick walls were built to amazing craftsmanship.

Unfortunately, a few years later, the bank would falter and close its doors in shame after the bank scandal of 1913 made the papers. The bank's young president, thirty-year-old Walter Lavancha, had been juggling deposits and record books so he could walk away with some money when he retired one day. When the bank examiners paid a visit to Mr. Lavancha, they discovered that the funds were indeed missing. Before Walter Lavancha could be held accountable for his actions, he took $10,000 from the bank's treasury, boarded a train, and departed for parts unknown. Never again would he be seen in Jefferson County. Reports eventually placed him in the Deep South.

Over the past forty years, the Buckley Building was converted into a five-story apartment complex which housed several of the town's residents. On this particular night, however, it was making history once again. On the rooftop stood a man in a black cloak overlooking the town and behind him sat Celeste Braxton, bound tightly to a chair and unable to break free.

As the Reaper observed the bright lights and the traffic below, Celeste tried to loosen the knots on her restraints. "Why do you think I'm a threat to you?" she yelled out to him pleadingly. "I'm not dangerous."

"All women are dangerous," the Reaper replied. "Besides, if something isn't dangerous…it isn't fun!" Then he reached behind his back and took out his stun gun with one hand and removed his hunting knife from his hip sheath with the other. "*This* is going to be a lot of fun, Celeste, I promise you."

"What are you going to do, Tim?"

The cloaked figure turned around to face her and hesitated, realizing for the first time that Celeste recognized who he was. Then Tim proceeded to turn away once more, acting as though he did not hear her question. He stepped back from the edge and shook his head as if preoccupied with unnerving thoughts.

Once he refocused his attention, Tim walked over to where Celeste was, removed his mask, and began to speak. "This place has a long and complex history. One that involved my father."

"Your father?" Celeste said with surprise. "What does he have to do with anything? *Who* is your father?"

"In many ways he wasn't much of a man—kinda like me, I suppose. He was a drunk who was so engrossed in self-pity that he became loathsome to my mom, so she left him."

Celeste kept her eyes upon him as she twisted the ropes that bound her.

"All his pain and suffering began here in this town," he continued. "Y'know, the day my mom took me and walked out on my dad I learned something. I learned the world was cruel, and people's hearts were cold. That day, I learned about suffering and struggle."

Celeste sounded very genuine. "I'm sorry for what happened to you and your family, Tim, but this isn't the way to change your life. Just because your father failed you, don't take your hurt and frustration out on innocent people."

"No one is innocent," Tim replied coldly. "Yeah, dad was a failure, but he was *my* father. That has to count for something…right?"

Celeste's eyes darted toward the ground.

"Dad may not have been there when I needed him, but then again, neither has anyone else in my life!" Tim paused to calm down. "His name was Russell…Russell Timmons. However, there's not much I remember about him when I was young. I remember more vividly my mother taking me to Louisiana with her and raising me on her own until I was taken away from her. When I tried to find her after I was released from the mental institution, I was told she died."

Tim paused briefly, shook his head again, and exhaled deeply. "I lived with relatives until I graduated from high school. After that, I went searching for my dad. During all of those years, I don't know if dad ever tried to find us—when I found Dad years later and asked him, he told me he did. I still don't know if I believe him. If he had, maybe we would've stayed together. Maybe I would've had a normal life, but then again, I doubt it."

Lifting her head, Celeste asked, "Why do you say that?"

"My dad was a troubled and restless kid right from the start. After his own father died, he and grandma were forced to move from town to town. The residents of Carthage turned their backs on my Grandmother and refused to help her because they suspected that her husband was the Reaper."

"The one from the 1950s?"

"Yes, that's him. My dad knew his father was the Reaper, too. Grandpa Timmons told dad it was their *special* secret and never to tell anyone."

Celeste tried to distract him and buy herself some time as she continued her questioning.

"Why did your grandfather start the fires and dress up as the Reaper?" she prodded.

"From what I understand, Grandpa Timmons did it to scare people away and buy their properties at rock-bottom prices—and the creation of the Reaper was essential in order to protect himself against being accused of insurance fraud for starting some of his own buildings on fire.

"Your Grandfather was the first Reaper?" she said as the reality was finally beginning to set in.

"Yes," Tim admitted. "He certainly had the skills to make the Reaper persona believable, and he played the part of a ghostly spectre with meticulous perfection. I've been told my grandfather was a champion track star during high school and held many State high-jumping and Triathlon records. He could run like the wind as a teenager and remained in excellent physical shape even in his forties! Because of his incredible speed and agility, he literally had people believing he was capable of supernatural feats."

Tim began to pace from side to side.

"As time went on, people in town were beginning to get suspicious of him, so my grandfather decided that it was time to move somewhere before the police decided to file charges against him."

Celeste kept her eyes focused on Tim's movements as she struggled with the ropes that were binding her wrists together. "So then, where did he plan on moving to after he left Carthage?" she asked in an attempt to keep his attention diverted.

"My father said grandpa went to Chicago to look for work and check out places for his wife and son to live. However, something happened to him on his trip, and when Gramps returned from Chicago, he was a changed man. Dad went on to say that grandpa seemed like a nervous wreck after his trip and constantly appeared as though he was worried about something. Shortly thereafter, grandpa told my dad he was going to stop being the Reaper for good."

"That's interesting," Celeste uttered, struggling mightily to free her hands from the tight restraints while Tim had his back to her and was lost in thought. "What happened to your grandfather in Chicago?"

"No one knows. Less than a week later, he died in one of his own fires. He got careless." Tim turned and faced her. "But my grandfather wasn't the first arsonist in my family; he was just carrying on a tradition."

Tim's last word caught Celeste's attention. "Tradition?" she inquired.

"Yeah, that's right," Tim continued. "As a matter of fact, my ancestors have been responsible for many of the mysterious fires that plagued this town. My great-grandfather was to blame for the great fire of 1888; he was just five years old at the time."

"What?" exclaimed Celeste. "How?"

"He was with some other kids who were playing with matches, and the flames started to spread. His friends ran off and left him there alone. At first, he was scared, but for some reason, he didn't run away. I suppose great-granddad stayed because he loved the rush. As he got older and more daring, he started more fires. Then my grandfather took it to a new level by inventing the Reaper persona."

"But didn't it stop there?" inquired Celeste. "You said your father moved away, right? What happened to your father after your grandma and him left Carthage? Was he bitter about how everyone in town treated him?"

"Initially he wasn't. He was too young to fully grasp what was happening in Carthage when he moved away."

Tim paused and kept his head low as he began to pace back and forth. "My father told me he came back to Carthage shortly before I entered the first grade, sometime in the early 1980s. Apparently, dad was thinking of relocating our family here and planned a short trip to Carthage to look for a house to buy. While he was in town, he wanted to reconnect with his roots and see some of his old childhood friends. But the happy little reunion my father expected to find was only a figment of his imagination. The townspeople looked down upon him because of resurfacing rumors about his father being the arsonist responsible for the fires of the 1950s.""

"People can be so cruel sometimes," Celeste muttered.

"How true, my dear Celeste. In fact, Dad was so angry that he left town again and never returned. However, before he departed, he ignited some fires over the span of several weeks that had the community in a panic. Dad was never caught though. He set up some dupe by the name of Bud Hopkins." Tim laughed slightly. "That poor bastard was convicted and sent away to prison for years, and he didn't have anything to do with the fires!"

"What a horrible thing to do!" Celeste blurted out, prolonging the conversation to stall for more time. "I'm surprised your mother, or any woman for that matter, would get involved with a man like that. Why didn't she turn him into the police? She must've known what he was doing?"

"My mother, Elizabeth, was a naïve young girl when she first met my father."

"She sounds like a woman who didn't have her head screwed on tight," Celeste retorted.

"Don't you *ever* mock my mother—Ever! She was a beautiful woman who was full of talent." His voice became tender and his eyes misted. "She sang me to sleep every night as a child…and I'll never forget how wonderful her voice sounded."

Celeste spoke in a gentle tone. "I'm sorry, Tim. I didn't mean to ridicule you or the memories of your mother."

Tears swelled in Tim's eyes and trickled down his cheeks as he said, "My mom was an excellent artist, as well as a poet and songwriter. She wrote several short stories that were published in the local newspaper, too. I swear…if it weren't for me draggin' her down, she could've gone far in life."

"I don't understand something, Tim. If your mother was as wonderful as you say, then why would she get involved with someone as troubled and dangerous as your father?"

"My dad was a charmer—a sweet talker—who knew just how to get her to do whatever he wanted. He got my mom pregnant, and they were quickly married by the Justice of the Peace. She stayed with him because she loved him. However, that all changed after he became a drunk. Eventually, she left him because she couldn't take his abuse and apathetic behavior any longer. I located him years later when I was a teenager; but by that time, my father was dying from liver disease. We sat down and talked for hours; he told me how sorry he was for being a bad father and then he told me all about our family's haunted history."

Celeste sat in silence, her body trembled as Tim laughed to himself.

"I guess it's like a 'rite of passage' for the men in my family," he said, looking out toward the river. Then he snapped out of his daze and turned to face Celeste as a crazed grin covered his face. "Are you still looking for the perfect ending for your novel, Celeste?"

That was an unexpected question which threw Celeste into a state of confusion. "I don't understand what you mean."

"I killed that old ferryman, Louis Ferr. I knew there were some strange things going on down at the waterfront; and one night, while walking on the trails along the banks of the Black River, I found out how deranged he really was."

"What makes you think he was any *more* deranged than you are, Tim?"

Tim's left brow rose slightly as he began to explain. "Working in a bar, I get to hear lots of gossip. I overheard Bucky and Roger talk about Mr. Ferr several times. I went down there to check it out for myself—the night Scott Patterson vanished to be exact."

Tim paused as his eyes met with hers.

"If you think I'm misguided, Celeste," he continued, "you wouldn't believe how crazy that old wacko was. I hid in the shrubbery across the river from the ferry service and watched Scott step on board the boat. Several minutes later, Louis Ferr raised his arms up to the sky and began chanting…from out of nowhere, a ghostlike dense fog emerged and smothered the ferry. I couldn't make out any images aboard the ferryboat through the fog; however, I did hear screams."

"Screams?" Celeste remarked.

"Yes, the agonizing screams of Scott Patterson as he called out for help—and soon afterward, he was screaming as if he was being tortured to death."

Celeste sat in horrified speechlessness.

"I knew right then and there that Ferr was a deranged psychotic, and I took it upon myself to thin out the ranks in this town." Tim smirked and then let out a spine-numbing laugh that seemed more like a shrill. "You can't have too many crazies on the street, you know. It just wouldn't be safe to leave your house at night!"

"So you planted the bomb at the ferry service," she whispered, having a moment of clarity. "And what about Pat Jordan? Did you have something to do with his death, too?"

"He was an insignificant boob!" Tim bellowed. "I remember how he came into the bar one night while I was working and bragged to me that he was single-handedly going to solve the mystery of the Reaper. Pat said he was compiling a file of information and he'd have it figured out in a couple of weeks."

"And did he figure it out?"

Tim spoke in a nonchalant voice. "Oh, I'm sure he would've if given enough time. I thought I covered my tracks, but I know now that I was wrong."

"What's that suppose to mean?"

Tim inhaled deeply before answering. "When I first came to town, I was nervous I might somehow get recognized. I knew that was utterly impossible, but I couldn't shake the feeling someone would find out who I was and stop me before I could carry out my plan. I went to the Carthage Library and found as many articles as I could that referenced my family, the original Reaper sightings, and the fires of the 1950s—then I destroyed them all. That way, there would be no way to connect me to anything."

"But what does that have to do with Pat Jordan?" Celeste asked, quite baffled.

"Well, apparently I missed an article or two because a few days after his ranting at Kitty's Bar, Mayor Jordan approached me while I was at work with a picture of my grandfather and said the resemblance was remarkable. Then he asked me why I had changed my name; he also mentioned that my grandfather was a suspect of being the Reaper before dying in a fire himself. When I had no answers, Jordan informed me he was going to have me investigated. I told him that it wouldn't be good for his safety if he didn't stop poking around. When he asked me why, I told him that he might find out that *I* was the Reaper."

"You actually said that! What did he do?"

"His face got all white, and he quickly left the bar," Tim answered, his tone becoming much more serious and harsh. "I closed down early that night and snuck into his house and murdered him. I searched his house from top to bottom looking for the alleged Reaper file but couldn't find it. Just to be on the safe side, I burned his house to make sure no one else found it either. When it wasn't discovered in his office, I figured I was in the clear. And just to be certain no one would ever come across that information again, I decided to torch the library."

Celeste was confused by Tim's actions. "But why would you just admit everything to Pat Jordan?"

"Ol' Mayor Jordan was getting too close in his pursuit. He would've kept digging around until he found out who I was and what my motives were. I couldn't let that happen; I couldn't let him stop me before I settled the score. I had been planning my revenge against Carthage for years and nothing was going to get in the way." Then he spat over the edge of the building and hollered, "Those sanctimonious fools had to pay for shunning my family and leaving us with nothing!"

A chill went down Celeste's spine. "What about Cristina Morgan, Tim? Did you kill her as well?"

"No," Tim emphatically stated. "I was at the library, setting it ablaze, the night Cristina died. Besides, I read the newspaper editorials about her death which mentioned she was the victim of a hit-and-run accident. Those articles also revealed the only lead the police had to go on was that someone saw a black van leaving the scene of the accident. And trust me, Celeste, I do *not* own a black van."

"You may not have been responsible for Cristina's death, Tim, but there's still one thing I don't understand. Why have you been killing the homeless?"

"Those lazy, inconsequential fools? I'm trying to purge the town of its undesirables as well as take revenge against the townspeople who turned their back on my family."

Celeste couldn't listen to his ramblings anymore and broke down crying. "I can't believe how one person could harbor so much resentment in their heart! Your living some deranged fantasy!"

"Everyone fantasizes. We all want to become something we're not, and subsequently, within each of us, often times, there dwells a mighty and raging fury." He smirked and stated, "For me, my anger and resentment was born in a sea of fire."

"Where did you hear that before, Tim? From watching the Incredible Hulk on television as a kid?"

"Why, yes I did," he chuckled. "Anyway, we are getting *way* off the topic. I researched this town for quite some time before coming here, and using the history of the town's mysterious fires, I decided that's how I would act out my revenge. I wanted to condemn Carthage to the same pain and agony my family went through. I've been slowly taking my vengeance on the residents here for years."

"What does that mean?" Celeste inquired. "Have you been starting the fires in town for the past few years? Tell me, Tim, how many other catastrophes have you caused?"

Tim ignored her direct question as he walked over to three jugs of gasoline that he'd brought up on the roof. He picked up one of the jugs, the one that rested closest to Celeste, unscrewed the top, and began to splash its contents over the rooftop. Next, Tim gathered the two other jugs and placed them at the other end of the rooftop, dumping most of their contents on the roof edge. With the jug that remained in his hand, he made a trail from the roof outskirts to a few feet away from Celeste.

"I'm sorry things have come to this," Tim said. "It may not seem like it, but I really do love you."

"Love?" shouted Celeste. "What could a deranged psychopath like you *possibly* know about 'love'?"

"I realize I've done some horrible things, Celeste," Tim replied in a soft, calm voice. "And I'm fairly certain I'll be going to Hell for everything I've put this town through. However, in spite of all my pain and suffering, you've been the one bright spot in my life. *You* are the closest to Heaven that I'll ever be."

With those words, Tim lit a match, gazed at the glow of the colors for a moment, and tossed it upon the ground. The flame ignited and began following the gas trail.

Tim's gaze shifted back toward Celeste as he said, "I really wanted it to work out between us. I honestly believe you could've subdued the rage I hold inside. A woman like you could have turned my whole life around."

"We never had anything going!" she screamed out. "Quite honestly, I don't know what I *ever* saw in you! You're not even half the man that either Bucky Morgan or Roger Fasick is!"

The mere mention of Bucky Morgan's name angered Tim, and he snapped at her in his grisly Reaper voice. "Be careful what you say, Celeste," warned Tim. "Remember, I can make this quick and easy for you, or I can make your death very painful. My word is law upon this roof. You cannot dispute my power!"

"Your word is *not* law!" Celeste screamed back. "You're just some demented psychotic who has an enormous need for revenge and an even bigger ego! You are no Reaper, Tim; you have no *real* power!"

"Maybe not, Celeste," he sneered. "But one thing is for sure. If I can't have you, no one will."

Flames started to surround the outskirts of the roof as Celeste watched in horror. Within moments, some of the old, dried out beams began to splinter.

"Tim!" she screamed. "Some of the wood has already started to collapse! We're going to die unless you…"

Tim interrupted her before she could finish her sentence. "Of course we're going to die up here, Celeste. That's what I want! An ending to these years of utter lunacy. A final peace to it all."

He paused for a moment and saw the tears running down Celeste's face.

"I never intended to hurt you, Celeste. But I see now that your life is as much a sad mistake as mine. This town is a noxious, evil place; you should be pleased to be leaving this pathetic life for something better." Then he turned, and with his back to her, he outstretched his arms to the sky and said, "Embrace the flames that frighten you, Celeste. Welcome the eternal peace of Death."

"No!" Celeste screamed. "I won't let you do this! I don't want to die!"

"Do not resist, my love," he said as he veered around and walked back over to her, stroking her cheek with his cold, coarse fingers.

Fear seized her. Celeste could no longer endure the horror of his touch, she screamed. Despite the sheer hopelessness, she threw her head from side to side and wretched at the unyielding restraints. She fought desperately to be free. Unfortunately, that was an impossible task, and for now, she had to be satisfied with dislodging the hand, which was stroking her face.

Tim saw the fear upon her face and the fierceness of her struggle, suddenly becoming empathetic.

"I'm sorry, Celeste," Tim said, stepping backwards as he gazed into her moist eyes. "I never intended for you to get involved in any of this mess. I especially didn't want to see you get hurt, but I guess it's gone too far for that."

He sounded genuinely ashamed of his wicked behavior, almost as if he were beginning to feel guilty for all the anguish and suffering he had inflicted upon the tiny town. There was no trace of the hysterical anger which he'd displayed only a moment ago. Only the look of sorrow and teary eyes were visible upon his sober face.

Celeste peered at him with a blank expression, appearing as though she was oblivious to everything around her and ignoring anything he was saying. Her hair was now dangling in her eyes, and there were large beads of sweat trickling down her forehead.

Tim pulled out the stun gun from under his cloak with his right hand and the hunting knife with his left. He stood and watched the flames spread across the roof. The stun gun hung heavy in Tim's hand, and he dropped it down before his feet. He sauntered over to Celeste and tears continued streaming down her face. Dropping the knife from his other hand, he touched her shoulder, and she flinched. His sinful touch was like a spider crawling on her skin. She attempted to pull away, but the rope was bound tightly and her restraints held her in place.

Tim lowered the dark Reaper mask over his face while Celeste watched Tim turn his back to her, glaring at the creeping blaze. Somewhere in the crackling of the flames, Celeste overheard Tim as he began chanting something she could not understand.

Chapter 46:

Final fate of the Reaper

Fire alarms rang and the firefighters raced to suit up and get to their designated trucks. These firemen have had more firefighting experience than they cared to discuss. Most of them were veterans of numerous fires in Carthage, and they'd all tell you that they've never seen so many fires in such a small town. A few of the men had resigned and left the department because of close calls with death themselves; they just couldn't take the stress any longer. Now, another fire was ravaging the tormented community; another historic landmark was going up in flames, and everyone was praying there would be no victims to grieve over.

It seemed to take forever for Bucky and Roger to reach the Buckley Building. Although it would take less than five minutes to travel from Bucky's house to the old building, those minutes seemed to drag on as hours.

Once they were within a mile away of the apartment building, both men remained in silence as different thoughts occupied their minds. Roger seethed of anger and wanted swift revenge. Bucky's thoughts were focused solely on Celeste and the fear of what may happen to her. He tried to remain calm so he could think clearly. The heavy pounding in his chest frightened him, but the nausea had subsided and there was no longer a trembling in his hands.

As Bucky and Roger approached the Buckley Building, they noticed the swarm of people gathered on the sidewalk across from the burning complex. Bucky hit the brakes a few hundred yards short of the blaze and pulled over to the curb. He killed the engine, started to get out.

"Why are we stopping?" asked Roger.

"The police barricade won't let me get much closer," Bucky explained. "We'll have to walk the rest of the way."

Roger stared at the flames. "Do you think they're still in there?"

Bucky glared across at his friend, perturbed at Roger's doubting tone. "You better believe it!" he told him. "And if we're lucky, we can get to Celeste before she gets hurt. Now let's stop jabbering and get moving!"

The street was jammed with onlookers standing in front of the Buckley Building, watching in disheartened awe. The densely-packed crowd was motionless. Nevertheless, Roger forced his way through, Bucky keeping tightly behind him. There were murmurs of annoyance as they shoved forward, complaints that were soon stifled by the sight of fury in Roger's eyes and the intense anger and panic on their faces.

Whereas most of the residents of the Buckley Building apartments were desperately trying to get out of the burning building, Roger and Bucky were rushing to get inside.

Just as the two men were making their way past the fire trucks, they were approached by Fire Chief Vincent "Vinnie" Montalvo. Vinnie was a short, wiry-looking fellow with a black moustache, a five o'clock shadow, and severe burn scars tattooed across his face.

Fire Chief Montalvo was dressed neatly in a white dress shirt, black tie, and a dark blue fireman's dress jacket with matching slacks. However, his knee-high rubber boots looked out of place with the rest of his uniform.

"Hold on!" Vinnie yelled out to them in a husky voice. "Where do you two think you're going?"

"I'm Bucky Morgan, the Mayor of this town, and we *need* to get inside that building," stated Bucky, pointing to the flame smothered structure.

"I don't care who you are, sir!" the fire chief declared. "No civilians are going back in there…for anything!"

"You don't understand," Roger exclaimed as he stepped in-between the two men and a hint of desperation in his voice. "The Reaper's up there, and we think he has a hostage!"

The firefighter looked astonished and his jaw dropped. "Who'd you say was up there?"

Bucky stepped forward, getting in the other man's face. "The Reaper!" he stated forcefully. "And he has Celeste Braxton up there with him!"

Vinnie's face became immediately pale. "Oh my god! I'll radio that information up to my men." Then he waived a finger in Bucky's face and said, "But I still can't let you up there."

As Fire Chief Montalvo reached for his radio, Roger turned to Bucky, giving him a wink and a nod. "I understand," Roger said in a calm voice to the firefighter. "But I also understand that…" Roger paused and shifted his attention toward the burning building. "Excuse me, sir. I think someone up there is trying to get your attention."

Vinnie veered around. "Who…?"

While his attention was diverted, Roger swung as hard as he could and punched the fire chief in the jaw, sending him to the ground and knocking him out cold.

"Okay, let's hurry and get up there!" Roger yelled.

Bucky looked down at the unconscious fireman. "I can't believe you just did that!" Then he smirked and said, "But it's a good thing you did or I would've had to!"

Roger and Bucky raced inside and reached Tim's apartment only to find that the door was locked. The two men backed up as far as they could and then sprinted ahead as fast as they could, slamming against the door with their shoulders. The force was so strong it broke the heavy oak door off its hinges.

Both men entered the dimly-lit apartment, greeted by the stench of burnt hair and a deathly silence. Slowly, they took a few steps inside and then stopped again to listen. More silence.

The apartment felt empty, almost lifeless. Bucky's apprehension intensified and a knot began to form in his stomach. Gesturing for Roger to follow, Bucky crept deeper into the apartment, looking for Celeste.

Bucky cautiously continued to walk through Tim's place until he reached the bedroom. Roger, on the other hand, began searching the living room and bathroom. Bucky scanned the bedroom, noticing the top of Tim's footlocker was open. Something inside caught Bucky's attention and he dashed over to see what the object was. When he got closer, his expression changed from curious to shock.

"Roger!" he hollered out. "You should come take a look at this!"

Roger rushed into the room and saw Bucky hovering over the wooden box. "What is it? Did you find something important?"

"Take a look at all of this stuff," Bucky said, pointing at the collection of items in the box.

Both men gazed at the paraphernalia lining the inside of the footlocker and the newspaper clippings that were strewn on the floor. They saw numerous articles about the town's fires, dating as far back as the late 1800s. Bucky and Roger sifted through dozens of articles, photographs, and even a few magazine articles describing fires, and even more shocking, obituaries of people who died in those fires. The more Roger and Bucky rummaged through Tim's collection of gruesome souvenirs, the more they realized what a deranged person they were dealing with.

Just then, they heard a woman scream and both men rushed back into the living room. They noticed that Tim's window leading to the fire escape was open. A closer look revealed a princess-cut, diamond studded earring was lying on the windowsill.

Bucky raced over and snatched the earring. "This is Celeste's," he said, holding it up for Roger to see.

Roger seemed unsure. "How do you know that?"

"Because *I'm* the one who gave it to her!" Bucky answered back. "It was for her birthday a few months ago. I wanted to let her know how much I appreciated everything she's done for Mikey and me."

Bucky leaned his head out the window to see if he could get a look at where the scream came from. "I think we should split up and head to the roof," he said as he started to climb up on the window sill.

"That's a good idea!" Roger responded in a rushed tone. "We'd better hurry; we don't have much time!"

"I'll take the fire escape up to the roof," Bucky announced. "You use the stairway, and we'll meet at the top."

Roger darted off, flinging the door open hard and running up the staircase, his shoes pounding the metal stairs. He moved with an intense quickness while his breathing became heavier as his lungs burned in his chest.

Swiftly, yet silently, Bucky climbed to the roof of the old building. A high-pitched cackle from the rooftop made him shudder. The piercing pain in his back and neck were beginning to cause him some discomfort, making his muscles sore and stiff while his head was feeling dizzy. His palms were wet with perspiration and slipped when he reached for a rung. He lost his balance and fell off the ladder, landing hard upon his back and momentarily knocking his wind out while his right leg twisted sideways.

"Aahhhh!" he screamed in pain. Trying to mask the sound of his screams, he quickly covered his mouth as to not attract any attention to himself.

Slowly, he got back up and grabbed onto a rung, pulling himself up. Bucky placed one foot on the ladder and dragged the other behind it, wincing with the effort.

Every movement caused him to cringe with aching pain and his heart to batter against his ribs. Bucky had to stop on each rung until the pain subsided and he was ready to take the next step.

When he reached the top, all he heard was the fury of the flames and the crackling of wooden beams. Everything else was silent, and Tim Matthews, the Reaper, was nowhere to be seen. The first thing Bucky saw was Celeste tied to a chair facing towards him with her hands bound behind her back and her mouth gagged. Celeste's head was moving to one side, almost as though she were trying to tell him something, or perhaps warn him of danger; unfortunately, Bucky either didn't notice her signal or he just didn't understand.

"Don't worry, Celeste!" he yelled to her. "Just hang on and I'll be right there! Everything's going to be alright!"

Just as Bucky began to walk toward Celeste, the Reaper jumped out from behind one of the large air vents and ambushed Bucky. Before Bucky could even react, an unnerving jolt of high-voltage energy surged through his body, dropping him to his knees.

"Yeeargh!" Bucky screamed in pain.

Bucky looked up and saw the Reaper standing over him, a stun gun sparked as he waved it in the air. The Reaper stood over him like a ghost, like a living nightmare; and for a moment, before Bucky regained his bearings, he thought it was Louis Ferr standing above him, back from the grave to steal his soul.

"Man!" Tim shouted, lifting up his Reaper mask. "That felt good! I've wanted to do that for a long time, Morgan. You pompous ass!"

Bucky groaned and rolled around in pain, too dazed to stand.

"You underestimate me, Bucky," Tim hissed in anger. "And you disappoint me as well! Do you believe me to be so ignorant that I wouldn't expect you coming after me? Did you think that once you and Roger discovered who was behind it all that I wouldn't be ready for you? However, that is not your worst mistake. Your biggest blunder was involving yourself in matters that don't involve you!"

Bucky rolled to his side, cringing as he tried to speak. "Don't involve me? You're causing horrifying havoc in my town, you've killed my friends, my neighbors, and now you're trying to kill the woman I love."

Tim scoffed at Bucky's remark. Then he leaned in close to Bucky's face, looking at him through squinted eyes. "I don't think you realize how much I respect you, Bucky—how much I admire your fierce determination, your resilience, and your ability to drive yourself to triumph. I know if I give you the chance, you will *not* give up until one of us is dead." Tim paused for a moment before saying, "I hold you in such high regard, it almost pains me to do this!"

Tim lowered his mask once again and grabbed a loose brick, whacking Bucky in the back of the head. Bucky landed forcibly upon his face; he was barely conscious and could hardly move. As he laid there on the roof, gasping for air and grunting in pain, Tim hovered above him. "In another place, maybe in another time...we could have been friends."

Roger opened the door to the roof and saw the Reaper standing directly above Bucky, taunting him with the brick in his hand. Roger immediately began thinking of what to do, knowing he didn't have much time. He needed a plan...Fast!

He crouched as he walked, making his way from smokestack to smokestack, trying to stay as inconspicuous as he could.

Roger had not moved very far before something struck fear in his heart. He watched as the Reaper raised the brick high above his head, ready to bring it down upon Bucky once again; this time, inflicting the finishing blow.

As the flames continued to soar, Roger gasped and his pulse quickened; he knew that he had only a few precious seconds to make his move. Head up, eyes still fixed upon the Reaper, Roger burst from his hiding place and sprinted across the roof.

Roger kept his body directly behind the Reaper's, out of his peripheral range of vision...or so he hoped. He was taking a big risk, hoping to reach him without being noticed. If the Reaper caught even a flicker of movement out of the corner of his eye, or if he happened to turn and look, his reflexes could bring the brick down upon Bucky's head. Roger had to be cautious because the Reaper could pull out his stun gun and drop him in his tracks before Roger even laid a finger on him.

Roger knew he had but one chance. He plunged forward and tackled the Reaper; nevertheless, the Reaper saw Roger a split second before he reached him. The Reaper turned just enough to throw Roger off to one side. Not knowing what weapons Roger had, the Reaper decided to make a quick getaway.

The Reaper darted to the stairwell door that led down to the next floor, but to his dismay, the door was locked. Immediately, he dashed to the fire escape, but he knew that would be a poor choice as there were a dozen police cars directly below. Now the Reaper was becoming anxious about the ever-towering flames that were rapidly spreading, and he also contemplated how he was going to escape.

The Reaper headed for the Penthouse, the small building on the roof that housed the elevator motors and cables which carried the elevator up and down the elevator shaft. In the back of his mind, the Reaper thought he might be able to climb down the cables; however, the door to the Penthouse was also locked. For the first time, the Reaper was beginning to panic, and he began running from one side of the roof to the other, looking for an escape route.

Bucky, who was still lying on his side, pulled his gun from its holster, which was stuffed in the back of his pants, and tossed it to Roger. "Take this," he grunted. "You're going to need it!"

Roger grabbed the gun, flipping the safety off. He cocked the trigger back and took off towards the Reaper, running faster than he ever had before.

When he caught up to the Reaper, Roger grabbed him by the shoulder and turned him around, their eyes flashing at one another. The Reaper's eyes flashed once again, and then his arm lashed out. Before Roger knew what was happening, the Reaper hit him hard in the chest. The blow caused the revolver to drop from Roger's hand, and he nearly tumbled off his feet. He stumbled backwards, landing against an air vent which resulted in the wind being knocked out of him.

Before Roger had time to react or recover, the Reaper lunged forward once again, attacking his midsection and punching the side of his head.

Wholly, instinctively, Roger pivoted on his right foot, and with all his strength sent his left hand straight at his attacker's face. His fist landed squarely on the Reaper's mouth, splitting his lip and breaking his top two teeth. Blood began streaming down the Reaper's chin.

The force of Roger's punch left the Reaper woozy and disoriented as he stumbled backwards, falling down to his knees. While down on one knee, the Reaper reached behind his back and drew out his stun gun. He stepped to his left and then stopped, changed direction and continued towards Roger on the right. While Roger was off guard, the Reaper reached in and zapped him directly in the chest, sending Roger stumbling backwards over a crate of roofing shingles.

As Roger laid in the rubble, the Reaper began to speak. "I'm sure you know by now who I really am. And you might also be aware there was a Reaper before me that killed your grandfather. My grandfather, Frank Timmons, was wearing this same mask back then. Jacob Gordon discovered my grandfather was the Reaper and responsible for the town's fires, so Jacob fired Frank and threatened to turn him in to the police. Grandpa Frank knew he was running out of options. He knew it would've only been a matter of time before ol' Jacob went to the cops and ratted him out. That's when Gramps figured he *had* to do something to silence Jacob in order to prevent going to jail."

"How?" questioned Roger.

"My grandpa telephoned Jacob and disguised his voice, pretending to be a potential buyer, and asked if he could look at one of the buildings Jacob had listed in his real estate business as 'For Sale.' When Jacob arrived, Grandpa Frank snuck up behind him and knocked his former business partner unconscious, and when Jacob awoke, the building was on fire.

While grasping his chest in pain, Roger managed to sputter out, "So, Frank Timmons left my grandfather in there to die."

"Oh, your grandfather still had a chance to get out of the burning building, but he heard a woman screaming from somewhere inside. I don't know who she was; I was told she was simply some woman who just happened to be working in the building. In fact, I believe she was the only person in the building at the time. Anyway, Jacob went after her; and alas, they both perished."

With anger seething, Roger stared at the ghastly Reaper.

"And now, I have taken my grandfather's place." The Reaper stopped to laugh. Then he veered around and watched the flames towering higher to the sky. "In keeping with tradition, I *also* caused havoc in your family's life."

Roger's eyes suddenly became very wide.

"That's right," the Reaper continued, not paying any attention to Roger. "I was responsible for Holly's death. I'm the reason for your anguish and guilt that breathes down your neck. You'll never know peace so long as I live, and when I die, I'll make sure you burn in Hell beside me."

The Reaper turned back once again and walked over to Roger, expecting to see a nearly unconscious person lying on the ground; however, when he looked at his victim, he saw that Roger was still alert and fighting to get to his feet. The Reaper stood for a short span of time, surprised that Roger had so miraculously withstood the blast to the chest. Then, having evidently decided to make up for the stun gun's failure, he drew his knife from the sheath on his hip and tested its point with his fingers while a wicked light shone from his squinting eyes.

As Roger finally stood up, the Reaper jumped toward him, swinging a swift, upward knife-thrust for his midsection. With surprising alacrity, Roger rotated his body and caught the wrist of his attacker. The Reaper was catapulted through the air, and his knife skidded harmlessly across the rooftop.

Roger slowly made his way over to where the Reaper landed. His body was in shock from the jolt of the stun gun, but in his mind, Roger felt nothing, nothing but vengeance seizing him by the heart. The same vengeance which dragged him down to the dark depths of hysterical strength. He grabbed the Reaper and ripped his mask off, exposing Tim Matthews's murderous face.

Rage surged through Roger's veins as he pounded on him, blow after blow, knocking him senseless. His anger fueled his ferocity as his punches got progressively more powerful, and the vengeance he'd harbored inside filled one last savage punch with such force it was nearly fatal.

Tim fell backward, crashing into the brick chimney near the edge of the roof.

There was a rumbling sound and then a shaking under Tim's feet. "The roof!" Tim stuttered. "It's beginning to give away." Just then there was a loud 'crack' and the planks collapsed as Tim began to fall.

"No! Help me! *Help me!*" he pleaded in desperation.

A blank expression covered Roger's face as Tim hung on for dear life.

"Come on Fasick!" yelled Tim, dangling on the edge. "You're a good and decent man—you won't let me fall!"

Roger hesitated for a moment; then he reached down to grab Tim's hand, pulling him up close to his face and looking straight into Tim's eyes.

"Whoever fights monsters should see to it that in the process he does not become a monster," Roger stated strictly.

Tim looked puzzled. "Huh? What do you mean?"

"My father told me that my inner demons would eventually consume me," he grumbled through clenched teeth. "It seems as though they finally have."

From the edge of the roof, Tim looked down at the street below him and the debris strewn about. His face contorted with fear. "Roger! No!"

Roger let go of Tim's hand and their fingers slipped past each other as Tim dropped.

"Ahhhh!" screamed Tim as he fell.

Roger closed his eyes but was unable to shut his ears to the blood-curdling scream and the thud as Tim hit the ground. Even then, the screaming seemed to continue, echoing back up the building like a wail from a grave. Roger opened his eyes and stood up, gazing upon

Tim's motionless body as he laid on the ground; covered in shingles, smoldering timbres, and other roof debris. Next to him, Tim's gasoline jugs were spilling onto the ground.

Roger shifted to his left side and grabbed Bucky's gun just as it was about to slide off the roof. Then, Roger stood and turned around to take one last look at Tim's body.

"May you rot in Hell, you bastard," he sneered.

While Roger was still engaged in battle with Tim, Bucky had made his way over to Celeste and untied her. They hugged one another tightly as they cried. When they released, Bucky fell to his knees as the blood trickled from his scalp and down his face. Celeste became very worried that Bucky was seriously injured, and she kneeled down next to him, cradling him in her arms. He gazed back at her and a silent communication passed between them. Tears fell from her eyes as she took his hand and guided it up to touch her cheek.

In that moment, Bucky realized he was wrong when he told her that he wanted to be alone. More than anything now, he wanted her in his life.

"Is it true what you said?" Celeste asked. "About you loving me?"

"Yes," he answered in a genuine, affectionate tone. Bucky tried his best to get up on his own. "I love you, Celeste," he said, stroking her hair and kissing her cheek. Then he let out a quiet laugh. "I was just waiting for a very memorable moment to tell you. That way, you'd never forget the first time I said it."

She grinned and laughed. "I guess you did."

Celeste hugged him tightly once again, resting her head upon his shoulder. Tears ran down her face and dampened the sleeve of Bucky's shirt.

"It's gonna take both of us a while to adjust to this," Bucky stated, "but if you're willing to be patient, I'm willing to try."

Pulling back so she could look him in the eyes, Celeste said, "I'm willing to take things as slow as you want. I think you're worth the wait."

At that moment, Roger rushed over to them, visibly distracted and somewhat shaken. He hung his head low as beads of water from the firefighter's water hoses splashed upon his head and shoulders.

"Roger!" Bucky yelled.

"Here you go, partner," Roger said, handing over the gun to Bucky. "This belongs to you."

"Thank you, Roger. I'm relieved you're alright!"

"Yeah, I suppose I am. How about the two of you?"

"We'll live," Celeste responded. Then she looked around. "What happened to Tim?"

"It's over," Roger announced. "He fell off the backside of the roof."

"Are you sure you're okay?" Bucky asked.

"Yeah, I think so," replied Roger. "Let's just get down from here while we still can."

The three climbed down the fire escape and ran to the other side of the yellow caution tape. They turned and watched as the flames soared high into the sky and how the firefighters were doing their best to extinguish it.

Roger, standing next to Bucky, said, "When Tim fell to his death, a part of me died at that moment as well. A part that's been searching for closure."

Bucky nodded. "Did you find the closure you were hoping for?"

"Yes. And now I can live peacefully knowing that Holly's killer has met the fate he deserved."

On a side street close by, a black van was parked, and a menacing raven sat perched upon it. As Bucky, Celeste, and Roger got to safety, a shadow appeared in-between the van and the nearby buildings. All of a sudden, there was a motion in the darkness and a strange figure emerged. It was the same figure wearing gray, leather gloves and a black, broad-brimmed hat who watched Bucky from the hospital parking lot the night Cristina died. Now, this mysterious stranger watched as the three friends were being examined by the medics at the fire scene.

Slowly, the figure made his way over to where Tim was lying and the raven fluttered past the stranger, landing next to Tim's bloodied body. The stranger stopped and stared. Suddenly, Tim's head moved and his eyes started to twitch.

Tim regained consciousness; however, he was badly broken up. His skull was fractured and his fingernails were torn off from clinging to the bricks so tightly. Blood was dripping down Tim's pants as the result of a compound fracture to his lower left leg, and every time he breathed, it felt like his chest was being pierced by a sharp sword. Tim strained to open his eyes and tilt his head up, but unfortunately, his vision was blurry.

Tim saw someone standing over him but could not make out who it was. "Who's there?" he asked in a broken, fading voice.

The stranger, hovering over him, said nothing.

"Mm...my...eyes..." Tim sputtered. "I can barely see anything. Who are you?"

"Someone who seeks your soul, Mr. Matthews," a deep booming voice said. "Or should I say 'Mr. Timmons'?"

"That voice...I know that voice."

"Yes, that's good. I *want* you to know who it is that takes what's left of your worthless life."

Tim rubbed his eyes again in an attempt to correct his vision.

The stranger with the deep voice said to him, "You did something you shouldn't have done, and now it's time for me to collect payment for your indiscretions."

Tim looked down just as his vision began to clear and noticed he was lying in a pool of gasoline.

"Is that gasoline I smell?" the stranger asked in a mocking tone.

"No, man! No!!!!" Tim pleaded.

The stranger picked up a piece of burning wood nearby and threw it upon the gasoline. Tim screamed as his gasoline drenched clothes went up in a burst of flames.

As the stranger walked away, the raven followed closely behind him. He climbed back into his black van, and suddenly, menacing red eyes began to glow through the tinted glass. The stranger then drove away, listening to the song *Sympathy for the Devil* by the Rolling Stones as it played on the radio.

Book 3

Revenge of the Reaper

'Reaper in the Wind'
By Marcus J. Mastin—August 2007

The Reaper's Return

When I was young, I would sit beside my mother
as she told elaborate tales to me and my little brother.
Her ghost stories had us on the edge of our chairs,
hearts beating wildly and nightmares full of scare.

Years later, I would be forced to confront my worst fears.
An ominous figure hell-bent on acquiring my soul appeared.
The Reaper attempted to drag me down to where he dwells,
but I vanquished the demon and sent him back to Hell.

Since that night, I am never as nervous as when darkness falls.
In the corner shadows, I hear the creatures of the night crawl.
Then, evil appeared again with a haunting message one evening.
A child possessed by a spirit sought me out to give warning.

(over)

"The Reaper is back," the child grinned and said,
"though you may want to believe this is just a dream.
You can try to run away from the undead,
but, alas, it will not help to scream."

Later that night, a chill overwhelmed me as the fog rolled in.
I glanced outside and there he was just as I remembered him.
His skull face glowed as he wore a black trench coat of wool,
standing near the cemetery gates by an old, abandoned school.

Within seconds, I heard his sickle scraping along my window;
a piercing sound reminiscent of fingernails on a chalkboard.
The searing noise caused jitters and goosebumps to arise,
my face cringed in excruciating pain as fear triggered my cries.

I sat and waited on the floor until the clock struck half past ten.
While I trembled by the door, the Reaper knocked again.
The menacing figure from my past came to settle the score.
With one last effort to flee, I busted out the back door.

After vanquishing him years ago, I thought he was gone forever.
I should've known from mother's tales the Reaper was more clever.
Narrowly escaping his clutches, I ran so fast my lungs began to burn.
The Reaper still seeks his revenge…and someday he will return.

By: Marcus J. Mastin
Still running from the *Reaper*
July 21, 2007

Before you embark on a journey of
Revenge...dig two graves.

—Confucius, 500 B.C.

PART ONE:
The End of a Killer...

Chapter 47:

Witness in the Shadows

On the night of August 27, 2006, the town of Carthage experienced another night of horror—and it was finally coming to an end. Dave "Bucky" Morgan and Roger Fasick (the same two local "heroes" who solved the mystery of Louis Ferr six years before) had uncovered a dirty secret that Tim Matthews desperately wanted to keep hidden. Though Tim had long been thought of as a weird but harmless loner, he also had a dark, twisted side to his personality.

During their research to solve the Reaper case, Bucky and Roger accidentally stumbled upon Tim's true identity. Tim was actually Matt Timmons, son of former Carthage native Russell Timmons. Despite Tim's shy personality, he was actually a deranged psychopath and for months had been terrorizing the town as the ghostly Reaper, a figure who was murdering residents and setting fires all over the community.

Tim's father, Russell Timmons, had been the arsonist who terrorized Carthage from the early 1980s. Bud Hopkins, another peculiar Carthage resident, had been framed for those fires and spent years in prison for Russell's crimes—similar to how Thomas Parker was going to be framed for Tim's crimes. Tim's grandfather, Frank Timmons, was the true original Reaper who horrified Carthage in the 1950s. Tim was following in his family's footsteps; however, the psychopath who rehashed his grandfather's Reaper persona and terror on the town was about to pay the ultimate penalty for his many horrendous sins.

On this night, Tim knew he'd been discovered, and with an absolutely insatiable lust for revenge, he wanted to make sure his sickening and horrifying deeds would be remembered in Carthage forever. In his demented mind, Tim decided the best way to instill a permanent terror into the people was to strike the very heart of the town: by setting the town's historical Buckley Building on fire and burning it to the ground, leaving only ashes in his wake.

Tim Matthews stood atop the five story apartment building where he lived, staring over the town he loathed while confessing his crimes to the world. It was an admission that wasn't necessarily meant to cleanse his soul, but an arrogant and prideful declaration to the world of what he had accomplished. Tim intended to take the building down, as well as himself, in an old fashioned funeral pyre. His twisted mind saw this as the perfect finale, an end to his revenge and the final step in stopping the lunacy that'd almost completely devoured his mind.

However, Tim wasn't alone on the roof where he was perched. He had a woman held hostage: a far too curious Celeste Braxton, who wanted to know about her date's mysterious background and accidentally stumbled upon the Reaper masks and robes. Celeste was going to witness the fiery destruction by his side and perish along with him.

This was a change in plans, because earlier that night Tim Matthews had donned the Reaper attire and botched an ill-fated murder attempt on the incarcerated Thomas Parker. Even though Thomas survived, the events which transpired directly resulted in the shooting of Officer Kenneth Johnson, who died in Josh Roberts's arms as Tim made his getaway. Tim returned to his apartment after the disastrous outcome at the police station only to find that Celeste had entered his apartment and discovered his terrible secret.

Tim rendered her unconscious with a jolt from his stun gun, but not before Bucky and Roger discovered Tim's hidden identity. They'd persisted in tracking down any information they could locate about the enigmatic Reaper (despite their differences and respective losses), and they were able to put the pieces of the puzzle together in time, learn of Celeste's capture, and mount a rescue attempt. During their final confrontation, Tim struggled and fought on the roof top with Roger Fasick. Without the element of surprise, or the aid of his stun gun, Tim Matthews, even in his demented insanity, couldn't overcome Roger or his rage.

After losing the struggle, Tim fell off the building to the ground, left laying in a bloody mess. It seemed utterly impossible he could possibly be alive, yet somehow he had survived the multi-story fall. Tim's broken body remained nearly motionless as the ash fell upon him, and his breathing was so shallow that his chest barely moved— but he did not go completely unnoticed.

The last time anyone had seen Thomas Parker, he was left in grave condition at the jailhouse. The Reaper entered the police station from one of the old, forgotten underground tunnels and attacked the incarcerated man. Thomas was zapped by the Reaper's stun gun, stabbed in the shoulder, and then left for dead in his jail cell under a pile of debris caused by an explosion from one of the cell walls. In the ensuing chaos, which led to the murder of Ken Johnson (as well as the sudden disappearance of the Reaper), Thomas was forgotten.

Miraculously, Thomas survived the ordeal, and after a short time, he regained consciousness. When he awoke, Thomas was still trapped beneath the rubble and a throbbing pain coursed through his head and limbs. Mustering all the strength left in his battered body, Thomas managed to wriggle his way from underneath the concrete and sheetrock fragments to freedom.

While all the other officers concentrated their efforts, in vain, on saving Ken Johnson's life, Thomas slowly made his way out of his jail cell and into the underground tunnel beneath the police station. Not familiar with the tunnel system, he wandered aimlessly through the tunnels underneath the streets of town trying to find a way to the outside world. After a half-hour that seemed like so much more time, Thomas staggered out of one of the entrances of the tunnel (the opening that led out from the smokestack on Tannery Island Boulevard), which was close to the Buckley Building—the same building where a blaze ignited by the Reaper was consuming it.

Dust from the sheetrock walls irritated Thomas's eyes, causing them to water and making it difficult to see anything. As if that wasn't bad enough, the gash around his right ear ran deep, making him dizzy and lightheaded as blood trickled down the side of his face and off his chin. Thomas wondered if he had a concussion. It certainly wouldn't surprise him after the chaos at the police station. The knife wound in his shoulder had coagulated and the bleeding stopped, but his arm still hurt and was stiff and numb—which was to be expected. There was a dull throbbing flowing through his body, but it exploded into an agonizing pain that shot through his nerves whenever an object bumped into, or brushed against, his wound.

Thomas stopped to catch his breath, explosions of yellow, orange, and purple spots appearing before him with every painful blink. He hid in the shadows of Clinton Street, a side street near the Buckley Building, unseen by anyone from the growing group of bystanders watching the fire from the street. Thomas stumbled into an alleyway and fell down, exhausted and beaten, face first in a pile of garbage.

The pain immersed him like crashing waves on all sides of his body, and even the massive rushes of adrenaline weren't nearly enough to counter the stress and exhaustion of that crazy day. Several minutes later, Thomas slowly lifted his head to try and get his bearings and check out his immediate surroundings.

The smell of the alley hit him first. A putrid, decaying, vomit odor. Rotten eggs and dirty diapers moldering in a wide-open dumpster on a humid summer night. The heat from the burning building brought out the disgusting stenches even more strongly, and Thomas could feel his stomach turn as the nauseating smells assaulted his senses.

After wheezing from the pain of broken ribs, Thomas stood up and stumbled a little further. His knees buckled after about thirty or forty feet and he dropped down to rest on all fours, desperately trying to catch his breath. Thomas's eyes adjusted to the darkness as he looked away from the burning building, and his blurriness had all but completely eased when he came upon something that, even in his injured state, tickled his curiosity.

A black van with tinted windows slowly pulled up and came to a halt at the corners of Clinton and Francis Streets, kitty-corner to the backside of the Buckley Building. A man appeared to be sitting alone in the black van, although Thomas had no way of knowing if there were more people sitting in the back. The stranger was trying in great detail to be discreet, and carefully kept his distance away from the commotion which was mounting nearby, and the inevitable crowds drawn to it like moths to the fire.

The stranger was slouched low in the driver's seat as the glare of headlights from passing motorists, and flashing lights from police cars and fire engine trucks, swept his windshield. They passed by without taking any notice of the man or his dark van.

After a few minutes, Thomas saw the shape of a tall man get out of the van and pass by the alleyway as he crossed a vacant, side street. The stranger moved stealthily, deliberately trying to avoid detection from anyone in the vicinity. He moved with an unnatural grace and silence that kept him from being seen by anyone else. Thomas could not see the person's face; the long, black trench coat the stranger wore and the broad-brimmed hat pulled down over his eyes overshadowed it.

The sight gave Thomas chills, and what transpired next would be permanently tattooed in Thomas Parker's memory forever. From where Thomas was slouched over, he had a clear view of the backside of the Buckley Building, far away from all the commotion in the front.

The tall man walked over to a pile of debris that had fallen from the roof of the flame engulfed building.

In the middle of the wooden boards and roofing shingles laid Tim Matthews, his Reaper costume ripped to shreds and his body twisted in positions that'd make a contortionist jealous. Thomas had assumed the Reaper must've been dead. But the stranger leaned over Tim's body, his head weaving from side to side as if carefully noting and inspecting the severity of each and every one of Tim's visible injuries. A few moments passed, and then Tim's head and arms slowly began to move. When Tim noticed the person hovering above him, his lips began to move as well.

Amazed and curious, Thomas narrowed his eyes to get a better view. Unfortunately, he was unable to hear any of the banter that transpired between the two men. He had made up his mind to stand up and move closer when he saw the man in black bend over with an outstretched hand. The stranger wore gray, tightly-fit driving gloves, and he did not flinch, scream, or exhibit *any* signs of pain as he picked up a flaming piece of board that should have burned him badly.

Thomas came to a sudden halt and crouched down, holding his position. The next thing Thomas saw was Tim's extended arm, twisted unnaturally, but still pushed up towards the stranger. He heard a faint yell of 'No!' as the tall stranger tossed the burning board onto the helpless man who laid before him. Within seconds, Tim's body was completely engulfed in a fiery inferno that consumed his body and all the debris pinning him down.

In his weakened and dazed condition, Thomas did not know what he should do. He wanted to move, to charge toward the man in the black coat and hat, but his legs were as solid as jelly, and he was not only badly injured, but shaken to his very core. He wanted to scream, but no sound could escape from his parched lips and throat. All Thomas could do was watch in horror, his mouth hung open and his body trembling.

Thomas's heart pounded wildly in his chest while he watched the stranger walk back to his van. His body began to ache and he suddenly felt faint, as if the world seemed to move right underneath his feet. Just then, a slight breeze picked up. The stranger was emitting a peculiar scent and it was heading in the direction of Thomas. It was the smell of copper and sour milk; the smell of death.

Too scared to move or utter any kind of a sound, Thomas kept his wide eyes glued to the frightening man in the black coat. A large, black Raven flew alongside as the stranger crept backwards. After he backpedaled about ten feet, the stranger suddenly stopped and turned around, slowly but steadily making his way back to his van and opening the driver's side door. Before he entered the vehicle, however, the man in black stepped into the light of a nearby street post for a brief moment, and even with just a passing glance, Thomas could see the man clearly.

When Thomas caught sight of the stranger's face, he lost control of his bladder and bowels, and yet didn't even notice when he soiled himself. All the color drained from his face and he became pale with fear. Thomas felt his legs buckle as he abruptly fell over onto his side. He laid there, alone and terrified, crouched into the fetal position and whimpering like a baby.

Chapter 48:

Night Ends

Meanwhile, on the opposite side of the Buckley Building, Roger and Bucky both stood next to a fire engine, nursing injuries and making sure their friend, Celeste, was all right after her traumatizing experience with the Reaper. A female paramedic was checking over Celeste and attending to her minor cuts and bruises. There was quite an impressive crowd gathered around police tape and fire trucks, but by the looks of the faraway stares on Roger and Bucky's faces, it was hard to tell if they even noticed.

Josh Roberts, ace reporter for the *Carthage Republican Tribune*, had left the police station after the Reaper attacked Thomas Parker in his cell. Kenneth Johnson was dead, the Reaper had fled, and there was nothing more that could be done there. When the police officers were called from the station to report to a fire and another possible Reaper sighting, he was out the door in a flash. As dramatic, frightening, and exhausting a day as it had been, Josh was still a reporter and he knew his editor would hang him if he missed out on scooping the Reaper story. After what happened at the station, he was eager to help in the capture of that psychopath.

Maybe Josh was distracted, or maybe the events had already numbed him to the point where he just didn't care, but at the scene of the fire he wasn't his normal self. Without even noticing, he bumped into a man, hard, on his way to the fire truck where Bucky and Roger were standing.

"Hey! Just because you're the Press, doesn't mean you have special privileges, Roberts!" the man yelled at him. "Get back behind the police line and cover the story like the rest of the reporters."

Josh turned around and saw his most hated competitor, a rival reporter named Jack Lavancha from the neighboring town of Watertown. He even wrote for the rival newspaper, *The Watertown Times*. Jack Lavancha was wearing a straw cowboy hat, tight-fitting blue jeans, and a green Hawaiian shirt. He also sported a thick brown moustache and had long pork chop sideburns.

Jack fit the traditional description of tall, dark, and handsome, but he was an emotionally stunted man. He was also very arrogant, cocky, and was driven by a desperate need to be a better man than his great-grandfather, Walter Lavancha.

The elder Lavancha was the bank president of the old First National Bank of Carthage many years ago. He wore the title and prestige with the type of arrogance you might expect from a small town fish who thought he was bigger than he actually was. After some time, his corrupt morals overtook his devotion for his family and he took off with $10,000 from the bank's treasury, triggering the biggest bank scandal in Northern New York's history. As a result, Jack always had a chip on his shoulder, always trying to live down his family's infamous reputation.

"Hello, J.R.," Jack said with a hint of sarcasm in his voice.

Josh's eyes flashed with anger. "Call me Josh, or even Roberts— but don't call me *J.R.!*"

"Whatever you say. Oh, by the way, I waved to you the other day as I drove through Carthage on my way back to Watertown."

"Yeah, I saw. You always wave with just one finger?"

Jack chuckled. "Only to you, Roberts."

"You really are a scumbag, aren't you?" Josh said with a scowl. "What the Hell are you doing here in *my* town, Lavancha?"

"I heard on my scanner the Buckley Building was on fire and that Reaper-guy was cornered on the roof. As much as I hate to come to this god forsaken town, this is news…and I cover the news." Noticing Josh didn't have his usual pad and pencil with him, Jack smirked again and asked, "Don't you cover the news anymore, Roberts?"

"Not that it's any of your business, Jack, but I just came from the police station and barely survived an attack from the Reaper. Others weren't so lucky."

Jack squinted his eyes and rubbed his chin. "You survived, huh? Damn, I guess there really is *NO* justice in this world."

"Why don't you go slither back under the rock you came from? You have no business in Carthage."

"Oh, I don't know about that." Jack's tone got sarcastic and condescending. "This place is starting to grow on me. Hell, maybe I have a future writing stories for this town."

"You have no future, '*Jack*'! You're an A-1 hack writer with a chip on his shoulder and a shitty attitude! Your methods are questionable at best and you have no clue what's going on in this town…so just stay out of the damn way."

"Come on, Roberts. There's no need to be hostile. If you know so much about the Reaper and what just happened here, why not give a fellow reporter a hand? Fill me in on what's going on. Who *is* the Reaper and what are his motives?"

"Sorry, Jack. You'll just have to read about it in tomorrow's news."

"Yeah…that's if you get your story done on time."

"Don't worry about what goes on in my life. I'll stay up all night if I have to. Believe me; my story *will* be ready by morning."

"Be careful, Roberts. You may just be scooped yet." Jack didn't lose a bit of arrogance, despite his obvious disadvantage.

"Go to Hell, Jack." Josh started to walk toward the fire trucks. "And get out of my town, too. You're not welcome around here."

Jack stared at him, hate smoldering in his eyes. "We'll be seeing each other again, Roberts. You can count on that."

Josh rolled his eyes and continued on.

Then, as they finished their conversation and Josh was walking away, Jack shouted out, "So long—*J.R.*!"

Josh turned his head as if to say something, but Jack was already gone. He watched as Jack headed off into the crowd of people to interview spectators while he was left standing there alone—fuming.

Moments later, before everyone left the crime scene, Roger was being escorted over to a police car to give his statement of events. Roger talked to a baby-faced officer named Nathan Barns. Officer Barns was a slight man with a build better suited for a horse jockey rather than a police officer. Roger was doing his best to answer the rookie's questions about the insanely strange and tragic night. While Roger was talking to the officer, Celeste made her way over to Bucky and grabbed him by the shoulder.

She looked intently at him and said, "Bucky, I have something to tell you."

"What is it, Celeste?" questioned Bucky, noticing the determination in her eyes.

The Historic Buckley Building

Celeste took a deep breath to get her thoughts together. "While Tim had me tied up on the roof, he confessed all his terrible sins. He admitted that *he* was responsible for Pat Jordan's death, as well as Holly's and all the homeless people in town. *All of them!*"

Bucky felt an uneasiness form in the pit of his stomach.

"Tim also said Bud Hopkins was *not* the arsonist in Carthage during the early 1980s," Celeste continued on. "It was Tim's father who started all those fires and killed those people. Bud was framed!"

Bucky was stunned by what Celeste had just told him. *Could it be the man spent most of his life in prison, marked as a felon, when he was completely innocent?* Bucky thought.

The idea of living as an outcast, of living through that hell, was too much to even imagine. "Are you sure of what you heard?" Bucky asked Celeste in disbelief.

"Yes. Tim told me every horrible deed he's done around town. He was bragging about it all. Tim even confessed to being responsible for the bomb at the ferry service all those years ago."

"The ferry service!" exclaimed Bucky. "So, Thomas *wasn't* the one who killed Louis Ferr after all."

Celeste gripped Bucky's hand firmly. "I think Tim was responsible for more devastation than we could ever have imagined."

Bucky sat perplexed. "I wonder why he would confess everything to you."

"I don't know," Celeste replied. "Maybe he needed to purge his conscience before he died. Nevertheless, I was shocked at the sheer amount of evil he caused. My mind was so rattled . . . I was so scared. I'm still not sure I understood everything he told me."

Bucky shook his head, completely shocked by the news. "Celeste, you know that you're gonna be asked to put your statement down on paper for the police. I hope you can recount *exactly* what Tim told you." He placed a hand on her shoulder for support.

"I hope so, too," Celeste said. "Maybe I should write it down now while it's still fresh in my mind. Do you think we should go to the police headquarters and give them all the information now?"

"No, not right now," Bucky replied. "This has been a hectic night already." He grabbed a corner of the blanket and wiped a smear of black ash from her forehead. "Whatever we have to say can wait. We'll go down to headquarters in the morning."

Celeste put her hands to her head. After the ordeal she had just endured with Tim Mathews, Celeste was feeling distraught and exhausted, not to mention completely overwhelmed. Her insides felt like an emotional pinball machine. Bucky pulled Celeste close to his body, trying to comfort her as they stood in front of the Buckley Building.

Bucky noticed how beautiful she looked, even after the haggardness of the last several hours. "Do you want to go back to my place and lie down? You look tired."

"That's all right, Bucky. I may be tired, but I'm not *too* tired."

"Oh no?" Bucky gave Celeste a sly grin. "Well, give me time. You will be."

After everyone had begun to disperse from the area, Jack Lavancha stayed behind to snoop around the ruins of the Buckley Building. He questioned some of the firemen and police officers, and also interviewed some of the bystanders along the street. Unfortunately, he received very little information which he could use, and left the scene frustrated, knowing he was missing out on something big.

Later on, Jack stopped at Potter's Liquor Store in the Freight Yard Plaza. After purchasing a quart of Jack Daniels Whiskey, he checked into the Imperial Hotel, located about a mile from the fire scene. He only drank that brand of whiskey because it was named for him, or so Jack told people whenever they inquired as to why he was frequently keeping company with 'Jack-in-a-bottle.' The response was usually brusque enough to keep people off his back while he partook in one of his more frequent indulgences—intoxicating himself with the amber colored liquor.

After Jack checked into the hotel and found his abode at the far end of the building, he entered the darkened room and threw his camera and shoulder bag on the bed. The camera bounced off the bed and hit the wall before making another 'thud' on the floor. Jack ignored it, then went into the bathroom and returned with a glass which he filled half full of Jack Daniels. He exhaled deeply before consuming the entire contents of the glass in one big swallow.

After he sampled the drink, he grimaced and said, "It needs something. Ice maybe."

Jack left his room with a plastic bucket in hand and headed off to the ice machine he passed on the way to his room. As he walked down the hallway, he passed a middle-aged woman with dyed red hair and gave her a flirtatious grin, but received no response. Once his bucket was full, Jack returned to his room and poured himself another glass half full of whiskey—this time with ice—and took a large gulp.

"Much better," he announced, grinning from ear to ear. "Always better on the rocks."

Although Jack was a heavy drinker, he was not an alcoholic. He started drinking heavy during his college days, and it wasn't *just* because of a broken relationship as many people have suspected. It always bothered Jack that he was expected to follow in his family's footsteps and become a banker. Jack knew he'd never measure up in the family's eyes, so he became a reporter and journalist—something he always wanted to be. Jack also knew how much his family wouldn't approve, and the cold shoulders and lack of contact from the rest of his family ever since confirmed that suspicion.

"Screw them!" he shouted to the empty room. "They don't pay my bills." Then Jack plopped down on the bed and poured himself yet another drink.

Jack was a good athlete in college. He played basketball and ran track as well as learning how to play the piano—which he would sometimes do as he drank. Another of his favorite pastimes was listening to the music of Tom Jones, but only to help him sleep better, he claimed. People who knew Jack said he reminded them of Rick

Simon from the old *Simon & Simon* television series because of his the way he dressed and also his personality.

Lately, Jack had been drinking even heavier than usual due to a heartbreaking and messy break-up with his longtime girlfriend, Megan Moser. One day, she packed up everything in their apartment and moved out, leaving him for another man. He prided himself on being sharp and observant, but that crushing blow had blindsided him. His situation was a classic example of the cliché, "Never even saw it coming."

Just after midnight, the whiskey finally did its work and Jack dozed off on the bed. About 3 am or so, Jack woke up, reached for his half empty bottle of Jack Daniels and guzzled down about a half glass full of the stuff. It burned his throat all the way down, and pooled in his stomach, but Jack just smiled in his stupor and had an amusing thought—even though he genuinely hated Josh Roberts, he did have much respect for him...but most of all, Jack certainly did enjoy irritating him for some reason. With that thought in mind, he dozed off...grinning from ear to ear.

Chapter 49:

The Professor discusses "The Poem"

Adam "Red" Richardson arrived home to his mother's house shortly after ten o'clock. He had spent the last several hours drinking away his sorrows at Kitty's Bar. A yellow cab pulled into the driveway and idled for a few minutes in silence. Inside were two men: Adam, not overly handsome but not ugly by any means, though he certainly looked like a ragged man who had spent a couple hours too many at his favorite watering hole. The other individual was the cab driver, Ben Reilly, a clean-cut young man in his mid-twenties with blond hair and hazel eyes.

Ben was something of a drifter, a lost soul who had been living in New York City for the past couple years. He was in excellent shape and appeared to have the body of a gymnast in that he was approximately 5'10" and weighed one hundred and sixty-three pounds. Ben had the odd timing of arriving in Carthage a little over a week ago, when the Reaper was still in full terrorize mode. Timing was never his strong point, and Ben always felt as though there was a bad-luck curse hanging over his head.

Tonight was Ben's first night on the job, and he was quickly finding out what most cab drivers would tell him: the job was never as easy as it looked, and it wore on you mighty quick. Although he was trying to be polite and keep his cool, the cab was sitting there idling…burning gas and wasting money. And unfortunately, the meter wasn't equipped to run at a $20 an hour 'waiting rate.'

It wasn't too long before Ben finally turned to the back seat and said, "Well, this is the right address, isn't it?"

"Yeah, I suppose it is," Adam mumbled.

"Well, are ya' gonna' get out, or what?" Ben asked gruffly. "I've got other places to go and other people to pick up tonight. I can't have ya in here throwin' up in my back seat or wastin' my time."

"All right, all right. Just give me a second to find my wallet," Adam apologized.

Ben rolled his eyes. "Have you tried your back pocket?"

"Oh, sorry," Adam uttered with a slight laugh. He pulled out a fifty dollar bill and handed it to the cabbie. "Here you go, man. You can keep the change."

Ben's demeanor softened when he realized how much of a tip he just made. "Thanks buddy!" he said, mood suddenly lifting. "I appreciate it!"

"Don't mention it," Adam grunted as he stumbled towards his house. "Thanks for the ride, dude."

It was late when Adam finally walked through the door. He plopped down on the couch, sunk into the cushions, and tried to relax. Then he reached for the remote to turn on the television and catch the remainder of the late local news. Just as Adam was about to push the power button on, the telephone rang.

Adam jumped involuntarily, and then laughed a little at himself for being antsy. Although he didn't really want to talk to anyone, he grudgingly rolled over and picked up the phone off the coffee table.

"Hello?" he answered in a halfhearted tone.

"Hi. May I speak to Adam Richardson please?"

"Yeah," Adam said as he exhaled heavily. "This is uh, Adam speaking."

"Oh, hello, Adam. Sorry to call so late, but this is Kyle Moody."

"Professor Moody!" exclaimed Adam. Adam sat up and rubbed his eyes. Then, he took a few deep breaths to get better focused. "Boy, what a surprise to hear your voice, Professor. How've ya been doin'?"

"Just fine, Adam," the professor replied in an upbeat tone. "I wasn't sure if you'd remember me."

"Sure I do, Professor...but why're ya callin' at this time of night?"

"I realize it's late," he stated, "but I was at dinner tonight with another professor who informed me of the recent goings-on in Carthage. He told me the terrible news about John Sears, and I wanted to express my condolences to you. I know how close the two of you were."

"Thank you, sir. That means a lot coming from you. To be honest, I'm still having a hard time getting over it."

"I completely understand, Adam," Professor Moody expressed in a caring voice.

After a brief period of dead silence, Adam coughed to clear his throat and then said, "Professor Moody, I'm really glad you called me. I've actually wanted to contact you for some time now."

"Really? What about?" Adam could hear the interest, and the concern, in Professor Moody's voice.

"Well, I remember how we once read a poem in your class titled 'The Ferryman,' or somethin' like that. I wanted to discuss it with ya to find out more about the person who wrote it. I think you mentioned the writer was an adventurer—a close friend of yours. Am I rememberin' that right, sir?"

"Yes, that's right. His name is Markus Batiste. We met back in college; working as part-time office cleaners for the same company in order to help pay for tuition. We also spent four years together in the French Foreign Legion."

Professor Moody paused, and Adam was in silent shock. He could imagine all the strange stares and murmurings Professor Moody must've encountered from people after revealing that fact of his life.

"We were kind of 'wild adventurers' back when we were young," the professor continued, "and we thought the Foreign Legion would be more exciting than the Peace Corps." Professor Moody laughed at the memory of his wild youth. "Markus now lives about an hour south of Canton."

"Here in New York? Really? Do you ever speak with him anymore?"

Professor Moody let out a sigh. "No, not as much as I used to. Then again, he hasn't kept in contact with many people over the years."

"Why is that?" Adam asked. "Is he a hermit?"

The professor laughed. "No, nothing like that. He's settled down. He has two small sons now, Jean-Sebastian and Tristan-Patrick. Their ages are 8 and 7 respectively. They're great boys, but they also have their father's adventurous and mischievous streak."

"Two young kids! That has to be tough on him. Isn't he married?"

"Well, he was. Markus's wife, Andrea-Jean, died in the Madrid Bombings in Spain a few years back. Although her body wasn't one of few the police were able to recover, we're certain she died in the blast." A lump formed in his throat as he added, "It's impossible to get complete 'closure' with an empty casket, you know?"

"Jeez, that poor guy. I can't even imagine how painful that is. I have a cousin whose wife died almost a year ago. He also has a small child, and I know how much he's been hurtin'. It's a very depressing situation."

"Yes, it is," Professor Moody replied solemnly.

"Was Batiste and his wife married a long time?"

"They were married for about ten years, but they knew each other since they were young children. Markus grew up next door to her grandparents, and she visited them quite often during summer vacation. They were good friends for most of their lives. Losing her was very hard for him." Professor Moody paused. "What's with all the questions about my friend, Adam?"

"Oh, sorry. It's nothing. It's just that, recently, John and I were discussing the poem Mr. Batiste wrote."

"Really? Why's that?" inquired the professor.

"I found his poem very interesting and I wanted to know more about the man who wrote it. I don't suppose you know whether it was based on a real life occurrence or not?"

"I believe so," the professor stated. "That was always the impression I got from the few times we actually talked about it. Not sure what type of experience would make a man write a poem like that, but then again, Batiste has always had a wild imagination. I wouldn't be completely surprised if it was something he totally conjured up in his mind."

"Did he ever tell you the specifics of how and why he wrote that poem?" Adam asked.

Professor Moody took a deep breath. "Well, let me think. It's been a long time since I've thought about that story—Markus wrote that poem during our younger days together. If my memory serves me correctly, I think Markus said he was visiting some of his Cajun relatives in Louisiana when he got lost in the woods. It wasn't completely swamp or bayou, but even for a Foreign Legion veteran, it wasn't the type of area you wanted to stay lost in. He stumbled across a small town seemingly in the middle of nowhere with a devilishly-looking ferryman. Apparently some type of altercation took place between the two of them and he barely survived. He's never been willing to go into more detail than that."

"Hmmm..." Adam mulled to himself.

"Unfortunately, that's about all I know on the topic, Adam," Moody continued. "I wish I could be more help to you, but I haven't talked to Markus about that subject in years and don't remember much about his adventures. I know that's one story he would rarely talk about."

"That's all right, Professor. You've helped quite a bit."

"I'm glad. Adam, if you ever need anything or if you run into trouble, don't hesitate to call me. Okay?"

"Okay. Thank you, Professor Moody."

After Adam hung up the phone, he stood up, went to his bedroom, and grabbed a notebook from his bookshelf. The conversation had rejuvenated him in a strange sort of way, and he didn't feel the effects of the alcohol from earlier that night. When he returned to the living room, he turned on the television and plopped down on the couch. He opened his notebook and thumbed through the pages until he found what he was looking for. Adam pulled out a piece of creased paper, unfolded it, and began to read:

> *The boat proceeds across the river ever so slowly,*
> *And frustration causes the stranger to become enraged.*
> *To the ferryman's dislike, we arrive with my soul unscathed.*
> *With a sigh of relief, I quickly run away as fast as I can.*
> *I've become just one of the few who survived a ride...*
> > *With the Ferryman.*

Adam stared at the piece of paper for a moment, and then he grabbed a pen off the coffee table and began to write in his notebook:

> *Dear Bucky,*
> > *Tonight I talked with an old professor of mine...*

As he was writing, Adam overheard a news reporter relating the breaking story about the Buckley Building going up in flames. After initially taking a passing glance at the television screen, Adam quickly sat up in full attention with his eyes glued to the screen when he saw Bucky, Celeste, and Roger standing next to a fire truck in the background. The trio were huddled up in blankets and wiping away the charcoal and soot that covered their faces.

"What the Hell happened to them?" Adam whispered.

Later on that night, just after 3 am, Bucky was at home in his bed with Celeste lying beside him. Bucky sat up in bed and was wide awake. The events of the evening were still running through his mind, and he couldn't calm down enough to sleep. He got out of bed, and headed to the sliding glass door ten feet away. Quietly, he opened the door and tiptoed onto the wooden steps. It was dark, with only the light of the moon helping him to see. Bucky closed his eyes and drew in a long breath of fresh air. The air was clean and crisp with a hint of autumn in it—peaceful, unlike Carthage's recent events.

A slight chill came over Bucky as he slowly opened his eyes. He glanced to his right side and saw an unfamiliar shape down toward the end of his property, right near the sidewalk which passed through his yard. Bucky squinted, trying to make out the shape in the dark. The figure appeared to be a tall person dressed in a long black trench coat and wearing a broad-brimmed hat.

"Hello?" Bucky yelled out. "Can I help you?"

The figure didn't answer, and didn't move. Bucky was sure the person heard him, and somehow Bucky knew the man was watching him, even though there was no way to see his face. After receiving no answer, Bucky leaned back inside his house and turned on the switch to the porch light. When he stuck his head back out the sliding glass door once more and looked toward the street, the figure was gone.

"What the Hell was that?" he whispered.

An unnerving chill shot down Bucky's spine and he quickly went inside, taking the time to lock the sliding glass door behind him and pulling the blinds shut.

Bucky hopped back into bed, but couldn't get back to sleep that night. He tossed and turned, trying not to disturb Celeste, staring at the ceiling. He knew how exhausted she was. Bucky was surprised she was even able to sleep in light of what she'd been through. For the remainder of the night, Bucky laid in bed looking at the ceiling with the image of the ghostly figure etched into his mind, trying to get rid of the feeling of eyes watching him.

Next to him, Celeste gripped the blankets tightly and opened her eyes.

Carthage Chronicles Volume I

PART TWO:

...And the beginning of another

Carthage Chronicles Volume I

Chapter 50:

New face at the News

The next morning, Police Chief Bernard Zimmerman drove his squad car up to an old motel in Deferiet, a small town located on the outskirts of Carthage. Deferiet was so small, in fact, that it was technically an "unincorporated village." Deferiet had twenty houses, just as many trailers, an unofficial bar which was once a farmer's barn, and the motel. That was everything to be seen in that depressing little town.

So despite the recent insanity in Carthage—the fires, the death of arsonist and serial killer Matthew Timmons, and the burning of the Buckley Building—when a body showed up in Deferiet, it was up to the Carthage police to handle the situation and investigate. Chief Zimmerman thought he was short handed to begin with; and now, aside from investigating all the crimes, helping prepare a funeral for Officer Kenneth Johnson, and being on shift for almost thirty hours straight, he had to come out to yet another body—now in tiny Deferiet.

Chief Zimmerman parked outside of the Northern Pines Motel, a cheap $30 a night place that barely lived off the occasional business that usually came in from out-of-towners who arrived for weddings, graduations, holidays, and funerals. It was a single-story building with dingy off-white paint chipping off the sides of the weathered shingles. The forlorn motel had only a dozen rooms available to rent, all of which smelled of moth balls stale beer.

Zimmerman finished off his now barely warm coffee and stepped out of the vehicle onto the gravel that covered the parking area in front of the motel. He was immediately approached by Officer Rick

Streeter, who was lucky enough to have been off duty the past weekend and get some downtime before all hell broke loose last night.

"Morning, Chief."

"What do we have, Rick?"

Officer Streeter motioned with his hand. "Come this way, Chief. No rest for the wicked."

"What's that supposed to mean," Chief Zimmerman grumbled, tired.

"No rest for the weary, then." Officer Streeter revised his last statement, not allowing himself to get sarcastic and disrespectful since everyone there was tired, irritable, and overworked.

"A female body was found by the water about 100 yards from the Northern Pines Motel," he continued. "The female was stripped of all clothing and no identification was found in the area. Her body was discovered by a jogger as he was passing the shallow side of the Black River. The corpse was caught up in an eddy right off the edge of the bridge. It was the only thing preventing the body from floating down the river."

"Lead the way, Streeter," Zimmerman instructed, steadying himself to see another corpse. It never got easier for him. "Oh, by the way, have you talked to anyone at the motel yet?"

Rick took a glance at the notepad in his hand. "Yes, I have. The person at the front desk isn't the one who worked the late shift last night. However, the woman in charge said that when she arrived this morning several sets of keys were lying on top of the front desk. That's apparently not uncommon. She did a check on the all the rooms rented last night and every single key was accounted for. Everyone who stayed there last night was gone by the time we got here this morning."

"So are we assuming this was a sexual assault?" Chief Zimmerman asked.

"Seems like a murder robbery," Officer Streeter said. "The man who found her is a local, older man. This one's weird. Doesn't seem related to anything in Carthage."

"I would hope not," Chief Zimmerman said as they arrived at the scene. "With the death of Timmons, that should be done and over with. Carthage has gone through enough torment to last a lifetime."

At the scene there were already crime scene investigators all over the area with their rubber gloves, plastic bags, and cameras. Officers were all over the area but were very careful not to disturb or contaminate the crime scene.

Two men were taping off the vicinity with yellow tape which read "Police Investigation Area: Keep Out" and another person was pouring a slurry mortar mix into footprints around the immediate area to preserve evidence. The rest of the officers were chewing gum like mad to get the smell of alcohol off their breaths from the night before. It had been a long several months for the officers, and many had turned to alcohol to forget about the murder and mayhem in Carthage.

As the two men were walking along, Officer Streeter asked, "By the way, Chief, what happened to Thomas Parker last night?"

"Parker was found by the firemen once they reached the backside of the building," C.Z. answered. "He was in an almost catatonic state of mind, so they called in a couple officers to come and get him. Parker was then transported to the mental ward section of the hospital for observation."

"Is he back in jail now?"

"No," Chief Zimmerman replied. "Since Thomas was obviously cleared of all arson charges, we really don't have any reason to hold him. He didn't pose a threat to anybody in the condition he was in, so I told the officers to drive Thomas home after the doctors released him. I think he'd be in better care at home with his wife instead of a jail cell."

When the men reached the riverbank, Chief Zimmerman looked down at a naked woman's body lying face down in the dirt. Her skin was a pale shade of gray and her lips were blue. The woman appeared to be thin and tall, with reddish colored hair and long, bright pink fingernails.

"No one local?" Chief Zimmerman asked.

"Nope," Officer Streeter answered. "At least it doesn't seem that way. We figure she had to have been from out of town. We're hoping her fingerprints might raise a flag somewhere, give us some kind of a clue."

"Did you say a jogger found the body early this morning?" Chief Zimmerman inquired.

"Yes, sir," Streeter answered.

Chief Zimmerman noticed the blue tint to the victim's skin and asked, "We've ruled out natural causes?"

"Sure, it could be natural," Streeter answered condescendingly. "If you call multiple stab wounds to the neck 'natural causes,' sir."

Zimmerman gave a quick glance to Streeter, letting him know to watch his mouth. "Anyway, do we know anything so far about this woman or who did this to her?"

"Not yet, Chief," Officer Streeter admitted. "Like I mentioned before, no identification of any kind was found on the body. I'm still waitin' to hear from some of the other officers who're checkin' the vicinity as well as the motel nearby."

"Nothing from the motel records?" Chief Zimmerman asked.

"They don't take credit cards, and as long as you can pay $30 cash, you don't have to sign nothin' either. Really small town—old fashioned, y'know?"

"I need to head back to Carthage and wrap up that Reaper disaster," Chief Zimmerman said. "It'll be a while before we're able to clean our hands of the bloody mess Timmons caused."

Then, just as he turned to leave, he voiced, "Keep me up-to-date on this, Rick. I have to help arrange Johnson's funeral…and hire a new officer at the same time. Make sure you check in with me periodically."

Officer Streeter nodded and watched the weary old man make his way back towards the motel, the seeming weight of the world bearing down on his shoulders.

Meanwhile over at the *Carthage Republican Tribune*, Roger Fasick was inside Josh Roberts's office, giving him a first-hand account of what happened upon the roof of the Buckley Building. Josh was scribbling down notes as Roger told his tale, and would occasionally turn to a keyboard and fix up a word or two on a rough draft, but Roger knew Josh was listening intently to every word.

After Roger finished his story, Josh held up a rough copy of the article he'd been working on about Tim Matthews (aka: Matthew Timmons), the Reaper, and the fires. It included the most positive note Josh ever wrote about Ken Johnson, whom Josh owed his life to. At least there was enough time in the end for a general understanding between the two men. Roger's account was amazing, and Josh knew he was given a once-in-a-lifetime story.

"I'm gonna be on TV; I'm gonna be giving interviews!" Josh exclaimed to Roger. "This is the kind of story that makes a career."

Roger was going to make a comment, but he was cut off by a voice that crept up behind him.

"Your report sounds most enlightening, Roberts. I can't wait to go over it with my red pen," Ty Harris, Josh's boss and a constant pain in the ass, butted in. "However, I think you'd better hold off on any television interviews or appearances."

Josh peered toward the doorway with a look of perplexity. Ty Harris was standing there, and after several seconds of intense stares between the two men, Ty made his way into Josh's office. "Roberts, I need to speak to you."

"Go ahead, Ty. I'm listening."

Ty looked down at Roger, who was still sitting in front of Josh's desk. Then he shifted his attention back to Josh and said, "I'd like to speak to you in private for a moment. It won't take long."

Roger smiled politely and said, "That's all right, Mr. Harris. I've gotta get goin' now anyway." Roger stood up slowly, his body still stiff from the events of the previous night, before heading towards the open door. He stopped before leaving, turned around and said to Josh, "If you need any more information, Josh, give me a call at home. I should be home the rest of the night. I'm expecting a call from an old friend of mine from Syracuse."

"Ahhh...would this happen to be a female friend?" Josh teased slyly.

Roger returned Josh's smirk. "As a matter of fact, it is. She's coming up here for a visit soon, and we're making plans to get together."

"Glad to hear it, bud. Have yourself a good time and we'll catch up later."

Once Roger was gone, Ty glared at Josh and said, "Come with me."

Josh stood up and followed Ty down the hallway. The two men entered Ty's office.

"What do ya want, Ty?" Josh asked gruffly.

Ty motioned toward a woman sitting in the leatherback chair positioned next to his desk. "I wanted to introduce you to Mary Powell. She's getting a little bit of a late start in life at the journalism business. However, her portfolio is very impressive for someone with so little experience. She's got an expert's eye for photography and she likes to sketch, as well. This paper can definitely use someone with her set of talents on our staff."

"That's great, Ty. It's nice to meet you, ma'am," Josh greeted her politely.

Sizing her up and down, Josh observed that Mary was an elegant looking woman. He assumed she was possibly in her late forties or early fifties by the wrinkles around her mouth and eyes. She also had small, perky breasts and bright red hair that was possibly getting some help out of a bottle—to help hold off the inevitable march of gray hairs creeping in.

Mary was about 5'6" tall and wore three-inch high heeled shoes which accented her shapely legs and calves. Her face was as fair as a snowy meadow and her pale complexion made her thin, red lips seem even redder. Mary carried herself with a quiet strength and confidence that could make her almost intimidating if she decided to push an issue. By the contours of her physique, Josh summarized she must've spent many hours in a gym in order to have such a tight body for a middle-aged woman. Mary didn't look like a wide-eyed newbie out of college, but like someone who has done and seen a lot...and would not be easily shaken by anything.

Josh hoped Mary was up for new challenges; therefore, other employees wouldn't have to babysit her while bringing her up to date on the events in town. Mary seemed competent enough; however, there was one nagging question that kept bothering Josh in his mind...Ty wasn't one to heap out praise, so how well did Ty *really* know Mary and why was he so eager to give her the job?

Josh nodded politely to Ms. Powell, not sure why Ty had interrupted his meeting with Roger. He was about to turn and walk away when Ty called out, "Not so fast, Roberts. You should know I've decided to hire Ms. Powell to be our newest photographer."

Josh turned back around to face the new hire. "Oh, well in that case, I believe 'congratulations' are in order."

"Why, thank you, Mr. Roberts," responded Mary.

Ty spoke up and said, "In time, she'll eventually be doing some reporting as well. Therefore, I'm pairing her up with you to learn the ropes—the day-to-day aspects of the business until she gets her feet wet."

"Ty, you can't do that! When it comes to reporting, I work alone. Not to mention, I'm busy wrapping up the Reaper story right now."

Josh turned and looked at Mary. "No offense," he added. "Besides, Ty, you were supposed to hire one new photographer and one reporter. You can't just lump them together so you can save money."

"First of all, I can do whatever I want, Roberts. Secondly, we all know the Reaper story is just about wrapped up. He's dead. After your next piece, that's old news."

Josh was baffled. "But..."

"Listen to me, Josh. There's nothing left to add. Once you hand in your finished draft to me, you'll have plenty of time to show Mary the ropes."

"So, when can I start?" interrupted Mary.

"You can start right away," Ty answered back.

Mary smiled proudly. "Thank you, Mr. Harris."

Just then, Josh butted in and said, "Pardon my interruption, Ty, but don't you wanna conduct a few more interviews? I thought you said you'd interview my brother, Jason, for the reporting job sometime this week."

"Josh, he's not even in the newspaper business. Didn't you tell me he's an at-home parent?"

"That's neither here nor there, Ty. The fact is...Jason is a talented writer and definitely needs the job. He's got one child at home with another on the way."

"I'm sorry, Roberts, but I'm satisfied with my choice. I don't need to do any more interviews. Though, I was *supposed* to interview another woman today." Ty glanced at his appointment book. "Beth Allen was her name. However, she didn't bother to show up for her nine o'clock interview this morning. Since this wasn't important enough for her to show, she's automatically disqualified."

Ty's eyes met with Josh's. The two men stared intently at one another.

"Don't argue with me, Roberts. Mary is hired, and that's final!"

Josh's face became red and he exited the office, being careful not to mutter anything he might come to regret.

Ty turned his attention back toward Mary and said, "Don't take it to heart, Ms. Powell, he's rude to everyone. By the way, Mary, do you have your driver's license or Social Security card with you? I need to send a copy over to Payroll for the W-2's and all that mess; you know how it goes."

Mary's eyes shifted away from Ty and toward the floor. She began fidgeting with her purse when she uttered, "Um, I have my Social Security card, but not my license. Can I get that to you another time?"

Ty waved her off. "Your Social Security card is fine for now, but the sooner you can get me your license the better," he announced. "Familiarize yourself with the building a bit and let Roberts cool off. Don't worry about him; everything will be fine."

"You know something, Mr. Harris," Mary said with a peculiar grin, "I think you might be right."

Chapter 51:

Coming to Terms

The day after the incident at the Buckley Building, Bucky drove over to see Adam "Red" Richardson in the early afternoon. Adam's mother, Rose, greeted her nephew with a warm hug and escorted him inside the house.

"Come in, come in. Make yourself right at home," Rose said, leading Bucky into the living room. Once they entered, Rose motioned for Bucky to sit down on a very comfortable couch. "It's good to see you, Bucky. I know you're busy being the Mayor and all, but you really should stop by more often. We're family; you know we're always here for you."

"I'm sorry, Aunt Rose. I promise to stop by with Mikey more often."

Rose smiled and gave him a peck on the cheek. "I'll go get Adam. You just relax, have a seat, and get comfortable."

Bucky sat on the couch and winced in pain as his sore muscles sank into the soft cushion. He tried to remember how often he visited his relatives, or didn't, and realized that although he saw Adam around town, he really didn't come around to visit him at home often enough. That was something he made a mental note of, and fully intended to change in the future.

As he glanced around, he noticed the living room was presentable, clean but not immaculate. Not obsessively so. Afraid he might get too comfortable and start to drift off after his sleepless night, Bucky stood up and paced around a little, swinging his arms to keep the blood moving. He looked out the window and admired his aunt's flower bed, noticing all the different types of flowers. Aside from the common carnations, she had some equally bright and colorful flowers such as Lilies, Daisies, and, of course, Roses. Some of her flowers were very rare, especially for the North Country.

Adam exited the kitchen area. He looked a little tired, as if he'd stayed up late, but he looked none the worse for wear. Bucky grinned when he saw his cousin. "Hey, Adam. I came to see how you're doing."

"The question is . . . how are you? I saw Celeste, Roger, and you on the news last night. All of ya were huddled by a fire truck next to that huge blaze at the Buckley Building."

"We all survived," Bucky answered with a sigh. "That's the best I could hope for."

Bucky noticed Adam had his jacket and sneakers on. "Did I catch you at a bad time? You goin' somewhere?"

"My mom gave me a lotto ticket and I won two dollars. I was gonna walk down to Potter's Liquor Store to cash it in. I can definitely use those two dollars."

Bucky tilted his head in confusion. "Why're you going all the way to the liquor store? You can cash your ticket at *any* convenient store."

"I was gonna use the two dollars towards the next bottle of Jack Daniels I intend on buying." Adam's voice was steady; his face showed no sign of joking, no sign of remorse, either. He just didn't care. His drinking problem had become ingrained as part of a routine now.

Bucky looked sadly at him and asked, "Can it wait? I'd really like to talk to you for a few minutes."

"I suppose so." Adam set the lotto ticket on the coffee table and then shifted his attention back to his cousin. At that moment, he noticed the bandage on Bucky's head for the first time. "Christ! What the Hell happened to your head?"

"Oh, I got whacked with a brick," Bucky answered surprisingly nonchalantly as he rubbed his head.

Adam cringed as he said, "Geez, man. It looks awful painful."

"Nah, not as bad as you might think. It's a little tender but I'll be okay."

Adam smirked and gave Bucky a pat on the shoulder. "Glad to hear it, cuz."

Bucky watched Adam open a can of beer and asked, "So, really, how are you, Adam? How're you handling knowing that it was Tim Matthews who killed John?"

Adam shrugged unconvincingly. "I'm learnin' to cope with that fact; just like I'm learnin' to cope with the loss of John. It's been hard not havin' that pothead around. Just knowin' that I'll never see him again, no matter how much I wanna party with the dude one more time, has been downright depressing."

"It's going to be a long while before you get over that type of pain. But in time, the hurt will fade and you'll learn to miss him a little less every day. It doesn't mean the pain goes away completely, but you get to the point where you can go on again."

"I can't guarantee that, Bucky," Adam stated. "I'm gonna miss John more than anyone will know. We did everything together. Hell, we both lost our virginity to the same girl at age fifteen, and I smoked my first cigarette in his tree house at age twelve." He paused to wipe a tear from his eye. "John was my best friend, Bucky, and he was closer to me than my own brother."

"Have you consulted anyone other than Jack Daniels about your feelings?"

Adam let out a chuckle. "Does Jim Beam count?"

Bucky smirked at his cousin's response. Despite the sadness, and scariness, of the situation, it was a pretty witty comeback. Bucky figured that if even a little bit of the old Adam he knew was still around, then there was a chance to save him. Bucky held out hope Adam would eventually find a way to crawl through the trap of alcoholism.

"That's not what I meant, Red. Have you talked to anyone, such as your mom, about the issues you're dealing with in your life?"

"No, I haven't," Adam confessed. "You know I don't feel very comfortable sharin' my feelings with other people—that includes both strangers *and* relatives."

"Oh, I see," Bucky said in a quiet voice.

Adam's face turned sad once again, and his eyes fell back to some unseen point of focus on the floor. "I just don't know what I'm gonna do without John, Bucky. He was the one person I could always go to without gettin' a lecture about how I should be livin' my life. Now it seems like I just don't have the answers to anything anymore." Adam finished off his seventh beer of the afternoon while he spoke. "I mean, after all…"

Bucky interrupted Adam. "Your depression isn't healthy, Red. I don't mean to butt in, but I saw this kind of behavior from Roger Fasick after his brother disappeared, and then again when he lost Holly last year. I don't care if you don't want to hear it, but I need to tell you—this level of depression is dangerous to your health and your well-being."

Adam exhaled deeply and nodded his head. "I believe you, Bucky. Depression *is* dangerous." Then he looked around the room and said, "Damn, I'm in need of an herbal remedy or somethin'."

"I think I have a bottle of green tea out in my car if you want some," Bucky offered.

With a smirk, Adam replied, "That's not the type of herb I was referrin' to."

"Very funny, wise-ass," Bucky voiced in a harsh tone. "Don't let me catch you smoking grass. After all, I'm the mayor of this town and have a reputation to uphold."

When it was obvious that no wise crack was coming in response, Bucky took a deep breath. "Normally I wouldn't recommend this," he continued, "but I think you should seek some professional assistance to help you cope and move on with your life."

Adam shook his head. "My depression isn't something new, Bucky. John's death was just the straw that broke the camel's back. Do you remember when I was thirteen and my brother died a month before I started high school?"

"Yes, I do. That was a very difficult time for all of us, Adam. Loren and I were very close as well."

Adam became choked up as he yelled, "It was a nightmare for me, Bucky! My brother killed himself on his 21st birthday...and why? Because he had another stupid argument with my father! They always fought; they never stopped. No matter what Loren tried to do to make them happy it wasn't enough—he couldn't keep his own life straight enough. My father always treated him like dirt—and my mother was nearly as bad. He shot himself because of our parents, Bucky. How can I ever forgive them for that?"

"You must first learn how to forgive before you will ever learn how to heal," explained Bucky.

Adam continued on as if he didn't hear Bucky's words. "And then, a few months later, the guilt became too much for my father to bear, so he committed suicide, as well. And in a blink of an eye...they were both gone."

Bucky's eyes misted as Adam continued to talk.

"And why did that happen? Because of some stupid dispute that no one can even remember! It was always like that between those two—having the same trivial arguments for as long as we could all remember."

"I know, Red. I know," Bucky whispered solemnly. "That's a painful subject for everyone and I never bring it up in conversation—

especially to you. I know you were utterly heartbroken over the whole. dilemma; that's why I avoid talking about it."

Adam wiped the teardrops from the corners of his eyes. "I still can't talk about it without breaking down. That's when my chance at a normal life ended and just waking up each day became a chore. Then again, maybe I never even had any chance to begin with. So, Bucky, when you tell me I should get on with my life, maybe you should take a good look at what kind of a life you're asking me to return to."

For a moment, the two men stood in silence, not knowing which direction to take the conversation. Bucky had known his cousin had problems, but he never imagined they ran as deeply as Adam had just finished describing.

Then Bucky spoke up and suggested, "Adam, you should start coming to the gym with me. It will release some of that anger and frustration as well as keep you out of a bar."

"Do you really think so?"

"Yes," he stated. "You just might forget your problems for a little while and relieve some stress in the process."

"Coming from the man who *always* seems to rise above any problems that come his way, your advice isn't all that helpful."

"Hey, I have problems too. The same as anyone else. But, whatever problems are going on in my life…they're overshadowed by the good things I've got. There's Celeste, my son Mikey, and I have scores of friends. It could be a lot worse." Bucky paused for a moment before speaking again. "You know what I think, Adam? I believe your problem is you need more confidence."

Adam let out a huff. "Coming from someone who's *always* right, that doesn't mean much."

"Y'know, Adam, Grandpa used to always say: Confidence comes not from being right but from not fearing to be wrong."

Adam crossed his arms and looked toward the floor.

"Maybe hanging out with me and going to the gym will help heal your weary soul," Bucky suggested. "You need to start somewhere."

"I don't know, Bucky. Exercise really isn't my cup of tea…that is, unless they serve whiskey on the rocks there."

"Not likely, wise-guy. Look, Adam, you need to straighten yourself out before you completely ruin your life. Come work out with me, cuz. Tomorrow you'll feel like a brand new man."

Adam sighed. "I'd settle for just feeling like a *man* again."

"So…?" prodded Bucky. "That's a 'yes,' right?"

"All right, Bucky," Adam said with a laugh that was half humorous, half resigned. "I'll give it a shot."

A few hours later, Bucky was leaving a meeting he had at the Carthage Area Hospital when he decided to visit Roger Fasick. He drove over to his Roger's house, flung open the front door, and announced, "Well, I just came from the coroner's office. Harry Moon has finished the autopsy and is putting together his report. It should be finished by this afternoon and handed over to the police department shortly thereafter."

"Did he say anything was peculiar about the cause of Tim's death?" inquired Roger.

"Funny you should bring that up. Harry mentioned that the firemen were able to put out the fire before it completely charred Tim's body, but it didn't really matter because he was already dead by the time the firemen arrived."

"Yeah, I wouldn't guess many people would survive a multi-story fall like that," Roger replied, walking in from the kitchen with a bologna sandwich in hand. "And besides, that doesn't fit into the category of 'peculiar' at all."

Bucky watched in awe as Roger chomped down his sandwich like a famished grizzly bear. After a few seconds, he shook his head and said, "That's true. But the most interesting part of it all is Harry Moon speculates that Tim might have actually survived the fall off the building somehow. He believes it was the flames from the falling debris which caught his clothes on fire and killed him."

"Oh, really? Why does the coroner think Tim survived the fall?"

"The bones in both of Tim's arms were shattered, which means he might've landed on them," Bucky explained. "That could've even protected him just enough to survive the fall. Tim's fingernails were dug into the cement as if he were alive and scratching and writhing around on the ground in excruciating pain when he died."

"Huh? That's strange."

"It sure is! And another weird thing about it all is that the firemen think they found faint traces of footprints around Tim's body, heading toward one of the side streets. So if he *was* alive, maybe someone was around him when he caught on fire and died."

"Well...that could've been Thomas Parker," Roger suggested. "I heard he was found near that area."

"Nah, couldn't have been him. The footprints they saw were different tread and shoe size than what Thomas was wearing," Bucky mentioned. "Apparently the tread was light—but the size was large. So, it must've been someone really tall, but without a lot weight,"

"Really?" Roger asked. "Did the police or firemen find any clues as to who the footprints belonged to?"

"No," Bucky answered. "The smell of burnt flesh and something else they couldn't identify was so strong in the air that Officer Streeter and a few other officers vomited right there in the street. It contaminated the whole crime scene! Now that the investigation is all but over, the last thing we have left to do is bury the bastard."

"Are you going to be attending his funeral?" inquired Roger.

Bucky nodded his head. "Sure, we all knew Tim. We may not have liked the guy, but as Mayor of Carthage, I feel like I'm obligated to go to his funeral. How I feel about it doesn't really matter—I think it's the right thing to do."

Roger, a little surprised by Bucky's comment, spoke up. "I won't be at his funeral, Mr. Mayor, but I'll send a letter approving of it. That is, if that's all right with you."

"You seem really hostile, Roger. And I noticed this is especially true whenever I bring up Tim's name. You always look very uneasy. Do you have something weighing on you that you wanna talk about?"

Roger turned away without saying a word.

"I'm right, aren't I? What is it? What's bothering you?"

Roger looked nervous. Without even thinking about it he raised his hand and rubbed the back of his neck, massaging the unseen weight that was weighing him down. When he noticed what he was doing, Roger dropped his hand back to his side and glanced around as if looking for spies who were following his every move.

"Well, what is it? What's bothering you, Roger?"

"Nothing, Bucky. Nothing. Are you sure it wasn't the fall that killed him?" Roger asked, hoping Bucky was right.

"Nothing is certain, but there's a lot of evidence to suggest Tim was still alive after he hit the ground...why are you so interested in knowing?"

Roger began recollecting the other night when they were on top of the Buckley Building. "I'll never forget the fear in his eyes as he fell from the roof."

Bucky listened to Roger's words, and then the pieces came together. "Oh my God...you did it, Roger! You pushed Tim off the building! You let him die, didn't you?"

Roger stopped dead, turned and faced Bucky; his eyes were unable to look Bucky in the face. He began to fidget with his hands and his feet moved as if his shoes were filled with cement.

"You did it!" Bucky said again, this time it was sinking in. "I can't believe you killed him."

"I don't know what to say, Bucky. It had to be done," Roger stated brusquely. "Tim would've gotten out of jail eventually and came back to do it again. That man didn't deserve to live. After what Tim did to this town…what he did to Holly."

An icy chill shot up Bucky's spine. "Roger, I realize you were hurting, but you must have faith in our justice system. We can't have vigilantes running around on the streets. Before you know it, they'll be dressing up in costumes like the freaks in New York City."

Bucky paused and took several deep breaths. "Now then, Roger, tell me what happened on the rooftop and explain to me why you did it."

"I let go of Tim's hand while he dangled off the building," Roger admitted, the words coming out in a stream.

Bucky stared in befuddlement. Hearing Roger confess was such a surreal feeling. He never expected his best friend was capable of committing such a heinous act.

"At the time, I didn't even fully realize what I was doing." Roger stopped. His face looked as if he was going to cry. "It was like I was outside of my body watching the events unfold…watching like a spectator as I let him fall." Roger closed his eyes and a single tear trickled down his cheek. "It's a strange and frightening thing, Bucky."

"What's that, Roger?" Bucky asked.

"To see yourself at your worst," he answered. "I…I think my dark side is starting to consume me. I can't take it anymore, Bucky, and each day is worse than the last. I don't know how much longer I can hang on."

"Listen, Roger, I sympathize as best as I can, but I honestly can't relate to what you're going through. I've never killed a man…but I'll admit I've read some obituaries that made me happy."

Roger looked over towards Bucky and smiled.

"I remember a quote I heard once, then again, maybe it was from a movie I watched. Anyway, I memorized it and keep those words close to heart. It goes like this…" Bucky started to paraphrase. "I believe there's a hero in us all, a certain quality that keeps us honest, makes us noble, and keeps us on an honorable path. And when our time comes, it will finally allow us to die with pride, even though it may mean we have give up the thing we want most in our life—even if it's our dreams."

"That's a nice quote. I want to believe it, but what happens when someone is pushed to the limits? Do they break down…do they become evil with no hope for atonement? Is there ever any way back?"

"What's with all the self-examination, Roger? After all, you did what you thought was right—whether it was the legal thing to do or not, it was probably for the best. I certainly can't blame you for it."

"Maybe you're right, Bucky. It's just that..." Roger's words trailed off.

Bucky could sense the conflict within his friend. "Is there something else, Roger? Something *more* you need to get off your chest?"

Roger stared at him with misty eyes. "There are those in life that get past all the bad things said and hurt feelings, and then there are those that let it seep and fester inside. They're the ones that go on shooting sprees. Which one am I, Bucky? I just don't know anymore!"

"I think you'll be just fine, Roger. You have many people who love you, bud. You just need to open your eyes and see that." Bucky paused and cocked his head. "Again I have to ask...what's with all the sentiment?"

"I don't want to be consumed by my hate." Roger paused as teardrops began trickling down his cheek. "I...I have a son, Bucky. And I want to be the best father I can possibly be for that little boy."

"What!?" Bucky yelped. "Whoa, wait a minute...did you just say that you have a son?"

Roger's shoulders drooped in shame. "Yes. I have a son. His name is Alex, and he wants to get to know me. I look at myself now after what I did...how I let Tim fall. I don't know what to do."

"A son?" Bucky uttered, still stunned at this very large piece of news. "When did this all come about? How long have you known? Who? How? What—why didn't you tell me about this?"

"There wasn't enough time," Roger explained. "I didn't even know myself until yesterday. Actually, I found out when I was coming back from my parents' house last night. I stopped at a gas station, and while I was there, I saw a little boy. He looked oddly familiar to me. The boy turned and ran, and for some reason I felt compelled to chase after. When I caught up to him, I came face-to-face with Nellie Spencer. She told me the little boy was hers...and mine. She was scared of my reaction, but ended up telling me everything."

Bucky stared off as though a thousand thoughts were racing in his head. "So...that night I found the pregnancy test at your house really *did* belong to her."

"It appears so," Roger concurred. "That's the reason I feel the way I do. I want to get to know my son...but I want to be a good parent, and not some evil monster."

Bucky put his hand on his friend's shoulder. "Roger, I can only tell you what my father told me. Don't dwell on the negative parts of life and be the best role model you can be. That's all you can do. Cherish your kids and cherish the moments you spend together because once those times are have passed, they're gone forever."

Roger nodded his head and grinned. "Thank you for those words of encouragement, Bucky. I really needed that."

Bucky simply grinned. After a moment, he asked, "So, when are you going to see your son again?"

"I talked to Nellie this morning. She's bringing Alex up for a visit soon. Nellie has a class reunion in the next couple weeks and agreed to stay at my place while they're in town."

"Are you comfortable with that?" questioned Bucky.

"Yeah, I suppose I am. I can't think of any better joy than having my own child sleep in the same house I grew up in. I actually have butterflies in my stomach."

"I'm happy for ya, buddy. Believe me, you're gonna love bein' a dad."

After a long pause, Roger let out a heavy exhale and smiled. Then he decided to change the topic by saying, "So, has there been a decision as to what's going to happen to Tim's body?"

"While I was talking to Harry Moon earlier, I think he mentioned that Tim's body will be ready for cremation by tomorrow or maybe the next day. I suppose he'll get around to it after all the tests have been finished and Harry is satisfied with his report."

"Seems oddly ironic in a way…Tim being cremated and all," Roger pointed out.

"I was thinking that myself," Bucky admitted. "Like the punch line to a really dark, unfunny joke."

Chapter 52:

The past comes clean

It was Tuesday, August 29, 2006, and the ruins of the Buckley Building were still smoldering, even after two days and 20,000 gallons of water. Whatever chemical concoction Tim Matthews had put together, it burned beyond normal gasoline. There was barely even a shell of the old building left. After the fire department knocked down the rest (so it wouldn't spread to nearby buildings), it was just a pile of smoldering rubble on the ground. The one positive aspect was that the smoldering was contained so there was very little threat of another flare up.

It was on this particular morning that Dave "Bucky" Morgan went to see Bud Hopkins to tell him what Celeste had discovered about Tim Matthews's past and his father's actions. Bucky also wanted to let Bud know that the *very* influential town council had been informed he was innocent of the crimes which had put him behind bars for nearly twenty years and made him a social outcast.

Bud Hopkins was born on a clay floor of a rundown shack that belonged to his family for many generations. The small decrepit building was all that was left of an old dairy farm that went defunct, leaving Bud's family dirt poor. The family fell into a degree of poverty they never seemed to be able to crawl out of; and sometimes, they didn't even have enough money to afford food, soap, or even pay for electricity.

Bud lived a hard life in that shack, and after the death of his mother from a tractor accident, Bud's father had a breakdown. From that point on, Bud was required to take care of his father and three siblings. Their clothes consisted of hand-me-downs and handouts, bringing occasional snickers and laughter from local kids, as well as many adults who looked down on Bud and his family. Sometimes the teasing resulted in a bare knuckles brawl, and more often than not it was Bud who received the harshest end of the treatment.

With his home life being so utterly desolate, one would've hoped that Bud could've went to school to get a break from his sadness and feelings of utter hopelessness. Unfortunately, trouble followed Bud wherever he went. The schoolyard bullies loved to torment Bud and his siblings on the playground and amuse themselves with practical jokes at Bud's expense every chance they could.

As the years passed, however, Bud began to mature and his body began to change as well. Once Bud turned thirteen, he grew rather tall, and because of all the physical labor he performed around his folks' place, he developed a rock hard physique, making him exceptionally strong for his age. Even though Bud had a slender build, he could run like the wind and over time he learned to handle himself very well in a fistfight. His frame was wiry, which made him quick on his feet and hard to manhandle.

After several encounters of having to defend himself from the bullies, most of the local 'tough guys' tended to avoid a fight with Bud because they knew that even if they managed to whip Bud (which wasn't exactly a sure thing, either), they'd have to fight him a dozen more times, or until Bud finally won. Although Bud didn't have much, he was very prideful and he never gave up...and more importantly, he would *always* get even. No offense ever went unanswered, no matter how much smarter it would be on his part to just walk away.

Having a tumultuous childhood would've been bad enough for most folks, but for Bud Hopkins his life only went downhill from there. In his early teen years, Bud had been accused, and even arrested, for several local petty crimes...none of which he actually committed, and he was later exonerated of the charges. However, because of his lowly status in the community, Bud was an easy mark to pin anything and everything on. Since Bud had been arrested several times, everyone assumed he was guilty, perpetuating the entire problem.

Years later, when a string of devastating fires erupted in Carthage during the early 1980's, Bud's problematic past made him seem like the perfect suspect for the crimes. That, along with no credible alibi, an eye witness account that was questionable at best (but in most people's minds, far more credible than Bud), and a series of critical news articles that all but accused him of the crimes, Bud's fate was sealed before the trial even started. He never had a chance, a hope, or a prayer.

Bud Hopkins spent over twenty years as a ward of the state, splitting his time between prison and the Ogdensburg Mental Facility, before being released. He had been convicted on charges of arson, attempted murder, and several counts of involuntary manslaughter for the deaths of those who were in the burning buildings that he had supposedly, yet erroneously, torched. Now, with his newfound freedom and his painful past behind him (as best as it could be), it seemed as though Bud's life might finally be taking a turn for the better.

While approaching Bud's street, Bucky couldn't help but notice how run down many of the houses were on his way to Bud Hopkins's apartment. A sad expression crossed Bucky's face as he looked around the area and thought how the job losses and lack of good high-paying careers had taken its toll in this community. Other parts of the upstate area were doing well because of the booming population of Fort Drum, but this wasn't one them.

As Bucky drove down North School Street, across the railroad tracks where the street merged into West End Avenue, he traveled a short distance further down and made a right turn on Parham Street. He went down two blocks and came to a **STOP** sign, then he crossed over to Adelaide Street, traveled about another half-block, noticing the squalor getting worse and worse as he went.

Bucky could hear the gravel crunch beneath his tires as he pulled into the driveway of the Calabria family. Gino Calabria, an elderly Italian immigrant, was renting a studio apartment above his garage to Bud Hopkins. Mr. Calabria was also one of the few people in town who would even make eye contact with Bud, let alone say more than two words to him.

Bud leased the apartment shortly after he was paroled. It was the only place he could find, or rather, Mr. Calabria was the only person that would rent to him once Bud put on his application where his last residence had been. After a person tells others they spent time in prison or a mental institution, not many doors are open to them. Because of that, Bud had a hard time getting a loan or his driver's license. However, Bucky suspected that possibly Mr. Calabria had a sordid past of his own from way back, and was more inclined to give someone a second chance...as long as the rent check kept coming in on time.

Bud couldn't afford a car and he kept getting the runaround at the DMV. Because of that, Bud didn't drive around town…and he didn't feel safe walking the streets all by himself. He didn't want someone giving him a hard time about being an ex-convict, or have an armed group of townsfolk decide on an old fashioned mob justice. On occasion, Bud used a bicycle he found at the dump and rode within a short vicinity of his apartment if he needed any essentials.

Bucky parked his tan-colored Chevy Blazer and sat inside for a few moments as he rehearsed what he was going to say to Bud. He took several deep breaths before gathering the nerve to climb the weathered, wooden stairs on the outside of the garage which led up to the apartment. Every stair creaked and bent under Bucky's weight, and he couldn't get to the top fast enough. He rapped on the window of the front door and waited, but no one came to the door.

After a few minutes, Bucky knocked again; this time, he heard movement from inside the apartment. Minutes passed again; then as Bucky was about to turn and leave, the door opened, and there stood Bud Hopkins with a cup of coffee in one hand and a butter knife in the other.

Bud was a slender man, with a thick moustache and several days' growth of whiskers. His hair was dark and slicked back, looking as if he used half a jar of Vaseline to get his hair to stay in that position. Although Bud was in his mid-forties, he was in excellent shape and fiercely strong from years of pumping iron in prison. It's been said that he could bend a quarter in half by the strength of his fingers. That might be a ridiculous rumor going around town, but Bucky could believe it from just looking at Bud's physique.

Bud had turned to weightlifting out of necessity more than anything else. It didn't take him very long to learn there were no friends in prison, and he had to exercise so he could defend himself against those who wanted to assault him—physically, sexually, and emotionally. Though Bud was one hell of a scrappy boxer, his fighting skills were still fairly amateurish. Being a scrapper wasn't enough behind those concrete walls.

Bud had kept mainly to himself since coming back to Carthage to live, and in all honesty, he preferred it that way. So it should come as no surprise that Bud was more than just a little stunned to see someone at his doorstep—especially when that someone was the Mayor of Carthage.

"Bud Hopkins?" inquired Bucky.

"Yeah?" stated Bud, glaring back at the stranger on his doorstep.

"My name is Dave Morgan. I'm the Mayor of Carthage, but you can call me Bucky."

Before saying anything more, Bucky waited for a response from the man in front of him, wanting to be quite sure he was talking to the man he went there to see.

Although Bud was annoyed to be bothered, he was curious why Bucky was there and bluntly asked him to state his business. "I know who you are, Mayor Morgan. Whatta' ya' want?"

"I just wanted to come by to introduce myself and see how you were making out. Do you need anything?"

Bud snapped at him with the first words that came to his mind. "How 'bout a new life? Or maybe ya can give me enough money so I can go someplace where no one knows who I am! Anything else ya wanna know, Mayor?"

Bucky's eyes popped out. He definitely wasn't accustomed to hostile sarcasm or being on the receiving end of excessive disrespect.

"There's no need to be so rude, Mr. Hopkins. I only came up here to help you. I think you can show a little more gratitude for my efforts."

"Oh, you do, do you? Well, I honestly don't give a rat's ass what you think, Mr. Mayor. The only thing I need from people like you is to be left alone...and maybe a few dollars to get away from this forsaken town."

"Money, huh?" Bucky said curiously. "Do you have any money, Bud? How're you paying for food and rent?"

Bud's eyes flashed. "Look, Mayor! How I pay my bills is none of your business. If ya came all the way up here to lecture me on staying on the right side of the law...you can save your damn speech. I do *not* steal if that's what you're thinking!"

"No..." Bucky answered as his face reddened with embarrassment.

"But just so you don't think I'm keeping secrets," Bud retorted with a sneer, "I'm living on the money I received when I got out of prison. Oh, I also received a small amount of life insurance when my father died, too."

"Your dad had life insurance?" Bucky mentioned, quite surprised.

"Apparently so. He sold our old house to a land developer during the years I was in prison. Dad bought a small run-down place in town, and he even managed to set aside some dough for a little life insurance. Dad's old accountant, Bobby-Jay Zehr, set everythin' up for me and my siblings. It's enough to keep me afloat for a while, but it won't last forever."

"Well, I may not be able to help you out with a new life, Mr. Hopkins, but maybe I can help you get on your feet."

"How?" Bud asked halfheartedly.

"I can find you a job to help out with your money situation," Bucky said, still trying to figure out the best way to broach the subject.

Bud scoffed. "Yeah, *sure* you can. Look, I don't mean to be rude, Mayor, but I don't have time to talk about nonsense right now. I'm not much for chit-chat anyway. So, why don't you get to the point as to *why* you showed up at my doorstep?"

"I'm serious, Mr. Hopkins. I wanted to talk to you about giving you a job."

In his mind, Bud thought Bucky was as phony as a three-dollar bill. However, Bud also wanted to find out the reason Mayor Morgan was so interested in his well-being.

"Why would the all-mighty 'Mayor of Carthage' wanna offer *me* a job?"

Bucky grinned at Bud once again and his eyes lit up. "If you would grant me just a few moments of your time, Bud, I can explain everything. May I come in?"

Bud thought for a moment as he debated what to do, and after some careful deliberation, he led Bucky into his apartment. After all, it wasn't like the mayor could really be any threat to him.

As Bucky entered, he took in his surroundings and noticed the apartment was very sparsely furnished. It was an ordinary studio apartment with dingy gray-colored walls and a petite kitchen with a tiny gas oven and a brown mini-fridge. A micro-sized bathroom was separated from the living room by no more than a frayed shower curtain. Just beyond the kitchen, by the only window in the entire apartment, Bud kept a miniature green house on his window sill to grow plants and several unusual kinds of flowers, including left-handed Honey Suckles, Lily of the Valleys, and even Venus Fly Traps.

The living room was also Bud's bedroom—having a hide-a-bed which doubled as the couch. A set of four TV trays was being used for a variety of uses. One was used as a lamp table next to the hide-a-bed, one was being used to hold his small 13" black & white TV, and one was used to eat his meals on, as there was no room for a regular table and chairs. On the last TV tray was an old copper ashtray with a half-smoked cigarette still smoldering and a partial pack of non-filtered Camel cigarettes. Also, next to the ashtray was a well-used wind-up alarm clock.

Bucky noticed Bud was wearing a tight-fitting white tank top T-shirt (sometimes called a 'wife beater'). Bucky often wondered how that type of shirt acquired such a derogatory nickname. After pausing for a moment, Bucky went on to observe the rest of Bud's attire. He was wearing a pair of worn-out dungarees from a second hand store and some blue and white loafers with no socks.

Bud didn't have a steady job, and purchased most of his apartment furnishings at flea markets and yard sales, or good old fashioned dumpster diving. Bud also bought the majority of his clothes at the Salvation Army Thrift Store—sometimes affectionately called the Sal-Boutique.

Just then, something caught Bucky's attention. On Bud's right upper arm was a tattoo of a heart with a halo of thorns hovering above it, and a bloody dagger piercing the center of the heart.

Bucky asked, "Does that tattoo have a story with it?"

The question was more to ease the tension Bucky could sense between Bud and himself.

"Yeah," mumbled Bud. "It signifies all my so-called friends who stabbed me in the heart, or the back if you prefer, when I needed their help." Bud took out a cigarette and lit it up. He puffed a cloud of smoke near Bucky's face and said, "That's the problem with good friends. You give 'em the shirt off your back and it shows 'em where they can put their knife."

Bucky's face became slightly flushed. He realized that was *not* the question to break the ice and ease the tension. He quickly tried another tactic. Bucky observed two pictures hanging on the wall. The first was a print of a sunset. The other was a picture of a distinguished looking man with a handlebar moustache. Bucky decided to ask another question, trying to sidestep his last inquiry which got a cool response.

"What's the portrait of?" Bucky inquired. "Is it a favorite place of yours or are you partial to sunsets?"

"No, not really. That picture is from my time spent in prison. I had no windows in my cell and I couldn't go outside for more than an hour a day. This picture hung on my wall in the joint—it was all I had."

"So why do you still keep it?" Bucky asked.

"I look at that picture every day of my life, and I will continue to look at this picture for the remainder of my life as a reminder of my time in prison."

"Oh," Bucky stated. "Well, how about the other picture? That's quite a distinguished-looking gentleman. Is he someone you know or a relative of yours?"

This time, to Bucky's surprise, Bud answered in a quieter and less hostile tone. "That was my father. It's one of the only pictures taken of him and just happens to be the only thing I have to remember my dad by. He was a great guy. A lot of people looked down on our family, but everyone liked him. To be honest, I wish I was more like him."

Bucky listened attentively as Bud talked more about his father and their relationship together. Bud talked for some time about his family before ending his story with, "That part of my life is history." And with that, Bud returned to his less-than-friendly attitude.

"Now then, Mr. Mayor," Bud said. "Aside from using me as an example of getting' tough on crime, I don't interact with too many mayors. Why would ya wanna to help me out? Don't ya know who I am? Don't ya know what I went to prison for?"

Bucky nodded politely. Bud's sneer became bigger as he had visions of backhanding the stupid grin off Bucky's face.

"Yeah, I know," Bucky stated matter-of-factly. "But I also know that you were falsely accused of starting those fires back then."

Bud's head snapped back and his eyes widened. "Is that so? Well, you're the only one who believes that. What makes ya so sure I wasn't lyin' about bein' framed? I *am* a bad seed and all."

"I was at the fire a few nights ago—the one that consumed the Buckley Building."

"Yeah, I saw your face on the news," Bud announced.

"That night, I discovered something that might be of interest for you."

"Oh really? What's that? Did the *real* arsonist finally come forward and admit my innocence?"

"Actually, yeah, something like that. My girlfr...I mean, my friend was on top the Buckley Building, trapped up there by the Reaper. She discovered that a local bartender named Tim Matthews was the person dressing up as the Reaper. But while Tim had her bound and gagged on the rooftop, he also confessed the rest of his family's sins to her."

In a blasé tone, Bud asked, "Are ya goin' somewhere with this story?"

"The point is...we found out who framed you for all those fires in town back in the early 1980s."

Bud gritted his teeth. "It was 1981 to be exact, Mr. Mayor."

"Uh...right," Bucky said with uneasiness. "Anyway, getting back to what I was saying. Tim Matthews was a sick individual, but before he died, he explained that his family was behind nearly all of the major fires which occurred in Carthage over the past one hundred years. Tim also said his father started the fires you were charged for, Bud. He framed you and then escaped out of town."

Bud's expression actually visibly changed; his knees began to wobble as well. He quickly braced himself on the counter and sat down in an old, rickety wooden chair next to the oven. Tears began to form in his eyes but he remained silent, refusing to cry, or maybe just not able to after so long.

"I'm sorry for everything that happened to you. I can only imagine how rough it was for you."

Bud's voice became choked up with emotion as he said, "You have no idea, Mayor. Just like you have no idea what it feels like to hear those words right now."

"It must've been a nightmarish ordeal for you. There are no special words to comfort, and no amount of money can fix what happened."

"You're right. It *was* a living nightmare, Mr. Mayor. I sometimes wonder how I survived all those years. Bad things happen behind those prison walls and the outside world doesn't know about it. It's true what people say—prison *does* change a man, but not always for the better. Hell, I'd wager *never* for the better."

"I guess it's safe to assume you weren't treated very well in prison, eh Bud?"

"Oh, sure!" Bud exclaimed sarcastically. "After a long and generous cavity search every mornin', the guards would gently escort me back to my less-than-comfy cell. After that, they'd tenderly shove their batons up my ass while they kindly banged my head off the cement walls on a regular basis."

There was an uncomfortable pause. Bucky didn't know what to make of Bud's dark humor and decided not to comment. The uneasiness of the subject was evident upon Bucky's face and he decided to change to topic in an attempt to relieve some tension.

Then, he noticed some scribbles on the back of Bud's right hand and asked, "Hey, Bud. What is that on your hand?"

"Oh, it's just a note."

"What does it say?"

"It says 'Milk'. I write notes on my hand or I'll forget. My mind is always preoccupied with a dozen different thoughts at one time."

"You know, that's why 'Post-It' notes were invented. So you wouldn't have to do that."

"I've tried using those...but I always end up losin' the little notes and I'm right back to square one again."

Bucky laughed and nodded his head. Then his tone became more business-like as he asked, "So, about this job I mentioned, do you happen to have any credentials that'd boost your resume?"

"Yeah, I have some education, Mr. Mayor."

"Well, I'd like to hear more about it. And *please*, call me Bucky."

"All right...Bucky. Well, I got my Associates Degree while I was in prison. I was lookin' to teach Criminology 101 as an adjunct at Jefferson Community College, but I guess that's just a dream."

"Why is that?"

"Well, you need a vehicle to get to Watertown, of which, I don't have."

"Is that all that's holding you back?"

Bud lifted his left pant leg and revealed the electronic monitor on his ankle. "This little piece of equipment doesn't come off for a few more days, Bucky. Besides, businesses usually aren't willin' to hire ex-cons who've just recently been paroled. It doesn't look good on the books, ya know."

"Just leave it to me, Bud. I'm sure I can find you something."

"You better not be pullin' me along Mr. May—Bucky. I wouldn't like that at all."

"I'm a man of my word, Mr. Hopkins," Bucky responded. "And I'll do what I can to see if there's a way to clear your criminal record. I don't know much about the law, but I figure with the confession and witnesses to it, we might be able to get you some kind of pardon or something."

"No fooling?" Bud asked suspiciously, trying not to get his hopes too high.

"I'll do my best on that, but I *can* guarantee I'll find you work. That's a promise!"

Bucky extended his hand. Bud hesitated, remembering a time in prison when a guy tried to shank him with his left hand after offering a truce, but he pushed that memory away and took Bucky's hand in a firm handshake.

"I'm gonna hold you to your word," Bud said.

"We'll get you on your feet yet," Bucky stated with confidence.

Bud thought about it and realized something—he actually believed Bucky had the best of intentions. And above all, Bud looked forward to the chance to prove his worth to a town that always doubted him.

Chapter 53:

Dark Side Revealed

It was the early morning of August 30th. Josh Roberts was at the *Tribune*, sitting in Ty Harris's office, and waiting for the editor to arrive. Josh looked around the room and noticed how clean and immaculate everything was—unlike the unkempt appearance of his own office. There were pictures of Ty's family, his two golden retrievers, and his former partner, Eric McGary, plastered all over the bright yellow walls.

Suddenly, Josh heard Ty's voice coming from down the hall as he was greeted by his secretary, Cathy Lee. Once Ty entered the room, he said, "Glad you could make it in so early, Josh. Sorry I was late for this meeting, but I got held up at the gym. The woman at the front counter said my membership had expired—which it hasn't." Ty shook his head. "Believe me, it was an exhausting argument!"

"I'm sure it was, Ty," Josh mumbled.

"Yes, well, what did you want to see me about so early in the morning?"

"I wanted to talk to you alone…without any distractions," Josh said in a serious tone. "Not only did I want to bring you up to speed about my article involving the Reaper case, which seems to be wrapping up nicely, but I also wanted to discuss my new and unexpected partner, Mary Powell."

"Alright then," Ty muttered as he pulled out a pink gym towel from his duffel bag and wiped the sweat from his clean-shaven face. "You have my full, undivided attention, Roberts. What's on your mind?"

"Ty, what do you know about this woman?" Josh asked.

Ty sat down in his chair and pulled a bottle of water from the mini-fridge that sat next to his desk. "Not much. She was a housewife for many years and worked as a secretary for her husband in his medical practice. Up until a year ago...when her husband died, in fact. Ever since then, I guess she's been pursuing a career in journalism."

"Are you sure?" inquired Josh. "You don't even have a photo ID of this woman. How do you know Mary is who she says she is?"

"What are you implying, Roberts? You think she has some sort of hidden agenda or something? I think that's a little farfetched...even for you."

"All I'm saying, Ty, is how do you know everything on her resume is the truth? Maybe she's feeding you false information just to look better in your eyes or to appeal to your sympathetic side."

Ty's nostrils flared and his cheeks became red with anger. "I don't have a sympathetic side!" he declared.

"Well, not towards me you don't. But it wouldn't be the first time someone fudged some information on their resume just to get a job in this office."

Ty nodded his head and unclenched his fists. "Listen, Josh. I'm sorry I didn't give the job to your brother. But you can't take out your frustrations on Mary, either. She's trying to move forward with her life after the death of her husband. She's taking a risk by trying a career change this late in life. Most other businesses wouldn't even give her a chance because of her age alone. I don't want to be one of those people."

Josh lowered his head and sighed. "It's just that she's so inexperienced and..."

Ty interrupted him by saying, "You can't be so skeptical of people all the time, Josh. Sometimes you have to give someone a chance."

"Being skeptical is part of my job. It's who I am."

"Maybe so," Ty responded, "but I don't think Mary should be penalized for getting a late start on life. Believe me; she is committed to doing whatever it takes to make sure this job works out."

"I appreciate how dedicated she is, but what makes you think she's qualified to do the work?" Josh pressed, still a little miffed at having his brother blown off after being more or less promised the job.

Ty sat up straight, presenting himself in a much more formal manner than before. He wasn't belligerent, but seemed unusually understanding and compassionate when dealing with Josh's somewhat pointed inquiry.

"I've seen her portfolio," Ty said. "She has an amazing flair for taking photos. I'd go so far as to even call it a gift. She had some journalism experience from when she was younger, and she can write a solid piece. She has too much talent to risk letting a competitor like Jack Lavancha or the *Watertown Times* to get a hold of her."

It was a blatant attempt by Ty to use Josh's feud with the competing reporter to get him to submit…but it worked, even though Josh knew exactly what his editor was doing. He sat back, resigned to the fact that Ty was going to get his way, and that he knew how to push all of Josh's buttons.

"I'm giving her a chance, Josh," Ty continued. "She has a lot of potential and I want her to learn from you. Learn how to interview people and learn how to write a column. I may not like to admit it, but you *are* the best reporter I have on staff."

"I don't suppose I can get that in writing?" Josh asked, touched by his editor's compliment, but also wanting to inject a little sarcasm in retaliation for Ty's remark about Jack Lavancha.

"Get back to work before I give her *your* job just for the hell of it." Ty tried to growl, but the usually gruff editor burst into a rare guffaw. However, that didn't stop him from shoving Josh out of the office and slamming the door behind him.

Instead of Josh heading back to his own office, he strolled over to the water cooler by the secretary's desk and waited. Ten minutes went by and Ty exited his office and walked down the hallway toward the restroom.

Once Ty was out of sight, Josh hurried over and snuck into Ty's office, searching through his filing cabinet. After that, he switched his attention to Ty's desk drawers as well as the papers lying upon his desk. Several minutes passed, and just when Josh was about to give up and exit the office before being caught, he came across the item he was looking for—Mary Powell's resume.

Around 9 am, Josh left the *Tribune* and drove over to City Hall to meet with Bucky. Mary wouldn't be on board until later that afternoon, and she still had to attend the new employee orientation class. Josh figured he still had a day or two before he'd have her as a second shadow. With that in mind, he took the opportunity to visit Bucky to find out what all was going on in town while he could still do so with relative anonymity.

Josh entered the building and walked over to the front desk to speak with LaTesha Prince. LaTesha was a beautiful Hispanic woman who, for the longest time, had to deal with an overabundance of attention from the opposite sex—but she also had the brains and strong independent personality to match her stunning looks. Although she was called plenty of names behind her back, all roughly translating to "ice princess," Josh liked LaTesha's no-nonsense attitude, and respected her for all the crap she had to put up with. Josh wouldn't get a chance to stay and chat, however, as LaTesha was already engaged in a conversation of her own with the town troublemaker, Edgar Polansky.

"Go jump off a bridge or something, Edgar. Stop hanging around my desk and go bother someone else!" LaTesha's eyes flashed with anger. "Why do you keep coming back all the time when you know you aren't welcome here?"

"To be honest, I enjoy looking at your body, LaTesha," Edgar said with bulging eyes. "And I must admit, you look very attractive today. I simply *love* women with your body type."

"Oh, really?" LaTesha asked in a rhetorical tone, one that she knew would invoke an answer, anyway. "And what type would that be?"

"Those of a *real* woman—and real women have curves. Admit it, LaTesha…underneath all that hostility you actually *want* me!"

LaTesha broke into a loud burst of laughter. "I hate to burst your bubble, Edgar, but I play for the *other* team now."

Edgar gasped in astonishment. "You mean you're a…"

LaTesha bared her pouty lips in a sneer that was half smile. "Yes, Edgar; I date women now."

Edgar looked confused. "I don't understand. Since when did *you* become a lesbian?"

"Since I got tired at looking at dirty, hairy asses all the time. I'm also fed up with 'little' boys and their immature games as well." LaTesha let out a huff. "Men don't want to be in a committed relationship; all they want is sex. Plain and simple. And as far as I'm concerned, men aren't even worth my time anymore."

That response caused Josh to burst out laughing. LaTesha tossed him a smirk and a glance, letting him know she heard, then went back to dealing with Edgar. Josh had limited time, and when he was done listening to those two exchange insults, he went straight up to Bucky's office where the Mayor and his good friend, Roger Fasick, were having a discussion of their own.

"What's going on, gentleman?" Josh bellowed as he thrust the door open.

"Hey, Josh!" Roger answered back. "We're just shootin' the breeze and such."

Bucky motioned for Josh to go ahead and take a seat. "I was telling Roger about my conversation with Officer Streeter yesterday. He informed me about the recent discovery of a body in nearby Deferiet."

"Oh, yeah," said Josh, making himself comfortable. "One of our writers, Jennifer Louise, wrote a short article about the incident. She told me there weren't many facts to go on, and the police were pretty hush-hush about the grisly details."

Roger thought for a moment and then turned to Bucky and asked, "Have you been able to wrangle any new information from the police? After all, Bucky, you *are* the Mayor, and Deferiet is fairly nearby."

"Not much," Bucky remarked dismally. "Unfortunately, the woman's fingerprints aren't in the data base, which means the victim didn't have a criminal record, and probably never worked for any government agency. Other than that, no ID has been located yet and she doesn't appear to be a local resident."

"I heard the body was found near Northern Pines Motel," Josh spoke up. "Have the police discovered any clues there?"

"Officer Streeter said there were a few women who stayed at the motel that night, but all paid for their room in cash. He wouldn't release the names of the people on the guest register either. Aside from that, there haven't been any eyewitness accounts or legitimate leads from call-ins."

"Legitimate?" Josh asked.

Bucky's face grimaced in an expression that Josh swore was something akin to contempt. "When I was a teenager, even the worst Hell raising didn't involve screwing with a police investigation. I know kids are prone to mischief, but this situation is far too serious for people to be phoning in with prank calls and false leads."

"You got that right!" Josh concurred.

Roger scratched his head as he thought aloud. "So there's an unidentified body—a murder victim nonetheless, in a nearby town with seemingly no evidence and no leads."

"This sounds fishy," Josh stated. "It's bizarre how an unidentified body just happens to appear the same time the Reaper is supposedly killed. Either this is really strange timing or the two situations are correlated in some way"

"It does seem a bit too coincidental," Bucky agreed.

Roger gave Josh a wink and a nod. "Josh, have you ever thought about being a cop? You sure sound like one."

A couple hours later, Josh was back in his office. He was grabbing some writing materials, as well as his tape recorder, and stuffing them into a black leather satchel. Josh appeared to be in a hurry, and just as he was about to walk out his office door, Ty strolled in with Mary Powell tagging along behind him.

"Are you going somewhere, Roberts?" he asked in a bellowing voice.

"Yeah, Ty. I'm heading over to Clinton Street. I want to see if there were any clues or information I can use to wrap up my Reaper story."

"Great!" Ty said exuberantly. "I think that's a wonderful idea. You can take Mary with you. She can get her feet wet by getting some photographs of the remains of the building." He turned to Mary and inquired, "Do you have your camera with you?"

"Um, yeah," Mary remarked. "I left it on the sofa in your office."

Ty turned back to Josh and smiled. "It's settled then. You two can get acquainted by going on this venture together."

"Yeah, just great," Josh remarked with a scowl.

Josh begrudgingly left the *Tribune* with Mary by his side and drove them over to Clinton Street in his bright-silver Lexus. For the entire trip, Josh neither spoke nor looked in the direction of Mary. He continued to stare straight ahead, smacking on some nicotine gum and listening to *Operation Mindcrime,* by Queensryche, screech from his custom-built speakers.

Once they arrived, he and Mary climbed out of the vehicle, and within a few minutes, were out picking through the garbage and investigating around the remains of the Buckley Building. The incineration had been near complete, and the burned out shell of the Buckley Building didn't seem to be offering many obvious clues. Josh was quiet at first, still not happy with being stuck with a partner. The lack of conversation was obvious and uncomfortable between the two, especially for Josh, with how outgoing he usually was.

Mary tried to break the uncomfortable silence. "I know you're not happy Ty pretty much *forced* you to take me along, but hopefully you'll see that this could be beneficial for both of us."

"Huh? How do you mean?" inquired Josh, still looking in the opposite direction.

"I just meant we could be a good team together, Josh. My pictures to go with your words. It could be a match made in Heaven. And, Hell, maybe someday, after learning from you, I might just get a by-line of my own."

"Anything is possible, Ms. Powell," Josh said neutrally.

"I'd really like to get to know you better, Josh. I'd like to learn more about this town and the tragedies which seem to have plagued it over the past few years. It seems we're gonna be working together whether you like it or not, and I'd really prefer it to be on friendly terms." Mary paused for a moment before suggesting, "Maybe we should hang out sometime and discuss things."

"Yeah," Josh said as he shifted his glance to Mary. It had seemed that Josh had finally realized she hadn't done anything wrong and there was no reason to hold a grudge. His *real* grudge was with Ty— as usual.

"Sounds like a good idea. I'd like that, Mary."

Mary grinned and left it at that.

"So, what're we doing here anyway?" Mary asked as Josh bent down and sifted through the debris.

"Tim Matthews lived in this building," Josh stated. "Maybe I can still find some of his belongings in the rubble."

"Who exactly was this Tim Matthews person?"

Josh looked up and laughed. "You don't miss a thing, do you? Well, he was actually a man named Matt Timmons. He was a psychopath who'd been terrorizing this town for the past couple years."

"No kiddin'? In this small town?"

"Yeah. Apparently, he blamed this town and these people for his family's problems and wanted to get revenge against all those he deemed responsible—which as far as any of us can tell, was everybody but himself."

"This Timmons guy sounds like he was completely filled with hate…like he couldn't feel joy or love at all," Mary commented.

Josh stopped and thought for a moment. "Actually, I do think Tim had a love of some kind, at least at first, but it was twisted by his anger and rage. He let it consume him. Almost everyone in town liked the guy, and he was very close with his co-worker, Celeste Braxton."

"Oh. I see," Mary said in a soft voice.

Mary was quiet after that, and Josh just shrugged it off. After a few seconds of deathly silence, Mary went in the other direction to look for clues. For some reason, Josh felt better after she was gone. He was trying to give her a chance, an opening to connect with one another, but they both seemed to have different vibes.

Minutes passed, and Josh sifted through the chaotic debris in deep concentration. With no one hovering over his shoulder, he was starting to feel at ease again. That was, until he came across the sight of Jack Lavancha again. Josh shook his head, and then he started to walk over to him.

"What brings you back to Carthage, Jack?" Josh asked.

"Hello, J.R.," Jack grumbled. "A dead body was found near Deferiet. It's a small town about ten miles away from here."

"I know where Deferiet is, Jack. I *am* the local here," Josh said sarcastically. "But what does a body in Deferiet have to do with *this* town?"

"Well, *Mr. Roberts...*" Jack inflected Josh's name with as much contempt as he could muster without spitting. "I want to find out if the Reaper case and the murder of this woman are connected."

"Doubtful, Jack," Josh replied with a sneer. "But go ahead and waste as much time here as you like."

Jack belched as he pulled out a cigarette and lit it up.

Josh smelled something in the air. He peered at Jack for a moment and then leaned over to take of whiff. "Is that whiskey I smell on your breath, Jack?"

Jack glared at his rival but remained quiet.

"Seriously, Jack. Whiskey before breakfast? What could you *possibly* be celebrating to be drunk so early in the day?"

"I'm not drunk!" Jack retorted. "Although it's none of your business, Roberts, the truth is I've been having a hard time since my wife left me for another man".

"Can't say as I blame her," Josh muttered in a mocking tone. "She sounds like a smart woman."

"Screw you, asshole!" roared Jack.

Josh's face flushed with embarrassment. "I'm sorry, Jack. I know we've had our differences since we were teenagers, but...well, *maybe* my remark about your relationship was a little insensitive."

"A little?!"

"Hey, I don't *have* to apologize at all! We may not like each other, but I can admit when I've crossed the line...and I was way over it that time."

Jack's demeanor softened. "Apology accepted, Roberts," he muttered.

"You should live by my philosophy, Jack. It'll get you farther in life."

"What's that, Roberts?"

"Never trust a woman."

As the two reporters were conversing, Mary Powell was about 100 feet away, examining the ruins and taking photographs. As she was strolling around, she observed a short, slobbish-looking man bent over exposing the crack of his ass. He stood up, adjusted his pants over his bulging belly, and brushed off some food crumbs that were hanging from his stubbly chin.

Shamus "Rusty" Hollinger, the landlord of the Buckley Building, was also sifting through the remains of the burned out building. However, he wasn't interested in photographs or discovering any new information about the Reaper; he was collecting the former tenants' possessions which were buried within the rubble. Rusty figured he'd better get there first before the representatives from the insurance company came around to go through the burned out remnants. He took off his worn-out Red Sox cap, wiped the sweat from his filthy forehead, and stuffed some trinkets into a faded green canvas tote bag.

"You can't do that!" yelled Mary. "That stuff belongs to other people!"

"Lady, I own this damn building and I can do whatever I want with this stuff!" Rusty said without apology.

Mary looked at him with eyes like ice but kept her remarks to herself. She gave a huff, stomped her feet, and then she darted off towards Josh and Jack.

Once she moseyed up to Josh, he turned to her and said, "So, did you find anything of importance?"

"Sorry, nothing new to report, Mr. Roberts."

Josh veered toward Mary and smiled. "You can call me Josh, Mary."

"Okay, thank you." Then she glanced at Jack and said, "So, Josh, who's your friend?"

Josh rolled his eyes. "He's *not* a friend of mine, Mary. But I'll introduce you anyway. Mary Powell, meet Jack Lavancha. He's a fellow writer in the upstate area."

"Pleased to meet you, Mr. Lavancha," Mary said with increasingly flushed cheeks.

"The pleasure is all mine, Ms. Powell. And truth be known, I'm actually a reporter for the *Watertown Times.*"

Mary raised an eyebrow. "The *Times,* huh? Never heard of it. Is Watertown close by?"

"It's a city about twenty miles from here. Are you new to the area?"

"Yes, I am. I just arrived in town a couple days ago."

"Well, in that case, maybe you'd like to go out with me sometime and I can show you around the area. And if you're interested, I can take you to Watertown one of these nights for dinner. They have the best restaurants in all the upstate area. You won't find a good meal in this rinky-dink town."

"Oh, my!" Mary stuttered and giggled. "A date offer already? We'll have to see."

Jack looked her up and down and uttered, "You look very familiar, Ms. Powell. Have we met before?"

Mary nodded her head. "We passed by each other at the Imperial Hotel. I'm staying there until I find an apartment."

"Oh, yes," Jack said, fairly convincingly, though Josh could tell by the body language that Jack didn't remember. "Good to see you again."

"You, as well," Mary agreed.

All of a sudden, Josh pulled Mary tightly by the arm and started walking away. "We've got to get going now, Jack. I'll see you around," he said curtly to the reporter.

"Oh, you can bet on that, J.R."

Jack grunted and went back to searching around the debris. Josh and Mary decided it was getting crowded with undesirables and left the scene of the Buckley Building. They hoped back into Josh's car and headed back toward the *Tribune*, leaving Jack behind to deal with the incorrigible Rusty Hollinger.

Chapter 54:

The Terror Begins...Again

That night, Tim Matthews's charred body lay on a long silver slab at the town coroner's. The aging hippie, Harry Moon, and his effeminate-looking assistant, Anthony Durgo, were preparing Tim's body for cremation. Harry shuffled his feet along the floor, dancing around in bellbottom blue jeans and untied high-top sneakers. He had long, black hair that hung down to the middle of his back, but he was as bald as a baby's bottom on the top. He was wearing wire-rimmed glasses over his bloodshot eyes and a worn-out T-shirt with a faded tie-dyed peace sign splattered across the front, which was barely noticeable under his surgeon's coat.

Harry was a former Vietnam veteran who spent two tours of duty fighting the Viet Cong back in the sixties. Back then, he was a naïve young man, full of hopes and high ideals. Ideals that were crushed once he saw the destruction and pain war can bring. After his time in the military, Harry became embittered with the government, the media, and all the white collar workers whose corrupt behavior was only outweighed by their insatiable greed. He returned to the U.S. and became involved in the counter culture at the time, experimenting with drugs and growing out his hair.

Across from Harry was his assistant, Anthony Durgo. He was born and raised in the North Country and looked like a clone of Anthony Perkins; only without the psychotic eyes. In high school, the other boys would beat him up every time they got the chance—for no other reason than he was different.

Anthony wasn't a jock, and he certainly didn't have a man's body either. The boys loved to tease him, calling him a 'girly man' in the hallways and even flushing his head in the toilet during one altercation in the locker room. At five foot six and all of 130 pounds, he was slender to the point of being anorexic. With shoulder-length jet black hair and skin as white as salt, his feminine appearance made the other boys uncomfortable and unfortunately singled Anthony out as a target for every bully in school.

In contrast, the girls in high school were actually quite friendly toward him. Maybe it was because he seemed more like them. Anthony was sensitive, kind, friendly, and didn't try to feed them a line of bullshit just to get them into bed—or so they thought. You see, Anthony wasn't as much of a victim as one might think. He manipulated the girls' feelings toward him and ultimately used their sympathy to his advantage. By the end of his senior year, he had slept with nearly every popular girl in the entire school.

As Harry and Anthony were conducting their work in the morgue, they were also grooving along to some Pink Floyd, *Dark Side of the Moon*, which was screaming over the intercom speakers. They were also munching on some pizza that was left over in the office from the day shift.

"Man, does this bring back memories," Anthony muttered.

"Why's that?" Moon asked.

Anthony smiled, a look of slight embarrassment sneaking up on his facial features. "Well, before I decided to work for the hospital, I was employed as a delivery driver for 'Two Fat Brothers Pizza.'"

Harry's eyes widened with surprise. "Wait a minute, *you* worked as a 'pizza boy'?"

"Yep," Anthony admitted.

"Wow, I'm really surprised."

"I know it's hard to believe I'd have a difficult time deciding whether to work the wonderful hours and glamorous life the county morgue offers," Anthony said with sarcasm, "but before this gig I delivered pizzas for six years. Eight, if you include part time to get through college."

Harry laughed. The two men talked for several minutes, making idle chit-chat in loud voices over the many eccentric sounds of blaring Pink Floyd.

On the outside of the office door, Officer Rick Streeter was standing. Streeter pulled out a bottle of whiskey from his coat pocket and poured some into his coffee, mixing it in for what his grandfather had always called an "Irish coffee," before entering the morgue. This wasn't a normal practice for Rick...at least not normal as in "daily."

But at that moment, Officer Streeter knew he needed something to take the edge off before he entered and saw any cadavers.

Officer Streeter took several deep breaths to calm down and gather his courage. After preparing himself for the sight of death (or at least the best prepared that he would ever be), Officer Streeter boldly walked into the room and said, "Harry, I'd like to discuss the Jane Doe that was brought in here the other day."

Harry stood up to greet him after taking a bite of some cold pepperoni and Canadian bacon pizza. "I've already showed you the body a couple days ago. Besides, you saw the chick when you were at the crime scene."

"I know, but with no identification and still no leads, I wanna look and see if there was somethin'...maybe just one detail that I missed."

Harry wiped his mouth with a napkin and motioned the officer over. "Come with me, Rick. The stiff is right over here."

The coroner led the way and Officer Streeter followed. Harry made a straight line to the sterile metal table holding the body, with the regulation white sheet covering the Jane Doe corpse. Harry pulled back the sheet, and took his pointer out of his lab coat pocket.

"Did you bring your notes and list of questions for the lecture?" Harry asked lightheartedly. His voice had dropped to a normal volume, as Anthony had been kind enough to turn down the Pink Floyd to a reasonable background level.

"Pulled an all-nighter studying," Officer Streeter replied jokingly. He tried to manage a smile despite the last line of the Pink Floyd song repeating over and over in his head: *and the worms ate into his brain...and the worms ate into his brain...*

Harry returned the smile, noticing obvious signs that Officer Streeter was uncomfortable, and being kind enough to ignore them. Harry began poking at the body and started the lecture. "Well to start, there seems to be a plethora of lacerations around the chest and throat areas."

Streeter cocked his head and asked, "Did you say 'plethora?'"

"Yeah. It means 'an exceptional amount.'"

"I ain't stupid, Moon. I *know* what it means," Officer Streeter said. "I just can't believe you said it. Are you planning to write a book or something?"

"I don't get what you mean," Harry said.

"Nobody talks like that, Moon."

"Sure they do," Harry countered. "I used to argue with several friends in college about that word. I always pronounced it 'PLEA-

THOR-A' and they were adamant that 'PLETH-O-RA' was the only way to say it. Sometimes, we'd debate the issue for hours."

Officer Streeter shook his head. "Just skip the flowery words and linguistical arguments and give it to me straight."

"Linguistical?"

"Shut up, Moon."

Harry laughed, and noticed that he even got a smile out of Officer Streeter. No small accomplishment considering they were standing over the corpse of an unidentified murder victim.

"Okay, then," Harry said. "In straight language, it appears someone stabbed her many, many times. At least thirteen. Might be more. The knife used was serrated, so it made one heck of a mess. It's hard to figure out exactly how many cuts and slashes there were."

As Officer Streeter was inspecting the dead body, he noticed something that Harry had overlooked. "What about this puncture wound to her left eye?"

"What about it?" Harry remarked.

"I didn't notice it the last time I saw her body. Her eyelids were closed and I didn't get a chance to do a thorough examination."

"Meh...I don't think it's anything to get excited about, dude. I saw it when the body was first brought in but disregarded it as nothing more than a superficial wound. It could've happened from a tree branch or a twig when her body was rolled down the hill into the river."

Rick covered his mouth with a handkerchief and leaned in for a closer look. "I don't think so, Harry. The wound is nearly perfectly round. It looks like she was stabbed with an object of some kind."

"Hmm..." Harry mused as he put on his glasses. "Well...I can't say I'm convinced with your assessment, bud. The wound doesn't match any of the other cut marks and puncture wounds on her body. It would've had to be a totally different weapon. How many killers pause in the middle of killin' someone and change weapons, Rick? I bet none of them do."

Harry touched the eyeball with his index finger and foul, yellow goo oozed out. The sight was nauseating to Rick who fought back the urge to vomit, and his face suddenly became pale. All of a sudden, Rick felt the whiskey in his stomach threaten to make its way back up.

Rick stumbled backwards as the coroner veered his attention to the officer. "By your complexion, I'd say you forgot to smear on your foundation cream," Harry commented.

Rick glared at Harry as he wiped the beads of sweat from his brow. "Not funny, wise-ass. I think I'm gonna be sick."

"Go ahead," Harry responded with a shrug, not happy with the shift in tone that Rick was using. "It wouldn't be the first time I saw you vomit."

"What the Hell are you talkin' about? I've never once come in here and got grossed out from one of your stiffs before now!" yelled Rick.

"No—but have you forgotten the time I took you on my fishing boat about a year or two ago? You became so seasick that your face turned green and you puked over the side of the boat about ten times."

"What's that gotta do with anything?" Rick responded in an irate tone.

"Oh, nothing. I just wonder how good of a cop you can be if you get sick every time you see a dead body. A habit like that is bound to contaminate some crime scenes. Maybe you don't have the stomach for this type of work, Rick. It could be you'd be better off as a car salesman or something else a little less dangerous and gruesome."

"Y'know somethin', Harry. Everyone has the right to be stupid at times, but some people abuse the privilege."

Harry straightened his body as his smiled faded away. "What's that supposed to mean, Rick?"

"It means your idiotic opinions and smart mouth are exactly the reasons why we don't hang out together anymore. How dare you question my ability as a police officer? And furthermore, I don't appreciate you cracking jokes at *my* expense!"

"I just meant that…"

Streeter cut him off. "I don't care what you meant. Maybe you've smoked too much weed in your life and it's warped your brain."

Harry's cheeks became flushed with anger. "I just call em' like I see em' dude."

By the expression on Streeter's face, Harry could tell how visibly annoyed he was. "I don't have time for this!" Rick snarled. "I refuse to have a battle of wits with an unarmed man!"

Officer Streeter stomped away. Rick exited the morgue in a sour mood, and not just because he hadn't learned a single thing from the morgue. He pushed the door open so forcefully that it slammed into the freshly painted drywall in the hallway, leaving a large dent.

Streeter took one look at the damage to the wall and shook his head in anger. "God damn it!" he roared. "Can't anything go right for me tonight?" Rick stomped down the hallway and began muttering to himself.

Rick slipped a pack of Marlboro Lights out from his overcoat, tapped the pack on the palm of his hand a few times, and pulled out a single cigarette. For a moment, Rick debated whether he should pop in a piece of nicotine gum instead, knowing his girlfriend would not approve if he came back to their apartment with the stench of cigarette smoke enveloped over him. Ultimately, he decided to give in to his cravings and light up the cancer stick.

Rick inhaled deeply and closed his eyes as if he was having a religious experience. "I *really* needed that," he muttered aloud.

As Rick put his lighter back in his pocket, he turned the corner and saw a 'No Smoking' sign on the wall. Rick simply disregarded the sign and rolled his eyes. However, a few seconds later it appeared as though a spot of guilt came over him, because after a few drags, Rick threw the cigarette down and mashed it into the floor.

With one disaster after another, it truly seemed like nothing in Carthage was going right—not in a long time. The toll was beginning to wear on everyone in town, especially the officers and firefighters. Streeter, for one, had been one of many who had succumbed to alcohol in order to take the edge off. Just as Rick made his way to the parking lot (and was certain no one was watching), he gulped down another Irish Coffee, minus the coffee.

Over at the Fasick home, Roger was sitting at his kitchen table with a half-eaten frozen dinner in front of him. A calendar was lying to his left side and the telephone pressed against his ear. He was conversing with Nellie Spencer and finalizing the plans for their upcoming visit.

"The following Saturday sounds like a great idea, Nellie!" he exclaimed. "I'll have the house cleaned from top to bottom and 'kid-friendly' by the time you and Alex arrive."

"Thanks again for letting me and Alex stay with you while we're in town, Roger. I really appreciate it—Alex is *very* excited to see you. I know my folks would rather us stay at their house, but it's too crowded in their little apartment and there's nowhere for Alex to play."

A huge smile beamed across Roger's face. "Believe me, Nellie; I'm just as excited as Alex is. I've got lots of activities planned for us to do together. This is my chance for us to bond and get to know one another."

"I'm looking forward to it, too," Nellie announced.

"If it's okay with you, Nellie, my folks would like to come by while you're in Carthage and meet Alex."

"I think that'd be a fantastic idea, Roger! Alex *should* get to know his paternal grandparents as well."

Roger let out a sigh of relief. "Thanks for being so understanding, Nellie. I think this could be the start of something wonderful."

"Me too," Nellie agreed. After a brief pause, she said, "Okay, then. I guess everything's all set for our trip. We'll be seeing you in about two weeks."

"I can hardly wait, Nellie!" Roger confessed. "Take care and tell Alex his Daddy misses him."

Just as Roger hung up the phone, there was a knock on his door. Since he wasn't expecting any company, especially at that hour, he cautiously walked toward the door and grabbed the baseball bat he kept by the coat rack. Sweat formed on his palms as he gripped the bat tightly. He took a deep breath, leaned toward the window by the door, and pushed the curtain aside. There, standing on his front steps, was Bucky Morgan and Bud Hopkins.

Roger exhaled and smiled. He set the baseball bat back down near the coat rack and opened the door. "What're you guys doin' here at this time of night?" inquired Roger.

"It's good to see you too," Bucky answered back. "I just wanted to stop by for a moment and introduce you to Bud Hopkins. He's going to be working at City Hall soon."

Roger extended his hand. "Pleased to meet you, Bud."

Bud shook his outstretched hand and said, "Same here, Mr. Fasick."

Bud seemed cordial enough to Roger, but there was something in his eyes, his cold empty stare, which made Roger feel uneasy. He disregarded the chill running down his spine and asked, "So what're you two doing out on the town this late?"

Bucky grinned and replied, "Well, I'll tell you if you decide to invite us in. I don't really want to have a conversation on your porch steps."

Roger stepped aside and uttered, "Come on in."

Bucky and Bud took a few steps inside as Roger closed the door behind them. When Bucky turned around, he noticed Roger's baseball bat next to the door. He turned his attention to Roger and observed his heavy breathing as well.

"What's wrong, Roger?" questioned Bucky. "You seem jittery for some reason. Are you all right?"

"No worse than usual," Roger mumbled.

Bucky looked sympathetically at his friend and asked, "Are you still shook up from our conflict with Tim Matthews the other night?"

"I suppose that's part of it," Roger admitted. "I know the ordeal is over, but I'm having a difficult time shaking it off." Then, Roger decided to change the subject and asked, "So, are ya gonna tell me what you're doin' driving around at this hour of the night?"

"We just left Kitty's Bar," Bucky said with a belch.

"It wasn't our intention to stay so late," Bud interrupted, "but there was a party goin' on and people kept buyin' us beer after beer."

"Party?" Roger said with surprise. "What kind of party?"

Bucky rubbed his belly as he spoke. "There was an engagement party going on for one of the bartenders. It was so busy that both Celeste and Travis Kull were needed to tend bar tonight."

Roger appeared confused. "Who was the party for?"

"Gary Wolff and his fiancée, Nancy Nettles," answered Bucky.

"I didn't even know Gary was dating anyone," Roger said as his eyes widened.

"I doubt you've ever asked him *any* questions about his personal life," Bucky stated. "Anyway, it was good to relax and enjoy the peacefulness of a quiet evening. It's been too long since things have been quiet in town. Let's just hope it stays that way for a while."

A little while later, back at the morgue, Anthony and Harry continued to work steadily as the clock was fast approaching midnight. The Pink Floyd had been turned up again, but it was still at a lower level than before. The music was well below blaring, low enough to make conversation fairly easy. As the two men talked, they were suddenly interrupted by a hard, thumping knock at the door.

"Maybe Rick forgot something," Harry said, a little irritated, but also feeling somewhat guilty for having pushed Officer Streeter further than the situation called for. "Go see if he's at the door, Anthony."

"All right, Harry. I'll be right back."

Anthony walked across the polished floor, through the dimly lit room, and opened the door. He stood for a moment, expecting to see Rick in the hallway, but to his surprise no one was there. He walked past the door frame and out into the dark, empty hallway.

"Hello?" Anthony asked, waiting for an answer.

Silence. Anthony strolled down the hallway a few more steps. He looked around, but didn't see anything. After a few more moments of deathly silence, Anthony turned back around, shut the hall door behind him, and walked back to Harry's desk.

"Who was at the door, and what did they want?" Harry asked as Anthony returned.

Anthony shrugged his shoulders. "I don't know. When I opened the door, nobody was there. I walked up and down the hallway, but didn't see a trace of anyone."

"Oh well. Probably just some troublesome rats from the basement, the wind blowing through the broken window in the hallway, or something stupid like that."

Anthony wasn't convinced of Harry's assumption but remained quiet.

"Anyway, I've got to go in the next room and finish completing my notes," Harry continued. "Stay out here and clean up a bit, Anthony. When I come back, we'll finish cremating Tim Matthews's body and call it a night."

Harry walked into the back room and closed the door behind him. "That should muffle the sound of the music so I can concentrate," he whispered to himself.

Minutes passed, and while Harry was sitting at his desk, he heard a faint buzzing sound. A moment later, there was a loud crashing noise. "What the hell is going on out there? Is everything all right with you, Anthony?"

There was no answer. Then, the music on the speakers abruptly stopped. Harry's brow furrowed. *Changing the music is one thing*, he thought, *but what's the cause of all the racket?*

"Are you changing the CD, Anthony?" Harry yelled.

Again, there was no answer.

Harry stood up and slowly walked to the door. He cautiously opened the door and entered the other room. He kept pushing away a nervous feeling, like something was terribly wrong. After taking a few steps, Harry saw the table which had Tim's body upon it. Only this time, there was a sheet covering the body, and a blood stain near the upper torso and neck area.

"What the hell is going on?" he uttered with chattering teeth. "There shouldn't be any blood in his body. Anthony, this isn't funny! Where are you?"

Harry inched his way over to the table and grabbed the white cloth. He took a deep breath, gathered his courage, and pulled back the sheet. In his horror, Harry's mouth dropped open as he gasped in fright—Tim Matthews's body was gone. In its place, lying on the table, was Anthony's corpse, staring wide eyed as if his last moments were among the most terrifying of his life. His throat had been slashed in a grotesque jagged smile that went from ear to ear, and he had chunks of pizza protruding out of his mouth.

"AHH!" Harry screamed as he stumbled backwards, tripping over his own feet and landing hard on the tile floor. He didn't even notice the loud cracking of bone and sharp pain in his wrist. He was too horrified by the site of his murdered co-worker's body.

The stereo speakers cracked and began playing Chopin's 'Funeral March' at a blaring, ear-splitting volume. Harry was terrified, and whipped his head from side to side, looking for the killer. He stumbled up to his feet, his knees still wobbly, and kept backing away until he came to his desk. He fumbled around for the phone and finally picked up the receiver. There was still a dial tone!

As he was about to dial 911, Harry heard a crackling noise behind him. He spun around and screamed like a child who just came face to face with the boogeyman. In front of Harry stood the Reaper—black, intimidating, and ominous, somehow appearing to coincide with the disappearance of Tim Matthews' corpse. It was as if the deceased man had risen from the ranks of the dead. The intruder was a terrifying cloaked form, and its face was as white and barren as a cold winter's storm.

"You will soon know how it feels to have your flesh cut from the bone," the Reaper hissed.

Harry's chest began to tighten up; it felt like the onset of a heart attack. With one hand clenching his shirt, he wheezed, "Wh…wha…what're you gonna do to me?"

"We're going to play a little game, Doctor," the spectre announced. "Unfortunately, it's a game you almost certainly won't survive."

As Harry stood in shock, his limbs were as stiff as a board. The Reaper waved a stun gun in one hand and a surgeon's scalpel in the other. Harry's eyes widened as his he followed the Reaper's hands move from side to side. Mustering his last bit of willpower, he tried to take a few steps backwards in a feeble attempt to flee. After only a few feet of backpedaling, Harry screamed as he tumbled over his chair and landed on his stomach. He tried to get back up but it was too late…the last thing Harry felt was the sting of the stun gun touching his neck and then all faded to black.

Chapter 55:

Carnage Aftermath

In the early morning hours on a brisk August 31st, Officer Rick Streeter walked into the coroner's office. The moment he stepped into the room, Rick was plowed over by a smell so rancid that it could sizzle a person's nose hairs. Streeter paced around without direction, still in shock at what he was seeing. From the moment he stepped into the room and witnessed the degree of the bloodbath, he had a surreal feeling of being in a Wes Craven horror film.

Large areas of the morgue's cement walls were splattered with blood, and several other smeared stains were seen across the floor. The cold temperature in the morgue made the chills running down Streeter's spine even more intense. Rick leaned against a gurney (where dead bodies are placed and stored) because a nauseous feeling was coming over him, but he immediately jumped back when his hand touched a sticky substance. He looked down to see his hand covered in blood. Rick veered his attention forward once again and nearly gagged as pieces of flesh and intestinal organs were hanging from the gurney.

How many hours ago had I been in here? he thought. *Anthony and Harry may not have been the best of guys, but no one deserved this.*

Officer Streeter did his best to appear studious, but in truth it was hard to keep his mind straight. Was the killer actually there when Josh came and inspected Jane Doe's body? Did the killer hear the whole conversation? Did Streeter just barely avoid the same fate as these other two? He inspected the crime scene for a few more moments, doing the best he could to concentrate on the situation at hand and focus his thoughts before walking over to talk to a young black officer.

"What do we know so far, Jules?" Streeter asked.

Officer Julius "Jules" Jackson pulled off his latex gloves and replied, "Well, Dr. Hiam Abyss found the two of them like this about an hour ago. Dr. Abyss said he was coming to speak to Harry about Tim Matthews when he came across Dr. Moon's corpse here."

"And where is Dr. Abyss now?" inquired Rick, wondering a little about the doctor's strange name. Streeter was also curious why Abyss was interested in the deceased Reaper, as opposed to the Jane Doe case they were still trying to get any type of a lead on.

The young officer pointed toward Harry's desk. "He's over there, sir. Giving a statement to Officer Lewis."

As Rick was talking to the young officer, he caught a whiff of something coming from the back room—a faint smell of smoke and ash.

"What's that odor, Julius?" Rick asked, sniffing at the air. "It smells like someone was having a fire around here."

"Harry's file cabinet was tipped over in the back room and the files were strewn about the area. It appears the killer started a fire to destroy the files, but the flames died out before the blaze could spread any further."

Rick nodded his head as he pondered this new development. Although Rick hadn't known Julius long, he trusted the young cop and admired his determination and work ethic. Julius was new to Carthage and had been hired by the police force just a little over a week ago. Chief Zimmerman was impressed by his credentials and letters of recommendation and hired him on the spot. Officer Jackson was the epitome of the perfect cop. Besides being tall (about six feet three) and very athletic, he was intelligent and very thorough at his job.

Julius had trained at the FBI school in Quantico, Virginia but failed his final physical due to an irregular heartbeat. That condition wouldn't keep him out of most police departments, but it *did* prevent him from working for the FBI. Aside from his stellar credentials, Chief Zimmerman was concerned about one thing—why would a young, black man from an upper middle-class family in Philadelphia, PA pick a small town in Northern New York to work? After all, he was far too qualified to take a job as a rookie police officer, particularly with his education and training.

As Julius wandered around Harry's desk, looking for clues, it was apparent by the queasy look upon his face that he was unprepared to witness such carnage. A bead of nervous sweat proved he was shaken to the bone by the strange occurrence—on the other hand, this was a lifestyle that most other officers in Carthage were becoming accustomed to.

Meanwhile, Rick had spotted where Dr. Abyss and Officer Lewis was sitting and started to walk over.

Officer Torri Lewis was a tall, thin woman with crystal blue eyes and hair so light it almost appeared white. Her complexion was generally pale and at times she would be mistaken for an albino. However, her creamy skin seemed even more pasty than usual as she apprehensively stood in the blood-spattered room.

As Rick approached them, he came up from behind and tapped the adjacent officer on the shoulder.

Torri's nerves got the best of her and she let out a slight shriek as she jumped in shock. She quickly settled down, took a deep breath, and turned to face Rick.

"Excuse me, Officer Lewis," Streeter said. "It wasn't my intent to startle you. I hate to interrupt your questioning, but I was wondering if it'd be possible to have a word alone with the doctor?"

"Sure, Rick. I think this is a good time for me to go out for a cup of coffee. I need to get some distance between me and this gore for a moment."

"Take all the time you need to collect yourself, Torri."

Torri tried her best to smile. "I'll come back to finish getting the doctor's statement in a few minutes."

Rick looked the doctor up and down before saying, "It was brought to my attention that you were the one who found the victims."

"That's correct, officer," Dr. Abyss said with his thick middle-eastern accent.

"Can you clarify what you were doing here?" Streeter asked.

"Well, as I was explaining to these other officers, I wanted to take a look at Mr. Matthews's file and discuss the findings in Harry's report. I was looking it over yesterday and there seemed to be some potentially interesting discrepancies. I was personally curious as what the *exact* cause of death was."

"I see," Rick voiced with doubt in his voice. He failed to see how the exact cause of death mattered, as long as you had the corpse of the serial arsonist and killer on ice. "And do you always satisfy such curiosities so early in the morning?"

Dr. Abyss watched as Officer Lewis returned with her coffee and placed it upon Harry's desk. The doctor smirked at the young female before shifting his attention back to Rick. The doctor seemed calm and complacent with the grisly scene surrounding him and undaunted by Officer Streeter's interrogative tone.

"For your information, officer, Harry works the night shift and I wanted to come in before *my* shift began," the doctor stated. "I knew he would've left the hospital by then...and I didn't want to wait all the way until the following night."

"Why not?"

"I was sure Harry had intended to cremate the body by then, and therefore, my visit would have been pointless." The doctor stared deep into Streeter's eyes and uttered, "There isn't anything wrong with me being here, is there, officer?"

Rick ignored Dr. Abyss's last words and nudged Officer Lewis with his elbow. Then he pointed at two officers bending over a few feet away with a plastic bag in their hands. "What're they doin' over there?"

Torri cringed as she replied, "Putting Harry's intestines in a bag. Everything is accounted for except for one finger."

"Finger?" repeated Streeter, feeling himself get a little queasy.

"Yes, sir," Lewis commented. "Apparently Harry's left index finger was severed from his hand and we haven't been able to locate it."

Rick shook his head in disgust. "What type of sick bastard are we dealing with?"

"I don't know, sir, but we've tore this place apart searching up and down for the finger. At this point, I think it's a good possibility the killer took it with him."

"I see," Streeter muttered. "Let me know if you come across any other strange findings."

"Beyond what we've already seen?"

Rick shot a glare back at her.

"I mean...we're doing our best, sir," she responded as her cheeks turned a shade of rouge.

Officer Streeter was just about to leave when he looked at the wall. There was a design of some sort; small yet conspicuous, painted in blood next to the filing cabinet. Streeter took a few steps closer to get a better view.

"That's friggin' bizarre. What the hell is it?" he wondered aloud.

"I don't know, sir," Officer Jackson said, walking up behind him. "I'll take a photo of it for you."

"Thanks, Julius. That'd be a good idea."

"I know what it is, officer," Dr. Abyss spoke up. "I spent some time in Egypt years ago. It's a scarab."

"What's a scarab doing on the wall?" Streeter inquired.

"A scarab is the Egyptian symbol for resurrection," continued Dr. Abyss. "In fact, it's the same symbol used for the resurrection of Christ."

Officer Streeter stood immersed in thought for several moments. He looked around and realized he had missed an important detail that would've jumped out instantly if not for the grisliness of the two murders. The charred corpse of Tim Matthews was missing.

"Where is Tim Matthews's body?" Officer Streeter yelled out.

Torri came over and stood next to Julius. "Um...well, that's just it, sir." Officer Lewis said, looking very uncomfortable. "We don't exactly know. It was missing when we arrived at the murder scene this morning."

"Are you trying to tell me the murderer took a charred corpse and a finger without being discovered?" Officer Streeter asked. "Or are you going to imply that a dead body stood up, killed two people, and walked away on its own?"

Rick glanced over at the symbol on the wall, representing resurrection. He felt chills rush down his spine as he stared at the symbol.

"Well maybe…" Officer Lewis said sheepishly.

"I don't wanna hear it!" snapped Streeter. By the looks on everyone's faces, Rick knew every single person in the room, even the generally unflappable Dr. Abyss, was feeling the same thing. That it just wasn't possible…was it?

As Officer Rick Streeter stood there in silence, several men walked behind him, taking Harry Moon's body out in garbage bags with a trail of blood dripping out behind them. Those in the room contemplated the terrifying, and worried about the impossible.

Over at the *Carthage Republican Tribune*, Josh Roberts was rushing into Ty Harris's office. Over the years, Josh had acquired many informants in town, and his connections usually kept him a step ahead of everyone else. This particular day would be no different. Josh had the scoop on the new story before the rumors had even begun to float out into the community.

"Ty, thank goodness you're here!" Josh voiced, gasping for breath.

"Roberts, what are you doing here," grumbled Ty. "I'm running a newspaper…*not* a jam session!"

"Calm down, Ty. I just got some news from one of my contacts down at the police station! You're not going to believe this, but he said that Harry Moon and his assistant were both gruesomely murdered at the morgue last night, and to top it off, Tim Matthews's body is missing!"

"This is bad news," Ty stated, "though it's good copy." Ty's eyes lit up as he came up with an idea. "Scratch that, this is *terrific* copy. We can sell truck loads of papers with this story!"

"Good copy?" questioned Josh. "What angle do you plan on spinning this article?"

Ty sat up straight in his chair and began waving his hands in excitement. "Think of it, Roberts. Three days after Tim's death and his body mysteriously disappears…it's just like Christ rising from the grave three days after *his* death! Only this time it's a serial killer coming back from the grave, and already leaving two bodies in his wake!"

Josh Roberts wasn't a man who often found himself speechless, but even he couldn't think of a rebuttal to Ty's illogical thoughts. Although Josh understood Ty's desire to twist tales in order to sell more papers, he was having a difficult time understanding Ty's reasoning…and principles.

Josh exited while Ty was still ranting on and trudged over to his office. When Josh was certain that he was alone, he opened up the bottom drawer to his file cabinet, reached behind all the files, and pulled out Mary Powell's resume. He sat down at his desk and perused it for several minutes. Then, after some careful thought, he picked up the phone and dialed one of the numbers listed as a reference on the paper.

After four rings, a gentleman with a deep, booming voice answered as politely as he could and said, "Hello, thank you for calling the *Conan Hills Gazette*. How can I help you today?"

"Excuse me, sir. I'm hoping to speak to the editor of the paper. A guy named Charles Flutie I think."

"This is Charles Flutie speaking. My secretary is taking a coffee break at the moment so I'm answering her phones. What can I do for you?"

Josh stammered. "My name is Josh Roberts and I work for the *Carthage Republican Tribune* over in Carthage—a few towns North of where you are."

"Yes?" the man said in a cautious tone. "I'm aware of your newspaper. Can't say as I'm too impressed though."

Josh let out a nervous laugh. "I can understand your position, sir. Our editor *has* published some questionable stories in the past." Josh cleared his throat and continued on. "Anyway, I'm calling today because we're contemplating hiring a woman named Mary Powell on our staff. As part of my job in Personnel, I've been asked to double check her references. Do you know her, sir?"

"Sure I do!" Mr. Flutie stated exuberantly. "Mary was an employee of mine for nearly two years."

"Mary worked for you for *two* years?" inquired Josh.

"Yeah, I think so. She wasn't here long, but Mary was a great woman and a joy to work with. She had a great work ethic."

"So, she was a quality employee, huh?"

"Certainly!" Flutie replied. "I would be glad to give her a flattering reference if you're looking for one."

"Actually, sir, I was wondering if you remember what she looks like."

The man paused for a moment. "That's a strange question to ask. Of course I remember what Mary looks like."

"Would you be willing to give me a description?"

"I guess so," Flutie responded with slight hesitation. "If that's what you *really* want."

"I apologize for the strange request, Mr. Flutie. I only work in Personnel; I don't come up with the questions."

"Alright, then. Let's see...Mary was a slight woman of average height with light complexion. But then, most people with fiery red hair have trouble getting and keeping a tan," he joked.

"Is there anything else? Anything about her features that stands out in your mind?"

"Well, aside from her distinct red hair, she liked to wear high heels a lot—the taller the better. She also had a fascination, almost an obsession, for bright red lipstick and nail polish." He paused and asked, "What's with all the questions regarding her physical appearance? Don't you want to know *anything* about her work habits, her attitude, or her personality?"

"Not really, sir. You're actually helping me quite a bit. I just have a couple more questions and that should wrap things up."

"Okay, what other questions do you have?"

"How does Mary handle problems, setbacks, and hardships? For instance, did she have a difficult time adjusting to the death of her husband?"

"What's that you say?" the man inquired.

Just then, Josh overheard a woman's voice in the background talking to Mr. Flutie.

"Hold on a moment, Mr. Roberts. My secretary just walked into my office." Flutie turned to the woman and asked, "What is it, Lois?"

"I'm sorry for the disruption, sir, but your nine o'clock appointment has arrived."

"Thank you, Lois. Please show them in." Flutie then put the receiver to his ear once again and said, "I'm sorry, Mr. Roberts. I have some important business to take care of. I hope I've been some help to you."

"You have, sir," Josh answered politely. "Thank you for your time."

Josh hung up the phone and sat in silence. He knew Mary had red hair, fair skin, and wore high-heeled-shoes. Strangely though, Josh had never seen her with any lipstick or nail polish on—ever!

Josh wondered aloud, "For someone who supposedly has an obsession for it, why wasn't she wearing any?"

Later that afternoon, Officer Streeter went to the police station. He was on his way to Chief Zimmerman's office so they could discuss the newest information regarding Harry Moon's murder. He wasn't looking forward to this meeting. So many weird things happened at the morgue, and he didn't even know where to begin. Rick had a feeling that discussing Tim Matthews's possible return from the grave to kill again wasn't going to sit well with the Chief.

Once Rick stepped inside Zimmerman's office, the Chief spoke up and said, "No time for pleasantries, Rick, I'm curious whether you have any information for me concerning the Jane Doe murder?"

"Uh...Chief, there's nothing significant to add to the report I filled out yesterday. So far, we've had men in Deferiet round the clock combing the area for clues. I just talked to Officer Jackson about an hour ago and he didn't have any additional clues or leads to pass on."

C.Z. kicked his feet out from under his desk and leaned back. He rubbed his gray whiskers with one hand and tapped his pencil on his leg with the other. His nostrils flared as he clenched his teeth.

"If you haven't had a chance to read my report yet, Chief, I can brief you on what I wrote."

"Oh, bullshit, Rick!" the old police chief snapped back. "I've already read the report. It contained *nothing*! What the hell do you think the taxpayers pay me to do?"

"Sorry, sir. No offense intended, I just meant that..."

"I don't care what you meant, Rick! The bottom line is I want answers, or at least, some type of deduction on your part." He stared intensely at the young officer and pointed. "Do you remember when you told me you could handle being the lead officer on this case?"

Rick nodded his head.

"You made me believe you were up to the challenge. So far, you haven't shown me much. I'm counting on you, Rick. It's up to *you* to get busy and catch whoever's responsible for the Deferiet murder."

"Yes, sir," Officer Streeter said with assurance. "I'll drive down to Deferiet this afternoon and look around for myself as well. I'll do some door to door interviews if needed, too."

Rick stopped and waited for C.Z. to say something. After a few moments of dead air, Rick spoke up and asked, "But don't you want me working on Harry Moon's death as well?"

The Chief shook his head with conviction. "I'm not putting you on that case, Rick."

Rick was floored by the news. "Why not?"

"You already have your plate full with the Deferiet homicide. I don't want you overloaded and neither case gets solved."

Rick desperately wanted to be put on Harry's death and pleaded his case. "But Chief, we're shorthanded as it is. And with Ken Johnson's death earlier this week, we need to double up on the workload more than ever."

Chief Zimmerman grinned. "I like your thinking, Streeter. If you feel that strongly about it, I suppose you can be in charge of Harry's murder as well as the Jane Doe case."

"Thanks, Chief. You won't regret this."

"Now that we've settled that, I have a question for you."

"Go ahead, Chief. Shoot."

"Is it true Tim Matthews's body is missing from the morgue?"

"Yes, sir. Some people are saying he rose from the dead and killed the two men."

C.Z. scoffed. "I have my doubts about that assumption, Rick. Let's think *non*-supernatural for a moment. My first guess would be to assume Tim had an accomplice, and this person is carrying on his murder spree."

"But from what I've heard, Tim Matthews was a loner. He had few friends and no girlfriend to speak of. I can't think of one person he could've got to help him pull this off."

Chief Zimmerman rolled his eyes and sighed. "Anyway, let's just focus on the logical theories before we go investigating the supernatural ones, okay?" He mashed out his cigar and asked, "So, Rick, what's your next course of action going to be?"

"Excuse me? I don't get what you mean, sir."

"Then let me spell it out for you. What're you planning to do to find out what the hell is going on in this god-forsaken town?"

Interesting choice of words, Officer Streeter thought, before giving the much safer answer of: "I'm doing all that I can, sir."

"Maybe you are, Streeter. You've always been one of the hardest workers here, right behind Ken. But Johnson's gone now, and this isn't a normal situation. I *need* you to do better, Rick. Now get out there and find our killer!"

"Chief, the fact remains that barely any clues have been found at all—at either crime scene! I don't think the two cases are connected, but both have been committed by careful, meticulous killers."

"Well, isn't this just goddamn great!" The Chief rubbed his temples before he muttered, "I came to Carthage from Watertown to get away from scum. Now, here I am...right back up to my knees in it." He took a deep breath before sitting up straight and saying, "As much as it pains me to do this, I don't have any choice."

"Choice?" Streeter inquired.

"I think you need a new job title for all the responsibility you'll be taking on from here on out."

"A new job title?"

"You see, before Ken Johnson was killed I was all set to move him from Sergeant to Detective and promote you to Sergeant. But all that's changed."

"I don't get what you mean, Chief," Officer Streeter said.

"I need you to take over Ken's place. *You* are moving up to Detective."

Officer Streeter was definitely taken aback by his sudden rapid promotion. "Oh my God! Thanks, Chief! You won't regret this—I promise."

"Now then, what facts do we know so far about Harry's murder, *Detective* Streeter?" asked the Chief.

"Nothing much, sir. The place was a real mess. Harry was killed with a scalpel and his assistant had his throat mutilated and stuffed with pizza."

C.Z. raised an eyebrow. "Isn't that ironic?"

"What's that, sir?"

"A coroner is killed with a scalpel and a former delivery boy is suffocated by pizza. Don't you see the irony in that? It's sick, it's twisted, but there's definitely some irony there."

"How do you know that Durgo kid delivered pizzas, sir?" Detective Streeter asked with heightened curiosity.

"He used to deliver to my house several years ago. He used to flirt with my wife back when she was in good health. That is, until I threatened to put a bullet in his 'manhood.' That stopped him from talking to my wife ever again. He was very professional after that."

"Damn, boss. I didn't know you were such a badass!" Detective Streeter said, looking at the old, often jolly looking, man in an entirely new way.

"Anyway, enough about that. Let's move on, Rick. I assume that whoever committed those murders knew something about both of those men and their past. It's not much, but maybe it'll give you something to work with," Chief Zimmerman announced. "That's your only freebie. You're a detective now, and I expect to see results."

Chief Zimmerman massaged throbbing temples with his fingers, and rubbed his already bloodshot eyes. He hadn't had a good night's sleep in days and the news seemed to get exponentially worse every time he did lie down, even for only a few hours nap. He wasn't as young as he used to be, and he knew this wasn't good for his health. He needed others to help share the burden, and Streeter was capable. There was no denying that.

"There is something else you should know about last night, Rick," Chief Zimmerman informed him. "Something *also* connected to the Reaper case."

"What else is there, Chief?" Streeter asked.

Chief Zimmerman bit down hard on his cigar and answered, "There was a break-in here at the station last night."

"Here? Was anything taken? How did that happen? Why wasn't I told?" Detective Streeter asked in a flurry of questions.

"The hole to the underground tunnels isn't fixed yet and someone came through. Whoever it was, they entered our evidence room, took some items, and exited just as quietly as they came in. I told the mayor two days ago we need to fill in all those tunnels, but I'm not pointing fingers. It's not Bucky's fault this happened—all the damage the Reaper caused has tied his hands, too. So, there's no telling when we'll get that wall fixed...but I digress. There *was* a robbery here last night."

Detective Streeter stood in shock. "What was stolen?"

Chief Zimmerman squinted his eyes and said, "All of Tim Matthews's Reaper equipment. The Reaper mask, his stun gun, and the hunting knife recovered from the rubble. All of it vanished."

At that moment, LaTesha Prince walked into Chief Zimmerman's office carrying a medium-sized square package wrapped in brown paper. She was about the only person who could barge into C.Z.'s office without knocking, but Zimmerman knew she was the reason everything ran as well as it did, and allowed these little special privileges.

She placed the 15x20 package upon the desk and spoke in an unusually giddy tone. "I found this on the doorstep, sir. There was no one around, but a note attached to the package says it's addressed to you."

The Chief's expression softened as he cleared his throat. "Thank you, LaTesha. I'll take it from here."

LaTesha gave the Chief a wink and seductively shook her hips as she walked out of the office.

Chief Zimmerman opened the bottom drawer of his desk, reached in, and pulled out a pair of latex gloves. After putting them on, he took a pocketknife from his pants and carefully cut the twine rope off. A few seconds later, he removed the brown paper. All at once, he saw in its entirety that the package was a freshly painted canvas.

But not just any kind of painting.

Someone had delivered a painting of Harry Moon in the last moments of his life. His eyes were bulging in terror, hands held up to ward off an unseen blow from an invisible assailant. And as a little bonus, taped to the backside of the canvas was a small cardboard box.

"What's that?" asked Detective Streeter, noticing the tiny package.

"I don't know," C.Z. answered, visibly shaken. After several deep breaths, he peeled off the tape and removed the box. "I have a bad feeling about this, Rick, but I think it's safe to assume we're supposed to look inside."

Chief Zimmerman's hands trembled slightly as he slowly opened up the package. He immediately took two steps backwards and gasped. Inside was a severed finger covered in blood, and fresh paint.

Chapter 56:

A Lull in the Storm
(September 4th - Morning)

Labor Day had finally arrived, offering a day off from work for most citizens of Carthage, but not for those connected to the Reaper case. Outside, the sky was filled with gray clouds that threatened a cold early autumn rain; but if you looked deeper, you would have noticed that there was also a distraction in the air; not only from the everyday worries and stresses of life, but also from the past months of tragedy. This ranged from the arson and serial murders of Tim Matthews' alter ego, The Reaper, to the recent killings in the city morgue.

For the residents of the village of Deferiet, it was a chance to enjoy the holiday and forget about the murder victim in their own town. Maybe the victim being an outsider made it a little easier, since there was always the chance that the unfortunate incident had nothing to do with any of the local residents.

Josh Roberts and Mary Powell were walking along the street by the remains of the Buckley Building. Josh knew there was little chance he would discover anything of significance since the police combed the area fairly well, and any evidence which might've explained Tim's murder spree was probably destroyed in the blaze. But, with the most recent murders still fresh on his mind, and Tim's body missing from the morgue, Josh wasn't ruling out the possibility of finding *something* within the ruins of Tim Mathews's former residence.

Josh stopped briefly and stood in awe at the sight of the ruins. As many times as he saw what was left of Carthage's oldest building, the magnitude of the destruction had yet to fully set in.

As Mary strolled next to him, she snapped a few pictures to take back to Ty and said, "So, Josh, what do you think is going to happen to this building? I know it's old and historic, but there's little more than a charred frame left now."

"I'm not exactly sure, Mary. As of this morning, the City Council was already planning a meeting to try to decide what to do with the area...whether to restore it, or go in a different direction completely."

While the two *Tribune* reporters continued their walk, Shamus "Rusty" Hollinger stepped out of his house, which was located diagonal from the backside of the building. Rusty was just another run-of-the-mill lazy moocher that people loved to hate. He never had a good word to say to (or about) anyone and he appeared to be in a state of constant dislike of the world.

Rusty was nearing his 50th birthday and was beginning to suffer from health problems from years of lack of exercise and unhealthy eating habits. His Diabetes made it painful to walk, and his 245 lbs put even more strain on his 5'5" frame. His slobbish appearance attracted snickers and heckles from some of the townsfolk, though none would tease him to his face—and not just because his body odor made him smell more dead than alive. Despite Rusty's beer keg belly, his nappy copper-colored hair (which probably hadn't been combed since the original Woodstock festival), and being bowlegged as hell, Rusty was as strong as an ox.

On this particular morning, Rusty bolted out of his house like he was a man on a mission. He had the usual unfriendly scowl on his whiskered face, brow burrowed in concentration on the task at hand. Rusty pulled a tattered aluminum folding table out of his garage and set it up in the middle of his driveway. Then, he wobbled over to the debris, picked through rubbish, gathered a few items, and wobbled back to his house.

Josh noticed Rusty's actions, but didn't think a whole lot of them. Rusty was always in a bad mood, and he was always up to some project or another. On the other hand, Mary watched him more intently, ignoring Josh's comments and staring at Rusty as he set up tables and puts items on them which belonged to the former residents of the burned-out building.

"What's he doing?" she asked Josh, her voice sharp and upset.

"Looks like he's having a rummage sale," Josh answered, seemingly indifferent to Rusty's insensitive behavior, as virtually anyone who spent any time around him was.

Mary shook her head in disgust. "What a horrible, tasteless thing to do! How can he possibly do that?"

"Yeah, well since he owns the building, he feels he owns what he finds in the debris. Believe me, Rusty has *always* been a scum bag, Mary," Josh commented.

"I believe it!" she hollered.

"Rusty's the original tightwad," added Josh. "He donates to nothing and helps no one. Rusty was once heard cursing some kids who were collecting for UNICEF. He said: 'I didn't have any help earnin' my money, and I don't need any help spendin' it, either.' Pretty nasty, huh?"

"Only a prick would do something like that."

"Don't get so worked up, Mary. Most of the people who've had to deal with Rusty have become desensitized to him." Josh let out a chuckle as he said, "Though a couple years ago he pissed off a guy who sent him to the emergency room for twenty stitches and a broken nose."

"I wish I could've seen that," sneered Mary.

"It was hilarious at the time, but the guy ended up in jail for aggravated assault. But don't worry, someday Rusty will piss off the wrong person and get what's coming to him."

Mary was silent and didn't respond, but Josh could feel the anger seething from her. She glared at Rusty so intensely that it appeared as though she was trying to permanently burn his image in her memory.

She's definitely been out of the real world a while if something as little as that sets her off, he thought.

Josh considered making a point to Mary about having to keep emotions hidden in order to be a good reporter, but decided to let it pass. She looked very angry, almost like she was personally offended by his actions, and Josh knew that part of being a good reporter was timing, knowing when to push and when not to. The talk could wait for another time.

Over at the Morgan residence, Bucky was inside vacuuming his living room and attending to other minor household chores to help him relieve stress, while whistling the theme song to "The Odd Couple" television show. Vacuuming was therapeutic for Bucky, and it gave him the opportunity to calm down and let his mind drift.

Bucky was getting the house cleaned for all the guests who were going to arrive later that afternoon. It was Mikey's fifth birthday and a party was just what everyone needed to take their minds off all the chaos in town. After all, any amount of return to normalcy felt like a break, even when his 'normal' schedule was still busy.

Celeste was having lunch at the Superior Restaurant with her mom, and Mikey was playing in the house with his Matchbox cars. Once Bucky was finished with his housework, he removed his apron, put the vacuum back in the closet, and placed the feather duster in a cabinet with other cleaning supplies.

Bucky walked over to where his son was playing, kneeled next to him, and said, "Hey, buddy. I have to go outside for a few minutes. I'm going to pull the Mustang out of the garage and give it a good wash-n-wax job before I put it away for the winter months."

"Okay, Daddy!" Mikey yelled out.

Bucky watched the boy smear the colors of the crayons all over his coloring books. Suddenly Bucky felt sorry that the boy had no one to play with. "Do you want to come with me and get some fresh air? It sure beats being stuck inside all morning. You'll probably be inside for the rest of the afternoon once your party guests arrive."

"Sure!" Mikey shouted. "That would be the best, Dad! Then I can play with my Power Rangers in the grass."

"Um…okay," Bucky mumbled.

As they stepped outside, Mikey looked toward the street and his eyes lit up. He turned to his dad, smiling with excitement, and asked, "Can I go to the green bench by the road instead and watch the cars go by?"

Bucky thought for a moment, looking down the yard. He decided that since the bench sat underneath a red Maple tree located approximately fifteen yards away from the shoulder of the road, it would be safe enough for Mikey to sit and watch the traffic. Besides, Mikey would still be in Bucky's sight, so he'd be able to watch over his son—just in case.

"Alright, son. I've got to put the yard tools and lawn ornaments in the garage before I pull the Mustang out. I've got to make some room to park the car in the grass before I wash it." Bucky gave his son a pat on the head. "I'll only be a few minutes, Mikey, but stay *out* of the road—no matter what your reason is!"

"Okay! I know that, Daddy. Thank you!"

Bucky smiled a nervous grin as Mikey ran down the yard. "Don't talk to strangers, Mikey," Bucky hollered out to him. "Or to anyone else on the street you don't recognize. There're some dangerous people on these streets right now and I don't want *anything* to happen to you!"

Mikey waved his hand up in the air to acknowledge his father's warning. Just as Mikey settled down on the wooden bench seat and placed his toy figures next to him, Bucky's cell phone began to ring.

Bucky rushed over to his phone, which was lying on the porch steps. He managed to grab it on the fourth ring and answered, "Hello? Bucky Morgan speaking."

"Hey babe!" Celeste shouted. "What's up?"

"Oh, hey pretty lady!" he answered in a flirtatious tone. "You sound as if you're in a good mood."

"I sure am! It's Mikey's birthday and I get to come to his party. I feel very happy that he invited me—that he actually *wants* me there."

"And why wouldn't he?" Bucky questioned. "You know Mikey cares for you very much."

"I know, Hun. I just don't want his feelings to change for me now that I'm staying with you. I don't want him to feel like I'm trying to take his mother's place."

Bucky grinned and spoke in a soft voice. "You worry too much, Celeste. Mikey loves you and so do I. Trust me; he *definitely* wants you at his party today. Besides, I couldn't have put this event together without your help."

"Thank you," she answered back. "So, how're things going at the house?"

"Fine. I have all the streamers taped on the walls for the party. Have you got the cake yet?"

"I'm still at the grocery store. They can't find the cake even though we put the order in over a week ago. The woman at the counter asked her manager and he told her the order was cancelled."

"Cancelled?" yelled Bucky. "How can that be?"

"I don't know. All she said was that a tall, older-looking man came in and told her to cancel the order."

Bucky's mind began to wander. "That's weird. I wonder who would've done something like that." Then, changing the subject, he said, "By the way, I forgot to mention that I talked to Chief Zimmerman last night."

"Oh, what information did he have to offer?"

"He was bringing me up to speed on the recent murders—the ones at the morgue. He said there was a painting delivered to his office by the killer."

A look of confusion covered Celeste's face. "Did you say the killer delivered a *painting?*"

"Yeah, an image of Harry Moon. The painting showed him being mutilated."

"I didn't hear about that on the news."

"And you probably won't, Celeste. Its one detail that C.Z. doesn't want leaked to the public just yet. And as if that wasn't strange enough, the killer painted the portrait with Harry's own severed finger!"

Celeste grimaced as an icy chill shot down her entire body. "That's disturbing."

"It certainly is."

"Who does Chief Zimmerman think is responsible for the murders? After all, it couldn't have been the work of the Reaper— Tim's dead!"

"Well, whoever killed Harry and his assistant wanted it to *appear* as though the Reaper did it," uttered Bucky. "But the Reaper who committed these murders did so in an entirely different way than Tim did. Besides, Tim was a bartender, not an artist. I'm *sure* it's a copycat trying to make us think Tim is still alive."

Celeste shook her head, not convinced by Bucky's hypothesis. "I wouldn't be so sure, Bucky. Tim actually was a very creative person. He said his mother was an artist and it's entirely possible Tim inherited some of her flare for the arts."

Bucky let out a groan. "Okay...so, what're you getting at, Celeste?"

"All I'm saying is don't think of him as some dumb country bumpkin. Tim was a diversified person, Bucky. He could make his own fireworks from scratch for Christ's sake! I've seen some sketch drawings he left in his apartment, and I'm almost certain he could've been a painter, too."

"You're right, Celeste. I can admit the guy had *some* talent. But…"

She interrupted him by saying, "And if *anyone* could find a way to come back from the dead to get revenge, it would be Tim."

"Maybe you've got a point, but then again, maybe someone knows of Tim's past. Maybe someone is trying to use that to their advantage and make people think Tim has been resurrected."

Celeste exhaled a heavy sigh, knowing she wouldn't be able to sway Bucky's opinion. "Aside from this new painting detail, is there any *other* reason why you don't think Tim survived the fall or has risen from the grave?"

"The lack of fires," Bucky explained. "Other than Harry's office, no further buildings have been torched. And another thing, whoever *was* in Harry's office did a piss-poor job trying to torch the place. It's not like Tim; this person is different." He paused for a second before saying, "Just so you know, Celeste; this information goes no further than you and me. Like I said before, Zimmerman hasn't released the fact about the painting, or the finger, to the public just yet."

"Okay, babe. I won't tell a soul."

Just then, a beeping noise echoed from the phone. "Hold on, Celeste. I have another call coming in," he informed her. Bucky checked the caller ID. "It's Bud Hopkins. Do you want to wait?"

"No, I'll just see you when I get back to the house."

While Bucky was talking on the phone, a black van with tinted windows pulled up along the curb next to his property—in front of Mikey. The passenger side window rolled partially down and a gloved hand extended from the vehicle.

"Hello, Mikey," a hushed voice said.

"Hi," Mikey replied.

"Come here for a moment, would you, please?" the voice said in a warm, friendly tone. "I'm afraid that I'm lost and need some help," the stranger explained.

"What kind of help, Mister?"

The stranger smiled from under his broad-brimmed hat, exposing his yellow, rotted teeth. "Can you give me directions to the park?"

"I can't," Mikey stated, trying to get a better glance at the stranger, but unable to get a clear look. "I have to stay over here. My daddy doesn't want me talkin' to strangers."

"That's very good advice," the voice said. "But I don't just need help with the directions; I have a present for you, too...but only if you can come over here and help me get to the park."

"A present! For me?" Mikey uttered with exuberant curiosity.

"Yes. It's a special present just for you on your birthday. Please...come a little closer so you may reach it."

"Hey? How'd you know my name...and how do ya know today is my birthday?" Mikey inquired, scratching his head.

"Young man...I know *everything*."

Just as Mikey was walking up to the window of the van, Bucky noticed the boy out of the corner of his eye. He put down his phone and hollered out to him, "Mikey, get away from the road and get back up here!"

Mikey stopped and turned around. "I'll be there in a moment, Daddy!" he yelled out.

Bucky's heartbeat quickened as he put the phone back up to his ear. "Bud, I gotta go!" he stated hastily.

Bucky quickly hung up the phone and returned his attention to his son, as well as the black van on the corner.

"Listen to me, young man!" Bucky yelled in his deep, booming fatherly tone. "You get up here this instant!"

The person in the van hurriedly gave Mikey a small package wrapped in tissue paper. Then, the passenger side window rolled back up, and the van quickly sped off, leaving some rubber on the pavement. Bucky tried to get a clear view of whoever was inside the vehicle, but the sky was gloomy from possible rain clouds and the windows of the van were darkly tinted.

Mikey hung his head down and his shoulders drooped as he begrudgingly trampled up the yard, package still in hand.

Bucky glared at the boy and asked harshly, "Mikey, what were you doing walking over to that van? What did I tell you?"

"The old man inside was askin' me for directions, Daddy," the little boy blurted out. "He was lost and wanted to know how to get to the Carthage Park." Mikey shrugged his shoulders. "I guess his driver didn't know either, but I know exactly where it is. He also had..."

"I don't care what he wanted, young man! Don't *ever* talk to strangers! Do you understand me?"

Mikey's upper lip trembled and tears formed in his eyes. He hung his head low once again and said, "Yes, I know. I'm sorry, Daddy. I won't do it again."

After closing his eyes and taking several deep breaths to regain his composure, Bucky calmed down enough to notice Mikey had a box in his hand.

"What are you holding, son?" Bucky asked. "Where did you get that?"

"The nice old man gave me a present for my birthday, Daddy."

Goosebumps formed on Bucky's arms and the hairs on the back of his neck stood straight up. "Bring that to me, Mikey."

The boy walked up to the house and handed the small package to his father. It was the size of a cigar box and wrapped in smoke-colored tissue paper. Bucky sat on the porch swing and carefully unwrapped the gift. His heart beat wildly as he removed the lid, reaching inside. His fingers trembled as he pulled out a toy ferryboat. It looked carved by hand and very old.

Bucky felt unnerved and a chill ran down his back. For a moment, he was completely fixated on the toy in his hand. Once the shock wore off, he shifted his attention back to his son and stumbled to speak.

"Listen, Mikey, I'm sorry for yelling at you. I'm just so scared that someone is going to steal you away." Bucky stopped and put his hand over his face as he took several more deep breaths to calm down. "Let's get out of here for a little while, son. You're party guests aren't arriving for a few hours; let's go for a ride."

"I like that idea, Dad!"

The two climbed into Bucky's Mustang and drove over to Intorcia's Doughnut Shop. Bucky seemed distracted the entire ride to the establishment, and kept quiet even though he had originally planned to talk to his son. When they finally arrived to the store, they parked in the last spot along State Street, exited the vehicle, and hurried inside to bite into one of Bill Intorcia's mouthwatering delicacies.

Upon entering the old-time establishment, the Morgan boys were intoxicated by the sweet aroma of fresh baked pastries—a smell that Intorcia's was quite famous for. Nevertheless, even though Bill's doughnuts were popular and in-demand throughout the North Country, the décor of the restaurant was far from modern. The doughnut shop would never have been mistaken for fancy; but the cozy, clean, and friendly atmosphere *more* than made up for any fashionable or structural imperfections.

The doughnut shop had been open for nearly fifty years, and during that time, few renovations had been done. The turquoise shag carpeting was old and frayed, as well as stained from many years of foot traffic and spilled coffee. The wallpaper, which had butterfly designs plastered from top to bottom, was still in relatively good shape. Although the wallpaper was once off-white when it was new, it was now stained yellow from decades of cigarette smoke and a poor ventilation system.

Bucky led Mikey along the right side of the room, beyond the twelve square-shaped tables, to the far end of the counter. As father and son sat upon the red cushion stools at the counter, Bucky asked, "Would you like to get a doughnut or some candy?"

"I'd like some candy! Can I have some taffy, Daddy?"

"Okay, Mikey," Bucky said with a sympathetic grin. Then he peered into the large window next to the counter which led into the kitchen area. Bill Intorcia was in the back, tossing some dough while his wife tended to the stainless steel oven baking the goods. Bill let out a yawn and was about to roll out the dough when he caught sight of Bucky. Bucky smiled and motioned for Bill to come over.

The elderly Italian moseyed over and twisted his moustache at the ends as he asked, "How're you two men doin' today?"

Mikey laughed and Bucky replied, "Fine, Bill. How're things with you? By the circles under your eyes, you look exhausted!"

"This is my busiest day of the week. The Mrs. and I always get up at three-thirty in the mornin' to start baking when we're expecting a big rush of people."

"I hope it's worth it, Bill. You look like you're going to pass out on your feet any minute."

"Ah, it doesn't bother me much anymore. I've been doing it for too many years to change now." He gave Mikey a wink and said, "What can I get for you today, little man?"

Mikey turned to his dad, hesitant to say anything. Bucky spoke up and replied, "Bill, could you please get Mikey some taffy?"

"Sure thing!" He shifted his attention back to Mikey and asked, "What flavor of taffy would you like?"

"Um…Teflon," he answered in his shy, quiet voice.

"Teflon flavored taffy?" Bill roared with a good natured laugh. "Why would you want that?"

"Well, I heard my dad say that nothing sticks to Teflon, and I don't want the taffy sticking to my teeth," Mikey said with the clean logic of a young child.

"Oh, I see," Bill said with a chuckle. "Well, I don't carry Teflon flavored taffy, but let me go look and see what kinds we *do* have."

Bucky laughed, cherishing the special moment with his son. But in the back of his mind, he couldn't get Mikey's gift from the stranger out of his mind."

Chapter 57:

Silence is Shattered

The following day, Detective Streeter was sitting with his feet upon his desk at the police station, rubbing his throbbing temples. An unrelenting headache was attempting to break his concentration, but he kept pressing on. His main priority at the moment was trying to get any leads on the corpse in Deferiet—the mysterious Jane Doe.

Rick was still unable to come up with any identification, there were few clues to follow-up on, and the sudden bloody mess at the city morgue had thrown everyone's focus out of sync. Although Rick had been initially thrilled about his promotion (and how it skyrocketed him up the department ranks), the heavy workload and mounting frustration was beginning to take its toll.

There were two new murders in Carthage, no sign of the Reaper's body, and Chief Zimmerman was now experiencing stress headaches. A condition brought upon from the intense pressure to restore order within the community and bring the killer to justice. And if the Chief was stressed, it meant that Streeter was *also* feeling the pressure. In addition to the mounting tension among the other officers, Rick had the displeasure of reporting to an already irate C.Z. that there weren't any encouraging signs in either murder case.

While focusing on Harry and Anthony's death at the morgue, Detective Streeter interviewed Dr. Hiam Abyss since he admitted to discovering the bodies. The questioning had lasted over an hour, but by the end of it, Streeter was convinced that Dr. Abyss wasn't involved in the murders. However, a seed of doubt kept nagging in the back of Rick's thoughts, and he wasn't entirely certain the doctor wasn't *really* hiding something.

It seemed strange how Hiam happened to be at Harry's office so early in the morning. On top of that, Rick thought how convenient it was that Hiam would know the meaning of the Scarab symbol and its connection to the resurrection of Christ. As coincidental as it seemed, Rick also realized that anyone with an encyclopedia or Internet connection probably could've found out the same things. But still, there was something about the doctor that just didn't sit right with Rick...he just couldn't put his finger on it.

Detective Streeter put his hands behind his head and let out a heavy sigh. *What is this killer trying to say? What is the missing clue that links all these events together?*

Rick didn't believe for one moment that Tim Matthews had returned from the dead. The deaths in the morgue were nothing like before, and serial killers weren't known to change their M.O. (modus operandi) in the middle of a killing spree. In other words, a serial killer who stabbed their victims didn't start using a gun, and an arsonist did *not* give up a torch for a surgeon's scalpel.

Whoever the killer was wanted to give the impression Tim Matthews was behind the mayhem and these new murders were of a supernatural occurrence...but that couldn't be, could it? Detective Streeter instantly dismissed the idea. He couldn't let Josh Roberts and the *Tribune* twist the details and spin a tale about Tim rising from the dead which would send the town into an all-out panic. Josh had already shown him the article he just wrapped up regarding the entire Reaper ordeal and Tim's psychosis—and he knew Josh would be anxious for more material to keep his readers happy.

"Damn that Josh Roberts!" Detective Streeter shouted to an empty room. He stopped himself before going on a complete tirade, rubbed his eyes, and walked from his desk over to the coffee pot for yet another mug of day old coffee.

Rick had been working like crazy to get any type of an edge on the case, but nothing was breaking. As much as he wanted to wring Josh's neck, Rick's conscience reminded him it wasn't right to vent his aggravations towards him. Roberts was a good guy and Streeter knew it. Rick's real thorn in his side was that of *Tribune* editor—Ty Harris. Ty was always pushing the reporters for bigger and better stories. At times, Streeter wondered if the guy was trying to turn the local paper into the little cousin of the infamous tabloid, *National Inquirer*.

Reporters could be really annoying, especially the good ones, and Josh Roberts was one of the best. Detective Streeter had to give him credit for that. Even so, Streeter would've liked to prevent leaks from inside the department and strangle whoever Josh's sources were. How Josh knew about the Egyptian resurrection sign and the missing body was beyond him. He just hoped that Roberts hadn't found out yet about the theft of the Reaper equipment at police headquarters or the grisly painting with the severed finger attached.

Speaking of Roberts, that was someone Detective Streeter thought he needed to sit down and have a talk with. Somehow Josh Roberts always seemed to be as informed as anyone else in town, and if anyone had any leads that the police weren't aware of, it would be him. Besides, he was the lone reporter from the *Tribune* who wrote the articles on the Reaper's exploits. Josh was also known to be an expert at research, so maybe he knew something none of the other officers had come across yet.

There was always the outside chance that maybe Josh was involved with the chaos somehow. Detective Streeter tried not to let that assumption creep into his thoughts, but no one would've pointed out Tim Matthews as a serial killer or that the elderly Louis Ferr was a sociopath either. And yet, the entire community suffered the wrath of those mistakes.

Detective Streeter sipped his bitter lukewarm coffee and tried to decide how to schedule the next few days. He obviously hoped there wouldn't be another increase in the body count any time soon, but sometimes with a serial killer, the only way to catch them was to keep waiting for bodies to pile up until eventually the killer makes a mistake.

With a lack of any other options, Detective Streeter decided the only logical next step was to go interview Josh Roberts. Rick leaned forward in his creaky chair and wrote a note in his calendar book to talk to the reporter as soon as possible. He desperately hoped a one-on-one conversation with Josh would lead to something—mostly because the thought of a Reaper copycat....or even worse, Tim's ghost...scared Detective Streeter half to death.

Optimism was in slim demand around the office, and Rick knew that if nothing new came from his chat with Josh, or from the autopsies on the latest victims, all they would be able to do was sit and wait. Streeter hated the thought of more carnage, but most of all, he hated that the department was still severely shorthanded. This inconvenience had everyone working double shifts, irritable from exhaustion, and jittery from fear.

That night, over at Kitty's Bar, Josh sat in a small secluded booth near the back of the bar. A basket of burgers and fries, as well as a longneck Budweiser were placed to his side. A large manila folder lay open in the middle of the table and a sea of notes was scattered in front of him.

Josh was waiting for Mary to arrive. He asked her to join him for a drink, away from the stress of the office, and planned on filling her in on the Reaper case. He figured it was about time he told her everything that had happened before she arrived in town. Then, if she had something new to offer, they would compare notes. In general, Josh was simply planning on bringing Mary up to speed, and hoping to make amends for coming across as a little bit of an ass the first time they met in Ty's office.

It was dead in the bar, especially for a Tuesday night. Since there was only a handful of patrons in the bar, Josh decided to play some soothing music to help him concentrate. He pulled out a couple dollar bills from his wallet and moseyed over to the juke box. After selecting a few songs, he returned to his table to find that Mary Powell had arrived.

"Hello, Mary," he said as he sat down. "I'm glad you could join me tonight."

Before Mary could answer, Mozart's "A little Night's Music" began booming from the speakers.

She cocked her head and said, "Did you select this?"

"Yeah," Josh responded. "Is there a problem?"

Mary grinned and nodded. "Not at all. I actually enjoy classical music. I'm just surprised *you* do as well."

"My dad was a big fan of Mozart and Bach. In fact, my middle name is Wolfgang. I grew up with an appreciation for the music and listen to it every now and then to help me relax and focus."

Once the ice was broken and Josh felt they were both relaxed and at ease, he decided this was a good time to bring up Mary's enigmatic photography skills. And if she didn't respond defensively, Josh also wanted to ask her a few personal questions.

Josh thought he'd catch her off-guard and begin the conversation by saying, "Mary, I spoke to Charles Flutie recently."

"Who?" Mary asked.

"Charles Flutie—the editor of the *Conan Hills Gazette*. He was listed as a reference on your resume." Josh studied her reaction for a moment and then continued. "You *do* know who I'm talking about, don't you?"

"Ohhh…yes," she replied. "Everyone in the office used to call him 'Chuck.' You caught me lost in my thoughts for a moment, that's all." She looked down at the floor while asking, "What did he have to say?"

"Well, for starters, he said that you were a hard worker and a decent person."

Mary lifted her head, looked him straight in the eyes, and smiled.

"But the strangest thing he told me was that you have an obsession about bright red lipstick and nail polish, and yet, I've never seen you wear either."

Mary took a large gulp of her beer and uttered, "Those are childish things, Josh. As we grow older, it's time to put those childish things away."

Josh nodded. "That's true, Mary. However, Mr. Flutie also said you worked there for…" All of a sudden, a spot of compassion came over Josh and he lost the urge to interrogate her. "Forget I even mentioned it. Let's just have a good time, okay?"

For the next twenty minutes, Josh and Mary sat at the secluded booth near the back corner of the bar and talked about the Reaper case. After a while, Josh's throat began to get dry.

"I'll be right back, Mary," he said as he stood up. "I'm going to get us another drink."

Mary nodded as she responded, "All right, Josh. I'll keep reading over your notes while you're gone." As Mary perused Josh's material, she noticed that his article seemed to be immensely biased. Instead of solid facts and quality writing, Josh's raw emotions had turned his Reaper editorial into a slander-filled personal attack against Tim's character and his mental health.

Josh went over to the bar and ordered up two beers from Gary Wolff.

Gary stood roughly five-feet-five and had the body of a young Bruce Lee. His amazing physique was chiseled from many years of wrestling during his high school and college years. Gary wasn't considered a pretty-boy by any means, but his deep blue eyes and confident smile could melt the ladies hearts every time. He always made certain his face was clean shaven, and he never had a strand of his tightly-cropped auburn hair out of place.

As a result of Tim's death, Gary was now the senior bartender at Kitty's Bar. Celeste was still only working part-time for Miss Kitty, basically just on the days when she would be needed most. However, Travis Kull, who had been hired by Miss Kitty as another part-timer, had been bumped up to full-time status due to the sudden surge in business and the bar being shorthanded on help.

"Hey Gary," Josh called out.

"Hi, Mr. Roberts," Gary answered in a polite, jovial tone. "What can I get for you tonight?"

"I need two draft beers in frosty mugs, bud."

"Coming right up!"

While Gary was fulfilling the order, Josh turned toward the jukebox and said, "I was noticing the new selections on the juke box. I'm glad Miss Kitty put a little variety in there."

"Yeah," said Gary. "I can tell by your song choices."

Josh removed his reading glasses and cleaned off the smudges with his blood-red colored silk tie. "Since when has there been classical music in a bar like this?"

"Oh, Miss Kitty just added a few classical songs for the older customers who come in during the day."

"Hey, you don't have to be old to appreciate good music. You should open up your mind to other styles of music other than just Hard Rock."

Just as Gary set the mugs on the counter, he glanced over and saw Adam Richardson stumble onto the pool table. "I'll keep that in mind, Mr. Roberts. Now, if you don't mind, I have some drunken idiots to tend to."

Josh picked up the beer and made his way over to Mary. As he brought the mugs back to the table, the song "Psycho" by Jack Kittel began playing on the jukebox. Josh smirked, wondering if anyone else in the bar appreciated the irony. Based on the bemused smile on Mary's face, Josh figured he wasn't the only one. He found himself warming up to her already.

Ten minutes later, Roger Fasick walked into the bar. Josh noticed him right away and stood up, waving him over to the table.

"Hey, Roger! How's everything going?"

"Can't complain too much," Roger uttered. "What's new with you?"

"I'm having a drink with my *new* partner; we're working on the Reaper follow-up story together." He veered his attention over to Mary and said, "Roger, I'd like to introduce you to Mary Powell. She's the newest addition to the *Tribune*'s staff."

Roger, as usual, made a good first impression. "Pleased to meet you, ma'am," he said in his most courteous voice.

"Pleased to meet you too, Roger."

Josh leaned toward Mary, his eyes now upon Roger, and said, "Mary, this guy is the hero of the Reaper case. He saved the town from that psychopath."

Roger's face blushed. "I'm nobody special, ma'am. Don't let him kid you."

"The boy is just being modest, Mary," Josh remarked. "By the way, Roger, what have you been doing recently? I haven't seen you in days."

Roger, who had been sizing up Mary and her demeanor, shifted his eyes to Josh and added, "Sorry I haven't been around much, but I've been busy at home. I'm getting my house looking clean and presentable; I have some company coming to visit from Syracuse very soon."

"That's all right, buddy. I've been busy myself lately. Training a new employee and researchin' the newest murders have been takin' up a lot of *my* time."

Roger grinned and then glanced at the door. "Hey, Josh, Bucky is supposed to be here tonight. Have you seen him around?"

Josh pointed toward the dart boards and stated, "No, Bucky isn't here...but we've all been entertained by watching his cousin over there."

"Oh, really? I better go see what ol' Red is up to. Take it easy, Josh." Roger nodded politely to Mary. "It was nice to meet you, ma'am. I apologize ahead of time that you got stuck with Josh. He really *isn't* a terrible guy once you get to know him, just mildly awful."

Mary laughed while Josh scowled. Roger was a natural joker, and he always seemed to have a one-liner that was one step ahead of any comeback Josh could imagine—which was impressive since Josh was pretty sharp and quick himself.

As Roger moved closer to the other side of the barroom, he saw Adam "Red" Richardson attempting to throw a game of darts. It was obvious by Red's wobbly legs and constant back and forth swaying that he was already inebriated and very unsteady. Adam tilted to his left side, and then back to his right. He went too far to the right, but before he tipped over, he threw a dart. The dart missed the board completely and wound up sticking in the sheetrock wall.

"Wow!" came a yell from Edgar Polansky. "You got that to stick in the wall! You must be working out."

Adam stood up and didn't even bother to brush the dust and dirt off his clothes. He turned toward Edgar, flexed his biceps, and told him, "The only thing I'm workin' out is my beer muscles. Can't ya see how big my forearms are gettin' from liftin' all these beers up and down?"

Adam chuckled a bit at his own joke before staggering over to a bar stool. He placed one hand on the back of the chair to steady himself, grabbed his empty bottle off the table, and headed straight back to the counter.

It can be said that most of the regulars thought of Kitty's Bar as a home away from home. That didn't change with the population explosion in town, especially since the military base had its own stores and bars. However, in the weeks after John Sears's death, Adam Richardson came to think of the Kitty's as his home—period. If the bar didn't close, he probably would've never gone home.

Gary noticed Adam out of the corner of his eye but did not acknowledge the man.

"Hey, bartender!" Adam bellowed, waving a ten dollar bill in the air. "I want a drink!"

Gary tried to avoid the drunkard, but after a few moments of Adam's pestering, Gary knew he wouldn't be able to ignore him forever. With his eyes flashing with anger, Gary let out a huff, gritted his teeth, and walked over.

"What'll it be, Red?" the bartender asked with disdain. "Do you want another beer?"

"I'm through with beer, Gary. The last few went down like water. I'll take a large Vodka on the rocks instead."

Gary hesitated before grabbing a glass. "Are you sure you *need* another drink, Adam? You've had more than your limit tonight. Why are you drinking so much anyway? If you keep drinking the way you are, you won't live to see your thirtieth birthday."

"Just get me my damn drink, Gary! My money is as good as anyone else's in here. Besides, I ain't drivin' home; I'm walkin' tonight." He leaned in closer to the bartender and announced, "For your information, I'm not lookin' to make it past Christmas."

At that moment, Bucky walked into the bar with Celeste. Celeste noticed Miss Kitty's purse sitting on top of the cash register and gave Bucky a quick peck on the cheek before stepping away.

"I'll be back in a little bit, babe. I need to go into the backroom to talk with Miss Kitty regarding next week's work schedule. Be a dear and go up to the counter to get our drinks."

While Celeste was heading to the kitchen area, Bucky saw his cousin, Adam, drunk at the bar and shook his head in frustration and disgust. Then, Bucky's face flushed with irritation, and he rushed over to Adam's side, grabbing him by the shoulder. He pulled his cousin off the barstool and stood within inches of his face.

"Adam, what the hell are you doing in here? You're supposed to be laying off the booze for awhile and going to the gym with me!"

"I'm sorry, Bucky." Adam's words came out slurred. "I just feel so damn depressed tonight."

"We had an agreement, Adam!" Bucky exclaimed in an unwaveringly tone. "I'm trying to be nice about things but I expect you to keep up your end!"

Bucky looked to his left and saw Gary standing with a Vodka drink in his hand. He wasn't mad at the bartender, he was sympathetic. There was only so much Gary could do, especially with his job.

"Cancel that order, Gary," Bucky instructed him.

He turned back toward his cousin. "Go home, Adam. Get something to eat and sleep it off. I'll be over to your house bright and early tomorrow morning."

"Tomorrow morning," moaned Adam. "How early?"

"Probably around 8 am or earlier. And I don't care how hung over you are, we're hitting the gym!"

Adam muttered something under his breath, but kept his eyes glued to the floor and his shoulders slumped. He nodded his head to the barkeep before heading for the door.

A few hours later, after everyone had left Kitty's Bar, strange events were about to transpire at the home of Shamus "Rusty" Hollinger. He was sitting on his couch in the living room, counting the wad of money he acquired from the large yard sale the other day—the left over belongings from his former tenants of the Buckley Building. It wasn't as much money as he had hoped for. It never was. But there was a nice little pile forming on the coffee table, so it was hard to be *too* upset with the results.

Just as he counted his last dollar, he heard a crashing noise come from the kitchen. Rusty froze and listened for any signs of an intruder. All was quiet except for the ticking of the wall clock and the drip of the kitchen faucet.

After a few moments of quiet stillness, Rusty's heart stopped racing and he allowed himself to breath once again. "Must've been a pile of dishes shifting in the sink, or something like that," he whispered quietly, trying to calm his frazzled nerves.

Just as he was beginning to relax, another crashing sound occurred. This time, Rusty decided to check it out and find what was making that noise.

Before walking into the kitchen, he took a brush from the fireplace, put it back, grabbed a shovel, put it back, and then grabbed a poker. He gripped it tightly and breathed a sigh of relief. A little smile appeared on his face. If some punk kid or former resident was thinking about causing trouble, Rusty was going to give them a lesson they would never forget.

"If I find out who's in here, I swear I'm gonna make you pay ya snot nosed punks!"

Once he stepped into the kitchen, Rusty noticed the window to the back entrance was shattered and the door was wide open. As he crept over to close the door, the phone rang. The robust man put down the poker and clenched his chest, panting from fright. Rusty looked at the clock—it read exactly midnight.

No one would be calling me this late unless there was some kind of an emergency, he thought. Rusty reached for the cordless by the sink and grabbed the receiver, placing it up to his ear.

"Hello?" he softly murmured into the phone.

All that greeted him back was silence.

"Hello?" Rusty asked again, a bit more brashly.

His fear had subsided and he was getting increasingly pissed off by the moment. Little by little, Rusty was becoming more certain that some immature teenagers were trying to make a fool out of him.

"Is anyone there?" he shouted into the phone.

This time, there was a loud crackling noise that blared in his ear—like the sound of a flickering stun gun. His head snapped back from the receiver of the phone, but the sound wasn't going away. It still filled his ears, buzzed through his skull like there was a hive of angry bees going nuts inside his head. It was at that moment Rusty realized the reason the sound wasn't dissipating was because the buzzing wasn't being emitted from the phone. The sound was coming from his own house...from right behind him, in fact.

The landlord tried to turn around quickly, but before he had a chance to defend himself, Rusty was zapped in the jugular with a stun gun. Rusty dropped to the ground in a heap, teeth chattering and throat seizing up as his muscles convulsed. A figure dressed completely in black, standing over the still-convulsive Rusty, appeared.

Though his body twitched in pain, Rusty was able to glance up toward the nightmare hovering above him and speak. "Wh...wh...who arrreee youuuu?" he sputtered out through clenched teeth.

"I am the Reaper!" the being stated in a menacing voice.

Coughing and wheezing, Rusty managed to ask, "Wh...what do y...you want?"

The Reaper stood silent.

"You can ha...have anything I own!" cried Rusty. "Just take wh...what you want and leave."

A frightening laughed echoed through the room. "There is nothing you *have* that I want, old man. I'm here to teach *you* a lesson!"

Rusty began to sob uncontrollably. "Wh...what're ya gonna do?"

The Reaper leaned down close to Rusty's face. "I'm going to give you exactly what you deserve."

As Rusty lay helpless upon the floor, the Reaper placed the stun gun up to the landlord's face and tasered him in the left eye, causing it to burst open. Rusty wailed in anguish, writhing around on the floor. The Reaper laughed again and reached for the poker lying on the floor. In one quick motion, the being raised the weapon high into the air and brought it down with a massive force, smacking Rusty in the back of the head.

The wound ran deep, and Rusty barely had enough strength to cover his head with his hands in a meager attempt to protect himself. While curled up in a fetal position, blood gushing from his face and skull, Rusty whimpered weakly as consciousness was rapidly fading away into the deep darkness.

The Reaper kicked Rusty in the stomach several times before rolling the injured man onto his side and removing Rusty's wallet from his back pocket. The impossible spectre in black then pulled several bills from the thick wallet and crumpled them in its hand.

"You've made a living feeding off the poor and needy," the Reaper muttered in a grisly tone. The Reaper then shoved the wad of money into Rusty's mouth, listening in pleasure as the old man gagged on the dirty dollar bills. "Here you go, Rusty. Feast on your harvest."

Rusty's right eye was bulging out as he choked to death. He tried to spit out the money but was too debilitated to fight back. One by one, the Reaper kept shoving dollars down the man's throat until Rusty's neck was fit to burst and there was no more movement in his body.

"Now then, that was money well spent!" laughed the cloaked figure.

The Reaper stood up and returned to the kitchen. After searching through the cabinets, the dark figure gathered several cans of Lysol, air fresheners, and other household cleaners...and stuffed them into the microwave. Next, the spectre walked out to the garage and looked around. He grabbed a full, five gallon jug of gasoline which was lying next to a busted weed whacker. To the right, on the floor, was a small cardboard box of fireworks. The Reaper reached under Rusty's cluttered work bench and picked those up as well.

With both arms full, the cloaked individual walked back to the kitchen and placed the items beside the microwave. After one more glance at the dead man in the living room, a gloved hand appeared from under the cloak and turned the microwave to ten minutes on HIGH.

The Reaper let out a fearsome snicker before escaping silently back into the night—well before the cans and the microwave exploded. However, the Reaper's actions hadn't been going unnoticed. From the moment the Reaper first passed by Rusty's window, watchful eyes were upon him. Just then, in the midst of a quiet, uneventful night in the community, a thunderous boom and shattering glass abruptly broke the deathly silence and rumbled through the neighborhood.

If anyone ever had thoughts of trying to rescue Rusty, their chances were immediately thwarted when the house burst into flames and quickly engulfed the front side of the house. The towering blaze was already lighting up the night sky even as the Reaper walked down the street, into the woods, and out of sight.

Chapter 58:

Chaos Ensues

The Carthage Fire Department arrived within minutes of receiving a call from Rusty Hollinger's neighbor—Martha Kreps. She was a frumpy woman in her late forties who had been a housewife with too much time on her hands. Martha was nosy, gossipy, and dispensed her narrow-minded opinions way too much. In other words, she was a busybody who everyone loathed. But sometimes, being a nuisance can be helpful, especially when it comes to witnessing a crime.

While washing some dishes in her sink, Mrs. Kreps peered out her kitchen window and glanced across the street. It was at that moment when she saw a flashlight beam sweep past Rusty's living room window. And although she wasn't certain, it appeared to be a cloaked individual inside Rusty's house. She was curious, so she dimmed down her lights and remained close by her kitchen window to find out what would happen next.

Martha had a difficult time seeing anything in the dark, so she went into the next room to get her binoculars. When she returned, Rusty's curtains were closed. Martha was not deterred and decided to pull up a chair and wait to see if anything peculiar would transpire. After roughly ten minutes of nothingness, her eyes widened as she saw a cloaked black figure walk out of Rusty's back door. A few minutes after that, she saw flames from inside the house.

After the firefighters extinguished the blaze, the officers discovered the dead body of Rusty Hollinger. The identification was possible because they caught the fire early enough so that most of the body was relatively untouched. The legs were badly charred, but the fire had not reached the corpse's upper torso. He was found with a wad of money stuffed down his throat, his face mangled, and stun gun marks all over his body. Just like the last victim, Rusty's left index finger was severed off and missing.

Detective Streeter was on the scene, helping two equally exhausted looking police officers set up police tape barriers before any late night gawkers could get too close and contaminate the crime scene. By the time the barrier was up, there was already one familiar face trying to get around it. Streeter groaned inside.

"I don't care if you're Press or not, Roberts, you keep your ass on the *other* side of the tape!" Detective Streeter yelled.

"Wouldn't dream of pissing you off, Detective," Josh Roberts answered, deciding not to press his luck because of the big bags underneath the officer's eyes. "And for what it's worth, congratulations on your recent promotion."

Detective Streeter grumbled. "No secrets left in this town, are there?"

"Only the ones we all wish we knew," Josh responded, still two steps ahead of the officer in the verbal sparring, and they both knew it. "Speaking of which, any early news on this one?"

Streeter looked exasperated. "You're not going to pester me for information like you used to do to Ken Johnson. I'm about solving a case first and answering questions later...especially when it concerns the Press!"

"Take it easy, Detective. I'm not your enemy here. I'm just trying to get to the bottom of this mystery the same as you are."

Rick nodded and his voice seemed less tense. "I'm sorry, Roberts. The stress of the job is starting to get to me."

Josh pulled his pen and notepad from his suit coat and straightened his tie. "Don't mention it, Rick. I had to put up with a lot worse from Ken for many years before we were finally civil toward one another." Josh put on his eyeglasses as he began to write. "Now then, do you think this is another Reaper attack?"

Rick let out a huff. "Look, we got a call from Rusty's neighbor and she informed us that she saw someone or something in a black cloak exit Rusty's house right before it went up in flames. She didn't mention whether or not she saw the person's face."

Josh's eyes lit up. "Have you done a thorough interview with her yet? Do you have her name and address? Maybe I can talk to the witness myself."

Streeter was beginning to get irritated once again. "Listen, Roberts. I'll let you know when I have more information to pass along to you." Then the detective glared at him and asked, "Are you always this big of a nuisance?"

"He is..." a very familiar and unfriendly voice answered from behind. Jack Lavancha walked up to the two men. "And from what I've been told, that's when he's at his best."

The two longtime rivals, and borderline enemies, exchanged less than courteous stares.

"I know it's early, Detective," Lavancha softened his gaze for the officer, "but is there going to be any type of an official statement by the Carthage Police Department prior to tomorrow morning?"

Detective Streeter reacted well to Lavancha's approach, which only grated Josh Roberts even more.

"For now you can quote me on this: Officially we have a murder at the scene of a fire. The victim's name is being withheld until family or next of kin can be notified. The cause of the fire has yet to be determined, although we are investigating the probability of arson, most likely by the same individual or individuals who committed the murder. That's all I can comment on for now, but Chief Zimmerman will make an official statement later tomorrow . . . or, I guess technically later today."

Josh scribbled down notes, like Jack, and swallowed his pride long enough to get the information, though he had no intention of leaving the story at that. He was going to be the first to break this story wide open—and there was no way Josh was going to get scooped by Lavancha.

Jack confirmed the spelling of Detective Streeter's name, and then Rick stepped away, leaving Officer Julius Jackson behind to make sure nobody crossed the police barrier. As Detective Streeter returned to the scene of the crime, Jack pulled out his disposable camera and began taking photos of the house and the surrounding area. Josh clenched his fist, irritated at himself for not remembering to bring a camera with him.

Jack turned toward Josh and smirked. "You're losing your edge, J.R. If you had brought that lovely-lookin' Mary Powell with you, she could've taken some photos for your sorry ass. But that's what you get for being impetuous and wanting to work alone."

"Just so you know, Jack, I *did* try calling Mary on the way here but couldn't reach her." Then his voice became more forceful as he said, "What're you doing here, Lavancha? Did you get kicked out of Watertown for being a pest again?"

"Use some common sense," Jack snarled. "What other huge story is there in this part of the state? My editor told me to keep him updated on the events going on around here, and that's just what I plan on doing!"

"You must have a fetish with coming in second place," Josh snapped back, "since you're always trying to compete with me."

Josh succeeded in getting under Jack's skin, and for a moment, he thought Jack was going to take a swing at him right there in front of the officer. Things were like that between the two men. There's an old saying that goes: 'The oldest burr itched the worst,' and that was certainly true in their feud. The whole mess started back in high school with a girl they were both interested in, and their quarrel exploded out of control beyond that, even long after the troublesome woman ceased being in either one of their lives.

"You may think you're good, Roberts, but all you are is lucky. And someday, your luck is going to run out. In my opinion, you're just a slimy, cowardly, back-stabbing bastard. As far as I'm concerned you're the scum of the earth, and that'll make it all the better when I put you in your place."

"Are you speaking of this story, or are you referring to Lana again, Jack?"

Jack's upper lip curled and he sneered, "Don't you *dare* mention her name to me, Roberts! You'd better change the subject in a hurry before I knock you on your ass!"

"I was eighteen years old!" Josh yelled back, "and if she was such a great catch, she wouldn't have strayed!"

Jack became enraged and his eyes narrowed. "She was my girlfriend, you asshole! I was going to propose to her."

"Then you should be thanking me for revealing her *true* character to you before it was too late," announced Josh. "An unfaithful woman is bound to break a man's heart eventually. If it wasn't me she fooled around with, it would've been only a matter of time before the floozy cheated on you with someone else."

Even in the relative darkness, Josh could see how red Jack's face was, and it wasn't from embarrassment. Once again, Josh wondered if Jack was going to clock him, and Jack was just big enough, and certainly mad enough to do it. Josh noticed the emotion in his rival's eyes, and suddenly, he felt a touch of remorse.

"Listen, Jack, I went too far with that one, but I *was* eighteen for Christ's sake! And it's not like either one of us has seen Lana in years. Is she really worth all this?"

Jack seemed to rein himself in and regain a little self-control. "So I should just drop everything—all the grief and hard feelings? And then you get to walk away with a guilt-free conscience, huh? What I get out of it? Peace of mind?"

Josh shrugged and said, "Well…"

"Go to Hell, Roberts!"

At that time, a flash from behind both of the arguing men caused them, as well as the officer who was nervously watching, to all jump. The three men all turned around at the same time and saw Mary Powell standing there with her expensive Sony digital camera with a telephoto zoom lens.

"Don't think that one's front page," she said with a relaxed smile. "I guess I should try another angle, huh?"

"Mary, what are you doing here?" Josh asked, as relieved as he was surprised.

"I figured that, as a *reporter*, if I just followed the action I'd be sure to find you. And the four police cars and three fire trucks I saw pass by the Imperial Hotel certainly counts as 'action' in my book."

Jack snickered at Mary's remark.

"Am I right, Jack?" Mary asked.

Jack nodded, his temper back in check—at least enough to hide any anger or discomfort.

Mary moved closer to Jack, put her hand on his shoulder, and said, "If I remember correctly, handsome, I believe you still owe me a night out."

Jack winked at Mary with a sly grin upon his face as he gazed affectionately into her eyes. "Well this isn't exactly my idea of a pleasurable date, pretty lady. Let's plan on something a little bit more romantic once things calm down around here."

The flirtatious couple pulled away from one another and Jack went back to writing notes in his pad. Josh grabbed Mary's arm and yanked her to the side as she continued to take pictures of the scene.

"What's with you and Lavancha?" questioned Josh, a spot of jealousy in his voice. "Are you *really* interested in that guy?"

"Not particularly," she stated, "but I figured I had to do something to diffuse the tension between the two of you. I could hear you guys arguing fifty yards away!"

"Sorry about that," Josh uttered in a quiet voice. "I was distracted by Jack's comments and let my temper get the best of me."

"Incidentally, what's with you guys, anyway?" she asked. "I've never heard such hostility between two esteemed reporters before."

"Bad history. Ask me another time." Josh pulled a handkerchief from his back pocket and wiped the sweat from his brow. His voice sounded tense as he asked, "Where were you, Mary? I tried calling your room on my way over here. I let it ring twenty-five times or more before I hung up."

"No need to get all paranoid on me, my dear. I was probably outside watching the emergency vehicles zoom by."

"We need to be able to reach each other on the spur of the moment—especially with all the commotion going on around town. I need your cell phone number, so if something like this happens again I have a way of getting a hold of you."

"Fair enough," Mary said simply, clicking another picture of the scene. "But I don't think we have to worry about the town suddenly becoming dull. It seems to me that *something* will happen around here again."

The hours dragged on until the sun rose, and then pushed on till mid-morning. Detective Streeter had moved from the scene of the crime to the police station after pulling an all-nighter on the case. At nine o'clock sharp, Chief Bernard Zimmerman entered the building and asked Rick to come into his office.

"I finally got the report back on the finger, Streeter."

"That's great, Chief," Josh said with a yawn. Did it belong to Harry?"

C.Z. pulled the file from his desk drawer and opened it. "Yes, it did. But that's not all."

"What else is there?" Detective Streeter asked, surprised at the fact that a severed finger had more news attached to it beyond being a severed finger.

"We also did a test on the painting to find out if there were any DNA samples on it. It was discovered that the picture was done in finger-painting style."

Rick sat down in a chair as a flood of speculative ideas raced through his mind. "That's quite interesting, sir. Did you run a match?"

"Yes, the fingerprints actually belong to Harry Moon."

Rick's jaw dropped in astonishment. "How can that be?"

"Whoever painted the picture, they used Harry's severed finger as their paintbrush."

While the two men continued talking, Detective Streeter informed the Chief of what little information they had on the most recent murder involving Rusty Hollinger. As he finished his account of what transpired, LaTesha Prince knocked on the widow to the chief's office.

"What is it?" C.Z. hollered out.

LaTesha opened the door and poked her head inside. "There's a package here, Chief. It's addressed to you."

The chief's eyes widened. "What kind of package is it, Ms. Prince?"

"One of the officers found it lying on the front steps a few minutes ago. It's wrapped in heavy brown paper and twine. Quite honestly, sir, it looks just like the last package that was left by the front door, sir."

A rush of adrenaline surged through Zimmerman's body. "In that case, bring it in right away!"

LaTesha carried in the square, 15x20 package into the room and placed it directly in the center of the Chief's desk.

They all stared at the bundle for a moment before C.Z. broke the silence. "Thank you, LaTesha," the Chief said, his eyes still fixated on the parcel lying before him.

"You're welcome, Chief," LaTesha answered, hovering over Zimmerman's desk as she waited for him to open the mysterious package.

C.Z. lifted his gaze and shifted his attention toward his secretary. "Is there anything else?"

"Um, no sir."

"In that case, you may leave now."

Although disappointed, LaTesha turned and exited the room, letting out a mild huff. The two men stared in awe, both deeply engrossed in their thoughts. For a moment, the office was as quiet as a tomb. A sense of dread overtook the room.

"Even lying innocently on your desk, it emits a sense of wickedness," observed Rick. "What should we do with it, Chief?"

C.Z. took a deep breath. "There's only one thing we can do…we're going to open it up."

Ever so carefully, Zimmerman slipped on the latex gloves he kept in his desk drawer and opened the package, careful not to contaminate any of the evidence. Once he peeled away the wrapping, he stepped back momentarily and stared in bewilderment.

Inside was another painted picture. This time the portrait featured an image of Rusty Hollinger's dead face with one eye missing and a wad of money protruding from his mouth. Included with the package, there was also another severed finger attached to the back side. And just like the previous occurrence, this finger was covered in fresh paint.

"Is this someone's sick idea of an M.O.?" the Chief wondered aloud.

"I don't know *what* this is supposed to mean," Detective Streeter declared. "How do you want to handle this, sir?"

"Run a test on this painting—and this time, put a rush on it!" Chief Zimmerman roared. Before Rick could take the painting and leave, C.Z. shook his head and motioned him back. "Wait a second, Rick. Before you leave…do you have any news to report to me? Any *good* news at all?"

Detective Streeter thought about it for a second and said, "Well, we know we're *not* dealing with Tim Matthews, so you can quash all those ridiculous resurrection stories."

The Chief was curious and confused. "How do you know that?"

"Rusty's house didn't burn all the way down. The person who started that fire wasn't nearly as proficient with flammables as the original Reaper."

"Rick, have you ever thought that may be exactly what the Reaper intended?"

Detective Streeter squinted his eyes and thought. "What do you mean, Chief?"

"Maybe the Reaper didn't want the fire to consume the entire house. It's possible he wanted Rusty's body to be found before the fire spread too much."

Rick cocked his head to the side. "I don't understand. Why would the Reaper do that?"

"If you remember, the Reaper did the same thing when Father Emerson was killed last month. At that time, Tim Matthews purposely set the fire in the furthest part of the church so the firefighters would be able to put out the blaze and find the priest's body intact."

"I recall the incident, sir, but I don't remember what Tim's motive was."

"Tim's reason was to make it appear as though Thomas Parker was the culprit." Zimmerman paused for a moment before continuing. "In fact, this instance only solidifies my hunch that Tim may *really* be behind the killings. Only this time, it's not so random. He's making it personal."

"What do you mean it's personal, Chief?"

"The first of the newest victims was Harry Moon and his assistant. The place where Tim would've risen from the dead. Then, the next victim is Rusty Hollinger, Tim's former landlord. I think we should start keeping tabs on Tim's former acquaintances."

"What about the dead woman in Deferiet?" Rick cried out. "Her body was found recently, too! How does she fit into all of this?"

The chief shrugged off his questions and replied, "We've already agreed that incident is totally unrelated to this case. Didn't we?"

"Not exactly," Rick uttered in a voice barely higher than a whisper.

"For the mean time, I want to divert our attention away from the Deferiet murder and focus on those who knew Tim Matthews the best. They could either be involved, or their lives could be in great danger."

Rick was flabbergasted. "Come on, Chief, we can't use *all* of our manpower to follow each and every one of Tim's friends."

"Sure we can, Rick. In fact, it's the best idea we have for catching whoever is doing this."

"But most of us are working double shifts as it is. You can't be serious!"

Zimmerman looked him straight faced and uttered, "As serious as you are about your promotion, Rick."

"Chief, you've never struck me as person who believes in the supernatural."

"Normally I'm not, Rick. However, I've seen some fairly strange things in the upstate area during my years on the police force—both in Watertown and here in Carthage. Not to mention, I've read the case file on Louis Ferr and the Ferryman incident which occurred in Carthage several years ago. After reviewing that information and talking to Bucky Morgan about what transpired, I don't disbelieve anything anymore."

"You may be right, Chief. But with all due respect, I still think we have a copycat killer on our hands."

Chief Zimmerman nodded. "Well...we always have to assume that whenever a case like this occurs. However, with the recent events and lack of solid clues, I'm not totally convinced...but keep working on that theory anyway. Whoever or whatever is behind the murders, the bastard is going to make a mistake sometime, and when he does, I want to nail the S.O.B.!"

PART THREE:
Legacy of the Reaper

Chapter 59:

The Compulsion for truth

More than two weeks had passed since the fire at the Buckley Building, and Thomas Parker had not spoken a word. On the night of the Buckley Building blaze, the police had found Thomas on the street in an almost catatonic state of mind. Once his wounds were treated and he was released from the hospital, Thomas was escorted home by the police and released into the care of his wife, Stacey.

Several days later, Thomas had yet to leave his property. On the rare occasion that Thomas got out of bed and stepped outside his home, he only went as far as his workshop, and then he rarely did anything—just kept staring in silence. Because of his odd behavior and his presence at the Buckley Building during Tim's death, Thomas's name was circulated once again as a suspect. In an effort to determine Thomas's sanity, an officer was assigned to track his moves and keep a watchful eye on his house at all times.

Thomas wasn't the only person still being steadily affected by that horrific night. Roger Fasick had quit his job as an investigator with the local law firm and was contemplating opening his own Private Investigator business in town. Ever since the night at the Buckley Building, Roger carried a gun with him everywhere he went. After the incident with the Ferryman several years back, and now the Reaper, Roger didn't feel as though he could function without a pistol close by. He would get the shakes in public, and see shady cloaked figures in the darkness whenever he turned around. Roger appeared as though he was constantly on edge; as if he was a time bomb waiting to explode.

On the other hand, Bucky had adjusted fairly well following the grisly events, and was trying to get a sense of normalcy back to his life. Mikey was beginning kindergarten and Bucky had to focus on getting his little boy dressed, fed, and ready for school every day. This was an important time in Mikey's life, and he couldn't waste time dwelling on his confrontation with Tim Matthews or the terror Tim had inflicted on the town.

Bucky was finally learning to cope with Cristina's passing, even though he still felt no closure regarding her death. Unlike Holly Boliver's murder, Tim had admitted to Celeste that he was *not* responsible for Cristina's demise. This fact weighed heavily on Bucky's thoughts, and he vowed that someday he'd track down the person accountable for his wife's hit and run accident.

Although Bucky still visited Cristina's grave every night on his way home from work, he was now willing to give into his feelings and let his relationship with Celeste mature and grow. Within days of admitting his love for Celeste, Bucky had asked her to move into his house so they could attempt to take their relationship to the next level—and she accepted.

Just like Thomas and Roger, Celeste Braxton also felt the effects from that horrible night. Since being held hostage atop of the flaming building by Tim Matthews, Celeste had trouble sleeping. Even though she felt safe in Bucky's home, Celeste was as jumpy as a cat on a hot tin roof. As a result, she spent almost every waking moment in his den working on her ferryman manuscript. Maybe it was a way to forget about her ordeal with Tim, or maybe it was a way to help calm her nerves, but whatever it was, Celeste was filled with ideas and kept writing nonstop.

In just over a week's time, Celeste had finished the remaining chapters to her newest mystery novel. She gathered up all her material, packaged it in a large yellow envelope, and sent the rough draft off to her publisher for perusal. With the completion of her manuscript, Celeste felt as though she had at least something positive to show for the ordeal she had been through. However, she would gladly have traded a few pages a day for less insomnia, and dreams that didn't end up as ominous omens or straight out terrifying nightmares.

It was approximately 9 am on Monday, September 11 at the Morgan residence, and Celeste was in the kitchen. She paced back-and-forth as she talked on the phone to her publishing company regarding her novel. After nearly an hour of talking shop, in addition to acquiring some painful shin splints from all her nervous pacing, she ended her call with Editor-in-Chief, Jody Monaghan. Celeste wrote something down on a notepad, tore off the sheet, and strolled into Bucky's den as he was getting his briefcase situated before leaving for work.

She plopped down in one of his black leather recliners and spoke in a laid-back tone, "Well, babe, my editor gave me an update on the manuscript I sent him."

"Oh yeah? Is Monaghan criticizing your writing again, or is he finally giving you the respect you deserve?"

"Aww...you're sweet," Celeste said lovingly. "Now quiet and shut up! First of all, he said that the last few chapters are excellent."

"No kiddin'? He actually used the word 'excellent'?"

"Yeah, but he also had some bad news."

Bucky snorted. "Of course he did."

"Jody said the last six chapters are perfect. I don't have to do a thing to change them...it's just that he wants me to do a short revision on the first fourteen."

Bucky's jaw dropped. "Whoa...what do you think about that?"

"I don't want to," groaned Celeste. "It'll take me months to complete it."

With a nod, Bucky replied, "I can understand your frustration, babe. I think you should tell 'em to take a hike."

Celeste raised a brow. "Y'know, I'm seriously thinking about it. He also believes it'd be best to change the title of my book."

Bucky shifted his glance toward her as he snapped his briefcase shut. "So...it won't be 'Beware of the Ferryman' anymore?"

Shaking her head with a sigh, she replied, "No, but my editor gave me two other alternatives." Celeste held out a piece of notebook paper with some words scribbled upon it. "Listen to this and tell me what you think. Tell me the first thing that comes to mind. I want your honest opinion."

Bucky stopped puttering around and his eyes met with hers. "Okay, you've got my undivided attention. Go ahead and lay it on me."

Celeste cleared her throat before reading it aloud. "The first one is, 'The Carthage Chronicles.' And I can pick that choice if I want to put more emphasis on the town aspect."

"That one is pretty cool, but also kinda bland," Bucky uttered with a slight grimace. "It works because the title tells the reader where the events take place, but it doesn't really allude too much of what the story's about."

"I agree," Celeste concurred. "The other title Jody suggested is, 'Don't Pay the Ferryman'. He told me to pick that one if I want to put more emphasis on the villain."

"Well, that one sounds menacing and it's very similar to your original title. Overall, I think it's a good title, but on the other hand, I *do* like the fact that the first option mentions Carthage in the title of the story. Is there any way you can combine the two titles somehow?"

Celeste jotted down Bucky's suggestion on her paper. "I don't know if they'll let me, Bucky, but that's not a bad idea. I'll have to look into it. Besides, we have plenty of time to haggle over the title. It might take a year or more before the book is on the shelves."

"A year!" Bucky gasped. "Why so long?"

"That's usually how long it takes before the manuscript is pristine and ready for print. There are many stages in the publishing process— such as revisions, edits, creating a cover design, and developing a market strategy."

"Oh, I had no idea it was so complicated."

"It's not as simple as you think. If it was, there wouldn't be any need for agents or editors." She paused as Bucky grabbed his long, black wool coat off his chair and slipped it on. "Speaking of stories, have you been reading the articles by Josh Roberts on the newest murders going on in town right now? Half the time I can't tell if I'm reading news or a horror novel."

Bucky smiled at her and nodded in agreement. "That probably has as much to do with Josh's editor as anything else. Ty Harris always tries to add some sensationalism into the paper. The other reason is that evidently there's just a lot of weird stuff going on with this new series of murders."

"So much for trying to downplay the events so the public doesn't become paranoid all over again."

"You got that right," Bucky agreed. "But, then again, Ty has never been one for tact."

Celeste exhaled loudly and asked, "Is this town cursed, or something?"

Bucky thought before answering. "Plenty of weird things have happened, that's for sure, but my father had a saying about curses: 'Curses are for Cubs and Phillies fans, and for keeping kids out of dangerous places, not for rational people.'"

Celeste laughed in response. "Yeah, I guess you're right. It does seem like a lot of crazy stuff happens here, though. Not a lot of it rational, either."

Bucky grabbed his briefcase, gave Celeste a kiss, and headed for the door. "That's true. Hopefully the police figure out the culprit behind these new murders...and soon. I hate the idea of another killer terrorizing our community. This town *needs* some peace!"

"You ain't kiddin', babe!" She stood up as Bucky grabbed the door handle. "What're you going to do today, Hun? Do you wanna get together for lunch at the Superior Restaurant?"

With a frown, Bucky responded, "I wish I could, but I probably won't have time to leave the office today. I have a meeting with Bud Hopkins in about an hour. We're going to discuss a job position at City Hall for him."

Celeste smiled proudly and said, "I think it's wonderful how you want to help Bud get acclimated back into society, Bucky. Not many people in your position would take two seconds out of their busy schedule just to give him the time of day."

Bucky grinned. "You have such a high opinion of politicians, Celeste. I don't know *how* you put up with me."

She blushed. "Well, I'm kinda fond of you, that why."

"Gee...thanks babe."

"So, have you decided which department do you plan on putting him in?"

Bucky nodded. "I've given this some careful thought, and I believe I've finally come up with the most logical choice."

"Which is...?" prodded Celeste.

"Being as how Bud isn't exactly a people person, I was thinking of trying him out in the Historical Records wing on the second floor. No one *ever* goes in there for anything. That way, I don't have to worry about Bud offending anyone."

Josh Roberts was sitting in a corner booth at Intorcia's Doughnut Shop, having a cup of Hazelnut coffee with Mary Powell. They were comparing their compiled rumors and notes, once again, on the recent happenings in Reaper case. Josh had to hand it to Mary, she was a quick study, and she seemed to be working her butt off to get photographs, interviews, and all other information they needed.

While she had her nose buried in her notepad, Josh took a sip of his coffee and said, "I'm not going to be around this afternoon, Mary. Apparently, Detective Streeter wants to ask me a few questions down at the station."

Mary quickly lifted her head and peered at him with wide eyes. "He doesn't think you're involved with these murders or anything, does he?"

601

"I don't think so," Josh replied, taking a bite of his plump, moist glazed doughnut. "However, if Streeter thinks this killer really *is* a copycat, then there probably isn't a 'non-cop' in this town who knows more about the Reaper or his M.O. then I do. Therefore, I guess by default, that would make me a suspect in this case until the cops find something to say otherwise."

"You're a reporter! It's your job to know a lot about the Reaper, isn't it?" questioned Mary.

"Yeah. More than likely, Rick just wants to see if I got any news the cops don't have yet. And if I'm lucky, he might be willing to feed me a few scraps for the article...and that's only *IF* I can provide him with some info. or connections he hasn't uncovered yet. Reporters and cops, Mary...we try to mutually help one another out, y'know."

Josh took another sip of coffee before continuing. "Those were good pictures of Rusty's house, Mary—especially having to work in the dark."

"Thank you, Josh," Mary said, slightly surprised at Josh's compliment. "That's very nice to say."

Josh swallowed hard before saying, "I'm sorry if I came across as a jerk the first time we met. Ty and I don't always get along, and it was more my frustration with him. No offense to you."

"None taken," Mary answered pleasantly.

"So...I, uh, was wondering..." Josh's words trailed off.

"Wondering what?"

Josh began fidgeting with his hands. "Did, um, you and Lavancha have that romantic rendezvous yet?"

Mary laughed exuberantly. "No, not yet. I don't know if we'll *ever* go out for a drink. Honestly, I wasn't all that serious anyway." Just then, a thought came to mind. "By the way, Josh, what's the beef between you two guys, anyway?"

Josh raised an eyebrow as he said, "We have a rock-kite relationship. I'm the rock; he's the kite."

"I'm being serious," Mary retorted. "Remember, Josh, you promised you'd tell me if I asked later. This *is* later."

Josh looked around, seeing if anyone else was listening to their conversation, but the place was empty. He couldn't think of a good excuse to wriggle out of answering her question, but at least there wasn't anyone nearby to overhear.

"It basically all goes back to a girl," Josh revealed.

"I should've known," Mary remarked. "It *always* has something to do with a woman!"

Josh cleared his throat and continued. "Don't get me wrong, Mary, there have been *many* other issues between Jack and I as well."

"Sure...like what?" scoffed Mary.

"Well, there've been jobs we both competed for; we attended rival colleges, and our feud has led to some missed opportunities in our careers."

Mary was starting to realize the degree of their feud. "Ohhh...I didn't know it was like that!"

"Like I said, there have been *a lot* of incidents between us...so many reasons for our rivalry, and yet, it all started with a girl named Lana."

"What a pretty name," Mary commented.

Josh nodded. "Jack and I have known each other since we were six years old. His grandparents were my neighbors and Jack visited them often. Back then, we were as close as brothers. We would build club houses in my back yard and get together to watch our favorite television shows at night."

A slight grin appeared on Mary's face. "Aww, isn't that cute. I bet you two were adorable."

"Um, I guess so. We got along so well because we were both interested in WWF Wrestling, the A-Team, Knight Rider, and Simon & Simon. During that time in our lives, we would've *never* let a woman come between us."

"I don't understand," Mary said with hesitation. "What happened to change all that?"

"Over time, Jack stopped visiting his grandparents on the weekends and we drifted apart. That was the turning point which would forever change our friendship."

"So...what happened after that? Did you guys not cross paths again until the whole mess erupted with Lana?"

"Actually, Mary, we saw each other again a few years later. As fate would have it, Jack and I attended the same high school for a couple years—back when I was living at my father's place in Watertown. My parents divorced after my freshman year and I transferred from Carthage High. I was the new kid on campus trying to fit in and make friends, and then my eye caught the attention of a girl. A breath of fresh air named Lana Sullivan. Unfortunately, she already had a boyfriend."

"Was it Jack?" inquired Mary.

"Yeah," Josh groaned. "And even though Jack and I weren't enemies at that time, he sure let me know that Lana was off limits. She and Jack had been going out for two and a half or three years…something like that. In high school, that would be considered an eternity."

Mary listened attentively to his words as Josh rambled on, staring out into nothingness.

"Lana was a stunning girl with bright blue eyes, long, flowing dark hair, a radiant smile, and the best pair of legs I've ever seen. She was as flawless as a magazine cover girl," Josh said as his expression softened. "She resembled a young Linda Carter from the Wonder Woman television series of the seventies."

Mary giggled at Josh's comparison.

"You could tell every guy in that school was infatuated with her. Every time she walked down the hallway, men's mouths dropped open and their eyes would become transfixed. I was completely in awe myself and she knew it. Lana flirted with me from time to time, sometimes right in front of Jack, but it was harmless. However, aside from those few conversations we had at our lockers, she never seemed all that interested in me." Josh paused and looked Mary directly into the eyes. "In fact, when I first met Lana, I intentionally refrained from making a pass at her out of respect to Jack."

Mary seemed confused. "If that's all there is to it, why is there so much bad blood between you two?"

"Oh no, Mary. There's more to the story…much more. Apparently, at some point during prom night, Jack and Lana got into a huge argument…and the long and short of it is that Lana came to me for consoling. Looking back on it now, she probably did it to get even with Jack for making out with her cousin. I heard she caught them underneath the bleachers after he was drunk from the pre-prom party."

"What do you mean by 'consoling,' Josh?"

"Listen, Mary. I was eighteen and immature. Jack and I may not have been enemies, but we weren't exactly friends anymore either." Josh took a deep breath and admitted, "I did what any other eighteen year old boy with raging hormones would do—I had sex with her."

Mary's expression turned to sadness once she heard Josh's admission. "Was it a one-time thing?"

"No. She led me on for a few weeks, all physical of course. I think she kept it going just to torment Jack. I didn't care; I couldn't say no to her."

Josh paused again. By the expression on his face, it appeared as though he was uncomfortable telling Mary all the humiliating details.

"That's one chapter of my life that I actually *do* regret. I can tell myself that was a kid and she was gorgeous, but that's still no excuse for my behavior. Even though Jack and I had drifted apart, it was wrong for me to do that to him."

"I think it's very noble of you to be able to look back at your life and admit your mistakes."

"Thank you, Mary. I still feel awfully bad because I think Jack was really head over heels in love with her. I don't know if Lana ever felt the same way back—if she did, she didn't show it." He let out a sigh. "Anyway, that's what started the feud between us. Jack and I got into a major fist fight and both of us were suspended. Ever since that time, it seems like we're always stepping on each other's feet. Plenty more incidents transpired over the years, but it all started with Lana."

"All that animosity because of some girl you both liked a couple decades ago?" Mary asked.

"Pretty much," Josh replied with a shrug. "It's at the point now where neither one of us can stand each other. And to make matters worse, we're both working in the writing field, covering the same stories for rival papers. It reminds me of a surreal yin-yang type thing."

"So that's why you guys are always at each other's throats," Mary said with clarity. "Have you ever thought about just leaving the area so you don't have to deal with it?"

Josh shrugged. "This place is home for me, just like it is for him. I think both of us just deal with it."

Mary was silent. They both sat staring straight ahead, drinking their coffee and enjoying the silence.

After a few minutes, Josh glanced at his wristwatch and said, "Well, I'd better head down to the station now, Mary. If I don't talk to you tonight, I'll catch up with you at work tomorrow."

Mary nodded, remaining strangely quiet as Josh left the doughnut shop, heading down the street for the police station and Detective Streeter's questioning.

Meanwhile, over at Kitty's Bar, Miss Kitty and Travis Kull were busy serving drinks, restocking their supplies, and preparing snacks for the customers. It had been somewhat of a busy night at the bar, and even though Travis was a relatively new hire, he handled the steady influx of drunken patrons like a seasoned bartender.

Travis had a long, wiry frame with elongated ears and light brown hair styled into a mullet. He was a former track star in college and barely carried more than 165 lbs on his 6'3" frame. Although Travis wasn't much of a drinker, he enjoyed working as a bartender since it gave him a chance to earn extra cash to put toward his soaring student loans. Travis also enjoyed working the night shift because it freed up his days, giving him the valuable time he needed to train for the New York Marathon.

On this particular night, Travis was at the far side of the bar preparing some chicken wings for the customers. The sweat was accumulating on his brow as he hovered over the hot mini fryer that Miss Kitty had set up next to the cash register. Over at the other end of the bar, Roger Fasick had wandered into the establishment and plunked down on one of the cushioned stools. He was sipping on a longneck bottle, talking to Miss Kitty about the events going on in his life as well as everything that was happening around town.

"I don't know what to believe anymore, Roger," Miss Kitty muttered, seemingly distressed. "I mean, whenever we think the worst is over for this town, something else comes along more evil than the last."

"Things will get better, Miss Kitty. They have to. No town can be cursed forever."

"Do you honestly believe that, Roger?"

"I have to, Miss Kitty. It's the only thing that keeps me going anymore."

Miss Kitty put her hand upon Roger's and said, "You were there at the Buckley Building, Roger. What's your opinion about the recent Reaper murders? Do you think Tim...I mean, Matthew Timmons is responsible." She shook her head in dismay. "I still have a difficult time getting used to that name."

Roger thought of how he let go of Tim's hand and watched him fall to his death, but decided not to mention it. "I honestly don't know what to think about the newest murders, Miss Kitty. It has me just as puzzled as everyone else."

Miss Kitty stepped back and looked intently into his eyes. "Do you think he's been resurrected like people around town have been saying? And if so, is Tim going to get revenge on those who he feels wronged him in some way?"

"I wish I had some answers for you, Miss Kitty. There are many nutcases in the world and they all seem to flock to Carthage. I wouldn't put it past someone to take up the guise of the Reaper...but to take Tim's body, too? That doesn't make sense."

Miss Kitty had fear in her eyes. "So there's either a sicko out there that's chillin' with Tim's dead corpse, or Tim Matthews has become the *real* Grim Reaper of Death."

"I know the idea seems impossible, but I had a run-in with Louis Ferr and lived to talk about it. I know there're supernatural beings in the world. And believe me, they *can* be dangerous, too."

Just then, the ever robust Edgar Polansky sauntered over, dropped his fat ass on a bar stool next to Roger, and interrupted the conversation. "I hear you two are talking about the Matthews kid."

"Yes we were," replied Miss Kitty tensely. "Do you have something to say about him, Edgar?"

Edgar glanced at her smugly. "I was just thinking how strange it is...him being resurrected after three days and all."

Roger rolled his eyes. "Now Edgar, there isn't any proof that he has risen from the grave."

"That's true, Edgar. Right now, everything is still just speculation."

"Just hear me out, Miss Kitty. Do you know who else rose from the dead after three days?"

"Who?" Roger and Miss Kitty said at the same time.

"Christ did," Edgar stated as he puffed out his chest.

Miss Kitty gasped. "Edgar, I hope you're not comparing Tim Matthews to Jesus Christ!"

"Not at all, ma'am. I just think it's a damn shame how out of *all* the people that could've come back from the dead, we had to have a serial killer be the lucky one."

Miss Kitty put her hand to her mouth and stared straight ahead. "I've prayed for this town. Prayed for an end to the horror and for a better tomorrow." She paused before returning her attention to the men sitting in front of her. "I may not be a practicing Christian, but I believe having a saintly figure like Jesus Christ would've been a better choice for resurrecting."

"Nah," uttered Edgar. "There are other people more popular than Christ. I'm sure the public would rather have someone else resurrected instead of him."

"Like who?" interrupted Roger. "Look around, Edgar. No one in this joint is going to go along with your ridiculous and illogical thinking."

"Is that so?" he retorted in a condescending tone.

Edgar turned and saw a strange woman sitting alone at a nearby table sipping a dry martini. She appeared to be in her late forties with short blond hair, large blue eyes, and dressed to the nines.

"Hey, lady!" shouted Edgar.

"Yes?" the woman answered in a soft impish voice.

Edgar whirled around on his bar stool and faced the woman. "Let me ask you a question. Who would you rather resurrect from the dead: Jesus Christ or Princess Di?"

The woman's eyes lit up as she smiled proudly and replied, "Ohhhh, I'd pick Diana for sure, sir."

"Thank you, ma'am. That's all I wanted to ask." Polansky veered around to face Roger once again. "There you go, Fasick. What do you think of that?"

"Just what're you trying to prove, Edgar?"

"Oh, nothing," he said smugly. "Just that Princess Di is more popular than Jesus."

"That's not even a fair assessment! Especially coming from you—you're Jewish after all. And the lady over there is dressed up like some sort of Princess Diana clone. I think your answer was completely biased!"

Edgar scoffed in his face. "You're just upset that I'm right. Isn't that true, Roger?"

"What you've just said is Blasphemy, Edgar!" Miss Kitty stated sternly. "You should go to Church right now and brush up on your sermons and commandments."

"Not to mention your manners!" Roger added.

"No thanks," Edgar retorted with a bit of a gloat. "If I'm ever in the mood for fairy tales, I just watch the Disney channel."

Roger could feel his cheeks becoming hot with anger. "Edgar, I think you're as big a piece of scum as your business partner, Stanley Spillanski."

Edgar's eyes widened. Roger's remark had come out of left field and confused the large obnoxious man. "What's your problem, Fasick? And why are you bringing Stanley into this? He's not here to defend himself, and I'm pretty sure he's never done anything to offend you."

"Josh Roberts told me Stanley was hitting on his brother's wife last year!" he exclaimed. "I don't think too highly of that. It shows poor morals. And if you want to desecrate Christ's name for a few laughs and compare him to an English princess that's been dead over a decade, then I think you have poor morals too!"

Edgar grabbed his cigar from the ashtray on the bar and began taking a few puffs. "Morals don't get you far in life, Fasick. If you really wanna make a name for yourself, you have to bend the rules every once in a while. Life isn't black and white, Roger. There are many shades of gray as well."

"I've hear that before, Edgar. And I think it's as much bullshit now as I did then." Roger's lip curled into a snarl as he said, "Listen to me, Edgar, and listen good. One of these days, your venomous words are going to get you in a mess you can't get yourself out of. And when that happens, I want to be there to see it. Mark my words, Polansky…you're time is coming!"

Chapter 60:

Deadly Admissions

Josh Roberts sat down in a narrow, wooden chair inside Detective Rick Streeter's office. The wood was weathered and splintered, and the seat cushion was stiff and lumpy. Even though Josh wriggled from side to side to get comfortable, the chair was about as comfy as sitting on a pile of steel marbles.

The office looked like it had just been moved in to, which, from how Josh understood Streeter's unexpected promotion, wasn't surprising. There were a couple boxes behind the desk with stuff Rick was moving into the office, while several boxes near the door contained Sergeant Kenneth Johnson's belongings that family members had yet to pick up. The office walls were dingy and bare, with lots of cobwebs and spiders taking up residence in the upper corners of the room. There were also several nails protruding from the sheetrock but no photos or diplomas hanging up on them.

As Streeter was gathering his paperwork together, Josh perused the room some more, remembering the last time he sat in that office— back when it belonged to Ken Johnson. Josh was feeling a bit depressed as he sat there, and with the current look of the office, he was almost too uncomfortable to do the interview there…but based on the recent events, he fully understood why there wasn't much time to spruce the place up.

"Sorry about the mess," Detective Streeter apologized. "I know that chair isn't worth a damn, either. Unfortunately, it's all I got at the moment."

"It's not that bad," Josh replied. "Better than being put in the interrogation room."

Detective Streeter laughed. "Yeah, well we're definitely not at that point yet."

"Yet?" Josh inquired, raising an eyebrow. "Do I need to find a lawyer?"

"Well, I'm kind of in a bind here, Rick." Sitting down in a chair, Detective Streeter let out a heavy exhale and replied, "I don't really believe you've done anything wrong, and we sure as hell don't have a shred of evidence saying otherwise."

"I'm sure I'd be sitting in a nice comfy cell if you did," Josh said with a smirk.

Streeter laughed, and even his natural laugh sounded stressed and tired. "Yeah, you got that right." Then, Rick's facial expression and tone of voice became much more serious. "I know you don't believe all that resurrection crap Ty Harris has been publishing any more than I do."

"It *is* a little far-fetched," Josh concurred.

"Nevertheless, there *are* some bizarre things goin' on throughout the North Country. You know of the scarab symbol someone planted at the morgue…and you know it's meaning, too."

Josh nodded his head. "That's true."

Rick shook his head and sighed. "And now someone is parading around town as a copycat killer!" Streeter paused as he reached for a piece of nicotine gum. "People are terrified out of their minds," he continued, "and I *know* Chief Zimmerman is feeling the pressure from all this chaos."

Rick Streeter stopped for a moment, rubbed his eyes and let those words sink in. Josh wasn't all that bad a guy, and Rick knew that despite some harsh words a couple nights ago, Josh would treat him well if Rick did the same. That was part of why Josh was such a great reporter; he was well respected by all his peers. Minus that whole Lavancha feud. Whatever was between them was before Rick's time in Carthage, and he had no intention of getting involved…unless it was to his advantage to solve the case.

"Look," Rick said, "we're all struggling here. The general way to deal with a smart serial killer is to wait until they make a mistake…but I can't afford to handle this situation with conventional methods. This town just got over one serial killer, and I'll be damned if I'm going to just sit around and wait for another dozen dead bodies to pile up before we get this perpetrator."

Josh sat impassively, waiting for Rick to finish. He still wasn't completely sure what was going on, but he was starting to get a basic idea of the direction their conversation was going.

Detective Streeter snatched the ceramic mug off his desk and sipped his coffee. Based on the expression on his face, Josh guessed that it was more than twelve hours old. It actually took some effort for Detective Streeter to wipe the grimace off of his face and continue with the discussion.

"You know the Reaper case inside and out better than anyone else outside of the police force, Josh—and even better than many of us in the department since you collaborated with Sergeant Johnson. He was responsible for a lot of the early detective work on that case."

"Yeah, we did sorta bond over the past few months. We exchanged some pertinent information in the weeks leading up to his death."

"Uh huh…well, I don't care who your sources are now, or how you get a lot of the information you get, but I need to know *everything* you know about this case, including everything that relates to Matthew Timmons," Detective Streeter demanded. "If you've found any type of a lead we may have missed, tell me now!"

"Right now I don't have much," Josh admitted. "I'd be happy to share anything I find out, but I'd like to know what I'm going to get in return."

Detective Streeter groaned. "How 'bout the general inside track on *any* story material I can get. Or did you have something else in mind?"

At first Josh didn't, but a sudden thought did strike him. "Yeah. In addition to this new Reaper case, I want all the information on the Deferiet murder you have in your possession."

"So, a two for one deal, huh?" asked the detective.

"Consider it fair market rate," Josh Roberts replied, happy to have an inside track on any information from the station. "So…what've you got on the Jane Doe in Deferiet?"

Detective Streeter actually smiled, and Josh knew that look well enough to know he was in trouble.

"Nothing," Detective Streeter said, enjoying the stunned look on Josh Roberts' face.

"Nothing?"

"Not a thing," Detective Streeter announced. "But the moment we know more, I'll personally let you know." Rick cringed as he took another sip of his coffee. "So, how about your notes on this new Reaper so far?"

"I told you…I'm still looking for my big break in this one," Josh stressed. "Besides, what information could I possibly have that's going to help you out? I probably don't have *anything* you don't already know."

"Well let's compare notes anyway," the detective replied, enjoying what he knew was going to be one of the few times he had distinctly pulled a quick one on the ace reporter. "You know, just in case."

That night Roger Fasick strolled into Kitty's Bar, figuring it was a good night for a beer and maybe some mindless chatter. He saw Celeste and Travis Kull were the two tending bar that night. Celeste was wiping the sweat from her brow with a dishtowel and the humidity was making Travis's mullet big and frizzy. The air conditioner in the bar was broken again, and the sweat from Travis's armpits was seeping through his Eddie Money t-shirt.

Roger wandered over and took a seat at the end of the bar, near the jukebox, while he searched his pockets for some quarters. He was thinking it'd be a good night to listen to some Tom Petty or Johnny Cash, which seemed to be the two artists that just about everyone seemed to like, regardless of their fierce alliance to either country or rock music.

"Roger!" exclaimed Celeste. "What're you doing here?"

Roger smiled. He was definitely in the mood for a Budweiser, but there was one *other* reason he made his way down to the bar as well. "Well, Bucky couldn't get out of the house tonight and he wanted me to stop by and check in on you. He's worried something might happen to you. I thought I could use a beer, too, so it was a convenient stop."

"He's so paranoid," Celeste said, rolling her eyes. "I'm in a bar surrounded by a bunch of friendly people—all of whom I know personally, albeit most are drunk off their ass. And to top it off, I have Travis working with me tonight." She glanced over and tossed him a wink. "He'll be a gentleman and walk me to my car when the shift is over."

"Yeah, but..."

"Trust me, Roger. I'm fine."

On the other side of the bar was Adam "Red" Richardson, having a few drinks of his own. He motioned for Travis to come over so he could order another beer. When Travis arrived Adam said, "I'll have another cold one, Travis."

"Are you sure? Don't you think it might impair your thinking...or your ability to make good decisions?"

"I don't need a babysitter, Travis!" roared Adam. "Besides, I've been sitting here thinking of philosophy tonight."

"Oh, really?" Travis replied, a little intrigued by this unexpected statement. "And what have you been thinking?"

Adam scratched his temple and asked, "Wasn't it Einstein who came up with the theory of Relatives?"

"Could be...then again, it might've been Darwin," Travis commented incorrectly. "Wait a second...did you say 'relatives' Adam?"

"Yeah, I remember now!" announced the drunkard. "He said: 'I think; therefore, I have relatives.'"

Travis stared at Adam dumbfounded and speechless. He had heard a lot of asinine conversations and proclamations over the years while bartending in Watertown, but this one took the cake.

Meanwhile, after a few drinks (and not just beer, Roger found that tonight felt like a whiskey night) Roger started to loosen up. Over the hours, the music had switched from the upbeat Southern twang of Tom Petty to a darker, more contemplative style of Johnny Cash. The music, the mood, and the whiskey were slowly becoming a dangerous combination. Like many men who've had something nagging on their thoughts—eating away at their insides—Roger wanted someone to talk to. And so, when the patrons at Kitty's Bar began to thin out and slow down, Roger's tongue suddenly became very loose, and he began telling things to Celeste that probably should've remained unsaid.

Roger cleared his throat and said, "Celeste, I was wonderin' if I could talk to ya for a moment. I, uh...I wanna tell you something."

"Sure, Roger," she answered with a smile. "You can always talk to me—just like when I used to babysit you. We had some great conversations back then."

Roger tried to grin, but the seriousness of the subject matter prevented him from doing so. "There's somethin' I can't get off my mind...somethin' I'm feelin' awfully guilty about."

"What could you *possibly* feel guilty about?" Celeste asked, coming over to listen and comfort her friend. "I've known you since you were just a little boy—running around your parents' house in those Superman pajamas. You're one of the sweetest guys I know."

Roger intended to tell only the basics to Celeste, maybe just allude to being a bad man; but as soon as the words started coming from his lips, they poured out like a river through a busted dam. Like a dying man searching for atonement of his sins, Roger felt compelled to confess everything to Celeste and couldn't stop himself from divulging all the details that transpired between him and Tim Matthews upon the roof of the Buckley Building.

Though Celeste let out a gasp and her eyes bulged, Roger continued on. He told her how much he hated Tim because of the fires...and Holly's murder. Roger said he always knew he'd probably kill whoever the Reaper was; that is, if he ever discovered the identity of the murderer. And then, Roger told Celeste the same bomb shell he dropped on Bucky—the one that shook him to his core—that Roger had a chance to pull Tim off the edge of the roof to safety, but that he let Tim fall off the roof. Roger let Tim die.

When Roger finished his story, a shameful silence fell over him.

"Roger, is this true?" Celeste asked, horrified.

"Every word," Roger admitted. "I wish I could say that if I was back in the same situation I'd save him, but I don't know if I would. To be honest, Celeste...I doubt I'd change a thing."

Off to the side, while acting busy wiping and cleaning glass mugs, Travis Kull listened attentively to every single detail of Roger's story.

Several miles away, over at the Morgan residence, Bucky was lying on Mikey's bed, reading his son a bedtime story. Once Bucky had finished, he stood and pulled the covers over the boy, tucking him into bed for the night.

"Here's your Pooh bear, Mikey. It's time to close your eyes and get some rest."

Thanks for reading me another chapter tonight, Daddy. This sure is a long book!"

"No problem, son. I wish I had time to do it more often. Don't worry though...we'll get 'Treasure Island' finished real soon."

"Can you read me one more chapter? Please..."

"Sorry, bud, it's getting late. It's after 10 pm and little boys need their sleep or they'll be grumpy in the morning."

Mikey groaned. "Oh, okay."

"Hey, I'll read another chapter to you tomorrow night."

Mikey's face lit up. "Yay!!"

Bucky chuckled as he walked over to Mikey's bedroom window to close the curtains. As he looked out to his back yard, Bucky saw a person standing next to a cedar hedge facing the house. Bucky squinted to get a better view but could only make out that the person was wearing a long coat...and possibly a hat of some kind, perhaps a fedora.

Just then, the person began waving to Bucky. Bucky's eyes widened. "What the hell...?"

"Daddy, you said a bad word!"

Bucky turned his attention to Mikey. "I'm sorry, son."

"You have to put a dollar in the swear jar, Dad!"

"I will," grinned Bucky. "It's just that…"

"Is something outside, Daddy? Is there a bear…or maybe a monster?"

"No…no…nothing like that, Mikey," answered Bucky, not wanting to worry his boy. "There's a chipmunk in our bird feeder again."

Mikey smiled and closed his eyes, hugging his teddy bear. Bucky shifted his gaze to his yard once again, but the figure was gone.

A few hours later, back at Kitty's Bar, Celeste had gathered up all the bowls of pretzels and peanuts, carrying them to the back room to be washed. Travis grabbed the broom next to the cash register and glanced at the clock hanging on the wall. It read 1 am.

"Closing time!" Travis hollered out.

"Aww…" all the patrons groaned.

"Hey, don't shoot the messenger people!"

"We don't wanna leave just yet!" yelled Edgar Polansky. "How 'bout one more beer for me and my pal, Stanley?"

Travis shook his head. "Sorry, Edgar, I ain't servin' anyone else tonight. You and Mr. Spillanski will have to clear out as well."

"But…but…" sputtered Edgar.

"Hey, I'm not saying y'all have to go home. I'm just tellin' ya you can't stay here! Now move those drunkin' asses of yours and leave!"

Within minutes, everyone had left the premises. Everyone, that was, except for the person watching the two bartenders from outside—peering into the window from the alleyway.

Shortly thereafter, Travis had finished sanitizing the bathrooms while Celeste wiped the tables clean and mopped the floors. Celeste put the mop and bucket back in the closet next to the restroom and said, "Well, I've finished all the cleaning duties, Travis. I'm going to head home now if it's okay with you."

"No problem, pretty lady," Travis replied. "I've got it all covered."

"Are you sure you don't need me to help you restock the fridge or close out the cash register?"

"Celeste, I used to work at the Time Warp Tavern in Watertown for two years. I think I can handle closing up by myself." He motioned his hand toward the front door and said, "Go ahead and slip out. I'll be okay."

"Are you working tomorrow night?" asked Celeste.

"Yup."

"Great! I'll see you then, Travis."

Travis gave her a nod as he smiled. "Bye, Celeste."

Celeste grabbed her cashmere sweater off the coat rack and walked out the door. As she stepped outside, the figure had disappeared from the window. After a few minutes, Travis was in the back room, putting half-full boxes of beer bottles away after he'd finished restocking the fridge. He was still back there when he heard a strange tapping noise that was impossible to ignore. Travis cautiously made his way to the front area and glanced around the barroom but didn't see anyone around…and the tapping had stopped.

A few moments passed, and then the tapping noise started again. This time Travis ignored it, assuming it was one of the new cuckoo clocks hanging on the wall. Travis looked over at the clocks and realized none of them were actually moving. Instantly, his eyes shifted to the window. Thinking that someone may have been tapping on the glass panes, Travis crept over to the back door leading to the alley, slowly opening it up.

Travis peered into the darkness and saw nothing. He reached for the utility shelf by his right side, grabbed a flashlight, and exhaled heavily. With his courage slowly returning and flashlight gripped tightly in hand, Travis took a few steps out the door, strolling up and down the lane a short distance to make sure no one was around. Once his knees stopped knocking together, he briskly walked back to the bar, grabbed the doorknob with trembling fingers, and forcefully closed and bolted the door as he reentered the building.

Travis took several deep breaths. After a minute or so, his heart rate started to calm down. "My imagination's gettin' the best of me," he said to himself.

Just then, a quarter could be heard as it was dropped into the juke box.

Travis turned toward the door which led to the front area. "Miss Kitty? Are you there?"

Silence.

Travis took several steps toward the front area. "Ce…Celeste?" he asked wearily. "Did you forget your purse or something?"

Again, there was silence.

"Gary?" he muttered through trembling lips. "Are you tryin' to play another practical joke on me, Wolff?"

Just as Travis was about to enter the front area, Chopin's Funeral March began playing over the speakers. Travis's heart began pounding wildly in his chest.

Travis turned around and ran back to the door leading to the alleyway. He unbolted the door and attempted to flee, but the door would not budge. He threw his shoulder into it, thinking the old wooden door had swelled in the humid air...but again, it would not open.

Travis peered out the window on the right side of the door and noticed that a steel bar was jammed up against the doorknob on the outside. Travis began to panic and turned around again. Only this time he came face-to-face with the Reaper (or rather face-to-chest, since the entity was distinctly smaller than him).

For a brief moment, Travis' body seized up from the shock; however, that would be all the time the Reaper would need. The spectre moved quickly, pulling a stun gun from underneath its frayed cloak. The Reaper placed the stun gun to Travis's chest and pulled the trigger.

Travis stumbled backwards, tripping over his own feet. After stumbling roughly ten feet, his body dropped to the floor and his head landed hard upon the base of the jukebox.

"Where is the girl?" the Reaper demanded.

"Wh...who?" Travis asked through clenched teeth. His entire body shook with fear, in addition to the massive electric jolt of electricity he had just received.

The grim entity leaned toward the incapacitated bartender. "Where is Celeste? The other bartender? She was just here a moment ago."

"She left already," whimpered Travis, trying to get his muscles to react to his mind's command to stand up, but finding his body too disjointed and unable to do so.

"Well then, I guess you'll have to do," the Reaper hissed.

"Don't ki...kill me!" Travis pleaded. "*Please*! If you truly are the Reaper...if you *are* the ghost of Tim Matthews, then you know I had absolutely nothing to do with what happened to you! We both know who's *really* responsible for your de...death! Let me go—*please*—and ki...kill them!"

"And who do you think that might be?" the cloaked figure inquired.

"It was Ro...Roger and Bu...Bu...Bucky!" he sputtered through chattering teeth. "They were the ones who rescued Celeste."

"Who?" the Reaper said with a slight pause.

"Bu...Bucky Morgan and Ro...Roger Fasick!" he sputtered once again. "They were the ones you fought in the fire atop of the Buckley Building!"

The Reaper cocked its head to the side while listening to the frightened man spill his guts.

"You shouldn't stutter so much," the entity growled. "It's hard to tell if you're simply scared and telling the truth, or if you're thinking of a believable lie in order to buy yourself some time."

"I swear; I *am* telling the truth!" cried Travis. "Roger was in here tonight and admitted to Celeste that he let go of your hand as you fell off the building. If you're back here to seek revenge, he's the one you want...not me!"

At that moment, the gruesome figure lowered the knife and spoke in a hushed tone, one that nagged Travis as being vaguely familiar. "You have a point."

"So...you won't kill me?" Travis asked, breathing a premature sigh of relief.

The Reaper picked up an empty bottle of Bud Light off the counter and smashed it upon the counter. The being held the broken, jagged pieces in its hand and stated, "Sorry, I just can't let you go."

Outside the bar, the quiet peaceful night was suddenly interrupted by the sound of a blood-curdling scream. It was the scream of a man at the point of death.

Chapter 61:

An Eye for an Eye

The following afternoon Bucky was sitting in his office, working on some paperwork. All of a sudden, his phone rang.

Bucky picked up the receiver after the third ring. "Yes, LaTesha? Is this important? I'm kinda busy at the moment."

"Bucky, Chief Zimmerman is here. He's with some other guy and they'd like to speak with you."

"C.Z. is here, huh? Okay, LaTesha. Send them up."

Bucky tidied his desk for a few minutes as the gentlemen made their way to his office. A moment later, C.Z. entered Bucky's office with a middle-aged gentleman Bucky had never seen before.

"Hello, Bernard," he said cordially. "What brings you here today?"

"Bucky, I'm glad you're in your office. I'd like to introduce you to Philip VanBuren. He'll be taking over Harry Moon's position as coroner."

"Pleased to meet you, sir." Bucky said as he extended his hand to shake.

"Same here," the man stated with a half-hearted smile. Philip wiped his hands with a handkerchief after shaking Bucky's hand.

Philip was a Bostonian who came from a family with 'old money,' which explained his snobbish attitude. He stood well over six-feet-tall and had a face full of deep wrinkles. His snow-white hair was well-groomed and his narrow eyes were black and piercing. Dr. VanBuren smelled of the very-pleasing BRUT aftershave, but his complexion was nearly as grey as some of his 'customers.'

Bucky stared at Philip for a moment, noticing his finely-pressed suit and starched white shirt. He rolled his eyes at the pretentious-looking man before shifting his attention back to C.Z. and asked, "So...was there anything else you wanted to talk about, Chief?"

"Actually, yes. There was another murder last night."

"Christ! This is getting ridiculous! Who was it this time?"

"One of the bartenders at Kitty's Bar. And yes, one of his fingers was missing, too. Same M.O. as the last two bodies."

"A bar...bartender?" inquired Bucky, becoming choked up. "From Kitty's Bar? Wh...who?"

"A kid by the name of Travis Kull. Do you know him?"

"Oh, shit," grimaced Bucky. "Actually, I do. And my girlfriend works with him!"

"Yeah, we're aware of that," the chief stated. "Look, we want to get to the bottom of this as quickly, and if possible, as quietly as we can. We don't need any vigilante on our streets scaring the townsfolk."

"I agree," Philip spoke up. "We never had vigilantes when I was growing up in Boston! My most recent job was in New York City, and in my experience, vigilantes can be just as dangerous as the criminals stalking the streets. Down in the city, there're people dressin' up in costumes, tryin' to catch the criminals."

"Costumes?"

"Yeah, one guy even dresses up like a bug or somethin'. The cops are none too about it, and the ordinary folk don't know whether these costumed creeps are doin' more harm than good to the community."

Just then, LaTesha knocked on Bucky's door and entered the room, her face was pale and her hands shook.

"Is something wrong, LaTesha," Bucky asked with a worried look upon his face. "Why are you shaking?"

LaTesha held up a small rectangle-shaped package that was wrapped in brown paper.

"Bucky, this package was found on the steps outside. It's just like the ones I delivered to the chief."

"Why did ya bring it in here?" C.Z. chimed in. "Go put it on my desk, LaTesha."

"Actually sir..." LaTesha stopped and turned to face Bucky once again. "Bucky, it's addressed to *you* this time."

With a look of confusion, Bucky said, "Me? Why me?"

Bucky took the package from LaTesha's hands and placed it upon his desk. After she left the room, all the men gathered around the mysterious object. Bucky put on a pair of latex gloves he kept in his desk drawer, grabbed his pocketknife from his jacket, and proceeded to open it up. Inside was another painting. A portrait of Travis Kull with a glass bottle protruding out of his neck.

A few hours later, Bucky was leaving his office when he bumped into Edgar Polansky in the parking lot.

"Hey Bucky. I heard about the Kull kid gettin' murdered at Kitty's. Too bad; he was a good bartender."

"How did you...?"

Edgar smirked. "I overheard some officers discussing the details when I was talking to LaTesha. He licked his lips and asked snidely, "How's your *wife*, err...I mean, your girlfriend holding up after the ordeal?"

Bucky's eyes flashed but he managed to keep a calm façade. "Not that it's any of your business, but she's fine. She doesn't know yet. By the way, how's your father doing?"

"My father?"

"Yeah, I heard he was arrested for trying to solicit sex from a girl scout by tempting her with candy and Barbie dolls."

Edgar's cheeks became red with anger. "You asshole! My father's been in a nursing home for several years...and you know that!"

"Oh, that's right," Bucky said. "I guess I was thinking about some other fat bastard."

Bucky grinned and walked away. Edgar stood silent and glared at Bucky with daggers in his eyes.

After his verbal joust with Edgar, Bucky drove home, wondering how he would break the news of Travis's death to Celeste. After parking his car in the driveway, Bucky walked inside his house and hung his jacket on the coat rack. He was tired, and it had been a long and frustrating day. He was definitely glad to be home. Another murder. Bucky was beginning to wonder if Carthage really was cursed. They certainly couldn't seem to catch a break.

Celeste ran over to give him a hug and a kiss but instantly noticed how distracted Bucky seemed.

"Is something bothering you, Honey?" she asked.

"I just came from my office," Bucky informed her. "While I was at work today Chief Zimmerman stopped by. We talked about the most recent murders and the shortage of police officers. He wasn't alone, though. Philip VanBuren was with him."

"Who's that?" Celeste asked, not remembering the name from her earlier years in and around Carthage.

"He's the new coroner at the hospital," Bucky answered. "Looks to be older than Harry was...and a very stiff, straight-by-the-book kind of man. Pretty much the complete and utter opposite of the hippy-style Harry was known for."

"Okay," Celeste said with slight hesitation, worried about any news that involved a coroner. "Why are you telling me this, Bucky?"

"C.Z. told me some very disturbing news."

Celeste appeared curious, but was cautious to ask him any questions. After all, the saying was, "Ignorance is Bliss," but she could see how visibly upset he was, and really wanted to share the burden of what he knew.

She mustered up enough courage to say, "What's wrong, Bucky?"

Bucky shook his head and let out a loud sigh. "Travis Kull is dead, Celeste. He was murdered sometime last night at the bar, probably shortly after you left."

Celeste felt like someone had just knocked the wind out of her. "Are you serious? When did he die? How did this happen?" she asked, noticeably shocked.

"He was stabbed in the throat with a broken beer bottle sometime after midnight. Based on the color of his skin and rigormortis in his muscles, the coroner has his time of death somewhere between one-thirty and two."

Celeste broke down in tears. "Oh my god, Travis."

"I know. That's around the same time you left the bar to come home. That means the Reaper could very well have been after you—not Travis! The killer might even have been there while you guys were closing down."

"I don't know what to think right now, Bucky," Celeste said, her tears streaming down her face as she tried to cope with grief and guilt of the news.

"Don't worry, Babe. I'll keep you safe," Bucky promised. "I won't let anything happen to you."

"I know you won't, Bucky."

As they hugged, Bucky said, "I wonder if there's any way we can figure out when and where the Reaper will strike next. We need to stop this psycho once and for all."

Meanwhile, at the *Carthage Republican Tribune*, Josh Roberts was entering his office when Ty Harris yelled to him. Josh tossed his coat on the chair across from his desk, rolled his eyes as he sighed, and made his way over to Ty's office.

"Josh, *what* the hell are you doing, and *where* the hell is Mary? Isn't she with you?" Ty inquired.

"No," Josh answered curtly. "I spoke with her early this morning and she was still in bed. She didn't get much sleep last night and was pretty worn out. Mary's not a young woman anymore, and I know how you 'old farts' desperately need your rest."

"Mock all you want now, Roberts. You'll be old, too, someday. That is, if someone doesn't bump you off first."

Josh glared at Ty. Murder jokes weren't funny with a crazed psychopathic serial killer running around town adding to the body count.

"Is there some reason you called me in your office?"

"Yes," Ty replied. "We have another murder on our hands. Well, the police department has a murder, we have a great story."

"Who was murdered?" Josh asked, ignoring Ty's glib comments about the dead.

"A bartender at Kitty's Bar. It happened sometime after the bar closed last night."

Josh's eyes widened and his heart skipped a beat. "Who was killed, Ty? Was the person male or female?"

"The victim's name was Travis Kull. Do you know him?"

Josh exhaled in relief. "No, not well, anyway. I'm just relieved to hear it wasn't Celeste Braxton."

"No, she's safe. She'd already left the premises by then."

Shaking his head in disbelief, Josh asked, "Ty, I don't understand...how did find out so much information about this before I did?"

With a sly grin, Ty responded, "I still have *my* sources too, kid. I still got what it takes to show you up from time to time." He chuckled to himself before saying, "Apparently, Miss Kitty found him when she entered the bar this morning. The kid was lying on the floor in the back room with a beer bottle sticking out of his neck. How's that for irony? Whoever heard of a bartender killed in a bar—with a bottle!"

Josh remained silent, speechless at his editor's last comment. It seemed like 'ironic' murders were happening a lot recently.

Later on, around nine-thirty, Roger was at home getting ready for bed. He usually wasn't one to call it an early evening, especially with everything still going on in town, but this was a special occasion. He wanted to get plenty of rest since Nellie was coming to Carthage in the morning, bringing Alex along with her so they could get to know one another. Roger had taken a shower, changed into his Haines pajama bottoms, and plucked his nose hairs. He still found it hard to believe he was old enough to worry about nose hair. The only thing left on his 'to do' list was shave his face.

He was standing in front of the bathroom mirror, listening to the sounds of .38 Special blaring from his stereo in the other room while applying the shaving cream. After a few moments, he began talking to himself.

"Nellie will be here tomorrow!" he said with glee. "And I get to see my son! *MY SON*! I still can't believe it!"

Roger was so engrossed in his thoughts that he didn't even notice that the music stopped playing in the bedroom. Just then, when he bent over to rinse his razor, a gruesome figure appeared behind him.

"Hello, Roger," the Reaper hissed.

Roger's head shot up. As he was beginning to spin around, he caught sight of a dark hooded figure over his shoulder. While he was doing so, the Reaper took the stun gun from his hip sheath and attacked—sending a jolt of electricity right into the side of Roger's neck.

Roger fell to the ground with a loud thump and wriggled around on the floor in pain. His hands and feet tingled wildly, and he was desperately trying not to choke on his own tongue. He winced to lift his head, but even through all the pain, he could tell the Reaper was standing over him.

"You killed me, Roger!" the Reaper bellowed. "And now, you *will* answer for the deeds you've done."

"I don't know who you are or how you got in here," Roger slurred, "but I'm going to find a way to stop you."

"I highly doubt it, Fasick," the Reaper hollered in a grisly voice, mispronouncing Roger's last name slightly by emphasizing the wrong syllable. "Look at yourself, Fasick. You can't even stand up! The only thing you'll be doing is going straight to Hell...and I'll be seeing you there."

The Reaper's gloved hand pulled a brick from under the ominous-looking cloak. "Do you recognize this, Roger?"

Roger squinted at the object and replied, "It's a friggin' brick. So what?"

Some feeling was returning to his fingers and toes, and he was hoping to be able to use one quick burst to surprise the Reaper. With a little luck and perfect timing, he was hoping to mount an attack and get out of this confrontation alive.

"I took this brick from the place where we last fought. The place where you let go of my hand and let me fall. You left me to die! Surely you must remember that?"

Roger felt himself go cold. Who else other than Bucky and Celeste knew he had let Tim Matthews fall to his death...other then, well...

"Why did you bring it here?" Roger uttered, wincing. "What're you gonna to do with it?"

Roger felt some movement return. He hoped it'd be enough to help defend himself and felt he had to make his move right away— before the Reaper could inflict any more pain upon him. With all the strength he could muster, Roger tried to lunge. He knees buckled as soon as he tried to stand and he landed harmlessly in front of the Reaper's feet.

"This is for you," the Reaper snarled.

The Reaper smacked Roger on the left side of his head just as he was attempting to stand again. The force threw Roger into the bathroom window and he crashed right through it. He fell twenty-five feet, bouncing off the side of his house and landed squarely on his back in the yard. A loud thud echoed in the wind.

The Reaper walked over to the window and looked down at the motionless body. The hellish being then tossed the brick down and it landed harmlessly on the ground next to Roger, though that wasn't an act of mercy.

As Roger was lying there, slipping in and out of consciousness, he had an unwavering intuit that Death was near. His gasps seemed to echo through the sky, and from out of nowhere, he felt the warmth of bright light upon his cheeks. Roger opened his eyes as best he could, and though his sight was hazy, he saw a shapely figure emerge from the illumination... and suddenly, a blonde angel approached him.

"H...H...Holly? Is...is that you?"

The lady, wearing only a white robe, leaned over him. She touched his cheek with the back of her hand and whispered, "Yes, darling. I'm here."

Roger smiled, his breathing was becoming slower. "I miss you so much, babe," he uttered as tears trickled from the corners of his eyes. "Am I going to die?"

The angel looked sympathetically at the wounded man. "No, Roger. It is not your time to leave this place."

Holly put her hands on his cheeks and kissed him softly upon the lips. "I have to leave, my love, but always know that I'll be watching over you."

The apparition began to disappear.

"No, Holly...I need you...please...don't go."

"I must, darling. Just remember...I love you."

The lady in white was gone. Roger's eyes closed as he lost consciousness.

At that moment, the Reaper, who was still standing in front of the broken window, lifted his gaze from the ground and saw Josh Roberts drive up the street. Within a few seconds, the reporter had pulled his vehicle alongside the curb next to Roger's driveway. Josh stepped out of his vehicle and looked up, viewing the fragments of the broken window. His eyes shifted over to the ground and saw Roger lying in a bloody heap.

Josh quickly rushed over to his friend's side to help. Once he got there, Josh looked up once more to the broken window and saw the Reaper standing there, looking down. Josh blinked and looked again, only this time, the Reaper had disappeared. Josh checked his friend's pulse to make sure he was still alive, and then ran to the house.

Josh rushed inside and bolted up the stairs. The Reaper was nowhere to be found. Just then, he heard a voice, maybe more, coming from downstairs. Josh dashed down the stairs and followed the voices into the kitchen. Once inside, he saw Detective Rick Streeter and Mary Powell standing by the door leading to the side patio.

"What are you two doing here?" Josh demanded. "Where did the Reaper go? *Where*?!"

Streeter put his hands on his hips and announced, "We received a call from one of the neighbors. She saw someone in the area— hanging outside of Roger's house—and I was following up on her call. What's this about the Reaper?"

"What about you, Mary?" asked Josh, ignoring Streeter's inquiry. "What's your explanation?"

"After we left the office tonight, I thought I'd stop by and get an interview with Roger. I wanted to ask him some questions about his experience on top of the Buckley Building. I just arrived a few minutes ago. When I arrived, the front door was locked, but I could hear a commotion inside. I came around the side of the house to see if I could get in from the kitchen door. As soon as I took a few steps inside, Detective Streeter came up behind me."

"Oh," Josh muttered. "I didn't see your car in the area."

"I parked a block down the street and walked up, Josh. Is there a problem with that?"

No...no problem at all, Mary," Josh said with hesitation. "Roger's hurt. We need to get an ambulance here right now. I know it was the Reaper...I saw him standing upstairs near the broken window."

Detective Streeter ran with Josh over to Roger's unconscious body. Streeter called the station for an ambulance, as well as every police officer available to come and search the area.

"Don't move him," Detective Streeter said. "Wait until the paramedics get here."

A flash caught both of the men's attention. Josh glared at Mary, who just snapped a picture. "Damn it, Mary! This isn't the time to be taking pictures for some friggin' news story!"

"Sorry, Josh," she said, "but *this* is the story."

Chapter 62:

Survival
(September 13th - Morning)

Bucky had raced to the hospital the moment he received the news of his best friend's near fatal run-in with the Reaper. In less than nine minutes from the time he hung up the phone, he was bursting through the doors of the Carthage Area Hospital's Emergency Room.

Josh Roberts immediately came up to him and said, "Bucky, I'm glad you came! I didn't know who else to call."

"I appreciate it, Josh. The guy is like a brother to me. I already called Roger's folks and Nellie Spencer's family on my way here."

"Nellie?" questioned Josh.

"Yeah, she's supposed to be coming up here to visit for a few days. Roger said she was staying at his place. I figured I should let her family know—I don't have her home number."

Josh nodded and grinned. "Ohhh....*she* was the one."

"So, Josh, what've you found out so far?"

"Wendy told me..."

Bucky cut him off in mid-sentence. "Who's Wendy?"

"My cousin," Josh remarked. "Anyway, Nurse *Lyndaker* came over and informed me that Roger's condition is *extremely* serious. The doctors are doing everything they can right now. He's better than he was when they brought him in. He's lucky to be alive—and he still isn't out of the woods."

Bucky moaned. "What condition is he in?"

"The Reaper messed him up pretty bad, Bucky. Nurse Lyndaker said that if Roger had lost much more blood, he probably wouldn't have survived the ride to the hospital."

Wiping the nervous sweat from his forehead, Bucky said, "I'm glad our ambulance squad is so proficient. The driver may have a lead foot, but I'd never reprimand him for speeding…especially now!"

"I'm thankful for their efficiency, too," Josh agreed. "I strongly believe that had it not been for the immediate 911 call by Roger's neighbor, he almost certainly would have died from the violent hemorrhaging his body went through after his head injury and trauma of the fall out the window."

Bucky turned away and groaned. "God damn, Reaper!"

A short while later, Bucky was pacing back and forth down the hallway, thinking about bumming a cigarette off from someone, even though he hadn't smoked since college. Even then, he was only a social smoker, lighting up a cigarette whenever he was at a bar with his frat brothers. Though smoking was just a phase for Bucky, he could see how the habit became addictive so easily for others.

Bucky kept pacing, hoping for any type of good news to come from the doctors. He had called Celeste to let her know the status of Roger's health, and then he told her to go to bed and get some rest— he'd call her in the morning if there was any change in Roger's condition. Bucky was lost in thought as he walked up one hallway and down another, and he was *still* lost in thought two hours later when, suddenly; Nellie arrived at the hospital with her son, Alex.

"Bucky!" Nellie said in a rushed tone. "Thank you for calling my folks. Mom telephoned me on her cell while you were still on the phone to my Dad. As soon as she told me about Roger, I knew I had to come right away."

"Nellie! It's great to see you." Bucky leaned over and gave her a kiss on the cheek. Then, he peered directly at her and said, "You look exhausted."

"I'm sure I do. We quickly packed up our suitcases and drove 80 mph from Syracuse the whole way just to find out what happened." Nellie glanced around the area and asked, "Are Roger's parents here somewhere?"

"Yes, they're by his side right now," Bucky replied. "I took the liberty of contacting them as soon as Josh Roberts informed me of Roger's accident. Hopefully, they'll come out to the waiting room soon and shed some light on what's going on with Roger." Just then, Bucky looked down at the boy clinging to Nellie's leg. "You must be Alex."

The boy nodded in silence.

"Your Daddy just recently told me about you. I have a son about your age, too. His name is Mikey...maybe the two of you can play together sometime."

Alex lifted his head and smiled. "Do you have any pets?"

"Um, yeah," Bucky replied. "Actually, we have a fat cat. He's a white, longhaired Himalayan and his name is Zack. Do you like pets, Alex?"

"I sure do!" the boy shouted. "I told mama I'd like to have a dog someday. Maybe a beagle or a yellow lab!"

"You don't have any pets, Alex?"

"Well...sometimes we have mice in the walls, but mama usually feeds them poison."

Bucky stared at the boy, noticing how his facial expressions mimicked his mother's. Alex may have looked like Nellie, but there was something in his face that just screamed Roger Fasick. Even at such a young age, he was a handsome boy...Alex was blessed to inherit the best features of both of his photogenic parents.

Nellie grabbed Bucky by the arm and said, "I don't want to seem rude and interrupt you, but I want to know how Roger is. Be honest with me, Bucky. How's he doing?"

Bucky grimaced as he shook his head. "I know very little, I'm afraid. The doctors aren't telling me much of anything, which is never a good sign."

Nellie exhaled heavily and put her hand to her mouth.

"I didn't mean to scare you, Nellie. I know for certain that Roger *is* alive, and he's breathing on his own. I just returned from getting a drink at the water fountain. While I was over there, I overheard Nurse Lyndaker telling the other nurses that Roger regained consciousness about fifteen minutes ago. If that's true, I'm pretty sure it's the first time he's opened his eyes since being brought to the hospital."

Just then, Dr. William Wiley came out of Roger's room with a chart under one arm and headed toward the nurses' desk. Bucky tried to read the doctor's facial expression, but couldn't quite interpret the old man's bizarre look. He quickly walked over to talk to the elderly doctor to ask him about his friend.

"Doc, how's Roger? Is he awake? Is he going to be all right?" Bucky asked, with Nellie and Alex right behind him.

"Maybe you should talk to his folks, Bucky. I've already told them all we know about Roger's current condition."

Nellie stepped in-between the two men. "Please, doctor!" she said with a tremble in her voice. "Will you tell me the extent of Roger's injuries? I think I'd rather hear the news from you."

631

The aged doctor with deep facial wrinkles looked at Bucky and Nellie for a moment and exhaled deeply before answering. "Very well, then. Roger *is* in rough shape," he stated. "Maybe not critical condition anymore, but still very serious. Most of his ribs are either cracked or broken; he had internal hemorrhaging that we managed to control, as well as several contusions around his head. He also has a severe concussion we're going to have to keep an eye on. Roger should be able to overcome most of this, but the worst of his injuries is that he has paralysis in both of his legs."

"Oh, my God!" gasped Nellie. "You mean he can't walk anymore?"

"I know it sounds bad," Dr. Wiley said, "but it's not nearly as bad as you think. The good news is that there isn't any actual nerve damage. He has something called nerve trauma."

"What does that mean?" asked Nellie.

"It means the paralysis is from shock, not from actual physical damage to the spine. With some time and therapy, and a little bit of good luck, he should eventually have a full recovery and be able to live a perfectly normal and healthy life." Doc Wiley adjusted the eyeglasses on his forehead and said, "That's about all I can tell you right now."

"May we see him?" Bucky asked immediately.

The doctor thought for a moment before answering. "I suppose so. However, his folks are already in there with him, so I only one of you in the room at a time. He's been through a lot, and he needs his rest."

"Thank you, Doctor," Nellie remarked.

Doc Wiley nodded and walked away.

"Bucky, maybe you should go in now," Nellie suggested. "I'll wait here for Roger's folks to come out of his room. I'd really like to talk to them in private first. And while we're waiting, Alex and I can sit and get some sorely needed rest."

"The two of you don't have to stay here all night," Bucky said. "You're both welcome to go to my house and get some rest. Celeste is there and she'd be happy to get you some food or fix you up with a place to sleep. And Alex would have a great time playing with Mikey."

"That sounds wonderful, Bucky. Just give me a minute to call my brothers; I want to tell them what's going on. Would you mind keeping an eye on Alex for me while I'm step away for a moment? I'd rather talk in private."

"Not at all," replied Bucky. "Take your time."

After a short while, Nellie returned and said, "All of my brothers were in shock. They're very concerned about Roger. My brother, Robert, sends his regards. And Joel and Toby want to come to town and see Roger. It'll take a week or longer to get their affairs in order and get here, but once that's done, they'll be here to stay for awhile."

"That sounds awesome," Bucky said. "I'll let Roger know the good news. It's been years since any of us saw your brothers. It'll be great to hang out together and catch up on what they're doing now."

Nellie smiled and leaned down, taking Alex by the hand. "Well, thanks again for letting us go over to your house. I'll be seeing you soon. If Roger's condition changes, please let me know right away."

"I will, Nellie. I promise."

Nellie continued down the hallway toward the Exit door, and then stopped as she walked past the gift shop. She took Alex by the hand and entered the store while Bucky made his way to Roger's room. Roger's folks were walking out as Bucky approached the door, and once the Fasick's saw Bucky, they all hugged and sobbed in silence. Mr. Fasick gave Bucky one last pat on the back before he entered Roger's room.

Bucky looked at his longtime friend with sadness, seeing a heavily bandaged head and battered body. Roger was breathing on his own, but there were tubes and needles going in and out of several parts of his body. Bucky walked over, sat down in a chair next to the bed, and placed his hand on Roger's arm.

Roger opened his eyes and turned his head slightly. "Bucky? Is that you?"

"Yeah, Rog, it's me. How're ya feelin' bud?"

"Like I got hit by a tractor trailer," Roger said, wincing in pain. "I'm not dead? How'd I get here?"

"Josh found you right after the Reaper attacked. It's a miracle you survived at all. I hate to ask you this Roger, but do you remember anything about the attack?"

"Not much," Roger muttered. "It happened so quickly. But I do remember the Reaper standing in back of me in my bathroom. He whacked me with a brick...he said it was from the Buckley Building debris. Whoever or whatever was in my house...was dressed exactly like Tim. And he knew. How did he know?"

"Do you think it was a person...or did the entity seem more like a ghost?"

"I can't be sure, Bucky. However, the Reaper did seem shorter than Tim was if that's any help to you."

"It is hard to think a ghost would have any reason to come back shorter," Bucky said. He looked over and saw Roger's eye lids fluttering shut. "Get some rest, buddy. I'll fill you in on everything else later."

As Bucky turned to leave, a tall, slender pale-faced nurse entered the room. She was holding a package, roughly two-inches in thickness, under her right arm. It was rectangle-shaped and wrapped in brown paper.

"Hey, Nurse Lyndaker," Roger uttered. "What're you don' in here?

"This package suddenly showed up on the nurses' desk," she responded. "It's addressed to you, Mr. Fasick."

Bucky's eyes widened. "Here, let me take that from you, nurse," he said as he grabbed the package and set it on the table next to Roger's bed.

Nurse Lyndaker turned and left the room. Bucky reached into his wallet and pulled out his pocketknife.

As Bucky unwrapped the package, his mouth dropped open and his face became as white as fresh snow. Roger noticed Bucky's frightened expression and veered his head toward the opened parcel.

"What is it, Bucky? What's inside the package?"

Bucky lifted the 15x20 canvas board off the table and turned it around to face Roger. It was a freshly-painted portrait of Roger lying on the ground, covered in blood and surrounded by broken glass…and a red brick.

With lightning speed, Bucky stepped into the hallway and ordered the officer who was standing guard outside Roger's door to come into the room and carefully remove the painting. Bucky instructed Officer Lewis to take the painting directly to Chief Zimmerman's office immediately.

The fright he received from the grisly painting was elevating Roger's blood pressure, and his heart began racing wildly. In fact, his breathing was becoming so erratic that Nurse Lyndaker had to come in and give Roger a sedative to calm him down.

A few minutes later, Bucky walked back into the hallway after watching Roger fall into an uncomfortable sleep. He wandered down to the lobby, looked toward the exit, and was surprised to see Nellie Spencer still at the hospital. Alex was leaning on her leg, holding her hand with both of his and scuffing his feet like he was bored. Nellie was talking to Josh Roberts and his new assistant, Mary something or other. Bucky couldn't remember her last name.

Bucky walked over and uttered, "Um…Nellie, I thought you were taking Alex over to my house."

"I still am, Bucky. I saw Roger's parents as we were walking outside and I stopped to talk to them." She paused as she shifted her attention to the two reporters. "After that, Josh approached me to give me a hug and introduce me to his partner, Mary Powell."

"Oh, I see," Bucky remarked. "Well, I hope neither of them is grilling you for information like reporters have been known to do."

Nellie laughed. "No, they're both speaking very kindly and politely to me."

"Good," voiced Bucky. "I'm glad to hear it."

Mary caught sight of Bucky and raised a hand in greeting. Bucky returned the salutation, and then veered his gaze to Josh. Out of the corner of his eye, Bucky saw Mary whisper something in Nellie's ear. Bucky didn't hear what Mary said to her, but Mary laid her hand on Nellie's arm and Nellie smiled in appreciation.

"You have a very beautiful boy," Mary commented as she kneeled and patted the boy on the head.

"Thanks," Nellie replied. "This was going to be the first time he really got to meet his father. I never really meant it to be this way, but sometimes things happen that are beyond our control, you know?"

Mary nodded in agreement. "Believe me; I understand."

"How's Roger doing?" Josh asked Bucky.

"He was awake long enough to talk a little, but I could tell how much excruciating pain he's in. Nurse Lyndaker gave him a sedative before I left his room. Roger needs his rest tonight, but we should be able to talk to him some more tomorrow."

"That's good," Josh said. "It's been one hell of a night. I'm still shocked the Reaper attacked Roger at his own house. I'm just glad I got there when I did."

"So are we," Nellie said.

"Did Roger mention anything about the attack to you, Bucky?" Josh asked.

"No," Bucky said, deciding to leave out the odd detail about the Reaper's height and the arrival of the painting. "He doesn't remember much of anything—just the sudden attack, some pain, and then blackness. Roger doesn't remember anything else."

Josh nodded. "Do the doctors have any idea when Roger can leave? I mean, he should be able to go home in a couple days or so, right?"

Bucky shook his head. "I don't know, Josh. We're still in the 'everyone's happy he's alive' mode."

Bucky looked at Nellie and Alex. "Come on, guys, let's get over to my house. You all look beat." He waved to the reporters and said, "Talk to ya later, Josh. Nice to see you again, Mary."

Josh and Mary nodded as the others walked out of the hospital. Mary looked down the hall toward Roger's room. Josh followed her gaze.

"If he didn't tell Bucky anything, then there's nothing here for us," Josh said. "I'm going home to crash on my couch for a few hours."

"You definitely look exhausted," Mary concurred. "Are you coming to the *Tribune* in the morning, or are you going to take the day off?"

"Nah, I'll be in to the office around noon. How about you, Mary?"

"I'll be there, too. I'm sure Ty wouldn't like it if I took a day off within the first month I was hired."

Josh nodded. "Yeah, Ty can be a pain in the ass over trivial things like that. Hey, do you have any plans for later on? Would you like to get some dinner after work and discuss the recent Reaper attacks?"

"I'd love to, Josh…but, Jack Lavancha already asked me," Mary answered, smiling. "Jack wants me to come to his hotel room after work so we can compare notes. But, if you'd like, you can come along with me."

"Mary! Are you crazy? You can't let a rival reporter know what information you have on a story. Don't be so naïve or you'll get scooped on every story you work on."

"Josh, I don't see the harm in talking to Jack. It's not like we have anything substantial anyway. We could definitely use a fresh outlook if we're going to try and get to the bottom of this. Besides, this isn't strictly work related. He wants me to have dinner with him in his room."

"I don't like the sound of this," Josh grumbled.

"Well, like I said, you can come if you want to."

Josh grimaced, grinding his teeth together in his mouth. But in the end, what choice did he have? He couldn't let his rival get the scoop on him. And so, Josh muttered some obscenities under his breath and followed Mary out of the hospital, not looking forward to the upcoming night.

Chapter 63:

Digging for Clues

It was the night of September 13th, and Jack Lavancha was in his room at the Imperial Hotel with Mary Powell, trying to eat pork fried rice with a pair of chopsticks. Josh Roberts was also in Jack's room, helping them research Tim Matthews's *complete* life history.

Josh was quietly aggravated, especially being so close to Lavancha for such an extended period of time. However, he managed to keep his feelings under the normally confident veneer in order to try and help things go smoothly.

The Historic Imperial Hotel

Jack seemed a little less concerned about appearances. He wore his frustration openly, though he hadn't went on a verbal tirade or lashed out at Roberts yet. Jack's constant glances over towards Mary only underlined the unease between the two men, which wasn't helped by the fact that Josh was caught glancing in her direction every so often as well. Mary reacted to everything by simply sitting in a chair, making as little eye contact with the two men as possible. She listened to the two men exchange remarks while quietly scribbling notes on a pad she kept on her lap.

Josh narrowed his eyes and peered at Jack as he said, "I talked to Bucky, Roger, and Celeste shortly after the Buckley Building incident. Celeste mentioned that Tim told her he was raised by his mother—Elizabeth."

Mary spoke up and said, "Is she still alive?"

"I don't know," Josh replied. "I did some research on the Timmons family and found that Elizabeth's last known address was somewhere in Black Bayou, Louisiana."

"Maybe she still lives there!" Mary said excitedly. "I wonder if there's a way to get in touch with her!"

"I can try, Mary. That's actually a good idea. I originally just wanted to find out what happened to Tim and his family...discover *why* he turned out to be the psychopath that he was. But I just realized something, too. If she *is* alive, I'm sure she doesn't know her son has just died. No one is looking for a *Tim Matthews*."

Josh took two cigars from his suit coat and handed one to Jack. Josh lit his stogie with his silver Zippo, inhaled deeply, and exhaled a large puff of smoke into the air. Jack lit his as well, and as he exhaled, a large pall of smoke descended upon the room.

Josh turned to Mary, pulled another cigar from his coat, and extended it to her. "Would you like one, Mary?"

"No thank you," she replied. "If I suddenly get the urge to smoke, I'll just breathe the air around me."

The two men laughed at Mary's remark and Josh opened a window to clear the air.

Jack leaned back in his chair, took a few more puffs, and announced, "I don't know if Tim's mother is still living in Louisiana, and quite frankly, I don't care." His words were a little more curtly than he intended. "I'm more interested in Tim's activities while he was in Carthage."

"Like what?" asked Mary.

"I'm curious whether he belonged to an occult or if he worshipped Satan," Jack said. "I'd like to know what force could bring a person back to life."

"I don't think it's a ghost, Jack," Josh countered. "It's probably some punk kid who idolized freaking psychopaths and is trying to copycat his hero."

Jack nodded slightly. "That's entirely possible, Roberts. Hell, maybe even likely...but I wouldn't dismiss the fact it could be a ghost. I remember hearing an urban legend of a musician who was killed along with his girlfriend in Detroit. A short time later, that man was brought back to life...by a bird of some kind I believe. The reason for his resurrection was *Revenge*! Kind of eerie how similar it is, isn't it?"

An eerie stillness came over the room. A few seconds later, Josh broke the silence by asking, "I'm going to the vending machine to get some more coffee. Does anyone want anything?"

"Nothing for me, thanks," said Mary.

"Nah," muttered Jack.

Josh walked down the hallway and arrived at the machine. Another gentleman was already putting in quarters when Josh arrived. The young blonde-haired man turned around and said, "I'm sorry, I'll just be a minute. I can't decide what I want. I'm not used to drinking coffee."

"No problem. Take your time." Josh looked at the man for a moment and asked, "Are you new in town? I don't think I've ever seen you around Carthage before."

"Yeah," the man replied. "My name's Ben Reilly. I just moved here a couple weeks ago."

"Oh, yeah?" Josh asked. "Well welcome to Carthage. Where are you from originally?"

"Well, uh, I grew up near Manhattan. I also lived in the heart of New York City for many years."

"Manhattan!" said Josh with exuberance. "Now there's a quality place. I love that whole area! My dad used to take me to see the Mets play when I was a kid. I couldn't get enough of it."

Ben grinned. "Yeah, I love baseball, too. In fact, one of my first memories is of Shea Stadium."

"So what the heck are you doing in Upstate New York? This place is *nothing* like Manhattan or any other upscale, trendy place."

"Actually, I've been traveling all over the world for quite some time. I lived in France for a while, and I've spent the past few years in the Catskills before deciding to come to the North Country."

Josh stared off and reminisced. "Ahhh...the Catskills *are* a beautiful area. I once did an internship down there."

"Yeah, and after seeing the countryside, I don't think I could *ever* go back to living in a big city. The rural setting is much more peaceful...and I don't want to be stuck in the middle of ten million people anymore."

"Can't blame ya there," agreed Josh.

"Anyway, I recently started driving a taxicab for the Yellow Cab business. I've been working there a couple of weeks now."

Josh squinted his eyes at Ben and said, "So...you just moved up here a few weeks ago, huh? That's an interesting timeframe if I do say so—that wouldn't happen to be around the same time the new Reaper arrived would it?"

"Is it?"

"Maybe I'll have to keep an eye on you...Ben, was it?"

Ben gave Josh a very weird look, grabbed his coffee, and walked away without saying another word.

"Take care, Mr. Reilly," Josh said as much to himself as to the departing man. "I'm sure we'll be talking again soon."

Inside Jack's room, Mary was sipping on her glass of Jack Daniels and looked slyly at the brooding man in front of her.

"So, Jack," said Mary, "tell me a little something about yourself. Do you have any family?"

Jack gave a slight smile, one that he figured fit in with his sarcastic, tough guy machismo. "I have a father I don't talk to. My mother died years ago."

"Are you married?" Mary asked, unfazed by Jack's initial answers.

Jack shook his head and scoffed. "Are ya kiddin', Mary? Marriage is an institution; if you believe in it, you belong in one yourself!"

"Why such the negative view on marriage?" Mary asked. "Were you married before? Do you have any children?"

"Nope," Jack responded nonchalantly. "I was engaged once, but that didn't work out. Hurt like hell, but I learned my lesson and didn't get caught again. For a while I had a live-in girlfriend, but that ended when she demanded marriage."

"And naturally you resisted..."

"Of course! What is marriage for? So in a couple years when she decided to find another flame, she could break my heart *and* take half of everything I own? No thanks."

"I guess it's safe to assume you don't have any children either, hmmm?"

"Nah, I didn't had any rugrats of my own. At least, not that I'm aware of. Y'see, I never had a good father, so I wouldn't even know where to begin. They would cramp my style and I don't have time for any anyway. It's just me going solo...and that's still just the way I like it."

"Why would you say that?" Mary asked. "You've never been lonely at night? Never wanted a child to call you daddy and carry on the family name?"

"Who needs a family, Mary?" Jack asked. "In all of my experience, I've come to the conclusion that they'll only let you down. Believe me; I'm saving any son of mine a lifetime of disappointment in me. Hell, maybe for us both."

"Why do you have such a chip on your shoulder, Jack? Did something happen in your family?"

Jack silently gave her credit. The girl wasn't just looks; she had a reporter's instincts and knew how to drive to the heart of a hidden story.

"I guess you could say that. Something happened many years ago. Somethin' that me and the rest of my family have been tryin' to live with for many generations."

"Like what?" Mary continued to press, taking one finger and playing with the single ice cube in her Jack Daniels. Lavancha found something about the motion very attractive.

"Well, it's like this, Mary. My family has a long history around these parts, and one thing about country folks is that they have a memory that spans generations, and if your great-great-great grandfather once insulted them, they won't let you forget it."

"Is that what happened in your case?"

"Pretty much, Mary. Y'see, there was a bank scandal in Carthage during 1913 that was plastered all over the upstate newspapers. The story even made its way down to the big New York papers."

"Wow!" exclaimed Mary. "The big newspaper companies from the city actually picked up on that story, huh? That *is* amazing."

"It wasn't front page material down in the city...their problems always seem much bigger. However, it *was* enough press to effectively humiliate Carthage."

"And how is that connected to your family?"

"The bank's president was a young, once promising, thirty-year-old man by the name of Walter Lavancha. He was my great-grandfather. Walter had been juggling deposits and record books in such a way so he could shave a little bit off the top each month without anyone catchin' him. From what I understand, the idea was that he'd be able to walk away with a big cushion of money when he retired one day."

Jack took a drink of his own whiskey before continuing: "When the bank examiners paid a visit to Walter, they discovered that the funds were indeed missing. Walter was better than the local bookkeepers, but not the big time examiners from New York City. They'd seen it all before."

Mary leaned forward with her elbows on the table. "What happened to him, Jack?"

"My great granddaddy knew the jig was up, and before Walter could be arrested and held accountable for his actions, he blatantly took $10,000 from the bank's treasury, boarded a train, and departed for parts unknown."

"Oh," Mary replied.

Jack Lavancha paused. "That may not sound like much now, but for a small-town bank back then, it was devastating. Walter would *never* be seen again in Jefferson County. Some rumors and reports eventually placed him somewhere in the Deep South, but no one had the ability to confirm it."

"Do you know if the Carthage Police went looking for him, or if they contacted any other departments in the South to try and locate him?"

"Doubt it. The police departments weren't connected back then the way they are now with the internet and such. My family's been considered the black sheep of the North Country ever since, and my last name is nothing but garbage. All because of something that happened well over fifty years before I was even born."

"I'm sorry to hear that, Jack," Mary said sympathetically. "So, your grandfather never got to know his dad? That's sad. Was there anything left behind to remember him by?"

"You mean other than his horrible legacy?" Jack asked, some definite venom in his voice as he thought about his family's history. "Yes, there were photographs. I saw one once...got to see what Walter looked like. It was an old, black and white faded photograph. My great grandfather was a tall, lanky man with a beard. Not even in the distinguished way, like Abe Lincoln. Nothing special."

"Oh, I see," Mary stated.

"How about you, Mary?" Jack asked, hoping to find out more about the attractive lady in his room, especially before Josh Roberts got back from getting coffee. "Do you have any family of your own?"

"I did. I was married for many years, but I'm a widow now. I married a wonderful man, and we had fifteen wonderful years together. He died just a little over a year ago," Mary confided. "We never had any children together."

"Look," Jack said, "I know I come across as somewhat crude, and maybe I am, but my dad made sure he taught me how to respect a woman." He paused to clear his throat before saying, "Y'know, I'm usually not attracted to mature ladies—"

"Oh, yeah? Prefer the young, stupid girls, huh?" Mary asked, teasing.

Jack leaned forward, his face coming within a few inches of Mary's. "It makes it easier to find someone who'll put up with me," Jack admitted with a smile. "But I really *am* attracted to you, Mary. After all this Reaper business, would you like to go out for a drink sometime? Just you an' me?"

Just then, with incredibly irritating timing, Josh came back into the room. "Boy, this Reaper is causing just as much havoc in Carthage as the last one," he commented. "Maybe even more!"

Jack jumped out of his chair. "Damn it, Roberts! You're always cramping my style. Why don't you go for a long walk or something? Come back in an hour or two...or better yet, don't come back at all!"

"Shut up, Jack, and listen for a moment!" bellowed Josh.

"What is it, Josh?" asked Mary.

"Well, the more I think about Jack's idea of resurrection, the more I'm beginning to wonder if the Reaper really *is* the ghost of Tim Matthews. It seems kinda eerie how closely everything follows, and that revenge theme Jack mentioned earlier definitely seems plausible."

"I told ya so!" hollered Jack.

"After all, aside from the sudden appearance of the 'murder portraits,' everything else is basically the same. The Reaper is targeting everyone Tim knew, still has the same cloak, and is still igniting fires. A copycat killer usually isn't as meticulous as this. They tend to get a little sloppy."

Mary and Jack sat scratching their chins.

"How about you, Mary? Do you believe in the myth of resurrection?"

"Well, all I can tell you is that every legend is supposedly based on fact. Every myth is grounded in some sort of truth. History proves that over and over again. City of Troy, the Great Flood...therefore, as strange and impossible as it might sound, I think it might very well be possible that he's been resurrected."

"I hope to hell we're wrong about the Reaper being a spectre. I'd prefer if it's just some wacko guy who will be caught eventually," Jack butted in. "Unfortunately, I don't have *any* idea who'd be pretending to be the Reaper. Other than Tim Matthews, do you have a gut feeling as to who it could be, Roberts?"

"Nothing yet," Josh said with a shrug. "Then again, maybe it's that Ben Reilly guy who lives down the hallway."

"The new cabbie in town?" asked Mary.

"What's that?" Josh asked, wondering how Mary knew who he was referring to.

Mary smiled broadly. "Are you talkin' about that good-lookin' blonde-haired guy from Manhattan?"

Josh's eyes narrowed. "Yeah, that's him. How do you know him, Mary?"

"Are you kiddin'? That guy's a hunk! I introduced myself to him an hour after I moved my belongings into my room." She exhaled deeply and said, "Seems like a nice, young man. I'm sure I could teach him a thing or two in the bedroom."

Josh stood in shock. He'd never heard Mary talk in such a way before. Jack was just as surprised, and his mouth dropped in astonishment.

"Um...I'm sure you could, Mary," Josh responded before changing the subject. "Anyway, I just talked to him at the vending machine and he mentioned that he's from New York City. Ben moved here right about the time the second round of Reaper attacks began. Makes ya wonder...what would a drifter from New York City be doing in Carthage?"

"Don't be so quick to assume it's *not* a local person, Roberts," Jack stated. "Neither Mary nor I are from Carthage, and we aren't homicidal maniacs. Maybe people from the city think differently than those from rural areas, but they're not *all* bad."

"I know," Josh admitted, "but..."

"Besides," Jack butted in, "the Reaper ordeal was a *huge* story for Carthage. Everyone on the East Coast who's picked up a newspaper within the last couple months knows what's been going on here."

Josh nodded. "Maybe you're right. Though Louis Ferr used a ferry business as a shield for his murderous actions, this could just be bad timing on Ben's part. Lord knows I wouldn't want to move into Carthage right now."

Josh took a sip of his coffee, and seemed to be thinking, brow furrowing as he did so. "But no matter who or what this Reaper is, I still don't have a clear cut opinion as to what the police should do when they catch the guy. The last Reaper eliminated several people on the police force…and the department was undermanned at that time! If the officers catch him and lock him up…" Josh stopped.

"What?" questioned Mary. "What're you thinking?"

"Well, if the case goes to trial, there's a chance this Reaper-person could be paroled at some point. And if he *does* get loose someday, I know he'll come back to Carthage and do it again."

Jack spoke up and offered his opinion. "I say they shoot him. Once in the head should do the trick. If the police don't want to do it, we can always resort to mob justice. That'll send a clear message to any punk copycat wannabe. Guarantee you wouldn't see another murderer show up in this town after that."

Mary scoffed. Jack veered his attention toward her.

"What do you think about this, Mary?" he prodded. "What would you do to the Reaper?"

"Nothing," she replied, looking somewhat offended. "I absolutely abhor violence."

Jack looked shocked. "Mary, are you implying that you don't think the Reaper has done anything—anything at *all* to justify killing him?"

"Well the answer to that question changes with every person's opinion. No, it's not that I think the person should get off the hook, but it's just that maybe the person isn't so evil after all. What's the worst that this Reaper has done? So what if the Reaper has sent some paintings of the victims to the police station with a severed finger attached to them?"

Jack's mouth dropped open again.

"Does that really make the actual killings any worse than if the men were shot during a war?" she continued. "Besides, off the record, from what I can tell, most of the victims so far were the types that live life just asking for trouble, anyway."

Jack looked surprised and asked, "What a minute, what did you say about paintings? How do you know about that?"

Mary's eyes darted away to the floor, then over to her whiskey, of which she took a sip, before her eyes returned to Josh's careful examination.

Jack Lavancha looked very interested, wondering why this painting information hadn't been mentioned to him yet, since obviously he was the only one out of the loop with whatever information this was.

Josh cocked his head to the side and studied Mary's demeanor carefully while he said, "Mary, that information hasn't been released to the public yet. I know because Roger heard it from the Mayor and he told me. So, how did *you* know that?"

Mary was fumbling for words. She blushed, as if embarrassed. "You're not the only one in this room who has sources, Josh."

"You haven't been in Carthage very long, Mary," Jack pointed out. "How could you have any sources...and if we're all working together on this one, why am I the *only* one out in the cold."

"Well, I do," Mary said firmly. "And apparently, they know *exactly* what they're talking about."

"Why didn't you tell me you knew about this, Mary?" asked Josh.

Mary stared him right in the eyes and remarked, "For the same reason you didn't tell me. You don't trust me, and until you do, I have no reason to trust you. A lack of trust is a lack of respect. Besides...what's the first thing you two would think of if I mentioned that I had sources this quick? Especially because I'm a woman!"

There was an uncomfortable silence in the room. Jack and Josh both looked at each other, and Jack had an amused smirk on his face, in part because of Mary's answer and in part because of how uncomfortable Josh obviously looked.

"You both think I slept with someone," Mary answered for them. "I'm a woman, not a whore. A little flirting goes a long way when you have breasts and a good smile. And sometimes, *women* will be more likely to confide in you than a man...especially if you meet the right one. Do you understand what I'm sayin' boys?"

Josh and Jack looked at one another and shook their heads.

"She's good," Jack said. "But honestly, Roberts, I know we haven't gotten along before, but if we're all withholding information, there's more of a chance this story's gonna slip right out of our fingers."

"I understand what you mean," Mary concurred.

Jack winked at her and then said, "Y'know, I realize you don't like my style, Roberts, but I'm guessin' we *all* have information the rest of us don't. Are we gonna to do this right, or aren't we?"

"All right," Josh said, gritting his teeth. He turned toward Mary. "I'm sorry for keeping information from you. I'm supposed to be mentoring you, and being deceitful is *not* the way for me to do a proper job. Please forgive me, Mary. It won't happen again."

"No problem, Hun," Mary said. "I'll be open, too, from now on."

Josh turned to Jack. "You're a pompous, disagreeable ass," Josh stated, "but sometimes your style *does* have its advantages. If I fill you in on the severed fingers, do you have any information to swap back?"

"Yeah," Jack said. "As a matter of fact, I do. I got more stuff about Louisiana and a few tidbits about Tim's family history. I don't have a lot of hard information to pass on, but I *do* have some interesting material that lets ya know there's more to this Reaper story than meets the eye."

"Before we go any further," Josh announced, "I wanna know one thing. What do you want out of all of this, Jack? You've never been known to help someone for nothing."

Jack smirked. "If we work together, I want all three of us get our names on the by-line…for both papers. Deal?"

"Works for me," Mary uttered, smiling.

"Deal," grumbled Josh. The two rivals glared at one another and begrudgingly shook hands to seal it.

Chapter 64:

Danger is Looming
(September 15th - Night)

Despite the impasse Detective Streeter encountered after all his investigative work toward the 'Resurrected Reaper' case (which is what the *Tribune's* headlines were now dubbing him), he kept pressing on. Rick was also continuing to gather information on the 'Jane Doe' murder in Deferiet.

Detective Streeter was active in his pursuit of solving both cases. However, if the Reaper investigation was going to drag on without achieving some type of resolution anytime soon, then Rick was determined to solve the other murder in the area and prove to Chief Zimmerman he *deserved* his promotion to detective. After hours of work came up empty with multiple dead-ends and endless runarounds, Rick decided to go for a drive and clear his head of the Reaper case for awhile. Rick drove an unmarked police car out to a wooded area in Deferiet and parked alongside the road.

Rick was walking along the decrepit lane where Jane Doe's body was found, inspecting every pothole in the road and every piece of trash that had accumulated in the ditches. After an hour of searching without success, Rick moseyed over to Deferiet's only bar—Hillbilly Heaven.

While gazing at the old rusty-colored bar from the outside, Rick had no idea what to expect. The building still had the appearance of a hay barn, except for the neon-lit beer signs which hung in every window. Rick took a deep breath to calm his nerves and gather the courage to enter. Streeter hoped that Hillbilly Heaven's notorious reputation for being a 'brawling bar' was overblown and cautiously opened the weathered oak door as he peered inside. The building stank of stale peanuts, burnt popcorn, beer, and urine…and Rick half expected to be assaulted by a bunch of plaid-wearin' rednecks as soon as he walked foot in the bar.

Holy shit! I feel like I've just stepped into a scene from the Deliverance film, Rick thought cynically. *No wonder all the hillbillies love it here.*

He made his way across the warped floorboards, down the middle of the room to a row of battered tables that were sticky with spilled beer. Rick went from table to table with a picture of Jane Doe's face in his hand and began asking the patrons a few questions. Most were unwilling to even talk to Rick, and more than one of the drunkards seemed to size him up, as if looking for a fight.

After Rick struck out with everyone sitting at the tables, he turned and noticed an elderly gentleman sitting at the far end of the bar near an old belly stove. The man sat in solitude, hunched over with several empty shot glasses stacked in front of him. Rick could tell by the pile of dollar bills the man kept next to his beer bottle that he was someone who enjoyed spending many hours at the establishment.

Rick approached the guy and said, "Hey old-timer! I'd like to ask you a question."

The stranger turned his rickety armchair to face Rick and squinted to see only a few feet in front of him.

Rick pulled out his picture of Jane Doe and waved it in the man's face. "Have you seen this woman before?"

The old man took the photo Rick held in front of him. He grabbed his coke-bottle eyeglasses off the bar and inspected the image.

"Uh…um…Yeah," the man said as he belched loudly. "I remember seein' her in here a while back!" His breath reeked of cheap whiskey that reminds you of kerosene. "Bright red hair—pretty girl, too."

"Are you sure it's the same girl?" questioned Rick. "Take your time and look at the picture for as long as you need."

"Sure I'm sure. I remember 'cause I was watchin' the TV at the bar when she came in. We wuz watchin' the news guys talk 'bout the big fire in Carthage."

"I think I know which night you're talking about," Rick mentioned. "And do you remember anything that happened after she entered?" he asked as he pulled out his notepad and began to write.

"Well, I turned 'round to tell a buddy of mine 'bout the TV and in that woman walked. She sat down at a table near the door, havin' a beer and eatin' some chicken wings with another lady."

"She wasn't alone?"

"Nah...both of 'em wuz frost queens if ya ask me. Wouldn't even talk to anyone else all friggin' night. Can you imagine that?"

For the benefit of getting information, and keeping his personal safety in mind, Detective Streeter decided to keep his derogatory retort to himself.

"Go back to the redhead's friend for a moment," Rick told the old man. "What did she look like?"

"Oh, I dunno," the drunkard replied. "When the redhead made it clear they weren't interested in anyone, I lost interest myself. I think the other woman had brownish hair, maybe a little auburn, I'm not sure. She was about the same height as the redhead—the girl there in your photo. The brunette was probably in her late forties, maybe early fifties. Pretty good lookin' herself...y'know, for an older chick an' all."

"What did the two ladies do while they were here?"

"They ate some chicken wings, drank a few beers, and chatted with each other. After an hour or two, they paid the bartender and left together."

"You didn't happen to catch either of their names, did you?" Detective Streeter asked, keeping his fingers crossed.

"Nope. Like I told ya, those two weren't interested in no one in here—they seemed too stuck-up for that. Although, now that I think about things, it did seem as though the brunette was just a little *too* interested in her friend."

That answer took Detective Streeter off guard. He wondered what exactly that meant, and so he asked. "What makes you think that?"

"Her eyes never seemed to drift away from the redheaded. Well, unless it was to watch the news on the TV. Like I told ya, we wuz all checkin' out the video of the Carthgae fire. I'm thinkin' it was some historic place called the Buckley Buildin' or somethin' like that."

Rick's eyes squinted in curiosity. "You're saying the brunette was ogling her companion. What's so strange about that? She could've been a lesbian."

"Well, her behavior was kinda eerie to me. She just had this look...looked at the redhead almost, I don't know, like a wolf or animal or somethin'. Way too intense. Would've made me nervous if I was on the other side of that stare."

"Anything else that sticks out in your mind?" questioned Rick as he jotted down notes.

"That's 'bout all I can recall. I was drinkin' a little bit that night— I do that a lot, lately."

"You've been more then helpful, old-timer," Streeter voiced as he tossed the man a twenty dollar bill. "Thank you for all the information."

Rick tucked his notepad back in his jacket pocket and exited the bar. The information he received wasn't going to break the case wide open, but it was a hell of a lot more than nothing...and at least he knew to be on the lookout for a newcomer in Carthage. Trying to spot a tourist or a newbie wasn't as easy as it used to be, especially because of Fort Drum's huge growth, but maybe this was a situation in which Josh Roberts or Jack Lavancha could help him out. Hell, why not both reporters? Whichever one could find the most usable information would get the inside track on the all the latest breaking news. That seemed fair enough to Detective Streeter.

On the way back to his vehicle, Rick took one last perusal around the crime scene, hoping for the one-in-a-million chance that he'd find something the forensics team had missed the first several times they were out there. After his search came up empty, he walked over to the Northern Pines Motel, hoping for any type of a clue that could put the pieces together for him.

Along the way, he was glancing around with his flashlight in hand when a sharp glint shined back at him. Streeter crouched downward, already drawing his gun, before realizing the object wasn't a knife or a gun...or a Reaper's scythe either. It was, however, something small and shiny, and the item was entangled in a pile of grass and leaves on the ground.

Detective Streeter walked over and bent down, pushing the grass aside with a pen he pulled from his pocket. This area was off to the right side of the motel, about fifty yards east of the crime scene. Strangely, it wasn't *so* far out of the way that this area wouldn't have been checked at least *once* already. Detective Rick Streeter looked in amazement as he discovered a fancy metallic fountain pen lying beneath the foliage...with traces of dried blood on the tip.

"How the hell did the other officers miss this?" he whispered softly. "I guess that's what happens when you work with an inexperienced crew."

Detective Streeter had put on plastic gloves and collected the pen, while also putting a yellow tag on the nearby tree to mark the spot for other officers. Luckily, Rick carried a few plastic Ziploc bags in his jacket pocket with him at all times, always as a 'just in case' precaution. It was a habit he'd learned from working alongside the recently deceased Detective Kenneth Johnson. Streeter called in ahead to the police station and reported his findings, as well as requesting a team to come back out to the scene the next morning at first light. After he finished perusing the area, Rick drove back to Carthage to inform Chief Zimmerman of the evidence he recovered.

At the station, Detective Streeter handed the Ziploc bag containing the pen over to Chief Zimmerman. C.Z. studied the pen and grunted with approval. After careful inspection, the chief called Officer Julius Jackson into the room and ordered him to take the baggie downstairs to the evidence closet next to their inadequate forensics lab.

After Julius left the room, Zimmerman said, "Good work, Rick. Maybe we'll get lucky and this pen will give us the break in the case we've been searchin' for."

With a proud smile, Rick said, "Thanks, Chief."

"At the very least, the dried blood is something the lab technician can do some tests on. On top of that, I've got some news to tell you about, too. While you were out in Deferiet looking around, I got an update on the dead woman."

"Really?" Streeter asked. "Like what?"

"Well, I'm getting a little ahead of myself," the chief retorted. "It's not an update yet, but I've got a friend in Watertown with better equipment and resources than we have in this rinky-dink police department."

Rick raised a brow. "A friend? Like who?"

"Police Chief Grant Morgan. The man who replaced me. Does it matter?"

"No," Rick replied. "I was just curious."

"Anyway, I sent him a copy of the dead woman's fingerprints this morning and Grant said he'd get back to me in a day or so if he finds any information. Even if Jane Doe is not a criminal, if she was *ever* hired as a government worker, or even just born in the area...we may still be able to get some results. Once we know who the victim is, we'll be onto the killer like a blood hound on a fox."

Rick threw a fist pump into the air. "That's great news, Chief. I'm ready to take down this psycho once and for all!"

"Oh, I think I should tell you that Mayor Morgan and I received some interesting mail this morning."

Rick cocked his head to the side. "Uhhh...okay."

"LaTesha found two letters lying on the front steps when she got to work. She brought them up to Bucky's office while I was in there talkin' to him. They were death threats."

Rick gasped. "Death threats! From who?"

"Apparently from the Reaper," C.Z. stated.

"Whoa...the Reaper has never done anything like this before. Seems like he's definitely making this string of murders more personal than anything he's previously done."

"I agree, Rick. And there's one other thing I should mention," the chief said as he itched his scalp. "Y'know that painting Bucky sent over here? The one Roger Fasick received from the hospital?"

"Yeah, Chief," uttered Rick. "I put the painting down in the storage closet with the rest of the Reaper evidence the night it came in."

C.Z. nodded. "Well, I'm sure you're also familiar with the fact that Roger did *not* have one of his fingers cut off."

"Yes, I was already aware of that, too. That's why this painting was such a head-scratcher for me. Without a finger, I figured it must've been painted with a brush this time."

"Actually, no," the chief answered as he leaned back and began stroking the whiskers on his chin. "It was still painted in finger-style painting."

Rick expression turned to shock. "It was? It had to have been the killer's own hand this time!"

"I'm not entirely sure about that, Rick. Y'see, I had the painting tested to see if there were any fingerprints on it that weren't smudged."

"Was there?"

"There was!" blurted the chief. "In fact, I just received the results back on the prints about an hour ago."

"And...?" prodded Detective Streeter.

Zimmerman took a deep breath and announced, "The fingerprints belong to Tim Matthews."

Later that night, Edgar Polansky walked into City Hall and approached LaTesha's desk. He had grease all over his pants resulting from someone's prank, and Edgar went to ask her which officers were on duty tonight so he could file a complaint. At that moment, Bucky came down the stairway leading from his office.

Bucky was just finishing another long, stressful day at work, which included fielding twenty calls an hour from infuriated residents who thought they were big shots in town and entitled to view every shred of evidence the police had on file. They screamed their frustration at Bucky, demanding to know what course of action was being done about the serial killings as well. By the end of the workday, Bucky's headache had mushroomed from a pin-sized annoyance into a full-fledged migraine. For Bucky, the worst part of the mayoral job wasn't the job duties and responsibility; it was all the bullshit he constantly had to put up with.

"I'm heading home now, LaTesha," Bucky said. He noticed Edgar standing at her desk with a scowl upon his face and asked, "Is this buffoon giving you a hard time?"

LaTesha rolled her eyes at the troublesome nuisance and shifted her attention to Bucky. "Nothing I can't handle, sir. Besides, I think he wants me to feel sorry for him so I'll agree to go on a date."

"Please!" Edgar hollered with a snort. "I wouldn't waste my time asking you out. Not with the way you look lately."

LaTesha slapped her hands on her desk and snarled, "What did you just say to me?"

"You've let yourself go, LaTesha. You used to be a gorgeous lady, but you don't take care of yourself like you used to. You're beginning to look like a frumpy old woman."

"Old woman! There's *nothing* on my body that resembles an old woman!"

"Well, your face is bit puffy. Looks like your packing on a few pounds of water weight. Oh, and your once tight ass is a bit saggy...as well as a bit of a turn-off."

A screeching noise erupted as LaTesha dug her nails into the top of her metal desk. "That shouldn't bother you, Edgar. After all, you should be used to saggy things. That's all you see when you look into a mirror!"

"Hey, don't shoot the messenger, lady! Haven't you ever heard the old saying, 'Guys don't make passes at girls with fat asses.'?"

LaTesha stood and screamed in his face, "The only one who's fat around here, Edgar, is you!"

Edgar stepped backwards and veered to face Bucky.

"Hey, Bucky, while I have you here, I wanted to find out if you got my letter in the mail."

Bucky stopped and thought. "Which letter is that?"

"The one stating how you stole my idea about installing new sidewalks at the park? You know I came up with that idea over a year ago, right?"

"Yeah," quipped Bucky. "Your note came in the mail. And, I gotta say, the letter arrived at just the *right* time."

Edgar looked puzzled. "What do ya mean?"

"I was sitting on the toilet when I was glancing over your letter. I looked to my side and noticed I was completely out of toilet paper! So...I used your letter to wipe my ass."

Edgar looked dumbfounded and appalled.

"What's the matter?" asked Bucky. "Was I not supposed to do that? You might still be able to fetch it out of my sewer if you need it back."

Bucky left Edgar standing in utter shock and entirely speechless. LaTesha roared in laughter as Bucky smirked and walked away.

Bucky tried to relax as he exited the building and let the thought of seeing Celeste, Nellie, Alex, and Mikey cheer him up. Even though his head was pounding like a jackhammer, Bucky was genuinely excited and eager to visit with everyone when he got home. In just the short amount of time Bucky had spent with Alex, he could already tell the boy was a good kid. However, Bucky could also sense that Alex had inherited the inquisitive and rebellious streak his father was famous (or infamous) for—depending on your interpretation. Roger would be very happy and proud.

Bucky let out a sigh of content and grinned. He had a strong feeling in his gut that some much-needed peaceful days were ahead for all of them—and they were certainly due for some good luck, too. Hell, just average luck would be sufficient at that point.

After stopping for a moment to inhale the cool night air, Bucky headed toward his magenta colored Mustang. His thoughts had shifted from the joy of seeing his loved ones to a much darker situation. The attack on Roger's life flooded his mind, and Bucky was also mulling over the bizarre note he received earlier that day.

While C.Z. was in Bucky's office, LaTesha had delivered two brown letter-sized envelopes—one addressed to each man. Inside the envelopes were death threats, comprised of words cut out of various magazines and glued onto home-made paper. Bucky's letter stated that he would die for his role in Tim's death, and Zimmerman's letter threatened his life for not bringing Tim's killers to justice. Bucky had been holding the note in his hand ever since.

Once in a while Bucky received a death threat from some crackpot playing a joke, but this time it seemed much more ominous than a childish prank, especially in light of Roger's attack. What's more, the Reaper actually told Roger he was claiming revenge for what happened to Tim Matthews.

After his past experiences, first with Louis Ferr, and then with the Reaper, Bucky knew better than to just blow off such a threat. On the flipside, he couldn't let fear run his life, either. He shrugged his shoulders, hoping maybe he could shrug off his disturbing feelings as well. Once he got back home, things would be better. Hell, maybe they could all drive to the hospital and visit Roger. That would be nice.

As Bucky approached the car, he placed the note inside his jacket pocket. He knew he'd have to tell Celeste about the death threat eventually, but now was not the time to worry her, or anyone else. They were all going through enough anguish as it was with Roger in the hospital, as well as the general fear imposed upon them by the vengeful Reaper.

Bucky pushed the button on his keychain for the automatic car starter when he was still about forty feet away. It was one of the few bits of modern convenience he really liked. When he clicked the button, however, the car instantly exploded into a gigantic ball of fire. Bucky fell backwards upon the pavement, banging the side of his head against the unforgiving surface, and feeling the air being ripped from his lungs. He heard a WHOOSH sound and felt hot air rolling over him from the initial explosion.

Bucky rolled over and inspected himself for injuries and burns before sitting up. Sore ribs. *Very* sore ribs; one or more of them was probably broken. Every time he breathed it felt like being stabbed in the chest. He touched his left temple and felt a deep gash on the side of his head; blood was trickling down his cheek. However, aside from that and a few other scrapes, Bucky was no worse for wear. After making sure he had all him limbs intact, Bucky glanced over at his car...all that was left of his beloved Mustang was a black, unrecognizable hulk of steel going up in flames.

Bud Hopkins and Ben Reilly were talking to each other on the street corner across from City Hall. The explosion had dropped them to their knees as well, and once they recovered, the two men came running over to Bucky's side. Ben had a cell phone that was issued to him by the taxicab company and began dialing 911.

"Are you all right, Bucky?" Bud quickly shouted as he approached the mayor. "Where does it hurt?"

Bucky was slightly dazed and his ears were ringing like church bells from the thunderous explosion, but he could still make out what the two men were saying.

"My ribs, Bud. They're hurtin' pretty bad."

"Don't move! I've called the police," Ben told him. "An ambulance should be here shortly!"

Bucky tried to stand but Bud put his hand on his shoulder to stop him. "The kid is right, Bucky. Just sit right there and keep still until the paramedics arrive. We don't know how badly hurt you actually are. You could have internal bleedin' or somethin' worse!"

"Calm down, Bud," Bucky replied, shaking off Bud's hand. "You two seem more hysterical than I do. I'm gonna be fine. In fact, I've been through a lot worse than this before."

Bucky's head began to clear and the ringing in his ears was fading as he heard a police siren getting closer. In a matter of a few seconds, the street was alive with Fire and Rescue trucks, police squad cars, and an ambulance.

Chapter 65:

Death waits in the Shadows
(September 16th - Night)

The following evening, Jack Lavancha and Josh Roberts met at Kitty's Bar to continue discussing the Reaper case. Even in just a span of twenty-four hours, so much had happened in Carthage, including the explosion of Bucky's car. Mary was invited to join the men at the bar but declined because she wasn't feeling well and wanted to rest in her hotel room. However, the two longtime rivals had seemed to find at least a temporary truce over a couple of beers and the increasingly bizarre story that was unfolding day-by-day right in front of their very eyes.

"I hear the mayor had an attempt on his life last night," Jack mentioned. "Do you know anything about it?"

"Yeah," replied Josh. "From what I was told, a bomb was hooked to the engine of his car. Someone rigged it up so that when the ignition was started, it'd automatically explode. Bucky got lucky that he had one of those automatic car starters. If it weren't for that, there's no way in hell he could've survived the explosion."

Jack shook his head and finished off the rest of his beer. "First, the Reaper attacks Roger Fasick, and now he tries to murder Bucky Morgan. Y'know, aside from Thomas Parker, who's been holed up inside his house since being released from the police, the only other *real* enemy Tim Matthews had in Carthage was you, Roberts. And nothing has happened to you...yet."

"Yeah, Jack. I know several of us have been the object of the Reaper's wrath," Josh commented in a weary voice. "I'm quite aware there's a connection between the targets as well. On the other hand, there's something about it all that just doesn't feel right to me."

"What do you mean?" Jack asked.

Josh was distracted by some raucous laughter across the bar. He glanced over and saw Edgar Polansky standing with a group of men.

Probably some racist or crude dirty joke, Josh thought. *Edgar is full of asinine little quips like that.*

While Josh didn't generally care for Edgar's sense of humor, Josh wondered what kind of joke could get a reaction like that.

"Roberts!" Jack yelled out.

Josh snapped out of his daze. "I'm sorry, Jack, what were you saying?"

"I asked ya what ya meant by your statement."

"Were you referring to the people being targeted, or everything feeling a bit too different with this Reaper?"

"How about both?" Jack asked. "Just let me know everything that's on your mind about this case."

Josh took another sip from the frosty mug. "Like you said, Jack. There've been murder attempts on Roger and Bucky within the past week. Both of whom were directly involved in the showdown with Tim upon the Buckley Building. And if we can assume that Celeste was the Reaper's *real* target here at Kitty's instead of Travis, that means everyone who's connected with the first Reaper's death has been targeted, right?" Josh paused before saying, "Everyone except me."

"Right," Jack agreed, having noticed the pattern himself, and half expecting he knew where Josh was going with this. However, he wanted to confirm his own suspicions directly from the horse's mouth.

Josh exhaled deeply and uttered, "Actually, Jack, that's not true."

"Huh, Roberts? What's not true?"

"I *have* been targeted by the Reaper. Y'see, when I arrived at the *Tribune* this morning, I received a letter which basically stated I'd pay with my life for the horrible articles I wrote about the Reaper and Tim Matthews—especially the offensive one I wrote the day after Tim's death."

"Damn, Roberts. That sucks! Are ya nervous?"

"I'm trying not to let it get to me," Josh told him. "However, it's kinda hard not to be worried. After all, I can pretty much be certain that whoever this homicidal maniac is...he'll eventually be coming after me."

"Bummer," Jack said after several moments of silence. It wasn't the response he wanted to give, but it was hard to come up with just the right words in lieu of '*I'm sorry a homicidal maniac, or possibly supernaturally resurrected serial killer who might not be able to die, is coming to cut your throat and set you on fire.'*

Josh took the comment in stride and laughed. "You can say that again, Jack. I know I'm a target, but I don't understand why. The Reaper and I exchanged words during his break-in at the jail, and I *have* written some derogatory articles, but I've never been any real threat to him."

"Maybe he's confusing you with someone else," Jack proposed. "Maybe he's not thinking straight."

While tapping his pencil upon the table, Josh said, "I know Ty's really pushing the supernatural angle, but I just don't think it's the same person. In fact, I'm almost positive it isn't. We're missing something here."

Jack nodded. "Yeah, this story's been driving me crazy, too. My gut says we're overlooking something huge. I got one question for you, though. What makes you so sure this Reaper *isn't* the resurrected corpse of Tim Matthews?"

"The way the murders are being done," Josh said. "Remember how Rusty Hollinger was killed, and then his house was set on fire?"

"Sure," Jack said. "But wasn't arson part of the original Reaper's M.O.? I mean, Tim was a serial arsonist in addition to being a serial killer, right? In my opinion, he seemed *more* like an arsonist who acquired a taste for murder rather than vice versa."

"Exactly my point!" Josh exclaimed, slapping his open palm on the table in excitement. He saw Jack's blank stare and quickly offered an explanation. "Tim Matthews was an excellent arsonist. Nothing he set on fire survived...unless it was the church. Even then, it was all part of his plan. If fact, even when Tim was upon the Buckley Building with Celeste, Roger, and Bucky...and everything was spiraling out of control, Tim made certain the Buckley Building still burned completely to the ground."

Jack nodded. "I think I see where you're going with this. Keep talkin'."

"Unlike the Reaper's other fires, Rusty's apartment was only half burned. It was an amateur job. After all, Aerosol cans in a microwave *will* cause a sudden explosion and flames, but they don't last. In fact, if Rusty's apartment had been cleaner, there's a chance the fire wouldn't have even reached the living room. A real arsonist would've left a trail of gasoline to make sure the fire spread and did its job."

With a hearty laugh, Jack bellowed, "Aerosol cans in a microwave? That's like some friggin' Hollywood crap you see on TV."

"Ridiculous, isn't it?" retorted Josh.

Jack nodded. "So, now you've got me wondering…how could this Reaper be the resurrected corpse of Tim Matthews and suddenly become really crappy at starting fires?"

"Precisely what I was thought!" Josh exclaimed. "Celeste said she could tell Matthews loved fire—way beyond being a normal pyromaniac. Apparently, he spoke about the burning buildings and arsons the way you or I might talk about the most amazing lover we ever had."

Josh noticed the unpleasant look upon Jack's flushed face. "Damn, Jack—sorry. Really bad analogy."

"Just keep going," Jack snapped, waving it off like it was no big deal, though his facial expressions said otherwise.

"Anyway, Rusty's apartment was on fire, but only the kitchen was completely burned out. The living room was barely charred, and most of the body was completely unburned. That's not a fire Tim Matthews would've set."

"Probably not," agreed Jack.

"In addition to that, I don't remember any throats being slashed by the original Reaper—he used a stun gun to inflict his pain. Now, all of a sudden, the Reaper is painting with severed fingers and sending death threats in the mail!"

Jack grinned as he wrote in his notepad. "I'm with ya so far, Roberts."

"The other conflict that's been bugging me about this particular situation," continued Josh, "is that Tim Matthews's original intent was burning Carthage to the ground for what happened to his family."

"Uh huh," commented Jack. "So, what's bothering you?"

"Why aren't *more* buildings being torched? And bombing Bucky's car? I guess technically that's fire based, but it just doesn't seem to fit with what I know about Tim Matthews, you know?"

"You've got the skills of a trained detective, Roberts," Jack said in a semi-sarcastic tone.

"Why is this recent string of revenge based around all the people Tim Matthews associated with?" Josh went on to say. "And what did those autopsy guys have to do with anything? This situation feels like revenge to me…but a crazy type of revenge. One that's spreading to kill anyone who's close by."

"Blind rage," Jack said, nodding his head in agreement and taking another long drink from his mug. "You've got a very good point there, Roberts. I was thinking along the same lines, but I couldn't put it into words the way you did."

The two continued to drink their beer as they sat in silence. Josh's thoughts were transfixed upon the letter which threatened his life. He was especially focused on the glaring fact Jack had pointed out—that Josh was the *only* one of Tim's enemies who hadn't been attacked at least once.

That detail made Josh more nervous than he had been in years. Granted, there were at least two survivors of Reaper attacks so far. However, Roger only survived because of Josh's good timing—and he just barely got there in the nick of time. Bucky's survival was by pure luck. Those weren't the types of odds that excited Josh.

After the two men finished their beers and put their notepads away, Jack pulled his wallet out of his pants pocket, set it on the table, and counted out a few dollar bills to tip the bartenders. Then the two slightly inebriated men exited the light of the smoke-filled bar and into the dark unknown of the night, not helped by the fact that some teenage vandals (who apparently weren't afraid of the Reaper) smashed half of the streetlights in the area.

The two strolled down the sidewalk at a nice easy pace. Goosebumps suddenly appeared on Josh's arms and the hair on the back of his neck stood straight up as a cold shivering sensation flowed through his veins like liquid nitrogen. A strange uneasiness suddenly overcame him, his heartbeat rose to a fast steady thumping, and he had the unshakeable feeling that someone was spying on him.

"Whoa...that's weird," Josh muttered, glancing around with a paranoid look upon his face.

Jack thought Josh's behavior was half funny, half nerve-racking.

"What's wrong, Roberts?" questioned Jack. "Y'know, aside from you talkin' to yourself. Are ya gettin' a psychic vibe or somethin'?"

"I can't explain it, Jack. There's a fear in me—cold and sharp as if..." Josh stopped halfway through his sentence and looked around the area once again.

"As if what?" Jack prodded.

"As if something bad were about to happen," Josh answered. "As if something *really* bad was coming our way."

Jack abruptly grabbed his rear end and yelled, "Damn, Nostradamus, you're right! Something *very* bad is about to happen! I got a feelin' someone's about to spend *my* money."

"Huh?"

"I left my wallet on the table back in the damn bar. I'd better go back and get it. You can wait for me if you want, Roberts. I'll only be a few minutes."

A minute later, as Jack was hustling back to Kitty's Bar to retrieve his lost wallet, Josh was standing on the sidewalk. Suddenly, he heard a distressed whimpering sound coming from the dark alleyway. He stopped dead in his tracks and waited for a moment, and then Josh heard the distressed sound again.

Although Josh was extremely hesitant to enter a dark alleyway, he couldn't ignore the whimpering. He surmised that someone could be seriously hurt down in the alley, and he wouldn't be able to live with himself if that person died from an injury simply because he hadn't tried to help them or call an ambulance.

Josh took a few steps into the alleyway and passed a garbage dumpster. The whimpering stopped. Josh listened for it to start again but didn't hear anything. A slight breeze passed over him. A jingling bulb, poorly attached to the side of the building, was all he had to see in the alley next to the dumpster.

"Hello?" Josh asked, jumping at the sound of his voice echoing in the narrow alleyway. "Is anyone there? Do you need assistance? I won't hurt you; I'm here to help."

Josh nervously took a few more steps forward, despite his brain and all his instincts telling him to get out of there as quickly as his feet would take him. Josh then heard a crackling noise behind him. With lightning speed, Josh spun around and instantly saw the Reaper standing before him. Josh tried to run, but his foot got caught on some scraps of garbage and he slipped, falling hard upon the littered pavement. The Reaper immediately pounced on top of him. Josh thought he could struggle free, but the Reaper grabbed a handful of Josh's hair and smacked his head on the cement. The Reaper laughed and slammed his head a second time for good measure.

Josh laid on the ground, motionless and woozy. The Reaper rolled Josh over onto his back so the reporter could view his attacker. The Reaper howled manically and waved a flickering stun gun in Josh's face. Bolts of electricity danced in front of Josh's eyes, and at that moment, he truly believed he was going to die.

Just as the Reaper was about to speak, Jack returned. It took a moment for Jack to fathom what he was seeing, but sure enough, there was the Reaper standing over an injured Josh Roberts. Jack noticed the stun gun in the Reaper's left hand, and the spectre's other hand was reaching for something from underneath his cloak.

Jack reached down, pulled up his right pant leg, and grabbed a full-sized boot knife that he always carried around in his sock. Jack kept it razor sharp, so he could gut a deer without a hitch during hunting season, and he was convinced the knife could do some damage to the Reaper as well.

"I may not like that bastard on the ground, but I ain't turnin' a blind eye on you, Reaper."

The Reaper spun, obviously surprised and taken aback by the interruption. Jack's knife glinted in the pale moonlight.

"Come on!" Jack challenged. "Come and taste some steel, you bastard! Come get some!"

"Stay out of this, Lavancha," the Reaper screeched. "You have no business interfering, and I have no quarrel with you...yet."

"Sorry, ugly, but you'd better back away from the jackass right now, or by God, I swear I'll cut you up!"

The Reaper laughed. "God has no place within this town! Just as facts have no place within organized religion!"

Jack took a few steps forward. "I warned you...now I'm making this *my* business."

The two glared at one another for an instant before the Reaper veered around and quickly sprinted down the alleyway, not pausing for even a moment. Jack noticed that Josh had recuperated enough from his injury to stagger to his feet, and after gripping the knife tightly in his hand, Jack began rushing down the alley. Josh grabbed a broken beer bottle lying next to the dumpster and went with him. The two men chased after the Reaper, turning the hunter into the hunted. Josh knew the streets of Carthage well, and he was hoping his knowledge would help them capture the Reaper, and then clobber the bastard into submission.

While Josh was hoping to give the Reaper some payback for nearly killing him, Jack kept thinking about the benefits that catching the killer would to his career. *If two reporters were to apprehend the area's most frightening serial killer in decades*, he thought, *now that would be a story!*

From one dark alley to another, the reporters continued their chase after the murderer, adrenaline pumping wildly. Unfortunately, Josh's injuries were slowing him down and Jack wasn't in any shape to be running lost distances.

As the time went on, and the initial spike in adrenaline wore off, they lost track of the Reaper and were unable to pick up on the spectre's cold trail. As much as they wanted to catch the serial killer and arsonist, it just wasn't going to happen. Not that night, anyway. Whoever the Reaper was, the individual obviously kept in great shape. Josh wasn't sure he could've kept up the pace even in his high school years.

Jack was huffing and puffing as he came to a complete stop, letting out a belch that smelled of beer. Then he lit up a cigarette and said, "Damn, I've got to stop smoking."

Josh stopped running as well. "I can't carry on the chase, either," he groaned. "I'm beat."

"Well, it seems like the Reaper has disappeared into the darkness again," mentioned Jack. "I don't see any traces of his presence to be found."

Josh leaned forward and vomited, feeling sharp stabs of pain in his head and chest as he did so.

After noticing Josh grimace in pain, Jack said, "Take it easy, Roberts. You probably have a concussion."

Josh knew he needed a doctor, and as much as he didn't want to admit it, he knew he owed his life to Jack Lavancha.

At least the smoking bastard had the decency not to bring it up, Josh thought as he struggled to keep the world from spinning out from under him.

Josh steadied himself and wiped his mouth with the back of his shirtsleeve. "I'm getting too close to this mystery. I must be making someone nervous."

Jack scoffed. "The only person you're making nervous is your physical therapist."

Meanwhile, unaware that another Reaper attack was taking place across town, Detective Rick Streeter was working yet another late shift. Rick had just returned to the police station after doing some investigative work at the hospital. He had his notepad gripped tightly in his hand and headed straight to Chief Zimmerman's office to inform him of the newest updates involving the murder in Deferiet.

He burst through the door just as Chief Zimmerman was putting on his trench coat. "Chief, I gotta tell you something. I talked to Kristen Coppering in the forensics lab tonight, and I just had quite an interesting conversation with the new coroner guy—Phil...uh, somethin' or other."

The chief put his car keys in his coat pocket. "Philip VanBuren is his name."

"Uh, yeah...that's him. Well, I was at Kristen's office, discussing the bloodied pen I'd found the other day. Afterwards, I paid a visit to VanBuren and talked about the circular puncture wound in Jane Doe's eye."

"Look, Rick, I really don't have time..."

Rick ignored the chief's words and kept talking. "Anyway, based on the information they've discovered, I've been able to determine a few things. First of all, the pen is the same exact size and shape of the victim's puncture wound, and the blood type *does* match that of Jane Doe's. Also…"

Chief Zimmerman quickly cut him off in mid sentence. "Good work, Streeter. I'm in a bit of a hurry and can't talk right now, but I expect you'll have a full report about your findings on my desk in the morning,"

"A full report?!" Rick blurted with eyes as wide as golf balls. "By tomorrow?"

"Precisely," C.Z. responded.

"Well, don't expect too much, sir," Rick countered. "Just don't expect too much."

"And why is that?"

Detective Streeter sighed. "Well even though I believe the pen is *definitely* the murder weapon, we were unable to lift even one fingerprint off from it. We did, however, find a strand of hair that might belong to our suspected killer."

"What's your next move, Rick?"

"We need to send it to a bigger lab to determine if we can get an actual DNA sample, Chief. And even if the hair *is* usable, there's no guaranteeing that person will be in the police system, either."

"What else do you have?" Zimmerman inquired. "Didn't you already get some information while talkin' to barflys at Hillbilly Heaven? Put the pieces of the clues together, Rick. That's what a good detective does."

"The only info I got about the 'mystery woman' at Hillbilly Heaven was from some old guy who was three-sheets-to-the-wind drunk! He gave me a basic description, but the rest of the patrons in there wouldn't even make eye contact with me."

Zimmerman sighed. "Rick, I shouldn't have to tell you that a 'basic' description is better than *no* description at all."

"Chief, all I know about the woman is she supposedly has brownish hair, maybe the same height as the victim, with no name and no identifying marks. The 'mystery woman' was described as anywhere in age from early forties to late fifties, with no knowledge of eye color. Not exactly someone who sticks out in a crowd."

Chief Zimmerman scowled. "I suppose I'm going to have to go outside our district for some help. Send the hair to Watertown first thing tomorrow morning for testing, and I'll call Grant Morgan again to see if he can use his influence to get the results back quicker."

"I'm sorry I don't have more to report, Chief."

"Don't sweat it, Rick. Listen, if there really *was* two women at the Hillbilly Heaven, or the Northern Pines Motel, than someone had to have seen the second lady at some point. People don't just disappear!"

"Damn straight!" hollered Rick.

"By the way," Chief Zimmerman continued, "what's the latest news on the attempt on Mayor Morgan's life?"

"I think we can safely assume the attack was initiated by the Reaper copycat," Detective Streeter announced.

C.Z. seemed surprised. "You seem pretty certain, Rick. Why is that?"

"The Reaper is stalking everyone who was associated with Tim Matthews, sir. I don't have any info on the bomb that was used on the mayor's car, yet, but I don't believe it's merely a coincidence that a bomb is planted on Bucky's car the same day he receives a letter threatening his life."

Zimmerman paced back and forth while stroking his whiskers vigorously.

"I know we're short on manpower, Chief," Josh uttered, "but I really think we should get a plain clothes detective to follow Josh Roberts."

"Roberts?" questioned the chief. "What does that reporter have to do with anything?"

"He called earlier and told me he received a death threat this morning. By the sounds of it, the note appears to be very similar to yours and Bucky's."

The chief's eyes widened. "That's not supposed to be public knowledge, Streeter! Who else have you told that I received a note?"

"I haven't told anyone, sir. I'm just saying that, aside from you, Josh is the only other person singled out by the Reaper who hasn't been attacked yet." Rick paused and waited for the chief to respond. "For some reason, C.Z., the copycat has obviously singled Roberts out. If we have someone watching him at all times, we have an excellent chance nabbing the Reaper when he strikes."

"Okay, let's do it," Chief Zimmerman ordered. "Get a hold of Roberts and see if he'll agree to being followed. I don't care if we have to search every closet in all of Carthage, we need to figure out who this maniac is—fast!"

"Yes, sir," Detective Streeter agreed, making his way out of the office to call Josh Roberts. Unfortunately, Rick was unaware the Reaper was already one step ahead of him again.

Chapter 66:

Going down to the Bayou
(September 18th - 2 days later)

Jack was watching TV in his hotel room while slumped in a chair, physically and mentally exhausted. Josh Roberts had decided to stay at his rival's room as well, especially after the attack on his life (which also had the added benefit to Jack of having someone to watch his back too—amazing how quickly paranoia could build like that). The two men even decided to sleep in shifts, though neither one got much sleeping done. In fact, Jack hadn't slept in nearly two days, and more importantly, he hadn't sipped even one drop of alcohol during that time as well. His hands trembled repeatedly, a side effect from being stone cold sober for one of the longest periods of his life since turning legal age.

Josh Roberts exited the bathroom and felt a chill upon his arms as a cool breeze passed through the room. He walked over to his duffel bag, put on a sweatshirt, and glanced at the television. On the screen, he saw a man creeping in what appeared to be a basement with Freddy Kruger's glove hanging on a wall behind him.

"What the hell are you watching, Lavancha? Is that a horror flick?"

"Yeah, it's Evil Dead. Part two, I think. I was watching it to get my adrenaline flowing and keep me awake."

"Are you out of your completely warped mind? With all the crazy shit that's happened recently and you want to watch a scary movie!"

"What?" Jack muttered with a shrug. "What's wrong with a few Goosebumps to keep us alert?"

Rolling his eyes, Josh replied, "Lavancha, you're sick! No, actually you're unstable...at best."

Jack laughed and turned off the television. He rubbed his tired, bloodshot eyes and yawned.

"Y'know, Roberts, I think we should take a couple days and get away from here," he suggested.

"And do what?" inquired Josh.

"We should take a trip and fly down to Black Bayou."

Josh cocked his head to the side. "For what?"

"Try and locate Tim Matthews's mom. Maybe we can interview her, or someone who knows her."

"You mean...together?" Josh asked.

"Of course that's what I mean," Jack said. "We should *definitely* go down to Louisiana. That is, if ya think ya can stand to be around me. I figure I can put up with your sorry ass for a couple more days...if I have to."

"Hell, I became friends with Ken Johnson. If I can do that, I can do anything," Josh declared. "But how about you? Are you willing to go all the way to Louisiana for an interview while the action is going on right here?"

"Why not?" bellowed Jack. "Maybe we *need* to get out of town in order to finally solve the mystery. Besides, Roberts, what could possibly go wrong?"

Josh rolled his eyes. "Famous last words."

Jack lit up a cigar and laughed.

"I'll talk to Ty right away," Josh announced. "Do you think the *Times* will give you money for a trip to Louisiana?"

"Not a chance in Hell," Jack roared. "I was there last year for the Hurricane Katrina story. I reported on the destruction, but I also partied with the locals while I was there. My editor wasn't happy when he had to bail me out of jail."

"So...can I definitely count you in or not?"

"After seeing the ruin of the Katrina disaster, and coming face-to-face with the Reaper, I'm up for just about anything. Let's see if Ty Harris is willing to let me tag along with you."

"Umm...okay. Don't hold your breath, Jack, but I'll give it a try. Hey, if we're gonna get a plane ride out of New York anytime soon, we need to go to Ty's office and get funding and permission as soon as possible."

Jack looked at him oddly. "Don't you have a credit card to use for necessary expenses from your editor?"

"Yes," Josh answered, "but he'll raise hell if I don't get something major like this approved first. Besides, I need to talk to Mary to make sure she's ready to cover my workload while I'm gone. What about you, Jack? Don't you have a credit card for expenses?"

"I used to," stated Jack. "Until I paid for a trip to Vegas last year and charged it to the newspaper. My editor stripped me of my card after that."

"Can't imagine way," Josh whispered sarcastically.

"You know, Roberts," Jack uttered with a devious grin and a glint in his eye. "It's a hell of a lot easier to apologize to your editor *after* breaking the story of the year than it is to ask for permission and possibly get turned down."

Josh grimaced. "I'm sure it is, Jack. That may be how you do things, but I'm not interested in being unemployed if we come back empty-handed."

Jack sighed. "Well then, I suppose we should both clean up if we're heading over there."

Josh looked Jack over. The reporter had three days of scraggly beard growth, disheveled hair, black bags under bloodshot eyes, and rumpled clothes...and Jack hadn't gotten the heavy bruising Josh received from having his head slammed into the ground by the Reaper. Josh could only imagine what *he* looked like in the mirror as well.

"I bet I look like shit, don't I?" Josh asked.

"Oh yeah," Jack said, laughing. "You've never looked better as far as I'm concerned."

"All right. I'll go wash up." As Josh headed back toward the bathroom, he turned and said, "I can ask Ty about funding the trip myself, Jack. Why do you wanna come to the *Tribune* with me?"

"To hit on that cute redhead at the office."

Josh rolled his eyes and let out a huff. Mary, of course. He turned once again and continued on to the shower.

"Don't act like that, Roberts," Jack hollered. "It's not like I got anythin' else to do before we board a plane, anyway."

Within the hour, Josh had showered, shaved, cleaned the gashes on his head and face, and drove over to the *Tribune*. While he made his way to Ty's office, Jack Lavancha hung out in the main lobby (he knew better than to butt into the editor's office of a rival paper). At that moment, Ty Harris was pacing back and forth as he relayed information to Mary about the death threat letter he received.

"I can't believe someone actually had the gall to send a threatening letter to my office," Ty announced.

"Are you sure it was meant as a threat," inquired Mary, "or perhaps it's just some cruel joke."

"Hardly a joke, Mary. The letter stated that I'm going to die a horrific death if I don't leave town. Well, I've got news for that so-called Reaper...I'm not going anywhere!"

Just then, Josh came barging into the room. He heard the tail end of their conversation, including Ty's blustery statement.

"You should take the threat serious, Ty," Josh warned. "Maybe getting out of town for a few days *is* the best option for you. I received a similar letter a few days ago and was attacked in an alleyway near Kitty's Bar. If it weren't for Jack Lavancha, the Reaper would've killed me too."

"Reaper?" Ty questioned. "Bah...it was probably some homeless guy trying to roll you for a couple of bucks to buy another bottle of wine."

Josh felt his face flush. "With a stun gun in his hand and talking about Tim Matthews? No, Ty. It *was* the Reaper. I saw the entity myself."

"Listen, Roberts," Ty Harris began. "There's no such thing as ghosts, and the Reaper is dead. Stop believing your own headlines—those are to sell papers until some teenage wannabe gets caught and story's over."

"I don't care if you believe me or not, Ty!" Josh shouted. "I *saw* the Reaper! I was attacked by the Reaper!"

"Son, you're the victim of an under-worked body and an overworked imagination," Ty insulted, keeping his voice in a low growl.

"Thanks for the vote of confidence, Ty," Josh said with sarcasm. Josh bit his lip to contain his emotions, knowing he was on the edge of saying something, or more accurately, calling Ty something that he'd seriously regret.

Ty looked over at the clock hanging near his window and noticed the time. Then he shifted his attention back toward Josh and said, "Roberts, what're you doing here anyway? You're supposed to be out on the street gettin' a juicy story for me to print."

"Actually..." Josh started to say.

Ty pointed toward the door. "Go get me another headline! I'm running a newspaper, not a jam session."

"Trust me; I wouldn't be here if it wasn't necessary," Josh muttered. "I need you to fund a trip to Louisiana."

"For what?" Ty asked, seemingly unnerved by Josh's request.

"Do you want me to come with you?" Mary interrupted.

"No, Mary. I need you to stay here," Josh replied. "You're gonna have to fill in for me while I'm gone. Besides, I don't think Ty would like it if we both left town anyway."

Mary nodded. "Okay, what can I do here?"

"Well, while I'm gone, go over to Roger's house and interview him."

"Whoa! Wait a sec—," Ty said before getting cut off in mid-sentence again.

"But, Josh, isn't Roger at the hospital?" Mary asked. "The last I knew, the police placed a guard near his door to keep anyone out except family—including the press?"

"He was until about an hour ago," Josh answered back. "Roger has recovered enough from his injuries in order to be released from the hospital."

"Ahhh...that's good news! Y'see, Roberts, that's where *you* should be going—" Ty interjected before getting interrupted yet again.

"Listen, Mary," Josh voiced in a direct tone. "Roger is doing better and is being transported home today. He's healing and getting his strength back, but the police are worried there might be another attack on his life."

Mary thought for a moment and asked, "If his life is still in danger, then why is he leaving the hospital?"

Josh shrugged his shoulders. "From what I've heard, the police seem to think it'd be better if Roger was supervised, taking his medications, and getting physical therapy all at his own house—therefore, he'd always be surrounded by friends and family."

"And by doing that, it'd make it harder for the Reaper to attack Roger," Mary added.

"Exactly!" bellowed Josh. "As an added bonus, some of Nellie Spencer's brothers are going to be coming to Carthage in couple of days. There'll be plenty of people around to watch Roger's back—I'd hate to be the Reaper if he tries to get past all of them!"

"Wait a minute you two!" Ty roared.

"Sounds like he'll be safer than a gator at a bunny convention," Mary uttered to Josh. "Don't you worry about a thing, Josh. I'll go to Roger's house and interview him while you're down in Louisiana."

"WAIT A DAMN MINUTE!" Ty screamed so loud, half the office stopped what they were doing and looked inside the editor's office. Ty noticed all the peering eyes, stood up, and slammed the open door to his office shut.

"I did *not* approve a flight to Louisiana, and guess what? I'm not going to! I've just about enough of you, Roberts. You are *both* going to Fasick's house and interview Roger first thing tomorrow...or as soon as he'll see you."

"Bu...but Ty—" Josh sputtered.

"I don't want to hear it, Roberts. No more chasing tails; I want solid results! Now get outta my office and don't ask me for anything more!"

Josh and Mary both walked out of the room. Josh was surprised with the calmness that Mary displayed—after all, even *he* was flustered after Ty's horrid outburst. The answers to this entire Reaper mess were in Louisiana. Josh was sure of it! If Ty *really* wanted the whole story behind this copycat Reaper, then Josh knew he'd have to go to Louisiana against his boss's wishes to get it.

"So, Roberts...how'd it go with your editor?" Jack asked quietly, strolling up to Josh when he was sure Ty's door was closed once again.

Josh grimaced and rolled his eyes. He then motioned to both Mary and Jack to move away from Ty's office (and possible ear shot) and over to Josh's desk. When they entered his office, Josh closed the door so they could speak in private. He placed his left hand over his eyes, rubbed his temples with his thumb and forefinger, and then looked up.

"Mary, you stay here and cover for me. It's easier to come up with excuses if you have a few planned up ahead of time, so think of some stories to give Ty whenever he wants to know why I'm not around."

Mary's eyes widened. "What are you planning, Josh?"

"I don't care what Ty said," he grumbled. "Jack and I are flying to Louisiana tonight and hunt down the roots of this story. I know the secrets to this new Reaper are hidden down in Louisiana."

Jack spoke up and remarked, "I'm willing to bet that everything we need to know can be found in the town where Tim Matthews was before he came back to Carthage."

"No problem, Josh," Mary said with a smile. "I'll call Roger's house tomorrow to set up a meeting, and I'll keep Ty off your trail in the meantime. But don't forget...I still want that byline with you guys when you break the story open!"

"You got it!" Josh exclaimed. "Thanks a lot."

"Is there anything else I can do for you?" Mary asked jokingly.

Jack stepped forward and kissed Mary on the cheek. She laughed and smacked him playfully in the chest. "Shoo. I'll still be right here when you get back."

Jack looked over at Josh and asked, "So, how exactly are we going to Louisiana without funding, Roberts?"

"I have a credit card for expenses," Josh mentioned, causing Jack to burst out laughing. "So, Lavancha…is it *always* easier to apologize after-the-fact rather than ask permission first?"

"Always," Jack uttered with a nod as he grinned slyly.

Josh pulled up the Syracuse Airport's website on his computer, and within minutes, the tickets were booked. In a few hours both reporters were sitting on a plane and on their way down to the dark and eerie bayous of Louisiana.

Later that night, after Jack and Josh left for Louisiana, Mary wandered back over to the Buckley Building. After strolling around the burned-out remains where the original Reaper perished for over an hour, she made her way over to the smokestack on Tannery Boulevard and stumbled across the entrance to the underground tunnels.

There was police tape up warning of a crime scene, but that had been up for two weeks and in all likelihood, the police were completely done with the area. Mary had heard a rumor from LaTesha Prince about strange art and murals in the tunnel that Tim Matthews had created. Mary wanted to see if this was true or not, and she chose to cross the police tape and walk inside.

Mary used a powerful halogen flashlight to see where she was going, and after wandering fifty yards or so, she noticed the artwork and scribbling on the walls. It was far different than anything she was prepared for. Her hand touched one of the charcoal scrawlings, trying to catch the mind and soul of the hand that created them, and she began to cry.

Mary witnessed hundreds of horrifying drawings splashed across the concrete walls and gasped in sheer astonishment for a moment before proceeding further down the dark tunnel into the unknown. After a few minutes, not even Mary's flashlight would be visible from the outside, as the darkness consumed even the tiniest bit of illumination.

Chapter 67:

More Revelations

Josh Roberts and Jack Lavancha left the New Orleans Airport in a taxi and rode for nearly an hour until they found a cheap $25 a night motel in the tiny, rarely visited town of Black Bayou, Louisiana. An additional $10 was required for an extra cot. The 'The Shady Swamp Motel' had a dirt parking lot and was more rundown than a dilapidated saw mill, but it was also the only place with a room to rent within a fifteen mile radius. The guys couldn't help but notice that the place was eerily similar in name and appearance to the motel where Jane Doe was murdered in Deferiet.

After a series of unfriendly stares from unimpressed locals, as well as the motel receptionist and the cleaning staff, the two men dropped their suitcases off in their room and walked down the street to the nearest gas station. The reporters decided it'd be safest to just buy some snack foods and eat in their room rather than go to one of the local diners to get a meal. It seemed quite evident the townsfolk were *not* fond of outsiders.

When they returned to the motel room and put their bags of goodies on the table, Josh went to the bathroom to wash his hands.

"This place is a pigsty," Josh complained. "Haven't these hillbillies ever heard of soap?"

"On the plus side," Jack yelled out to him, "we don't have to worry about rats comin' around."

Josh wiped his hands with a towel and asked, "How do you know? This place looks like it'd be infested with them."

Jack sat at the table and started to eat. "Nah. Got plenty of rattlers and water moccasins to take care of them."

"And how about the rattlers and water moccasins?" Josh asked, definitely far less comfortable than Jack was in their new surroundings. "What takes care of them?"

Jack shrugged. "Plenty of gators roamin' the area, too."

"Ain't that just friggin' wonderful," Josh commented, wondering if the warped plywood door and cracked floorboards would be strong enough to stop anything from coming in.

Josh and Jack went to bed early so they could be fully alert and completely prepared for whatever they'd have to face in the morning. Just after sunrise, after a continental breakfast consisting of dry, flavorless doughnuts and watered-down orange juice, the two reporters took a taxi ride over to Empire Car Rentals in the neighboring town of Sorrento. After ninety minutes of filling out paperwork and standing in line, Josh was able to rent a 1989 lime-green Chrysler LeBaron.

As they walked out of the rental office, Jack announced, "I'm driving, Roberts. Hand over the keys."

"I don't think so, Jack! The car is *my* responsibility. If anything happens to it, I'm the one who has to pay for it!"

"I told ya, Roberts, I was here just last year. I think I know my way around this area a little bit better than you do."

Josh exhaled heavily. "Fine!" he grumbled. "But if you get just *one* scratch on it…"

"Calm down, Roberts," Jack uttered, rolling his eyes. "I know what I'm doing."

Once they left Sorrento, they headed back to their motel room and grabbed Jack's portable GPS machine. The men stuffed some snack food and a couple bottles of water into a duffle bag and drove away. As they traveled down the narrow roadway, a six-foot-long object that was lying on the side of the road suddenly dove into a pond of swamp water.

"Was that what I think it was?" Josh yelped, jumping halfway out of the passenger seat.

"Yep," Jack mumbled, a little nervous at how close the alligator was. "Not a big one, though." He glanced alongside the road and mused, "Wonder where the momma gator is."

The two men decided to best way to start their investigation was to drive out to the house where the Timmons family used to live. Maybe the mother was still around, or at the very least, maybe whoever was presently living there could give them some useful information.

"I'd be willing to bet there're still some of Timmons's relatives living around here," Josh commented as he peered out the side window.

Jack chomped on a toothpick and muttered, "Oh? Why ya say that?"

"Seems like this area has been desolate for many generations. It doesn't seem like the type of town where a lot of people move in and out of with any frequency."

"That may be true," Jack said, "but let's not get carried away with the stereotypes. There are plenty of places in New England where if you haven't lived there for a minimum of three generations you're considered an outsider. There're places in West Virginia you just can't travel to without risking your life. And Indiana was the least friendly state I ever went to! Then again, I did have a pony tail and tie-dyed t-shirt at the time…possibly a cocky attitude, too."

"I know I'm basing my judgment on a few bumpy dirt roads and a handful of rundown houses," Josh admitted begrudgingly. "Still, I'm not sure I'd wanna spend much longer here than I absolutely had to."

"This town seemed a bit eerie at first, but actually it's kinda lame," Jack stated. "If you want excitement, Roberts, I heard there's a town in Alaska where almost every tourist who visits there ends up disappearing—or maybe it was they died a horrible death. I can't remember which."

"That's a great urban legend to try and debunk if you're looking to get rid of your spouse," joked Josh. "Makes ya wonder…who'd ever travel all that distance just to confirm something so absurd—so ominous?"

Jack laughed in agreement. "I bet I've got a few exes who'd like to take me there." Jack eased off on the gas pedal and focused straight ahead. "Hey, there're several side-roads ahead. What's the name of the one we have to turn on?"

"It's called the Kaine Road," Josh answered.

"Looks like we're here," Jack said, slowing down and turning the steering wheel to the right.

"Just great," sighed Josh. "*Another* dirt road!"

"Yeah, and this one looks more like an ATV trail than a county road," Jack asserted.

A few hundred yards further down the dirt road, Jack came to a stop in front of a heavily rusted mail box with a faded pink flag (that was most likely colored red at one time).

The once gravel driveway was overgrown with grass and moss. A small water snake darted into some nearby cattails while Josh noticed how the cypress trees and willows seemed to overwhelm the home more and more all the way up to the Timmons's doorstep.

From their first glance, it was obvious the house was abandoned, and had been for some time. While most of the homes near the town were far away from marshy swamplands, this one was so close that the swamp water and wildlife had started to overrun the property again.

"Whoa," Josh uttered in shock. "This place is a wreck. I doubt this house could be repaired or become usable again."

"Yup," Jack interjected. "It's a shame to see a three-storied antique home just slowly rotting away."

The abandoned Timmons house was surrounded by long prairie-like grass and the glass panes in all the windows were knocked out. There was also an eight-foot wire fence that surrounded the property on all sides. Although most of it was standard 12.5-gauge high-tensile wire, some particularly old looking strands near the top looked like rusty barbed wire.

"How're we going to look around?" Josh asked, not sure he wanted to jump into chest-high grass without being able to see anything that was around him.

"Let's start climbing, pretty boy," Jack ordered.

The sound of large boots crunching on gravel caused both Jack Lavancha and Josh Roberts to turn around. Out of the grass a large man emerged, dressed in black knee-high boots, muddy overalls, and a white t-shirt that had long since turned brown. The stranger towered over the two reporters, standing a minimum of five inches taller than either Jack or Josh, and he easily outweighed them by a hundred pounds or more.

Even though some of the stranger's bulk came from an oversized belly, there was enough mass in his arms, legs, and chest to make Josh think they were screwed if the swamp man decided to pick a fight. Aside from his hulking physique, the stranger was also holding a sawed-off shotgun in his arms.

"Can't you city boys read?" he asked in a thick drawl that was Southern, but also something else, something extra that made it seem more Cajun-like.

"I most certainly can, sir," stated Josh. "Why? Would you like me to read something for you?"

Jack's face grimaced, even as he was trying to keep from smiling. Josh was proving he wasn't quite the stiff that Jack had always taken him for, though Jack was keenly aware that Josh had picked a horrible moment to break out of his shell. Jack knew they were likely to come out of this situation just fine; but as a general rule, a person's chances dramatically increase if they don't piss off the guy pointing a gun toward their head.

"Very funny, wise ass," the angry swamp man grumbled. "Are ya tryin' to piss me off, city slicker?"

"Uh, no..." replied Josh.

"I would think not! Don't ya realize I could kill you two right where ya stand? Look around, punks! There's a place to stash your bodies where no one would ever look only five feet away...everywhere around this area!"

Josh and Jack glanced at each other nervously with widened eyes.

"This here is private property," the swamp man continued. "And all the signs on the fence and trees say, 'No Trespassing.' Since y'all seem to need translatin', it means keep your ass away unless ya got permission."

"Who are you, sir?" Jack asked, not sure whether to add the 'sir' or not, but deciding it was better safe than sorry.

"I'm the caretaker of this here piece of land. And I know ya ain't got permission to be here 'cause I never seen either of you two 'pretty boys' before."

He spat chewing tobacco in front of the two reporters and Josh could feel the contempt this man had for the both of them. Not a 'meanness' per se, but a definite contempt.

"Can we ask you a few questions about the former owners of this place?" Jack asked politely.

The old man sat down on a tree stump. He set his shotgun across his lap, removed a large straw cowboy hat, and wiped the sweat from his forehead with a dirty blue handkerchief.

"I'm listenin'. But make it quick."

"My colleague and I were doing some research and found this address as Elizabeth Timmons's last known place of residence," Jack explained.

The snarl upon the swamp man's face disappeared as he raised a brow.

Josh decided to let Jack handle the questioning since he had a much better rapport with the swamp man than Josh could've hoped for at that point.

"It looks like she just disappeared," Jack added. "Do you know her, or whatever happened to her?"

"Oh, yeah," the backwoods swamp man said, a friendly smile actually appearing on his face. "I sure do remember sweet Elizabeth.

She was a beautiful woman. Good figure, but always dressed nice and appropriate, like every day was a church Sunday."

"Was she a farmer?" Josh inquired. "Or was she self-employed in some way?"

The stranger shook his head. "Nah, but she *was* an excellent artist. Actually, she had a lot of talent for all sorts of artsy things. I think she even wrote a children's book, if my memory is correct, but it never quite made it to publication."

"Sounds like she was an exceptional woman," Jack added.

"She sure was," he bellowed. "If only her book coulda got published…maybe she could've gotten a little bit of fame. Maybe she coulda got outta this hellhole." The backwoodsman paused and let out a sigh. "But I guess gettin' rejected by a book company was the *least* of her problems at the time."

The reporters' ears perked up at the swamp man's last words.

"Y'know, she could've gone far in life, but her hopes and dreams were cut down by those son-of-a-bitch'n snobs in town. Never had a chance, really. Poor Beth never had a chance."

"Beth?" Josh asked, interrupting. Both he and Jack glanced at each other.

"That's what a lot of her friends used to call her," the man said. "She never used her full name, and she wasn't huge on Liz or Liza as a nickname, either."

"You don't say," Josh voiced in an inquisitive tone.

"Yeah, but 'Elizabeth' was her God given Christian name, and she always felt obliged to use at least part of it. For me, I always liked the nickname 'Lizzie' better, though."

"Is it possible Beth still lives near town?" Jack asked. "We'd really like to speak with her if she does."

The swamp man studied Josh and Jack. He pulled out a rolling paper that somehow remained clearly white and stuffed it with tobacco from a pouch to roll up a smoke.

"Either of you boys want one?" he asked in a tone that indicated a willingness to be hospitable, but not necessarily a desire to roll another cigarette.

Both men got the point and shook their heads no.

"Why would either of you boys wanna know about Elizabeth Timmons?" the man asked, lighting the smoke with a wooden tipped match. "What're your intentions? You lookin' to hurt her or somethin'?"

"No," both the men said at once. Josh nodded to Jack, telling him to keep speaking.

"We don't wanna hurt anyone," Jack stated. "We're from Northern New York—the city of Carthage. Her son lived there with an assumed name, but...well, we have bad news for her."

"Bad news?" the old man inquired. "Like what?"

"There've been some weird things going on where we're from," Josh replied.

The stranger leaned forward. "Uh huh...go on."

Jack shot Josh a stern glance to keep silent and continued talking. "Her son died in a fire...arson, actually."

"So...you've come so y'all can tell her in person?"

"Well, not exactly," Jack said. "Y'see, there've been some unexplainable occurrences in our hometown ever since his death. We're trying to track down Mrs. Timmons to see if she can help us figure out what's going on."

The swamp man let out a long exhale and studied the men hard. "What do ya think she'd know that could help you two fellas out?"

Josh and Jack looked at each other. What was there to say? Could they really ask about the supernatural without sounding insulting?

"Did either Elizabeth Timmons or her son practice voodoo, witchcraft, or anything like that?" Jack asked.

The swamp man snorted. "Not hardly. They were a church-goin' family, even though they mostly attended on Sundays. Of course, they quit goin' to church altogether after the town scandal, for obvious reasons."

"What obvious reason?" inquired Josh.

"Beth's son was taken away from her after the priest from their church declared them liars. The boy claimed the priest molested him, but the townsfolk didn't believe him. When her son was taken away and committed, Beth went insane."

Jack's eyes widened. "Insane?"

"Yup. Right off the deep end, too. In fact, she had to be committed herself. I've been watchin' over this property since then."

"Wait, so Matthew Timmons was taken away from his mom?" Josh asked.

"And committed," the swamp man said. "Beth had a difficult time coping with the loss and eventually had a nervous breakdown. They committed her to an asylum in Baton Rouge."

"Is she still there?" Jack asked.

The swamp man rubbed out the last of his cigarette on the stump and stood up. The action reminded both reporters of just how much bigger the man was than they were, and how intimidating he could be if he chose to be so.

681

He placed the straw hat back on his head and finally said, "Sir, I don't know where she is. Papers said she died, and that became the official report with the police and all that...but I wouldn't be 100% certain of that."

"So, what're you saying?" Jack asked. "She *didn't* die?"

"Well, being next of kin and all, I was informed that she committed suicide—set herself on fire," the swamp man said. "Now, I never got to see the body or nothing, so I can't tell you for sure, but I did read the report which the facility sent to me".

"Was there something wrong, Mr...?" Josh asked.

"Call me Jacques. I ain't no gentleman, and I don't plan on being one. But to answer your question, yeah. The body they found didn't seem to match her description. How's that for something being rotten in Denmark?"

Both Josh and Jack looked at each other, openly surprised and stunned at the Shakespearean reference. There was a lot they could have expected, but a direct quote from *Hamlet* wasn't one of them.

"So, what do you think happened to her?" Jack asked, the first to recover.

"I...uh, don't know anything else." Jacques started to get misty-eyed. "And to be honest, I don't feel like talking about it anymore. Now then, if you two gentlemen don't mind, I think it's time for you both to git goin' and leave."

"Please, sir. If you know something else, you must tell us," Josh pleaded, even though he knew he was on shaky ground. "There has been a string of murders in our town recently by her son, and even after he died the same murders and fires kept going. People are dying. Some of our best friends have barely survived, and any information you could give us could help."

Jacques bowed his head and gripped his hat tightly, trying to hold back his emotions. "We don't betray kin. But then again, if it really were either one of them...they haven't been back in so long it's hard to call 'em family any more with a straight face." He exhaled deeply and said, "Call the mental hospital Beth was sent to."

A smile appeared on Josh's face. "We certainly will, Jacques. Do you know the name of the facility?"

"Of course I do! It's called the Baton Rouge Mental Facility. It's 'bout an hour or so from here if you stay of the main road and don't try any shortcuts."

Jack butted in and asked, "Who should we talk to?"

"Ask to speak to Dr. Gebo. He's the one who sent me the file. He's also the one who hinted that Elizabeth did *not* commit suicide.

He's probably the only one who might know the information you're looking for…he'd definitely be the only one who'd actually talk about it."

"Thanks, Jacques," the two reporters said.

"Now seriously, boys, turn around and get out of here. I've given you all I'm willing to! And with all due respect, if I see either of you two snooping 'round here again, I'll feed ya to the gators. Let the dead stay dead. Nothing good comes out of bringing 'em back."

Back in Carthage, at the police station, Chief Zimmerman walked out of his office and yelled to Rick Streeter, "Hey, Rick. I just got a call from someone living near Tannery Island Boulevard. He saw some type of light coming from the entrance to the underground tunnels."

Rick shifted his attention to Zimmerman and asked, "What do you want me to do, Chief?"

"I need you to go down there and check it out. There could be some kids or some other vandals inside. We don't need anybody getting hurt in those tunnels."

"I'm on my way to Roger's house, Chief. Can I go there in the morning?"

"Nevermind," the chief mumbled in an annoyed tone. He whistled over to Officer Lewis and yelled, "Torri! Go over to the tunnel entrance near Tannery Island Boulevard and check it out. There might be some vandals runnin' around in there. Got it?"

Torri jumped out of her desk chair and grabbed the keys to her squad car. "Yes, Chief. I'm on it!"

C.Z. turned back toward Rick and said, "Y'see, that's how you get things done."

Thirty minutes later, Torri entered the tunnels. As she cautiously walked inside, Officer Lewis had one hand on the gun holster on her hip and the other was holding a flashlight.

"Hello, this is Officer Lewis of the Carthage Police Department. Is anyone in here?"

All she heard in response was her words echoing back at her. She progressed further down the tunnel, taking small steps. As she walked, a foul smell kept getting stronger. It stunk as if someone had thrown a hunk of deer meat on a campfire and left it out to rot. About one hundred yards down, the beam of her flashlight passed over a long, narrow object that was lying on the ground. She made her way over and saw a black tarp on the ground, covering something the size of a human being.

Torri's hands trembled and she tried to use her walkie talkie, but the batteries were dead. She grabbed her cell phone and tried to call the station, but she was unable to get any reception. Reluctantly, Torri inched closer to the black tarp. She came up to it and kneeled down. The beam of the flashlight quivered across the ground and she grabbed the corner of the tarp, taking a few deep breaths to calm down.

Just as she was about to pull the tarp back, Torri heard heavy breathing coming from behind her. She quickly spun around and gasped. Just as she was reaching for her gun, the Reaper lunged forward and sliced Torri's throat with a scalpel. Torri fell backwards and grabbed her neck, trying to apply pressure to contain the bleeding.

The Reaper pounced upon the helpless officer and began cutting at her face and chest. Within moments, Torri was lying motionless in the mud and gurgling as blood erupted from her mouth.

Chapter 68:

Truth comes to Light
(September 20th – Morning)

The next morning, the two reporters woke up bright and early. They ventured down and bought some candy bars from the vending machine in the main lobby and took them back to their room to eat for breakfast. Once they were finished stuffing their mouths with sugar and empty calories, they took turns washing up.

Josh returned from the bathroom after taking a quick, three minute shower and shouted, "That was the worst damn shower I've ever had! There's not a drop of hot water at all!"

"You got a problem with a cold shower, Roberts?"

"Yeah!" snapped Josh. "Cold does to a man's penis like water did to the Wicked Witch of the West."

Jack shook his head and turned away.

Twenty minutes later, after both men finished getting as clean and presentable as they could manage, they left the small town of Black Bayou and drove the rental car toward the mental institution in Baton Rouge, discussing the case and their findings along the way.

"I've been nervous ever since we talked to the swamp man yesterday," Josh Roberts confessed. "Did it shake you up when he told us to 'let the dead stay dead'?"

Jack nodded, even as he kept his eyes on the road.

"Hey, you might need to slow down around these curves," Josh reminded him, watching as the road seemed to close in as the Cypress trees came closer and closer. The long silk-like strands acted like a drape that came just short of dusting the top of the car. "Do you know where you're going, Jack? You sure this road leads to Baton Rouge?"

"Positive," Jack answered. "I took a roadmap from the motel lobby. It's like this for another half mile or so, and then we'll hit the freeway. From there, we can head straight to the asylum."

"Sounds good to me," Josh remarked. "We'll just keep nose to the grind and see what we can find in Baton Rouge. Eventually, we'll *have* to stumble across something."

"Trust me…the answer we're searching for is down here, Roberts. I'm sure of it."

The Cypress trees finally gave way, and the roughly paved and worn road connected at a T-intersection with a much better maintained highway. Jack made a left-hand turn heading north towards Baton Rouge.

"I just hope we figure out this mystery before it's too late for Roger and Bucky," Josh mentioned.

"What do you mean by that?" inquired Jack. "Do you think they're next on the Reaper's hit list or something?"

"It would stand to reason that they are," stated Josh. "After all, we're *both* down here in Louisiana. Who else is left in Carthage for the Reaper to hunt down?"

After that solemn statement, Jack pressed the accelerator down and sped up to about twenty miles-per-hour over the posted speed limit. For the rest of the drive, the two men rode in grim silence, wondering what secrets were still left to be revealed. The warnings of the swamp man still echoed in both of their heads—especially his rant about letting dead things remain dead, about the danger of dredging them back to life.

When the two men arrived at the Baton Rouge asylum, they were greeted by an ornery receptionist with an enormous brown mole on the left side of her nose. The mole was so large, in fact, that it made her eyeglasses sit crooked upon her face. Jack knew he shouldn't stare, but that thing got to him. Even if he tried to ignore the blotch and make eye contact with the receptionist, a large chunk of it remained in his peripheral view, sprouting in all its putrid glory.

"She doesn't look very polite," Jack whispered, eyes fixated on the unsightly blemish on her face. He couldn't believe how hard it was to look away.

"Don't worry," Josh assured his longtime rival. "I've had many conversations with the not-so-pleasant LaTesha Prince. I know all there is to know about dealing with unhappy women and overcoming problematic hurdles."

"Who?" Jack asked, unfamiliar with the name.

"The Mayor's receptionist," Josh replied. "LaTesha was hired to keep undesirables out, and to do it with enough temperament so they'd think twice before coming up and trying to bother the Mayor again. And if I can handle her, than I can handle talking to anyone."

"Are you sure?" inquired Jack. "This lady here looks like she's a real bulldog."

"Well, I can tolerate talking to and spending time with you...and God knows that isn't easy. Dear Lord, the patience, the punishment, the penance..."

"Get on with it, Roberts!"

"Anyway, I've had lots of practice dealing with difficult people. Being around you has conditioned me for this type of situation."

"Screw you, you prick!" Jack retorted.

Once the two men approached the desk, the woman looked up at them with eyes as cold as ice, and they were already shooting icicles into both men as if they were heathens strutting onto the holiest of grounds.

"Can I help you?" she uttered in a low, monotone voice that somehow seemed to growl while conveying utter indifference.

"Hello, ma'am. We'd like to see Dr. Gebo if he's available," Josh said politely.

"You would?" she voiced in a sarcastic tone. "I'd like a Porsche, but I don't see that happening anytime soon on this salary."

The two reporters looked at the receptionist with confused expressions upon their faces.

"You want to see Dr. Gebo, huh? And I don't suppose either of you have an appointment to see the doctor, do you?"

"No, but it's an important matter, and we must talk to him directly!" Jack interjected.

"That's what all the salesmen say. We're not interested in buying any pharmaceuticals. We're an asylum, not a drug testing lab."

"Excuse me, ma'am," Josh said, trying to smooth things over. "We appreciate the job you're doing, and this is my fault for not introducing ourselves properly. We're working on an investigation of a series of recent murders in upstate New York that we believe may involve a former patient of Dr. Gebo's."

The receptionist leaned back in her chair and crossed her arms upon her chest.

Josh glanced at Jack for a moment before continuing on. "We believe he may have information and expertise to help our investigation that no one else can provide. We won't take much of his time—twenty minutes at the most. Would you please check to see if we can speak with him voluntarily? We find everyone is generally much happier that way...and please excuse my partner's rudeness. He's new."

Jack glared at Josh, not believing that big pile of bullshit had any chance of swaying the ugly woman's stance...and he didn't appreciate the cheap shot, either. However, he kept his tongue in check when he realized it looked like the mole lady was actually considering letting them through.

The receptionist peered at the two men in silence for a few more seconds before she stood up from her desk and said, "Hold on a minute. I'll check to see if he's available to talk to visitors. However, you must understand that he's a *very* busy man. Even if he does agree to see you, don't expect more than twenty minutes."

"Twenty will be plenty, ma'am," Josh replied graciously. "Thank you."

After the receptionist left her desk and walked down a dingy gray hallway lit by white fluorescent bulbs, the two men stood around and inspected the décor of the institution. The main reception room wasn't as bare, or as desolate, as Josh imagined it would be. He wasn't sure what he'd been expecting, but the utter bleak scenery from the film *One Flew over the Cuckoo's Nest* was more of what Josh had envisioned.

There was a dull green carpet with some worn red trim. A couple of certificates of certification hung on a wall behind the desk, and the dingy gray paint was peeling badly along the ceiling molding. Psych wards weren't an area of heavy funding—not during the Reagan administration and not any time since. At least this place was still going...mole lady receptionist and all.

After a few minutes, the receptionist returned and said, "Dr. Gebo would like to know what your purpose for being here is. Why do you *need* to speak to him?"

Just as Josh was about to speak, Jack grabbed him by the arm and interrupted him by saying, "Tell him it's in regards to a former patient here—Elizabeth Timmons."

Josh glared at Jack for butting in, but Jack understood that Josh's smooth talking had them in the door, and now was the time to set the hook. Josh's facial features relaxed once the woman turned and walked back through the door to enter the institution, without a glare or another word.

The two reporters let out a sigh and looked at each other. Scary as it was, they could tell they were both thinking the same thing: *We could make a really good team if the other guy wasn't such an ass...*

Ten minutes later a tall, slender, man with slick gray hair parted to the side came out from the door. He looked through thick framed glasses that seemed disproportionate to the thinness of the lenses, but he oozed confidence and authority.

The man walked up to both of the reporters and said, "Hello. My name is Dr. Dan Gebo. I was told you gentleman would like to talk to me regarding Elizabeth Timmons."

"Yes, sir," the two reporters said at the same time.

"Follow me then. We'll have more privacy in my office to discuss this potentially delicate matter."

Dr. Gebo led the men through the door of the institution and down the hall to his office. As they passed the cafeteria area, Josh looked inside and caught a glance of a man who resembled Thomas Parker. Josh quickly stopped and did a double take.

"What's wrong?" Jack asked, noticing his comrade lagging behind.

"Nothing," Josh replied, snapping his head forward. "Nothing at all."

After all the men were in Doctor Gebo's office and seated, the doctor announced, "Okay, you have my undivided attention, though I get the feeling you're not really with the police. What did you two wish to discuss with me today?"

Jack was quick to ask, "Dr. Gebo, can you elaborate on what happened to Elizabeth Timmons?"

"She died," he answered emphatically. "I'm sorry you had to come all the way down here to learn that. A little research, or a phone call, could've saved you a lot of trouble on that one."

"Yes, we know that's what everyone was told," Josh retorted, picking up right where Jack left off. "But we had a talk with Jacques Timmons yesterday—"

"Morissette," Dr. Gebo corrected.

"What?" Josh asked.

"Jacques Morissette—the next of kin. He was Elizabeth Timmons's stepbrother, not her blood relation or a brother-in-law," Dr. Gebo explained in a snotty tone of voice.

Josh was beginning to get a gut feeling that he just didn't like this guy. Jack took over where Josh left off this time.

"Anyway, Jacques Morissette told us to come talk to you," Jack told him. "He said you gave him the impression Elizabeth Timmons didn't commit suicide and that you were the only one who might be willing to help us. We need to know what happened; and if she's alive, we need to know where she might be. It might be a matter of life or death to a lot of people."

Dr. Gebo seemed unmoved, but he answered in a steady voice, anyhow. "She was mainly a patient of my colleague, Dr. Kevin Allen. Elizabeth was very withdrawn at first. She remained sullen, and would stare out into nowhere for hours. She never did anything violent, or have any run-ins with other patients that would make me think she was dangerous, so her file is clean. But...there was definitely a hard edge underneath."

"Go on," Jack encouraged.

"She never really did warm up to anybody but Dr. Allen, and shortly after her apparent death, he left the facility for another hospital upstate," Dr. Gebo explained. "It raised a few eyebrows about his timing, and started some rumors about Dr. Allen's potential breach of ethics, but no one had anything but gossip to back it up."

"So why do you believe she didn't commit suicide?" Josh asked.

Dr. Gebo wiped his spectacles with a part of his lab coat and sighed. "The cause of death said she burned to death, and it's true, the body had been burned—especially the face. However, the woman's hair was different and the shape of the body didn't seem right."

"Can you elaborate on that," questioned Jack.

"Well, the shade of auburn brown was off, and the woman's height seemed suspicious. Elizabeth was somewhat tall for a woman, and the corpse looked average height. The clothes and bracelet may have said Elizabeth Timmons on them, but I've always had some serious doubts."

"What do you think happened?" Josh interjected.

"Before I tell you that," Dr. Gebo said, "I need to know who I'm talking to and whether this is on or off the record."

"We're people who will never bother you again," Jack assured him.

"And who have a vested interest in making sure our friends don't become victims of a serial killer who seems intertwined with the Timmons family," Josh added. "We need to know who were facing, and we think the key to solving our mystery is here in Louisiana."

"And this is all off the record," Jack declared. "We won't quote a thing you say and we won't mention any part of this conversation."

Dr. Gebo studied the two men and then nodded. "I believe Dr. Allen and Elizabeth Timmons, or Beth, as I heard him call her once, were having an inappropriate lover's tryst. I think she manipulated him and drew him in, and underneath that supposedly innocent exterior, I think there's darkness inside her as sharp as any machete you can find."

"Do you think Dr. Allen was somehow involved in her *supposed* death?" questioned Josh.

After a long, deep exhale, Dr. Gebo replied, "I've never said this to anyone before, but...I think Dr. Allen found a woman who was close enough in appearance to pass for Elizabeth and killed her."

A look of sheer shock covered the two reporters' faces.

"I believe Dr. Allen was so completely obsessed with Elizabeth that he would've done anything, and *everything*, to get her out of here. From the time the body was first discovered, I thought Kevin helped Elizabeth escape while using the other girl's corpse to cover up the entire thing. I don't think Elizabeth ever died, and I don't think she was insane—at least not in the way that she wanted everyone to think she was."

"What do you mean by that?" Jack asked cautiously.

Dr. Gebo appeared distressed. "I think Elizabeth was a smart, calculating person and not the meek, withdrawn woman she wanted us all to believe she was." The doctor paused and leaned back in his chair, looking at the ceiling as he reminisced. "Y'know, there was a young woman who disappeared from a nearby town the same week Elizabeth died. The only reason I know this is because I was dating a lady at the time that lived near there. The girl who disappeared looked similar to Elizabeth Timmons, except she was a little heavier and shorter. The authorities said the girl ran away from home, and I guess she had a history of doing so, but I always wondered."

"Are you saying—?" Josh began before biting his tongue.

The doctor veered his attention back to the two reporters and said, "It wouldn't surprise me if Elizabeth had Kevin murder that young girl and set the body on fire. If I'm right, Elizabeth Timmons is *more* than capable of killing again. She believes society has wronged her family...and if she could be so coldblooded toward one victim, I have no reason to believe that she couldn't do it again. If she's the one you're looking for, be careful. She's capable of anything."

While the reporters had been investigating, more action was transpiring over a thousand miles away in Carthage. Police Chief Bernard Zimmerman was sitting at his desk when he saw Detective Rick Streeter pass by his doorway. The chief whistled to get Rick's attention and waved him in to his office.

Rick stepped inside the room and asked, "Do you need something, Chief?"

"Hey, Rick. I just wanted to let you know that I got a call from my buddy, Grant Morgan, over at the Watertown Police Station."

"Was he able to find any information for us, sir?"

"Yeah, Rick. He said the fingerprints of our Jane Doe match those of a woman named Mary Powell. Apparently, she was booked on a misdemeanor charge in Watertown several years ago."

"Mary Powell? Isn't that the name of the woman working with Josh Roberts over at the *Tribune*?"

"Yes…and that's what I told him. But then Grant gave me some more chilling news."

Rick's eyes widened. "What's that, Chief?"

"A missing person's report was filed in his office last week. The description matches that of our Jane Doe…and the name of the missing person was Mary Powell."

"Holy shit, Chief! What do we do now?"

"I've contacted Mary Powell's relatives in Watertown. They're supposed to be faxing me a picture of Ms. Powell any moment now."

Rick was filled with excitement. "This could finally be the break we've been looking for!"

"Not only that, but I just got a call from Officer Jackson."

"What did he have to say?"

"I sent him to back to the Northern Pines Motel. He talked to the person running the front desk on the night Jane Doe was killed. Jules said that two women left the motel and went toward Hillbilly Heaven. One woman matches the description of our Jane Doe—aka: Mary Powell. The clerk told Jules that other woman was someone who signed in using the name Beth Allen."

"That's great news, Chief! Where is Jules now?"

"I think he's on his way back to town. I told him to check out those underground tunnels one more time before heading back to the station, though. I might also have Jules stop by Torri's house, too. I haven't heard from her all day. Her shift was supposed to start over six hours ago."

Back in Baton Rouge, the two reporters were standing outside the asylum. Josh began pacing back and forth and put his hands in his coat as let out a heavy sigh. Then, he took out a cellular phone and checked for a signal.

"Who're ya callin'?" Jack asked.

"Detective Streeter. Maybe with what Dr. Gebo told us, he'll be able to put some pieces of this mystery together. With his training, perhaps he can use this information to get a bigger picture of what the heck is going on."

Josh found four bars and speed dialed the number that went straight to Detective Streeter's cell phone.

"Hello?" a voice answered from the other line.

"Detective Streeter, this is Josh Roberts."

Streeter sounded irritated as he said, "Roberts! I told you not to call me on my cell unless it was an *emergency*!"

"It is, Rick! Jack Lavancha and I came down to Louisiana and there's something important that you need to know! Tim's mother didn't die."

Rick shook his head. "What're you talkin' about?"

"Tim Matthews! His mother's name is Elizabeth Timmons and she's still alive!"

"Do you think she's dangerous, Josh?" Rick asked.

"Absolutely! She killed a local girl down here in Louisiana, staged an escape from a mental institution, and then she disappeared! It's possible our 'resurrected' Reaper is Elizabeth Timmons looking for revenge!"

Streeter scratched his head. "Are you sure?"

"Positive," Josh responded. "Elizabeth Timmons is alive, and in all likelihood she's killed before. The doctor at the mental institution certainly seemed to think so."

Just then, Office Nathan Barnes ran into the room and handed a file to the detective while he was still on the phone. "Detective Streeter, we have an ID on the body. The dead woman in Deferiet *is* Mary Powell."

"Oh my god, not Mary!" Josh uttered, overhearing the conversation. Suddenly, he felt incredibly guilty about the suspicions that had been creeping up on him all week.

"It's not what you think, Josh," Detective Streeter stated. "Mary was the name of the Jane Doe we found in Deferiet the other week."

Josh's jaw dropped wide open. "What? That can't be. I've been working with her for weeks."

"No, I'm afraid not," remarked Rick. "We believe the woman you have been working with is a woman by the name of Bethany Allen. She also checked into the motel the same night that Mary did. On top of that, the two of women were spotted having drinks at the Hillbilly Heaven bar that night. At least, that's the information we've got so far."

"Who is this Beth Allen?" Josh asked. He put the cell phone on loudspeaker, to let Jack listen in easier.

"Not much is known. A background check revealed that she's a widowed woman. She married a man, a Doctor Kevin Allen, about fifteen years ago."

Jack could not believe his ears. "Did you say her husband's name was Kevin Allen?"

"Yup. After Dr. Allen died a little over a year ago, she's been working as a freelance photographer," Rick mentioned.

Both of the reporters' eyes were becoming as wide as golf balls.

"Doctor Allen?" Jack exclaimed. "Where did they live?"

"Somewhere in Louisiana."

"Bethany...like Beth?" Josh muttered to himself. "Eliza*BETH*! Oh my God! Mary is Elizabeth Timmons! She has to be...she even showed up right when the murders started! It's her, Rick! Mary's the Reaper!"

"What's that, Josh?" Detective Streeter asked, listening to the alarm in Josh's voice.

"Rick! Beth Allen is Tim's mom—Elizabeth Timmons! She's the one who murdered the real Mary Powell to take her place, and she's the one who's re-started the murders. She's the Reaper! Roger's life is in great danger! You've got to get officers over there right now!"

"I'm on it!" Detective Streeter told Josh. Rick hung up the phone and motioned to several officers standing near him. "Go to the gun cabinet and grab the shotguns. Get all the ammo you can carry, too. Drive your squad cars over to the Fasick place—Now!"

"Are you coming, sir?" Officer Barns inquired.

"I'll be right behind you, Nathan. I'm going to inform Chief Zimmerman of what's going on."

Chapter 69:

Seeking an old Friend

Once Josh ended his phone call with the police, he immediately called Roger's house. No one picked up the receiver, and the answering machine was turned off. Refusing to be deterred, he hung up and dialed again. After several more rings without any success, Josh slammed the receiver down in frustration. Jack looked on in silence, concerned, while Josh re-dialed for a third time. After ten more rings, he decided to give up and called Bucky's house instead. This time, someone *did* answer the phone.

"Bucky! This is Josh," he said in a hurried voice.

"Hey, Josh," Bucky replied as he took a bite of a bologna sandwich. "What's goin' on?"

"Listen, Bucky, I know this is gonna sound crazy, but I think Roger's life is in great danger! You need to get over to his place right now!"

The terror in Josh's tone grabbed Bucky's attention. "What's going on, Josh? What's got you so upset?"

"I was talking to Detective Streeter a few minutes ago," Josh explained, "and we've come to the conclusion that my partner at the *Tribune*, Mary, may not be who she claims to be. In fact, we're certain she's *not* Mary Powell."

Bucky placed his sandwich on the kitchen table and began pacing through his house until he entered his den, looking for his car keys and a jacket. He didn't know the severity of the situation, but anything that involved his friend Roger was a *big* deal.

"I think Mary is actually Tim Matthews's mother, Elizabeth Timmons. There's also strong evidence to suggest this woman killed the *real* Mary Powell and took over her identity."

"Are you serious?" asked Bucky, shaking his head in disbelief.

"Yes!" he yelled hysterically. "She's the Reaper, Bucky! Mary is the murderer! She's Tim Matthews' mother *and* she's the Reaper! You have to stop her!"

Bucky didn't know what to make of the information. "But Josh, Celeste talked to me about Tim's mom weeks ago. She told me that while he had her captive atop of the Buckley Building, Tim told her that his mother was dead. She died when he was a teenager. How can Mary Powell be Tim Matthews' mother if she supposedly died years ago?"

"He was wrong, Bucky," Josh stated. "He thought she was dead, but he didn't know the whole story. Jack and I are in Louisiana right now. We talked to the doctor at psychiatric facility she was in, as well as one of her surviving relatives."

"Calm down, Josh. What information did you manage to dig up?"

"Tim's mother murdered a girl and burned her body to cover up the crime. Elizabeth Timmons is still alive and I think she's going to try and kill Roger. She's the Reaper!"

There was stunned silence on the line. Josh couldn't tell if Bucky believed him or not, but he needed to know that Bucky was acting quickly, whether he took Josh's warning seriously or if he thought Josh was being overzealous.

"Don't you understand, Bucky?" Josh yelled. "Roger's life is in danger! Mary's supposed to be heading over there sometime today!"

Even though Bucky was hesitant about the validity of Josh's story, it seemed way too crazy to possibly be true, he thought about everything else that had happened in Carthage and conceded to ease his mind by saying, "Okay, Josh. I'll go down to Roger's house and keep an eye on him until Mary...err, Elizabeth is located. Luckily, someone is always home with Roger. He should be safe from any danger until I arrive."

Although Bucky was skeptical, he knew from previous experiences never to rule anything out. Bucky didn't like the idea of taking a weapon, but just in case trouble arose, Bucky needed a back-up plan. He walked over to his desk, pulled out Jim Draven's pistol from his top drawer, and headed out the door. It was better to be safe than sorry.

Bucky was unaware of the actual danger Roger was in, and wasn't in as much of a rush as he should've been. He figured that since there were many people in Roger's house, there shouldn't be a problem if he took a detour first. After all, the Reaper tended to strike isolated people when they were in a vulnerable state.

After he left his house, Bucky decided to drive over to Thomas Parker's home on his way to 'protect' Roger and ask Thomas for some assistance. As Bucky pulled up the driveway, he saw Stacey in the yard, walking toward the front door. Bucky ogled at the way she looked. It was difficult not to. Even though Stacey was getting older, her $20,000 "career enhancers" were as perky as the day her doctor implanted them, and she kept the rest of herself in good shape to match. Thomas was a lucky man in that regard.

Once Bucky stepped out of his vehicle, he observed that Stacey was leaving the house with her daughter. The car was loaded with furniture and it looked like the two were moving. Bucky walked up to the front door just as she was coming back out.

He stopped dead in his tracks and asked, "Where are you going, Stacey?"

"We're in a bit of a hurry," Stacey informed him. "I've been preoccupied all day and now I'm in a rush to get Penny over to the west side of town in the next fifteen minutes. Sorry if I seem rude, but we need to get going if we're going to stay on schedule."

Bucky cocked his head and asked, "For what? Is there a PTO meeting tonight? If there is, I wasn't made aware of it."

Stacey shook her head. "No, it's nothing like that. We have an appointment at MACS Hair Salon over in the Freight Yard Plaza."

"Oh, is there a special occasion?"

"Penny takes dance lessons at *Amy's Dance Studio* on Liberty Street. She has a recital at seven o'clock and she wants tonight to be extra memorable. We both do."

A look of surprise covered Bucky's face. "There's a dance studio on Liberty Street? Is that new?"

"No," Stacey responded mockingly. "It's been there several years."

"Really? Where on Liberty Street is it located?" asked, not quite getting the hint.

Stacey started to get annoyed that Bucky was holding her up, but she tried to maintain her composure. "Right next door to Kitty's Bar," she muttered while trying to make her way out the door.

"Wow! I've never noticed it before," Bucky commented, genuinely surprised at that bit of information.

"Why would you, Bucky?" she said in an aggravated tone. "There aren't any beer signs hanging in its windows."

Bucky could tell from her sarcastic remark that she wasn't in the mood to chat. "Oh, I apologize for upsetting you. Anyway, I won't keep you then. I was just wondering if Thomas was here. I could use his help."

Just as Stacey was brushing her way past Bucky and making her way out the door, she stopped and turned around. Her eyes narrowed as she said, "Help? Help with what?"

"I'm going over to Roger's house to keep an eye on him. There's a chance the perpetrator might make another attempt on his life. If so, I was wondering if Thomas wanted to come along for the added back-up. He's helped us out in the past and I thought this could possibly give us the edge we need to capture this *new* Reaper."

Bucky paused and looked into her bleak eyes.

"Y'know, Stacey, it'd *also* be a good way to get Thomas out of the house and maybe out of the funk he's been in recently," he remarked.

"Well, I'm sure he'd jump at the chance to help you if he could but...he's not here, Bucky," Stacey uttered, her voice still surprisingly insensitive.

"Why? Where is he?" Bucky asked.

"Baton Rouge," Stacey said emphatically.

Bucky's eyes widened. That was certainly a coincidence. "In Louisiana? Why?"

"That's where his mental hospital is located. He's been committed again and the psychologist at Carthage Hospital thought it'd be best for him to be with familiar doctors in a familiar setting. Of course, being in Louisiana didn't do a lot of good the last time he was there."

"What?" Bucky uttered in astonishment. "Committed to a mental hospital? Wh...why?"

"I had a psychologist stop by here last week to talk to Thomas, and it was his opinion that Thomas had a mild breakdown because of something traumatic."

"Traumatic?" Bucky wondered aloud.

"Ever since the fire at the Buckley Building, Thomas has been a living vegetable. He just stares straight ahead with a blank expression on his face, muttering nonsense. Sometimes he gets so bad that he screams hysterically at a wall or a shadow. The psychologist said Thomas should be treated professionally, and I agreed."

"Everyone was traumatized by Tim Matthews, Stacey. Thomas will snap out of it just like he always does."

"I don't think so, Bucky. Not this time, anyway. In the days that've followed since his encounter with Tim Matthews, Thomas has kept to himself—far more than usual. Trust me, whatever it was that spooked Thomas, he's not saying. He'd be sitting quiet on the couch or in bed, nearly catatonic, and then suddenly he'd explode."

Bucky raised a brow and asked, "Explode?"

"Yeah. He'd start screaming like a kid terrified from a nightmare. But he wouldn't talk about it once he stopped. He'd just stare off again like a zombie."

Stacey paused for a moment; she seemed genuinely distraught. Eventually, she regained her composure and continued on. "The psychologist told me that if Thomas's condition didn't change soon, he would eventually be found to be incompetent—and he'd be sent away to a mental institution, anyway. As painful as it was, I figured I'd better set up everything for Thomas to go back to Louisiana. I believe it's for his own good. And for ours, too."

Just then, Bucky looked past Stacey and saw several suitcases lying on the floor of the living room, even more than what were already packed up in the vehicle. "What's with all the suitcases?"

Stacey exhaled deeply and said, "We're going away for a while. The kids and I are leaving tomorrow. Tonight is Penny's last dance class and she's pretty emotional about it. I hate to do this, but I have to think about all of us. It'd be hard enough to handle everything if it were just me."

Bucky looked confused. "You're leaving? Why? How long will you be gone for?"

Stacey lowered her head and her shoulders drooped. "I'm leaving Thomas, Bucky. It's just too hard. Like I said before, it'd be a hard situation to cope with if it was just me, but I've gotta think about the kids, too."

In another flurry of questions, Bucky asked, "You're leaving him? Permanently? Where will you go?"

"I've contacted Thomas's first wife, Catherine. She said we can come out to California and stay with her until we get back on our feet. Besides, all the kids can live closer to each other now." She paused for a moment as tears swelled in her eyes. "I can't keep living like this anymore, Bucky. Life is too short not to be happy, and I can't have the kids scared of their father. It's better this way."

Bucky hung his head for a moment before responding. "You know, Stacey, I thought of leaving Cristina once, but my dad gave me some good advice. The hardest thing to do and the right thing to do are usually the same thing. Make sure you know what you're doing before you do something that can't be taken back."

"I know you're right, Bucky," Stacey admitted. "Why can't it be easier?"

"I'm sorry, Stacey. '*Easy*' doesn't enter into the adult world," Bucky repeated the sad truth he knew all too well.

With a heavy heart, Bucky walked outside. Before he went back to his SUV, Bucky took a stroll out back of Thomas's house and glanced at the old workshop Thomas had spent many hours in.

The building looked so desolate next to the dead Maple tree which stood next to it. Some of the boards were beginning to rot and fall off the side of the building. A substantial amount of peat moss was growing on the shingles and the roof appeared as though it was ready to collapse. It was just the type of shed the Unabomber would feel cozy in. Bucky opened the rickety door and stepped inside to see the workshop one last time.

As he walked around, Bucky didn't notice a letter lying on the counter. On the outside of the envelope was Bucky's name. But as he brushed off the thick layer of sawdust that covered the workbench, the letter, and the desperate warning it contained inside, got lost in the mix. The envelope fell harmlessly into the wastebasket where its desperate cries could not be heard.

Meanwhile, over at the Police Station, Detective Streeter had walked into Chief Zimmerman's office and caught him on the phone, deciding he had to update the Chief quickly before taking off with half of the active force.

The officer stood silent as he overheard Chief Zimmerman say, "I don't care what he said. I want him!"

Zimmerman stopped talking and glanced at Streeter as he stood in the doorway. The Chief covered the phone with one hand and scowled. "Yes, Streeter? What do you want?"

"I just got a call from Josh Roberts. He thinks Tim Matthews's mother is actually the Reaper and that Roger Fasick's life is in danger. Mary Powell—the fake Mary Powell that is—she's the one."

"I thought we were looking for someone named Beth Allen," the chief exclaimed.

"The woman known as Beth Allen is in fact Elizabeth Timmons…Matthew Timmons mother. She's our Deferiet murderer *and* the Reaper."

"Oh, Christ…" Zimmerman muttered solemnly.

"I have all available units on the way to Roger's house," Streeter announced. "Could be dangerous, Chief."

Chief Zimmerman hung up the phone and roared, "Let's get there, NOW! We're going to end this bloody mess once and for all, and I'll be damned if this Reaper gets another kill on my watch!"

Zimmerman rose and grabbed his trench coat off the coat rack. He slipped it on, slid his pistol into his holster, and removed a box of bullets from his cabinet.

Just as the two men headed toward Zimmerman's door, the chief's phone rang. "Damn it!" C.Z. shouted. "Well, I guess I should answer it…maybe it's important."

On the other end of the phone was Officer Julius Jackson. "Sir, it's Jules," he said as C.Z. answered the phone.

"What is it, Jackson? I'm just on my way out to go catch the Reaper."

"Chief, I've located Torri…" he uttered as his voice trailed off.

C.Z. cleared his throat and asked, "Well, is she alright? She was supposed to come in to work today."

Julius began to sob. "No, Chief. I found Torri's mutilated body in the underground tunnels. She's dead, sir."

Zimmerman gasped and dropped the phone.

Chapter 70:

The Reaper's Revenge

Mary broke into Jack's hotel room and stole his car keys. His Pontiac smelled of cheap cigars and was low on gas, but Mary didn't care. She only needed it for one more mission.

She stuffed a frayed, barrel-shaped duffel bag into the trunk of the car and drove over to Roger's house, relishing the opportunity for what was to come next. Now that Jack and Josh would run into nothing but dead ends in Louisiana, she was free to do what she had to…and no one was going to get away with taking her son away from her. Not again.

Mary loosened her grip on the steering wheel, realizing she was gripping it far too tightly and needed to calm down. Breathing deeply and steadily, she returned to a place of tranquility, imagining the satisfaction she would feel when her quest for revenge was over.

By the time Mary arrived to Roger's residence and pulled up alongside the curb, she was calm. A pleasant grin appeared on her face, and she exited the car with a stun gun and a few other necessities she grabbed from the duffel bag and hid inside her purse. After ringing the doorbell twice, Nellie answered the door.

Mary smiled warmly and said, "Hi there! How're you doing, Nellie?"

Nellie's face lit up as she replied, "Oh, hello, Mary! It's good to see you, again. Roger told me you'd be stopping by sometime today." Nellie stepped to the side and said, "Come on in."

Mary gripped her purse tightly with both hands as she entered the house. "So, are you doing okay, Nellie? Seems like it'd be kinda stressful around here."

"I'm doing as well as can be expected, you know. It's hard seeing Roger in so much pain. I'm worried all this turmoil is going to affect Alex in a negative way, too."

Looking from side to side, Mary inquired, "Where is little Alex today?"

"Alex is over to Bucky Morgan's house hanging out with his son, Mikey. Celeste is playing with the boys while Bucky finishes some paperwork. I just love that family; they've been so helpful!"

"That's nice," Mary remarked with a smile. "So, it's just you and Roger here right now?"

"Yes," Nellie responded. "Would you like to sit down and have a cup of coffee with me?"

Mary shook her head. "No, thank you. If it's not too much trouble, I'd like to talk to Roger. That is, if he's feeling all right."

"Sure, Mary," Nellie said as they walked into the kitchen. "He's up in his bedroom relaxing." She took a seat at the breakfast nook and asked, "Since you're here, were there any questions you wanted to ask me, Mary?"

"None that I can think of," Mary replied. "I'd really like to do an interview with Roger and discuss his encounters with the Reaper—if he has the energy. I promise I won't take too much of his time; I know he needs all the energy he can get if he hopes to have a speedy recovery."

Nellie grinned as she chuckled.

"However, I'm sure the readers would be very interested in what Roger has to say…and maybe there's something in his story that can help the police catch that terrible 'Reaper' person. Once he's behind bars, you won't have to worry about the safety of your loved ones anymore."

Nellie nodded in agreement. "I think that's a wonderful idea. Roger's eager to have some visitors, and his health has been getting better each day, too."

"I'm glad to hear it," Mary commented.

"You can go upstairs and talk," Nellie instructed. "He'll enjoy the company. That will give me some time to go get Alex from Bucky's house. I'll take him over to the grocery store and buy some milk and bread while we're in town. Also, it'll give you some privacy to interview. I'll keep my cell phone on in case Roger needs me."

"Thank you," Mary said, making her way upstairs while Nellie slipped on her jacket and exited the house.

Roger was lying on his side in the bed. He had taken some pain meds about an hour ago, and they were beginning to kick in. Roger focused on his window, watching the dark clouds roll in and the sky turn to dusk. He was trying to rest, but a storm was approaching. The rumble in the heavens and the rain pellets slapping the window kept Roger from sleeping.

Just then, a creak in the floorboards alarmed him. "Hello?" he called out. "Who's there?"

Mary rapped on the open door before walking into Roger's room and announced, "Hey, Roger. I'd like to interview the hero of the Reaper mystery and get your thoughts on Tim Matthews."

"Lady, I'm no hero," Roger grumbled as he lied on his bed, his face contorted from the unrelenting pain. "And in case you haven't noticed, the Reaper is still prowling the streets…so, there's not much to celebrate just yet."

"Nonsense," Mary retorted. "You're just being modest. You stopped Tim Matthews from killing an innocent woman. Just because someone else wants to finish off where *Matt* left off doesn't mean we can't celebrate your heroics."

Roger suddenly felt uneasy in Mary's presence. The hairs on the back of his neck stood up, and he wondered where Nellie was.

"No offense, Mary, but I'm not feeling very good right now. Maybe we can do this another time."

"I'm sorry, Roger," Mary uttered in a monotone voice, "but we're going to do this right now."

"What's going on here? Who *exactly* are you?" Roger asked, unable to place Mary's face with anyone he knew, yet in some weird way she seemed vaguely familiar.

"Who am I?" she repeated mockingly. "I'm the person who's going to kill you because of your sins."

Mary reached into her bag and pulled out the Reaper mask, and the stun gun. As she revealed who she was, Roger quickly reached for the HELP button, and pressed it repeatedly.

"Nellie!" Roger yelled toward the doorway. "Call the police! Run!"

"Your little button won't save you, Roger. There's no one who can hear you."

"How can you be the Reaper," shouted Roger. "What do you have against me?"

Mary looked at him with madness in her eyes.

704

"Who *are* you and why are you doing this?" Roger stammered, panic rising up in his chest. The realization that he was still too weak to effectively defend himself was beginning to set in.

Mary pulled the Reaper mask over her face. "You're right, Roger. I can't kill you without you knowing exactly who I am."

Roger squinted his eyes and his lip curled.

"My name is *not* Mary Powell. The *real* Mary was the poor woman killed in Deferiet. Unfortunate, but necessary."

Roger's breathing became more rapid. His chest and back started to ache as Mary began inching closer to Roger's bed.

"My *real* name is Beth Allen...or you may know me by my former name—Elizabeth Timmons."

"Ti...Timmons!?" Roger stuttered in a surprised shout.

"Yes, Roger," she voiced with a sharp tongue. "Matthew was my son."

The color drained from Roger's face. "Whoa...are you serious?"

"As serious as a heart attack," she answered through clenched teeth.

Roger squinted again and glared intensely at his attacker. "So, Tim *hasn't* come back to life! It's you! You're responsible for all the murders in town, aren't you? You've been the one dressed as the Reaper!"

"That's right, Roger. I'm responsible for you lying in this bed, and now I'm going to finish what I started. This time, no one can save you!"

Roger's eyes darted around the room, looking for a weapon to defend himself with. He kept bombarding Mary with questions as he searched.

"But why...why did you kill the others? I'm the one who killed Tim! I'm the one who let go of his hand as he dangled off the building. Take your anger out on me!"

Mary stopped inching forward. "Why did I kill the others? Isn't it obvious, Roger? I did it go get revenge on all those who wronged my little boy."

"Revenge? What type of revenge did Travis Kull deserve, Mary?" Roger asked, trying to buy some time.

"He took over my son's job—a job Travis didn't deserve. Tim was the best bartender that place ever had. I would *not* let my son's reputation be ruined by that worthless ape of a lackey. Besides, I was *actually* looking for Celeste. Travis was just a bonus for me."

"Do you have a reason for everyone you killed?" Roger pressed, continuing to stall.

"Actually, I do," Ms. Timmons answered, her voice reflecting a righteous indignant rage that made her all the more terrifying. "I killed the *real* Mary Powell because even though my portfolio had better writing and better pictures, her credentials were far superior...and I knew she'd get the job at the Tribune over me." Mary paused briefly before saying, "So, after we had a beer at the bar, I invited her over to my room to show her some of my sketches. On our way back to the motel, I stabbed her with one of my micron pens. She was standing in the way of justice, and that was unacceptable."

"Justice?" Roger blurted out. "What sort of justice?"

"I saw the news report of my son's death on the night he died. I was so excited to come to Carthage and see him...to hold him. And in a split second, all my hopes and dreams were crushed. I'm sure some psychiatrist would tell you that something inside my mind simply snapped. I think I was destined to come here and avenge my son's murder."

Roger quickly changed the topic and said, "I don't understand something, lady. How did you take over Mary Powell's identity?"

"I put my photos and sketches in Mary's portfolio and stole her resume. I guess I should've been more careful with the references she listed. I didn't know Josh Roberts would follow-up with them."

"That's despicable!" roared Roger. "You may have had a messed up reason, but you didn't have to go and kill Harry Moon or his assistant."

"They were cutting up my boy!" Ms. Timmons hollered back. "They were desecrating his body. I don't care if he is dead; I was not going to let them slice open my son!"

"Speaking of your son..." Roger said. "Where exactly did you put his body?"

"He's safe. I put his body in a secluded spot in the underground tunnels," Ms. Timmons revealed. "That's a proper burial, like the pharaohs of old. I go see him every night, to tell him how beautiful he is, how special my baby boy is."

"Special?"

"Yes. I talk to him and let Matt know that I'm going to get revenge for every person who wronged him...who wronged us both! You, Roger Fasick, deserve to die for what you did to him!"

"He was a murderer and an arsonist!" Roger replied angrily.

"Matt was only getting revenge against those who wronged our family!" bellowed Mary.

"He killed an innocent woman who had nothing to do with that!" Roger yelled back. "And he would have killed more just because he was a blood thirsty monster!"

Ms. Timmons slapped Roger with an open palm, her fake fingernail gashing a cut across his cheek.

"My son was a sweet boy!" Mary screamed. "He was taken away from me because that priest in Louisiana was a pedophile—a monster! My boy told the truth! But I'll show you who the *real* monster is. I'll show you all!"

Chapter 71:

It all Ends Here

On the way to Roger's house, Bucky saw Bud Hopkins walking on the street. Bucky pulled his Chevy Blazer over to the side of the curb and rolled down the window. "Hey, Bud. How's everything?"

Bud stopped walking and looked over his shoulder. "Oh, hey Bucky. I'm just out for a little stroll. I don't get to walk as much during the day since you got me that desk job. I do appreciate it, by the way."

"Glad to hear it," grinned Bucky. "How're things working out in the Records Department?"

"Great," Bud answered. "I'm a little overwhelmed by the amount of paperwork involved, but I'm getting' the hang of it. Supervisors seem content enough, so I guess that's all that really matters."

Bucky nodded and announced, "Hey, I'm on my way to Roger Fasick's house. Do you want to come with me? We can talk on the way over."

Shrugging his shoulders, Bud replied, "Sure, why not? I ain't got nowhere important to be right now."

Bud stepped off the sidewalk and slid into the passenger's seat of the vehicle while Bucky continued chatting with the man he'd recently helped climb his way off of the scrapheap.

At least one person has been helped out during this Reaper fiasco, Bucky thought. He smiled at his passenger and the two talked and cracked jokes on their way towards Roger's house.

Meanwhile, Mary Powell had revealed herself to Roger as being Elizabeth Timmons, and she had donned the identity of the murderous

Reaper as naturally as her sociopathic son had. It seemed this was a family full of psychopaths and serial killers, and if there was ever a clan that dedicated themselves completely to a cause, it seemed like this was just the brood. Roger half expected Louis Ferr to jump out of the closet and reveal himself as Elizabeth's biological father.

Roger's right hand was down by his side, pressing the HELP button repeatedly. He was trying to be as inconspicuous as possible, but it was hard to hide his intentions in plain sight. He knew the pager in the kitchen had to be buzzing loudly, but he didn't know if anyone was downstairs to receive the signal.

Elizabeth raised her mask over her face and stared at Roger. She noticed Roger's hand movements and remarked, "Nellie's not in the house right now, Roger. Don't worry though…she's unharmed, for the moment."

Roger glared into her cold, dark eyes. He desperately wanted to believe her words…but could he trust her? He grimaced and quickly pressed the HELP button again.

"I already told you that button won't do you any good, Roger," Elizabeth said sharply. "What's the matter…don't you believe me?"

Roger remained silent.

"Believe me; Nellie went to the market to get a few items and *no one* else is downstairs. I suppose you could try calling her cell phone, but you *won't* make it that far. She thinks I'm interviewing you for the *Tribune*, and she's decided to give us some privacy."

Elizabeth Timmons broke out in a loud high pitched laugh. "You see, Roger, I have you all to myself. And when I'm finished with you, you'll finally know what it's like to feel unbearable pain—just like the pain you put me through after you killed my son."

Roger sat up straight and yelled, "If you want a piece of me, lady, come over here and givge me your best shot."

"You sure have a fighting spirit, don't you?" Elizabeth uttered in surprise. "Y'know, Roger, after I'm through torturing you, I think I'll cut you where I know it'll hurt the most."

"What the hell are ya blabberin' about, you friggin' psycho?"

Elizabeth grinned from ear to ear. "In this type of situation, I think an 'eye for an eye' is appropriate. After all, you killed my son…so it's only fitting that I kill yours."

Roger eyes flashed. "If you lay one hand on my boy, I swear I'll beat you within an inch of your life."

Elizabeth laughed. "You'll do nothing, Roger. In fact, I'll make certain little Alex suffers just like my son did. That's only fair, right?"

Roger clenched his teeth.

"Just be thankful you've had the time with him that you did, Roger. I never got to see my son before he was murdered."

"That's your own fault, lady!" Roger yelled.

"Yes, I guess that's true," Elizabeth admitted. "I faked my own death thinking Matt would be better off without me."

Roger noticed Elizabeth's slight hesitation and decided to prod her on the topic of her son. "Why did you have to fake your death for that?" he asked, still stalling, desperately trying to think of what he could do to defend himself against an attack.

Elizabeth stopped dead in her tracks, feeling somewhat obligated to explain her reasoning why she abandoned her son at a young age. "I changed my name and faked my death so that I could start over. I needed to get away from that town and the institution without being sought after." Elizabeth took a few steps backwards and uttered, "You see, after the church scandal in which the town priest was unjustly exonerated and my son was taken away from me, even though it was the priest who was as guilty as the sin he committed, I had my life threatened constantly and was warned not to press charges."

Roger fought to keep his eyes open and his reflexes sharp as the pain medication worked its way through his system.

Elizabeth's eyes looked far off into the distance, her face scrunched in a mask of rage over the incident, even though she was nearly thirty years removed from the memory. "I was threatened daily by the townsfolk...and I was even physically assaulted on more than one occasion."

"Come on, lady. You expect me to believe that?" gabbed Roger, egging her on.

"It's true, Fasick. I had a nervous breakdown and was committed to a mental hospital in Baton Rouge...roughly forty miles from Matt's facility. I knew there was no way to go back, and there was no way I'd be able to help my son. I was resigned to the fact he'd have to make his own way in life without me. I needed to get out, and maybe later in life there would be some way we could be reunited again."

"Seems to me that all the treatment you received in the mental hospital didn't do a lick of good," countered Roger.

Elizabeth scowled. "Half the doctors in that hospital weren't any better than the devious priest who was the cause of our troubles. They groped whoever and whatever they wanted to feel...and those bastards deserved to be locked up more than any of the patients in the facility. I escaped with the help of a kind doctor and never went back. Years later, that wonderful man helped me get better, and eventually, we got married."

"So, you went all these years letting your son believe you were dead? What did your husband think of that?"

"I never told my husband the whole story, Roger. He never knew what happened to Matt. When my husband died, I fell to pieces and was looking for something good in my life. Then, when my life was stable, I finally got the courage to find Matt. I came to this town only to discover that he was already dead, murdered by a couple of so-called heroes. Thanks to you and your friend, Bucky. You two stole my chance at a future with my son, and slandered his good name in front of the whole town. You're going to pay. All of you are going to pay."

"We didn't—"

Elizabeth cut his off in mid sentence and screamed, "You're very shrewd, Roger. You've got me monologuing in order to buy yourself some more time."

"Yeah, I'm shrewd..."

"No more talking, Roger," Elizabeth bellowed, slipping on the mask of the Reaper once again. "It's time for you to shut up and die!"

Sparks flew from her stun gun. Roger tried to struggle, but in his weakened condition, he was no match for his assailant. As the Reaper placed the stun gun to Roger's neck and pulled the trigger, everything went black. Roger fell into unconsciousness while trying to yell his son's name.

Just then, Bucky and Bud pulled into Roger's driveway and noticed Jack Lavancha's vehicle parked alongside the curb. An ill feeling formed in his stomach as he abruptly stopped the car and the tires screeched to a halt.

"Oh God, no," Bucky muttered.

"What's wrong?" Bud asked, peering at Roger's house.

"That's Jack Lavancha's car," Bucky explained. "And he's in Louisiana with Josh Roberts."

"Is there a problem with that, Bucky?"

"Mary Powell must've stolen it and driven it here, Bud. She must be in there right now!"

"You didn't mention anything about Mary on the way over her, Bucky. What's wrong with her being here?"

"Josh Roberts thinks she's the one masquerading as the Reaper and believes Roger's life is in danger."

"Holy shit!" exclaimed Bud. "Well, if she's inside right now, we'd better get in there!"

With lightning speed, Bud unlatched his seat belt and flung open his door as he rushed to get out of the vehicle, not bothering to slam the passenger door shut behind him.

Both men bolted from the vehicle and ran into Roger's house. After a quick perusal, they noticed that no one was on the lower level of the house and quickly ran up the stairs to Roger's bedroom. Bucky grabbed the doorknob and turned but it would not budge.

"The door is locked!" Bucky exclaimed. "Roger! Roger can you hear me?"

"Well, there's only one thing we can do," Bud stated as he started to back up. "Get out of the way, Bucky."

Bucky stepped to the side. Bud ran at a full sprint and brought his leg up, slamming a kick perfectly into the middle of the door, just off to the side of the lock. Bud knew this was the best place to kick in a door, and the power of a kick was much better than a shoulder to force a locked door to open. Bud slammed hard into the door, and the force busted the lock and knocked the door in.

Bud followed his momentum forward and tripped as the door bounced back off the wall from the force of his kick. Bud fell face-first on the floor, knocking the wind out of him. Before Bud could get to his knees, or Bucky could even enter the room, the Reaper pounced upon Bud, zapping him repeatedly in the chest with the stun gun.

Bucky was caught off-guard and hesitated for a brief moment. Bud screamed in agony, but he refused to give up. Having been beaten several times during his stint in prison, Bud's willpower gave him the strength to fight back against Elizabeth, who wasn't expecting any type of resistance.

Bud's screams caused the initial shock Bucky experienced to wear off. He raised his pistol, aimed with two shaky hands, and shot Elizabeth in her left shoulder.

She fell down, and Bucky rushed to check Roger, who was still unconscious. Elizabeth stood up, and before Bucky could turn around, she shocked him in the back of his neck with the stun gun.

"Now I can finish both of you off," the deranged woman screeched. "I'll teach you to never mess with my family!"

Elizabeth reached into her purse and pulled out Tim's hunting knife. Just as she was about to stab Bucky in the back, Detective Rick Streeter arrived at the house with back-up following behind him.

Rick already had his gun drawn when he entered Roger's bedroom and yelled, "Freeze! Don't move another muscle."

The Reaper stopped.

"We know who you really are, Ms. Allen. Or should I say...Elizabeth Timmons?"

Elizabeth pulled her Reaper mask off and asked, "How did you find out who I am, Detective?"

"We discovered the *real* Mary Powell is the dead woman in Deferiet. And with Josh Roberts's help, we were able to deduce that *you* are Elizabeth Timmons."

"Very good, Detective," she said slyly. "I thought it'd take you *much* longer to put the pieces together than it actually did."

Rick took a deep breath to calm his thumping heart. "You seem pretty intent on getting revenge on this town, lady. Tell me then...why did you go and kill Ms. Powell? After all, she's not from Carthage and she had nothing to do with your son's death."

As Elizabeth inched closer to Bucky's limp body, she said, "We were on the same bus that brought us to the Deferiet bus stop," she explained. "We checked into the motel at the same time, and after realizing we were both going for the same job, we decided to have a late dinner together and talk."

"That doesn't clarify very much, lady," Detective Streeter stated.

"As I told Roger earlier, I saw the newscast about my son while we were eating. When it was reported that he fell off the Buckley Building, I knew he was dead. And I knew I would get my revenge on those responsible for his death."

"And that meant killing Ms. Powell?" questioned Rick.

Elizabeth ignored Rick's question and stared at Bucky's body. After a few seconds, she shifted her gaze back to the detective and continued on. "When we finished our meal and were on our way back to the motel, I passed by a river and got an idea. We went for a walk toward the riverbank, and when we got close, I pulled my micron pen out of my purse and stabbed her in the eye."

The hairs stood straight up on the back of Rick's neck.

"While she was writhing around on the ground, I pounced on top of her and kept stabbing her." Elizabeth smirked and said, "When I knew she was dead, I took her room key and went back to the motel. I stole her resume and portfolio and spent the rest of the night editing her resume to include my credentials. I also dyed my hair to match hers the best I could. The next morning, I put both room keys on the desk and left the village by bus."

For a second, there was dead silence as the killer and the detective locked eyes. Elizabeth thought for a moment and then decided to make her move. She knew she would never have another chance to get revenge on her son's killer, and she didn't care about dying. These men had to die. They *had* to suffer.

Detective Streeter saw her muscles tense, and he knew she was about to plant the knife in Bucky's back. Just as Elizabeth raised her knife and lunged toward Bucky, Rick aimed and shot her in the other shoulder. Elizabeth wailed in pain as she staggered backwards.

Elizabeth was running solely on adrenaline, and charged straight at Detective Streeter with an insane fury that sent chills down his spine. Rick paused for a split second before he squeezed the trigger and fired again. The bullet hit Elizabeth in the chest, and the force of the bullet drove her back into the bedroom window.

Just as the glass was about to shatter, she regained her footing and screamed as leaped forward one more time. Detective Streeter fired one more shot, hitting Elizabeth squarely between her eyes. This time, Elizabeth spun around, crashed through the window, and fell. She landed in a pile of broken glass in Roger's back yard.

Detective Streeter rushed to Bucky and took his pulse. He was unconscious, but the pulse was steady. Rick looked over at Bud, who had staggered to his feet.

"You all right, Bud?" Streeter asked.

"I've been better," Bud groaned, standing on wobbly legs. Bud was hunched over with his hands upon his knees to give support as his heart slowly returned to a semi-normal rhythm.

"What're you doing here anyway?" Streeter wondered.

"I rode over with Bucky. I broke down the door and then that friggin' psycho attacked me." He looked at Bucky lying on the ground and asked, "Is he gonna be all right?"

"I think so," Streeter muttered.

Chief Zimmerman walked in behind the other officers and surveyed the scene. He glanced at Bucky and Roger for a moment before strolling over to the broken window. Once he was finished perusing the area, he turned around and walked over to Bud.

"We're going to need to get a statement from you, Bud," Chief Zimmerman informed him. "We've got an ambulance on the way here. Make sure to get checked out, okay?"

Bud nodded his head and groaned.

Chief Zimmerman took his radio of his belt and spoke into it. "This is Chief Zimmerman. We're gonna need a forensics team at the Fasick residence right now."

Chief Zimmerman pointed at a couple of the new officers and told them, "Get downstairs and check the yard. Secure the body and don't let anyone get near it." He shifted his attention to Dective Streeter and said, "Good job, Rick. Go out front and wait for the paramedics to arrive. I'll take it from here."

A few minutes later, Nellie and Alex arrived back at the house, only to see yellow police tape, two ambulances, and every available police officer in Carthage occupying the yard. Nellie was in shock, but she kept Alex by her side and remained out in the yard with the other officers. Nellie and Alex were instructed to stay out front while the officers walked to the backyard and covered up the lifeless body of Beth Allen—aka: Elizabeth Timmons.

There would be no more resurrections for the Reaper. This nightmare was over.

Chapter 72:

Loose Ends
(September 21st - Afternoon)

The following afternoon, Jack and Josh returned from Louisiana. Josh was standing by the desk in his office and Jack was hanging out there as well. Waiting at Josh's office was Detective Streeter, who then proceeded to brief both men on everything that had occurred in town while they were gone. On his way to the *Tribune*, Josh had stopped by the Fasick residence to talk to Bucky and Roger while Jack went to the police station and attempted to get statements from Julius Jackson, Nathan Barns, and Chief Zimmerman.

On the plane trip back the New York, the two reporters co-wrote a story that was not only going to be featured in each of their respective newspapers—but was also going to be picked up by half the papers around the country, including *The New York Times*. It was decided that each would write their own follow-up stories, but the success of their little partnership ensured neither one of them would ever need to worry about finding a job again.

As Josh was straightening up his desk, he asked, "So, what're you going to do next, Jack?"

Jack placed his cowboy hat upon his head and remarked, "I'm headin' back to Watertown."

"What for?" Josh inquired. "I thought you'd want to stick around town for a few more days and bask in all the celebrity-like attention you've been getting."

"My editor wants me back 'cause some spooky shit has been happenin' around there," Jack said nonchalantly.

Josh stopped in his tracks and raised an eyebrow. "What kind of spooky stuff?"

"Not sure," Jack responded. "He said somethin' about an 'eater of souls' runnin' loose."

"A Soul-Eater?"

"Yeah, I guess so. My editor wasn't very informative on the phone. Editors are amazing, aren't they? You break the story of the decade, and a day later they're pissed because you're not already on the next lead."

"Well, good luck with that," uttered Josh. "I have my hands full with all the peculiar events that go on around *this* town."

"So, I guess this is it then," Jack muttered and he walked toward the doorway.

"Hold on a sec…" Josh hollered before Jack exited the room.

Jack stopped and turned around.

"After spending the last few days with you, Jack, I think my feelings have changed about you."

"Oh yeah?"

"Yeah," Josh confessed. "I like you, Jack…but *only* when you're asleep."

"Very funny, wise-ass. Hey, I will admit, I *do* have respect for you, Roberts. But don't think that just because we went to Louisiana and worked on solving a mystery together mean we're friends or anything."

"Don't worry, Jack. I didn't think that for a second," Josh assured him with a laugh.

Jack tipped his hat as he started toward the exit. He turned to face Josh one more time and said, "You were right, Roberts."

Josh looked surprised by Jack's admission. "I was? About what?"

"You told me to never trust a woman. This is one time when you were correct." Then Jack smiled and said, "Well, sometime next year I'll have some overdue vacation time coming to me. If you're interested, I know of a New York publisher who'd be real interested in a book about the Reaper and all we went through. We could probably split six figures. Just something to keep in mind if you're interested."

"I may have to take you up on that," Josh replied.

"Well, see you around, *J.R.*" Jack Lavancha shouted with a smirk as he headed out the door.

Jack exited and Josh was left standing at his desk, fuming at the ears. He hated it when someone used his old nickname from high school. Bastard.

As Jack was leaving town, he was almost broadsided by another vehicle. Jack scowled and honked his horn as he glared into the dark tinted windows. Although he couldn't see the driver, Jack observed that the vehicle was a black van which was speeding out of Carthage and down the interstate—far away from the North Country.

Over at the Fasick house, Bucky was upstairs in Roger's bedroom, talking to his friend when Nellie entered the room. Walking in behind her were Alex and her two brothers, Joel and Toby Spencer.

Although Joel was only 5'6" tall, he was built like piece of steel. The muscles in his biceps were as big as a grown man's waist and Joel's chest was as round as a barrel. With his red hair buzzed close to the scalp and a goatee nearly six inches long, Joel looked every bit of a badass. Toby, on the other hand, was a gentle giant. He stood well over six-feet-tall and weighed close to three hundred pounds. Toby kept his black hair long, just past his shoulders, and walked with a bit of a limp—the remnants from an injury he incurred while working at a paper mill many years ago.

"Hey there, Roger!" Joel yelled. "How're ya feeling? Looks like you got roughed-up pretty good."

"I'm hanging in there, Joel," Roger groaned, managing a smile. "I'm really glad you guys could come."

Toby sat at the foot of the bed and said, "We wouldn't have missed seeing you, bro. You've always been a good friend of ours."

"I appreciate it, Toby" Roger replied. "I'm just glad to have some visitors here that aren't trying to kill me. Sit down and make yourselves at home."

Joel put his hand on Roger's shoulder. "I was shocked when Nellie called and told us you were nearly killed by the Reaper. We knew we had to get here as soon as possible."

"Yeah," Toby interjected. "We were all worried, Roger."

"There was no need to worry, Toby. I had things under control."

"Really? It didn't look like it when I entered the room," quipped Bucky.

"I had a strategy, Bucky. Y'see, Mrs. Timmons fell prey to the one major weakness of *all* villains."

"Oh?" Nellie remarked. "And what weakness was that?"

Roger smirked and replied, "The tendency to ramble about their plans before they are executed."

Everyone in the room laughed at Roger's response. Roger glanced at Nellie and smiled, receiving the same in return. He was enjoying having Nellie stay at his house, and most importantly, he *needed* her in his life. Roger knew he wasn't ready to settle down and start family a few years ago, but as he looked upon the tender face of little Alex, he thought maybe now he was ready...to love again.

Across town, at the police station, Rick Streeter was entering Chief Zimmerman's office just as Officers Julius Jackson and Nathan Barns were exiting.

"Hey, Chief. LaTesha said you wanted to talk to me."

C.Z. nodded and replied, "Yes, Rick. Have a seat."

Rick plopped down in a wooden chair and asked, "What did you want to talk about?"

"I was about to close my investigation on Jane Doe, Mrs. Timmons, and the Reaper. I was wondering if there're any further details I should know about before I file all the paperwork away."

Rick thought for a moment before saying, "Well, we recovered Tim's corpse in the underground tunnels."

"That great!" C.Z. answered with a grin. "I guess it's safe to assume that we've tied up all the loose ends on this case."

Rick shook his head. "Well, there's still one thing I don't understand about the whole situation though."

Zimmerman rubbed the whiskers on his chin and asked, "What's got ya stumped, Rick?"

"On the night Tim Matthews died, his mother was in Deferiet."

The chief looked perplexed by Rick's comment. "That's not a question, Rick. And it certainly isn't something that should confuse you."

"Just hear me out, Chief. Thomas Parker was found lying on the street near the Buckley Building...he acted like he was nearly scared to death that night!"

"Hmmm..." mused the chief. "You're right, Rick. What's your assessment of his peculiar behavior?"

"I think he saw something that made him go crazy after witnessing Tim's death!" Rick revealed. "However, I don't think he was frightened simply because he saw Tim's mom walking along the streets. I just don't know *what* it was."

Chief Zimmerman leaned back and his chair and exhaled deeply. "Y'know somethin', Rick. That just might be a question which never gets answered."

Turn the page to read the secret ending...

Hundreds of miles away, at the Baton Rouge Mental Facility in Louisiana, Thomas Parker sat at a gray wooden table in the middle of a blank white room. His hands were folded in his lap and his eyes appeared to be glazed over, staring in the distance at nothing in particular.

Moments later, Dr. Dan Gebo, the middle-aged medical doctor with slick gray hair parted to the side and thick glasses, entered the room. He took a quick glance at the one-way mirror on the wall before sitting down and placing a folder on the table.

The doctor opened the folder and began perusing the paperwork inside. After a few seconds, he shifted his attention to Thomas and said, "Hello, Thomas. How're you doing today?"

Thomas continued to stare and remained quiet.

"My name is Dr. Gebo, Thomas. I'm going to be talking with you today."

Thomas said nothing. However, his eyes shifted downward and settled upon the doctor. His pupils seemed to come into focus.

"I understand you were a patient here many years ago. We tried locating your file but somehow it was either lost or stolen." Dr. Gebo let out a small chuckle. "I'm just kidding around, Thomas. I'm sure one of the nurses misplaced it and it'll turn up eventually. If not, it's no big deal. We have everything backed up on a computer anyway.

Thomas blinked but stayed silent.

"Our facility is still sorting out the mess that was caused by Hurricane Katrina last year," continued the doctor, "but rest assured, we will still provide the highest quality of service we can."

Thomas glanced at his hands, which began to fidget in his lap. He seemed uncomfortable with the situation.

"I'm here to help you, Thomas," the doctor commented. "I'll do my best to help you get better. But first, you have to tell me what happened in Carthage. It seemed like you were doing well. A loving wife and a great family…you have a lot to live for and be proud of. What drove you over the edge? Was it because of all the murders in your hometown?"

Again, Thomas sat in silence. His hands began to shake even more vigorously.

Dr. Gebo pulled out an article he printed from the Internet regarding the events which transpired in Carthage. "Look at what I'm holding, Thomas," he said, pointing to the paper. "This article says that the killer in Carthage was stopped. It was a person by the name of Beth Allen—her real name was Elizabeth Timmons. Apparently, she was the mother of someone named Tim Matthews."

Dr. Gebo waited for a response, but his patient still would not speak. The doctor let out a huff and continued on.

"Anyway, she was killed by the authorities and can no longer hurt anyone ever again. The Reaper was human, Thomas. It was a deranged woman and now she's gone. Nothing more."

Thomas's vacant eyes suddenly showed signs of life and they became fixated on the article that was laid in front of him. It was a copy of the story written by Josh Roberts and Jack Lavancha.

The doctor noticed the change in Thomas and his eyes widened with excitement. "Was it *this* woman you saw the night of your nervous breakdown?" the doctor inquired, pointing at a picture of Elizabeth Timmons. "Is she the one who had you so frightened?"

Thomas's eyes faded once again and he bowed his head, staring back at his folded hands.

"Please, Thomas, say something. Say anything. Anything at all," the doctor pleaded with his patient, hoping to get any type of a reaction.

"Ferr," Thomas uttered.

"What? What did you say?" the doctor asked.

Thomas raised his head as his eyes widened. "It wasn't a woman I saw kill Tim Matthews...it was Louis Ferr."

About the Author

Marcus Mastin is an American writer and author of the "Carthage Chronicles" mystery series based in Upstate New York. Marcus was born in Carthage, New York in 1975, and is the youngest of six children. He grew up in a rural, wooded vicinity five miles outside of Carthage and has lived in the surrounding area most of his life.

Mr. Mastin has been a stay-at-home dad for his son and daughter for over nine years as well as working part-time as a daycare provider during that time. He currently resides in Watertown, NY with his wife, Christina, and their two children, Sebastian and Alana-Raven.

July 5, 2008

Made in the USA
Charleston, SC
16 April 2013